WHITE SPIRIT

A NOVEL BASED ON A TRUE STORY

Lance&James
MORCAN

WHITE SPIRIT

Published by:

Sterling Gate Books
78 Pacific View Rd,
Papamoa 3118,
Bay of Plenty,
New Zealand
sterlinggatebooks@gmail.com

Copyright © Lance Morcan & James Morcan 2017

National Library of New Zealand publication data:

Morcan, Lance 1948-
Morcan, James 1978-
Title: White Spirit
Edition: First ed.
Format: Paperback
Publisher: Sterling Gate Books
ISBN: 978-0-473-37226-2

AUTHORS' NOTE:

This novel was inspired by historical accounts of the true-life story of Irishman John Graham, who, in 1825, was transported by convict ship to the British penal colony of Australia. While that in itself was nothing out of the ordinary—after all Graham was but one of an estimated one hundred and sixty-four thousand convicts shipped 'Down Under'—it's what followed that sets him apart . . .

"THOSE WHO LOSE DREAMING ARE LOST."

—Aboriginal proverb

PART ONE

GATEWAY
TO HELL

PROLOGUE

BIG RED BRUSHED FLIES FROM his face as he studied the distant billabong from the cover of trees and dense foliage. Long grass hid the freshwater pool from sight, but he knew it was there even though he'd never been in these parts before. He could smell water even from a hundred yards distant.

Normally, Big Red began each day with a cool drink to assuage his thirst, but on this particular day he'd been harried by Aboriginal hunters who had ambushed him as he approached his usual watering hole. That had been a while back—at dawn. He'd easily evaded the hunters, but their presence had forced him to journey some distance to find water. Already the morning sun was high in the sky, it was hellishly hot and he was dying for a drink.

The approach to the billabong looked clear, but still Big Red hung back. Long experience evading men who wanted to kill him had taught him patience. Besides, he could sense danger.

From his hiding place, he studied the hilly terrain. To his left and right, the rainforest continued, uninterrupted, north and south toward distant horizons while directly ahead, miles beyond the billabong, the blue waters of the ocean could be seen, sparkling in the sunlight. Those waters, he knew, marked the eastern edge of the vast continent that was home for him and his fellows. That's where he was headed today, but first he *had* to drink.

Between Big Red and the billabong was a solitary tree stump. The remains of a once-proud, towering gum tree, it had been charred almost beyond recognition—a result of some long forgotten bushfire or lightning strike. Something about it bothered him. It stood there, like a lone sentinel, and that struck him as a bad omen. He debated whether to seek water elsewhere.

Finally, his thirst got the better of him, and he cautiously emerged from the trees and approached the billabong.

Behind the charred tree stump, a solitary Aborigine stood stock still, his spear clasped close to his side. Moilow had been standing there, unmoving, since dawn. He'd been about to give up when he sensed a presence in the rainforest beyond his hiding place.

A respected member of the local Kabi tribe, Moilow was, in many ways, typical of others of his race. Intelligent, dark, deep-set eyes peered out from beneath furrowed brows; his broad nose protruded above full lips, and he wore a black, matted beard to complement his bushy hair, which he'd tied in a knot; his coal-black skin glistened and his near-naked, wiry frame oozed strength and robustness—the end result of fifty thousand years' evolution in this unforgiving, inhospitable land; his chest and limbs were scarified as a result of his following the age-old practice of lancing the flesh with shells; and his nakedness was covered only by a skimpy loincloth fashioned from the skin of a dingo, the native wild dog that ranges over much of the continent. The loincloth, once yellow like the dingo that wore it, had browned with age.

In other ways, Moilow was not typical of his race. For a start, he was taller than most Aboriginal men, and his legs were well formed, not skinny like the majority of his fellows. He was also a solitary figure, preferring his own company to that of others, which explained why he was here now, alone.

His desire for solitude, even when hunting, had brought him to this very spot after separating from his hunting companions in the darkness of the pre-dawn. He'd assumed he wouldn't have long to wait until one or more kangaroos arrived for their first drink of the day in keeping with their daily routine.

To his surprise, he'd been proven wrong. By mid-morning, apart from a harmless carpet snake that slithered by, no creature had shown itself. That was about to change.

He identified the creature as soon as it emerged from the trees. It was a prized red kangaroo—a big buck. Moilow estimated the roo was at least a full head taller than himself.

Now, as the big red cautiously approached, Moilow willed himself to remain still. No easy task considering he'd maintained the same frozen position for several hours, and his legs were beginning to cramp.

The mid-summer sun beat down on him unmercifully, and, in the high humidity, sweat streamed from every pore. He had to fight against wiping the sweat from his eyes, and he had to ignore the myriad of flies that had settled on his face. Some crawled into his ears and one began exploring his left nostril. Still he resisted the urge to swat them away.

In fact, Moilow wasn't totally still. His eyes constantly moved, flicking from left to right as he waited to catch another glimpse of his quarry; and the fingers of his free hand caressed the shark's tooth that hung from a shell necklace on his chest—a habit he'd gotten into ever since his wife had gifted it to him at the end of the wet season before last.

Moilow loosened his grip on the spear he held. He'd been clasping it so tight his right hand was cramping. The spear, which he'd fashioned from the tecoma vine, was longer than himself by some two feet. It was encased within a woomera, or spear-thrower, which he'd secured in a trade with a fellow hunter. The woomera, traditionally made from mulga wood, had several useful functions; on this occasion it would be used for its main purpose—to launch the spear with considerably more power than Moilow could summon from his strong right arm alone.

The lone hunter couldn't see or hear his intended prey, but he daren't risk even a quick peek in case he gave himself away. He guessed the roo had stopped to graze or to check out the surroundings. Not for the first time he cursed that he hadn't covered himself in mud from the billabong when he'd had the chance. Without the protective mud, he was aware there was a chance the roo would smell him. Fortunately, the air was still so there was no breeze to carry his scent.

Big Red had stopped. He was close enough to see the water now, but still he couldn't bring himself to hop the last fifty yards or so to assuage his thirst. The charred stump still worried him, standing there like the sentinel it was between himself and the billabong. He looked around, sniffed the air and his big ears twitched as he brought all his senses into play to check for danger.

Finally, he threw caution to the wind and bounded toward the billabong, each mighty hop carrying him around twenty feet.

Moilow heard him coming before he saw him. As the big roo drew level with the stump, the hunter stepped out from behind it and, in one fluid movement, raised his woomera and launched the spear.

Big Red saw the danger too late, and veered away in mid-stride. The spear caught him side on. Such was its force it went right through his body, its barbed tip protruding out the other side.

At first, Big Red felt no pain. He bounded away, oblivious to the weapon that had just skewered him.

His elation at having escaped was gradually replaced by another feeling: a niggly pain that extended from his chest to his limbs. His coordination started to go—and then the pain hit. It was a white hot pain than almost caused him to fall.

Now conscious of the black man following him, he tried to keep moving, but he was done. He collapsed in a heap and lay there panting and pawing at the air, trying in vain to regain his feet. Blood flowed from his wounds and bubbled from his nose and mouth.

Moilow arrived to find his prey close to death. He stooped to pull the spear from the dying animal. It took several attempts to pull it free.

Big Red could only watch as the black man raised his spear. He heard foreign sounds coming from the man's mouth. He wasn't to know the man was addressing him.

"You are free now, great red one," Moilow said as he drove the spear home. Its barbed tip pierced the big red's heart, killing him instantly. "You can now join the others who have gone before you." Breathing hard from the sudden exertion, Moilow immediately cast aside his spear and used the woomera to saw open the roo's chest. For this task, he used a piece of quartz rock inserted into the spear-thrower's handle for just this purpose. As he finally cut through the breastbone, he reached in, grasped the big red's heart and pulled it out, then, without hesitating, he held it tight against his chest and close to his own heart.

Eyes closed, and oblivious to the blood that dribbled down his chest to his groin, he recited another respectful chant to honour his prey.

It was late afternoon before Moilow caught up to his hunting companions. The big red, which he carried over his shoulders like a backpack, had slowed him down even though he'd removed its guts and innards. It was the biggest roo he'd killed in some time.

Moilow saw the others before they noticed him. A glance told him they hadn't fared as well as himself, and they looked noticeably downcast. Between them, the six

Kabi hunters carried an assortment of game, including a python, several goannas, possums and wallabies, but not a roo between them. Still they hadn't noticed the newcomer.

A mischievous grin crossed Moilow's face. "Is that all you fellas managed to catch?" he asked.

The others looked around and saw their fellow hunter who was now grinning hugely. Their eyes rested on the big red, which now lay at his feet.

Pointing at the kills his companions carried, and then looking pointedly at the big roo, Moilow said, "You would have had more luck if you had sent the women in your place."

The hunters tried to hide their embarrassment behind rowdy banter, which they directed Moilow's way.

"We killed a dozen big reds earlier," said one.

"Yes we tired of waiting for you so we cooked them and ate them," said another who rubbed his stomach exaggeratedly.

"Why do I not believe you?" Moilow asked.

The good-natured banter continued as Moilow hoisted his kill over his shoulders once more and joined the others as they resumed their trek home.

Moilow surveyed his companions. Like himself, they were all bearded, and their physiques were lean and scrawny yet impressive at the same time. They'd been hardened by the harsh land and by the unforgiving elements they had to contend with year in, year out. And, like Moilow, their chest and limbs were scarified, and they wore their bushy hair tied in a knot atop their heads. Unlike Moilow, several used the knot as a repository for spare spear heads and other useful items.

The hunters were led by Mirritji, one of the Kabi clan's senior elders whose advanced years had slowed him down, but not prevented him from enjoying the thrill of the hunt on occasion. Moilow studied Mirritji as he walked ahead of the others, his impossibly bowed legs covering the ground with surprising speed for someone so bandy and so aged. As always, Moilow's heart went out to him. The elder had been like a father to him, and the younger man had nothing but respect for the old man.

Following close behind Mirritji was Gabirri, an experienced hunter and respected warrior who had proven himself numerous times in skirmishes with the Kabi's enemies. Gabirri was followed by Moilow's best friend Turo, a big, raw-boned warrior who had more kills to his name—human kills that is—than any other man in the tribe.

Turo, who carried a dead adult python over his broad shoulders with effortless ease, dropped back to join Moilow. "Good kill," he mumbled, looking at the carcass his friend carried.

"I got lucky," Moilow said.

They walked in companionable silence until they reached their encampment. The site was a grassy knoll overlooking a sandy beach. Beyond it, the blue of the vast ocean merged with the blue of the cloudless sky, rendering the horizon invisible to all but the keenest eye.

The encampment was home to around a hundred Kabi, the region's predominant tribe. It comprised an assortment of lean-tos and bivouacs fashioned from driftwood, branches, brush and grass, and had a very temporary feel to it—temporary because, like all Aborigines, the Kabi were a nomadic people who were constantly on the move in search of food.

Mirritji's clan had been here less than a week, and they would depart within a few days if the hunting didn't improve soon. Unfortunately, the fishing had gone poorly also, and clan members were hungry.

Excited children, all naked, greeted the hunters as they strode into the camp. Adults—some naked, some semi-naked—hid their disappointment as best they could as they viewed the hunters' slim pickings. They reserved their heartiest congratulations for Moilow whose sizeable kill impressed everyone.

Moilow made his way to his bivouac where he was greeted by his wife Mamba and their two young children. Eight-year-old Murrowdooling jumped into his father's arms and four-year-old Carravanty clung to his father's leg as Moilow lowered the roo carcass to the ground.

Mamba, a pretty woman with sparkling brown eyes and noticeably finer features than any of the other women, greeted her husband with a smile. "You did well today, Moilow," she murmured.

"Yes," a proud Moilow agreed. "We will eat well tonight at least."

Flames from a huge communal cooking fire lit up the night sky, casting shadows over the assembled clan members. The fresh carcasses hung from a makeshift spit above the fire, their flesh rapidly turning a golden colour in the heat.

All eyes were on the carcass of the big red Moilow had killed. It was as big as all the other carcasses combined. Though unskinned when it was placed over the fire, the roo's pelt had soon been burnt off. Hot coals placed in the animal's gut would doubly ensure the meat would be tender in the extreme when finally ready to eat.

As was the custom of the Kabi, proceeds of the hunt were shared amongst the clan members. The one-for-all, all-for-one philosophy was the only one that worked for these people, for they relied on each other for their very survival.

Women dispensed the cooked meat to the menfolk first. Mirritji and the other senior elders were given the best, juiciest and most tender cuts; next best went to Moilow and the other hunters who had provided the food; the next best cuts were dispensed to the other men, and finally the women and children shared what was left.

Moilow and Turo sat side by side, deep in discussion, as they ate. While they talked, Mamba watched her husband with pride. She knew she was the envy of the other women, some of whom openly lusted after Moilow, and she silently thanked her totem for sending her such a handsome man—and a good provider to boot.

Turo caught Mamba's eye and flashed her a sly smile. She quickly looked away, ever-aware of Turo's unbridled lust for women—especially for those already spoken for, like herself. Mamba believed four wives was more than enough for any man, and so, Moilow's friend should be satisfied and stop looking to add to his harem.

5

Mamba returned her attention to Moilow. Her heart rejoiced when she observed him fondling the shark's tooth that hung from the necklace she'd given him. It was a habit she found endearing, and she was delighted he was so attached to the necklace. He'd worn it permanently since receiving it.

As soon as the last of the food was demolished, the womenfolk and their children withdrew to their bivouacs, leaving the men to talk. The discussion, which was led by the elders, concerned the availability of food, or, more accurately, the shortage of food. It was agreed they would mount one more hunt, leaving at first light next day, before deciding on whether to stay at the current campsite any longer.

One by one, the men retired. Moilow and Turo were among the first to withdraw. They planned an early start, before dawn, to make the most of the next day's hunt. Guided by the light of a full moon, they weaved their way through the camp.

Moilow bade Turo goodnight as he continued past his friend's bivouac. Turo's makeshift home was one of the biggest in the camp. It had to be, to accommodate his wives and thirteen children.

As Moilow neared his own bivouac, which was located a little way from the others, he found he was hurrying. He realised he suddenly *needed* to be with Mamba.

Moilow stooped and entered the bivouac. He was pleased to find Mamba still awake. Their sons lay nearby, fast asleep.

"Mamba—"

"Sshhh!" she whispered. "Do not wake the boys." She grabbed his hand and guided him down onto her.

Moilow was pleased to discover Mamba was naked beneath him. He was even more pleased to discover she needed him as much as he needed her. She guided him into her and they proceeded to make love. Wild, urgent love.

•E———3•

Next morning, Mamba was woken by the first rays of the sun as they streamed into the bivouac and chased the darkness away. Looking around, she realised she and the boys were alone. Moilow had departed before dawn to hunt, as he'd promised.

Mamba smiled to herself at the memory of their night of lovemaking. She found she was already looking forward to another night like the one just gone.

While the men were away hunting, Mamba and the other women took turns to look after the children and attend to their daily chores. The chores included gathering fruit and berries in the surrounding bush, and collecting mussels, oysters and other shellfish from the rocks and rock pools along the shore.

Those children who were old enough either helped their mothers or amused themselves by playing games or swimming in the sea. In the heat of the day, when it became too hot to remain outside, they slept in the shade.

For Mamba, the day passed slowly, as the days tended to do when Moilow was away. She was always anxious when he was away and completely content when he was with her. On this occasion she was unaccountably anxious for some reason.

Mamba relaxed when she saw Turo emerge from the rainforest beyond the encampment. She knew Moilow wouldn't be far behind.

The first she realised something was wrong was when cries of alarm carried to her. She looked up to see a woman running toward Turo who had fallen to his knees. The woman was Turo's youngest wife.

Mamba and several other adults in the immediate vicinity hurried to investigate. Only as she drew near did she notice Turo had suffered a nasty shoulder wound. Blood flowed freely from it.

"What happened?" Mamba asked. She looked toward the nearby rainforest and then back at Turo. "Where is Moilow?" She experienced a sinking feeling when she noticed Turo was looking at her strangely. "Where is my husband?" she demanded.

Turo struggled to his feet and looked squarely at Mamba. "Moilow was killed," he said simply. "We were ambushed by our enemies . . . the Noonuccal."

The mere mention of the Kabi's long-time enemies prompted Turo and other men close by to spit on the ground, such was their hatred of the Noonuccal—a tribe known and feared for its cannibalistic practices.

Turo added, "Your husband fought bravely and died like the warrior he was."

Mamba looked from Turo to the other women, as if to solicit a response from them that would make everything alright. They had no such response. They could only look away. Finally, she asked, "What did they do with him?"

Turo hesitated. "They dragged his body away," he murmured.

Mamba screamed and ran back to her bivouac. Distraught, she gathered up her two sons who had been sleeping, and held them tight to her.

The oldest, Murrowdooling, sleepily asked, "Where is Moilow?"

"Hush, child," Mamba sobbed. She couldn't bring herself to tell her sons their father was dead. Not yet.

Her grief was all the greater because she knew why her husband's body had been taken. Only cannibals claimed the bodies of those they killed. If Moilow hadn't already been eaten, he would be soon. Of that she had no doubt.

Mamba raised her head skyward, and screamed. It was a long, heart-wrenching, primordial scream that came from her very soul.

1

—❦———❦—

A WIRY ABORIGINAL TRACKER RAN fast through the undergrowth, following tracks only he could see. He carried a spear in one hand and a nulla nulla, or club, in the other. Wearing only a loincloth, he covered the ground with effortless ease, his bare feet hardly touching the sun-baked earth.

This was Barega, one of the last surviving members of the mysterious Joondaburri, a tribe whose menfolk were renowned up and down Australia's east coast for their superior tracking abilities. In the language of his people, his name meant *the Wind,* which was appropriate for he ran like the wind. To the British soldiers who employed him, he was simply known as *the Tracker.*

Although only average height, Barega's legs were out of proportion in that they were unusually long in relation to his torso—a fact that gave him a distinct advantage in his chosen occupation. Few men, black or white, could match him for speed in a cross-country foot race, and, like others of his tribe, he could run all day long, seemingly without tiring or succumbing to the relentless heat.

The tracks he followed were those of three convicts who had escaped custody earlier that morning. They were heading west, away from the coast and away from Moreton Bay—the site of Britain's newest penal colony and home to two hundred or so convicts and soldiers. The route was leading deeper into the tropical rainforest that hugged this part of the coast. It became progressively steeper as the hills gave way to mountains.

Barega was accompanied by three soldiers who followed him on horseback. He glanced back at them from time to time to ensure they remained in contact. Though their horses were doing most of the work, it was clear to him the men were having a hard time of it in the heat. They stopped every so often to drink from their water bottles.

Leading the way was Lieutenant Desmond Hogan, a dashing Englishman who was a career soldier through and through. Hogan's ambition to succeed in his chosen career was hinted at by his senior ranking, which was an achievement in itself for one so young. He was only twenty-six. His rapid rise up the ranks had undoubtedly been influenced by the fact that his father and his father's father had both been high ranking army officers, and he was candid enough to acknowledge that, but that didn't change the fact he was a man of some ability whose promotion had largely been based on merit.

Hogan caught Barega's eye. "How close, Tracker?" he asked.

Pulling up, the tracker pointed at the sun, which at that moment was to the northeast, and then he pointed dead north. "Soon, Mister," he said by way of explanation, though no explanation was necessary.

The young lieutenant had used Barega so often he could readily understand the other's hand signals. On this occasion, the tracker had indicated they'd catch up to their quarry by mid-day when the sun would be where he'd indicated—dead north. By Hogan's reckoning, that would be in an hour's time give or take. He glanced around at his two men. "Another hour should do it," he said.

"Thank Christ," one of them muttered.

Like their commanding officer, the two soldiers—both privates—had removed their red tunics, which now hung loosely from their saddles. It was the one allowance Hogan made for the heat, but only when out of sight of the penal settlement as it bucked the army's rigid dress code.

Behind the pair, in the distance, Hogan could still see Moreton Bay. Trees concealed the penal settlement that had taken its name from the bay, but from the current vantage point there was an unobstructed view of the bay itself. And beyond it, the blue of the Pacific Ocean merged with the blue of the sky. It was a sight to behold.

Hogan and the others weren't here to admire the view, however. They'd been tasked with capturing the runaways, and to a man they were aware the sooner they accomplished that the sooner they could return to base and enjoy some well-earned refreshments—and escape the accursed heat and humidity.

Ahead of them, Barega had resumed running. His black skin glistened with sweat as he picked up the pace. It was clear he sensed his prey were close now.

The soldiers followed, staying close to the tracker so as not to lose touch with him in the dense rainforest. Vines and creepers clawed at them, threatening to unseat them from their mounts, as they proceeded. Despite their discomfort, the soldiers were grateful the convicts had opted to keep to a well-worn trail carved out over the centuries by nomadic natives. They knew if their quarry had opted to deviate from the path, the horses would be no use to them and they'd have been forced to follow on foot.

Lieutenant Hogan knew something his men didn't know, however. He alone knew they weren't expected to bring all of the runaways back alive. Before setting out, the penal settlement's commandant had made it very clear to Hogan privately that he'd be upset if more than one escapee survived.

Lord Bertram Cheetham's reputation for cruelty had preceded him before he took up his new posting as Moreton Bay's commander-in-chief four months earlier. Since then, Hogan and the other officers had come to see Cheetham's reputation was well deserved; he viewed the convicts as animals and expected the soldiers under his command to treat them as such. As a result, floggings had become a daily event, the overworked convicts were starved and regularly beaten, and the dysentery and other ailments that plagued them and some of the soldiers, too, had reached epidemic proportions. Nearly every single convict had at least one serious illness or injury and, to make matters worse, medical care was basic to say the least. Despite this, as long as a convict could draw breath, he was forced to endure sixteen-hour days of hard labour, seven days a week.

So harsh were the conditions—reportedly as harsh as those at infamous Norfolk Island—a few convicts had opted to commit suicide rather than serve out their sentences, and more than a few others were contemplating such drastic action.

Another consequence of the cruelty was barely a week passed without one or more convicts attempting to escape. Where they hoped to escape to was anyone's guess because Moreton Bay was many hundreds of miles from the nearest civilization. Convicts escaping overland risked death by heatstroke, thirst, starvation, snakebite or unfriendly natives, and escape by sea was out of the question because the only vessels visiting Moreton Bay were those servicing the penal settlement.

Rebellion was inevitable, of course, and since Lord Cheetham's arrival illness, escape attempts and deaths amongst the convicts were all increasing. This had only served to infuriate Cheetham whose solution was to work the convicts even harder and to impose harsher punishments for any transgression.

Attempts by Hogan and the other officers to appeal to the commandant's common sense, if not his humanity, had fallen upon deaf ears. Hence Cheetham's private instructions to Hogan earlier that morning—to make an example of these latest escapees and ensure only one of them was returned to Moreton Bay alive. So desperate was he to deter the other convicts from attempting to escape.

Such instructions didn't sit well with Hogan, but he felt his hands were tied. Experience had taught him if he returned the three escapees alive, the eccentric Cheetham was likely to order the execution of all three, and possibly one or two others as well. He'd seen that happen before.

In a clearing, Hogan glanced behind him and was distracted by the sight of a sailing ship some two or three miles offshore. She was far to the south—so distant that he wouldn't have noticed her had it not been for her billowing white sails. They could easily have been mistaken for clouds had it not been a cloudless day. The young officer knew immediately the vessel was *the Hoogley* for she was the only one scheduled to visit Moreton Bay this week. She was bringing another shipment of convicts from the Parramatta penal settlement near Sydney Town. A regular occurrence these days. Had Hogan not been prevailed upon to supervise the capture of the escapees he'd have been tasked with greeting *the Hoogley* and her cargo of convicts. As it was, that particular chore would fall to his commanding officer on this occasion.

Though compassion and sympathy didn't figure highly in his make-up, the lieutenant almost felt sorry for the men incarcerated in the hold of the schooner he was observing. Almost but not quite. He was aware that convicts unlucky enough to be shipped out to Moreton Bay, or to the other hell-hole that was Norfolk Island, were considered the most incorrigible of the convicts. *Beyond Repatriation* was the army's official term for these men. As far as the military was concerned, they were unlikely to taste freedom again let alone ever return to their countries of origin. As far as Hogan was concerned, they deserved to rot in hell.

Hogan's horse stumbled on the protruding root of a tree, forcing him to focus on the task at hand. He realised he'd lost sight of the tracker, and dug his heels into his mount's flanks, encouraging the horse to move faster.

Offshore, *the Hoogley* was making hard work of it as she plied north through high, rolling seas. The conditions were the lingering aftermath of a storm, which, up until the previous evening, had battered the three-masted schooner without let-up since she'd departed Sydney Town six days earlier. Her timbers creaked in protest as her bow rose and fell alarmingly, and the waves that crashed over her threatened to tear the sails from their masts. In the rigging, high above deck, riggers hung on for dear life as they carried out their death-defying duties.

Below deck, the conditions were scarcely any better. As well as putting up with the rolling motion of the vessel, the forty mainly Irish convicts and their guards had to contend with the constant sea spray and saltwater, which poured through the portholes and open hatches, and which ensured the men remained permanently wet.

The convicts had the worst of it for they had been confined below deck for the entirety of the voyage. Permanently shackled, their ankles were secured by chains, which, in turn, passed through a longer chain bolted to the hull's interior at each end of the hold. Their condition wasn't helped any by the lack of adequate food and water throughout the voyage, nor by the temperatures, which soared in the confined space by day and dropped to near-freezing by night.

The overpowering stench of urine and shit combined with the ever-present bilge water that sloshed about in the bottom of the hold was all pervasive. An outbreak of dysentery early in the voyage had swept through the vessel, affecting convicts, guards and crew alike, adding to the misery of all.

Not all the convicts had survived the voyage. One, a sickly young man from Belfast, had succumbed to pneumonia. His body had been unceremoniously dumped at sea two days earlier. And several others were critically ill. Their condition wasn't helped any by the fact there was no doctor or even any rudimentary medical facilities on board.

Harsh though this voyage was, it was nothing compared to the three or four-month journeys these convicts had originally endured out from England. In some cases, fatalities had been as high as forty per cent, and on one ship fatalities had topped sixty per cent.

Two survivors of that hellish voyage aboard the most notorious of prison ships were now aboard *the Hoogley*. Twenty-eight-year-old John Graham and the slightly younger Noel Thomas whose date of birth was unknown—unknown to Noel at least—were chained together toward the rear of the hold. Originally from Dundalk, in County Louth, Ireland, they were boyhood friends. The former had been sentenced to seven years' transportation to Australia for stealing ten pounds from a shady employer he alleged hadn't paid him, while the latter—hackneyed though it may sound—had been sentenced to five years for stealing a loaf of bread.

The two friends were a study in contrasts. John was broad-shouldered and taller than most of his companions, and certainly better looking. His unruly black, shoulder-length hair framed a pale but interesting face that women invariably found attractive. What really set him apart, however, was his startling blue eyes. Ever-alert, they missed nothing. Even here, chained in the hold of a ship, John constantly surveyed his fellows and the guards who watched over them.

Noel, on the other hand, was short and wiry, and not overly handsome. Nevertheless, he had an engaging manner and a cheeky wit that endeared him to all—all except his jailers that is. His cheekiness constantly landed him in trouble, with fellow convicts and guards alike, and John had had to come to his rescue more than once.

Chained alongside them was elderly Dubliner who was ailing rapidly. Leith Donovan, who claimed to be forty-five but looked to be all of sixty-five, had been ill even before departing Parramatta. He began throwing up as soon as the schooner set sail and was still throwing up now. In the last six days he'd lost damn near half his bodyweight.

"Hang in there, Leith," Noel urged as Donovan disgorged the last of the meagre rations he'd managed to keep down. The remains of those rations, including vestiges of cabbage and corn, ended up on Noel's leg.

"Sorry, Thomas," Donovan mumbled as he made a half-hearted attempt to wipe the mess from his companion's leg with his hand.

John glanced at Noel. His friend's expression signalled that he thought it likely Donovan's journey would end soon—an opinion that John shared.

Noel waved to the nearest guard to catch his attention. "We have a sick man here," he said.

The guard, a callous Englishman who took every opportunity to show his contempt for the Irish, just grinned at Noel. He quickly looked away when he noticed John staring at him.

John Graham's startling blue eyes had that effect. Few men could hold his gaze. There was something behind those eyes that unnerved them.

•€•———•3•

At the same time, in the hinterland behind Moreton Bay, the three convict escapees were so exhausted they had slowed to a walk. While they'd started out full of running in the cool of the pre-dawn, the exertion, heat and thirst had quickly reduced them to a slow shuffle. They weren't helped either by the leg irons they wore. The heavy shackles made running almost impossible, and the *clinking* noise they made gave the convicts' whereabouts away to anyone within fifty yards or so. Only the thought of what awaited them back at Moreton Bay should they be caught kept them going. To a man, they'd rather die than return to the place they called hell.

They were a mixed bunch. About all they had in common was they were English convicts with a shared yearning for freedom. And they were armed. The older man carried a tomahawk and the two younger men carried knives.

Tim Brady, the ringleader, was the oldest of the three by some years. A forty-five-year-old Cornishman, he was considerably shorter than his two companions, but he was almost as wide as he was tall. What he lacked in height he made up for with strength, and it was widely accepted he was the strongest of all the convicts—and all the soldiers, too, for that matter—at Moreton Bay.

Brady's companions, both Cockneys and both in their early twenties, naturally

12

looked to Brady for guidance. After all, the escape had been his idea. Unfortunately for them, Brady was now out of ideas and so exhausted he was no use to them or to himself for that matter.

The two Cockneys pulled up when they realised Brady had fallen behind.

"Hurry up Brady!" the younger man shouted.

Gasping for breath, the Cornishman tried to run, but his legs gave out from under him and he crashed to the ground. "Water," he mumbled. "I need water."

"We all need water, Brady!" the older Cockney said. "We 'ave to keep movin.'"

Brady slowly pushed himself to his feet and stumbled forward to catch up with his companions.

The two Cockneys looked at each other.

"He's slowin' us down," one mumbled.

"Yeah fuck 'im," the other said.

The pair took off, leaving Brady to fend for himself.

"Wait, you bastards!" Brady called. He hurried after them, desperate not to be left behind.

The first the Cornishman realised they had company was when the tip of the tracker's spear skewered him from behind. He saw its tip emerge from his chest before he felt any pain. And what pain he felt was only fleeting as Barega's nulla nulla smashed his skull, killing him moments after the spear had entered him.

Barega stopped only long enough to retrieve his spear then resumed running after the other two. Behind him, the sound of horses' hooves told him the soldiers were close by. Ahead of him, he could hear the two Cockneys' clinking leg irons as they crashed through the undergrowth.

Although less than fifty yards ahead of their pursuers, the surviving escapees had no clue they were about to be captured, or worse. For the moment, they were blissfully unaware of Brady's untimely end or the fact that their freedom could now be measured in minutes, or less.

The first they realised the game was up was when the sound of the horses reached them. They immediately hid in dense bush and waited, their knives drawn.

Looking through the foliage, they were confused by a series of movements too quick for the eye to follow. Barega moved with such speed and stealth he gave the impression there were two or even three of him.

In the confusion, the younger Cockney moved, revealing his hiding place. It was the last thing he ever did. The tracker's spear went straight through his throat, pinning him to a tree.

Terrified, the surviving convict took off, running blindly through the trees.

Not for the first time that day, twenty-three-year-old Frank Patterson pondered the wisdom of attempting to escape. In fact, he had regretted his decision almost immediately, but he'd made his choice and had to keep going.

Patterson didn't see the nulla nulla that flew through the air, striking the back of his head and stunning him.

Barega retrieved his weapon and prepared to finish off the stunned Cockney. He was distracted by the arrival of Hogan and the others. His hesitation gave Patterson time to retrieve the long-bladed hunting knife he'd dropped. Barega brought his nulla nulla down hard, shattering his victim's forearm and causing him to scream out in agony.

The tracker looked on, amused, as the desperate convict retrieved the fallen knife with his good hand and shaped up to attack again.

To Patterson's surprise, Barega suddenly lay prone on the earth. The young Cockney glanced up to see the two soldiers with Hogan had their muskets pointed his way. Two shots rang out as a single volley. Such was his shock Patterson fell to the ground, convinced he was dead. It took him a moment or to realise he'd been spared. He looked up to see the soldiers were laughing at him.

"Welcome back to the land of the living, lad!" one of the soldiers shouted, prompting more laughter. They'd pulled the same trick on other escapees, aiming their weapons high or wide of their would-be victim, though Patterson wasn't to know that.

Grinning, the tracker rose and pulled the long-bladed knife from the Cockney's grasp, claiming it for himself. Such spoils were his as of right. That was the arrangement he'd made with the British. Barega beamed at Hogan who motioned to him to lift the relieved but still shocked survivor to his feet and start marching him back to Moreton Bay.

2

CAPTAIN TOM MARSDEN AND HIS wife Vera looked on amused from the shaded veranda of their cottage as their daughter chased her younger brother around the giant trunk of the Moreton Bay fig tree that occupied pride of place on their front yard.

Nineteen-year-old Helen Marsden was furious Matthew had scrawled an unflattering remark on a letter she'd been painstakingly drafting to a former classmate—a boy—back in London. "I am going to thrash you when I catch you, Matthew!" she shouted.

Eleven-year-old Matthew was shrieking with laughter as he led his sister on a merry dance round and round the towering tree. "Helen loves Samuel!" he taunted, referring to the boy he suspected Helen still carried a candle for.

"You little—" Helen caught herself when she remembered her parents were within earshot.

"Don't tease your sister, Matthew!" Missus Marsden shouted, her accent revealing her middle class upbringing.

The boy took no notice of his mother, and continued his teasing.

Tom Marsden chuckled to himself. He never ceased to get pleasure out of watching his children interact. Despite their age difference and their not infrequent tiffs, they were usually the best of friends. But not today.

Helen finally tired of trying to catch the elusive Matthew. It was a brutally hot afternoon, and, lithe and athletic though she was, she'd run out of energy. "I will get you later," she promised her brother as she sat down in the shade of the tree, her back resting against its trunk.

Disappointed the fun was over, the irrepressible Matthew skipped over to his parents. "Can I have a cold drink, mama?"

"Can I have a cold drink *what?*" a stern Tom Marsden asked. His accent was not dissimilar to his wife's. A little more working class perhaps, no doubt roughened by fifteen continuous years of military service in some of the British Empire's farthest flung colonies.

"Can I have a cold drink *please*, mama?" Matthew asked.

"That's better." The boy was the apple of Marsden Senior's eye, but he wasn't about to ease up on disciplining him when required.

"Of course you can," Missus Marsden said. "Ask Orana to pour you a glass of lemonade, and one for Helen one, too," she added, referring to the Aboriginal maid who had become the fifth member of their little family since they'd taken up residence here.

Matthew pulled a face at the mention of his sister and disappeared inside.

"He's a good boy," Missus Marsden said—more to herself than to anyone else—as she returned her attention to the book she'd been reading before Matthew had started teasing his sister.

Helen, who had been lip-reading what her mother was saying, shouted, "You are too lenient on Matthew, mama!"

Tom Marsden nodded to show he agreed with his daughter.

"Nonsense," Missus Marsden said. "He's just being a brother."

Helen looked to her father for support. Marsden just shrugged, indicating he supported her morally at least.

An exasperated Helen shook her head, signalling to her father she was not impressed by his tepid support then she closed her eyes and willed herself to go to sleep. She had learned that Moreton Bay, in early January, was so hot that sleeping in the shade was one of the most effective ways of escaping the summer heat. She'd also learned she had to fight her own battles where Matthew was concerned because her parents, like parents everywhere, invariably sided with the younger sibling in disputes. Despite that, she did love her young brother. Most of the time.

Matthew reappeared around the corner of the house with a full glass of lemonade in each hand, and hesitantly approached his sister. "Sis," he murmured. "You awake?"

Helen opened her eyes and smiled when she saw her brother had come bearing gifts. She patted the ground next to her, indicating Matthew should sit. He did. Then she playfully reached out and tweaked his cheek before taking a glass from him and sipping from it.

Relieved he'd been forgiven, Matthew sipped from his glass. In no time the pair were chatting away like the good friends they were.

Observing the siblings, Marsden marvelled for perhaps the hundredth time at how well they got on despite their age-difference. He gave Helen much of the credit for that. Where many young women would be too busy to give of their time to so boisterous a young brother, Helen was a giving person who always put others first—siblings included—no matter how annoying they were.

Marsden was proud of his daughter. She was growing into a beautiful young woman—inside and out. With her blonde hair and sparkling blue eyes, her golden tan and trim figure, she was a true beauty. That was something she was becoming aware of. And most certainly the soldiers in the nearby penal settlement were aware of it. Several young officers had already served notice of their interest in his daughter.

Not for the first time, Marsden questioned his wisdom in bringing a beautiful young woman like Helen to Australia. Not only Helen, but his whole family in fact. Australia, after all, was nothing more than a fledgling penal colony situated at the bottom of the world, and the Moreton Bay convict settlement was some four hundred and fifty miles north of Sydney Town, the nearest civilization. As one confidant uncharitably described it, Moreton Bay was located "at the arse-end of nowhere." That same confidant had referred to it as "a place suitable only for savages and blowflies where no white man in his right mind ought to live."

"Penny for your thoughts?" Missus Marsden asked, interrupting her husband's reverie. She'd been observing him for a moment without his realising.

"Oh . . . I was just wondering once again if I have done the right thing bringing you all out here," Marsden said.

Missus Marsden lowered her book to her lap and removed her reading glasses. "We have been through that, Tom," she lectured. "This posting was too good a career opportunity for you to pass up, and there was no way we were going to be separated from you."

Not convinced Marsden added, "And I worry about Helen." He asked, "What career or marriage prospects does a place like this offer a young woman?" Though he was proud to be a soldier and to serve with the British Army, he didn't want his daughter to end up a soldier's wife. And realistically, a soldier's wife she'd be if she stayed here.

Missus Marsden didn't respond immediately. She'd been having the same thoughts of late. Content though she was in her marriage, she more than most understood the sacrifices an army wife had to make, and she didn't want that for Helen either. Eventually, she said, "I think the day is coming we will have to send her back to London to stay with your sister."

"Or to Sydney Town perhaps," Marsden said, referring to the fast-growing coastal settlement south of Moreton Bay.

"Heaven forbid!" Missus Marsden said. "That place is a den of iniquity. Full of drunks, reprobates, thieves and prostitutes."

"I'm not sure London is much better, my dear," Marsden gently reminded his wife. "Remember one of the reasons we established penal colonies around the world. To—"

"I know, I know," Missus Marsden sighed. "To rid Britain of her undesirables."

The conversation lapsed—as it usually did when they discussed Helen's future. Neither wanted their daughter to leave the roost, but they knew the time was fast approaching. There was no future for her here. Missus Marsden wanted her to return to London where she could stay with her aunt while Tom Marsden preferred she move to Sydney Town where old family friends had offered her bed and board, and training as a junior teacher in the school they'd established. At least there she'd be in the same continent, he reasoned.

Marsden studied his wife as she buried her nose in her book once more. Initially, he had feared she wouldn't cope with life in the new colony. She was, after all, frail of build and genteel by nature—better suited to the life of the lady she was in London than to the harshness of, first, India, and then Africa, and now Australia. But she'd proven him wrong each time. Uncomplaining, she embraced all that life threw at her and greeted every problem as an exciting challenge. Home-schooling Matthew had been a case in point. Though well educated, Missus Marsden had no teaching experience when she took it upon herself to home-school the boy. Despite her husband's early reservations, she'd proven to be a natural teacher, and Matthew's education was progressing better than either could have hoped.

The man of the house stood and stretched, aware it wouldn't be long before he had to report for duty. Though only of medium build and height, Marsden's forty-year-old frame exuded strength and vitality, and his piercing grey eyes reflected an inner steel that matched his cool temperament. Certainly the men under him knew not to cross him. Even so, he had a reputation for fairness and straight-talking, and his men respected him.

Marsden looked around at the place they now called home. Their three bedroom cottage, which had been constructed using convict labour, sat atop a rise overlooking the penal settlement some two hundred yards distant.

It was a view Marsden never tired of. All around, sun-drenched hills stretched to distant horizons. Some had been burnt bare while others were covered in dense bush. And the rolling plains that linked the hills with the coast were dotted with stands of eucalypts, or gum trees, as far as the eye could see. The flowering gums were popular with Matthew and the handful of other European children in the settlement because they were home to the cuddly koala bears, which could often be found chewing on the eucalyptus leaves while perched precariously in the trees' branches.

Between the cottage and the settlement were unfenced fields of corn, potatoes, cabbages and other hardy vegetables. They'd been broken in and planted by the convicts soon after the settlement had been relocated from a less suitable site further to the north some two years earlier. To date, only the corn had taken; the other vegetables weren't faring at all well. Marsden wasn't sure how much that was attributable to climate and the state of the soil and how much to the slackness of the convicts tasked with tending the crops. He had his suspicions.

The settlement itself comprised a motley collection of wooden huts and barracks along the near bank of a major but as-yet-unnamed river that emptied into the bay beyond. The huts housed two hundred convicts—soon to number two hundred and forty—and the barracks accommodated the soldiers.

Adjoining the soldiers' barracks were rudimentary offices for Marsden and the handful of clerical workers in the army's employ, a building that accommodated a soldiers' mess and a separate convicts' mess with kitchens for both those facilities, a single ablutions block divided into two to accommodate soldiers at one end and convicts at the other, a workshop, three storage sheds, a hay barn, two water tanks, stables for the horses and a shed to facilitate the resident blacksmith. And, as Marsden well knew, behind those facilities and conveniently concealed from sight was a whipping post and a set of gallows, both of which had been well utilised in recent times. Too well utilised for his liking.

On either side of the settlement, the beginnings of what could only be described as a shanty town were taking shape. Local Aborigines—members of the predominant Quandamooka tribe—had taken to residing close to the white newcomers. It was an arrangement that suited both parties. The Aborigines scavenged food and liquor from the soldiers while the latter made use of the former's tracking and food-gathering skills, and, on occasion, their women. This arrangement had its disadvantages of course. Drunkenness and disorderliness among the Quandamooka was increasing, and soldiers vying for the attentions of native women often came to blows.

Marsden wondered at his fellow soldiers' taste in women. Especially the men of lower ranks who were, it seemed, a different breed, and he had to agree with the observation of one wit who once famously observed, "They'd shag anything on two legs."

Marsden's eyes were drawn to a flock of black-crested cockatoos that flew past the cottage, screeching. They were heading in the direction of the fledgling town of Brisbane, a quarter-of-a-mile upriver.

Brisbane Town: population forty-seven adults—thirty-five males and twelve females to be precise—and half a dozen children.

The township had evolved, seemingly out of the dust, as a service centre for the expanding penal settlement and the soldiers stationed there. Its menfolk were primarily involved with the provision of essential services and supplies while a hardy few were trying to break in the surrounding countryside with a view to eventually farming it. Marsden wasn't sure what the single women did to survive, though he had a theory or two on that.

Officially, Brisbane Town and greater Moreton Bay were part of the state of New South Wales. It would be another thirty-two years before they became part of a new state that would be known as Queensland.

The only building of note in the township was the house Lord Cheetham called home when he wasn't required in Sydney Town for meetings with the Governor of New South Wales. *Home,* in this case, was something of a misnomer. It was a three-storeyed colonial mansion so grand it wouldn't have looked out of place in Cheetham's home county of Essex, in Mother England. The mansion wasn't visible from the Marsden homestead, hidden as it was behind the inevitable gum trees, but Marsden was very familiar with it, having been summonsed there for staff meetings too often for his liking.

The captain looked downriver, beyond the penal settlement to the quarry where the convicts spent much of their time breaking up the rocks that would be used in local roading and construction projects.

At that moment he could see a group of thirty or so convicts being escorted under armed guard to relieve a similar number of convicts who were currently toiling in the quarry. They kicked up little clouds of dust as they shuffled over the red earth. Their leg irons, combined with the heat, ensured the four hundred-yard trek from the settlement to the quarry would not be a speedy one despite the encouragement of the mounted soldiers escorting them. That *encouragement* included constant verbal abuse and the frequent lash of a whip. Even from here, Marsden could see the convicts looked exhausted, and their shift hadn't even begun.

"Papa!"

Marsden glanced up to see an excited Matthew pointing out into the bay. He looked around and saw the three-masted schooner sailing toward the river mouth.

"It's the Hoogley," Matthew said.

"Aye, I see it," Marsden said with considerably less excitement than his son. The vessel's arrival meant an immediate return to duty for him. Lieutenant Hogan's absence dictated that his services were required.

Strictly speaking, it was Marsden's role as the senior officer and, by default, the head warden, to welcome the new arrivals. In reality, he was head warden in name only. That role, though officially his, had been usurped by the all-powerful Lord Cheetham who had taken it upon himself to meddle in Marsden's affairs. Unfortunately for Marsden, complaints to higher authorities in Sydney Town had fallen on deaf ears. Cheetham had been given free rein to run Moreton Bay as he saw fit, and he was taking full advantage of that.

Marsden reluctantly donned his red tunic, which his wife had thoughtfully hung by the front door. "I shouldn't be too late, my dear," he said. "Back soon after dark."

Missus Marsden immediately jumped up and ran inside only to emerge moments later holding her husband's regimental hat, which she placed lovingly on his head before straightening his uniform. It was a routine they'd gone through many times in many different locales. "You look fit to lead an army," she said proudly. It was a refrain she'd repeated many times as well.

Marsden smiled nevertheless. "Thank you, my dear," he said. He gave her a peck on the cheek and waved to his children before descending the steps and striding off down the hill. "Be good, you two!" he shouted.

Matthew and Helen waved at him. The boy then executed a snappy salute, which his father returned with equal professionalism. Yet another ritual neither party tired of.

Before Marsden had gone more than a few paces, a soldier rode out from the settlement, leading a spare horse at the gallop toward him. The soldier, a young corporal, pulled up just short of his senior officer. "Sorry I'm late, Captain," the corporal said, saluting smartly.

Marsden returned the salute and mounted the spare horse without so much as a word to his subordinate who was several minutes late returning his horse from the blacksmith's where it was being re-shoed. His silence signalled to Corporal Angus Davies he wasn't impressed by his tardiness. The chastened soldier followed his senior officer back toward the settlement at a slow trot.

Finally, Marsden glanced around at Davies. "Has Lord Cheetham been advised of the Hoogley's arrival, Corporal Davies?"

"Yes, sir!" Davies responded. "Private Withers is fetching him now."

"Very good." With that Marsden dug his heels into his mount and, with his subordinate following close behind, galloped along a track that veered right and took him along the riverbank toward the wharf where the schooner would soon berth.

At that moment, at the mansion that was home to Lord Bertram Cheetham, or *Bertie* as the soldiers called him behind his back, Private Jonathon Withers was pulling on the pretentiously oversized doorbell that hung from the front door.

Everything about the mansion was pretentious—from the ornately carved balustrades that lined the ground floor and first floor verandas to the ornate Italian chandeliers visible through one of the upstairs windows to the English-style country garden that extended a good fifty yards beyond the back of the house. Two elderly Aboriginal gardeners were tending the grounds at that very moment. In the heat, they seemed to be working in slow motion.

For Withers, this was his first visit to the mansion. The wide-eyed private couldn't believe how out of place the structure looked—located as it was amongst the scattering of modest dwellings, stores and workshops that made up the fledgling township that was Brisbane Town.

Withers was about to ring the bell again when footsteps alerted him to a presence within the mansion. The door opened to reveal an Aboriginal girl who looked no older than sixteen. She was, Withers guessed, one of the many local Quandamooka girls he'd heard visited the commandant's mansion when summonsed.

"Master will be down soon, Mister," the girl mumbled, revealing several missing teeth.

Despite the absent molars, she was by no means the ugliest Aboriginal girl Withers had seen in the short time he'd been in Moreton Bay. Before he had a chance to respond to the girl, Lord Cheetham himself appeared in the doorway.

The commandant looked beyond Withers to the waiting horse-drawn cart before returning his gaze to the young soldier standing before him. Unimpressed a lowly private had been sent to collect him, Cheetham muttered something unintelligible to the girl and then, with some difficulty, descended the front steps and walked unsteadily toward the cart.

Following close behind, Withers wondered if the older man was drunk. In fact, Cheetham *was* intoxicated, but alcohol wasn't to blame. Though he was certainly partial to the odd tipple or two—gin being his preference—it was opium that was the cause of his present state. He'd spent the afternoon smoking it. His penchant for the drug was an open secret, and some considered he was on his way to becoming an addict.

This was the first time Withers had seen Cheetham up close. A short, rotund, pompous-looking man conspicuously overdressed for the environment and the conditions, he did, in Withers' opinion, need only the addition of a monocle to complete the English gentry image he so obviously wanted to portray. Withers thought he looked like he belonged within the hallowed walls of some London gentleman's club, not out here in the harsh Australian sun.

Cheetham needed assistance to climb aboard the cart. Instead of asking Withers to help him, he simply fixed the private with a steely stare. Withers jumped to and helped the older man aboard. This was achieved after some considerable huffing and puffing. Only now did he note his passenger carried a folded umbrella—a mauve sun umbrella of all things.

By the time Cheetham was seated near the tailboard, he was already sweating like a pig. "Let's go, man!" he snapped. "We can't keep His Majesty's forces waiting."

"Yes, sir . . . ah . . . no sir," Withers replied as he jumped aboard. After releasing the cart's handbrake and urging the two horses to start pulling their fare, they were on their way.

As they followed the track back to the penal settlement, Withers glanced behind him and was amused to see Cheetham shading himself beneath his now open sun umbrella, clearly oblivious to how ridiculous he looked.

3

T HE HOOGLEY'S MASTER ENSURED THE schooner entered the river mouth
equidistant from the left and right banks to avoid the unseen sandbanks
hard-earned experience had taught him were there, just beneath the surface.
Squinting into the late afternoon sun, the captain spotted a huge saltwater crocodile
just before its distinctive snout disappeared under the water. Directly ahead, about
half-a-mile distant, he could see the wharf that marked journey's end.

The schooner's arrival had been delayed by an unhelpful outgoing tide, which
forced the vessel to anchor out in Moreton Bay, or *the bay* as locals called it, for
several hours. Ships could only enter the river mouth during an incoming tide or,
better still, at full tide. More than a few ships' masters had paid the price after
disregarding this unwritten rule.

From below, the captain could hear shouting as his men readied the vessel's cargo
of convicts for the next chapter in their brutal lives. The shouting was coming from
the guards who were busy unshackling the convicts.

Below deck, John Graham and Noel Thomas awaited their turn to be unshackled.
All around them, convicts gingerly pushed themselves to their feet as their chains
were removed. The chains had left their ankles bruised and sore, and the skin around
them red and raw. For most of the men, it was the first time they'd been able to
stand in six days. For some, standing was a bridge too far; one poor sod fainted and
others had to be propped up by their fellows.

A guard finally arrived in front of the two Irish friends and their ailing Dublin
companion Leith Donovan, and he bent down and unlocked the chain that secured
the ankles of all three. "There you go, me lovelies," he chuckled as he walked away.
"You're free now . . . until you get topside."

Only as he wandered off did John and Noel recognise him as the same
Englishman who had refused to help Donovan earlier. They rubbed their ankles to
get the blood flowing before struggling to their feet. Standing was beyond their
companion so between them they hauled him to his feet.

Throughout all this the guards were haranguing the convicts, urging them to get
topside. "It's time to get the hell off our boat!" one of them grumbled. Six days
aboard the rust bucket that was *the Hoogley* had clearly gotten to the guards and crew
almost as much as it had the convicts.

Before John and Noel had taken a single step, Donovan slumped to the deck.
None of the others noticed. The guards were too busy unshackling the last of the
convicts, and the convicts themselves were too busy with their own problems to
worry about anyone else's.

Noel quickly checked Donovan's breathing. "Feck! I think he's dead," Noel said.

"Check his pulse," John suggested.

Noel checked the older man's pulse. "He's gone," he said simply.

"Poor bugger," John muttered. After a quick glance to confirm no-one else was looking his way, he reached into Donovan's trouser pockets and pulled out two coins. His and Noel's eyes lit up when he saw he was holding two gold sovereigns. The men realised these represented the deceased's life savings, which he'd somehow managed to keep concealed from the guards.

Noel held out his hand expectantly, but John shook his head. "Finders keepers," he grinned.

"Feckin' bastard!" Noel muttered as John pocketed the coins. He was miffed because, where money was involved, friendship came a distant second as far as John was concerned.

Ever the opportunist and blindingly oblivious to Noel's annoyance, John's eyes were drawn to a silver crucifix hanging from Donovan's neck. He reached down and tugged it hard. The crucifix and the chain it hung from came away in his hand, and he quickly pocketed his ill-gotten gains. Sensing Noel's critical eyes upon him, he muttered, "Never know . . . I might be able to trade it for some rum . . . or maybe for some time with a god-fearing whore."

Noel nodded glumly, still pissed at his friend's selfishness.

John looked around for the nearest guard. "We have a dead man here!" he announced. When the guards showed no interest he repeated his announcement, only louder.

Finally, the same guard who had unshackled them approached. After a cursory inspection of the deceased, he asked another guard to unlock a trapdoor in the hull. He then turned to the two Irishmen. "Grab a leg each," he ordered. With that, he bent down and grabbed Donovan under the armpits.

John and Noel looked at each other then did as they'd been instructed, each grabbing one of Donovan's legs. With that, the unlikely trio shuffled toward the now open trapdoor. Through it they could see the river.

Only now did Noel realise what was in store for Donovan. He looked at the guard. "Do ye not think he's worth a Christian burial?" he asked.

The guard looked around at his fellow guards. "Did you hear that?" he asked. When he saw he had the attention of the others, he said, "One of these Irish bastards asked if we should give this'n a Christian burial. What d'ya think?"

The other guards thought that a great joke. "Sure," one of them said, laughing. "And maybe we should 'ave a wake for 'im, too!" This prompted more laughter.

"And we could invite the fuckin' Governor," another suggested.

Still more laughter.

By now Donovan's body was in front of the trapdoor. The same guard who had been helping carry Donovan uttered an oft-quoted blasphemous prayer that was a favourite of the guards, advising God and all within earshot that "Here comes another Irish goodfernothin' for Ye to send straight to hell, Amen." And with that he pushed the body through the opening.

Before the trapdoor swung shut, John and Noel caught a glimpse of a large saltwater crocodile grab the body in its jaws. Both men automatically closed their eyes and made the sign of the cross. Suddenly anxious to escape this place of death, they joined the other convicts and climbed topside.

Above deck, the glare of the sun almost blinded them. Here, they noticed, guards had been joined by armed Redcoats who lined the convicts up in rows and supervised the shackling of their charges. The soldiers watched as leg-irons were secured to the ankles of each convict. The new arrivals got the distinct impression that escape was out of the question, which was the exact impression the authorities wished to instil in them.

There were chaotic scenes as convicts stumbled about, unable to cope with standing upright after so many days chained below deck, while soldiers and guards shouted at them. Two convicts fainted and several others would have keeled over had they not had the support of their fellows.

As their eyes became accustomed to the glare, John and Noel took in their new surroundings.

The first thing John noticed was the British ensign, which fluttered proudly in the faint breeze above the schooner's stern. The breeze only served to distribute the afternoon heat, so it brought the convicts and soldiers no respite. They were all sweating profusely.

The first person John noticed was Captain Tom Marsden who sat astride his horse on the riverbank. Marsden, like the other Redcoats around him, was resplendent in his smart uniform. John watched him as he calmly relayed orders to his men who, he observed, carried out those orders without hesitation. It was obvious the captain ran a tight operation.

Further along the bank, John saw a collection of bivouacs and lean-tos that obviously belonged to the Quandamooka who had taken up residence. Some of the natives, he noted, sat or slept in whatever shade there was; others wandered about listlessly, and a few speared fish along the riverbank. They were, he decided, a sorry looking lot. Some of the menfolk appeared drunk, and one or two of the women, too.

Rowdy Aboriginal children played a game John didn't recognise. The children at least seemed happy enough. To John's dismay, some of them frolicked in the river, or, rather, at the water's edge, seemingly oblivious to the ever-present danger of crocodiles. He wasn't to know the children, and their parents, were very aware of the potential danger, but had developed a sixth sense that warned them when a croc was in the vicinity. Most times at least.

Beyond the Quandamooka, he could just make out the buildings he assumed belonged to the penal settlement. Their dilapidated condition didn't inspire him, and he hoped he was mistaken in his assumption.

A white cottage on a rise above the settlement caught his attention. He couldn't help thinking how out of place it looked.

Observing the new arrivals from the riverbank, Marsden considered they looked a sorry lot—haggard and unshaven. Worse than the usual batch of convicts he took delivery of from Parramatta. He put that down to the stormy conditions the schooner's master had advised him they'd encountered en route.

Marsden's gaze rested on John Graham. One look at the Irishman told him he would be capable of putting in a good day's work—always a priority for him when assessing the likely worth of new arrivals. John looked stronger and fitter than most of his fellow convicts. He looked determined, too, surveying his surroundings through those startling blue eyes.

John chose that moment to look directly at Marsden. The two held each other's gaze for one long moment before John finally looked away.

4

AFTER A SHAMBLES OF A roll call—prolonged somewhat by the duty clerk's having to record the name, age, nationality and occupation of every convict—the new arrivals filed down the schooner's gangplank.

Soldiers on horseback escorted the convicts to the penal settlement. There was some urgency because the shadows were lengthening and Marsden wanted the newcomers squared away in their quarters before nightfall. And he knew Lord Cheetham was awaiting them.

Although only a quarter-of-a-mile, it seemed more like a hundred miles to men weakened by sea-sickness, hunger, thirst, dysentery and a dozen other ailments. Their every step was marked by the clink of chains and leg-irons. That aside, the only other sounds were the obligatory curses from the soldiers, the clip-clop of their horses' hooves and the occasional crack of a whip. The convicts were too exhausted even to complain.

Mercifully, Marsden had ordered a generous ration of water for the newcomers before they'd disembarked from the schooner, and that was welcome relief for men whose throats were parched dry.

John considered the captain's thoughtfulness bode well for their stay at Moreton Bay.

Marsden rode at the head of the caravan of soldiers and convicts. Every now and then he glanced around to observe the new arrivals. Each time he did so, John noted, he studied the faces of the convicts as if to assess and memorise them. Once, he looked directly at John who held his gaze a second time. This time it was Marsden's turn to look away.

Along the route, the Quandamooka, or those of them who were awake at least, surveyed the latest batch of convicts with little more than passing interest. It was a sight they were well used to.

The resident convicts showed considerably more interest in the new arrivals as they walked along the riverbank. Leg irons aside, the former were easily distinguishable from the soldiers. All wore long-sleeved, grey-blue shirts and breeches, wide-brimmed hats and work boots. Some were returning from the nearby quarry, though the newcomers weren't to know that. They marched with an escort of guards and foremen, also on foot, and soldiers on horseback. A horse-drawn cart followed, piled high with shovels, pick-axes and other tools.

Other convicts were engaged in a myriad of other tasks around the settlement, repairing huts, erecting fences, digging in new vegetable gardens and weeding established ones, constructing stone paths and sinking a well. A teenage convict staggered amongst the work gangs, free of leg-irons but hampered by the two heavy water buckets he carried. He stopped every so often to dispense a mug-full of water to a grateful convict and, when the guards weren't looking, to gulp down a mouthful himself.

Everywhere, the crack of whips could be heard as soldiers exhorted their exhausted charges to work harder and faster. Kind words, apparently, weren't as effective.

John's first impression of Moreton Bay's convicts was they appeared undernourished, haggard and dispirited—even more so than their counterparts at Parramatta.

Grumblings could be heard from every quarter. The convicts complained about the soldiers and anything else that came to mind, and the soldiers complained about the convicts and just about everything else.

John was able to detect a dozen different accents—possibly more. Amongst the soldiers these included accents covering all the home unions excepting Northern Ireland with English being predominant followed by Scottish and Welsh in that order; and amongst the convicts there were a good number of English and Irish accents, a few Welsh and Scottish accents, and even an American accent.

John identified the owner of the American accent as an African-American who was as black as any Aborigine and who, he'd learn later, had lived in Birmingham until he'd been found guilty of murdering his white lover's husband—a crime, which, for some strange reason, he'd proudly admitted to. How he had avoided the death penalty was anyone's guess.

Switching his attention back to the soldiers, John noticed that while those of lower rank carried the familiar smoothbore muskets that had served the British Army so well for so long, those of senior rank carried a musket-like weapon he'd never seen before. He wasn't to know the weapon was the *Infantry Rifle*, a flintlock rifle used with some success during the Napoleonic Wars. The army, in its wisdom, had decided to test the rifle's effectiveness in one of its penal settlements—and Moreton Bay had been chosen. The *Infantry Rifle* would be phased in to replace the musket in the coming months.

As they approached the settlement, the duty sergeant launched into a dissertation that would continue until they reached their destination. Sergeant Charlie Benson, a burly veteran who brooked no tardiness from the convicts or from the soldiers under him, began by assuring the new arrivals in the strongest of Devon accents they'd be flogged unmercifully if they broke any of the settlement's rules, and he finished by telling them they'd be flogged unmercifully if they broke any of the settlement's rules. In between those two gems of information, he warned the convicts what the future held for them.

"If ye thought Parra was hard, ye'll soon change yer minds, I can promise ye that," Sergeant Benson barked, referring to the soft lives he considered the convicts had led at Parramatta.

"What's dat Englishman talkin' about?" one wizened old Irish convict asked his companions.

"Fecked if I know," another Irishman said.

This brief interchange prompted laughter amongst men who hadn't had a lot to laugh about over the past week.

Benson rounded on the Irishmen, his already sunburnt face bright red with anger. "Shuddup you men or I'll have ye drawn and quartered!" he shouted.

When the convicts concerned threw more cheek the sergeant's way, a soldier grabbed the whip that hung from his saddle and tried to lash the nearest offender. Unfortunately, the whip landed across the shoulders of an innocent party who immediately protested and who received another lash because of it. This sparked yet more laughter, prompting the soldier with the bad aim to start lashing all convicts within range.

"Enough!"

It was Marsden who spoke. Glaring at the convicts, he said, "The next man to step out of line will receive a hundred lashes."

The warning was delivered so quietly, the men had to strain to hear him, but they got the message. None of them said another word.

Having recovered his composure, Sergeant Benson resumed his speech. John tried to block him out, but wasn't successful. He was alarmed to hear the words *flogging* and *lashing* and *whipping* featured in every second sentence, and they were said with relish.

On arrival at the settlement, the convicts were surprised to find there was no boundary wall in sight. Not even a solitary guard tower. There didn't even seem to be any sentries on duty, although armed Redcoats could be seen in every direction. Several convicts commented on this amongst themselves.

John sensed that walls and sentries weren't required for a prison that was many hundreds of miles from civilization and surrounded by an immense unexplored continent on one side and an even more immense ocean on the other. But he kept those thoughts to himself.

Noel glanced at John and noticed he was busy studying the timber huts that obviously served as accommodation for the convicts. "Well, this place sure looks fit for a king," he observed with more than a touch of sarcasm.

Neither man was impressed by what they saw. The ramshackle dwellings, which the pair would soon learn were referred to as *lodges* by the army, were little more than hastily erected shacks. Each only appeared to have one barred window—small but big enough to let the rain in, not to mention the creepy-crawlies—and a tin roof, which would no doubt heat up like an oven whenever the sun shone. And the huts were small. Surprisingly small given the number of convicts they had to house.

"How many huts can you see?" a concerned John asked his friend.

Noel scanned the settlement. "I can only see six," he said.

"Me, too. And how many men would each hut take, do you reckon?"

"I dunno. They're bloody small."

"I reckon they'd hold twenty men maximum."

Noel concurred. He and John looked around them, trying to establish how many convicts resided at Moreton Bay. After some arguing they agreed there must be close to two hundred, counting their lot.

They were partly correct. There *were* two hundred convicts at Moreton Bay, but their arrival had just boosted the convict population to two hundred-and-thirty-eight.

And they were correct to have misgivings about their accommodation. The huts, which were designed to sleep twenty men, each had to accommodate thirty-three on average. Today's new arrivals would swell the numbers allocated to each hut to nigh on forty.

John did the math quickly in his head. "Christ, it's gonna be standing room only in there." He nodded to the nearest hut.

Noel looked at the unoccupied hut John had indicated. Its front and only door was open, and he could see through to the hut's rear wall. His assessment was there was hardly room to swing a cat inside. He looked up at the cottage that had caught John's eye earlier. "Perhaps they'll billet us up there," he said hopefully.

John managed the faintest of smiles. "Yeah and perhaps the Pope will invite us to board at the Vatican."

For John and Noel and the other new arrivals it was now very evident that Moreton Bay penal settlement was a shanty town compared to where they'd come from.

At the Marsden cottage that had caught the Irishmen's eye, Helen and Matthew were standing on the veranda watching their father and the other soldiers escort the newly arrived convicts into the penal settlement below. Dusk was fast descending, and the soldiers and their charges were barely visible in the gloom.

"Mama!" Matthew called. "Come and see papa."

"Too busy, child," Missus Marsden said. She and her Aboriginal maid were in the kitchen at the rear of the cottage, peeling freshly dug potatoes in preparation for the evening meal.

"Mama!" Matthew whined.

"Mama's busy, Matthew," Helen said. A movement to her right caught her attention. She looked around to see Lieutenant Hogan emerge on horseback from the bush beyond the cottage. Adorned in his red tunic, he looked as dashing as usual.

Hogan noticed Helen and executed a respectful salute in her direction. The young Englishwoman returned his acknowledgement with a shy wave. She considered the lieutenant quite handsome, but she wasn't about to let him know that.

The interchange was noticed by an observant Missus Marsden who, unbeknown to her children, had come to the front door to see whatever it was that Matthew had summonsed her to look at. An admirer of Lieutenant Hogan, she waved at him. He returned the older woman's greeting with a smile.

Unaware her mother had left the kitchen, and thinking Hogan's smile was for her, Helen returned the smile. Her smile faded when the other members of the lieutenant's hunting party emerged from the bush.

The two soldiers who had accompanied Hogan on the hunt for the escapees were escorting their prisoner, the young Cockney Frank Patterson, who was tethered by rope tied to the saddle of one of their horses. The exhausted Patterson was bloodied and bruised, and almost unrecognisable after surviving the exhausting trek from the interior. Having been dragged behind the horse for much of the journey, he'd been stripped of all his clothing and was covered in scratches.

Missus Marsden and her children were shocked by the sight. She hurriedly pulled Matthew inside and called to her daughter to follow.

Helen couldn't move. She was transfixed, and her heart went out to the captured convict who was clearly on his last legs. At that moment, Patterson lost his footing and was now literally dragged behind the soldier's horse.

Finally, the tracker appeared. In addition to the weapons he carried, Barega was lugging a kangaroo he'd killed on the trek back to the bay. He dropped the carcass to the ground beneath the fig tree then turned to Helen. "Tell Captain I get later," he said, pointing to the carcass.

Helen nodded and hurried inside. She had no time for the tracker. Something about him frightened her. Unfortunately, she had to see a lot of Barega as he was a regular companion of their maid Orana, and the pair lived together in an annex to the shed behind the cottage.

5

THE LIGHT HAD ALL BUT faded when the newly arrived convicts found themselves in a large, dusty courtyard in the middle of the settlement. Situated behind large stables, it was concealed from the view of settlers or other passers-by—and for good reason. It was the setting for frequent floggings and hangings. Here, the convicts were greeted by the sight of a heavily perspiring, overdressed Cheetham, unashamedly sitting beneath his mauve sun umbrella even though the last of the sun's rays had disappeared. To be fair, it was still hot and humid, but the umbrella was altogether unnecessary. The pompous commandant was reclining atop the same horse-drawn cart he'd arrived in earlier.

To complete the bizarre scene, the cart was parked between the whipping post and the gallows. A rope noose hung from the latter, and the blood of untold numbers of hapless convicts, still faintly visible in the gloom, stained the former.

Cheetham's sweaty face looked like thunder. He never liked being kept waiting at the best of times. To be kept waiting by *a bunch of lowly rabble,* as he called the convicts, was especially irksome.

Private Withers stood next to the cart, as Cheetham had ordered, trying his best not to faint in the heat and trying harder still to look invisible to the men now facing him. He was acutely aware how ridiculous the eccentric commandant, and himself by association, must appear to them.

In their exhausted state, the convicts didn't know what to make of the extraordinary sight. One or two thought they might be seeing things, and said as much, too.

"Quiet in the ranks!" Sergeant Benson bawled.

The convicts and their military escort waited in silence while Marsden rode over to report to Cheetham.

As he approached his superior, Marsden willed him to stand to greet him. After all, military and civilian etiquette demanded that, and it would demonstrate to the men—the soldiers and convicts alike—that he was respected here. But he knew there was no hope of that. Cheetham considered he was above such courtesies and viewed everyone else at Moreton Bay, from Marsden down, as his inferiors.

When Marsden reined in his horse in front of the cart, Cheetham executed a limp-wristed, wish-washy salute so lacking in enthusiasm that the captain wondered whether to even return it. In the end, he delivered a snappy salute, which he hoped would serve as an example to his men.

"What kept you, Captain? Cheetham asked.

"Sorry, my Lord," Marsden said. "The Hoogley was a little late and—"

"Never mind," an impatient Cheetham interjected. Looking at the convicts, he asked, "Where is this lot from?"

Amazed his opposite could ask so stupid a question, Marsden was tempted to say "From the moon, sir." Instead he said, "From Parramatta, sir, via Sydney Town."

"Ah, yes . . . of course." Cheetham glanced over at the assembled. "More Irish, eh?"

"Afraid so, sir," Marsden concurred. "Most of them at least."

"Ah well . . ." Cheetham clearly wasn't enthralled by that bit of news.

Looking into the commandant's glassy eyes, Marsden could tell at once he'd been indulging himself again. It was common knowledge Cheetham used opium whenever he could lay his hands on it. Eccentric at the best of times, he was impossible when under the influence. And he was clearly under the influence now.

After a long almost embarrassing silence, Cheetham motioned to the captain to proceed. "Carry on, Captain," he mumbled.

"Yes, sir." Marsden turned and nodded to Sergeant Benson who was now on foot and standing close by.

Benson turned to the assembled convicts. "You prisoners of His Majesty's are now residents of the Moreton Bay Penal Settlement," he announced in a voice that all could hear. He then formally introduced Cheetham and Marsden to them before verbally delivering, from memory, a depressingly long list of the settlement's rules—much of it a repeat of his earlier dissertation. As before, his delivery was punctuated by frequent profanities and constant assurances the convicts would be flogged if they broke the rules.

Throughout the sergeant's address, the convicts glared at the armed soldiers guarding them, and the soldiers glared right back. Some mouthed insults at their opposites, and the odd obscene gesture was surreptitiously flashed in the direction of certain individuals. It's fair to say there was no love lost at all between the two factions. Aggrieved parties made a mental note to avenge the insults later.

John noticed Noel had entered into a staring contest with a cherubic-faced English corporal who looked like he should still be at school. Neither man was prepared to back down. John nudged his friend to suggest he behave, but Noel remained steadfast. Only the announcement there was to be a roll call brought the contest to an end. The corporal had to help out so he hurried off, but not before promising Noel via sign language that he'd deal with him later. Noel blew the corporal a kiss as he departed.

The same harried clerk who had conducted the shambolic roll call aboard *the Hoogley* began calling out names from the manifest he'd prepared earlier. "Step forward when you hear your name!" he shouted. "O'Neill, Seamus."

Irishman Seamus O'Neill stepped forward.

The clerk continued, "Kennedy, Pat. Donovan, Luke. O'Driscoll, Sean. Thomas, Noel. Graham, John."

The aforementioned stepped forward as their names were called.

"Donovan, Leith," the clerk said to the amusement of the convicts. Leith was the Dubliner who had died a short time earlier aboard *the Hoogley* and whose name had miraculously reappeared on the clerk's list.

Several convicts laughed out loud. "It seems Donovan has to serve out his full term whether he likes it or not!" one wag shouted.

"Perhaps he didn't like the look of hell and decided to come back to us!" another said.

More laughter.

"Quiet you lot!" Sergeant Benson shouted. He turned to the clerk and indicated he should resume.

In the convicts' front ranks, John studied the silver crucifix he'd removed from Donovan's person and which he now wore round his neck. He fondled it admiringly.

Cheetham opted to climb down from the cart as the roll call ended. He achieved this, to the amusement of the assembled, only with some considerable assistance from Private Withers. Aware he now had everyone's attention, the portly commandant strutted up and down theatrically, his hands clasped behind his back. "I am Lord Cheetham," he reminded them, "king and emperor of all that you see around you." He walked along the front rank of convicts, looking each man in the eye and ever-oblivious to just how ridiculous he looked and sounded.

It was a routine the soldiers had witnessed many times. So many times it almost seemed normal to them.

Looking on, Marsden wondered yet again how such an incompetent had ended up running the penal settlement. It irked him that he, Marsden, was holding this place together, yet it was Cheetham who received all the credit. He noticed as the commandant reached John Graham he momentarily hesitated, as if mesmerised by the Irishman's startling blue eyes.

Cheetham walked on for a few steps then turned around and pointed to Marsden. "As head warden, Captain Marsden oversees the everyday running of the settlement," he said. "He can be your best friend, or your worst enemy. It is up to you." Cheetham let the statement hang.

The impact of this little bit of theatre was weakened somewhat by the arrival of Lieutenant Hogan's hunting party. Still on horseback, Hogan rode into the compound closely followed by Barega, the two soldiers and their bloodied, bruised and still naked prisoner.

Convicts and soldiers alike watched in shocked silence as Hogan acknowledged Cheetham and then rode to Marsden's side to report on the day's events. A grim-faced Marsden listened as his fellow officer explained how the tracker had killed the other two escapees before he could be stopped. Hogan stressed that Barega had gone against orders in acting as he had. Marsden wasn't convinced, but determined to have it out with his subordinate, and with Barega, too, at a more appropriate time.

Cheetham, who was anxious to regain the attention of his audience, coughed pointedly to signal that now was not the time for a mission debrief. The two officers took the hint and separated.

Turning back to the assembled convicts, Cheetham surveyed them coldly then looked over at Patterson who had just fallen to his knees. "What splendid timing," he said. "This wretched chap is living proof of the perils that await you beyond this settlement. This country is like nothing you could imagine. The dangers it holds are too many to mention."

As the speech continued, John and the other convicts couldn't take their eyes off the long-legged tracker Barega. Though he'd obviously travelled on foot, Barega looked as fresh as a lily. He still carried the traditional weapons he had used so effectively in the bush. Covered only by a loincloth, the only concession he made to European influence was the long-bladed hunting knife he'd taken from Patterson. It now hung from his waist.

The tracker, now aware he was the object of the convicts' attention, grinned malevolently their way. He looked directly at John, and his grin widened.

Cheetham continued, "For all intents and purposes, you are now in hell. And for those of you foolish enough to try to escape"—he nodded yet again toward Patterson—"that is what awaits you." Then, pointing at Barega, he added, "Or if you are unlucky you end up as supper for that one's cousins."

The tracker's malevolent grin widened still more when he realised he'd been mentioned.

Cheetham turned back to Marsden. "Over to you, Captain." The commandant then snapped his fingers in Withers' direction and weaved his way unsteadily back toward the waiting cart.

As Private Withers hurried to assist Cheetham up onto the cart, Marsden ordered the same two soldiers who had dragged Frank Patterson in to take him to the cell block for the night. He then ordered Sergeant Benson to get the new arrivals settled in.

The captain was about to leave when he saw the master of *the Hoogley* enter the compound, carrying a large package. The seaman walked straight over to Cheetham, who was now seated atop the cart, and handed the package up to him. Given the eagerness with which the commandant accepted the package, Marsden had a pretty good idea what it contained.

For the convicts who arrived aboard *the Hoogley*, their first night at Moreton Bay was a continuation of the nightmare that had begun with their incarceration aboard the schooner six days earlier. The awful deprivations they'd suffered at sea continued, albeit in different ways, here in the middle of nowhere.

Before the night ended, another three new arrivals would die—one from exhaustion, one with a mystery ailment and another who was already near death but was helped on his way by violent convicts he'd inadvertently offended—and half a dozen more came down with a variety of serious complaints, which included diarrhoea and influenza.

The night began well enough for each man with a quick shower in the ablutions block. *Block* was something of a misnomer for it comprised nothing more than a fenced-off area beneath one of the settlement's two huge, free-standing water towers. Small holes punched into the bottom of buckets that hung suspended beneath the tower ensured a generous supply of cold water escaped, and a clever piping system ensured the buckets were automatically refilled as soon as they emptied.

The soldiers made use of an identical system beneath the second tower while the officers had use of a private bath, complete with hot water, in their quarters.

No soap was supplied for the convicts to use, but at least the water was refreshing for men who hadn't showered in over a week. They would learn later that summer showers were something of a luxury at Moreton Bay: unseasonal rains had recently filled the towers' tanks, which were often near-empty this time of year.

Unfortunately, water from the nearby tidal river was unsuitable for drinking or showering. Being so close to the sea, it was more saltwater than fresh, hence the presence of saltwater crocs. Not even the residents of the township a quarter-of-a-mile upstream could drink the water—not when the bay was at high tide at least.

Showering was hardly a private affair either. The area beneath the convicts' water tower wasn't screened off, so the men were exposed to all and sundry. Consequently, they became the butt of many a joke cracked by fellow convicts and soldiers who happened to be in the vicinity.

The guards had unshackled the new arrivals so they could undress before showering. After showering, the still naked men were herded to a storage hut where army stores personnel handed out new clothes, wide-brimmed hats and work boots for all. It was a mad grab to claim items that looked like a reasonable fit. Not everyone was happy. Some ended up with ill-fitting clothes or boots, or both. Fighting broke out as dissatisfied men tried to claim what they felt was rightfully theirs, and at one point guards had to step in with batons in hand to establish the peace.

Fortunately for John and Noel they got in quicker than many of the others, ending up with new clothes and footwear that fitted reasonably well. Noel's hat was the exception: it was several sizes too small to the amusement of his companions—one of whom observed it looked like a pimple on a pumpkin.

Next, each man was issued with cutlery, which comprised a well-used knife-fork-spoon set plus a tin bowl for porridge and soup, and a tin dish for main courses. The dishes had obviously been used before, the congealed remains of meals still visible in the bottom of many.

"If ye lose these, keep in mind there are no spare dishes or utensils," the head storeman announced. "So I suggest ye write your name on each item and don't lose it."

The guards then shackled their charges once more, attaching the familiar leg-irons to each man.

In their shackles and their blue-grey breeches and long-sleeved shirts, the new arrivals were now almost indistinguishable from the other convicts. Almost. The older hands stood out because the clothes that covered their gaunt frames were little more than tattered rags, and their work boots were long past their use-by date. The old hands also had that unsettling thousand-yard stare the newcomers had yet to acquire.

Next for the new arrivals came the eagerly-awaited evening meal. Again, for men who had been on starvation rations for the past week, they were looking forward to a half-decent feed.

It was about this point the evening deteriorated. Dinner was *served,* for want of a better word, in the convicts' mess. The mess was actually an annex to the stables, and the smell of horse shit and manure coming from the adjoining stables was overpowering. It was a smell they'd have to learn to tolerate because it never went away.

Looking around, John could see that except for those preparing the food they pretty much had the mess to themselves. He guessed the other convicts had eaten. At a pinch, he estimated, there seemed to be seating for around half the convict population.

Those doing the cooking were resident convicts fortunate enough to have been allocated soft kitchen duties over heavy outdoor labour. There were two of them on duty. Their idea of serving was to scoop modest portions of reheated food from a large, cast-iron cooking pot and throw the portions into each man's tin dish. It was a hit-and-miss process with some men ending up with smaller helpings than others. Complaints were met with abuse, which, in turn, attracted anger which threatened to turn into something more. Only the presence of guards prevented violence.

As for the food, it could only be described as slops. Almost unpalatable, it only vaguely resembled the stew it was meant to be. Despite that, the newcomers wolfed it down and lined up for seconds. They were disappointed to learn there were no second-helpings served in this mess. Not ever.

The elation felt by one Welsh convict who, for some reason, had ended up with more food on his plate that anyone else, was short-lived when he discovered a dead mouse in his watery stew. To the mirth of his comrades, he held the rodent up by the tail and rounded on the convict who had served him, demanding to know who the chef was. When those concerned laughed at his plight, he released a stream of profanities—first in English and then, when he'd exhausted them, in Gaelic—and then threw the dead mouse out the open door.

While no-one commiserated with the unlucky Welshman, each made a mental note to check his food before eating it in future.

With dinner now out of the way, the guards ordered the new arrivals to line up in half a dozen separate groups. John and Noel joined Seamus O'Neill and Pat Kennedy, two Irishmen they'd befriended at Parra, and they roped in another couple—Irishman Sean O'Driscoll and Scotsman Angus McPherson—whom they'd established a passing acquaintance with.

That done, guards then escorted each group to separate huts—the rationale being it was better to split up the mainly Irish convicts throughout the settlement and thereby reduce the likelihood of rebellion. Good in theory at least.

John's group was escorted toward one of the nearest huts. Its door was open and the faint lamplight within revealed it was already very overcrowded.

"Holy mother of God," O'Neill mumbled when he saw what awaited them.

"She's not gonna help us," Kennedy observed.

"Where they gonna put us?" John enquired of one of the guards, a surly

Northerner.

"Shuddup Irish!" the guard snapped.

John was about to respond with a wisecrack, but thought better of it. The Northerner was holding a rifle in one hand and a baton in the other, and he looked keen to use either one or both.

Another guard strode ahead of the small group and stopped in front of the open doorway. "Make way for the new men, you lot!" he barked at the hut's residents.

Grumbles from within signalled the residents weren't happy about having to welcome more men to their already overcrowded quarters.

"Where you expect us to sleep with this lot on board?" one convict asked.

"That's your problem!" the same guard responded.

"It's standing room only in here!" another convict shouted.

Ignoring the complaints, the guards unshackled John and the others then bundled them through the open doorway and slammed the door shut before locking it.

"Sleep well me hearties!" the Northerner shouted. He and the other guards walked off, the shouts and curses of angry convicts ringing in their ears. All around them, the same familiar routine was being repeated as small groups of convicts were introduced to their new quarters.

6

I NSIDE THE FIRST HUT, JOHN and his companions literally had to push their way through the throng of convicts, so congested was it. They finally emerged into a clear area in the middle of the dwelling where at last they had some breathing space.

The first thing the newcomers noticed, besides the seething mass of humanity crowding around them, was the oppressive heat. With only one small barred window for ventilation, and a tin roof that continued to act like an oven well after the sun had gone down, the hut was unbearably hot and stuffy. So stuffy it was hard to breathe.

Silence prevailed as the hut's residents assessed the uninvited newcomers who had ended up in their midst.

"Bloody Irish!" an English convict said.

"How do you know that?" another Englishman asked. "They haven't even said a word yet."

"We don't need to hear 'em speak to know they're bloody Irish," yet another convict retorted.

"Well I certainly ain't Irish!" the non-Irish member of John's little group pointed out. Big Angus McPherson took exception to being labelled Irish. And his heavy Scottish brogue left no-one in doubt as to where he originally hailed from.

"Just what we need," an unseen Englishman called out, "another bloody Scotsman!"

This prompted some laughter amongst the assembled, which helped relieve the tension a little.

"Where you lot from?" a Cornishman asked.

"Ireland," O'Driscoll said.

"I realise that," the Cornishman replied. "I mean where was yer last stop?"

"Parra," Noel said, using the preferred abbreviation for Parramatta. "Where else would we be from?"

"There's bin talk of a shipment of lads from Norfolk Island sometime soon," a middle-aged Cockney said.

At the mention of the infamous Norfolk Island penal colony, several convicts gave the sign of the cross.

"I heard they learned how bad it is here and changed their minds," one comedian suggested.

This sparked more laughter.

John assessed the new faces around him. He could see they were a mixed lot, ranging in age from the teenage water boy they'd seen earlier to an elderly, toothless Liverpudlian who looked all of seventy. Many carried injuries, including sprains and bruises suffered in the course of their work or as a consequence of getting offside with over-zealous guards; as many again were ill with ailments ranging from minor colds and dysentery to what appeared to be serious viruses and pneumonia; some men had permanent, hacking coughs, and coughing could be heard coming from every hut throughout the settlement.

What stood out for John was that all the men looked worn out—more so than the convicts they'd left behind at Parra. Their gaunt faces were burnt and chaffed by the sun, their backs were bowed by hard labour and their hands were cracked and calloused. And then there was the thousand-yard stare he'd noticed earlier. *What did you poor bastards see that made you like that?* he asked himself. "Are there any other Irish here?" he asked. "Or are we it?"

"I'm Irish," a skinny little Dubliner announced. He stepped forward, hand extended, to introduce himself to John. "Paddy O'Donnell at your service."

John reluctantly accepted the other's hand. "And where were you when we needed a friendly smile?" he asked, referring to the frosty welcome he and his companions had received moments earlier.

O'Donnell mumbled something that sounded like an apology of sorts and backed away, unable to hold John's gaze.

More men stepped forward and introduced themselves to the newcomers. News was exchanged as the Parramatta lot relayed the latest events of note back there and in Sydney Town while the locals explained how things worked here at Moreton Bay.

As the men got to know each other, John surveyed his new quarters. He could see the dwelling comprised one large, single room. The dim lighting was supplied courtesy of a solitary lantern hanging just inside the door.

John caught sight of two large buckets sitting side by side in one corner of the room. One was labelled PISS BUCKET and the other labelled SHIT BUCKET, so he didn't need to ask what they were for.

A notice scrawled on the wall above the two buckets read:

> *Please pull chain after use, my dear boy.*
> *Signed*
> *Your Mother*

The shit bucket, John noticed, was close to overflowing, and the smell was putrid.

Extending out from the wall opposite the makeshift ablutions were three rows of wooden slat bunks stacked five high so the top bunks ended just shy of the ceiling, leaving little room for whoever drew short straws and ended up there. John counted fifteen bunks in total and, he estimated, there must be at least forty men in the overcrowded hut.

Out of the blue, as if he'd been reading John's mind, big Angus McPherson asked, "So where do we all sleep?"

No-one answered. There was some movement toward the rear of the room. Heads turned and the ranks parted to make way for a man so big he towered over everyone present.

Londoner Dan Green was, John decided, not only the biggest man in the hut, but quite possibly the biggest man he'd ever seen—and he'd seen some big bastards in his time. He realised Green must have been seated until now, otherwise he and the others would most certainly have noticed him.

Green stood all of seven foot tall, and, unlike fellow convicts who were mostly gaunt and haggard, he was one solid mass of prime beef. The Londoner's face was at odds with his huge physical presence. Rather than looking as though it had been carved from stone like his body, his face was round and chubby, and clean-shaven, too, more like an English office worker's face than a convict's. But the eyes were something else altogether. They were cold and cruel, and looked like they belonged in someone else's face.

Right now, Green's cruel eyes were fastened on McPherson—and John, like everyone else in the hut, immediately sensed trouble.

"Everyone sleeps where I tell 'em to sleep," Green said in an accent which revealed his working class upbringing. His was also a high pitched voice that surprised those who were meeting him for the first time.

"Is that a fact?" McPherson replied, seemingly unfazed by the bigger man. "And where would ye be thinking I'd be sleeping?"

Green's top lip curled into a snarl and he pointed to the shit bucket. "You can sleep on the shit bucket tonight," he said, his voice rising several octaves higher.

This prompted some nervous laughter from Green's allies. It also prompted McPherson to swing into action, his theory being if he acted first and got a lucky punch in he might get the jump on the giant standing in front of him. The Scotsman swung a mighty roundhouse right hook Green's way.

Fast though McPherson was, the Londoner was even quicker. Unbelievably quick for so huge a man. Green evaded the swinging fist and threw a right of his own that landed flush on McPherson's jaw, felling him. Stunned, the Scotsman could only lie there, looking up at the huge form hovering over him. The coup de gras was delivered courtesy of Green's left boot, which he stamped down hard on McPherson's nose, breaking it and rendering his victim unconscious.

The violent chain of events had happened so quickly it took everyone by surprise. Only now did John and his fellow Irishmen act. As one, they rushed Green, taking him to the floor beneath their combined weight. Two of them rained punches down on him while the other three stamped on him in their new boots.

Green managed to clock a couple of his assailants with his ham-sized fists, but he was getting the worst of it.

Throughout the assault, John was conscious of the other convicts—especially Green's friends. He decided they must be fair weather friends as none came to his rescue. Truth be known, the so-called friends were pleased to see the giant get what was coming to him.

Formidable though he was, Green was no match for five irate Irishmen, and he soon succumbed to the onslaught. When they were through, two of them—Noel and O'Driscoll—were displaying shiners that would be black and blue by morning.

John suggested they lug the now unconscious, bloodied Green over to the shit bucket he'd referred to earlier. This they did with some enthusiasm, and with some difficulty, too, hoisting him up into a sitting position atop the bucket. All this to the cheers of the other convicts.

The bully didn't look so formidable now. Chin on chest, his huge body seemed to have shrunk a little as he lay slumped, his back resting against the wall and his legs splayed out in front of him. His allies, or former allies perhaps, were looking at the unconscious Green differently now. He'd been proven human after all—even if it had taken five Irishmen to prove the point. Tomorrow may be a different story, after he'd recovered, but in the meantime they planned to enjoy the new dynamic that existed inside their tiny world.

There was no doubt the mood in the hut had suddenly changed. Everyone sensed a power shift had just occurred. The old hands crowded around the newcomers, slapping them on the back and welcoming them like old friends.

As soon as they could extricate themselves from the clutches of the others, John and Noel knelt down beside McPherson who was just regaining consciousness. Green's boot had left the Scotsman's nose broken and misshapen, and both eyes blackened. Despite that, he was still able to flash a faint grin.

"Did I give as good as I got?" McPherson asked.

"Aye, you should see 'im now," Noel chuckled.

The Irishmen helped their Scottish friend to his feet and immediately pointed to his attacker across the room.

It took McPherson a moment or two for his eyes to focus. Then he laughed when he saw the unfortunate Dan Green who was still atop the shit bucket and was only now starting to come round. "Did I do that?" an incredulous McPherson asked.

"Aye, you did," John confirmed with a straight face.

"We had to pull you off before you killed him," Noel added. He said it with an equally straight face, and McPherson didn't know whether his friends were pulling his leg or not. If they weren't, for the life of him he couldn't remember beating up the unfortunate Green, but he was happy to take the credit.

The sudden *clanging* of a baton on the bars of the hut's window announced the arrival of a guard.

"Lights out, me lovelies!" the guard shouted. "Get all the sleep ye can. You'll need it for what's ahead of ya, I can promise ye that."

One of the old hands hurried to extinguish the lamp, and the hut's interior was plunged into darkness. He and the others had learned to their cost that any delay in extinguishing the lamps at lights-out earned a flogging for every member of the hut concerned, so that was one task they carried out promptly.

The same guard could be heard chuckling to himself as he walked off to the next hut.

As the convicts' eyes adjusted to the semi-darkness, they could see well enough to move around and bed down for the night without stumbling over unseen objects. They were aided somewhat by the moonlight that filtered through the small window. Exterior lamps that had been hung up between the huts also provided some light for the huts' residents and for the guards on night patrol.

While sentries were considered unnecessary by day given there were always numerous soldiers on duty in and around the settlement, the nights were a different story; there had been a number of escape attempts after dark, and Captain Marsden had established a roster for night-time sentries soon after taking up his post.

The newly arrived convicts quickly realised that the old hands had the night-time routine off pat. Some bedded down on the bunks—oftentimes two per bunk—and the rest made themselves as comfortable as they could on the floor. At best there was one worn blanket per bunk, more often none at all. And there were no blankets for those who had to sleep on the floor. Convicts substituted spare clothes, towels, rags and whatever else they'd managed to scavenge as bedding. There were half a dozen pillows, but these had been commandeered by the hut's *top dogs*. Green was *the* top dog, of course, or at least he used to be.

No allowance was made for the newcomers. It was a case of *last in, last served*, as one convict explained. The same convict advised them, rather unnecessarily, that a pecking order had been established in each hut, and it was up to newcomers to find their own place in that order. It had been the same at Parramatta, and, they had no doubt, it was the same at every penal colony the world over. Until the convicts, prisoners, inmates—call them what you will—climbed the ladder, so to speak, they'd sleep on the floor.

There was one difference to the usual routine this night, however. Dan Green's bunk was unoccupied as the giant was still ensconced on the shit bucket he'd been deposited upon a while earlier. Green was obviously not with it. Badly concussed, he sat there, groaning, unable to work out where he was and what had happened to him.

"He won't be needin' his bunk tonight," Noel observed.

"Aye, he's away with the fairies," John agreed.

Noel turned to McPherson who was still poorly after the hiding he'd received, and was having trouble breathing through his broken nose. "C'mon Angus, let's get you to bed," he said. He and Kennedy helped the big Scotsman to the spare bunk and, after pumping the pillow, laid him down to sleep.

No-one tried to stop them or to claim Green's vacated bunk for himself. Already, it seemed, the pecking order in this hut at least was changing.

After the convicts climbed into their bunks, the newly arrived Irishmen joined a dozen other men on the floor, taking their lead from the older hands and sleeping as far away from the smelly buckets as they could. Even so, the stench followed them.

Despite the alien surroundings, the hardness of the timber floor beneath them, the stuffiness and the heat, the new arrivals fell asleep almost as soon as they lay down. Except for John. He remained wide awake.

Whether it was the fear of what the future held, or the snores and farts of his new sleeping companions that was keeping him awake, he wasn't sure, but whatever the reason he couldn't sleep.

Looking up at the bunks, he could see at least two thirds of them were occupied by two men. They lay top and tail, so each man had his companion's smelly feet in his face. Regardless, it seemed to work for them. Everyone was asleep—except for two men in one of the top bunks who, if John wasn't mistaken, had opted for an alternative to the top-and-tail position. In fact, if he wasn't imagining it, they were currently in the *doggy position*. This was confirmed almost immediately when their groans of passion carried to him.

John couldn't identify the pair in the dark, but he made a mental note which bunk was theirs so he could establish their identities in the morning. It was a security issue for him. He liked to know who was behind him whenever he had to bend down to pick something up.

Peace and quiet returned inside the hut, and John focused on trying to identify the sounds of the world outside. He identified the distinctive *hoot* of an owl away in the distance, and thought he heard the footsteps of a sentry doing his rounds. Somewhere, a dog barked. There were other faint sounds, too, but he couldn't make sense of them.

Curses and angry mutterings from the direction of the shit bucket alerted him to the fact that big Dan Green had finally worked out where he was, and he sounded none too impressed. Across the room, he could just make out Green's huge form. He'd just slid down onto the floor, having lapsed in and out of consciousness atop the bucket over the last hour. Now, he was trying to climb to his feet. That turned out to be beyond him, and he slumped down again.

Whether Green was asleep or unconscious, John couldn't tell. He didn't care either.

Lying here in the stifling Moreton Bay heat, exhausted after the hellish voyage from Sydney Town, listening to the snores of his fellow convicts and the sound of rats scurrying across the ceiling, flicking cockroaches and other bugs he could feel crawling over him, and being attacked by blood-sucking mosquitos, he wasn't feeling at all confident he would last the remaining five years in his seven-year sentence.

⊷ε•——•3⊶

John didn't know how long he'd been asleep when he sensed a movement behind him. He looked around and saw the giant form of Green standing over the bunk he considered his. The Londoner was looking down at the sleeping McPherson who was snoring contentedly.

Sensing trouble, John shook the two Irishmen on either side of him. Noel and Kennedy quickly took stock of the situation and joined John who was already on his feet.

"Don't even think about it," John warned the big Londoner.

Green slowly looked around at John and his companions. The giant appeared to be considering reclaiming his bunk, but finally thought better of it.

Even in the dark, John could tell Green wasn't himself. He'd been badly concussed and looked ready to topple over at any moment. Green seemed aware of his fragility and so weaved his way unsteadily across the room and lay down again—this time some distance from the two buckets.

John and his companions breathed a collective sigh of relief and bedded down once more. This time, John fell asleep immediately, his fingers around the silver crucifix he'd acquired.

7

◆⟶⟶◆

MORETON BAY'S CONVICTS WERE WOKEN by the dawn chorus of kookaburras. The unique birdcall, which sounds uncannily like human laughter, was a call the new arrivals were familiar with as they'd gotten to know it well at Parramatta.

Almost immediately, in John's hut, the sound was drowned out by the clanging of a guard's baton against the window's bars.

"Wakey, wakey, girls!" a gruff voice called out. "Time to rise!"

The wake-up call was greeted by curses and grumbles. Early risers dressed quickly and queued to use the piss bucket before it overflowed as it invariably did come dawn. Others waited for a guard to unlock the door so they could take their first leak of the day behind the hut. They didn't have long to wait: a guard soon obliged, and those who needed to poured outside and did their business.

John awoke to find he was still holding the silver crucifix that rested on his chest. Its touch no longer felt foreign to him and, in a strange way, it gave him hope. *False hope no doubt,* he thought.

Tired though he was, he had the presence of mind to look up at the top bunk that had accommodated the shenanigans he'd observed after lights-out. Only one occupant remained in the bunk. In the grey light of dawn, John identified him as Rhys Jones, the Welshman who had found the mouse in his evening meal. The Irishman determined to keep a wary eye on this particular Welshman in future.

All the new arrivals were so tired they remained where they were—half asleep on the floor; in McPherson's case, he remained fast asleep on his bunk. His broken nose had swollen during the night, his breathing sounded ragged and his face was badly bruised as a result of the punishment Dan Green had dished out.

John cast an eye around to look for the man responsible for the Scotsman's injuries, half expecting to see Green where he'd last seen him—with the other unfortunates on the floor. He wasn't entirely surprised to see the giant Londoner had commandeered another bunk for himself. It was a bunk formerly occupied by Paddy O'Donnell, the skinny little Dubliner who had somewhat belatedly introduced himself to his fellow Irishmen the previous evening. O'Donnell had ended up having to sleep on the floor and, judging by the way he was now stretching to ease his aches and pains, he hadn't enjoyed a good night's sleep.

John could sympathise: he felt stiff and sore all over, and was convinced he'd hardly slept a wink. And looking around at his companions nearby, he was certain they'd fared just as poorly.

As for Green, his huge frame was now perched on the edge of his bunk and he

44

was in deep discussion with one of his allies, Don Henderson, a surly Englishman. Every now and then one or other glanced in John's direction, leaving the Irishman in no doubt the pair were talking about him and his fellow Irishmen.

John noted with satisfaction the Londoner's face was still a bloody mess as a result of the beating he'd sustained. He caught Green looking at him and couldn't resist flashing a cheeky grin the big man's way. Green glared at him and resumed talking to Henderson. John immediately regretted his cockiness, fearing he could pay for it later. *Christ, Graham!* he silently chastised himself. *Think before you act, man.*

Four convicts the newcomers hadn't seen before filed into the hut. Each one resembled a robber or bushranger, having tied a handkerchief around his face to cover his nose. Ignoring the jeers and lewd comments being directed their way, they headed for the now overflowing piss bucket and the near-full shit bucket, which were being buzzed by a cloud of angry flies, and between the four of them carried their stinking loads from the hut. The smell, the flies and the heckling followed them out the door.

"Don't be too hard on them, boys," an older convict warned those doing the heckling. "It could be your fuckin' turn next week." The same convict advised John and the other new arrivals that four convicts were assigned latrine duties each week. "Your turn will come soon enough," he added.

By now, everyone was on his feet except for the new men. An old hand walked amongst them, kicking their feet to rouse them. "C'mon you lot!" he said. "It's the lash for ye if ye sleep in."

Grumbling, the Irishmen pushed themselves painfully to their feet.

In the gloom, John noted the shiner that Noel had sustained in last night's skirmish had turned an ugly purple. Their mate Sean O'Driscoll sported a shiner to match.

Noel realised he and O'Driscoll were the object of John's attention. "I know, we could be feckin' twins," he mumbled.

"Ugly twins at that," John said.

"You can say that again," Pat Kennedy agreed.

As the four Irishmen exchanged verbal jabs, their countryman Seamus O'Neill was shaking McPherson, trying to rouse him from his slumbers. "Hey!" O'Neill called to the others. "Angus ain't lookin' too good."

Noel and Kennedy joined him and found the Scotsman was unresponsive to O'Neill's efforts.

"Looks like he's in a coma," Kennedy said.

"Best get him to the infirmary," a concerned Noel said.

"What infirmary?" one of the old hands asked. "You'll find no infirmary here. Not for us convicts at least."

"Aye, there's a sickbay and doctor on hand for the Redcoats and the settlers, but not for us," another convict confirmed.

"Fuckin' Redcoats!" a Cockney convict cursed. He spat on the floor to emphasise his loathing for the soldiers.

The lack of medical care for the convicts came as sobering news for the newcomers. Even the Parramatta penal settlement, harsh though it was, provided at least a basic standard of medical care for its convict population.

Loud banging on the hut's door alerted those still inside the hut they were needed outside for the first roll call of the day. An armed guard was motioning to them with his thumb. "Outside you lot!" he ordered.

John walked to the door, but his friends remained where they were, beside McPherson's bunk. He looked back at them as he stepped outside. "C'mon lads," he called, "leave him be."

Ignoring John, Noel looked at the guard. "We have a man here in need of medical attention," he said.

The guard unshouldered his rifle and entered the hut. "I'll check on him," he said. "Meanwhile, you lot outside."

Noel and the others joined John outside the hut where they found several more armed guards watching over them and their fellow convicts. They saw the same scene was being repeated outside the other huts, and the shouts of angry guards and grumbling convicts could be heard throughout the settlement.

The guard who had been checking on McPherson emerged from the hut and said something to one of the other guards. He then turned to the Irishmen and said, "No-one's excused from work at Moreton Bay. Get the Irishman up and ready."

"He's not Irish, he's a Scot," Noel complained, "and he's too sick to work!"

The guard pointed his rifle at Noel. "I don't care if he's a bloody Hottentot!" he cursed. "Get him ready for work or I'll have you and him both flogged."

John steered Noel by the arm and led him back into the hut. "Watch your temper," he murmured, "or you'll be the death of us."

Inside the hut, they found McPherson still asleep. It took some effort to wake him. McPherson mumbled incoherently and was clearly having trouble breathing through his shattered nose. It was very evident to both Irishmen he was in bad shape. Both suspected he was concussed, though neither said as much.

"Let's get you outside," a sympathetic Noel said to McPherson as he and John lifted him off the bunk and, with quite some effort, half carried him to through the open door to join the others. Fortunately, the big Scotsman had bedded down fully clothed and was still wearing his boots, so at least they hadn't had to dress him.

Outside, Kennedy and O'Driscoll took over, supporting McPherson between them.

"What happened to him?" another guard enquired.

John and Noel recognised him as the surly Northerner who had abused them whilst escorting them to the hut the night before.

Noel looked around for Green then pointed directly at him. "Ask him," he said accusingly.

Green greeted the accusation with a sneer. The guard, James Whitelock, then walked over to speak to the Londoner. To the surprise of the new men, Whitelock laughed at something Green said before playfully punching the giant on the shoulder and moving on.

O'Donnell noted the surprised look on the faces of his fellow Irishmen. "Green's a convict-warden," he whispered.

John and his friends knew what that meant. Parra had had its share of convict-wardens, or convicts who curried the favour of their guards by acting as de facto guards or wardens. They were hated and feared by the other convicts who collectively referred to them as *lowlifes*. All too often, these lowlifes performed their duties zealously, and they had a well-deserved reputation for being as cruel as the official guards.

In return for helping keep their fellow convicts in line, the convict-wardens were rewarded with softer duties and extra rations and privileges. At Parra, those privileges had included free time with the settlement's prostitutes, or *comfort girls* as they were fondly called.

Here, at Moreton Bay, prostitutes wouldn't arrive for another two or three years. Until then, the convict-wardens had to content themselves with any local Quandamooka females who were prepared to exchange sexual favours for half a bottle of watered-down rum—as did the soldiers who had first pick of course. Some of the native girls who entered into such trades only looked about thirteen or maybe fourteen, but Marsden and the other officers turned a blind eye to that, so resigned were they to keeping the men happy.

As the guards shackled the waiting convicts and applied the accursed leg-irons to their charges, O'Donnell explained to the new arrivals what lay ahead of them on this, their first day at Moreton Bay. "Chances are you'll spend the day in the quarry," he said. "The captain likes to test newcomers on their first day—to see who is gonna last the distance."

The guards then conducted what would prove to be the first of several roll calls that day. They looked relieved that no-one from this hut had died or escaped during the night, and that all personnel were present and accounted for—even if there were a few walking wounded amongst them.

"Move out!" Whitelock shouted.

To the familiar *clink* of their shackles, the convicts then shuffled toward the mess where their first meal of the day awaited them. The new men hoped breakfast would be more enjoyable than the hastily prepared slops they'd had for dinner. The older hands knew better.

As they walked, John noticed convicts from a nearby hut digging a hole close to the hut's rear wall. Two convicts emerged from the same hut, struggling to support the weight of a fellow convict they carried between them. It soon became obvious the poor fellow was dead, and the hole was to be his final resting place. Sure enough, the convicts dropped the deceased into the hole, and, without further ceremony, those wielding the shovels began shovelling dirt over the body.

Nearby, other gravesites—each one marked by a small pile of stones—served as a graphic reminder that the life expectancy of Moreton Bay's convicts was depressingly short.

Looking around, John noticed numerous gravesites dotted around the settlement.

He counted forty such sites before he gave up, but he estimated there was probably that many again.

John surveyed his fellow convicts. On one side, he could see O'Driscoll and Kennedy were struggling to support McPherson who appeared to be delirious and whose movement was severely hindered by his shackles. Nearby, Green's status as a convict-warden was confirmed for John when he noticed the Londoner walked freely and unshackled. He also noticed that, unlike other long-serving Moreton Bay convicts, Green's uniform and boots appeared to be brand new.

Noting the current object of John's attention, the ever-alert O'Donnell said, "There's one like Green in every hut."

"A giant you mean?"

"No. A convict-warden." O'Donnell added, "I tried to warn you about him last night, but I didn't get the chance before you boys bashed him."

John didn't respond, but he now looked at Green in a new light and realised he and his friends may live to regret their actions of the previous evening. Or they may not.

8

Breakfast turned out to be even more chaotic and hardly more satisfying than dinner. The mess was overflowing with convicts from at least half the huts in attendance, and there was only just enough seating to accommodate everyone. Convicts from the various huts, it seemed, stuck together, in most cases eating at the same long table.

The first course was a watery substance that only faintly resembled the porridge it was meant to be. No-one discovered a mouse in their food, but Noel was one of a number of diners who found a bug or insect of some description in theirs. In Noel's case, it was a large cockroach whose legs were still moving. His displeasure was noted by one Terry McIntosh, a hardened Scottish convict, who sniggered openly at Noel's discomfort.

John quietly studied McIntosh, who, he observed, could have passed for McPherson's older brother. Big and raw-boned, he had the no-nonsense look of a clansman from the Scottish highlands. John wondered why McIntosh hadn't come to the aid of his fellow countryman last night.

As if reading John's mind, O'Donnell leaned over to the Irishman and whispered, "That's Terry McIntosh, and in case you're wondering, he and Angus hate each other's guts." When John didn't respond, he added, "Something to do with a girl in Edinburgh I believe."

By now it had occurred to John the ever-present, ever-alert O'Donnell had taken it upon himself to act as something of a mentor, or guide perhaps, for the new arrivals in his hut, or for those of them who were Irish at least. He found the skinny, little runt somewhat annoying, but resisted blowing him off because he realised he could learn from him what made this place tick and how best to survive. He looked at O'Donnell and asked, "And how long have you been here at Moreton Bay, Paddy?"

O'Donnell, who was flattered by John's sudden interest in him, proceeded to relate to his new friend his entire history since arriving in Australia. It turned out he'd been at Moreton Bay eighteen months, or, in his own words, long enough to know what made this place tick.

Porridge was followed by a mug of tea and two slices of toast per man. The toast, which was invariably either burnt or underdone, was faintly covered by some unidentifiable spread—apricot jam perhaps—and the tea was tepid and, in the opinion of one wit, was as weak as bees' piss.

Noel and Kennedy took turns to feed McPherson who was too feeble and uncoordinated to feed himself. They were sitting opposite John who was dying to say

49

something about the attention they were lavishing on their patient. The amount of time they were spending looking after the Scotsman was starting to agitate him.

It was Noel who first noticed John's agitation. "If you've got something on your feckin' mind John Graham, say it," he mumbled.

That was the opening John needed. "I don't know why you're wasting your time on that Scotsman," he fired back. "He clearly isn't gonna last the day."

"So we should just give up on him, is that what you're saying?" Noel shot Kennedy a look as if to indicate he sometimes despaired of his friend.

"What I'm saying Noel Thomas, is in this foreign land we each have to look out for ourselves and not worry about the next man," said John. "Otherwise it could be the last thing you ever do."

Noel shook his head sadly. "You really can be a selfish bastard sometimes," he said.

John shrugged. "And maybe I'm still alive because of it."

Somewhere outside the mess a bell rang, signifying the end of breakfast.

"Assemble back 'ere in ten minutes!" a guard shouted at the convicts. "And don't be late."

John turned to O'Donnell who had been listening to the exchange between the two friends with interest. "What now?" he asked

"We get ten minutes to use the latrines if we need to," O'Donnell said.

John stood and tagged along behind forty or so others who were heading for the ablutions block. There, John and several other stragglers had to queue while convicts defecated behind a screen comprised of sacks hung out over a line. The line extended from the base of the water tower to the side of a barn. There were insufficient sacks to screen everyone from view, and several convicts could be seen doing their business as they squatted above a freshly dug trench. They seemed unconcerned either by the lack of privacy or by the clouds of flies that buzzed them.

Pages torn from old newspapers and yellowed by age served as toilet paper. These were dispensed to the queuing convicts by a young convict who looked even younger than the water boy John had seen yesterday.

Glancing at the paper now in his hand, John saw he was holding a page torn from the January 25, 1820 edition of the London newspaper *The Sunday Times*. Its date and masthead were still clearly legible, and the page was headed *Births, Deaths and Marriages*.

Idly running his eye over the columns John noted that one Anne Brontë, daughter of Irish clergyman Patrick Brontë, had been born on January 17th in West Yorkshire, and on January 23rd Prince Edward the Duke of Kent had died.

The *Marriages* column was illegible, but an advertisement at the bottom of the page caught John's attention. It had been placed by a London publishing house and it advertised the publication of English poet John Keats' poem *Lamia,* which the Irishman recalled had been a favourite of his dear departed father. Truth be known, he'd never met his father, but his mother assured him his father was a dear—before he'd run off with a neighbour's wife, that is. After that sad event, John's mother had changed her mind about John's father, calling him something else altogether.

The advertisement John was now looking at included verses from Keats' famous poem.

It read:

When from this wreathed tomb shall I awake!
When move in a sweet body fit for life,
And love, and pleasure, and the ruddy strife
Of hearts and lips! Ah, miserable me!

John felt as though the poem could have been written for him. The moment was made all the more memorable for him by the arrival of the first rays of morning sun. They escaped the eastern horizon and bathed the paper he held in golden light. He took that as a good omen for the day ahead.

A place behind the sack screen became available as a convict finished his business. John hurried forward to claim the vacated spot. As he did, he tore the advertisement out, folded it and placed it in the pocket of his new-issue shirt, vowing to read all the verses later.

The ringing of a second bell alerted John to the fact he was running behind schedule. He and a few other stragglers hurried from the ablutions block to the mess where they found their fellow convicts already lined up in rows beneath the critical gaze of Sergeant Benson, the Devonshire veteran who had escorted the new arrivals from the wharf the previous day.

For their tardiness, a couple of stragglers behind John received a blow or two from batons wielded by guards who circulated amongst the convicts.

Sitting astride his horse, Benson studied the newcomers amongst the two hundred and thirty odd convicts assembled before him. They stood out in their clean, new clothes. The sergeant didn't seem at all impressed by what he was looking at. "I hope you lot are well rested," he said with more than a hint of sarcasm. "You have a demanding day ahead. But first, we have a lesson in store for you." He smiled grimly and paused to lend weight to what awaited the assembled. "It's a lesson that should need no explaining."

With that, Benson turned his horse and ordered the convicts to follow him as he headed past the stables to the nearby courtyard where the newcomers had assembled the previous night. And as was the case then, Captain Marsden and Lieutenant Hogan were there, also on horseback, in front of the whipping post. On either side of them, two platoons of armed Redcoats stood at attention.

Barega the tracker lounged nearby, looking bored and fondling the long-bladed knife he'd acquired the previous day. Only Lord Cheetham was conspicuous by his absence.

Benson rode up to Marsden. "All present and accounted for, Captain," he said, exchanging salutes with his superior.

"Any casualties amongst the new arrivals overnight, Sergeant?" Marsden enquired.

"Yes sir," Benson said. "Three deaths. All from various ailments. And half a dozen others have complained of illness, but I think they are exaggerating the severity of their complaints, sir."

John, who overheard the exchange, wondered if McPherson's sorry condition had been brought to the sergeant's attention and, if so, whether he considered the Scotsman's complaint an exaggeration. Looking around at McPherson now, it seemed increasingly unlikely the man would survive the day without medical attention. For that reason alone, it irked him to see Noel and his mates were still supporting McPherson.

Silly bastards.

John shot them a glance to signal he considered they were wasting their time. He was all for helping a man in need, but not when the man was a lost cause.

John was distracted when he caught sight of Dan Green who was now standing a little removed from his fellow convicts. He got no small pleasure from the fact that the giant Londoner's face was now bruised black and blue as a result of the bashing he'd received the previous evening. The look on Green's face told him he got no pleasure from it either. He'd joined five others who, although not as big as the giant Londoner, shared a number of similarities: they were all big, tough-looking men and, unlike the other long-serving convicts, they wore clothes and boots that were new or near-new. None were shackled and, like the official guards, all carried batons.

Noting John's interest in the six men, O'Donnell leaned over and murmured, "Lowlifes."

"Convict-wardens?" John asked.

O'Donnell nodded.

Benson called for quiet in the ranks. Those who didn't immediately quieten felt the wrath of the guards in the form of a well-aimed baton or the lash of a whip.

By now, John and the other new arrivals had worked out that Moreton Bay was a different proposition to Parramatta. The Parra penal settlement had been a holiday camp compared to this. They didn't know it, but they were about to witness an event that would drive that point home.

Another platoon of soldiers approached on foot. They could be heard long before they appeared around the far end of the stables. As the platoon approached, John noted each and every man in it carried the new-issue Infantry Rifle he'd noticed upon arrival yesterday. He wasn't to know the weapons arrived aboard *the Hoogley*. The lucky recipients would test the unfamiliar rifles on the army's practice range over the coming days.

John also noticed the soldiers were escorting a convict. It wasn't until they pulled up in front of the whipping post opposite he recognised the convict as the young Cockney escapee who had been dragged back to the settlement the previous evening.

Barefoot and topless, Frank Patterson was in better shape than he had been twelve hours earlier. He was no longer bleeding, although the cuts and bruises he'd suffered were still raw and ugly. Mentally, however, the twenty-three-year-old was highly stressed. He was clearly aware of what awaited him.

The platoon members stood at attention as they awaited their orders.

Marsden surveyed the scene before him through impassive eyes. He knew it was important to portray an image of professional indifference. Since his arrival at

Moreton Bay he'd had to preside over numerous floggings, and it was one part of the job he abhorred. He considered the punishment a necessary evil. After all, escape attempts from Moreton Bay were becoming an almost daily scourge. In the past month alone there had been twenty-six attempts—and this despite the punishment of one hundred lashes for those who were caught.

It never ceased to amaze Marsden the convicts seemed undaunted by their lack of success. It was no secret that those who hadn't been killed by Aborigines or who hadn't died of thirst, hunger or snake bite had all been caught.

The captain had suggested to Cheetham there must be more humane and effective ways to deter the convicts from trying to escape, but this had fallen on deaf ears. When he'd pressed him, the commandant had threatened him with demotion if his orders weren't carried out to the letter. It was no idle threat either, for Cheetham had the ear of New South Wales' Governor, and the captain was very aware of that.

Unfortunately for Marsden, the dramatic increase in escape attempts had occurred since he'd arrived at Moreton Bay to take over as Cheetham's second-in-command. He felt that was entirely coincidental for he'd learned the discontent amongst the convicts had been building for some time. For all he knew, the commandant's hard line could be the right approach. Even he had to admit something had to be done to curb the ever-rising number of escape attempts.

However, that didn't change the fact deep down that flogging men to within an inch of their miserable lives for trying to escape the hellish conditions they were forced to endure didn't sit well with him.

As if on cue, Lord Cheetham himself arrived by horse-drawn cart. Marsden watched him over the heads of the assembled convicts as he pulled up behind them. Cheetham looked every bit as foolish as he had the previous evening beneath his ridiculous mauve sun umbrella. He delivered a sloppy salute in the captain's direction and motioned to him to proceed.

Marsden eyed the assembled convicts. "This man's doomed escape was his second attempt in as many months," he said, looking down at the quivering Patterson. He added, "The punishment for that is one hundred lashes."

On hearing this, Patterson began hyperventilating. His condition didn't improve any when, from the soldiers' ranks, stepped the army's official flogger.

Amongst the convicts' ranks, a Welshman murmured, "Meet Old Bumble, gentlemen." That announcement was for the benefit of the new arrivals. The older hands knew this particular flogger very well, many of them having personally experienced the flogger's wrath.

Old Bumble was a sturdy Englishman with a muscular torso that was somewhat incongruously perched atop of a pair of deformed legs, which he'd been cursed with from birth. As a result, his gait resembled a bee when he walked. His nickname wasn't entirely apt, however, for he was a youthful thirty-seven.

As two soldiers tied Patterson to the whipping post, Old Bumble walked up and down, testing the multi-tailed whip he held in his right hand. For a minute or two, the only sound in the compound was the ominous crack of the whip.

Observing the flogger, John thought he'd have been better named *Old Crabby,* for his gait, to the Irishman's eyes at least, better resembled a crab as he walked. He noticed Old Bumble's whip was a variation on the cat o' nine tails: five tails had been removed, so it was in effect a cat o' four tails. However, the tails were leather, not rope, and each one, John noted, had been tied in knots, which, he estimated, were spaced at five-inch intervals along the length of each tail. He could only imagine the damage they would inflict.

The convicts remained hushed as Old Bumble went to work. Each lash was delivered with forceful ease, and was counted off by a young private who had been *volunteered* by Sergeant Benson.

To Patterson's credit, he didn't cry out, but he grunted with pain with each and every lash.

"Fifty," the young private said as Old Bumble delivered the fiftieth lash to the offender's back.

Now halfway through his punishment, Patterson was a bloody mess. With every lash, the knotted leather tails of the whip tore flesh from his back.

Old Bumble was almost as bloodied as his victim, and blood flecked the face and shirt of the private, too. The young soldier had only belatedly realised he was in the firing line and had moved out of range, but too late to avoid being bloodied. He'd turned deathly white, and appeared to be close to fainting.

The count continued. "Fifty-one, fifty-two, fifty-three . . ." The private's voice was now faltering noticeably. Without further warning, he fainted.

Sergeant Benson quickly stepped in, and took over the counting. "Fifty-four, fifty-five, fifty-six," he called, ignoring the unconscious private at his feet.

Within the ranks of the latest batch of convicts, someone began murmuring the Lord's Prayer. Others joined in.

John and Noel watched, ashen-faced, as the sergeant's count slowly climbed to seventy.

"Feck, he's not going to survive this," Noel whispered.

John silently agreed with his friend. Patterson hadn't moved or uttered a sound since the punishment reached the halfway mark, and the count still had a long way to go.

"Sixty-four, sixty-five, sixty-six." The count continued.

"Keep your chin up, lads!" someone called out in the thickest of Scottish brogues. "Don't let them see it bothers ye."

John turned around and saw it was Terry McIntosh, the other Scotsman who shared his hut.

McIntosh's outburst seemed to rally Noel and the others. John, however, was now staring across at Barega who appeared blithely unaffected by what was taking place. He'd obviously seen it all before. The tracker caught John's eye and grinned.

At seventy, Marsden wanted to stop the punishment. He looked across the heads of the convicts to Cheetham who, he saw, was looking directly at him and who appeared to have read his mind. The commandant firmly shook his head, indicating the punishment must continue.

Finally, after what seemed an age, the count reached one hundred.

Before anyone had time to express their relief, Cheetham called out from the back. "Another twenty lashes, Captain."

Marsden looked at the commandant, and wondered if he'd heard right.

Cheetham nodded his way, indicating he should carry out the order. "Another twenty lashes," he repeated for good measure.

Marsden hesitated. The captain was aware even ten more lashes could kill the offender—that is if he wasn't dead already. He'd seen men survive two hundred lashes before, but not when the punishment was delivered by Old Bumble and his unique variation on the cat o' nine tails. He debated whether to carry out the order.

After a long, drawn-out silence, Marsden nodded to the flogger. "Twenty more lashes," he said. He silently asked for God's forgiveness.

And so the punishment continued.

When it finally ended, Patterson was almost unrecognisable as a human being. He was saturated in his own blood, and better resembled a carcass in an abattoir than a man. Flesh had been stripped from his back, and parts of his ribs and spine were exposed. The bones gleamed white in the early morning light.

Soldiers untied the offender and unceremoniously dragged him away. Some of the new men assumed he was being taken to the infirmary, but they would learn later there was no infirmary for them, only for the soldiers. Patterson, *if* he'd survived, would be expected to report for work the following day. If he didn't, they learned, he'd be flogged again. Such was life at Moreton Bay.

Marsden was about to order his men to escort the convicts to their respective workplaces when he realised Cheetham had joined him.

Without bothering to explain himself, the commandant addressed the convicts. "That fool"—he glanced in the direction Patterson had been dragged—"paid the price for attempting to escape," he said. "I doubt he will try that again."

As Cheetham droned on, the newly arrived convicts couldn't take their eyes off Old Bumble. The flogger had just finished washing blood from his whip in a can of water. To the newcomers' amazement he then raised the can to his lips and greedily gulped down the contents.

John looked around and realised that the older hands hadn't even seemed to notice the flogger's actions. They were very familiar with his peculiar ways.

Cheetham continued, "Be warned, from now on *any* escape attempt will be punishable by death." He emphasised the word *any*.

This got John's attention, and everyone else's, too.

Marsden couldn't believe his ears. Cheetham hadn't consulted him regarding introducing the death sentence for first-time escapees. Until now, only recidivist escapees had been hung.

The commandant continued, "And for any of you foolish enough to try to escape"—he glanced pointedly at the gallows to his right—"that's what awaits you." With that, Cheetham marched off without any further acknowledgement of Marsden.

A stunned Marsden looked at Hogan as if to ascertain whether he'd received any warning such an announcement was to be made. The lieutenant shrugged, indicating he was as much in the dark as his opposite.

9

THE ONLY SOUND TO BE heard, apart from the occasional squawk of a cockatoo or rainbow lorikeet, was the clink of chains and the clomp of horses' hooves as the convicts were escorted to their workplaces. There was no talking. The memory of Frank Patterson's flogging was still raw in the minds of each.

John and Noel and the others from their hut, along with the inmates of two other huts, were heading for the quarry on the settlement's outskirts where, they'd been told, they would labour until nightfall. Doing what exactly the newcomers weren't sure. Whatever awaited them, they sensed wouldn't be enjoyable—especially not in this heat. The sun was still low in the sky, having not long risen, but it was already brutally hot. Though no hotter than Parramatta at this time of year, it was far more humid, and convicts and soldiers alike were already sweating profusely.

Around six mounted soldiers accompanied each gang of convicts.

John, who had a penchant for figures, and not only feminine figures, wondered just how many soldiers were based at Moreton Bay. He did the math to fill in the time. *If there's six gangs with six Redcoats per gang that totals thirty-six soldiers currently guarding the convicts.* He'd been told the soldiers' days had been divided into two shifts. *So that equals seventy-two soldiers. Allowing for another eight either away or engaged on other duties . . . that amounts to eighty Redcoats, which, in turn, roughly equals one for every three convicts. Not good odds for convicts intent on escaping.* He dismissed that thought as soon as he had it. *Only an idiot would try to escape from here.*

John's calculations weren't too far out. In fact, there were only sixty-four soldiers stationed here, or almost one for every four convicts. Still not good odds—especially not if the guards, convict-wardens and Aboriginal trackers were taken into account.

While Barega was the main tracker, he was ably assisted by local Quandamooka men who were also highly adept at tracking escapees.

As for the guards, there were eighteen of them—three per hut—employed by the army. Recruited in Sydney Town, they were a mixed lot. Some were former soldiers, others had previously been unemployed and a few were ex-convicts. With two or three notable exceptions, all were cruel in the extreme, seemingly thriving in the brutality of life at the bay. Their cruelty easily matched that of the most brutal of soldiers currently stationed in the settlement, and was perhaps exceeded only by the convict-wardens whom soldiers and convicts alike despised.

The convict-wardens, for the most part, performed easy albeit mundane tasks in the settlement, while the guards were primarily responsible for guarding the settlement—its convict population in particular—at night, thereby all but eliminating the need for soldiers to work the night shift.

Marsden was considering changing that roster system given most escapes occurred at night, but for better or worse that was the situation for the time being.

In addition to their escort of Redcoats, today each gang had been assigned a guard and a convict-warden to watch over them. Like the soldiers, the guards were on horseback, but the convict-wardens were on foot, albeit unshackled. The old hands knew from experience the extra manpower was a show of force designed to keep the new arrivals in line and nip any problems in the bud before they festered.

It was no surprise to John to see the inmates of the various huts had, for the most part, been kept together. One group had remained in the settlement where they were already at work, attending to various repair jobs and constructing a stone fence to mark the settlement's boundary; another group was being escorted downriver to the wharf where they would attend to repairs of that facility; yet another group was also at work, harvesting corn in one of the fields between the settlement and Marsden's cottage, while the other three groups were now nearing the quarry. Nor was it a surprise to John to see the giant Dan Green was the convict-warden assigned to his group.

Although only four hundred yards from the settlement, the trek to the quarry felt more like four miles to the shackled convicts. Especially for those weakened by the voyage from Sydney Town. And for those labouring with illness or injury, such as the ailing Angus McPherson, it seemed much further.

As they walked, John observed his surroundings. He couldn't help but be impressed by the area's beauty. The red earth contrasted with the green of the bush and gum trees that covered most of the rolling hills and plains around the settlement, while to the east the waters of the bay shimmered in the early morning sunlight. On the higher hills, especially to the north, bush gave way to the tropical green of the rainforest that covered much of the coastal regions in these parts.

To his left, John studied the banks of the nearby river. Through gaps in the trees he could see clumps of white lilies growing in the tidal mud. On the far bank, he spotted two large crocs sunbathing. He idly wondered if one of them was the brute that had devoured the old Dubliner the previous day.

Along the near bank, the shantytown that was home to the local Quandamooka was coming alive as men, women and children emerged from their makeshift bivouacs and greeted the new day in a variety of different ways. Spear-wielding men wandered down to the river's edge to spear fish while others cast nets, presumably to snare fish or eels or other such creatures; the womenfolk chaperoned the children or busied themselves collecting branches to use as firewood, while some of the younger women talked to a group of off-duty soldiers who were showing more than a passing interest in them.

One of the soldiers escorting John's group had also noticed the interchange between his fellow soldiers and the Aboriginal women. "Watch that ye don't catch a dose of the Quandamooka Clap, you bastards!" he shouted at the off-duty soldiers. *Quandamooka Clap* was the term the soldiers used for venereal disease contracted through sexual liaisons with these particular native women—an all too common outcome.

The off-duty soldiers looked around, and one of them flashed a lewd sign the comedian's way. They were too far away, in John's opinion, to have heard exactly what the heckler was saying, but they evidently caught the gist of it.

Comments from some of the convicts in John's group called his attention to a small mob of kangaroos drinking from a billabong up ahead. The roos bounded away as the group neared, but not before the men noticed the head of a Joey, or baby roo, protruding from its mother's pouch. The Joey appeared to look around at the convicts as it was whisked away, sparking laughter from men who hadn't laughed in a while.

Surveying his companions, John noticed that Kennedy and O'Neill were making hard work of supporting McPherson whose condition had further deteriorated since they'd departed the settlement some ten minutes earlier. The two Irishmen were struggling to support the big Scotsman's weight even though they'd only just taken over from Donovan and O'Driscoll.

Noel also noticed his countrymen were struggling. Turning to John, he said, "We better help 'em or they're not going to make it."

"To hell with them," John said. "We need to conserve our energy or none of us will survive what the British have planned for us today."

Noel was rendered speechless by his friend's selfish attitude. All he could do was flash a scathing look his way.

The look wasn't lost on John, who added, "The Scotsman's a lost cause." When he saw his friend wasn't convinced, he said, "Look at him. He's had it."

"Quiet in the ranks!" a sergeant bellowed.

Sergeant Christopher Rogers, a strapping Birmingham man, was, John thought, a dead ringer for Sergeant Benson. Of similar age, appearance and bearing, only his accent differed from that of the Devonshire sergeant. John would soon learn that wasn't the only difference: where Benson had a reputation for harsh discipline, Rogers was known for his brutality.

The convicts fell silent once more. They were approaching the quarry's entrance, which had been carved from the side of a hill so high it dwarfed them. It made them feel like ants scurrying, or shuffling at least, to work.

The quarry itself reminded John of the crater of an extinct volcano. It looked bare, barren and hot, with nary a tree nor anything else in sight that would provide any degree of shade. Bare rock glistened in the sun, and everywhere were the signs of previous work parties—broken spades, discarded pick-axes, horse troughs, the remains of perhaps a thousand cooking fires, discarded clothing and other incidentals.

"Welcome to paradise, lads," one of the soldiers chuckled.

As they negotiated a steep, rocky incline leading to the quarry's entrance, Terry McIntosh began reciting from a popular ballad the convicts knew only as *Moreton Bay*. "I am a native of Erin's island," the Scotsman said, "but banished now to the fatal shore, they tore me from my aged parents and from the maiden I do adore."

"You tell 'em, Terry!" an English convict yelled.

"Quiet!" Sergeant Rogers ordered.

Undeterred, McIntosh continued, "I've been a prisoner at Port Macquarie, Norfolk Island and Emu Plains, at Castle Hill and cursed Toongabbie. At all those settlements I've worked in chains. But of all those places of condemnation, in each penal station of New South Wales, to Moreton Bay I've found no equal, excessive tyranny there each day prevails."

John and the other newcomers would soon learn that McIntosh knew the ballad by heart, and recited excerpts from it daily. It resonated with the convicts and, strangely, with the soldiers, too. As a result, the soldiers and guards begrudgingly tolerated the Scotsman's recitations. One or two, truth be known, even looked forward to them. Entertainment was hard to come by at Moreton Bay.

A movement in a field to John's right drew his attention. He saw two women picking wildflowers, which they placed in the baskets they carried. A young boy was climbing a gum tree just behind them. The younger of the women struck John as being a real beauty although she was so far away he couldn't be certain. He guessed she and the boy were the older woman's children.

Just then, the boy appeared to find himself stuck in the tree. The two women tried to help him down, but were unsuccessful. Then the older woman looked around and waved out to someone who was apparently following behind the convicts.

John looked behind him and saw a young officer he'd noticed twice before in the settlement's courtyard. The officer was Lieutenant Hogan. He'd been riding alongside a horse-driven cart that was also heading for the quarry. It was laden down with tools, food, water and other supplies the convicts would need for the day ahead.

The last John saw before filing through the opening to the quarry was the Redcoat galloping off to rescue the boy and no doubt impress the young beauty.

Hogan arrived just in time to rescue young Matthew Marsden before he lost his grip on the branch he was holding. Standing tall in his stirrups, the lieutenant grabbed the boy by his braces and lowered him to the ground.

"I could have climbed down by myself!" an embarrassed Matthew protested.

"I'm sure you could have," Hogan agreed.

"Come now, Matthew," Missus Marsden scolded the lad. "You thank Lieutenant Hogan.

"No need for that Missus Marsden," Hogan assured her.

She ignored the lieutenant and scowled at Matthew.

"Thank you, Lieutenant," Matthew mumbled.

"There now, that wasn't hard, was it Matthew?" Helen said, ruffling her brother's hair good naturedly.

Only now did Hogan look at Helen. He tipped his cap and smiled at her, and was pleased to see she responded with a shy smile, which, if he wasn't mistaken, seemed to light up the very air around her. Hogan considered that progress as the young woman had rarely acknowledged him before.

Missus Marsden interrupted this silent exchange by suggesting Hogan join the trio for a cold drink. She pointed to a picnic basket lying in the long grass nearby.

"Oh, no need, Missus Marsden," Hogan assured her. Glancing at Helen, he added, "A dance with your daughter at the Governor's dinner will be quite sufficient thanks."

Helen could feel herself blushing. She hoped it didn't show.

"I am sure she'll be delighted," Missus Marsden said.

"Mother!" Helen protested.

"Good, that's settled then," Hogan said, smiling at Helen again. He winked at Matthew before pulling his horse around and galloping off to re-join the other soldiers.

As soon as he was out of earshot, Helen rounded on her mother. "Mama, did you have to volunteer me to dance with Lieutenant Hogan?"

"Oh, but he is such a dashing young man," Missus Marsden gushed. "He so reminds me of your father when he was young."

"That is hardly the point," Helen said. Again she found herself blushing.

Missus Marsden resumed gathering flowers, the discussion already forgotten. Her mind was on the Governor's dinner, which was shaping up to be the social event of the year in Moreton Bay.

10

CAPTAIN MARSDEN HAD TO BITE his tongue as he waited for his opposite to start the meeting. He had a busy day ahead of him, and Cheetham had already kept him waiting an hour before calling him to his office. And now the old man was searching his desk drawers for a box of cigars he'd misplaced.

The duty clerk, Corporal Cedric Dunstan, who sat ready to take notes on Marsden's left, sympathised with the captain. These weekly meetings were a real pain in the arse. They used to be a daily event, but the commandant had soon discovered daily meetings were too taxing, so he'd reduced them to twice weekly and then weekly. No-one, except Cheetham himself, was in any doubt daily meetings were too taxing because the man was usually in an opium daze.

Weekly meetings suited Marsden just fine because any more than that and he was sure he'd snap and pull his pistol out from its holster and shoot Cheetham between the eyes. Such was the effect the overbearing commandant had on him. He couldn't hold his tongue any longer. "My Lord, I really do have a lot to do today—"

Cheetham held up one hand to signal he'd found what he was looking for. He drew out a cigar, sniffed it like the expert he considered himself to be then proceeded to light it. No thought was given to offering a cigar to his subordinates. Finally, he looked across the desk at Marsden. "Very well, captain," he mumbled. "What is the first item on the agenda?"

A relieved Marsden turned to Corporal Dunstan who handed him the agenda he'd written up earlier that morning. Marsden referred to Item Number One. "The first item concerns a discussion I understand you had with Lieutenant Hogan," he said, looking directly at his superior.

"Go on," Cheetham said.

Marsden suspected the commandant knew what was coming. "Lieutenant Hogan informed me last night that you ordered him to ensure only one escapee returned to the settlement alive yesterday," he said.

"I gave no such order," Cheetham said, "and I do not appreciate your accusatory tone."

"I am not accusing you. I—"

"I simply mentioned to the lieutenant it was imperative at least one escapee was returned alive—to serve as a lesson to the others," Cheetham interjected. "If he misconstrued that to mean he was to have two of them killed that is not my fault."

Looking into Cheetham's eyes, Marsden was surprised to see they seemed clear—certainly clearer than they'd been the previous day. So he'd obviously refrained from smoking opium since then. Then it occurred to him that Cheetham was cleaning his act up in preparation for the Governor's visit, which was now only a day away. The difference was as noticeable as night and day. The old boy's eyes were clear and his gaze focused.

"What's next?" Cheetham asked.

Realising he'd get no further pursuing Item One, Marsden's eyes dropped to Item Two. "The blacksmith's assistant died of pneumonia two days ago," he said. "We need to hire another one."

"There is no allocation in the budget for another such appointment until next year," Cheetham said.

"Then I will have to appoint an assistant from within the convicts' ranks. I understand there may be one or two smithies among the new arrivals."

"Do that. Next item."

Marsden referred to the next item. Alongside him, the clerk dipped his feather quill into an open ink bottle and scribbled away furiously as he recorded in longhand the most important points covered so far. "Item Three," the captain said, "is a request that our doctor's services be extended to include the convicts."

Cheetham looked up sharply. "We covered that last week," he said, carelessly blowing cigar smoke toward his opposites.

"Yes we did, and since then another nine convicts have died of various illnesses and, at last count, another forty-two have fallen ill. Sergeant Benson reports twenty-seven serious cases of dysentery, ten cases of scurvy, three cases of pneumonia and two cases—"

Cheetham interjected yet again, this time with a dismissive wave of the half-smoked cigar he held. "Most of them minor complaints, I'd wager, and—"

This time it was Marsden's turn to interject. "Dying is hardly a minor complaint, sir!" he shouted.

Cheetham was so surprised by his subordinate's outburst he nearly dropped his cigar. Recovering his composure, he said, "My first duty here is to *my* men. Not to men who are the scum of the earth."

"The men you refer to *sir* are human beings, and they deserve basic care at the very least."

"They are barely more human than the savages who frequent this sorry land, and they deserve no more than they get." Almost as an afterthought, Cheetham added, "Besides, Doctor Andrews has a full schedule looking after the soldiers and any townsfolk who need his services."

Marsden knew that to be true enough. Doctor Phillip Andrews, who had formerly served as a surgeon at Edinburgh Hospital, in Scotland, was struggling to cope with his present workload. But Marsden also knew one reason for that was the good doctor was an alcoholic who was barely sober long enough to meet the needs of Moreton Bay's soldiers. Which was why he, Marsden, had long been pushing for the appointment of a doctor specifically to look after the convicts. God knows they needed one.

The two officials sat glaring at each other across the desk. Each knew where the other stood on the issue, and neither was prepared to back down.

Speaking for the first time, Corporal Dunstan endeavoured to break the stalemate. "Lord Cheetham, if I may," he said.

"Yes, what is it man?" Cheetham fixed the clerk with a critical gaze from beneath his bushy eyebrows.

A nervous Dunstan said, "Captain Marsden raises a very good point, sir."

Cheetham audibly sighed.

Undeterred, Dunstan continued, "We all agree we need to expand our convict population to meet the growth planned for Moreton Bay, yet the new convicts arriving barely make up for those who have died or who are too ill and feeble to put in a good day's work."

"My point exactly," Marsden said. "Not appointing a doctor to look after the convicts is false economy."

Cheetham pondered that. Finally, he promised to come back with a decision at a later date. Neither man believed him. He'd made the same promise last month and the month before that.

If Marsden had to bet, Cheetham would never appoint a doctor to service the convicts. The commandant viewed the convicts as animals, and he treated them as such.

What Marsden didn't know was that Cheetham had arranged with the Governor of New South Wales to greatly increase the number of convicts being shipped to Moreton Bay. The extra numbers were required to achieve a projected convict population of two thousand within the next few years to help meet the expansion Dunstan had so astutely referred to. But Cheetham preferred to keep that quiet for the moment. The Governor had told him in no uncertain terms he wanted to announce that himself.

"Anything else?" a fidgety Cheetham asked. Whenever he started fidgeting, his subordinates knew his patience and his powers of concentration were coming to an end.

"The next item," Marsden said without even referring to the agenda, "concerns your decision to hang first-time escapees." He had been brooding about the commandant's decree that all returned escapees would be hung ever since the unexpected announcement had been made. "And I must object that you chose to deliver such a decree without consulting myself. I am, after all, head ward—"

"We have been over this, Captain Marsden!" a furious Cheetham exploded. Now on his feet, he said, "Since your appointment, the convicts have taken to escaping like never before. They treat it as they would a hobby. Something to do in their spare time. Floggings have proven no deterrent." Then he played his trump card. Looking squarely at Marsden, he asked, "What would you suggest we do to deter future escape attempts, Captain?"

Marsden looked off into space. He considered the obvious answer was to increase the number of soldiers in the settlement, but he'd already fought that battle—several times—and lost. As always, it came back to budget. And there was no budget for more soldiers. Not until the convict population rose. So he remained silent.

"And there's my answer," a triumphant Cheetham said. He savoured his little victory for a moment then, in a more conciliatory tone, asked, "Is everything in order for Wednesday?" He referred, of course, to the Governor's visit and the dinner that had been planned for him two days hence.

"Yes, my Lord," Marsden said. Aware time was marching on, and anxious to extricate himself from Cheetham's presence before he gave in to his desire to shoot the man, he stood up. "If you will excuse me, I must check on my men. Corporal Dunstan can update you on the latest plans for the Governor." He hurried from the office before his superior could object.

11

J OHN AND THE OTHER NEW arrivals wondered what they'd struck as they laboured alongside the long-serving convicts in the quarry. It was only mid-morning and already the temperatures were scorching. Heat stroke was a very real danger for all.

In all there were one hundred and fourteen convicts toiling in the quarry and, as always, they were watched over closely by soldiers and guards. The convicts performed a variety of tasks, ranging from digging rocks from the barren hillside to smashing those same rocks into smaller pieces to loading the resulting rubble onto carts. They were rotated from one task to the next at set intervals, and any who lagged in their efforts felt the lash of a whip wielded by the guards who circulated amongst them.

No matter what the task, it was back-breaking work, and the new arrivals in particular suffered. They were severely hampered in their efforts by their leg-irons, which, by now, seemed to weigh a ton and were hot to touch.

One of the busiest convicts was the water boy assigned to dispensing water to his fellow convicts. Fifteen-year-old Billy Morris was the same lad John had noticed dispensing water to his fellows the previous day. He alone was permitted to work unshackled. A slip of a lad, Billy was struggling to carry two large buckets of water from one group of convicts to the next. The buckets hung from hoops attached to either end of a rod, which he balanced on his shoulders. As the buckets' contents were emptied, he returned to refill them from one of three water barrels that sat atop the horse-drawn cart that had accompanied the convicts to the quarry.

It was so hot the convicts, and the soldiers and guards, too, had to drink constantly to assuage their thirst and help keep heat stroke at bay. However, the latter gentlemen had the added benefit of a canvass shade awning they'd erected in the quarry entrance upon arrival. Those not out in the sun, checking on their charges and dispensing punishment when required, rested in the shade, swapping jokes, playing cards and sometimes napping—much to the resentment of the convicts.

Beyond the soldiers, the river could be seen, shimmering, in the distance. Even though the penal settlement itself was only a quarter-of-a-mile away, it was just out of sight to the west, or left, of the quarry; and the sparkling waters of Moreton Bay, away to the east, or right, of the quarry were also hidden from view.

Also out of sight was the army's practice range. However, constant gunfire could be heard coming from it as soldiers familiarised themselves with their new Infantry Rifle. It was a sound the convicts would become used to in the coming days and weeks. Captain Marsden demanded high standards, and his men would be drilled exhaustively in their use of the new weapon.

On the quarry floor, the sight of a death adder basking on a rock in the morning sun, seemingly oblivious to all the industry going on around it, alarmed some of those closest to it. Only a well-aimed stone thrown by Rhys Jones, the Welsh convict, prompted the deadly reptile to relinquish its sunbathing spot and slither off through a hole in the rock.

"One bite from that and you're dead in thirty minutes," Jones said.

The newcomers took note of that piece of sobering news. It was yet another reminder of how dangerous this land could be. Death adders hadn't been a problem at Parramatta for, like the crocs, they couldn't survive the cooler winters any further south than Moreton Bay.

John and Noel were assigned to the group tasked with smashing rocks as they were prized from the quarry face by convicts working above them. The pair attacked the rocks with pick-axes and sledgehammers—no easy task considering some of the rocks were big enough to crush a man. Already their hands were blistered and sore.

"Look out!" John shouted as a dislodged rock tumbled toward them from the quarry face above. He pulled Noel safely to one side, and they watched as the rock bounced past them and came to a rest nearby.

"Jesus!" a relieved Noel mumbled. "That was too feckin' close."

John agreed wholeheartedly. The rock had been dislodged by one of the forty or so convicts responsible for prizing rocks from the quarry face. Pick-axes in hand, they swarmed all over the face, making use of narrow tracks that had been carved out by legions of convicts before them. The tracks stopped some way short of the summit—a security consideration to prevent convicts from attempting to escape.

"Did you see who was responsible?" Noel asked.

John surveyed the convicts directly above him, but none was owing up to their carelessness. He noticed one looking a little sheepish, and pointed him out to his friend. "I'd wager it was him," he said.

The clomp of horses' hooves and the appearance of a shadow on the ground in front of the pair alerted them to the arrival of a soldier on horseback. Squinting up into the sun, they saw it was Sergeant Rogers. He brandished a whip, which he appeared ready to use.

"Get back to work, you two!" Rogers bawled, his distinctive Birmingham accent bouncing off the quarry walls, prompting other convicts to look around.

John and Noel quickly resumed smashing rocks, their sledgehammers rising and falling almost in unison.

"Feckin' English!" Noel muttered. He cussed softly, but it was loud enough for the brutal sergeant to hear.

Noel didn't see the whip's thong fall, but he felt it as it ripped open his shirt and tore a strip of flesh from his back. "Aaagh!" he grunted, dropping his sledgehammer.

Rogers, who was beside himself with rage, raised his whip again, all the while directing a barrage of curses and insults at Noel.

John stepped between his friend and the irate sergeant, and stood staring up at him, as if daring him to strike him.

"John!" Noel hissed, alarmed to see his workmate tempting fate so.

Rogers needed no second invitation. As he prepared to employ his whip a second time, he was distracted by the sounds of a commotion behind him. He turned to see convict-warden Dan Green laying into one of the other convicts with his baton. The convict on the receiving end of the vicious battering lay unmoving at his feet. Looking back at John, the sergeant snarled, "I'll deal with you later." He then pulled his steed around and galloped over to investigate.

Only then did the two Irishmen see who Green's victim was: it was Angus McPherson. They were alarmed to see the battering continued unabated, and the Scotsman still wasn't moving. The beating only stopped when Rogers reached Green's side.

From where they stood, John and Noel could only catch snatches of the conversation between the sergeant and the convict-warden. It soon became clear to them that Green had been angered by the ailing Scotsman's inability to pull his weight and do his fair share of work, and so had dispensed punishment as he saw fit. It was very evident he'd made no allowance for McPherson's fragile state, and had seized the first opportunity to avenge the beating he'd suffered at the hands of the Scotsman's friends.

"The feckin' bastard!" Noel cursed. "I think he's killed Angus."

John concurred. McPherson still wasn't moving.

The Irishmen were concerned to see that Rogers appeared to condone Green's violent actions. That was confirmed for them when they witnessed the two men share a joke before the sergeant turned and barked orders at a group of convicts working nearby. Four convicts each grabbed a spade and began digging a hole that looked suspiciously like the beginnings of a grave.

By now, all the convicts had stopped to observe the grim scene unfolding on the quarry floor. It was obvious to everyone that McPherson was dead. They assumed Green had killed him. In fact, *he had,* but not just as a result of his latest assault on the Scotsman. The severe concussion McPherson had sustained from the beating Green gave him the previous evening had, without the intervention of skilled medical assistance, been a guaranteed death sentence. It was only a matter of time before the swelling in his brain caused him to have a stroke or some other fatal event. This morning's bashing had simply hastened that.

So hard was the rocky, sun-baked earth, it took the four convicts wielding the spades some time to dig even a shallow grave.

"That'll do," Rogers said. "Drop 'im in it."

The convicts downed tools and unceremoniously manhandled McPherson's body into the grave. As they shovelled dirt over him, Green looked around at the other convicts. His gaze rested on John and Noel, and he smiled maliciously in their direction. The intent behind it wasn't lost on the pair either.

"I swear I'm gonna to kill that Englishman," Noel murmured.

"Which one?" John asked, looking at both the sergeant and the convict-warden.

"Both," Noel said.

"Don't waste your energy," John cautioned. Referring to McPherson, he added,

"No Scotsman's worth putting yourself on the line for."

Noel didn't respond. Not for the first time he wondered at his friend's coldness and his lack of empathy for McPherson—and for others for that matter.

As the last lump of dirt and rock was shovelled onto the grave, Rogers blew two sharp blasts on a whistle that he carried on a cord around his neck.

Bemused, John and Noel looked at each other.

"That's the signal to go back to work," the ever-present, ever-reliable Paddy O'Donnell advised them and other new convicts standing within earshot.

John and Noel resumed their labour, ignoring the glares that both Rogers and Green directed their way.

The Irishmen sensed trouble would coming their way sooner or later, and probably sooner than later.

For the new arrivals toiling in the quarry, time had never passed so slowly. Not since the long weeks and months they'd spent in the holds of the transport ships at least. By mid-morning, the quarry was like an oven; by mid-day, it was like a furnace. The convicts, new and old, felt as though they were being baked alive. They perspired so much their clothes were saturated.

The guards and soldiers were feeling it, too, but at least they could retire to the shade of the awning they'd rigged up when they needed respite. And they could drink from the water barrel whenever they liked as opposed to having to wait for young Billy the water boy to reach them on his rounds.

Three sharp blasts of Sergeant Rogers' whistle announced it was time for a meal break. The old hands greeted this development with murmurs of appreciation.

"That's the signal for lunch," O'Donnell advised the newcomers. Pointing at the supply cart, where convicts were already starting to queue, he downed tools and headed for it as fast as his leg-irons would allow. Over his shoulder, he yelled, "Follow me. If you're too feckin' slow you could miss out."

The newcomers followed him as fast as they could manage, anxious not to be last in line.

The mid-day meal—for the convicts at least—comprised little more than one cooked potato served cold and two slices of stale bread per man. Sandwiched between the slices were aged cabbage leaves and something that tasted like dripping, or lard, though the men couldn't be sure. Dessert was an apple, which, all too often, was either rotten or worm-infested, or sometimes both. Unappetising though the food was, the convicts agreed the mid-day meal was the best meal of the day. It was washed down with generous helpings of water, which was the only item on the menu not in short supply at this time.

Though the refreshments and the short break from work were appreciated by all the convicts, they'd have willingly traded the food for some shade. The sun, which was at its zenith now, beat down upon them mercilessly. For the older hands, who had already been burnt nutmeg brown, it was difficult to endure, but for the new arrivals it was akin to being fried alive. Already the exposed skin of those in the latter category resembled that of lobsters, and it was obvious most if not all were in for a painful bout of sunburn.

Besides the incessant heat, the men were besieged by clouds of flies attracted by the food. Flies were a scourge from dawn to dusk, but at meal times they appeared in force, intent on driving all men, regardless of their rank and status, to distraction.

John and Noel ate with a small group that included fellow Irishmen O'Neill, Kennedy, Donovan and O'Driscoll, the water boy Billy Morris and hardnosed Scotsman Terry McIntosh. They were, naturally enough, discussing the fate that had befallen McIntosh's countryman Angus McPherson.

"That was murder plain and simple," Kennedy complained.

"Aye it was that," O'Neill agreed.

"That big oaf will get what's comin' to him," Kennedy said, referring to the giant Londoner who was responsible for McPherson's death.

"And who is going to see big Dan Green gets what's comin' to him?" McIntosh asked. "You?"

"Aye, it just might be me," Kennedy said, rising to the challenge.

The conversation lapsed as each man in his own way remembered McPherson. Few could bear to look at the Scotsman's freshly dug gravesite just a short distance away. It only served to remind them of their own mortality.

It was John who broke the silence. Looking at McIntosh, he said, "I thought it would be you wanting to avenge the murder of your countryman."

"He may have been my countryman, but he was no friend of mine!" McIntosh snapped back.

John could see that McPherson's death had no more affected McIntosh than it had himself.

A shrill blast on a whistle drew the convicts' attention to Sergeant Rogers. "Five minutes!" Rogers shouted when he saw he had his audience's attention, meaning they had five more minutes to enjoy their break.

"That's generous of him," Noel said. He turned to John and saw that he was reading something he'd just fished out of his shirt pocket. "What's that you're reading?" he asked.

John was in a world of his own and wasn't even aware his friend was talking to him. He was reading the same verse from John Keats' poem *Lamia* that had so caught his fancy earlier.

When from this wreathed tomb shall I awake!
When move in a sweet body fit for life,
And love, and pleasure, and the ruddy strife
Of hearts and lips! Ah, miserable me!

John absentmindedly fingered the silver crucifix as he read the poignant passage a third time. He felt the words contained a hidden message just for him, but for the life of him he didn't know what that message was.

"What's that you're reading?" Noel asked again.

Only now did John hear him. "I found this, this morning," he said, handing Noel the piece of paper he'd torn from *The Sunday Times* newspaper. He immediately took

69

it back, remembering that Noel couldn't read. "It's one of Keats's poems," he said.

"Read me a verse," Noel demanded.

Suddenly aware all his companions were listening, John mumbled, "Later."

"Read it now," Donovan said. His companions nodded encouragingly. Apparently, they, too, wanted to be entertained.

"Okay," a somewhat reluctant John said. His eyes went to the next excerpt from *Lamia,* and he began reciting. "Ah, happy Lycius," he said. "For she was a maid. More—"

"Put some oomph into it, man!" McIntosh urged. "Ye are starting to put me to sleep."

The Scotsman's companions agreed, exhorting John to be a tad more enthusiastic.

Embarrassed, John started over. "Ah, happy Lycius!" he said with as much enthusiasm as he could muster. "For she was a maid."

"That's better!" McIntosh said.

John continued, "More beautiful than ever twisted braid, or sigh'd, or blush'd, or on spring-flowered lea. Spread a green kirtle to the minstrelsy. A virgin—"

"A virgin purest lipp'd, yet in the lore, of love deep learned to the red heart's core," McIntosh interjected, taking up the refrain he knew by heart. The Scotsman continued, "Not one hour old, yet of sciential brain. To unperplex bliss from its neighbour pain."

"Bravo!" O'Driscoll enthused. His companions also expressed their appreciation of the Scotsman's literary prowess. Even John was impressed though he took care not to show it.

"Did I get it right?" McIntosh asked.

John quickly re-read the verse the Scotsman had quoted then looked up. "Word for feckin' word," he confirmed.

McIntosh gave a mock bow as his companions congratulated him on his prowess.

Two shrill blasts on the sergeant's whistle signalled that meal-time was over and the afternoon shift was underway. It was with much grumbling, and stretching of aching limbs, that the convicts reported to their work stations. A few lagged behind to relieve their full bladders. They pissed out in the open on the quarry floor. As always, stragglers were treated to lashes from soldiers' whips and blows from guards' batons.

The commencement of the new shift coincided with another rotation of duties. In the latest rotation, John and his companions found themselves in the gang tasked with carrying the smashed rocks to carts that were now lined up, minus their steeds, in the entrance to the quarry. It was hard work—every bit as back-breaking as smashing rocks albeit without the jarring to hands and arms that that job had entailed.

The convicts talked amongst themselves as they toiled. Some carried rocks from the quarry face to the carts while others returned to the face for their next load. A few had the luxury of heavy-duty wheelbarrows to support their loads, but these proved unwieldy on the rocky, uneven ground and there were a number of spills. Each spill was punished by a lashing, which was delivered by the nearest soldier.

John and Noel, who were a little away from the others, were in deep discussion as they carried yet another load of rocks toward the nearest of the empty carts. The latter had broached the subject of escape, and the former wanted nothing to do with it.

"Did you hear what I said?" Noel asked, barely able to contain his excitement.

"I heard the sun talking," John said. "Are you mad?" he asked. "Or do you just fancy the end of a rope?"

"I'm telling you, I can get us in on an escape," Noel insisted.

John looked more than a little incredulous. "You're crazy," he said. "Have you forgotten escaping is now a hanging offence for first-timers?" He added, "And *we* are first-timers."

Both men had stopped walking now. They faced each other, trying as best they could to ignore the weight of their loads.

Their fellow convicts shot glances their way as they walked by. McIntosh was among them. They didn't know it, but he had a vested interest in the conversation between the two friends. Looking at John and Noel, he asked, "What are you Irish goodfernuthins up to?"

"None of your business, Scottie," Noel shot back.

McIntosh laughed. Turning to the others, in a voice so loud everyone could hear, he announced, "Look at these two Irishmen. Always together like a couple of lovebirds!"

This sparked laughter amongst his companions, and they directed lewd comments toward the pair.

Ignoring the others, Noel said, "They reckon their plan is fool proof."

"And who is *they* exactly?" John asked.

"Ah . . . Terry, the Scotsman," Noel said. He glanced at McIntosh, confirming that was who he referred to.

"Oh, that's alright then," John said with as much sarcasm as he could muster. "Anyone can see he's a genius." He looked around until he saw who he was looking for—Dan Green and the other two convict-wardens who had been assigned to guard duties in the quarry. They were playing cards in the shade of the awning at that moment. He nodded toward them. "That's the job I want," he said. "Easier than this shit."

Noel glanced over at the trio. "Terry says we should give them a wide berth," he said at length.

"Tell me something I don't know," John said, indicating he'd already worked that out for himself. He and Noel noticed Green looking their way. They immediately resumed walking, resisting the temptation to drop their heavy loads.

"I'll tell you what's no good," John said, straining to avoid giving in to the temptation. "Breaking our backs carrying these feckin' rocks!" He hurried ahead to unload the rocks into the tray of the cart.

McIntosh, who was now returning for another load, approached Noel. "Is he in?" he asked.

Noel answered him with a shake of his head.

12

TWO ROTATIONS LATER, JOHN AND Noel found themselves smashing rocks once more. Neither was speaking. Not that they were still having a tiff. They were just too exhausted to talk.

The hard labour and the heat were taking their toll, and all the convicts were suffering one way or the other. Many had heat stroke to varying degrees, some were physically sick and two fainted. Everyone seemed to be working in slow motion.

Soldiers and guards also suffered in the heat, and they invariably took their discomfort and their frustrations out on the convicts. Their whips and batons worked overtime as the afternoon dragged on, and the convicts' output slowed even more.

The sight of an officer approaching the quarry on horseback proved a momentary distraction for all. The Redcoat was leading a spare horse that trailed behind him, and both horses kicked up little puffs of dust as they traversed the dry terrain.

As the officer drew closer, John recognised him as Lieutenant Hogan whom he'd observed following the convicts out to the quarry that morning. The last he'd seen of him was when he galloped off to assist the boy stuck in the tree. He noticed the spare horse was saddled, and he idly wondered who it was for.

Hogan galloped into the quarry and pulled up alongside Sergeant Rogers who at that moment was close to where John and Noel toiled. After exchanging salutes with the sergeant, Hogan asked, "Is there a blacksmith by the name of Samuel Thompson in this work party, Sergeant?"

Rogers conferred with his second-in-command, a nuggety corporal, then turned back to the lieutenant. "No, sir," he said. "I'm informed Thompson died a week ago."

"Damn it," Hogan swore. Muttering to himself, he said, "Seems there's a curse on smithies at Moreton Bay." He made a mental note to discipline the army's clerk for not updating the personnel records.

"What's the problem, Lieutenant?" the sergeant asked.

"Captain Marsden ordered me to second Thompson to assist the smithy in the foundry," Hogan said. "His assistant has just died."

John, who had overheard the entire conversation, sensed an opportunity. He stepped forward. "I'm a smithy, sir," he lied. *It's only a white lie,* he reasoned. *I was a smithy's labourer after all.* "I ran my own foundry in Ireland."

Hogan looked at John long and hard. "Is that a fact?"

"It is, sir."

"What's your name, Irishman?"

"John Graham, sir."

"How long were you a smithy, Graham?"

"Ten years, sir."

"And what crime sees you here?"

"I . . . stole five pounds from my . . . uncle."

It was ten pounds, and I took it from my employer, but hopefully they won't have a record of that here at Moreton Bay.

John hoped his employment records weren't here either as they would show he was only a smithy's assistant, and then only for one year, not ten.

Hogan studied John closely. He wasn't aware he shared the same misgivings Marsden had about the Irishman with the startling blue eyes. John Graham had rebellion written all over his face. Against his better judgement, Hogan asked, "Can you ride, Graham?"

John met Hogan's steady gaze.

I can't ride, but I'm a fast learner.

"Yes, sir," he said, his reply oozing confidence.

A touch of the blarney never hurts.

Hogan turned to Rogers. "Unshackle him," he ordered.

"Yes, sir," the sergeant replied.

As Rogers unshackled John, Hogan turned to the nearest mounted soldier—a young private. "What's your name, soldier?"

"Private Henry Askew, sir," the soldier said.

"I want you to accompany me, Private Askew." As an afterthought, he added, "To keep a close eye on *him*." He nodded toward John. Then, addressing the Irishman, he said, "Mount up."

Noel, who was standing nearby and had heard the entire discussion, looked on in amazement as a now unshackled John prepared to mount the spare horse Hogan had brought with him. He alone knew that his friend from Dundalk, in County Louth, was never a smithy and, to the best of his knowledge, had only ever sat on a horse once or twice—and a pony it was at that. Noel had to control himself so he didn't laugh out loud.

Hogan and the other soldiers directed strange glances John's way as he tried to mount the horse, a skittish mare, which appeared to sense the Irishman didn't know horses. The mare tried to kick him. When that didn't deter him, she tried to bite him.

"It's been a while," John mumbled by way of explanation as he finally managed to mount the horse.

It was immediately obvious to Hogan that John Graham couldn't ride. Wondering what else the Irishman had lied about, he grumbled, "Follow me." With that, he galloped from the quarry, his horse's hooves sending up clouds of dust.

John flashed a nervous glance Noel's way then kicked his horse's flanks and held on for dear life as the mare bolted after Hogan's mount. Private Askew followed close behind John, keeping an eye on him as ordered.

The last Noel saw before his friend and his escorts disappeared from view was he'd relinquished his grip on the reins and was lying forward with his arms wrapped tight around the horse's neck.

Convicts working in and around the settlement gaped at the sight of one of their own riding, unshackled and on horseback, into the settlement. Their amazement had as much to do with John's highly unconventional riding style as his unshackled state.

No-one was more amazed than John that he'd galloped the quarter-mile between the quarry and the settlement without falling off. He breathed a sigh of relief as Hogan reined in his horse alongside the stables, and motioned to him and the young private to follow suit. Only Askew's timely intervention prevented John's mare from riding off into the sunset with her rider still on board.

John's dismount from the frisky mare was as entertaining as mounting her had been. She reared up and struck out at him with her front hooves, narrowly missing his head. The Irishman was about to give her a tongue-lashing, but thought better of it.

As Hogan observed the interaction between man and horse, his misgivings about John intensified, but he, too, held his tongue. "Follow me," he said curtly.

John and Private Askew followed the lieutenant through a doorway at one end of the stables. It was the end farthest away from the convicts' mess where John had now eaten twice. The Irishman had assumed the doorway led into the stables, but was surprised to find this end of the building accommodated the settlement's foundry.

Hogan marched straight over to the resident blacksmith who was busy hammering a plate of red hot steel he'd not long removed from the forge.

Only now did Irish smithy Jonathan O'Shea, himself a convict, realise he had company. He dropped his tools and studied the new arrivals as they approached.

"O'Shea, this is John Graham," the lieutenant said, nodding toward John. "He claims to be a smithy and is interested in replacing Thompson as your new assistant." He looked hard at O'Shea. "Will he do?" he asked.

John's heart sank. He'd thought the job was his, and only now did he realise he was still auditioning for it. His confidence wasn't helped any by the way the smithy was now looking at him.

Holy Mary. He's seen right through me.

John flashed his most engaging smile at O'Shea.

As the smithy assessed the younger Irishman, John assessed him. He figured O'Shea was all of fifty, possibly older. Despite his age, he looked as hard as nails, his lean arms defined by sinewy muscle, no doubt a legacy of plying his trade over many years. His keen eyes missed nothing as he looked John up and down.

O'Shea didn't need to question John to know he was no smithy. "Where were you a smithy?" he asked.

Only now after hearing O'Shea speak did John realise for sure that he was Irish.

He suddenly felt hopeful. "In Dundalk, Count—"

"I know where Dundalk is, laddie," the smithy interjected. "I also knew all the feckin' smithies in County Louth." He glared at John.

John's heart sank once more.

"Who did you work for?" the smithy asked.

"I . . . worked for myself."

The question-and-answer exchange continued for several minutes under Lieutenant Hogan's watchful eye. At length, O'Shea looked at the lieutenant and simply said, "He'll do." With that, the smithy turned and resumed hammering the steel plate he'd been working on.

Hogan, who was as surprised as John by O'Shea's response, motioned to John and to the young soldier to accompany him outside. As they departed, none noticed that the smithy was quietly chuckling to himself. He'd liked the look of the young Irishman and intended to take him on from the outset.

Outside the foundry, Hogan looked at John and shook his head. Finally, he said, "Well, I guess you were telling the truth Graham. The job's yours." Turning to Private Askew, he said, "Shackle him, Private."

"Yes, sir." Askew said. He retrieved a set of leg-irons he'd noticed hanging just inside the foundry door and quickly fitted them to John's ankles.

"You two can travel in that cart." Hogan said, pointing to a horse-drawn cart parked outside the mess at the opposite end of the stables.

"Yes, sir," Askew said as he escorted John toward the waiting cart.

"Follow me when you're ready," Hogan called out as he mounted his horse.

"Sir."

As John was being escorted to the Marsdens' cottage, Marsden himself was busy supervising half a dozen soldiers who were in the process of unloading caskets of rifles from a large crate that had been deposited on his front yard that morning. The rifles, along with other items, had been unloaded off *the Hoogley* the previous day. "Store those in the barn around the back," he ordered his men.

The soldiers worked in relays, carrying the heavy caskets around to the barn.

Marsden was already in a bad mood following his frustrating meeting with Lord Cheetham, and having to store army property at his homestead was doing nothing to improve his mood. Storage space in the settlement was at a premium and, until planned new facilities were built, he was expected to help out by storing materials and equipment—and now weapons—at his residence.

The captain's mood deteriorated further when he noticed his daughter flash by on horseback. He had no qualms about Helen riding: she loved horses and was a skilled rider. However, she was under firm instructions—as was Matthew—never to venture from the vicinity of the cottage without himself or one of his soldiers being present. Marsden had instilled in them that the convicts and Aborigines, not to mention the snakes, crocs and other such creatures, couldn't be trusted.

Helen flashed past again. This time she saw her father, and waved. Marsden waved her over to him, but she didn't notice. Either that or she pretended not to notice.

Despite his annoyance, Marsden couldn't help but be proud of his daughter's horsemanship. She rode as well as any woman he'd seen ride, and better than some of his soldiers. Almost as well as himself, in fact.

Corporal Davies, the young soldier who had accompanied him to meet *the Hoogley* yesterday, approached Marsden. "The caskets have all been stored, Captain," he said.

"Safely locked away?"

"Yes, sir." Davies handed his superior a key. "In the storage room at the far end of the barn." His eyes settled on a dozen or so cartons that remained in the bottom of the crate. "Can we carry those inside for you, sir?" he asked.

"No, that will be all, Corporal," Marsden said. "You and the men are dismissed."

The pair exchanged salutes, and Davies and the other soldiers, who by now had worked up a good sweat-up, headed back to the settlement on foot.

Marsden looked at the cartons the corporal had referred to. They contained personal items, and much as he would have liked to ask the soldiers to carry them into the cottage, he preferred not to use them for personal chores as strictly speaking that was against army regulations. And he was a stickler for the rules.

No sooner had his soldiers departed than his daughter returned. Still on horseback and astride her favourite steed Benjie, she reined in, in a cloud of dust, only a few feet away from her father.

"I swear if Benjie was any faster we'd be flying, papa!" she said breathlessly, her flushed face full of excitement after an exhilarating ride.

Any plans to deliver a tongue-lashing to his daughter evaporated as Marsden studied her. She'd never looked more alive, or more beautiful, to his eyes than she did now. Even so, he knew it was his fatherly duty to caution her. Adopting as stern a look as he could muster, he said, "Helen, you know you mustn't ride alone. I told you—"

"Papa, you fuss too much!" Helen declared, laughing gaily as she dismounted her steed. She planted a kiss on her father's cheek before he could remonstrate with her any further. Only then did she notice the cartons in the crate. "Are those what I think they are?" she asked wide-eyed.

Marsden nodded, confirming they were what Helen thought they were—gifts he'd ordered from Sydney Town.

"Wonderful!" Helen gushed. "I'll get Benjie brushed down and then I will come and help you unpack."

"No need, I'll get the tracker to look after Benj," Marsden said. He turned and called, "Tracker!"

Before Helen could object, Barega appeared around the corner of the cottage. As always, when he wasn't out tracking or hunting, he wore European clothes. Only his feet were bare: he never could get accustomed to wearing the white man's shoes. He grinned at the young woman when he saw her. Helen quickly looked away.

"Look after the horse, will you?" Marsden asked.

"Yes, Mister," Barega said. Without another word, he took the reins from Helen and led Benji around to the barn that also served as his living quarters.

"I don't like that man," Helen murmured as soon as the tracker was out of earshot.

"Don't let Orana hear you say that," Marsden cautioned, referring to their Aboriginal maid who lived on the property with Barega.

From inside the house, Missus Marsden could be heard calling to her daughter. Helen skipped inside, leaving her father alone.

The captain was about to pick up the first of the cartons when he noticed a horse-drawn cart approaching. It was being escorted by Lieutenant Hogan who rode on horseback ahead of the cart and its driver and passenger.

Hogan pulled up opposite his superior and dismounted. No sooner had they exchanged salutes than Private Askew arrived aboard the cart, stopping close by.

Marsden knew who John was even before Hogan introduced him. Not by name, but by sight. He remembered that rebellious face and those incredible blue eyes from yesterday when he saw him at the wharf.

"This is the blackmith's new assistant, Captain," the lieutenant said. Referring to the smithy, he added, "O'Shea's happy enough with him."

Marsden fixed John with a steely gaze, which John met. "Bring him to me, Private," Marsden ordered Askew without taking his eyes off the Irishman.

"Yes, sir!" Askew hurried to assist his shackled passenger down from the cart.

Moments later, John found himself standing before Marsden.

"Your name?" the captain asked.

"John Graham, sir."

The accent confirmed for Marsden that John was Irish. That came as no surprise. He was aware many of the latest batch of convicts were Irish, so it was odds on that this one was. Irish, that is. That aside, he thought the convict's nationality kind of went with his rebellious look. Marsden proceeded to give John the same grilling that both the smithy and the lieutenant had before him.

John, who was very aware Hogan was listening closely to his answers, made sure his latest responses matched his earlier ones. *Holy mother of God, how do I get myself into these pickles?* he asked himself. He tried hard to appear relaxed, but that only made him feel more tense. Fortunately, it didn't show, and his responses did match his earlier ones.

13

MARSDEN STUDIED JOHN ASTUTELY FOR a moment. Though still wary, he couldn't help but be impressed by the Irishman's confidence. Finally, he said, "It's rather serendipitous you are here." He added, "If you hadn't turned up, I would have had to send to Sydney Town for another blacksmith."

John nodded with all the sincerity he could marshal to convey he shared in the captain's concern that the settlement could have been left a smithy short.

Heaven forbid that should happen.

Not for the first time he thought he may have missed his calling.

I should've been an actor.

Marsden turned back to Hogan. "Thank you, Lieutenant." Before dismissing Hogan, he had a thought. "Perhaps Private Askew could wait behind while Graham helps me get these cartons inside," he said. While the captain didn't ask army personnel to undertake personal chores, he wasn't averse to ordering convicts to help out on occasion.

"Certainly, sir," Hogan said. He saluted his superior and then relayed the captain's orders to Askew before mounting his steed and riding back toward the settlement.

Marsden turned to John and pointed to the cartons. "Bring those through to the dining room, Graham," he said. He disappeared inside, leaving John to follow, and leaving Askew waiting by the horse-drawn cart, as ordered.

From inside the cottage, John heard Marsden say, "Show Mister Graham where to go, Matthew."

Moments later, young Matthew emerged from the cottage and, bold as brass, introduced himself to John. "Hello," he said, "I'm Matthew."

"Hello," the Irishman smiled. "I'm John Graham." He noticed the lad couldn't take his eyes off the carton he was holding.

"This way, Mister Graham," Matthew said, disappearing through the front door.

John followed the boy down a dark corridor to a doorway that opened into the dining room. His leg-irons clinked on the floorboards as he shuffled along. En route, through another open door, he noticed the Marsdens' maid Orana peeling potatoes in the kitchen. He guessed she was preparing for the evening meal.

"Through here." Matthew's voice carried to John from the dining room.

The Irishman entered the room where he found the boy waiting with his parents.

"Put it there," Marsden said to John, pointing to an alcove built into the far wall.

John nodded respectfully to Missus Marsden then shuffled toward the alcove. Suddenly aware of his sweaty body and his dirty clothes, not to mention his clinking leg-irons, he could sense the Marsdens' eyes on him as he deposited the carton and shuffled out to collect the next one. Behind him, he could hear Marsden telling his wife that he was the smithy's new assistant. He thought he heard Missus Marsden say something like "I hope he has a little more luck than the last two blacksmiths" but he couldn't be sure.

When John carried the final carton inside, he found he had the dining room to himself. The voices of family members carried to him from elsewhere in the cottage. After placing the carton alongside the others, he took a moment to catch his breath, and to survey the room.

It was, he decided, a simple but tastefully furnished room. Lace curtains framed latticed windows that afforded a spectacular view of the settlement, the river, and the hinterland and hills beyond; a large oak dining table with seating for six people occupied the centre of the room while comfortable chairs were dotted here and there, conveying a feeling of casual elegance.

Framed portrait paintings of people young and old adorned the walls and lined a mantelpiece that protruded above an open fireplace. John guessed the portraits were family members—many of them departed judging by the faded images.

He didn't need to look any further to realise the cottage couldn't be further removed from the tiny, one-room hut he shared with his fellow convicts. Being here, now, filled him with envy, and with a sense of loss. Loss for a life that had somehow passed him by—a life he doubted he'd ever experience.

Suddenly depressed, the Irishman felt an urge to distance himself from the dining room and from the cottage. He quickly shuffled from the room. As he proceeded down the corridor toward the front door, he noticed a bedroom door ajar that hadn't been open earlier. The sweet sound of a young woman humming a lullaby carried to him.

Drawing level with the open door, he peered in and saw Helen. She was sitting in front of a dressing table, combing her hair. The late afternoon sun shining through a nearby window cast her in a golden glow, making her blonde hair sparkle and creating an aura around her. She'd obviously just bathed for her hair was wet and she wore only a bathrobe. Oblivious to John's presence, she continued humming to herself.

John was immediately struck by her beauty. He recognised her as the young woman he'd seen with her mother and brother in the field that morning. Close up, she looked even more beautiful.

Only now did he notice a bookshelf against the room's far wall. It was so large it covered the entire wall, and every shelf was packed with books. The books' titles revealed Helen's reading tastes were wide and varied.

Beautiful and intelligent.

John couldn't help but be impressed.

Something made Helen look around. Her eyes widened when she saw John, but she didn't cry out. In fact, she kept humming and she kept combing her hair. Although outwardly calm, inwardly she was out of control, mesmerised by the startling blue eyes that stared out from the stranger's sunburnt, unshaven face.

The mood was broken when a nearby door slammed, causing both of them to jump. John flashed a cheeky grin at Helen and resumed shuffling toward the front door, his chains clinking once more on the wooden floorboards.

Alone again, Helen wondered who the stranger was—and why she hadn't heard the clinking chains earlier. She realised she must have been daydreaming. That was something she'd been doing a lot of late.

Matthew suddenly burst into her room.

"Matthew!" she scolded. "I told you to knock."

"Come look!" Matthew said, ignoring his big sister's scolding. "The presents have arrived." Excited, he grabbed her hand and started to pull her from the bedroom.

Helen resisted for a moment. "Who was that man?" she asked.

Matthew had to think for a moment. "Oh, that was Mister . . . Mister Graham I think he said it was." Anticipating Helen's next question, he added, "Papa got him to bring the presents inside." He couldn't wait any longer. "Come on, sis!"

Helen allowed herself to be pulled from her room by her excited brother. As she was dragged into the corridor, she looked through the front door, but was disappointed to see the stranger had gone.

In the dining room, they found their parents had already started to unpack the cartons.

"Wait for me!" Matthew shouted, running to inspect the cartons' contents.

Observing his son's enthusiasm, Marsden glanced at his wife. "If only he moved that quickly for his lessons," he lamented.

"Be careful not to break anything, Matthew," Missus Marsden warned. "There is no rush."

Matthew got the message and restrained his enthusiasm as best he could.

"One gift each," Marsden advised his children. "The remainder are for Christmas," he added. "Now close your eyes."

The happy pair did as they were asked. Marsden reached into one of the cartons and drew out two gift-wrapped packages. "Alright you can look now," he said.

Brother and sister opened their eyes and took the offerings from their father.

Matthew tore the paper wrapping off his gift to discover a pile of new books. The top books comprised a selection of history and nature books, which didn't excite him too much. However, the next lot of books were boys' own tales, complete with colourful diagrams, which more than made up for his earlier disappointment. "Thanks papa!" he said.

Helen opened her parcel and pulled out a black evening gown. "Oh father, it's beautiful," she gushed. The young beauty held the gown to her breast, momentarily overcome.

"I thought perhaps you could wear it at the Governor's dinner this week," Marsden said.

"I will," Helen promised. "It's lovely. I'm going to try it on." She hurried from the room, studying the gown as she left.

Missus Marsden looked tenderly at her husband. "You chose well, my dear," she murmured. "That will mean a lot to her. Her first-ever evening gown." As an afterthought, she added, "That gown will surely please Lieutenant Hogan at the Governor's—"

"Mother!" Helen called from her room. She'd overheard her mother's comment.

Missus Marsden smiled at her daughter's reaction. Her husband, however, did not.

"He shall be there . . . in all his barbaric splendour, no doubt," Marsden said, unimpressed by the young lieutenant's interest in his daughter.

His wife looked at him critically. "Tom!" she rebuked him.

"What? It's true. All the lieutenant is good for is the hunt."

"Sounds familiar." Missus Marsden thought the two men shared a number of things in common, including a love of hunting. Although to be fair her husband hunted wild game whereas Hogan hunted men.

It irked Marsden to think that Hogan was interested in Helen. While he considered the lieutenant had the makings of a good officer, he didn't necessarily think he'd make a good husband. Not for his daughter at least. It was Hogan's cavalier attitude toward the wellbeing of those he considered beneath him—such as Moreton Bay's convicts—that Marsden didn't admire. Yesterday being a case in point when it was obvious the lieutenant had turned a blind eye as Barega set about killing two of the convicts they were pursuing. The captain marvelled that one of the escapees had been returned alive.

Marsden's expression softened and he reached back into the open carton, drawing out another gift-wrapped parcel. "And for my lovely wife," he murmured as he placed the parcel in Missus Marsden's hand.

"Tom, you shouldn't have."

The captain chuckled. "You don't even know what it is yet." His wife unwrapped the present to reveal an ornate hair pin.

"Oh, Tom it's . . ."

"Beautiful. Just like you." He gently placed the pin in his wife's hair and kissed her forehead.

Helen chose that tender moment to return. She was resplendent in her new evening gown. It clung to her slim figure, making her look more beautiful than ever.

The sight moved her mother to tears. "Darling, you look radiant," Missus Marsden said. "Don't you agree, Tom?"

Marsden could only nod in agreement. He couldn't trust himself to speak, so overtaken was he by his daughter's radiance.

Dusk was falling as the convicts employed in the quarry headed back to the settlement. The return trek was considerably slower than the outward one had been thirteen hours earlier, and more painful too—especially for Noel and the other new men. They were sunburnt, thirsty, hungry and aching all over. Above all, they were bone weary and yearning to rest their tired bodies.

Even the soldiers were subdued. For them, too, it had been a long, hot day. Much like the previous day, and the one before that, and, as they well knew, the one awaiting them tomorrow. At the bay, some things never changed.

As they shuffled along, their leg-irons clinking, the long-serving convicts wondered what culinary delights would be served up in the mess this evening, so famished were they, while the new arrivals could think of nothing other than sleep, so spent were they.

Amongst the older hands, Paddy O'Donnell looked around for Terry McIntosh. When he saw the big Scotsman, several rows behind, he shouted, "Terry, give us another verse or two!"

"Aye," Rhys Jones said, "give us another verse."

McIntosh needed no excuse to recite another verse or two from the *Moreton Bay* ballad. "Alright, alright," he said, pretending to be annoyed. "Here goes . . . For three long years I was beastly treated, heavy irons on my legs I wore. My back from flogging it was lacerated, and often painted with crimson gore—"

"You'd know all about that, McIntosh!" a soldier shouted.

"Aye, he would at that," another soldier agreed."

Undeterred, McIntosh continued, "And many a lad from downright starvation lies mouldering humbly beneath the clay—"

"Would you look at that?" Sean O'Driscoll said, interrupting the Scotsman in mid-verse.

O'Driscoll and the others gaped in amazement at the sight of John reclining on the tray of the horse-drawn cart that was transferring him from the Marsden cottage to the settlement. Their paths wouldn't have crossed had the cart not been delayed after suffering a minor mishap shortly after departing the cottage. John was now resting against the cart's tailboard, his eyes closed and his hands clasped behind his head as Private Askew steered the cart past their surprised audience.

"Looks like he's on bloody holiday," Luke Donovan observed.

"Aye, he does at that," Pat Kennedy agreed.

Noel, who was sandwiched between Kennedy and Donovan, chuckled to himself at the sight of his mate lording it up.

Only now did John deign to open an eye. He fastened it on his fellow convicts, gave them a cheery wave, and closed his eye again.

"Talk about the luck o' the Irish," English convict Don Henderson grumbled.

John heard the grumbles, but he didn't react. Listening to the comments of his fellow convicts, he was glad he'd been delayed. It warmed his heart to hear them complaining about his change of fortune for it reinforced the conclusion he'd reached since laying eyes on the Marsden girl—that this Irishman's rotten luck could be about to change for the better.

On entering the settlement, one more surprise awaited John and his fellow convicts.

They saw nothing untoward until they bypassed the compound en route to the mess for their evening meal. There, hanging like a rag doll from the gallows, was the lifeless body of Frank Patterson, the Cockney who had been so publicly flogged for attempting to escape. Bare-chested and bloodied, the marks left by the flogging he'd been subjected to were visible for all to see.

The convicts and their escorts alike were shocked into stunned silence at the sight. To a man, they'd assumed Patterson had already been punished, and they couldn't fathom why he was now hanging from the gallows.

John's escort, Private Askew, conferred with another soldier who, it turned out, had witnessed the hanging earlier that afternoon. On returning to the cart, Askew advised John that Patterson had been captured trying to escape yet again, and the luckless convict had been hung on Cheetham's orders by Lieutenant Hogan. "Death by suicide they believe it was," Askew confided.

John understood what the soldier was saying. *Death by suicide* was a term ascribed to those convicts who opted for death ahead of serving out their sentences. He'd witnessed the practice once before, at Parramatta, and he'd heard it was common at Norfolk Island. He was soon to learn it wasn't uncommon at Moreton Bay either. Looking back at Patterson as they continued to the mess, John asked, "Are they going to leave him there?"

"Aye," Askew said. "Apparently Cheetham wants him left there overnight to serve as a warning for the rest of you."

For John and the other newcomers their second night in the settlement was but a blur. More tired than they'd ever been, they were almost literally asleep on their feet as they assembled in the mess for their evening meal. The meal, which was no more edifying than the previous night's dinner, consisted of onion soup so lacking in onions it was little better than warm water; it was followed by tiny portions of underdone kangaroo meat swamped in re-heated gravy so congealed a knife and fork was needed to cut through it.

The convicts were then escorted from the mess to their respective huts where they were unshackled and interned for the night.

In John's hut, as was the case in all six huts, the long-serving convicts had no sympathy for the newcomers' aches and pains. Worse, they delighted in throwing off at the new men and they took every opportunity to poke fun at them.

The banter was borderline malicious, and it was one-way traffic as the newcomers were too exhausted to respond. Much of it was led by the giant Londoner Dan Green who was now almost fully recovered from the beating he had received the previous night—although his bruises were still plainly visible—and he'd regained any confidence he may have lost as a result of that.

Much of the banter was directed John's way as a result of his sudden good fortune in being appointed assistant to the smithy. There was some feeling behind it, too, because the others realised the appointment meant John would no longer have to slave away beside them from dawn till dusk in the quarry. To their annoyance, the comments all went over the Irishman's head. He was too buggered to care.

The only incident of note occurred when the convicts first entered the hut. John had made a beeline for the bunk formerly occupied by the now deceased Angus McPherson. One or two of the older hands who had been relegated to sleeping on the floor considered they should be first in line to claim the spare bunk—in particular

Don Henderson, one of Green's allies.

Henderson recruited Green to help him *persuade* John to relinquish the bunk he'd claimed, and only some fast talking by the cheeky Irishman had averted a beating, or worse perhaps. John had reminded them that smithies were in short supply at Moreton Bay, and neither Lord Cheetham nor Captain Marsden would be at all happy if the new assistant blacksmith was too incapacitated to report for work in the morning.

14

*T*HE *HOOGLEY*, THE SCHOONER THAT had delivered John and his fellow convicts to Moreton Bay two days earlier, also delivered back copies of newspapers for the reading pleasure of the settlement's military personnel and settlers. Among these were copies of *The Sydney Gazette,* and it was the most recent edition of this, Australia's first ever newspaper, that Marsden was reading now.

This issue was dated December 20, 1826, so the news was only two weeks old, which made for a refreshing change. That was one advantage of the growth of Moreton Bay's convict population: shipments of convicts to the settlement were becoming more frequent, and with them came little luxuries that made life easier for the settlement's non-convict population at least. Luxuries such as letters from home, and liquor, sweets and reading material from Sydney Town.

Reading was something of a treat for Marsden. He was usually too busy, or too tired, to read. However, he made an exception for *the Gazette,* reading it from front cover to back, and usually over breakfast, as he was doing now.

On this occasion, the newspaper helped take his mind off Patterson's execution the previous day. The hanging had taken place without his knowledge whilst he'd been tied up supervising the unloading of supplies at the cottage. Marsden couldn't help thinking Cheetham had taken advantage of his absence in sanctioning the execution. In his absence, the commandant had ordered Hogan to do the deed. It was carried out, in Marsden's opinion, with indecent haste, and he vowed to have it out with Cheetham.

Breakfasting with his children was also something of a rarity for Marsden as he usually reported for duty in the settlement at daybreak, before they were up and about. However, on this occasion he'd promised them they could ride into the settlement with him and accompany him on his morning rounds, so he'd delayed his departure time.

Matthew and Helen were discussing the Governor's dinner, which was now only a day away, but their father was in a world of his own, so engrossed was he in his reading.

Nearby, Missus Marsden fussed about like the mother hen she was. "More tea, my dear?" she asked as she hovered over her husband, teapot in hand.

Marsden mumbled something in the affirmative and raised his near-empty cup, which his wife promptly filled. The article that so preoccupied him was the front page lead story whose banner headline read: "Convict rebellion on Norfolk Island."

The headline caught Missus Marsden's eye. She gasped, "Lordy! A convict rebellion."

This got Matthew's attention. "A rebellion?" he asked, alarmed. "Here?'

Only now did Marsden look up. "No, it was at Norfolk Island," he said.

"When was this, Tom?" Missus Marsden asked.

"Four months ago."

"What happened, papa?" Helen asked.

"It seems fifty convicts overcame their guards and killed a soldier."

"Could the same thing happen here, papa?" Matthew asked.

"No fear of that, son," Marsden chuckled.

"Moreton Bay's convicts are too starved and weak to even think of rebelling," Helen piped up. Treatment of the settlement's convict population had long been a sore point with her, and she wasn't slow to remind her father of this whenever the opportunity arose.

Marsden scowled at his daughter as he tried to think of a suitable response. His thinking was interrupted by the chiming of the grandfather clock that occupied pride of place in the hallway, reminding him he needed to get moving. "Come on you two," he said to his children, "it's time to see to the horses."

Helen and Matthew needed no extra encouragement to ride with their father. Riding was Helen's passion, and it was fast becoming Matthew's, too. They jumped up, bade their mother goodbye and hurried outside, leaving their parents alone for a moment.

"They do so enjoy it when you take them riding," Missus Marsden said, helping her husband into his red tunic.

"Don't fuss so, my dear," Marsden complained half-heartedly. As he always did whenever his wife fussed over his uniform, Marsden feigned impatience, and, as she always did, she ignored him.

"There you go," Missus Marsden said, satisfied he now looked the part. "Are you prepared for your big meeting this afternoon?" The meeting she referred to had been called by Lord Cheetham late the previous day. Its purpose was to go over final arrangements for the Governor's dinner.

"As prepared as I'll ever be."

"Well, I am sure it will go fine." She knew her husband planned to discuss more than the dinner arrangements with Cheetham. He was still fuming about the hanging, news of which they'd kept from their children. "Good luck," she said, kissing him as he headed for the back door.

"Thank you, my dear."

Outside, Marsden was greeted by the sight of his children preparing to mount their steeds, which had already been saddled for them by Barega. The tracker was standing nearby, holding the reins of the captain's horse, which he'd also saddled. It was a routine Barega repeated every morning—when he wasn't away tracking or hunting, that is.

Matthew's mount, which he'd received for his eleventh birthday and had named *George,* was a pony. George looked like a miniature of Helen's steed Benji, but that's where the similarities ended. The pony was so docile he looked half asleep, and he was so lethargic he could barely break into a gallop. Matthew often complained about this to his father, but the complaints fell on deaf ears for Marsden had insisted his son's first mount be of passive temperament.

Marsden took the reins of his horse from Barega, mounted it and looked around at his children. "Ready?" he asked.

They nodded, their faces full of anticipation.

"Move out!" Marsden ordered in military parlance, leading the way toward the settlement.

"Yes, sir!" Helen and Matthew said in exaggerated unison as they followed their father down the hillside.

Behind them, Barega observed their progress. His deep set, black eyes missed nothing as he watched the trio ride off. He shifted his gaze to the riverbank beyond, and he frowned at the sight of the Quandamooka men spearing fish from the riverbank. The tracker and others of his Joondaburri tribe had no time for the Quandamooka. They were ancient enemies.

Barega was distracted by a movement behind him. He turned and noticed Orana, the Marsden's maid, emerge from the cottage. Orana saw him and flashed a knowing smile as she walked toward the annex she shared with Barega. The tracker returned her smile and hurried to join her. It was a routine they both enjoyed.

Orana was of Quandamooka blood, but Barega was prepared to overlook that. His concubine gave him too much pleasure to quibble about her heritage.

◦ξ────3◦

Smithy Jonathan O'Shea looked on as his new assistant poured molten steel from the furnace into an iron vat. He'd only needed five minutes with John to confirm his earlier suspicion that the young Irishman was no more a qualified blacksmith than he was a professional ballet dancer. Despite that, O'Shea could see John was a quick learner, and he seemed agreeable enough, so he was prepared to persevere. His previous assistant, though highly skilled and proficient, had been as disagreeable as John was agreeable, and he'd vowed to look for other attributes in his next appointment.

As for John, he was elated to be working in the foundry and not out in the hot sun, breaking his back smashing rocks. However physical smithing may be, it was nothing compared to working in the quarry. Not that the foundry didn't have its drawbacks: even at this early hour, before the sun was up, John noticed the heat from the furnace was fierce. He could only imagine how hot it would be come mid-day. Little wonder he and the smithy were already perspiring.

Sensing O'Shea's eyes on him, John asked, "What's this molten steel for?"

"It's to make sleeves, like those"—the smithy pointed to a dozen curved metal sheets stacked end on end against the foundry's far wall—"for the posts supporting the old wharf," he said. "To strengthen 'em."

That made sense to John. He'd observed the wharf was in a serious state of disrepair. Only now did he note his opposite wasn't shackled or restrained by leg-irons. He wondered if O'Shea was a convict-warden, but dismissed that thought almost immediately.

Sounds from outside signalled to them they were about to have company.

Moments later, Marsden walked in. He was carrying two damaged horse shoes, which he handed to O'Shea. "Fix these will you?" the captain asked.

"Yes, sir," O'Shea said. He took the shoes from Marsden, and busied himself repairing them while, nearby, John poured the last batch of molten steel into the vat.

Marsden observed John at work as he addressed O'Shea. "How is the new man working out?" he asked.

"A bit early to say, sir," O'Shea mumbled. "But I think he'll be fine."

Marsden smiled to himself. Coming from the hard-bitten smithy, he knew that was high praise indeed for the new assistant.

At that moment, Helen and Matthew walked in. They were arguing about who was the better rider, and didn't notice John immediately. When they finally saw him, they fell silent.

John had noticed the pair as soon as they'd entered the foundry. More to the point, he'd noticed Helen, and yet again he was struck by her beauty. *If only I was ten years younger,* he thought. *And not stuck in this place.* He flashed a conspiring smile at her.

Helen returned smile and found herself flushing. Those blue eyes of John's affected her so. She glanced at her father and hoped he hadn't witnessed the silent exchange. He hadn't.

John wondered if Helen would look so happy if she'd seen Patterson's body hanging from the gallows the previous day. Fortunately, the body had been removed during the night. He wasn't to know that Marsden had ordered its removal after convincing Cheetham it had been left hanging long enough to teach the convicts a lesson.

As John wheeled the heavy vat of molten steel on a trolley toward a workbench, some of the steel splashed over the lip of the vat, cooling as it settled in a pool on the earth floor. His progress was seriously hampered by his leg-irons.

Marsden noticed John was struggling. "Graham!" he shouted. "Wait."

John pulled up and waited as Marsden approached him. The captain produced a bunch of keys hanging from a large steel key ring on his belt. He selected a master key. "This should do it," he muttered. With that he bent down and tried to unlock John's leg-irons. "Damn!" He realised he'd selected the wrong key. After two more unsuccessful attempts, he found the matching key and, a moment later the smithy's assistant was unshackled.

The surprised Irishman was rendered speechless.

Noting John's surprise, Marsden said, "You have all the tools in this foundry to bust out of those leg irons anyway, Graham." The captain added, "Best you're free to work unhindered." He made a mental note to advise the guards of John's new status later.

John mumbled his thanks and resumed wheeling the vat across the floor. He moved much more freely now and had a spring in his step.

As the two Irishmen worked at their respective tasks, Marsden conducted a quick tour of the foundry, noting where improvements were required, while Matthew buried his head in a new book he'd brought along with him. Helen pretended to study some fancy iron railings that were stacked against the near wall whilst surreptitiously observing John. The younger of the two Irishmen intrigued her.

Matthew came across a word he couldn't decipher. He trotted over toward his father, holding out his open book. "Papa, what is this word?" he asked.

John, who was closer to the boy than Marsden was at that moment, said, "Here, let me see."

Matthew hesitated. He looked to his father who had noted the interchange between the two. Marsden nodded. Emboldened, Matthew held the open page up to John's face, his forefinger pointing at the strange word. "This word," he said.

John glanced at the page. "Honorary," he said. "It's like being given something without really owning it."

Matthew was impressed.

So, too, was Marsden who looked at John in a new light. "You're a blacksmith and you can read?" he asked.

"My family's landlord was also our benefactor," John explained. "He insisted all his tenants' children receive an education." That much at least was the truth. What he didn't divulge was his mother had shrewdly arranged the free lessons for her children in return for performing certain favours for the landlord. It was, he recalled, an arrangement that seemed to suit his mother as she also received fashionable clothes and other gifts in return for allowing the landlord to share her bed on occasion.

"Ah, a piece of good fortune for the Grahams, I'm sure," Marsden said.

"Yes, sir," John said.

Marsden realised Helen had been uncharacteristically quiet since entering the foundry. He looked around and observed she seemed enchanted by the smithy's new assistant.

Suddenly aware of her father's stern gaze, Helen excused herself and left the foundry, saying she would check on the horses.

Meanwhile, Matthew repeated the new word he'd just learned, and practised using it in various ways. "My sister has an honorary brain," he said. When he got no reaction, he repeated it, only louder.

"I heard that!" Helen shouted from outside the open door.

O'Shea chose that moment to announce he'd finished repairing the horse-shoes. "All yours, Captain," he said, handing the shoes to Marsden.

"Thank you," Marsden said. He nodded to O'Shea, and then to John, before departing. Over his shoulder, he called, "Come on, Matthew."

The boy smiled at John and ran after his father.

Father and son emerged from the foundry to find Helen deep in discussion with Private Withers who had not long arrived on horseback. Marsden recognised him as the young soldier Cheetham often used as his coachman whenever he needed a chauffeur. To his annoyance, the captain observed the soldier was so enamoured by his daughter he hadn't even noticed him.

It was Helen who first saw Marsden. "Papa, Private Withers has a message for you," she said.

Withers sat bolt upright in the saddle when he finally noticed his superior. "Sir!" he said, executing the smartest salute he'd ever delivered.

Marsden returned the salute. "If you have a message for me, I suggest you deliver it to me and not to my daughter, Private," he grumbled.

"Yes, sir," Withers stammered. "Sorry, sir."

"Very well, let me have it."

"Lord Cheetham has asked if you could bring forward your afternoon meeting to this morning, Captain."

"When exactly this morning?" Marsden asked.

"Ah . . . he mentioned straightaway, sir."

"If he mentioned straightaway, you should have said that, Private." Without waiting for a response, Marsden turned to his children. He could see the disappointment in their eyes.

Matthew groaned audibly, resigned to his morning ride ending early.

"I'm sorry, Matthew," Marsden said. "We will do this again, I promise." Turning back to Withers, he said, "Escort these two back to the cottage will you, Private?"

"Certainly, sir," Withers said.

Marsden didn't need to look at Helen to know she was rolling her eyes at the thought of being escorted to the cottage by someone other than himself. She considered an escort beneath her. Especially one who was barely older than herself. After all, as she constantly reminded her father, she was a woman now.

The captain bade his children goodbye, and watched as they mounted their steeds and trotted off toward the cottage with their escort in tow.

Marsden wasn't the only one observing Helen and Matthew at that moment. Lieutenant Hogan, who was off duty today, had noticed the pair when he'd walked his horse from the nearby stables. He was planning to spend his free day hunting in the hills above Moreton Bay. Hunting was his love, and he didn't mind what he hunted—roos, wallabies, wild pigs or possum. Or convicts for that matter.

Hogan watched as Marsden and his children went their separate ways. He noticed his captain following the cart track upriver, and guessed he was going to meet with Cheetham. There was no other good reason to ride into Brisbane Town. The township's motley collection of commercial establishments—stables, a food store, a farm supply outlet, a farrier's, a postal depot and a drinking tavern—was hardly an attraction for the army's officers as they had all of those facilities and more right here in the penal settlement.

The lieutenant saw that Marsden's children and their escort were already halfway to the cottage. Hogan immediately mounted his horse, dug his heels into its flanks and galloped to catch up to the threesome. He caught up to them as they neared the cottage. Reining in alongside Withers, he said, "I'll take over from here, Private."

"Ah, the captain told me to escort them to the cottage, sir," Withers said, returning his superior's salute.

"And the lieutenant is telling you, you are dismissed, Private Withers," Hogan said evenly.

Though Hogan hadn't raised his voice, Withers could tell he was angry. Uncertain, he looked at the cottage and realised it was so close he'd all but carried out the captain's orders anyway. "Yes, sir," he said, turning his horse around.

As the private rode off, Hogan reined in alongside Helen, and doffed his riding hat. "Morning Miss Marsden," he smiled.

"Good morning Lieutenant Hogan," Helen replied, taking care to hide her sudden shyness behind a confident smile. The dashing young lieutenant always managed to cut right through her coolness and throw her off balance. She wasn't sure if it was his good looks or his worldliness. It was probably both if she was honest. To make matters worse, he seemed to sense the effect he had on her. The disarming smile he flashed at her now only served to confirm that.

Hogan finally took his eyes off Helen and glanced across at her brother. "And good morning to you, too, Master Marsden," he said.

"Good morning, lieuten-an-ent," Matthew said, stumbling over the word.

Helen corrected her brother.

Hogan pretended he hadn't noticed. "And where are you two heading?" he asked the boy.

"Home, sir," Matthew said, opting to use the shorter, easier title this time.

"I meant where after that?" Hogan asked, his question directed at Helen this time.

"Where would you propose we go, Lieutenant?" Helen asked. She immediately regretted her response, realising it sounded forward.

"Please, it's Desmond," Hogan said.

"Desmond," Helen murmured. The word felt strange to her ear. It was the first time in her life she'd ever used that name.

"I thought you might like to ride up to the lookout with me," he said. "The view is spectacular up there."

"Ooh yes!" an excited Matthew shouted, believing the invitation extended to him as well.

Hogan chuckled. "I don't believe your father would approve of your riding so far from home, young man," he said. Looking at Helen, he added, "The invitation is for your sister only."

Matthew lapsed into a sulky silence as they reined in alongside the cottage.

Helen's mind was racing as she considered the lieutenant's invitation. On the one hand, she loved the idea of riding up into the hills. She'd done that often, but always in the company of her father. On the other hand, she wasn't totally sure of Hogan's intentions, although she had a pretty good idea. Sneaking a glance at him, she was reminded of his good looks and his presence. Their eyes locked for a moment, and she swore he was reading her mind right then. She blushed something fierce, and he looked away so as not to embarrass her further. Finally, she said, "Alright."

"Alright?" Hogan asked, hoping he'd heard her correctly.

Helen nodded. "I will just let my mother know," she said, dismounting Benji.

"Of course," Hogan said. He waited while Helen ran inside. It was only then he remembered Matthew was still there. He turned to the boy. "How old are you, Matthew?"

"Eleven, Lieuten . . . Sir."

"Perhaps when you turn twelve you can ride up to the lookout with me."

Matthew's eyes lit up. "Yes, sir," he grinned.

Helen reappeared at the front door. She was accompanied by her mother who waved to Hogan as soon as she saw him.

"Don't keep her out too long, Lieutenant," Missus Marsden shouted.

"Certainly, Missus Marsden," Hogan assured her. He asked, "All set for the Governor's dinner tomorrow night?"

"Oh, yes," Missus Marsden said. "Wouldn't miss it for the world."

As Helen walked over to Benji, Hogan saw she'd changed her top. She now wore a loose-fitting shirt, which, although not as feminine as the blouse she'd worn earlier, was more alluring for its top buttons were unbuttoned, revealing the barest hint of a cleavage between her pert breasts. Hogan had to tear his eyes away as she mounted her steed.

"Be careful, you two," Missus Marsden said, waving the pair off.

The young couple returned the wave and trotted off toward the bush behind the cottage. They followed a steep track that would take them deep into the hills to the lookout Hogan had referred to.

15

-⟨E⟩———⟨3⟩-

LORD CHEETHAM AND CAPTAIN MARSDEN observed each other coolly above the respective rims of the teacups each man held. They'd been arguing since the meeting began twenty minutes earlier, and only the arrival of the commandant's maid—the young Aboriginal girl Private Withers had been so taken with—caused them to cease hostilities for the moment at least.

The maid, whom Cheetham referred to as Lucy, was in the process of serving cake to each man. Having already spilt tea into the saucers when pouring it a few moments earlier, she was now dropping crumbs onto the floor as she served the cake, prompting Marsden to ascertain she wasn't kept on because of her superior waitressing skills. This was confirmed when, out of the corner of his eye, he observed his superior affectionately stroke Lucy's bottom.

Lucy smiled shyly at Marsden as she left. Her smile, he decided, would light up any room if it weren't for her missing front teeth. He wondered if they'd been knocked out by one of the Quandamooka men, upset perhaps that she'd transferred her affections to the lord of the manor.

Cheetham chuckled, as if to hide any embarrassment he may have felt, but Marsden gave no sign he'd noticed anything untoward.

Observing his opposite, Marsden noticed a change in him since their last meeting. Cheetham was no longer as clear-eyed. He now looked unfocussed, and, if Marsden had to bet, was back on the opium. Certainly the pungent albeit faint odour he detected would account for that, although he thought he could be mistaking burning incense for opium. He hadn't been around opium long enough to be familiar with its smell, and he had noticed sticks of burning incense in the hallway when he'd arrived. The thought did occur that the incense could be used to hide the smell of opium.

They were meeting in Cheetham's den on the ground floor of his mansion in Brisbane Town. Marsden had attended several meetings here since his arrival at Moreton Bay, and each time the den—like the palatial house itself—seemed even grander. It was a big as Marsden's dining room, and far more sumptuously furnished; the mahogany desk, at which they sat now, was bigger than Marsden's dining table; exquisite Arabian carpets all but covered the kauri floor; the furnishing themselves were collectors' items sourced from various parts of Europe, and expensive paintings hung from the walls. A portrait painting of England's reigning monarch, King George IV, occupied pride of place on the wall facing the den's doorway.

Ostensibly, today's meeting had been called to review final arrangements for the Governor's dinner. New South Wales' Governor, General Sir Ralph Darling, was arriving by ship the following morning, and the dinner was scheduled to be held in the mansion tomorrow evening.

Cheetham was understandably on tenterhooks, anxious to create a good impression. However, he and Marsden were both aware that wasn't the main reason for today's meeting: the commandant wanted Marsden's assurance he wouldn't take advantage of the Governor's visit to push for improved treatment of, and conditions for, Moreton Bay's convict population.

So far, Marsden hadn't given any such assurance.

The captain had known what was on his superior's mind as soon as Cheetham had called the meeting, and he'd discussed it at length with his wife. Fortunately, she agreed with him that the humane treatment of convicts must over-ride any career aspirations he may have, and she had given him her blessing to stand up for his beliefs and to speak out on the matter. Patterson's execution had been the last straw for Marsden.

As for Cheetham, he sensed Marsden was a lost cause. Fine military man though he may be—for his record surely attested to that—he had a soft streak, which, in his view, wasn't a good fit with running a penal settlement. Fortunately, Governor Darling's opinions of convicts mirrored his own: like Cheetham, the Governor had made no secret of the fact he believed convicts were animals and should be treated as such. The commandant determined he'd have a word in the Governor's ear before Marsden got to him.

The men were momentarily distracted by a commotion outside. Through the den's window they could see a convict gang struggling to erect the marquee that would be used for the Governor's dinner. A sizeable marquee, it covered much of the mansion's backyard. Marsden estimated it would hold at least a hundred people—more than enough for tomorrow evening's function. A pole had collapsed and the convicts were attempting to extricate themselves from the canvas awning that had enveloped them. The guards were adding to their misery by flailing at them with whips and exhorting them to work faster.

"Moving on," Cheetham said turning back to Marsden, "we need to give some urgency to upgrading the wharf to cope with the ever-increasing number of vessels." He paused to allow his opposite to comment. When no comment was forthcoming, he added, "I want you to pull the smithy out of the foundry to work with our carpenters to ensure a speedy completion of the wharf extension."

"My Lord, I must object," Marsden said. "The smithy can't even fulfil all his jobs in the settlement—"

"I understand he now has a new assistant."

"Yes he does, but—"

"Then put the assistant onto the wharf job. He's needed to handle all the steelwork."

Marsden could see Cheetham was adamant. "Very well, sir." He wisely decided to keep his powder dry to fight the bigger battle that was coming. "I will get the new man onto it straight away." Thinking the meeting was over, he began to stand. "Will that be all, my Lord?"

"Yes . . . Oh, one more thing," Cheetham said. "The Governor will be bringing his own entourage of course, but I'd like you to spare two of your men to assist with dishwashing duties at the dinner tomorrow night."

This was the last straw for Marsden whose patience had already reached its limit. "I cannot authorise that, sir," he said firmly. "My men are not available for dishwashing duties at a private function."

"They are not *your* men, and this is not a private function," Cheetham said.

By now, both men were standing, glaring at each other across the huge desk.

"Nevertheless, I will not order soldiers to do your dishwashing," Marsden said.

Cheetham, whose normally pink complexion was now bright red, said, "Damn it, man! I should have you demoted for insubordination."

"Nowhere in the rulebook does it say soldiers must—"

"Alright, alright," Cheetham said, conceding that his subordinate had a point.

"If I can suggest," Marsden said, "I can organise two of the convicts to help out."

"Can they be trusted?"

"The two I have in mind can be, yes my Lord." In fact, Marsden had only one suitable candidate in mind. He was confident he could find a second one before tomorrow night.

As Marsden's testy meeting with Cheetham concluded, Helen and Lieutenant Hogan had not long reached their destination—the place locals referred to as *the Lookout*. They were sitting together in the long grass, admiring the panoramic view, while their horses grazed, untethered, behind them.

The Lookout was some four miles from the settlement. Hard riding over steep country, and through dense bush, had seen the pair arrive here thirty minutes after leaving the cottage. Although still only mid-morning, it was already hot, and they were both sweating and still a little breathless after their recent exertions.

"It's beautiful," Helen said, admiring the view.

"It certainly is," Hogan agreed.

Helen suspected her companion wasn't referring to the view for she could sense his eyes were firmly on her. "I never tire of coming up here," she said, determined not to let him see he unsettled her.

"Anyone who tired of this view would have to be tired of living, I suspect," Hogan said.

The conversation lapsed as they took in the view, or, more correctly, the *views*. From where they sat, they had three hundred-and-sixty-degree views. Below them, in the distance, they could just make out the penal settlement and the river whose bank it occupied. To their right, the waters of Moreton Bay merged with the blue of the Pacific Ocean, and to their left, bush-covered hills stretched toward the continent's interior—like a sea of green.

The silence dragged out.

"I wonder how far inland the rainforest extends?" Helen asked at length. "It looks like it goes on forever." She spoke only to break the silence. The silence between them unsettled her.

"That's only an illusion. It ends at that mountain range on the horizon." He pointed at a range whose distinctive peaks reminded Helen of glasshouses she'd seen in England. "Beyond that there's nothing for many hundreds of miles."

"Nothing?" Helen asked.

"Nothing for us white folk," Hogan assured her. "Only the darkies can survive out there."

Helen wasn't comfortable about the way her companion spoke of the Aborigines, but she said nothing. In her experience, most, if not all the soldiers referred to the natives in such disparaging terms.

Again the conversation lapsed.

Finally, Hogan asked, "Do you ever tire of Moreton Bay?"

"No, not really," Helen said. "I miss the old school friends, and the theatre and outings we had in England, but I love the open spaces out here. And the riding." She asked, "What about you, Lieuten . . . ah. .Desmond?"

Hogan smiled. "I *was* beginning to tire of this place . . ." He left the sentence unfinished, but its meaning was clear to the young woman next to him.

Helen wasn't at all sure of how she felt about the lieutenant. She certainly thought him attractive, and she found his company stimulating, but she wasn't certain if there was anything more than that, or even if there ever could be. Not yet at least. Besides, she couldn't get the Irishman John Graham out of her mind. She could still see his startling blue eyes boring into hers. He'd been all she had been able to think about since seeing him in the foundry earlier.

The young woman risked a quick glance at Hogan. That was all the encouragement he needed. He leaned across, intending to plant a kiss on her lips. She averted her face at the last moment, and his lips connected with her cheek.

If Helen wasn't sure of her companion's motives before, she was now. She didn't know whether she should feel flattered or insulted. Confused—about her own feelings more than anything else—she jumped to her feet. "I'm sorry!" she blurted. "I have to go."

"No, I'm sorry," Hogan said, jumping to his feet. "I shouldn't have rushed things so."

Helen could see her companion was mortified by her reaction to his advances, but she offered no comforting words to ease his guilt. Instead, she mounted Benji and set off toward Moreton Bay at a slow trot.

Hogan quickly mounted his horse and caught up to her. They rode side by side for a good mile in deafening silence.

Finally, it was Helen who extended the olive branch. "Do you still want to dance with me at the Governor's dinner, Lieutenant Hogan?" she asked mischievously.

"Well, only if you promise me you won't slap my face."

"I didn't slap you before, did I?" Helen couldn't keep the laughter out of her voice.

"No you didn't," Hogan chuckled. "And please call me Desmond."

"Alright," Helen laughed. "Desmond it is." She looked slyly at Hogan. "Last one home is a stuffed turkey!" With that, she dug her heels into Benji and, still laughing, galloped down the hill at breakneck speed.

"Women!" Hogan shouted. "I'll never understand them." He galloped after her.

They were both laughing now.

16

JOHN COULDN'T BELIEVE HOW HIS life had changed so in the space of one day—or less if the actual hours were calculated. This time yesterday, he'd been labouring, shackled and under the whip, or under threat of the whip at least, in the quarry. Now he was unshackled and working more or less unsupervised at the settlement's wharf. Not quite unsupervised for an armed soldier had been posted to keep an eye on him to ensure he didn't shirk or try to escape.

If the smithy's assistant wasn't mistaken, the soldier—a private—was shirking in *his* duties because, far from keeping an eye on his solitary charge, he seemed to snooze most of the time.

The latest momentous change in John's routine had transpired earlier that morning when Marsden had returned to the foundry and advised him he was now required to relocate to the wharf to work fulltime on the upgrade of the sub-standard facility. This announcement had been met with strenuous objections from smithy Jonathan O'Shea, but his objections had been to no avail.

Within minutes, John had found himself being driven aboard a horse-drawn cart to the wharf. The cart was laden with loose bricks and the same steel braces he had seen stockpiled in the foundry. On Marsden's orders, John and his escort had been accompanied by a grumpy O'Shea who spent an hour instructing his assistant on what needed doing before he returned, on foot and grumpier than ever, to the foundry.

John's first task was to construct a kiln alongside the wharf to serve as a forge to facilitate the steelwork required for the job ahead. He was doing this now, using the bricks he'd brought with him from the foundry. It was heavy work, and hot, too, under the sun, but he paid no mind to that. He relished his comparative freedom, working unshackled and unbothered by anyone but the sleepy soldier who, between snoozes, would occasionally swear at him or offer similar earthy encouragements to help justify his existence.

Looking around, John observed his arrival had been noticed by the Quandamooka who had made their home along the riverbank. The natives gazed at him openly, watching his every move. They seemed friendly enough for they smiled and waved when he waved at them. A small group of Quandamooka women showed more than a passing interest in him. They gathered together, giggling whenever the Irishman looked their way.

The women weren't to know they were wasting their time. John had already assessed them, and decided they weren't for him. Their spindly shanks and sagging breasts didn't remotely appeal. "They have to be the ugliest women I've ever seen," he said to himself with more than a tinge of regret. The thought of a comely native maiden to help him while away the hours had been a nice one while it lasted.

Heads like cannonballs and faces like the back end of an Irish Moiled Cow.

"I ain't that desperate," he muttered.

Further along the riverbank, he noticed some of the men fishing. Most fished traditionally, using spears. One group cast for fish, using a net, which John thought looked suspiciously like those he'd seen European fishermen use. He guessed it had been secured in a trade.

A disturbance in the water nearby reminded John—and the fishermen, too—that crocs resided in the river. Those fishermen who were in the water jumped out as fast as they could. Safely on the bank, they laughed at their close call.

The Quandamooka weren't the only ones to have noticed John: his fellow convicts had taken special interest in seeing one of their own arriving for work, unfettered, and by all accounts left largely to his own resources. Those not working in the quarry were engaged in various heavy labour duties around the settlement and in the fields, and it was John's assessment none of them seemed happy about his change in fortune.

"Graham!"

John looked around and saw the soldier beckoning to him, indicating it was time to break for the mid-day meal. The food turned out to be a repeat of yesterday's mid-day meal, but for some reason the Irishman found it more edifying.

Must be gettin' used to this place.

That wasn't his only surprise. The soldier allowed him to spend his break in a small hut that adjoined the wharf. This facility, complete with desk and chairs, was used by an army clerk whenever a ship arrived or departed. John discovered if he lined the chairs up in a row, he had himself a makeshift bunk, which allowed him to lie down and have a snooze during the break. The soldier didn't seem to object.

Yes, it had so far been a day of surprises. Strangest of all was the announcement that he'd be helping out with dishwashing duties at the dinner at Lord Cheetham's mansion. That bit of news had been delivered by Marsden who also advised John he had to nominate a fellow convict to assist him at the mansion.

John's second workday at Moreton Bay ended much as his first workday had: he was driven back to the settlement aboard a horse-drawn cart and, as had happened yesterday, he was seen in all his glory by his fellow convicts as they were returning from the quarry. He spotted Noel and his other Irish mates among them.

As before, John reclined on his back atop the cart, and he attracted the same amount of catcalls and jeers he had the first time. The only significant difference this time was he was now unshackled. He took great delight in raising his feet up in the air to show his fellows he was unhindered by leg-irons. As expected, this attracted more jeers, only louder than before.

It was dark by the time John was dropped off at the foundry. He was surprised to find O'Shea still at work, and not looking at all happy. The smithy insisted John help him tidy up before reporting to the mess for dinner, and he didn't appear at all concerned his assistant would miss his evening meal if he was delayed. John assumed O'Shea was grumpy because his new assistant was now employed elsewhere.

John's concerns he'd miss the evening meal were well founded. Thanks to O'Shea, he arrived late at the mess where he was advised by an over-zealous convict-warden there would be no food for him this night.

So, John was somewhat grumpy himself when he finally joined the others in his hut.

He entered the hut to find the convicts gathered around big Terry McIntosh who was amusing them with a yarn. None of them noticed the late arrival immediately.

The first thing John noticed was how different they looked. After another long day in the quarry, they looked tired, dirty and unkempt. By comparison, he looked fit and fresh, and he felt that way, too.

Ah well, that's my luck and their loss.

He looked around for Noel.

Convict-warden Dan Green was the first to notice John. "Well, will ye look what the cat's dragged in," the giant Londoner said.

The others turned to see what Green was referring to. The catcalls and jeers resumed when they saw it was John. And the tone of the heckling, to his ears at least, wasn't the friendliest. There was clearly some ill feeling toward his change of fortune.

McIntosh immediately broke from his yarn. Sitting on his bunk, he hitched up his trousers to reveal the angry red welts the leg-irons had left around both ankles. He then extended both feet toward John and asked, "Oh, Mister Blacksmith, do you think ye could make me a new set of leg-irons? Perhaps some lovely blue ones to match me lovely blue eyes?"

This only served to encourage the others—especially the non-Irish convicts—who directed similar retorts toward John. The new arrival had the decency to look embarrassed, and a little guilty, too, which probably saved him from a beating, even if it was all an act.

John elbowed his way through the assembled convicts and flopped down on his bunk, doing his best to ignore the comments that continued unabated. He looked around. Catching Noel's eye, he nodded, indicating they needed to speak.

Noel sidled over to his friend. "You best sleep with one eye open tonight," he warned.

"Why's that?"

Noel looked around at the others then turned back to John. "Why the feck d'you think?"

John just shrugged, indicating it was of no importance what anyone else thought.

"They're unhappy about the way you're flaunting your sudden change of fortune," Noel explained. It was clear to him he was wasting his breath. He asked, "What are you working on now?" Before John could answer, Noel said, "Wait. Let me guess. You're not working. You're on holiday."

John grinned. "Close," he said. "They've got me doing the wharf upgrade." He spent the next few minutes filling his friend in on what his new duties were, oblivious to the glares still being directed his way by the others.

One of those most upset by John's good luck was English convict Don Henderson. He was in a huddle with others whose number included McIntosh. Watching the two Irish friends talking in hushed tones, Henderson asked, "Why the hell does Noel Thomas have so much time for that Irish weasel?"

"I believe John Graham looked after him on the journey out," McIntosh said. He'd been told as much by Pat Kennedy earlier that day. The journey he referred to was the hellish voyage the Irish friends had endured from England to the colony two years earlier.

A one-eyed convict, Englishman William Harrison, nodded knowingly. "Aye. One of those Irish bastards"—he nodded toward another group whose number included O'Neill, Donovan and O'Driscoll—"told me Noel Thomas owes 'im his life."

The mood in the hut slowly returned to normal as tired men prepared their aching bodies for what they hoped would be a good night's sleep.

John and Noel were still in deep discussion. "I have some news for you," John whispered.

"I'm all ears," Noel said.

"Lord Cheetham's hosting a dinner party for the Governor tomorrow night, and Captain Marsden said he needs a couple of dishwashers," John murmured. He added, "Me and you."

"The captain asked for me?" Noel asked somewhat incredulously.

"Well, not you personally, but he said I could choose anyone I trust."

"Trust to do what? Not break a dish?"

"Not to try to escape." John added, "There will be food, proper food, there."

"Cheetham's scraps."

"Scraps you can share with your mates." John looked pointedly over at McIntosh. "Why not check with His Highness before you give an answer?"

"Not feckin' funny, John." Noel thought about the offer then shook his head. "Thanks but no thanks. After a day in the quarry, last thing I want to do is spend the night washing dishes in some fat Englishman's castle."

John wasn't deterred. He smiled mischievously. "Oh, I meant to mention . . . we'd get the day off to prepare. Marsden doesn't want overworked, smelly convicts covered in dust and grime going anywhere near the Governor's dinner." He added, "Then again, I know how attached you are to breaking rocks . . ."

Noel suddenly smiled at the thought of a free day. And the possibility of being able to scavenge some fancy food to eat whilst at the big event appealed as well. He was, after all, a scavenger without equal. "Okay," he said, "What the feck . . . I'm in."

"Good. And I'm tired." John said, rolling over to face the wall.

Noel took the hint and retired to his own bunk.

The familiar clanging of a guard's baton against the window's bars signalled lights out, and the hut soon fell quiet.

"My Lord, I have been here almost two years," Lieutenant Hogan said. He felt his pleas were falling on deaf ears, but he plodded on. "I feel it is time—" Hogan broke off when his opposite held up one hand. If it wasn't clear before, it was now: he was getting nowhere with Cheetham.

"You are invaluable to me here at Moreton Bay, Lieutenant," the commandant said.

"Sir, there are plenty of men who could replace me. I ask for your recommendation for a position in Melbourne or Sydney Town as . . ." Hogan trailed off when Cheetham's Aboriginal servant girl, Lucy, entered the room. She carried a tray containing Oriental cutlery, a spatula, an oil lamp and a distinctive pipe, which Hogan immediately recognised as the tools of opium users. Lucy set the tray down on the desktop and expertly set about preparing the pipe with vaporized opium.

As this impromptu ceremony progressed, Cheetham observed his opposite across his desktop. Hogan sat where Marsden had sat earlier that day—in the mansion's study. Except for the moonlight that now streamed through a gap in the curtains, the study looked exactly as it had during the day. To his credit, Hogan showed no surprise or discomfort at what was happening right in front of him. This only served to raise Cheetham's opinion of the lieutenant even higher in his eyes. The commandant had long considered Hogan a future replacement for Marsden, and he was quietly grooming him for that role.

Hogan was annoyed Cheetham was allowing his opium addiction to take priority over this meeting. He'd requested the meeting several days earlier, and he'd stressed its importance. The lieutenant saw no future for himself or his career in Moreton Bay. He considered it a backwater, and desperately wanted a transfer to one of the colony's larger, established settlements to the south. Today's ride with Helen had only strengthened his resolve. He'd decided to court her with a view to proposing marriage, and felt he'd be a more attractive proposition to her, and to her protective father, if he could announce he'd be pursuing his military career in Melbourne or Sydney Town, or anywhere but here.

Lucy indicated to Cheetham the opium pipe was now ready. The commandant playfully smacked her bottom then whispered something in her ear as he sent her on her way.

None of this was lost on Hogan who waited, taking care not to show his impatience.

Cheetham placed the pipe in his mouth and inhaled. He closed his eyes as the powerful opiate entered his bloodstream. After exhaling, he opened his eyes and extended the pipe to his subordinate, indicating he should smoke it. Hogan shook his head, making no attempt to hide his disapproval.

That went straight over Cheetham's head. "Funny thing, Lieutenant . . . Before arriving in this colony, I was employed by the East India Company, delivering opium from Bengal into China . . ." He placed the pipe in his mouth and prepared to inhale again. "I made the mistake of smoking it just once . . . And let me tell you it was heaven on earth . . ." The older man's eyes opened wide as he inhaled, deeply this time. "And now, I cannot stop . . . not even if I wanted to . . ."

As the opiate worked its magic, Cheetham's eyes went dead. He continued smoking, trance-like and oblivious to Hogan's presence before he slumped down in his chair, all but out to it. Smoke now engulfed the study.

An annoyed Hogan left, determined the raise the matter of a transfer with Cheetham again—when the man wasn't under the influence. In the passageway outside the den, he passed Lucy who was hurrying to check on her master. It was obviously a routine she was familiar with.

As the lieutenant stepped outside, the faint sound of thunder carried to him, and clouds covered the moon. A storm was coming. He hoped that wasn't a bad omen for the Governor's visit—or for his own ambitions.

John was woken by a raging storm. Lightning flashed continuously, bathing the hut's interior in bright light, all to the dramatic accompaniment of rolling thunder. The thunderclaps were so loud they caused the entire hut to vibrate, waking most of the inmates.

Lying there, in his bunk, John observed those unlucky ones who had been relegated to sleeping on the floor. It was a pitiful sight. As always, they'd bedded down as far away as possible from the shit bucket and the piss bucket, and as a result they were huddled so close together there wasn't room to turn over—unless they all turned over at once. Fortunately, the buckets hadn't overflowed as they had the first two nights, but the stench nevertheless was overpowering.

John didn't doubt it was the same in all the huts. It was his assessment the plight of Moreton Bay's convicts was worse than ever. There had been another two deaths, dysentery was sweeping the settlement, more convicts had fallen ill and several, it seemed, would be lucky to survive another day. Before the storm's arrival, the groans and cries of those worst affected could be heard throughout the settlement.

Groans of a different kind carried to John between the thunderclaps. He looked up to the top bunk where he'd observed Rhys Jones indulging in unmentionable hijinks with a fellow convict two nights earlier. A flash of lightning illuminated the pair, and he identified the Welshman's partner as Don Henderson.

The top bunk shenanigans eventually ceased and, quite coincidentally, the storm eased and the lightning was replaced by moonlight as the clouds rolled away.

Try as he may, John couldn't get back to sleep. As he often did, he fondled the silver crucifix on his chest, thinking back to his former life in Ireland.

A face from the past came to him. A girl's face. Then her name came to him.

Milly Flanders.

John hadn't thought about her in years. The daughter of a baker in his hometown Dundalk, Milly was his first sexual conquest.

He couldn't recall accurately whether it was his conquest or hers.

Probably hers if I'm not mistaken.

From memory, she'd seduced him, not the other way round. He was fifteen at the time and she was sixteen, or so she'd claimed. He'd learned later she was only fourteen—and he'd had her, or she'd had him, in the storeroom of her father's bakery.

Such fine breasts, he recalled. *And what an arse!*

John smiled at the memory of Milly's father finding them in his storeroom and chasing him down the road, threatening blue murder. John had departed the storeroom in such a hurry he'd left his trousers there. They could still be there for all he knew.

Milly's face faded in John's memory. He tried to retrieve it, but another face came to him. It was Helen's.

17

T HE MARQUEE BEHIND LORD CHEETHAM'S mansion overflowed with people. Ninety of the colony's finest gentry had assembled for the long-awaited Governor's dinner—their numbers boosted considerably by Sir Ralph Darling's entourage, which comprised senior members of his own staff, and high ranking army officers from Sydney Town and Parramatta. Many of the staff members and officers were accompanied by their wives, so there was a good mix of men and women in attendance.

A string quartet was also part of the Governor's entourage, and they were now entertaining guests in the marquee. Some couples had already taken to the temporary wooden dance floor, and they were dancing to the strains of a Viennese waltz. The flooring had been laid earlier by workmen from the township.

Among the few outsiders to have accompanied Sir Ralph was one Timothy Hershaw, deputy editor of *The Sydney Gazette*. Hershaw was armed with ink bottle, feather quills and other tools of his trade, and, judging by the look of enthusiasm on his face, was evidently expecting to depart Moreton Bay with some major news for his newspaper's readers.

Lanterns provided lighting inside the marquee, while outside flaming torches lit up the surrounding lawn, and light shone from every window of the nearby mansion.

Fortunately, the weather had remained fine since the storm of the previous night had passed by, and a gentle breeze wafting in from the bay ensured the mid-summer temperatures were bearable at least.

The Governor and his entourage had arrived late morning aboard a brig that would remain anchored at the wharf until her passengers boarded for the return journey in two days' time.

Also among Governor Darling's staff members were his two personal chefs and three waiting staff. The former were currently engaged preparing dinner in the mansion's kitchen while the latter were circulating amongst guests, plying them with wines, ales and other refreshments.

The Moreton Bay penal settlement's main contribution to the evening was the food—supplied courtesy of the army's collection of livestock holdings, vegetables from the vegetable plot, fresh fish and lobsters from the bay, and fruit and nuts from the nearby rainforest. Two cows and half a dozen pigs had been slaughtered, and these, along with the lobsters Moreton Bay was fast becoming famous for, would feature on tonight's menu.

Conspicuous by their absence were the guest of honour, Sir Ralph Darling himself, and his host, Lord Cheetham. They were currently next door in the mansion, ensconced, deep in discussion, in the commandant's study.

Both officials were resplendent in their ceremonial uniforms, which were adorned with medals and ribbons. In the Governor's case, the adornments paid tribute to his distinguished military service; in the commandant's case, they acknowledged the fact he was from one of southern England's wealthiest and most influential families, but not much else. Truth be known, he'd been an embarrassment to his family, and his appointment to one of the empire's farthest flung colonies had been seen as an effective way to minimise the possibility of his causing further damage to the family's good name.

Cheetham's eyes were remarkably clear and his wits sharp considering he'd indulged his opium habit just the previous evening. That was largely due to the fact that, upon arising, he'd spent a good hour bathing in a tub filled with cold water followed by consumption of a vile beverage of unknown herbs administered to him by Lucy's elderly mother. Lucy had assured him her mother was a healer and knew what she was about. He assumed she wasn't lying because his hangover had gone by the time the Governor arrived.

"I hope you haven't said anything about the projections for Moreton Bay, Bertie?" Sir Ralph mumbled.

"Certainly not, Ralph," Cheetham assured him, mindful that the Governor alone wanted to have the honour of making so important an announcement.

The commandant was as proud as punch to be hosting Sir Ralph. It was the Governor's first visit to Moreton Bay, and the occasion couldn't have started any better. The Governor was clearly impressed by what he'd seen so far, and he'd said as much.

Sir Ralph was an imposing chap. Middle-aged, but with the height and bearing befitting of an army general, he commanded respect. His only weakness, from Cheetham's perspective, was he was Irish-born, but the commandant was prepared to overlook that. So, it was with some trepidation that he broached the subject that had been occupying his mind of late. "Ralph . . . I wanted to raise something with you . . . before dinner," he said.

"Go on."

The Governor's attention seemed focused on the pipe he was now in the process of lighting, but Cheetham knew the man was listening. What he didn't know was how he'd react to what he was about to say. "It's about Captain Marsden . . ."

"Ah, how is Tom these days?"

"Oh, he's fine. It's just that . . . well . . . I'm not certain he's the man for the job."

"Nonsense. Captain Marsden has a fine military record." The Governor jabbed his pipe in Cheetham's direction to emphasise his point.

That wasn't the reaction the commandant had been hoping for. He realised he'd need to choose his words carefully. "No question about that, Ralph. But he is . . . shall we say . . . soft . . . in his treatment of the convicts."

"Ah, I thought you were building to that." Sir Ralph smiled. "I picked up on that from your monthly reports . . . and from his reports, too, when I read between the lines."

Cheetham breathed a sigh of relief. His relief was short-lived when the Governor said, "That's why I appointed you to this job, old chap."

"I'm sorry?"

"Look. I've known for a while Tom has a soft streak where the convicts are concerned, but don't let that fool you. He has a backbone of steel. Believe me, I've seen it." Sir Ralph eyeballed his opposite. "If push comes to shove, he'll do the right thing. Besides, I think you two complement each other."

Cheetham was nonplussed by his opposite's reaction. In the two years since taking up his post as the seventh Governor of New South Wales, Sir Ralph had earned a reputation for cruelty—amongst the colony's convict population at least. Cheetham knew it was a reputation well deserved, too, for he'd personally witnessed him torturing prisoners at Parramatta. The commandant had thought Sir Ralph would at least sympathise with him regarding *the Marsden issue,* as he thought of it. He considered pursuing it, but restrained himself when he noticed the Governor's mind was elsewhere. He'd been distracted by the sight of guests coming and going from the marquee outside.

Cheetham turned and looked out the window. He could see the dusk had faded into night, and the torches now cast their flickering shadows over the backyard. "Well, I suppose we had better join them," he said, feeling more than a little deflated by the Governor's response to the little speech he'd been preparing these past few weeks.

"Lead on, my good man," Sir Ralph said.

Without another word, the pair stood and departed the study.

Cheetham led his guest down the passageway, past the large kitchen where the chefs were hard at work, to the backdoor. Their arrival at the mansion's back steps coincided with the arrival of horse-drawn cart being driven by Private Withers.

The commandant guessed the two passengers atop the cart were the convicts Marsden had appointed to assist with dishwashing duties. Cheetham was relieved to see they wore clean, fresh-pressed clothes and looked halfway presentable at least. However, as they disembarked from the cart, he was alarmed to see one of them, John, was unencumbered by leg-irons. He hoped Sir Ralph would assume the unrestrained convict was a settler, for the Governor, like himself, preferred the colony's convicts remain permanently shackled regardless of the occasion. Cheetham vowed to take the obvious oversight up with Marsden later.

As Withers escorted John and Noel into the mansion, the Governor and the commandant headed for the marquee. An army bugler stationed at entrance heralded the pair's arrival and, inside the marquee, they were greeted by a standing ovation.

"Three cheers for the Governor!" an officer shouted. "Hoorah! Hoorah! Hoorah!"

As the cheers and applause died down, Cheetham escorted Sir Ralph toward the table of honour at the far side of the marquee. Weaving their way through the assembled guests, they stopped every few paces to exchange pleasantries with various individuals.

The Governor deviated a little when he spotted the Marsdens amongst the guests.

107

"Good to see you, Tom," he said, grasping Captain Marsden's extended hand.

"You, too, Governor," Marsden said.

Sir Ralph nodded to Lieutenant Hogan, who shared the Marsden's table, then smiled at Marsden's wife. "And good to see you again, Missus Marsden," he said, kissing the back of her hand like the gentleman he was.

"Please, Governor. It's Vera," Missus Marsden insisted.

Observing the interchange between the pair, Marsden couldn't help but feel proud of his dear wife. Her poise and her fragile beauty set her apart from most of the other women. His eyes were drawn to the ornate hairpin he'd recently gifted to her. Like her, it sparkled in the light.

Sir Ralph was about to move on when he noticed Helen. She looked stunning in her new black dress. Elegant beyond her years, she had been the centre of attention as soon as she'd entered the marquee.

"My daughter," a proud Marsden said, introducing the Governor to Helen.

Sir Ralph was clearly taken with the beautiful young woman who curtsied before him. Addressing Helen, he said, "I see you have your mother's beauty, young lady."

Helen and her mother both blushed. Before either could respond, Cheetham ushered the Governor to the top table.

As soon as everyone was seated, Cheetham formally welcomed the Governor to Moreton Bay and then invited him to speak.

Sir Ralph stepped up onto a raised platform and surveyed the assembled. At well over six foot, he cut a fine figure. A plumed hat and ceremonial sword complemented his uniform, and he looked at ease as he prepared to speak.

Though the Governor was now the centre of attention, Hogan's eyes were on Cheetham. The young lieutenant couldn't believe the commandant was the same man he'd observed in an opium-induced stupor only the night before. He'd been convinced Cheetham would be a cot case today.

Sir Ralph's oratory skills were such he had his audience in the palm of his hand. He began by thanking his hosts, and congratulating Moreton Bay's senior command for the fine job they were doing. Cheetham and Marsden were singled out for a special mention, and Missus Marsden glowed with pride to hear her husband praised in such flattering terms.

Whenever the Governor made a key point, he glanced at the Gazette's deputy editor, as if to underline its importance.

Then came the announcement he'd been building to. "Finally, ladies and gentlemen," he said, "it is with pleasure I inform you our government in its wisdom has approved my plans to fast-track growth in Moreton Bay." Although he addressed the guests, his gaze rested on scribe Timothy Hershaw for he understood the importance of getting his message out far beyond the confines of Moreton Bay.

Hershaw scribbled furiously, determined to capture every word the Governor uttered.

Sir Ralph continued, "For the township, we project an influx of free settlers, starting with the arrival by boat of fifty-eight men, women and children in

September." This prompted enthusiastic applause. "For the penal settlement, the projection is for an additional two thousand convicts arriving over the next two years." Ignoring the gasps of disbelief prompted by that statement, he added, "This expansion will commence next month with the arrival of one hundred-and-eleven convicts from Van Diemen's Land." He referred to the island south of mainland Australia that would one day be known as Tasmania.

The applause was more muted than the Governor had hoped. It was obvious the most enthusiastic applause was coming from his own entourage, and from Cheetham who welcomed any expansion because he considered it a reflection of the faith Sir Ralph had in him personally. The reaction from Moreton Bay's officers was somewhat restrained as they couldn't imagine how the settlement could cope with any more convicts. Marsden in particular was horrified by the thought.

As if reading their minds, the Governor said, "To accommodate this growth, we will embark on major roading and building projects here in the very near future." He scowled at Hershaw as if to emphasise the importance of his capturing every word.

While the Governor addressed the guests, John and Noel were earning their keep in the mansion's kitchen. They worked side by side, placing entrée dishes the chefs had prepared on trolleys for the waiters who arrived at regular intervals to wheel out to the marquee.

Private Withers, who had remained outside, kept watch on the two Irishmen through the mansion's rear door. It allowed him a clear view through to the kitchen.

The soldier was unaware that while he was watching John and Noel, he, too, was under observation.

Beyond the light of the flickering torches, Barega observed Withers. The tracker had been asked to remain with the cart and horses that had transported the Marsdens to the mansion. Bored, he studied the rifle that hung from Withers' shoulder, and idly wondered whether the young white and his gun would be any match for him and his spear.

18

COUPLES TOOK TO THE FLOOR to dance as the waiters cleared the last of the mains dishes from the tables and served dessert. By now, any inhibitions had long been set aside: loud debate and laughter almost drowned out the strains of the string quartet, and the Governor and the commandant wandered from table to table, renewing old acquaintances and generally ingratiating themselves with one and all.

It wasn't long before the two officials ended up at Marsden's table. Cheetham, who had evidently had one or two drinks too many and was now slurring his words, sat next to Marsden while Sir Ralph sat next to Missus Marsden. Sharing their table were half a dozen officers and their wives from Sydney Town, and Helen and Lieutenant Hogan. The young couple had found themselves sitting together thanks to some earlier meddling in the arrangement of the seating places by Helen's mother, though neither was aware of that.

Up to now, discussion between Helen and the lieutenant had been somewhat inhibited. The memory of Hogan's little indiscretion on their recent ride was still fresh on the minds of each.

"About yesterday," a tentative Hogan said.

"I have already forgotten about that," Helen smiled.

"So all is forgiven?"

"There is nothing to forgive."

A relieved Hogan asked, "Well then, may I have this dance, Helen?"

"Ah . . . maybe later," Helen said, "when the food has gone down perhaps." She patted her tummy to convey she'd eaten too much.

"Of course." Hogan looked a little deflated.

Helen wasn't sure if she wanted to dance with the lieutenant or give him any reason to suspect his obvious affection for her was being returned. Handsome, dashing and eligible though he was, she still wasn't certain of her own feelings toward him.

Further along the table, Cheetham, who was now more tipsy than ever, had taken it upon himself to entertain the guests with an impromptu poetry recital. "Small cheer and great welcome makes a merry feast!" the commandant spouted. "Full fathom five thy father lies. Of his bones are coral made. Those are pearls that were his eyes."

Sir Ralph, who was rather merry himself, was suitably amused. "Bravo, Bertie!" he said. He failed to notice the underlying tension between Cheetham and Marsden who, so far this evening, had ignored each other.

Buoyed by the Governor's support, Cheetham continued, "Nothing of him that doth fade, but doth suffer a sea-change. Into something rich and strange." He became distracted by the sight of his now empty wine glass, and held it out to a passing drinks waiter.

Missus Marsden looked along the table and was concerned to see Helen and the lieutenant didn't appear to be talking. She caught Helen's her eye, signalling her to make conversation.

The exchange was noted by Marsden. He was aware his wife was rather taken with Hogan and he was concerned she seemed intent on fostering a romance between the young officer and their daughter.

Not wishing to make things too difficult for her dinner partner, Helen turned to Hogan and said, "It must be a great honour to have this posting at such a young age, Desmond."

"Well, that's one way of looking at it," Hogan said, surprised that Helen had engaged him in conversation after her latest brush-off. "I guess it suits me here as I like to hunt."

The comment was overheard by a chubby woman who sat opposite the young couple. She and her officer-husband were part of the Governor's entourage. Having just eaten her dessert, the chubby woman was now helping herself to her husband's dessert, oblivious to the cream that dribbled down both sides of her mouth. She asked, "Really? What is it you hunt, Lieutenant?"

"Men," Hogan said simply. He added, "If you could call the wretched beasts that."

Helen glanced at the lieutenant, surprised by his harsh tone. She wasn't to know his response had been for her benefit. He was annoyed by her off-handedness, and wanted to shock her.

The chubby woman's inquisitiveness was now well and truly piqued. She asked, "Natives or escaped convicts?"

"Convicts." Only now did Hogan notice he had the attention of everyone at the table.

Cheetham piped up, "You will be interested to know Madam, the lieutenant captured one only two or three days ago. A convict that is."

"Really?" the woman said, stuffing the last of her husband's dessert into her mouth.

"We hung him," Hogan said, quietly enjoying the discomfort he knew Helen must be experiencing.

"You hung him?" a disbelieving Helen asked. "For what?"

Cheetham said, "For escaping, young lady."

"And for that you would kill a man?" Helen asked.

Concerned his daughter was about to remonstrate with his superior in front of the Governor, Marsden flashed a warning frown her way. "Helen," he murmured.

"Surely, father, you do not agree with this?" Helen asked.

"It is complicated, Helen," Marsden said, annoyed that the lieutenant had raised the subject, and even more annoyed that Cheetham had stirred the pot. He just hoped Helen would remember where she was and in whose company she was in.

"I would have thought it simple," Helen said, undeterred. "Punishment, yes. But death?" She looked around at the men who shared her table, her eyes ablaze. "Would not any man held in captivity seek his freedom?" she asked defiantly. "It would be as instinctive as breathing. Surely?"

"Instinctive or not, my dear, there are rules," Sir Ralph said, joining this latest discussion. "And civilized society cannot function without rules."

"And Moreton Bay cannot function without them," Cheetham added. Raising his glass, he said, "To rules!"

All except Helen raised their glasses. She was about to remonstrate further when she caught her father's eye. The steely look he gave her dissuaded her. She glanced at Hogan who studiously ignored her as he studied the bottom of his wine glass.

Suddenly needing to be alone, Helen stood and headed outside. She walked to the rear of the marquee, but pulled up when she saw Barega standing there. The tracker stared at her. She did an about-turn and hurried back the way she'd come.

As she prepared to re-enter the marquee, she noticed John and Noel through the mansion's rear doorway. They were washing pots in the kitchen and, when they thought no-one was looking, they scoffed down leftover food. Every now and then, Helen noticed, one of them would wrap items of food and stuff them into their pockets—no doubt to share with their mates later.

Intrigued, Helen wandered over to the mansion and entered the kitchen. Ignoring the other kitchen staff, she walked up behind John. "Well, well Mister Blacksmith," she said, "I didn't know you had other skills as well." She looked knowingly at the latest parcel of food John was about to deposit in his pocket.

Surprised to find himself in the company of the captain's beautiful daughter once more, John asked, "Can we help you, miss?" He surreptitiously dropped the food parcel into the sink behind him.

"Helen. And no, I am fine, thank you." She watched, amused, as John and Noel finished washing the pots and busied themselves drying and polishing silverware.

John became aware that Helen seemed in no hurry to leave. He wondered what her game was, and he hoped her father wasn't around. The Irishman could imagine what the captain would think of his daughter fraternising with convicts.

And with Irish convicts, to boot!

He put all his energy into removing a spot from the silver spatula he was currently polishing.

"It's Mister Graham, isn't it?" Helen asked, knowing full well who it was she was talking to.

"My name's John." He kept his eyes firmly on the spatula.

"I heard father talking to mother about you. He is fascinated that you can read."

John finally looked around at Helen. "Must be smarter than I look," he grinned.

Noel nudged John and whispered, "You'll get us both flogged!" He'd noticed the chefs were giving John strange looks.

"You must miss your family?" Helen asked.

John studied her for a moment. As before, he was struck by her beauty, though he took care to show no sign of that. "No family to speak of, Helen," he said at length.

"No wife?"

John shook his head.

"What did you do to be sent here?"

"My employer didn't pay me wages. So I took what he owed."

"And they sent you here for that?"

"There's never an excuse to take the law into your own hands, Miss Marsden," Hogan said. The lieutenant had appeared without warning in the kitchen doorway. He stared at John who avoided his gaze and returned his attention to the silverware, as did Noel. "You two," he said, addressing the pair coldly.

The Irishmen looked around at Hogan.

"See that the tracker gets a meal," the lieutenant said.

Noel hurried over to the nearest chef to request a tray of food for the tracker.

Hogan stared coldly at John a while longer then turned to Helen. "Allow me to escort you back to your table, my lady," he said.

Helen took Hogan's arm. As the pair departed, she looked back at John. Their eyes locked for a moment, and then she was gone.

Meanwhile, the chef quickly prepared a tray of food and handed it to Noel who returned to John's side. Without a word, Noel stirred some of the silverware polish he'd been using into the food, taking care to ensure he wasn't being observed from either inside or outside the kitchen. John hid a smile as Noel left the mansion to find the tracker.

Outside the backdoor, Noel explained to the ever-watchful Private Withers the food was for Barega. The soldier escorted Noel to the rear of the marquee where they found the tracker waiting. Without a word, Noel handed him the tray of contaminated food then returned to the kitchen, whistling an Irish ditty as he walked.

⋅⋅⋅

It was past midnight when kitchen duties ended for the two Irishmen. As Private Withers escorted them to the horse-drawn cart to return them to their hut, they had the satisfaction of seeing Barega bent over and throwing up behind the marquee. The tracker was obviously distressed.

"He won't be chasing any convicts for a while," John observed dryly.

Noel chuckled.

Withers observed the Irishmen. He couldn't help wondering whether they had something to do with Barega's current condition.

⋅⋅⋅

It was well into the early hours when John and Noel arrived back at their hut. Except for Paddy O'Donnell, all the other inmates were asleep.

On entering the hut, John sensed something was different, but he couldn't put his finger on it.

O'Donnell quickly put him out of his misery. Whispering so as not to wake the others, he said, "Big Dan Green and the other convicts have been relocated elsewhere."

"Why?" John asked, relieved to learn the giant Londoner no longer shared their hut.

Clearly excited, O'Donnell said, "Turns out there was an attempt on the life of one of the other convict-wardens."

"Jesus!" Noel said.

"Shhh!" O'Donnell cautioned. "Marsden ordered all the convict-wardens to evacuate the huts and sleep in the barn's storeroom from now on." He added, "He knows how much we hate those lowlifes."

"Not before time," John said, yawning. "I got to turn in," he said, collapsing onto his bunk.

The other two followed suit, and soon all of the hut's occupants were fast asleep.

Creaking floorboards woke John. It was still dark and he didn't have a clue how long he'd been asleep. He determined to get back to sleep when the sound of whispering carried to him.

John propped himself up on one elbow and saw half a dozen convicts gathered beside Terry McIntosh's bunk. He noticed Noel, Donovan and Kennedy were among them. They and the big Scotsman were obviously planning something. Intrigued, he climbed off his bunk and walked over to investigate.

It was only when he joined the men he noticed several floorboards had been prized apart below the Scotsman's bunk. The convicts were so engrossed they hadn't noticed John.

It wasn't until McIntosh squeezed through the new opening in the floor and disappeared from sight that John realised he was witnessing an escape attempt. He was about to caution McIntosh when, to his astonishment, Noel squeezed through the same opening and disappeared. John pushed his way through the other men. "Noel!" he cried. "Don't be a bloody fool!"

Noel's head re-emerged through the gap. "Shhh! The guards will hear you."

By now most of the hut's occupants were awake.

Lowering his voice, John asked, "Have you forgotten escaping's a hanging offence?"

"It's fine," Noel grinned. "Terry has it all feckin' planned."

John was rendered momentarily speechless. Grasping at straws, he said, "It's too close to dawn." He didn't know what the time was, but he guessed dawn wasn't that far away.

Noel wasn't to be deterred. Smiling, he looked up at his friend. "I never did thank you for saving my bacon on the journey out," he said. And then he was gone.

"Noel!" John cried, more alarmed than ever.

"Shhh!" Kennedy said.

John rounded on Kennedy and the others. "How long have you known about this?" he asked. He couldn't believe Noel hadn't confided in him earlier.

"It was a last minute decision," an aggrieved Kennedy said. "He only decided a few minutes before you woke up."

Shaking his head, John instinctively touched his silver crucifix as Kennedy and the others quietly repositioned the floorboards.

The sixth member of the group, a one-time professional pugilist from Merseyside, in England, turned to John. "He'll be fine, me ol' China," he said, smiling.

Not convinced, John asked, "So how're you planning to get around the count?"

"Another two names get marked as deceased on the infirmary list," the Merseysider said. The *infirmary* he referred to was a brand new facility the army's carpenters had built two days earlier in anticipation of the Governor's visit. He continued, "Then in the morning two men from the infirmary sneak over and get counted on our list while the guards are distracted."

"Distracted?" an incredulous John asked. "How?"

John didn't see the Merseysider's big fist connect with his jaw. The Irishman was out for the count before he even knew what hit him.

19

IT WASN'T DAYLIGHT OR THE chatter of kookaburras that woke John. Nor was it the clanging of the guard's baton against the window's bars. It was the large volume of water he received full in his face. He woke, startled, to see a guard standing over his bunk, empty bucket in hand. Behind the guard, he noticed a concerned Sergeant Benson looking at him.

"Who did this to you, Graham?" Benson asked.

"Wha . . . ?" Dazed, John shook his head to clear his senses. Only now did he realise his head hurt and he was sore all over. If he had a mirror, he'd have seen he sported a black eye, a cut lip, a nasty head gash and bruises all over his face. He'd learn later that after the pugilistic Merseysider had knocked him out, he'd continued to bash him about the head while he was still unconscious.

"I asked who did this to you, Graham?" the sergeant asked again.

John looked through the hut's open door and saw his fellow convicts shackled and lined up in rows as they awaited the first roll call of the day. He looked for Noel then remembered his friend had scarpered.

"Graham!" Benson shouted.

"Ah . . . I don't know, Sergeant," John said. He wasn't lying. He really didn't remember.

Benson questioned him some more. When he could see he was getting nowhere, he ordered the nearest soldier to fetch Marsden then he turned back to John. "You stay there Graham until the captain sees you," he ordered. The sergeant then left the hut to await Marsden and watch over the roll call that was about to commence.

Neither Benson nor the guards were aware that two convicts from the infirmary had quietly mingled with the others from John's hut soon after they'd stepped outside. The roll call was completed without incident. The number of convicts present tallied with the guards' records, and the disappearance of Noel and McIntosh remained undiscovered.

Benson then ordered the convicts to stand easy to await the arrival of the captain.

They didn't have long to wait. Marsden and the soldier who had been sent to fetch him arrived on horseback within a few minutes. The captain was somewhat disgruntled, having had his breakfast interrupted. Benson quickly briefed Marsden on the morning's developments before he entered the hut to check on John.

The captain was shocked to see the state the injured Irishman was in, but he hid his concern. "Are you fit enough to work, Graham?" he asked.

John nodded, but Marsden wasn't convinced. Turning to Benson, the captain said,

"Get this man to the infirmary." Without another word, he strode outside and, from the hut's top step, surveyed the waiting convicts. "Sergeant Benson informs me no-one admits to knowing anything about what happened to John Graham," he said. None of the assembled convicts could look him in the eye. "I assume I will get the same response if I ask the same question"—he let the statement hang for a moment—"so I won't ask."

The pugilistic Merseysider thought about owing up, but he decided against it. After all, it hadn't been his idea that John should be the scapegoat to distract the guards and cover for the disappearance of two convicts.

Turning to the guards, Marsden said, "These men are now on half rations for the next twenty-four hours. See if hunger pains may jog someone's memory." With that, he mounted his horse and rode off, oblivious to the grumbles coming from the convicts behind him.

Benson demanded silence and then asked for volunteers to assist John to the new infirmary. Ironically, the two imposters who had snuck over from the infirmary volunteered. As the others were escorted to the mess for their first rationed meal of the day, the two volunteers assisted John to the infirmary that was located conveniently close by.

While John's injuries were being attended to by the army's doctor, Marsden was back at the cottage finishing his interrupted breakfast in the company of his wife. The couple treasured these rare moments when they could be alone during waking hours.

"All set for the big tour this morning?" Missus Marsden asked. She referred to a tour of nearby Brisbane Town that Cheetham had arranged for the Governor and members of his entourage. The commandant and Marsden were hosting the tour, which had been organised so that Sir Ralph could see for himself what the fledgling settlement was lacking by way of facilities and infrastructure.

"Don't remind me," Marsden said gloomily. The prospect of spending an entire morning in Cheetham's company hardly enthralled him. Putting on a brave face, he asked, "And what have you planned for this morning, my love?"

"I promised Matthew he could do his studies in the meadow this morning," Missus Marsden said. She added "It's a good excuse for me to get out in the fresh air."

Marsden frowned. "Is that boy applying himself to his studies?" he asked, ever-anxious that his son wasn't disadvantaged by not attending school like other boys his age.

"Oh, yes," his wife assured him. "I make sure of that."

Marsden knew that much was true. He was aware, and thankful, that his wife valued education as highly as he did, and was equally determined their children would be well equipped for whatever life had in store for them. "And what about Helen?" he asked.

"She's a regular bookworm," Missus Marsden said. "She . . ." Her voice trailed off. "But you know that don't you," she told him. She knew her husband was only being over-protective of their beloved daughter.

"Yes," Marsden smiled. He had no cause for concern about Helen's attitude or her scholastic abilities. She had received an excellent education in London, and she'd continued studying of her own accord since coming to Australia. The captain said, "I was merely asking what she has planned for today."

"Oh," Missus Marsden said, "I believe she is going riding this morning."

"Remind her she is not to leave the cottage without an escort."

"Oh, Tom. You fuss too much." Before Marsden could object, his wife added, "And that's one of the things I love about you." She leaned over the breakfast table and kissed him tenderly.

Marsden returned the kiss with equal tenderness. Not for the first time, he quietly congratulated himself on his choice of a life partner.

John was at his new workstation, alongside the wharf, by mid-morning. Still not a hundred per cent recovered, and still looking like he'd gone twenty rounds with—well, with a Merseyside pugilist—he nevertheless felt a whole lot better since the doctor had tended his wounds. His split lip had been stitched, his gashed head had been bandaged, and his headache had eased.

Having had time to ascertain how he'd ended up in such a state, he'd finally worked out that he was the "distraction" the Merseysider had referred to just before he'd knocked him out. He reminded himself to have a word with the man about that at the earliest opportunity.

It wasn't his physical injuries that bothered him, however. John was consumed by worry for Noel, and for perhaps the twentieth time that morning he cursed his friend's foolhardiness, and McIntosh's, too.

Damned idiots! You won't last a day.

He knew it was only a matter of time before the pair's absence was noticed and the tracker was sent after them.

And then it's the hangman's noose for you.

He tried in vain to push all thoughts of Noel's capture and likely execution from his mind.

John's guard for the day was a young private he'd never seen before. He guessed the soldier was new to Moreton Bay, and probably new to Australia. John could always pick the newcomers amongst the soldiers, and amongst the convicts, too. They had a look about them.

A look that says what the hell am I doing here?

John noticed there were more distractions at his workstation on the riverbank than there had been the last time he'd worked here. The biggest distraction was the vessel which had brought the Governor's party to the settlement and which was now tied up alongside the wharf. A three-masted brig named *the Southern Cross*, she made a fine sight even with her sails furled. Crewmembers clambered over her, repairing the rigging, scrubbing decks and attending to a multitude of other maintenance tasks.

On the wharf itself, a six-man carpentry team was now working on the wharf extension. The team comprised the army's three resident carpenters and three handymen recruited from the nearby township.

Two armed Redcoats patrolled the wharf—a round-the-clock practice Marsden had insisted on whenever a ship berthed. To remove the temptation for convicts to stow away on board no doubt. The sentries, John noticed, carried the new-issue Infantry Rifle. He'd heard the final shipment of rifles had arrived aboard *the Southern Cross,* which effectively meant the army's muskets were now obsolete, at Moreton Bay at least. As if to prove the point, the sound of gunfire carried to John as soldiers familiarised themselves with their new weapons on the practice range. The gunfire would continue with seldom a break until sunset.

Nearby, Quandamooka fishermen speared fish from the riverbank, and nearer still John noticed three natives preparing a fire so that they could cook a dozen freshly caught, live eels for their morning meal. He watched the trio closely as they tried to start the fire.

The older of the three split a branch, placed it at his feet and inserted narrow wooden wedges to ensure the crack remained open and the branch remained firmly secured to the ground.

John had seen Aborigines use this method in Parramatta, so he knew what was coming next.

The youngest of the three natives then stood astride the branch to further secure it while the third man placed dry roo dung in the crack then lay down his woomera, or spear-thrower, so that it was above the dung. He held one end of the woomera while the oldest native bent down and grasped the opposite end. The pair then used the woomera as they would a saw, pulling it back and forth between the legs of the other native who was still standing astride the branch.

In less than a minute, John noticed smoke rising from the dung inside the crack. The pair holding the woomera ceased their sawing and began blowing on the smouldering dung while the other native added dry grass that acted as tinder. Satisfied, the oldest man transferred the burning tinder to the dried leaves and branches that would serve as the cooking fire.

In no time, a fire was blazing. The youngest native then skewered the live eels and hung them from a branch he'd laid horizontally over the fire. The writhing eels soon succumbed to the heat, and it wasn't long before they were ready to eat.

John reckoned the entire process had taken less than five minutes.

Suddenly aware the soldier guarding him was observing him wasting time, he busied himself, firing up his new kiln and preparing to manufacture more metal sleeves for the wharf's posts. This seemed to satisfy the young private who wandered onto the wharf for a closer look at the brig.

John took advantage of the soldier's inattention to watch Missus Marsden and her son whom he'd observed arrive in the same field he'd seen them in with Helen the other day. He guessed the pair were on another picnic. They were a good hundred yards away. Matthew was running around in the long grass while his mother was reading on a blanket.

At the same time, he noticed Helen ride by on her steed. She was accompanied by a middle-aged corporal whom the Irishman guessed was her escort for the day.

Lucky bugger.

John would have liked to change places with the soldier. *Best learn to ride first,* he reminded himself.

Helen must have noticed him for she immediately changed direction and galloped over, her escort in tow.

John pretended not to notice the captain's daughter approaching. He only looked up as she pulled Benji to a halt a couple of yards shy of the kiln at which he laboured. The corporal escorting Helen reined in close behind her. Helen flashed a warning glance his way, indicating he should keep his distance. The soldier took the hint and backed his horse up a little.

Helen dismounted Benji and looked directly at John for the first time that morning. "My God, look at your face," she gasped. When John didn't respond, she said, "They told me you were sick."

"Aye, I was," John said. "Sick of being punched."

Helen smiled. Examining his face, she spontaneously reached out and touched his cheek.

"Still beautiful?" John asked, ignoring the angry look Helen's escort was directing his way.

"Yes, but it seems they beat the modesty right out of you," Helen laughed. Looking into the Irishman's eyes, she found herself being drawn to him.

A wary John took a step back. Helen was confused by his guardedness. She was about to say something when she noticed the young private tasked with guarding the Irishman approaching, his rifle unshouldered.

"Back to work, Graham!" the private shouted.

John spun around and saw the young soldier looked both angry and confused that his charge was talking to a beautiful young woman instead of working. The private, who had yet to learn that Helen was the captain's daughter, was also confused that the corporal escorting her had allowed the fraternisation he'd just witnessed. The corporal nodded to him, indicating everything was under control.

Not wanting to get John into trouble, Helen quickly mounted her horse, flashed a disarming smile at the private and trotted off along the riverbank, her escort in tow as before.

The corporal urged his horse forward until he was level with Helen. A glance her way told him the Irishman's reticence had upset her. "It's not chivalry that stops him, Miss," he said. "It's fear of messing up the good thing he has going with your father."

Helen looked sharply at her escort.

Undeterred, the corporal added, "Fear will make many a scoundrel decent."

Helen reined in Benji in front of the corporal's horse, forcing its rider to pull up. "How dare you address me in that fashion, Corporal," she said. "Perhaps I will tell my father what you said. Then we'll see who is afraid."

The corporal realised too late he'd overstepped the mark. He tipped his hat respectfully and fell in behind Helen as she dug her heels into Benji's flanks and galloped ahead.

Behind them, the private was gazing after the blonde beauty who had just smiled at him. He was already in love with her and had completely forgotten about the convict he was meant to be guarding.

As for John, he busied himself pouring molten steel into a vat. Replaying Helen's visit over and over in his mind, he wasn't sure what had just happened between the young Englishwoman and himself.

The tour of Brisbane Town by the Governor and members of his entourage wasn't proving as painful as Marsden had feared. Not so far at least. Cheetham had been a little more subdued than usual—possibly as a result of having over-indulged at the previous night's dinner—and had left most of the talking to Marsden who found, to his surprise, he was enjoying the experience. It was a welcome break from the tedium of his everyday duties.

Sir Ralph's entourage on this occasion included an architect, two draughtsmen, a town planner, a roading engineer, an army general and Timothy Hershaw, from *The Gazette*. They, along with other members of the entourage, were staying in the commandant's mansion while most of the visiting officers and wives were being accommodated in the officers' quarters in the penal settlement.

The township's commercial enterprises and dwellings were so few the tour was almost over before it started. Marsden couldn't help thinking it was a waste of time, but Sir Ralph was generous in his praise. There was little doubt his praise was more for the benefit of Hershaw than for his hosts, but neither Marsden nor Cheetham challenged him on that.

20

JOHN WATCHED WITH INTEREST AS the young soldier guarding him retrieved several sheets of paper from the nearby clerk's hut then climbed down the riverbank and disappeared beneath the wharf where he obviously planned to defecate at the water's edge. The soldier had evidently yet to learn there were crocs in these waters. John thought of warning him, but the thought passed as quickly as it occurred. *Could be one less soldier to worry about soon,* he thought. He returned to his work.

The sun was high in the sky now, and it was hot. John felt like he was burning up. He was only thankful he wasn't still working in the quarry with the others from his hut. Thinking of them reminded him of Noel.

Where are you now, you silly bastard?

He looked westward, toward the interior, and wondered whether Noel and McIntosh had gone that way.

A child's screams attracted his attention. He looked around, toward the meadow, and realised it was Matthew who was screaming. The boy was standing stock still, and bellowing at the top of his lungs. He was joined moments later by his mother who also started screaming.

John acted almost without thinking. He raced to the rear of the hut where the soldier's horse was tethered to a hitching rail. Untying the rope that held it fast, he scrambled onto the horse. Now that he was mounted, he wasn't sure what to do next.

As soon as the horse sensed its rider's hesitation, it reared up, dislodging the Irishman. John landed hard on his back. The wind was knocked out of him and his headache returned with a vengeance, but he gave that no thought as he scrambled to his feet. The screams from the meadow continued unabated, and his only thought was to get to the boy and his mother as quickly as he could.

To John's great surprise, the horse didn't bolt. Rather, it just stood there, looking at him as if daring him to try again.

"Alright you," John said, taking up the challenge. He mounted the horse, steadied himself and shook the reins. To his great relief the horse trotted off in the direction he was trying to steer it—toward the distressed Matthew and his mother. He ignored the shouts now coming from the soldier who had just noticed him riding off on his horse, and he hoped he wasn't about to be shot. He crouched low in the saddle just in case.

The source of the Marsdens' alarm was a deadly King Brown snake. Matthew had stumbled across it while playing in the long grass. It had struck out at him, twice, each time burying its fangs in the protective boots that Marsden had insisted his son wear whenever he ventured outdoors. That measure, so far, had saved Matthew's life for the fangs hadn't pierced his skin.

Now it was coming at the terrified boy again, hissing and threatening to strike a third time. "Mama!" Matthew cried out.

To shield Matthew, Missus Marsden began hitting the King Brown with a fallen branch she'd found nearby. The aggressive snake turned its attention to her and it struck out, burying its fangs into her exposed calf. It had been so quick, neither Missus Marsden nor her son saw the actual strike, but she felt it. A searing pain shot up her leg. She dropped the branch and staggered backwards in shock.

"Mama!" Matthew cried.

Only now did John arrive. He clumsily dismounted his borrowed horse, stumbling in his haste as his feet touched the ground, and he picked up the branch Missus Marsden had dropped. The snake turned its attention to him, and he began hitting it for all he was worth. He'd recognized the reptile as a King Brown as he'd seen them on several occasions at Parramatta. The Aborigines there had told him this particular snake's bite was almost invariably fatal.

John was so busy fighting for his own life he didn't see that Missus Marsden had collapsed behind him, but he could hear Matthew who was now crying. "It's alright, Matthew," John said reassuringly. He spoke with a confidence he didn't feel.

"I think it bit mama!" the boy whimpered.

Breathing hard, John risked a quick look behind him and saw Missus Marsden was unresponsive to her son's efforts to wake her. The persistent snake struck out at him again and he only just managed to parry it. "Try to wake her, Matthew!" John shouted, his attention now fully back on the King Brown, which was at last showing signs of losing the will to fight. He struck the snake yet again and it finally slithered away, disappearing in the long grass.

John hurried to Missus Marsden's side. He saw she was groaning and starting to come round.

"Is she going to be alright?" Matthew asked, still crying.

John didn't answer. He'd just noticed the ugly red fang marks in the woman's right calf. They were weeping, discharging droplets of some fluid he'd never seen before. He assumed the fluid was the snake's venom. The sound of horse's hooves carried to him. He looked around as the young private whose horse he'd taken arrived on a mount he'd borrowed from one of the carpenters.

The soldier, who had quickly ascertained that John wasn't trying to escape, pulled up close by. He looked at Missus Marsden who was now deathly white. "Snake bite?" he asked.

John nodded. "King Brown," he said. "Fetch the doctor. Quickly!"

The soldier switched mounts and galloped off, on his own horse this time, toward the settlement, leaving John and Matthew alone with Missus Marsden.

"Mama, talk to me!" Matthew cried as his mother lapsed back into unconsciousness.

John checked the woman's pulse. It took him a while to find a pulse, it was so weak. He didn't like her chances.

Matthew seemed to sense his mother was dying. He looked at John through tortured eyes. "Is there anything we can do for her?" he asked.

John shook his head. "Just pray for her, son."

Matthew dissolved into tears.

Looking at Missus Marsden, John wracked his brain, trying to recall how the Parramatta Aborigines treated snake bite victims. He remembered they'd used some herbal concoction, but he hadn't a clue what it was made up of.

John checked Missus Marsden's pulse again. It was no stronger, and her breathing was now very shallow.

To the Irishman and his young companion, the passing minutes seemed like hours. Finally, John noticed three horsemen galloping at speed out from the settlement. As they drew closer, he identified them as the young soldier, the doctor and the captain.

"Papa!" Matthew shouted when he recognised his father.

Marsden was first to arrive. He dismounted before his horse had even stopped, and he ran to his wife, pushing John aside. "Vera!" he said, shaking his wife. The captain was alarmed by her lack of response. He looked around at John. "You are sure it was a King Brown, Graham?" he asked.

"Yes, sir," John said. "No doubt."

Marsden looked back at his wife, calling out her name over and over, determined to elicit a response. He turned back to John as a thought occurred to him. "Did you suck out the poison?"

John realised he hadn't even thought of that. Guilt registered on his face and he could only shake his head.

Cursing, Marsden reached to his belt for a knife that wasn't there. Frantic, he looked around for a substitute. His eyes rested on the same decorative hairpin his wife had worn to the Governor's dinner. It reminded him she mentioned she'd never go anywhere without it. He'd thought she was joking. The captain seized the hairpin and buried its sharp point between the two fang marks. Pulling the pin out, he then sucked blood from the wound.

John and Matthew looked on helplessly as Mrs Marsden failed to respond.

Only now did the doctor arrive. Doctor Andrews was no horseman, and his dismount from his steed was barely more impressive than John's had been. Breathless, and sweating profusely, the Scotsman retrieved the medical bag attached to his saddle and hurried to check on the patient. "Move aside, Tom!" Andrews ordered.

Marsden finished sucking out the poison and reluctantly made room for the doctor.

John thought he detected the faint whiff of whisky on Andrews' breath. He glanced at Marsden to see if he'd noticed, but the captain was too distraught to observe such things.

"What will happen to her, papa?" Matthew asked, staring wide-eyed at his unresponsive mother.

"We don't know, Matthew," Marsden murmured. He held his son tight and glared at John as they awaited Doctor Andrews' verdict.

A guilty John wondered why he hadn't thought to suck out the poison. Then he remembered the Aborigines at Parramatta had scoffed at the very suggestion, claiming that was useless for treating snake bites. He recalled they used some herbal concoction, but hadn't a clue what it was made up of. A thought came to him. Addressing the doctor, he said, "Perhaps the local Aborigines have a cure for snake bite."

Andrews, who had spent the last minute trying to encourage his unconscious patient to ingest medicine from a dispenser he'd brought with him, rounded on John. "Surely you're not suggesting the hocus pocus treatments used by the savages are as effective as the medicines developed by Europe's finest doctors?" he asked scathingly in a Scottish brogue so thick it would have rivalled Angus McPherson's.

John had trouble understanding the doctor—and not only because of his brogue. It sounded as though he was slurring his words, and for the second time he wondered if the Scotsman had been drinking. He'd heard Andrews had a penchant for drink, and he did look flushed, although he was aware that could be attributed to the heat. John looked to Marsden for support for his suggestion they consult the local natives for help, but the captain's pained expression told him he considered his suggestion equally ridiculous.

"Perhaps if you'd thought to suck out the poison straight away," Marsden said, "my wife would not be in this state."

They looked back at Andrews who was now checking Missus Marsden's pulse. The doctor looked up at Marsden, grim-faced, and, almost imperceptibly, shook his head.

21

"PRECIOUS IN THE SIGHT OF the Lord is the death of his saints," the army chaplain said. "Yes, we are of good courage, and we would rather be away from the body and at home with the Lord." With these words, the chaplain closed the well-thumbed copy of the bible he'd been reading from and motioned to the assembled pallbearers to lower the coffin into the grave.

The six pallbearers, who were soldiers of various ranks, braced themselves as they took up the weight of the casket containing the body of Vera Marsden. Though heavy clouds covered the sun, the humidity was oppressive and pallbearers and mourners alike sweated profusely.

Captain Marsden and his children watched, grief-stricken, as the coffin disappeared from their sight. Helen and Matthew sobbed uncontrollably and held tight to their father. It was almost twenty-four hours to the minute since their mother had died, and they still couldn't believe it.

Lieutenant Hogan hovered close by, offering what emotional support he could to the family and to Helen in particular.

The hastily dug grave was located atop a hill a short distance from the Marsdens' cottage. It was an idyllic setting that commanded a view of Moreton Bay and the ocean beyond. The view from the hilltop was such Missus Marsden had once told her husband she wanted to be buried here should anything happen to her. In fact, she had made him promise she'd get her wish. Now, standing here, the bereaved captain vividly recalled that prophetic discussion. He wondered if his wife had had some kind of glimpse into the future.

Marsden was thankful for the heavy, grey clouds above. He considered the gloomy day appropriate. It was, he thought, nature's way of acknowledging this sombre occasion. Somehow, bright sunshine would not have been appropriate.

The crowd attending the funeral was the largest gathering of soldiers and townsfolk ever seen at the bay. Their numbers were bolstered by the Governor's entire entourage. Sir Ralph had been so moved by Missus Marsden's passing he'd postponed appointments and delayed his departure for Sydney Town by one day so that he could attend the funeral.

Marsden could have delayed the funeral to allow for a period of adjustment before committing his beloved Vera to the earth. However, that would have meant the Governor wouldn't have been able to attend as he had urgent appointments to keep at home. Also, he knew how much it would have meant to his wife to know Sir Ralph had attended her funeral, so it had been an easy decision in the end.

One of the pallbearers, Sergeant Benson, nodded to Marsden to indicate he should drop the first sod into the open grave. The captain stepped forward, leading his children by the hand. Benson handed a spade to his superior and stood back as Marsden turfed a spade-full of red earth on top of the coffin. The captain then handed the spade to Matthew and watched as his son, and then his daughter, each followed suit. That done, Marsden handed the spade to Sir Ralph who did his duty before handing the spade to Lord Cheetham, the next person in line.

Marsden didn't wait for the grave to be filled. Holding his children close to him, he walked slowly back to the cottage.

John had kept one eye on the funeral ceremony as he operated his kiln alongside the wharf. Now, as he stopped for his mid-day meal break, he watched as mourners began filing back to the cottage. From here, they were mere dots on the hillside.

At one stage, he thought he saw Hogan comforting Helen, but they were so far away he couldn't be sure.

The funeral had added to John's gloomy disposition. Already depressed at the thought of what fate awaited Noel when he was finally captured, the funeral only heightened the guilt he felt over Missus Marsden's death. For the thousandth time, he asked himself if he could have done more.

One bright spark on an otherwise gloomy day was that the disappearance of Noel and McIntosh hadn't yet been noticed. John knew that every hour that passed put them an hour closer to freedom.

That is if the natives haven't already got 'em.

He tried to remain positive, but it wasn't easy.

As he retired to the clerk's hut for his break, he noticed a horse-drawn cart approaching. It was being driven by Jonathan O'Shea, the smithy. He was escorted by an armed soldier on horseback. The cart was full of steel rods, which John guessed were for the wharf.

O'Shea hailed his assistant as soon as he saw him. "Help me unload these," he said, referring to the rods.

"It's my meal break," John protested.

"You can have your break after we unload these," the smithy said as he climbed down from the cart and began unloading the rods. That was his way of letting John know he'd brook no argument today.

John reluctantly went to O'Shea's assistance, trying as best he could to ignore his rumbling tummy.

When O'Shea finally spoke, it was to advise his assistant they had to swap workplaces for the afternoon: his skills were required on the wharf upgrade while John had a job awaiting him back in the foundry. John learnt the job entailed cleaning, which did nothing to improve his already gloomy mood.

By mid-afternoon, most of the mourners had returned to the settlement, having paid their respects at the cottage. With the assistance of the army's cooks, and the Marsdens' maid Orana, the captain had put on a modest spread of sandwiches and refreshments for the mourners. Now, only Sir Ralph, Lord Cheetham, Doctor Andrews, the Gazette's Deputy Editor Timothy Hershaw, Hogan and two other high ranking officers remained.

The men were assembled in the dining room, drinking whisky. Cheetham and Andrews had had a head start on the others, and they were now well under the influence. The sunlight, which had not long broken through the cloud cover, was kept at bay by the curtains, which Orana had drawn at Marsden's request. As a result, the room was almost as gloomy as the atmosphere.

Hershaw had been invited on Sir Ralph's gentle insistence. The Governor had suggested to Marsden that the scribe pen an obituary on Missus Marsden for *The Sydney Gazette,* and the captain had reluctantly agreed to the request. That had entailed allowing Hershaw to interview him in the privacy of his study. As it turned out, Hershaw had handled the assignment thoughtfully and with dignity, and talking about his wife had proven something of a cathartic albeit painful experience for Marsden.

Marsden's children were conspicuous by their absence. Helen and Matthew had opted to indulge their grief in the privacy of their bedrooms, so the menfolk had the dining room to themselves.

"It's an unforgiving country," Sir Ralph said to no-one in particular as he helped himself to another shot of whisky.

A listless Marsden could only manage a grunt in the affirmative.

"No real place for a lady," Cheetham piped up.

"Especially a lady such as she," Doctor Andrews agreed.

Marsden nodded morosely and helped himself to another drink. He'd lost count of the number of drinks he'd had. The whisky warmed his gut, bringing a measure of relief to his grief-stricken state, but other than that it had no effect.

Sensing the captain's mood, the Governor said, "I hope Mister Hershaw handled the interview with some sensitivity, Tom." He made no allowance for the fact that the scribe was sitting only a few feet away.

"He was very professional," Marsden said, catching Hershaw's eye and raising a glass in his direction.

Hershaw returned Marsden's silent toast by raising his own glass.

"Good," Sir Ralph said.

The conversation lapsed once more, and the men studied the bottom of their respective drinking glasses with more intensity than they'd normally give to so mindless a task.

Marsden's attention was drawn to the hallway as Helen emerged from her room. He was surprised to see she was in her riding outfit, and she was obviously heading out for a ride. "Helen!" he called. In the quick glimpse he'd had of her, he saw she was still crying.

"Back later, papa," Helen called as she headed for the backdoor. She'd adopted a forced lightness in her voice, but her father wasn't fooled.

"Helen!" Marsden stood up and prepared to go after her.

Sir Ralph restrained him. "She needs to be alone, old boy," he said.

"But . . ." Marsden didn't finish the sentence. He knew the Governor was right.

"Here, let me top you up," Cheetham said, topping up the captain's glass.

A resigned Marsden sat down and allowed the commandant to do the honours. He didn't like the idea of Helen riding alone, but he was prepared to make an exception this time. God knows, he understood she needed to be alone.

Like Marsden, Hogan also didn't like the idea of Helen riding unescorted. He sidled up to his superior. "Should I escort your daughter, Captain?" he asked quietly.

Marsden hesitated for a moment then nodded. "Thank you, Lieutenant," he murmured.

Hogan excused himself and hurried outside. He arrived at the backdoor as Helen was preparing to mount Benji. "Wait up, Helen," he said. "I'll keep you company."

Company was the last thing Helen wanted. "I need to be alone, Desmond," she informed him. She quickly mounted Benji and galloped off.

Undeterred, Hogan hurried over to his tethered horse. He'd only just mounted it when he noticed a soldier galloping toward the cottage at speed. As the soldier neared, the lieutenant recognised him as Private Henry Askew. He noticed the young private was riding with urgency, so he galloped to intercept him.

Moments later, the two horsemen pulled up only yards apart.

After exchanging hurried salutes, Hogan asked, "What is it, Private?"

"Sir, two convicts have escaped!" a breathless Askew said.

"When?"

"Two . . . possibly three days ago, Lieutenant."

"Two, possibly three? Can you be a little more specific, Askew?"

The young private shook his head. "The guards can't say exactly when, sir." He hurriedly added, "All they know it was well planned."

Hogan questioned Askew further, learning a few more details including the names of the escapees, before dismissing the private and hurrying back inside. He entered the dining room to find the curtains had been opened and the men were looking at him expectantly.

"Well, Lieutenant?" Marsden asked, "What is it?" He and the others had seen the lieutenant talking to Askew, and they could tell something was up.

Hogan quickly relayed what he'd learned.

"Two convicts?" Marsden asked.

"Yes, Captain," Hogan replied.

"Names."

"McIntosh and Thomas."

"Noel Thomas, the Irishman?" Marsden asked.

"Yes, sir."

22

JOHN WAS ALREADY MISSING HIS wharf job even though he'd only been back at the foundry a couple of hours. Cleaning the grubby premises from top to bottom was not his idea of a good time.

It was his assessment the foundry had never been cleaned even though the smithy had assured him it was cleaned monthly. Having swept the concrete floor and then mopped it clean, he was now scrubbing the walls with a wire brush to remove the congealed soot that remained as a result of the smoke from the furnace and kiln. It was hard going. *It's better than slaving in the quarry,* he kept reminding himself.

Working alone, John actually missed the companionship, such as it was, of the carpenters working on the wharf and even the Quandamooka fishing and going about their lives along the riverbank. At least there, there was always something to look at.

The depression he'd felt earlier hadn't lifted either. It anything it was worse than ever. Missus Marsden's death and Noel's escape consumed his thoughts. Still he blamed himself for the former's plight, and still he worried about the latter's fate.

John was so engrossed in his thoughts he wasn't aware he had company until he heard a footfall behind him. He turned to see Helen, her tear-stained face full of anguish.

"I . . . I didn't know where else to go," she sobbed.

John dropped his brush and removed his work gloves then walked toward the young woman. He stopped a few steps short.

The two stood there, looking at each other for several drawn-out moments. John's heart went out to Helen. He could see she was grief-stricken. The sight of her only served to intensify the guilt he already felt.

Helen suddenly went to him and buried her face in his chest as she dissolved into tears. "I . . . I'm sorry," she blurted. "I—"

"It's alright," John assured her. "I'm glad you came." He held her close to him until her sobbing subsided.

Helen finally regained her composure and separated from John. Drying her eyes, she asked, "Can I stay a while, John Graham?"

"Of course you can, Helen." He removed some items from a bench and they sat down, so close they were almost touching.

"Thank you," she whispered.

They sat in companionable silence for some time. It didn't feel forced or unnatural. In fact, to each, it felt totally normal—despite the abnormality of the situation.

John couldn't help thinking Helen had never looked more beautiful than she did at that moment. He could see she was completely vulnerable, and he wished he was a few years younger. *A few years younger,* he thought, *and not a bloody convict.* He looked at her and waited for her to speak when she was ready.

Out of the blue, Helen said, "Father believes I should return to England." She added, "He feels this is no place for a young lady."

"Perhaps he has a point."

That wasn't necessarily what Helen wanted to hear.

Again they lapsed into silence. John looked away, pensive.

Helen reached out and turned his face to her. "What's wrong?" she asked. "Do you want me to go?"

John didn't answer. He desperately wanted to tell her, but he couldn't find the words to explain the guilt he felt. Not to the dead woman's daughter.

Helen finally worked it out for herself. "You blame yourself, don't you?" she asked. It was more a statement.

"If I had sucked the poison out, your mother would still be—"

"*Could* still be alive, John," Helen interjected. "Not *would* still be alive . . . No-one knows for certain. Not you, not me, not my father. Not even the doctor."

"I thought of doing it," John confessed. "Sucking the poison out, that is, but I remembered the Parramatta Aborigines scoffed at the very idea." He was in full flight now. It felt good, too, getting it off his chest like this. He continued, "And I recalled the army's medical people at Parra had no luck using that method with snakebite victims, but I should have tried at least . . ." His voice trailed off.

Listening to John, Helen hadn't realised until now how much he blamed himself for her mother's death. She could see he was a tormented soul at that moment.

John was shaking his head. "I should have tried—"

Helen cut him off with a kiss, tentative at first then more passionate. Surprised, John responded with equal passion. Helen lay back on the bench, pulling him down on top of her. They began tearing at each other's clothes.

John suddenly rolled off her. "This isn't right, Helen," he said, hardly able to believe he was turning down an open invitation from the beautiful young woman before him.

"Why not?" Helen asked. She, too, was standing now.

"I'm a convict for Christ's sake! And this"—he gestured around the foundry's grubby interior—"isn't good enough for you."

Helen was lost for words, and John could see she needed a better excuse than the one he'd just given her. "I told you I didn't have a family to miss," he said at length.

She nodded.

"Well, that's not true," John said. "I do. Have family, that is. And I miss them . . . although they certainly don't miss me."

"I don't understand."

"They disowned me years ago. They knew what I was like, Helen . . . I've spent my whole life putting myself first. Making sure I got the best deal for me. You don't want . . ."

Helen went to argue the point, but the look on the Irishman's face cut her short.

"Just go home, Helen," John said.

Fighting back more tears, Helen straightened her riding clothes and prepared to leave. She hesitated when the sound of horses carried to them from outside.

John hurried to the door. He peeked outside and was alarmed to see Helen's father and the lieutenant tethering their horses near the foundry's entrance. It was obvious they planned to enter his workplace. John quickly returned to Helen's side. "It's your father and Lieutenant Hogan." Ignoring the horrified look on Helen's face, he asked, "Where did you tether your horse?"

"Behind the stables."

"Good. They don't know you're here then." John just hoped they hadn't come from behind the stables, otherwise they would have seen Helen's horse and they'd certainly guess she was here. "This way, quick!" he said, pulling her toward the rear of the foundry. Pushing her into a tiny storage space behind a cowhide curtain, he whispered, "Not a sound." Satisfied she was hidden from view, he hurried back toward the entrance, picked up the wire brush he'd dropped earlier and resumed scrubbing the near wall.

John heard Marsden calling to someone. Moments later, a three-way discussion carried to him. He couldn't discern what was being said, but he ascertained he was about to have three visitors.

When the two officers entered the foundry, John saw they were accompanied by one of the guards—James Whitelock, the Northerner. His heart sank when he noticed Whitelock was carrying a set of leg-irons, and by the angry look on Marsden's face, he could tell the leg-irons were for him.

Marsden glared at the Irishman then turned to the guard. "Shackle him," he ordered.

Whitelock immediately stepped forward and attached the familiar leg-irons to John's ankles.

While this was happening, John's attention was on Hogan who was now walking around the foundry, inspecting the facility.

Marsden looked at John and came straight to the point. "Your friend Noel Thomas has escaped," he said.

"I didn't know," John protested. "I wasn't aware Noel—"

"Do you think I'm a fool?" an irate Marsden asked. "I know you and Thomas are thick as thieves!"

John was alarmed to see Hogan approaching Helen's hiding place.

"Look at me when I address you, Irishman!" Marsden shouted.

John looked back at the captain. "Yes, sir."

At that moment, Hogan drew the cowhide curtain aside. Helen let out a cry of dismay. The others looked around to see the young woman staring out at them from her hiding place.

Marsden couldn't believe his eyes. "Helen?"

Helen could only cover her face with her hands.

Marsden turned and looked hard at John. The Irishman could see there was murder in his eyes, and in Hogan's eyes, too.

"I . . . I can explain, Captain," John said.

Marsden shaped up to strike John then he thought better of it and looked back at Helen. "Did he lay a hand on you, girl?" he asked.

Her face still hidden, Helen shook her head. "No, papa," she murmured.

Not convinced, Marsden turned to Whitelock. "Take him to the cells," he ordered.

Whitelock frogmarched John from the foundry.

The last glimpse John had of Helen was Marsden standing over her, demanding an explanation.

Outside, Marsden's words carried to him. "How could you, Helen?" the captain asked. "Your mother's body not yet cold in the ground."

John couldn't make out Helen's mumbled reply, but he could hear the guilt and pain in her voice.

Inside the foundry, Marsden hadn't finished with Helen. He glanced at Hogan who took the hint and left father and daughter to themselves.

When they were finally alone, Marsden turned back to Helen. He'd finally come to a decision. "You shall return to England on the next ship, young lady," he said.

◆⋲⋅━━━⋅₃◆

John lay curled up on the concrete floor of a tiny cell. It was one of half a dozen cells in the army's prison block.

Moonlight filtered through the cell's solitary barred window, revealing there was no bedding or furniture of any kind. The only concession to any sort of amenity was a bucket for toileting. It was half full of urine left by the previous occupant, and, judging by the smell, it had been there for days if not weeks.

The Irishman wasn't sure how long he'd been here. Whitelock and another guard had roughed him up a little before leaving him in solitary. Since then he'd dozed intermittently, and had lost track of time. As far as he knew, he was the cell block's only occupant.

Every so often, to amuse themselves, the guards would walk through the block, trailing their batons against the bars of each cell. The only purpose to this that John could see was to ensure he couldn't sleep for long.

On cue, two English guards he'd never seen before entered the block and began their little ritual. When they reached John's cell, which was at the far end of the block, they indulged themselves further by making jokes at his expense.

The nearest guard peered through the bars at John. "Couldn't fuckin' help yourself, could you," he said. Turning to the other guard, he added, "He blew that sweet deal with the captain. All for a wee sniff of his daughter."

John didn't give them the satisfaction of knowing he was awake. They eventually

133

tired of their little game and wandered off.

Fingering the silver crucifix he wore, John closed his eyes and thought back to the last time he was alone in a prison cell. It was the day of his trial in the London Courthouse. He'd been sentenced and was awaiting shipment to Australia in the cells behind the grim establishment.

On that fateful day, guards had escorted him and nine other felons on foot down to the docks where they were interned along with two hundred-and-forty others aboard the barque *The Northern Lights,* one of five converted convict ships bound for Australia. There, they were confined below deck in the hold, and there they remained for another three weeks until the vessel departed and then another four months until their arrival at Sydney Town.

For much of the voyage, John recalled, they remained shackled below deck. Usually, the only convicts allowed above deck during convict voyages were those poor souls who had died. Their bodies were, of course, consigned to the sea. Certainly, he and Noel never left the hold until they reached their final destination.

The conditions, he recalled, were atrocious with harsh discipline, dysentery, typhoid and scurvy claiming one hundred and forty-seven lives before the voyage was completed. Noel had almost become the one hundred and forty-eighth victim, and only John's support had kept him alive.

The memory faded, and John finally drifted off to sleep.

John was woken by the arrival of another prisoner. In the dark, the prisoner's limp form, which was supported between the same two guards who had taunted John earlier, was just a shadowy figure. But John didn't need to see his face to know it was Noel. His leg-irons rattled as he was dragged along the concrete floor.

"Another Irishman to keep you company, Graham," one of the guards announced.

The guards bundled Noel into the cell adjoining John's then slammed the cell door shut and locked it. A grunt from Noel as he landed hard on the concrete floor told John his friend was alive at least.

"It's the hangman's noose for you," the same guard said to the new prisoner as he and his companion walked off.

The other guard cracked a joke that was indiscernible to John. Their laughter echoed throughout the cell block.

As soon as the guards had departed, John reached through the bars of his cell and grabbed Noel's arm. "Noel! You alright?" he asked. In the moonlight he could see the younger Irishman was in a bad way—as to be expected for someone who had been on the run in the harsh Australian wilderness. He was cut and scratched, and burnt by the sun, and his clothes—or what was left of them—were in tatters. And, John could see, he'd been savagely beaten. More concerned than ever, John shook his friend's arm, harder this time. "Noel!"

"Leave me be," Noel mumbled, turning away.

Sensing Noel didn't want him to see him in such a state, John relinquished his grip on his friend's arm and lay back down. "When you're ready," he murmured. "No rush." He'd noticed Noel's voice was dry and raspy, and imagined he was thirsty.

After a long, long silence, Noel said, "We didn't run far enough . . ."

John looked at Noel through the bars. He saw that his friend was now staring at him, his face illuminated in the moonlight.

Noel continued, "We ran and we ran, but . . . the tracker still found us."

"Which way did you go?"

"West. Always west."

That told John they'd headed inland. He considered that a mistake, but didn't voice his opinion. "What's the terrain out there?" he asked.

"Desert. Nothing but feckin' desert. No water. Not even a drop."

John guessed Noel's Scottish companion hadn't survived the escapade. He waited for him to volunteer what had happened. When nothing more was forthcoming, he asked, "What happened to McIntosh?"

"They . . . they snuck in during the night and cut poor Terry's throat!" Noel choked back a sob.

"Jesus, Mary and Joseph."

"I didn't even wake up . . . They waited until I woke and found Terry like that . . . They laughed at me, John." Noel gave in to his emotions and sobbed. As his sobbing subsided, he sat upright and looked around his cell. "Water," he gasped. "I need water."

"There is no water in here," John said.

Resigned to remaining thirsty, Noel lay back on the concrete.

The two friends didn't speak again that night. They lay there, only a few feet apart, each wide awake and each alone with his thoughts. Each knew this would be Noel's last night. And for all John knew, this could be his last night, too.

John clasped his crucifix tightly. On a sudden impulse, he pulled it from around his neck and threw it to his condemned friend. It landed on Noel's shoulder. Noel said nothing, but he slipped it around his neck.

23

AT DAWN, TWO DIFFERENT GUARDS came for John and Noel. The former was marched toward the cell block exit while the latter was prepared for his execution. There was no time for goodbyes.

The army's idea of preparation for an execution was, as Noel was about to discover, a change of clothes for the condemned man, a drink of water and a verse from the good book half-heartedly recited by a chaplain who, on this occasion, was annoyed he'd been woken so early for what he considered so mundane a task.

Meanwhile, outside the cell block, John was marched to the compound where he found his fellow convicts already assembled in front of the gallows. Between the gallows and the whipping post, Marsden and Hogan sat astride their horses. Both glared at John as he was left standing in the front row of the convicts.

Staring back at the two officers, John could see the hatred in their eyes. Especially in Hogan's eyes. For one awful moment he wondered if this was to be the day of his own execution as well as his friend's.

Nearby, the ever-present Barega studied John with casual indifference. Looking cool, calm and collected in his adopted European clothing, the bare-footed tracker showed no sign of having spent the last day or so tracking escapees through the wilderness.

Some distance beyond the tracker, John noticed the Governor and his entire entourage—even the officers' wives—had turned out for the occasion. *Like the vultures they are,* he thought. They sat atop horse-drawn carts—the same carts that would transport them to their waiting vessel as soon as proceedings came to an end.

Sir Ralph was accompanied by Lord Cheetham. The two officials sat side by side, silently observing proceedings.

Even from where John was standing, he could see Cheetham wasn't happy. He could imagine the commandant was angry, and embarrassed, too, by the latest escape attempt. After all, the timing couldn't have been worse coming as it did during the Governor's visit. What John didn't know was Cheetham was suffering withdrawal symptoms, having refrained from indulging his opium habit since Sir Ralph's arrival at Moreton Bay. His craving for the drug was, by now, causing him excruciating discomfort, and he was counting down the minutes until the Governor finally departed.

Looking around at his fellow convicts, John could see their attention was on the gallows. They'd heard Noel had been captured, and they knew what was coming. John just hoped they weren't here to witness two hangings.

The beating of a drum announced the arrival of Noel's escort. It comprised a platoon of Redcoats. They were led by the army's head drummer who beat a steady tattoo on his drum. Noel was in the middle of the platoon, so John only caught glimpses of him.

Only when the platoon pulled up in front of the gallows could John and the other convicts see Noel clearly. To his credit, the condemned man stood tall, looking proud and unafraid. John just hoped he'd be as brave when he faced his own death. He also hoped that wouldn't be anytime soon.

At a nod from Marsden, two soldiers escorted Noel to the gallows' steps. They led him up the steps where the hangman offered him a blindfold. Noel steadfastly shook his head, refusing the offer.

Observing Noel through tear-filled eyes, John took great pride from his friend's composure. Only now did he notice Noel wore the silver crucifix he'd given him. It glinted in the early morning light. "God be with you, Noel," he whispered.

Marsden looked around at Cheetham then turned back to face the convicts. The captain said, "This man tried to escape," he said. "The punishment for that is death."

Without warning, Noel started singing a popular rebel song. "It was early, early in the spring, The birds did whistle and sweetly sing . . ."

"No singing, prisoner!" Hogan shouted.

Noel defiantly continued, only louder now. "Changing their notes from tree to tree . . ." For the first time, he looked directly at John as if commanding him to join with him.

John needed no second invitation. He lent his voice to the refrain.

As their singing reverberated throughout the compound, a murmur ran through the ranks of the convicts. Several Irish voices joined with Noel and John. "And the song they sang was Old Ireland free . . ." they sang at full volume.

"No singing!" a furious Hogan shouted. He turned to Marsden who nodded, indicating it was time to bring proceedings to an end. Hogan pulled a lever and the gallows' trapdoor flew open.

Noel was still singing as he dropped through the opening. John was the last person he saw before the rope cut short his fall. Mercifully, the fall snapped his neck, thereby circumventing the final struggles and twitches associated with many hangings.

By now, all the Irish convicts were singing.

John's voice rose above them all as he belted out another verse from the song Noel had started. Only when soldiers circulated among the convicts, striking them with their rifle butts and threating to shoot them, did the singing subside.

John was so overcome by the loss of his friend he had to turn away. However, he looked back when, out of the corner of his eye, he noticed the tracker approach Hogan. Barega motioned to the silver crucifix around Noel's neck. Hogan nodded and the tracker reached up astride his unusually long legs and grasped the crucifix, tearing it from Noel's neck, before walking away, admiring it.

If John hadn't been shackled, he'd have gone after Barega.

Watching from afar, the Governor had seen enough. The spontaneous outburst of singing had, for him, been the last straw, and he indicated as much to an already embarrassed Cheetham. The harried commandant ordered Private Withers to take them to the wharf. As they departed, with the Governor's entourage in tow, Cheetham promised himself he'd make life even more miserable for the convicts in future.

Marsden watched as the last of the Governor's entourage departed the compound. The captain had largely remained silent in the build-up to the execution. He'd surprised himself how at ease he felt overseeing Noel Thomas's hanging. While the concept of hanging convicts for attempting to escape still didn't sit well with him, he felt no guilt or shame over this particular execution. Looking down at John Graham, Marsden wondered if the deceased's friendship with John had anything to do with the way he felt. It probably did, he thought. Helen's recent indiscretion only served to strengthen his strong dislike of the Irishman. With that in mind, he knew he'd get some perverse enjoyment out of what he planned to do next.

The captain turned to Sergeant Christopher Rogers, the Birmingham soldier. "Bring John Graham to me, Sergeant Rogers," he ordered.

"Yes, Captain," the brutal Rogers said. He pulled John from the convict's ranks and stationed him in front of Marsden.

The captain fastened his steely gaze on John and then looked at the assembled convicts.

John tensed as he awaited Marsden's next words. He was suddenly sure he was about to be hung.

Marsden stared long and hard at the convicts then said, "For aiding and abetting in the escape of a fellow convict . . . John Graham shall receive fifty lashes."

John's initial reaction was one of relief. Only after his shirt had been torn from his back and he'd been tied to the whipping post, did his initial elation subside. His spirits plummeted even further when Old Bumble appeared, cat o' nine tails in hand, alongside him. The head flogger cracked his knotted whip several times in anticipation of what he was about to do.

To John's surprise, Marsden himself administered the count as Old Bumble went to work.

The first lash landed, sending shockwaves through the Irishman's entire body and causing him to strain at the bonds that held him.

"One," Marsden said, commencing the count.

The lashing continued and the count rose so slowly John thought time must be standing still.

With every crack of the whip, the assembled convicts flinched. It was a macabre sight: one of their own being flogged beneath another who hung from the gallows.

Later that morning, Marsden and Matthew stood hand in hand, looking down at Missus Marsden's grave atop the rise near the cottage. It was marked by a simple white cross.

Father and son watched in silence as a stonemason from the township took measurements for a permanent gravestone Marsden had ordered. The stonemason, an elderly Welshman who had served his time as a convict in Van Diemen's Land, went about his work with a quiet dignity, which impressed the captain.

"Shall we go back now, papa?" Matthew asked.

"Let's do that," Marsden smiled. He thanked the stonemason then walked back toward the cottage with Matthew's little hand still in his. The captain was taking advantage of special leave—*Sympathy Leave* the army called it—to help him get over his wife's death. At the suggestion of the Governor, Cheetham had insisted he take some leave, and Marsden had readily agreed. So, from today, he'd decided, he would take time to be with his children whenever his duties allowed. For the next few weeks at least.

"Do you think mama is in heaven yet?" Matthew asked.

"If she's not yet, she will be soon," Marsden said.

Matthew's face lit up at that news.

Observing his son, Marsden marvelled at how quickly youngsters recovered from tragedy. Matthew still hadn't really come to grips with his mother's death, but already he was showing signs of getting on with his life. Which was more than could be said for Helen. She was taking her mother's death hard, and had rarely ventured from her room since he'd dragged her back to the cottage in shame the previous day.

So he was surprised when he noticed Helen outside the cottage. She was talking to Hogan who was astride his horse. The lieutenant noticed his superior approaching and waved to him before bidding Helen goodbye and riding off.

To Marsden's further surprise, Helen waited for Matthew and himself. As they neared her, she rounded on him. "How could you flog him?" she asked, hands firmly on hips.

"This is not your business, Helen," Marsden replied.

"That man saved my brother's life," Helen reminded him. "Whatever else he may, or may not have done . . ."

"He aided in the escape of two men. What would you have me do?"

"I would have you show compassion."

Marsden stared at her.

"You cannot blame John Graham for mother," Helen said.

"That has nothing to do with it. I cannot allow the whims and fancies of the heart to run a prison. Your mother understood—"

"Stop it! Matthew cried. "Both of you, stop it." Close to tears, the boy turned and ran toward the cottage's front door.

"Matthew!" Marsden called. His son kept running and disappeared inside. Alone now, he turned back to Helen. "John Graham is not the man you think he is," he said. "He's an Irish rogue and a convicted thief."

Father and daughter stared at each other. After a long silence, Marsden reached into his pocket and drew out a small parcel, which he handed to Helen. She debated whether to accept the parcel. Finally, she took it and removed the wrapping to find it contained the ornate hairpin her father had given her mother.

Helen's eyes filled with tears. "Oh, papa." She flung her arms around Marsden. "I miss her so!"

"I miss her, too, my dear."

Soon they were both crying.

After recovering their composure, Marsden led Helen to the front veranda of the cottage. Here they had their first meaningful talk since the funeral.

"We are sitting where you and mama always sat," Helen observed.

Marsden smiled at the memory. Helen was quite right. He and his wife often sat here, overlooking Moreton Bay.

After a moment's silence, Marsden looked at his daughter. "I was serious about sending you back to England, you know?"

"I know, papa."

"Moreton Bay is no place for a young woman."

"So you keep telling me," Helen smiled.

"I have lost the love of my life," Marsden said. "I don't want to lose another loved-one." When Helen didn't answer, he continued, "I have learned the next London-bound ship is scheduled to call in here in three weeks."

After Helen digested that bit of news, she turned to her father and grabbed both his hands in hers. "Papa, would you mind if I boarded with the Browns in Sydney Town?" she asked. She referred to the Marsdens' long-time family friends who had relocated to Sydney Town from London about the same time the Marsdens had arrived in Australia. She reminded her father that William and Thelma Brown had offered her bed and board, and had offered to take her on as a teacher in the school they'd established.

Marsden considered Helen's suggestion. Tempting though it was, he considered the entire colony, not just Moreton Bay, unsuitable for a young woman. He shook his head. "No Helen. My mind is made up—"

"There is something else I need to tell you," Helen interjected. She'd debated whether to share her news with her father, but, if she was to get him to agree she could move to Sydney Town rather than London, she knew she must play her trump card.

"Oh?"

Helen steeled herself. "Lieutenant Hogan was here earlier," she said.

"Yes, he waved to me," Marsden reminded her.

"Yes. He . . . ah . . . he likes me." When her father didn't comment, she continued, "He came to tell me he plans to propose marriage when the time is right."

"Marriage?" Marsden asked, askance. "To you?"

Helen smiled. "Yes, papa," she said with exaggerated patience. "Who do you think I was referring to?"

Marsden wasn't overjoyed by this news. He had reservations about Hogan, and he had reservations about his daughter marrying him, or marrying *any* soldier for that matter.

Helen was very aware of her father's reservations. She'd overheard him expressing them in private discussions with her mother. She pressed home what she hoped would be the clincher. "You know how much mama liked the lieutenant," she said.

Marsden wasn't sure how to respond. He *was* aware how much his wife thought of Hogan. She'd said as much, and she'd hinted how well suited she thought the lieutenant and Helen were, but he wasn't sure how much she'd been influenced by his dashing style and his ready smile. He'd seen another side to Hogan—a side that neither his wife nor daughter had seen to his knowledge.

"Papa?" Helen was anxious for an answer.

"One minute." Marsden needed more time to think. If he was honest, he did prefer the idea of Helen being on the same continent as himself. If she returned to London, it would almost be like he'd lost her. He had already lost his wife; he didn't want to lose his daughter too. There was also Matthew to consider. He and his sister were close, and Marsden didn't want them to grow up oceans apart.

While he considered Hogan's interest in Helen was a complication he could do without, Marsden had to admit she could do worse. The lieutenant was, after all, a high achiever and clearly had a good future ahead of him.

Marsden looked at Helen with an intensity she'd never seen before. "Do you love Mister Hogan?" he asked.

Helen had been expecting that question. Without hesitating, she said, "I honestly don't know how I feel about him, papa. But I do know if he is here and I am in London, I will never find out." She added, "At least if I am in Sydney Town I will be able to see him occasionally, and I am sure in time I will be able to answer your question."

Marsden considered what Helen had just told him. She had obviously given her proposition a lot of thought, and, he suspected, she'd somehow outmanoeuvred him. At length, he turned to her and nodded.

"Oh, papa!" Helen hugged him tight and kissed his cheek.

141

PART TWO

NEW BEGINNINGS

24

JOHN SWUNG HIS PICK-AXE in a steady rhythm as he attacked the quarry wall. Six months' hard labour at Moreton Bay had hardened him and conditioned him to life as a convict in this, one of the colony's most notorious penal settlements.

The Irishman was coping with his lot better than most. The attrition rates within the settlement's convict population had risen alarmingly in recent months, and convicts were dropping like flies. If the tuberculosis, dysentery, typhoid or whooping cough didn't get them, the cholera, scurvy, smallpox or influenza almost invariably did.

Doctor Andrews was still the only doctor in the settlement for either the convicts or the soldiers—and of course the soldiers received priority treatment. It didn't help anyone either that the good doctor was drinking more than ever these days.

Added to that was death by injury or misadventure—*misadventure* being the army's euphemism for the harsh, often fatal punishment meted out by soldiers and guards alike.

It was John's assessment if it wasn't for the new convicts arriving in ever-increasing numbers, the original two-hundred-and-thirty or so who had been here when he arrived would now number scarcely more than a hundred. As it was, frequent shipments from Sydney Town, and some from Van Diemen's Land, too, had boosted the convict population to five hundred with more arriving by the week. And as always the new arrivals were the hard cases—or *the scum of the earth* as the soldiers called them—whose natural inclination was to resist army-style discipline.

Unfortunately, construction in the convict settlement wasn't keeping pace with the rise in convict numbers. Only two new huts had been built to accommodate the extra convicts, and as a result the accommodation had become even more overcrowded with many more men now sleeping on the floor than in bunks.

Illness and injury weren't the only reasons for the high attrition rates. More and more convicts were opting for death by suicide, such were the conditions at Moreton Bay. Death was considered a merciful release. As a result, escape attempts continued to rise—and so, too, did the hangings. The tracker had never been busier, and since Noel's execution twenty-eight convicts had died trying to escape and a further eighteen had been hung.

The men realised their chances of escape were slim, and their chances of remaining free should they manage to escape were even slimmer. But that only served to encourage those who had given up on life.

It wouldn't have surprised John and the others to learn the Moreton Bay penal settlement was earning a reputation as *the hell hole of the colony*. It was regularly referred to as such by the newspapers.

One man could be blamed for that state of affairs: Lord Bertram Cheetham. His cruelty knew no bounds. It had been heightened by his continued use of opium. The Governor was aware of this, but it suited Sir Ralph Darling to turn a blind eye to Cheetham's addiction and his harsh managerial methods. His eye, after all, was on the end goal: to fast-track Moreton Bay's growth—and Australia's growth, too. That's what the politicians back home demanded of the Governor, and that's what he intended to deliver.

A good example of Cheetham's cruelty was an incident involving, of all people, one of the soldiers. Private Joseph Sudds, who was considered a simpleton among his peers, foolishly believed seven years as a convict would be preferable to serving out his twenty years with the army—and so he'd stolen valuables from Cheetham's mansion.

As Sudds had anticipated, he'd been caught and imprisoned. What the simpleton hadn't anticipated was Cheetham sentencing him to wear a permanent, spiked, steel choker, or collar, and be put to work in the quarry alongside the convicts.

Unfortunately, the steel collar became red hot in the sun, burning Sudds' flesh and causing him immense pain. His fellow workers felt such pity for him they implored their guards to remove the collar, but their pleas were ignored. After several days, Sudds' neck swelled to the extent he couldn't breathe, and he eventually suffocated. It was a long, slow and terrible death.

As a final insult, Cheetham consigned the soldier's body to the river where the crocs took him.

There were many other gruesome incidents, but that was undoubtedly one of the worst.

How John had remained fit and healthy through all of these dramas, he couldn't say. Although overworked and constantly hungry, he felt surprisingly strong. The exposed parts of his body had been darkened by the sun, his hands were now permanently calloused and the muscles on his lean frame were hard and sinewy. He could work all day while others dropped around him.

John climbed higher on the quarry face to attack a rocky outcrop that was only a few yards from the summit. He noticed the rock above him sloped outwards. The angle was ever so slight, but it was sufficient to dispel any thought he may have had of escape. Not that he'd once seriously considered escaping. His aim was to serve out his seven years and then return to Ireland. God how he missed Ireland. He missed its green fields, its continuous rain and its cooler temperatures.

And its women!

My how he missed Irish women.

At least the temperatures had cooled in Moreton Bay for it was winter now. Midwinter in fact. Even so, it was still warm, but it was pleasantly warm, and the humidity levels were now almost negligible.

Below John, on the quarry floor, convicts used sledgehammers to smash rocks he and others had prised from the rock face. Looking down, he identified the promiscuous Englishman Don Henderson and Welshman Rhys Jones, Henderson's boyfriend. They were working alongside Dubliner Paddy O'Donnell and the one-eyed Englishman William Harrison. Young water boy Billy Morris scurried amongst them, dispensing water from the buckets he carried. Billy had survived despite contracting typhoid in the autumn. Not even in Doctor Andrews' sober moments could he explain how the lad had gotten through that.

On the rock face alongside John were his countrymen Seamus O'Neill, Pat Kennedy, Luke Donovan and Sean O'Driscoll. The Irishmen, along with O'Donnell, had formed a tight little unit in the past six months, and they worked together as often as the guards allowed.

John became distracted when he noticed two officers approaching the quarry on horseback. As they neared, he recognised them as Captain Marsden and Lieutenant Hogan. Whenever he saw them, he thought of Helen. He hadn't seen the beautiful young woman since she'd departed for Sydney Town four months earlier. He'd heard on the grapevine she'd gone to board with family friends there, but he had no idea whether she intended to return to Moreton Bay or whether he'd ever see her again. He somehow doubted he would.

The Irishman watched as the two officers consulted with soldiers in the quarry. He observed the pair were as professional and business-like as ever, and not for the first time he wondered whether there was some tension between the two. To his eyes, the relationship between Marsden and Hogan appeared strained, but he put that down to the differences in their ranks and ages.

The officers finally rode off, and John went back to work.

The Irishman found himself working alone on the rock face, some distance from his companions. A fissure in the rock caught his eye. He'd seen it before, but had never ventured into it. He entered the fissure and saw it offered easy pickings in the form of loose rocks, which he thought could be easily removed, so he took to the nearest rock with a mighty swing of his pick-axe.

To his surprise, a large slab of the rock came away, revealing another fissure—narrower than the first one. John looked behind him and realised he was out of sight of the others. He inched his way along the narrow opening in the rock, holding the pick-axe close to his chest. It became darker as he progressed deeper into the cleft.

Progressing largely by touch, he prayed he wouldn't encounter one of the death adders he knew frequented the quarry. As he negotiated a tight turn, he noticed the darkness was becoming lighter.

Before he knew it, he was standing in bright sunshine on the hillside outside the quarry—a free man. "Holy Mother of God!" he muttered. He saw the opening had delivered him to the western side of the quarry, away from Moreton Bay and more importantly away from prying eyes. Ahead of him, as far as the eye could see, scrub and bush-covered hills extended all the way to the western horizon.

It took him a moment or two to take stock of the situation he'd unexpectedly found himself in. And when it did sink in, he realised he had a decision to make. He looked all around him, still not quite able to believe he'd escaped the quarry and was totally alone.

Almost without thinking, he began running downhill as fast as his shackles would allow. It never occurred to him to drop his pick-axe as he planned to make use of it soon. He'd often thought—on those rare occasions he'd idly contemplated escape—he'd use a pick-axe to free himself of his leg-irons. And right now, that was his first priority.

John soon reached the cover of the bush. He immediately slowed, knowing that for the moment at least he was out of sight. Pushing through the undergrowth, he soon found what he was looking for—a rock. He sat down and draped his legs over it, ensuring the chain that linked his metal ankle braces was stretched taught. Then, raising his pick-axe high above his head, he brought its flat, steel edge down hard, severing the chain.

Next came the tricky task of severing the press-studs that held fast the two metal braces, or clasps, encircling his ankles.

John altered his grip on the pick-axe to bring the narrower of its two blades into play. Taking careful aim to minimise the risk of hitting his left ankle instead of the metal clasp, he brought the pick-axe down. "Bull's eye!" he exclaimed. His aim was true and the blade disengaged the stud holding the clasp. It fell from his ankle. "One down, one to go," he mumbled.

The right hand clasp proved more problematic. On the first attempt, he missed the stud. The blow sent shock waves through his leg, and for a moment he thought his ankle may have been broken. Two further attempts met with the same result, and he regretted he hadn't brought a more suitable tool for the job. By now he was in considerable pain. He gave it one more shot, and thankfully that was enough. "Got you, you feckin' bastard!" he muttered. The stud sprang open and the second clasp fell off.

John pushed himself slowly to his feet. Although still in pain, he relished the feeling of freedom that came with being unshackled. He shaped up to throw the pick-axe away when he had a thought. On an impulse, he jammed the pick-axe handle into a cleft in the rock so that the tool was left in an upright position. He then hung his discarded shackles from its steel blades.

Something to remember me by.

He knew Barega would find it sooner or later—later, he hoped—and it was his way of saying "Come find me" to the tracker.

The Irishman set off deeper into the bush, anxious to distance himself from Moreton Bay.

Although no longer encumbered by leg-irons, his right ankle was so sore it caused him to limp quite badly. He just hoped he hadn't caused himself any permanent injury.

As he hobbled along, he calculated his odds. The sun, which was barely visible in the dense bush, was on his right—due north—confirming for him that it was close to noon, which meant his fellow convicts would soon be stopping for their mid-day meal if they hadn't stopped already. "Thirty minutes at most before they know I'm gone," to told himself. He was in no doubt his disappearance would be noted after the headcount, which always followed the mid-day break.

Allow another thirty minutes until they set the tracker after me, that gives me an hour's start if

I'm lucky.

An hour didn't sound very long to him.

Noel and McIntosh had roughly a day's start, and even that wasn't enough.

Thinking of Noel and the Scotsmen, and the fate they met with, forced him to move faster. He was soon breathing hard and sweating profusely, and his ankle was really hurting now.

25

MID-DAY MEAL-BREAK OVER, SERGEANT BENSON supervised as three soldiers conducted a headcount of the convicts in the quarry. The hundred and twenty-three convicts working there this warm July day had been split into three groups of forty-one men for the sake of the count.

O'Driscoll, Kennedy, Donovan, O'Donnell and O'Neill stood side by side as Private Henry Askew counted the men in their group. When the young soldier came up a man short, he conducted a second count—for the same result. He immediately brought the discrepancy to his sergeant's attention.

As the two soldiers conferred, Kennedy looked around at the other convicts in his group. He caught the eye of Donovan, the man on his left, and grinned. "It's Graham," he whispered.

Donovan nodded. 'The bastard didn't even say goodbye." He, too, grinned.

A worried Benson commenced a more thorough count of the convicts in the group, calling out the names of each man and ticking them off as they answered.

As the roll call continued in the quarry, Marsden surveyed the seventy or so convicts who had been employed to fence off the corn fields between his cottage and the penal settlement. From astride his horse, he had an uninterrupted view of his charges. Half the convicts were carrying rocks from six horse-drawn carts lined up in a row nearby. They worked in relays, delivering the rocks to those convicts tasked with actually constructing the stone fences. As carts were emptied, they were hauled back to the quarry for another load.

There was similar activity in the settlement where more convicts were building stone fences and paths. And, Marsden was aware, still more were engaged in projects in the nearby township, constructing fences and working on a new road that would eventually connect Brisbane Town with the penal settlement and the wharf, and, eventually, with the bay beyond.

The wharf itself had undergone a transformation, too. The old wharf's timbers had been replaced, and the facility was now three times longer than when John briefly worked on it.

Marsden glanced up at the cottage and was pleased to see Matthew doing his schoolwork in the shade of the veranda. The boy was being home-schooled by one of the settler's wives. She was a former teacher from Edinburgh and, although still on trial, Marsden was more than satisfied with her. Matthew seemed to be responding well to her tuition and even looked forward to her weekday visits.

The captain's eyes wandered to his late wife's resting place. Her grave on the hilltop was now marked by a permanent gravestone. It was, he thought, a fitting memorial to a fine woman.

Thinking of his wife invariably reminded him of their daughter. Helen, according to her latest letter, was enjoying her new life in Sydney Town. She had recently started work as a trainee teacher at the junior school run by family friends William and Thelma Brown with whom she boarded. And, according to William Brown's latest letter, Helen had all the hallmarks of being an excellent teacher.

Marsden still had misgivings about his daughter's interest in Hogan, but he'd adopted a more fatalistic attitude regarding their relationship, and regarding life generally, since his wife's passing, and so was now more relaxed about the possibility of marriage.

The captain had become more fatalistic about the penal settlement and his role in it, too. While he didn't condone the cruel regime Lord Cheetham had established at Moreton Bay, he'd gone along with it—to an extent at least.

Marsden had softened his stance on the treatment of convicts after the Governor's visit six months earlier. That visit had brought home to him that Sir Ralph fully supported Cheetham's methods, especially his harsh treatment of convicts.

The danger of not supporting the commandant had been brought home to him loud and clear three months ago when he'd received a personal letter from the Governor warning that his career was at risk if he didn't fall into line. It was evident Sir Ralph had received a complaint, or more likely complaints, about him from Cheetham although the Governor never said as much. After much soul-searching, Marsden had taken Sir Ralph's advice and fallen into line. It still didn't sit well with him, but his decision had been made and he had learned to live with it, and with himself.

Marsden noticed a soldier galloping toward him from the quarry. Sensing some urgency, the captain galloped to meet him. As the gap between them narrowed, Marsden identified the soldier as Private Askew.

Thirty minutes later, Marsden and Hogan emerged from the stables on horseback. They were followed by two soldiers, also on horseback, and by Barega, who was on foot and looking eager for the hunt.

The soldiers, both privates, were the same pair who accompanied Hogan when he and Barega successfully tracked Frank Patterson and his fellow escapees all those months ago. They'd formed a successful team since then, apprehending many escapees, and so the captain used them as often as he could.

Marsden was in the middle of briefing his lieutenant. "Graham has at least an hour's start," he said.

"That might as well be a five-minute start, Captain," a cocky Hogan said, glancing in the tracker's direction.

"Don't be so sure," Marsden warned. "This Irishman is smart."

Hogan wasn't convinced, but he said nothing.

Marsden continued, "And remember Lieutenant, I want him taken alive."

"Yes, sir."

"Make sure the tracker understands that."

"Yes, sir."

Only now did the officers notice Cheetham approaching from the direction of the township. He was on horseback, which was unusual for him, and he was accompanied by Private Withers.

The commandant reined in close to his subordinates. Marsden and Hogan saw that he was breathing hard and sweating profusely despite the absence of any humidity. They guessed Cheetham had been indulging his addiction again. Either that or he'd been drinking, or both perhaps. This was confirmed for them when he spoke.

"I hear another Irishman has escaped," Cheetham said, slurring his words.

"Yes, sir," Marsden said. He glanced at Withers, realising the young soldier must be under orders to alert the commandant as soon as there was news of an escape. That would also explain why Cheetham had unexpectedly turned up soon after the previous two escapes had been discovered.

Withers couldn't meet the captain's gaze.

"I want that Irish bastard back," the commandant said.

"Of course, sir," Marsden said.

"I want him back dead or alive."

"I have ordered Lieutenant Hogan to return him alive."

"*Dead* or alive!" Cheetham snapped. He glared at Marsden then switched his glare to Hogan. "Is that understood, Lieutenant?"

Hogan glanced at Marsden before answering, "Ah . . . yes, Lord Cheetham."

"Lord Cheetham! I must—" Marsden was about to protest when his superior galloped back the way he'd come.

"Dead or alive!" Cheetham yelled over his shoulder before he disappeared around the corner of the stables.

Marsden felt humiliated that he'd been undermined in front of his subordinates. That was happening too often for his liking. He debated whether to countermand Cheetham's orders. In the end he turned to Hogan and said, "You heard the commandant, Lieutenant."

"Yes, Captain," Hogan said.

The pair saluted and Marsden rode off, leaving Hogan and his men to their own resources.

Hogan had a quick word with his two soldiers before heading out of the settlement at a steady trot. The tracker led the way, his deep-set eyes on the western horizon and his long legs covering the ground with effortless ease.

Barega was back in his element, doing what he loved. He clasped his spear and woomera in one hand and a bone nulla nulla in the other. The bone looked suspiciously like a human femur, and it was obvious it could crush the thickest of human skulls. Hanging from his loincloth was the hunting knife that had once belonged to Frank Patterson, and around his neck was the silver necklace he'd taken from Noel Thomas's body. The crucifix that hung from the necklace bounced against his chest as he ran.

26

J OHN WAS IN FRIGHTFUL PAIN now. His right ankle had swollen up, and he had been reduced to a painful hobble. He was thirsty, too, and desperately needed a drink.

The Irishman was breathing hard as he climbed a steep hill covered in dense rainforest. In the last little while, the bush had given way to rainforest, and vines and branches had reduced his clothes to tatters; his face and hands were covered in scratches. Somehow his hat was still atop his head, but it was also tattered.

It was with some relief he neared the top of the hill. Emerging from the gloom of the rainforest, he found himself in a clearing on the hilltop. And there, in front of him, was a billabong. "Praise the Lord!" he muttered. He stumbled over to the small watering hole and plunged into it, taking in mouthfuls of water to assuage his thirst.

After a few moments, he reluctantly left the coolness of the billabong and surveyed his surroundings. Only now did he realise the hilltop offered three hundred and sixty-degree views. His first thought was how far he'd progressed from Moreton Bay. A quick glance left him feeling deflated. Though he couldn't see the quarry from here, he could see the penal settlement. It was, he thought, depressingly close. He estimated at most he'd ventured two or three miles from the quarry. "More like two miles," he mumbled. The sun's location told him it was mid-afternoon.

Three hours to darkness give or take.

He knew he had to stay ahead of those tracking him until nightfall.

John was in no doubt they were coming for him. His disappearance would most certainly have been noticed after the mid-day meal break, and the inevitable search party would have been on its way within half an hour of that. And he was in no doubt the tracker was a member of that search party. He'd seen Barega in the settlement just that morning, so he knew he wasn't on walkabout or otherwise engaged.

Almost on cue, John saw a puff of dust between the settlement and his current position.

Horses!

In the distance he could make out three horsemen. Their red tunics identified them as soldiers. They were trailing a lone Aborigine who followed John's tracks on foot. "Barega," he whispered. Though the others were too far away to identify, John recognised the tracker by the abnormal length of his stride.

Barega's spear glinted in the sunlight, prompting the fugitive to be on his way. He turned around and struck off downhill, heading further inland.

"Ow!" he gasped. Pain shot up through his right leg as he took his first step. In his haste, he'd forgotten about his injured ankle. He forced himself to slow down and watch where he placed his feet.

More haste less speed.

That thought kept coming to him. He pulled up and told himself he needed to think about what he was doing. "I need a plan." He realised he'd been running blind since finding himself outside the quarry.

What am I doing and where am I going?

The thought of the hangman's noose helped him focus his thinking for he was in no doubt that's what awaited him should he be caught.

I'm heading west, but Noel said there was nothing there. No people, no water. Only desert.

The realisation dawned he'd have more chance evading his pursuers here, in the rainforest, than in the Australian desert, or *the Outback* as the locals called it.

At least here there's food and water . . . and places to hide.

He realised if he wanted to stay in the rainforest that meant remaining close to the coast, for the rainforest, as far as he knew, hugged the coastline. "So the question is . . . do I head north or south?" he asked himself.

If he had a coin, he'd have tossed it. Finally, it was a bird call that decided it for him. It was a bird he'd never heard before, and its foreign, trumpet-like sound startled him. The call came from a tree to his left, on the edge of the clearing, so he headed in the opposite direction. "North it is," he said to himself, hoping like hell he'd made the right decision.

Before he re-entered the rainforest, he looked back toward Moreton Bay for a final glimpse of his pursuers, but they'd disappeared from view. The sobering thought occurred that he probably wouldn't see them again until they caught up to him. This thought gave him renewed energy, and, ignoring the pain in his ankle as best he could, he pushed on through the trees.

Barega stopped running when he came across the pick-axe John had left. The shackles hanging from its steel blade left no doubt the fugitive was conveying a symbolic gesture to his pursuers.

The tracker followed his quarry's tracks a few more paces and stopped at the point where John had veered off to the north some thirty minutes earlier. He waited patiently for Hogan and the other soldiers to reach him. In the rainforest, they'd been reduced to walking their horses, so he had some more time to himself before they caught up to him.

Barega fingered the silver crucifix he'd acquired. He held it up to the sunlight that filtered through the canopy of trees, and he marvelled at how it glinted when the light caught it.

Hogan was first to arrive. He'd removed his red tunic to avoid the risk of it being torn by the branches. His shirt and breeches had already been torn, and his face and hands were scratched. Droplets of blood mingled with sweat on his face.

The lieutenant had seen the pick-axe and shackles as soon as he'd arrived, but he pretended to ignore it. Sighting the symbolic gesture had only served to harden his resolve. As far as he was concerned, John Graham was a dead man.

The two privates arrived, and they were faring no better than their commanding officer. They, too, were scratched and bloodied. All three soldiers were keen to apprehend the escapee as soon as possible so that they could be back at Moreton Bay before dark.

Barega, on the other hand, still looked as fresh as when they'd started out.

"How close?" Hogan asked the tracker.

"Close now," Barega grinned.

"Exactly how close?" Hogan knew from experience that his tracker's idea of *close* or *nearby* or *soon* was quite different to his. Previous searches had taught him Barega's idea of *close* was anywhere within a hundred miles.

"Before dark, Mister," Barega said.

"Good enough," Hogan said, ignoring the groans that came from his men. Like him, they'd been hoping for an earlier outcome.

Barega pointed to John's tracks. "Irish injured," he said. The tracker knew enough about his quarry to know he was Irish though he didn't comprehend what that meant. He assumed that was the escapee's first name.

Hogan studied the tracks, but couldn't determine how the tracker had deduced their quarry was injured. However, he didn't doubt Barega. If the native said the Irishman was injured, he was injured.

Barega ran on ahead. Before the trees swallowed him up, Hogan had to yell out and remind him not to get too far ahead otherwise he'd have to mount a search for them as well.

John had no idea how long it had been since he'd struck off to the north. The rainforest was so dense it allowed very little light to penetrate its canopy, and he'd lost all track of time. Consequently, he didn't know how long it would be before darkness fell.

The escapee had become obsessed with remaining free until nightfall. He knew not even the tracker could follow his tracks in the dark.

Finally, a gap in the canopy let the sunlight through. John was disappointed to see how bright it was. "Damn!" he cursed. It was so bright he estimated dusk was still a good hour away. He reckoned it would be touch and go whether he could stay ahead of his pursuers until nightfall—especially as his injured ankle was proving more and more of a problem.

John pushed on, trying as best he could to ignore the pain the injury was causing him. His progress wasn't helped any by the damp underfoot conditions. Even though it had hardly rained at Moreton Bay for some months, here, in the rainforest it was different. The rainforest had its own microclimate, and here it rained more frequently. And because the sun scarcely penetrated the forest canopy, the ground remained damp and often muddy, causing John to slip and slide while negotiating the terrain. His progress wasn't helped either by the huge surface roots that extended out, like writhing snakes, from some of the trees. They conspired to trip him, or so it seemed, as he pushed on.

Not for the first time, a thought kept coming to him.

Death by suicide.

He kept pushing it away, but it always returned.

Thinking back to the moment he found himself on the hillside outside the quarry, he asked himself what was going through his mind when he decided to flee.

I could have just as easy returned to the quarry and no-one would have been any wiser.

He wondered whether he'd subconsciously decided he wanted to be caught trying to escape. If he was honest with himself he was fed up with his life as a convict, and Noel's execution had left him feeling depressed and more homesick than ever. He thought of Ireland and the friends he'd left behind. And he knew he wanted to live— if only to see them and his homeland again.

"I want to live!" he said, pushing harder through the trees.

A roaring sound carried to John. Soon, he was able to identify it as a river, and by the sound of it, it was running high.

Minutes later he found himself on the bank of a fast-flowing river. The sun was hidden behind hills on the far side of the river, but he could tell it was low in the sky. "Dusk can't be far off, surely." He couldn't even hear himself speak, so loud was the roar of the river.

Looking downriver, he could see rapids, and beyond them he could just make out what appeared to be a waterfall. A cloud of spray marked the location of the falls.

John scrambled along the bank. As he did, the thought occurred he could shake his pursuers once and for all if he could somehow cross the river. Closer inspection of the raging waters told him that would be suicidal, so he dismissed that thought.

The Irishman screamed in pain when he slipped on a moss-covered rock, and his right boot became jammed. He finally managed to extricate his foot, nearly losing his boot in the process, and continued along the bank in more pain than ever.

As he neared the falls, the river's roar became deafening and he was drenched by the spray. Something made him glance behind him and he was alarmed to see Barega. The tracker was standing on the same rock John had slipped on just a few minutes earlier and, although he was a good fifty yards distant, the Irishman could see he was grinning.

Barega seemed to be in no hurry to catch up to his quarry. John guessed he was waiting for his masters. Sure enough, the tracker was soon joined by the three Redcoats he'd seen earlier. They were now travelling on foot, having found the rainforest and steep terrain unsuitable for their horses.

Only now did John identify Hogan as one of the soldiers. That didn't surprise him. He guessed Helen's interest in him had made this personal for the young lieutenant.

At a word from Hogan, Barega began walking along the bank toward John, his spear and club in hand. The soldiers followed, unshouldering their rifles as they walked.

John looked around wildly. He reckoned he had, at best, two minutes of freedom left.

Make that two minutes to live.

The Irishman was in no doubt the men hunting him weren't planning to take him alive. He scrambled over the rocks as fast as his injured ankle would permit. Now oblivious to the pain, he was solely focussed on one thing: his survival.

Barega was now so close, John was aware he was within range of his spear. In fact, he could see the tracker was so close he could spear him even without using his woomera.

For the second time that day, John knew he must make a life-changing, or possibly life-ending, decision.

Wait for the tracker to kill me or take my chances in the river.

He looked into the raging waters and wasn't at all sure he'd have the courage to jump in. Then he looked back at Barega and saw the native was in the process of inserting his spear into the woomera. He also observed that Hogan had caught up to the tracker and was showing no inclination to prevent him from throwing his spear.

"God help me," John mumbled as he prepared to launch himself into the river.

Not twenty yards away, Hogan raised his rifle in John's direction as he realised what the escapee was about to do.

Barega was already in the process of launching his spear. The woomera sent it on its way with enough power to send it a hundred yards or more.

John felt the wind from the spear, or perhaps it was from the waterfall, as he dived into the river. When he entered the water, it felt as though he was suspended there for a moment, and then the river grabbed him and flung him over the falls.

It was only as he was tumbling head over heels that he wondered how high the falls were. A lifetime later, or so it seemed, he landed in the water at the foot of the falls. Mercifully, he didn't strike a rock, but he did nearly drown before he managed to resurface. Even then, he wasn't out of danger. The force of the waterfall kept pushing him under, and it was only by diving deeper and swimming underwater, away from the torrent, that he was able to survive.

When he finally surfaced, choking and spluttering, he gratefully sucked in several deep breaths. Despite his near-death experience, he had the presence of mind to realise he'd lost his hat.

Below the falls, the river widened and the current soon slowed. He was able to float downstream on his back. Only now could he see how high the falls were. "Jesus, Mary and Joseph!" he mumbled. He estimated the falls were all of a hundred foot high, maybe more.

Before overhanging branches from trees along the near bank concealed his view, he caught sight of Barega staring down at him from a rock at the top of the falls. For one awful moment he thought Barega was going to dive in after him, but the tracker showed no inclination to do that.

"Come and get me, you bastard!" John shouted, shaking his fist at Barega. He realised he couldn't be heard above the roar of the falls, but he felt better nonetheless and couldn't stop from laughing.

The lazy current carried him around a bend in the river. It was only then he noticed dusk was falling. The realisation set in that he was going to achieve his immediate goal and survive until nightfall. He let out a scream of triumph. The scream was cut short when he swallowed a mouthful of water.

After he'd regained his breath, he saw a sandy beach between the rocks along the near bank. He prepared to swim over to it, but changed his mind at the last moment. His survival instincts told him the tracker would keep searching for him until dark, and so he resigned himself to remaining in the river as long as possible. That way, he could distance himself from his pursuers better than would be possible on land—especially the way his ankle was.

Floating along on his back, staring up at the darkening sky, he idly wondered whether there were crocs in this particular river. He wasn't to know there were, but they were further downstream, nearer the coast.

John remained in the river as long as he dared.

It was almost pitch dark when he finally dog-paddled over to some low-lying rocks he'd spotted along the far bank.

Climbing onto the rocks took all of his remaining energy. Having floated for perhaps an hour in the river after having spent the earlier part of the afternoon fleeing through the bush, and not forgetting he'd spent the morning doing hard labour in the quarry, he was exhausted. He was also cold, hungry and frightened. Frightened because he wasn't certain he could survive the night, and he was even less certain he could survive the next day.

As if all that wasn't serious enough, his right ankle had now swollen up like a balloon, and he was convinced it was broken.

A mile upriver, above the falls, Hogan had resigned himself to spending the night in the rainforest. He and his companions hadn't expected the Irishman to remain free until nightfall, so they hadn't come prepared for a night in the outdoors. That's to say, the soldiers hadn't come prepared. Barega, on the other hand, was always prepared. He could sleep standing up if he had to.

Faced with a night out in the open with few rations and little gear, the soldiers were frustrated and grumpy. Hogan in particular was angry John had given them such a run-around. The lieutenant had no reason to like the Irishman, not after the incident involving Helen, and he hadn't been at all disappointed when Cheetham countermanded Marsden's order not to kill John Graham. Come tomorrow, he promised himself, if the tracker didn't kill him, he most certainly would.

27

JOHN HARDLY SLEPT A WINK despite having found a sheltered place to spend the night—in a cavity in the trunk of a huge fig tree. Old fig leaves from the previous Autumn covered the floor of the cavity, providing a mattress of sorts that was comfortable and warm at least. The makeshift sleeping quarters with its leafy mattress was certainly cosy, but not so much that John could forget the pain he was in. His swollen ankle was so sore he couldn't sleep more than a few minutes at a time.

When he found the sleeping place, the thought had crossed his mind he should check it first for snakes. He recalled warnings that snakes frequented holes in tree trunks, but he was so tired it was all he could do to collapse onto the leaves. As it turned out, he had his sleeping quarters to himself.

In addition to the pain he was in, he found himself listening to the foreign sounds of the rainforest. He heard sounds he'd never heard before, and was convinced every snake, scorpion, spider and wild animal in the vicinity was coming for him.

As for the mosquitos, they had attacked him as soon as he'd scrambled from the river, and they never let up. He recalled the Quandamooka natives often smothered themselves in mud to repel the pesky insects, which were a problem for Moreton Bay's residents as well. However, the energy it would have taken to extricate himself from his sleeping quarters and hobble back to the riverbank to collect some mud would, he decided, be more trouble than it was worth, and so he put up with his blood-sucking companions.

Sleep finally came just before the grey light of dawn filtered down into the gorge. Unfortunately for him, he didn't wake until sunlight streamed into his little sanctuary. "Damn!" he admonished himself for allowing himself to sleep in.

To add to his woes, he discovered the mosquitos that had feasted on him during the night had left him covered in bites, and he was itchy all over.

The dawn chorus of Kookaburras seemed to be laughing at his misfortune. At least it seemed that way to him.

Daylight arrived as quickly as nightfall here in the tropics, or in the sub-tropics at least, and he cursed himself again for not remembering that. He was well aware his pursuers wouldn't have slept in. In fact, he was surprised they hadn't already found him.

With difficulty, he extricated himself from his leafy sanctuary and gingerly tested his right ankle. He was relieved to find the swelling had almost completely subsided and he could at least stand on his right foot without too much pain.

Thankful for one small mercy at least, he headed back toward the nearby river, scratching his mosquito bites, which were now driving him crazy.

As John was embarking on his second day of freedom, Barega was half a mile upriver, searching for his quarry's spoor. Hogan and his two men followed, waiting for the tracker to signal that he'd found John's tracks.

Barega was checking both banks every fifty yards or so for some sign of his quarry. This entailed entering the river and drifting diagonally with the current over to the opposite bank. After a quick reconnoitre of the far bank, he'd repeat the process and check the near bank. His plan was to work his way back upriver if he had no luck soon. And that's exactly how it turned out.

A hundred yards upriver from where John had finally gone ashore the night before, Barega began retracing his steps back toward the falls. It was slower going because he now had to swim against the current each time he crossed the river. His methodology drew complaints from Hogan, but the tracker continued his search undaunted. He knew if John was still alive, he'd find his tracks—sooner or later. Besides, he was in no rush to get home. He was right where he belonged out here in the wilderness.

John was so exhausted, he felt as though he was in someone else's body. He was just going through the motions now. Even if he managed to evade his pursuers, he hadn't a clue how he was going to survive this wilderness experience. Never once in his life had he been hunting or trekking. Nor had he indulged in any outdoor pursuits—other than enjoying some rough and tumble with a buxom farmer's wife in a hay paddock on the outskirts of Dundalk. But he wasn't sure that counted.

Despite his exhaustion, he'd had the wherewithal to realise the river still offered his best hope of escape. In the river, he didn't leave tracks, he wasn't disadvantaged by his injured ankle and he could travel quicker than those following on foot could. Much quicker. And so he'd returned to the river.

By the time the morning sun reached the river at the bottom of the gorge, John estimated the current had carried him a good two miles from his overnight resting place. He began to allow himself to believe he'd eluded his pursuers. At the same time, he kept a wary eye out for them—and for crocs.

A familiar roaring sound carried to him from downriver.

Waterfall!

The last falls had been loud. These ones were deafening even though they were still some way off. At least he thought they were some way off for he'd yet to see the tell-tale spray that marked their location.

When he finally did see the spray, he noticed it carried all the way to the top of the gorge hundreds of feet above. The sighting coincided with the current noticeably quickening. Not wanting to risk being swept to a certain death, he quickly swam to the near bank, which happened to be the opposite bank to that which he'd last seen his pursuers occupy.

He planned to continue along the bank and climb down the side of the falls. However, a quick inspection of the steep terrain revealed that wasn't possible, and he was forced to head away from the river.

Upstream, Barega had retraced his steps to the foot of the first waterfall, and had still found no spoor. This only served to strengthen Hogan's conviction that John had died. The lieutenant had scarcely been able to believe the fugitive had survived the jump over the falls, and thought it likely he'd sustained fatal injuries and had probably drowned.

The tracker wasn't convinced, pointing out that if the escapee had drowned, they would more than likely have found his body by now. He talked a reluctant Hogan into allowing him to continue searching.

And so Barega headed off downriver a second time, leaving Hogan and the other two at the foot of the falls to await his return.

Now on their own, with nothing to do but wait, the privates let Hogan know they weren't happy. The prospect of spending another night in the wilderness with few supplies didn't appeal to them. Nor did it appeal to Hogan. He assured them he would only give the tracker until early afternoon and then they'd return to Moreton Bay.

Early afternoon came and went, and Barega hadn't yet returned. Still Hogan and his men waited.

"You said we would leave by now, Lieutenant," the older of the two soldiers reminded him.

"Another ten minutes, Private," Hogan said.

Ten minutes came and went. After twenty minutes, Hogan finally gave the order. "Alright, time to move out," he said. He got no argument from his men. They jumped to and followed him back to where they'd left their horses.

The soldiers hadn't travelled more than a few hundred yards when Barega caught up to them. Breathing hard, his black skin glistening with sweat, he said, "I found Irish."

"Where?" a surprised Hogan asked.

Barega quickly explained he'd found John's spoor heading away from the river immediately before the second waterfall.

If Hogan understood the tracker correctly, the second waterfall was a good three miles downriver. He was about to suggest they return to Moreton Bay for more men and supplies when Barega advised him he knew where John was heading and he also knew a shortcut they could take to head him off.

Exactly how Barega knew all that Hogan couldn't say, but he knew the tracker well enough not to doubt him.

In fact, Barega had realised the route John was taking away from the river followed another narrower gorge whose sides were too steep to climb. So, unless the escapee turned back he would emerge at a place the tracker knew well not five miles distant. The shortcut Barega had referred to would take them out of the rainforest and over grasslands, so the soldiers could ride most of the way. With any luck, they'd still be back at Moreton Bay before dark.

That was the theory at least.

First, they needed to swim their horses across the river, but that didn't faze Hogan. He and his men had done many a river crossing.

Barega's calculations had been spot on in every respect except John reached the end of the narrow gorge shortly before his pursuers arrived, so he avoided the trap they'd planned. However, that was of little consequence for the tracker quickly picked up his spoor.

When John had arrived on the plateau, he'd been struck by the beauty of the scene. The gorge opened out onto a plateau from which the coastline could be viewed. White sandy bays fringed by trees on one side and ocean on the other stretched up and down the coast as far as he could see. Perfect sets of waves lined up, awaiting their turn to crash onto the shore.

John had been tempted to walk down to the beach and bathe, but the thought of capture had deterred him. Although logic told him he'd escaped his pursuers, for so much time had passed, he kept going, pushing on through his pain, ignoring his overwhelming desire to rest, his need to sleep and his hunger pangs.

A mob of kangaroos—big Reds—grazed in the long grass alongside a billabong. The sight of the meaty marsupials reminded the fugitive he hadn't eaten since breakfast yesterday, and he hadn't tasted meat in over a week. The so-called *stew* the convict-chefs served most nights at the penal settlement was little more than slops— an unappetising combination of reheated gravy, mouldy bread and dripping with the occasional mouse, cockroach or blowfly thrown in for good measure. *Little wonder I'm not fat*, he thought.

John was walking alongside a bush-covered hill. On a whim, he entered the bush and continued on, albeit a little slower now that he'd left the plateau.

A few moments later, from a clearing, he looked back and did a double take when he saw the tracker emerge from the gorge he'd left a short time earlier. He realised Barega would have had to have taken a shortcut to reach the plateau so quickly.

How did he know I'd come this way?

He wondered if the soldiers had accompanied the tracker.

His question was answered almost immediately when Hogan and the two privates rode out onto the plateau. They reined in their horses near the same billabong where John had seen the roos grazing, and they waited for the tracker to pick up their quarry's spoor.

"Damnation!" John cried. Looking skyward, he asked God, "Why are you doing this to me? What did I ever do to you?"

It didn't take Barega long to find his quarry's tracks. Setting a fast pace, the tracker followed the spoor, and the soldiers fell in behind him at a steady trot.

John estimated they were less than half a mile away. He took one last look at them before continuing up the hill. It became progressively steeper, and the bush became ever more dense as he climbed.

At the top of a knoll, he pushed his way through heavy undergrowth and before he knew it he was standing knee-deep in a stream. Faced with the decision of following it uphill or down, he opted for the former. He made sure he stayed in the water so as not to leave tracks.

An overhanging branch caught his eye. He clambered up onto it then climbed from tree to tree in the hope that he'd lose his pursuers once and for all. Only when he could climb no further did he drop back down to the ground. After checking to ensure he'd left no tracks, he ran deeper into the bush.

The afternoon sun was high in the sky by the time Barega located John's exit point from the stream. Crumpled leaves and scratched bark gave the escapee away. Others would have missed the signs, but not Barega. His keen eyes missed nothing.

Hogan and his men, who were still on horseback despite the difficult terrain, had resigned themselves to spending another night in the open. To a man they now focussed their frustrations on John. All they wanted to do was find him, kill him and return to the comforts of Moreton Bay.

It didn't take long for Barega to find where the Irishman had climbed down from the trees and resumed his trek through the bush. The route he took soon became too steep for the horses, so the soldiers tethered their steeds and followed the tracker on foot.

"Fuck!" the younger private cursed. "Where the hell are we?"

"Damned if I know," the older private said. "I can't tell which way's north and which is south."

By now they were having to hold on to branches to help haul themselves up the hillside, so steep was it.

Hogan, who was just in front of the privates, was concerned he'd lost sight of Barega. "Tracker!" he called. "Tracker!" he called again, only louder this time. Turning back to his men, he said, "That bloody tracker is going to be the death of me."

With that, the branch the lieutenant happened to be holding snapped, sending him crashing down the hillside. The privates tried to arrest his fall, but Hogan kept rolling and didn't stop until he crashed into a rock.

The others hurried to the lieutenant's side. They could see he'd been knocked out, and his left leg was twisted at an awkward angle.

"Fuck me!" the older private said, staring at Hogan's twisted leg.

The lieutenant's breeches had been torn above and below the left knee. His tibia, or shin bone, had snapped, and its shattered ends protruded some distance through the skin.

The younger private recoiled at the sight. "Shit!" he mumbled. He looked at his companion. "What do we do now?"

"We get him home," the older soldier said. "That's what we do, lad."

A hundred yards up the hill, Barega had crept to within thirty yards of where he believed John was hiding. He'd followed his quarry's spoor up a steep track that led to a cave near the summit. John had made a crude effort to cover his tracks by brushing the ground with a leafy branch, but Barega wasn't fooled. His quarry might as well have left arrow signs signalling which way he went.

The tracker was tempted to enter the cave and deal with John himself, but Hogan had left him with firm orders to report to him when he located the fugitive. So it was with some regret he retraced his steps down the hillside.

Barega reached the others just as Hogan was coming around. The lieutenant was groaning and obviously in pain.

When the older private saw the tracker, he said, "The lieutenant's leg is broken. We have to go back."

"I found the Irish," Barega said, pointing up the hill. "Up there."

"Forget him," the young private said. "We're going back."

Ignoring the two soldiers, the tracker turned and headed back uphill.

"Hey!" the older private shouted.

Barega kept walking. Over his shoulder, he said, "You carry boss back. This Irish close. I get him."

By now, Hogan had regained his senses. He looked around at the departing Barega and shouted, "Tracker! Come here! That's an order." The effort of shouting was so much, Hogan had to lie back and close his eyes. He gritted his teeth against the pain as his men set about applying a bandage and splint to his shattered leg.

Only now did the tracker stop. He looked longingly up the hill toward the cave where he was now convinced his quarry was, and then reluctantly returned to the others.

A hundred yards away, in the darkness of the cave, John breathed a sigh of relief when he saw his pursuers finally make their way back down the hill. He'd witnessed the lieutenant's mishap, and realised that event more than likely meant the hunt for him would be called off—for the time-being at least.

Not wanting to hang around in case Barega returned, he emerged from his hiding place and set off up the hill as fast as he could go.

28

NIGHT WAS FALLING AS JOHN reached the top of the hill. Now facing his second night without food, he was desperate to eat. His hunger pains were starting to consume his every thought, and he found he was starting to make irrational decisions. "Man can survive weeks without food," he reminded himself in a moment of clarity. "I need to forget about my belly and focus on finding a place to sleep."

The fugitive knew enough about the wilderness to know it was no place to overnight out in the open. Even though the region had a reputation for being *the winterless north,* as some called it, the nights could be cold as he'd discovered the previous night. If it hadn't been for his bed of leaves and his sanctuary in the trunk of the fig tree, he'd have been very uncomfortable, and cold, too. Thinking back on that experience reminded him he'd almost been eaten alive by mosquitos, and the bites they'd inflicted were still driving him crazy.

Daylight had all but faded when John found the opening to yet another cave. He would learn the hills in this area were dotted with caves and grottoes. This particular cave was near the top of the hill and, he could see, it afforded views out over the plateau below and the ocean beyond. In the fading light, the sea was recognisable only as a purple band between the brown plateau and the darkening sky above. Stars could already be seen in the eastern sky, and a full moon was rising, its golden light reflected in the ocean.

Before entering the cave, he wisely scouted around for mud with which to coat himself before the mosquitos could make another meal of him. They were already seeking him out. He found some mud in a ferny grove nearby. It was a fortuitous find for the ferns hid a natural spring, which he took advantage of to quench his thirst.

Coating his face, neck and hands in mud, he returned to the cave and cautiously entered it. The moonlight revealed the cave's rear wall was only a few yards in from the entrance, and it appeared he had the place to himself. That was until the feint fluttering of wings alerted him to the fact it was home to a colony of bats. The dark, furry creatures of the night flew from the cave, startling him as they passed within a few feet of his head.

Before entering the cave, he had also thought to gather up some fallen ferns and leafy branches to fashion a rudimentary bed for himself, and he ensured he had enough leaves with which to cover himself to keep warm.

Inside the cave, he made himself as comfortable as he could. He'd have given anything for some food for his tummy was rumbling more than ever. "What I'd give for a helping of Gerty's roast beef right now," he mumbled.

Gerty, or Gertrude, was one of his girlfriends in Dundalk. She would always have a special place in John's heart as she had some memorable skills of which cooking roast beef was one. He'd enjoyed the company of some willing lasses since then at the Parramatta penal settlement, but they were prostitutes, and so he didn't really class them as girlfriends. Like himself, they were convicts—shipped out from England to provide relief for the male convicts. Gerty was a seamstress and also the best friend of the baker's daughter in whose father's bakery he'd left his trousers after a somewhat hurried departure.

John realised he'd give anything for a fire as well. Not just for the warmth it would provide, but for keeping the snakes and other creepy-crawlies at bay. Snakes in particular scared him. The very thought of them made him shiver. He was aware almost every poisonous snake known to Man was to be found in plentiful abundance throughout Australia, and he was understandably anxious to avoid being bitten.

If there was one silver lining in the cloud of hopelessness that threatened to engulf him it was the mud pack he'd applied to his exposed skin seemed to be working. The mosquitos were holding off—for the moment at least. The dried mud also soothed his bites, and he observed they were no longer itching. That was his last thought before he drifted off to sleep.

John felt the morning sun on his face long before he opened his eyes. He'd slept right through the night and was enjoying his lie-in so much he didn't want it to end. So he just lay there, soaking up the warmth of the sun.

Suddenly, he sat bolt upright. He'd just remembered he was still on the run. Wiping the sleep from his eyes, he looked out from the cave, half expecting to see Barega and the soldiers standing there. He relaxed and lay back down when he realised he was worrying about nothing.

Before he knew it, he drifted off back to sleep.

He didn't know how long he'd slept in when he next opened his eyes. Judging by the sun, which was now high in the morning sky, it had been two or three hours. He stretched and luxuriated in the feeling that came with having slept so well after having been on the run without let-up for so long.

For the first time, John looked around the cave that had served him so well this past night. Human figures painted on the rear wall alerted him to the fact he hadn't quite had the cave to himself. He had in fact shared it with other people, or with historic drawings of others at least.

Painted in ochre, the colourful drawings depicted Aborigines engaged in a variety of activities ranging from hunting and cooking to eating and copulating.

John marvelled at the detail. The fugitive hadn't a clue how old the paintings were, but he guessed they were at least several hundred years old. He wasn't to know they were several thousand years old, and would be heralded as a historic find when the cave he occupied was officially discovered a century from now.

A rumbling tummy reminded him he *had* to eat. Pushing himself to his feet, he took one final look at the paintings then emerged from the cave and gratefully relieved his full bladder. It was his first piss in over fifteen hours—not that he was counting. That done, he set off down the hill, heading back to the plateau. He followed a zigzag route, looking for fruit and berries, or anything remotely edible, as he descended. To his disappointment, he came up with nothing.

John recognised a number of trees and shrubs—fig, apple, plum and tree tomato included—which bore no fruit. This brought home to him the downside of traveling overland in New South Wales in winter. While he benefitted from the cooler temperatures winter brought, he was faced with the seasonal scarcity of edible fruit and vegetables.

Not for the first time, he cursed himself for his impulsiveness in fleeing the quarry.

Serve you right, Graham.

No sooner had that thought occurred than he came across a raspberry bush. He recognised it immediately for he'd often helped himself to raspberries when out with other convicts collecting firewood for the soldiers at Parramatta. The bush confronting him now was small, but it was laden with ripe berries. "Hallelujah!" he muttered. He helped himself to the raspberries, cramming them into his mouth.

When he'd had his fill, he set off again, feeling more satisfied than he had for some time. He now wore a bonnet-like covering he'd fashioned from ferns to cover his head and to protect him from the sun. It was similar to head coverings he'd seen the Quandamooka wear on hot days at Moreton Bay—except theirs didn't look as ridiculous as he was sure his must look. He'd secured it by tying two palm fronds together beneath his chin.

Down on the plateau once more, he continued ever-northwards, his rationale being that sooner or later he'd come across a trading ship bound for either China or England. He'd heard such vessels called in to these shores from time to time—to replenish their supplies of freshwater and to attend to repairs and the like. Whether the master of such a vessel would believe he was a shipwreck survivor and not an escaped convict was another problem, but he'd face that when the time came. His first action, he decided, would be to strip naked and hide his boots and his convict clothes, or what was left of them, and try to convince his rescuers he was who he said he was.

To improve his chances of encountering a vessel, he realised he'd need to remain close to the coast. And therein lay another problem: he'd been told the main concentration of Aboriginal tribes in this part of the world was to be found along the coast—first and foremost because the sea offered them a bountiful, year-round harvest of shellfish and other seafood to complement what they scavenged from the land. He was also aware many if not all the tribes—the Quandamooka aside—should be avoided at all costs. The colony was rife with horrendous tales of whites falling foul of the natives. There were rumours of cannibalism, too. He wasn't sure how many of the tales were true, but he didn't want to put them to the test.

His alternative, clearly, was to keep well away from the coast, but that would mean he wouldn't encounter any ships, and that would defeat the whole purpose of his heading north.

So, he decided, he would compromise: by day he'd keep to the hills, sleeping as required and scavenging for food in the rainforest, and by night he'd trek along the coast.

The need to rest up and remain hidden by day, he realised, needed to be tempered by the more pressing need to distance himself from Moreton Bay, for he was in no doubt the tracker would return to look for him. Therefore, he resigned himself to taking advantage of the daylight to put as many miles as he could between himself and the penal settlement. And so he remained out in the open for the time being.

The afternoon sun was past its zenith before John traversed the plateau and reached the hills on its northern edge. He didn't know how many miles he'd come since setting out in the early morning, but he guessed he'd put another twenty or so miles between himself and Moreton Bay.

Throughout the day he'd seen a variety of east coast wildlife, including the dragon-like goanna, other lizards he'd never seen before, a harmless carpet snake, wallabies, koala bears perched in the numerous gum trees and bird varieties too numerous to mention.

One bird that did catch his eye was the Australian brush turkey with its distinctive featherless red head, yellow wattle and black body. It was a fair size, too, and he could imagine it would make a good meal. He was pleased to see the bird abounded in these parts.

Even more mouth-watering for someone who couldn't remember when he'd last eaten cooked turkey or chicken, or any type of fowl for that matter, was a solitary emu, which he saw running east to west across the plateau not a hundred yards ahead of him. It covered the ground in mighty strides as it weaved its way between giant ant hills that dotted the plateau. The big bird was almost as tall as the ant hills, and John could only imagine how many cooked dinners it would provide.

The sight of so many edible birds reminded him he needed to prepare early for the coming night, and hopefully find or catch something that would serve as dinner.

Leaving the plateau behind, he found himself climbing scrubby, bush-covered hills, which, if nothing else, offered good hiding places and protection from prying eyes. Not that he'd seen any sign of human life since he'd shaken his pursuers the previous evening, but he remained ever-alert. The last thing he wanted to do was stumble into an Aboriginal encampment or hunting party.

John soon found what he was looking for—a sheltered spot beneath an overhang in a hillside—that would provide a good place to sleep. It was near a billabong and, more importantly, it was screened by ferns and bushes, and so offered reasonable security.

Satisfied he'd found a suitable place to overnight, he set about finding food. The memory of the brush turkeys was still vivid in his mind, so he armed himself with two sizeable stones and crept through the bush in search of one of the big birds.

The shadows were lengthening and John hadn't come across a solitary turkey, or any type of bird that could make a meal. He imagined the cockatoos and kookaburras, which he could hear but not see in the dense bush, were laughing at him and at his amateurish hunting skills. "You're for it if I see you!" he shouted at his unseen tormentors.

The hunger he'd experienced earlier had returned with a vengeance.

I have to eat soon or I'm dead.

Giving up on his plan to kill a turkey for supper, he threw away the stones he was holding and retraced his steps to the sleeping place he'd found. As he neared it, he heard a foreign *tapping* sound. It was coming from the direction of the nearby billabong. Fearing he may have human company, he crept forward to investigate.

On the edge of the bush, he saw a mob of kangaroos drinking from the billabong and grazing alongside it. Two of the larger adult marsupials were rhythmically tapping their rear legs on the ground—as they do when they come out to graze in the approaching dusk.

John's belly rumbled as he studied the roos. His gaze rested on the largest of the adults—a big buck—and his mouth watered at the thought of cooking it on a spit the way he'd seen the Quandamooka cook roos. He reminded himself to fashion a spear sometime soon so that he could better take advantage of such opportunities in future.

Suddenly spooked, the roos took off, leaving the fugitive alone once more. He watched forlornly as they bounded away, and wondered whether it was his rumbling tummy that had spooked them so.

John realised he needed to lower his sights somewhat if he was to eat that night.

Forget about roos and turkeys and home-cooked dinners tonight John boy.

The Irishman looked at the red earth beneath his feet and recalled the Aborigines sourced much of their food from the ground. He immediately set about finding edible roots and grubs to satisfy his hunger.

It didn't take long before he found three large, white grubs, which he correctly assumed were witchetty grubs, a well-known favourite of Aborigines throughout Australia. Further searching revealed they were edible and in plentiful supply in these parts.

Studying the grotesque-looking grubs now squirming in the palm of his hand, he wished he had a fire to cook them over. He'd seen the Quandamooka, and the Parra Aborigines before them, cook grubs and beetles, and he recalled they seemed to enjoy the taste.

"It's eat or die," he reminded himself. Closing his eyes, he rammed the squirming grubs into his mouth and started chewing. It took all his willpower not to spit them out. The initial taste, to his taste buds at least, was awful. Gradually, after swallowing, the aftertaste became more palatable.

Almost like scrambled eggs.

To aid his digestion, he hurried over to the billabong and gulped down several mouthfuls of water. Then he waited for his belly to reject the grubs. He was pleasantly surprised to find he experienced no compunction to spew out the contents of his stomach, so he went in search of more.

His immediate hunger was soon appeased. The main course of witchetty grubs was followed by more raspberries, which he found on a bush near the billabong. The berries here weren't as plentiful as those he'd found that morning, but there were sufficient to provide a dessert of sorts.

Returning to the billabong for a final drink before retiring to his sleeping place, he studied his reflection in the still waters. He almost didn't recognise the face that stared back at him. The beginnings of a beard covered his normally clean-shaven features, and his face—or the exposed area of his face at least—had been burnt nutmeg brown by the sun. Only his eyes seemed familiar to him. Even in the fading light of dusk, those startling blue eyes looked as keen and alert as ever.

John jumped when his still reflection was distorted by ripples in the water. Moments later, a creature emerged—so strange it was beyond belief. In fact, he wondered if he was dreaming. He wasn't to know he was looking at that strangest of all Australia's, and possibly the world's, animals—the platypus.

Sometimes known as the duck-billed platypus, this semi-aquatic mammal, which was endemic to the colony's east coast, was favoured by Aborigines for its fur and would soon be hunted almost to extinction by European hunters for the same reason. This particular platypus stared back at the Irishman, seemingly unperturbed, then lazily swam over to the far bank. In somewhat clumsy fashion, it clambered up onto the bank and meandered off, disappearing behind rocks.

Before it disappeared, John had noted other unusual characteristics, not the least being its beaver-like tail and its otter-like feet. So unusual was its appearance, he wouldn't have been surprised to learn it was the only mammal that started life as an egg.

John hurried off to relocate his overnight sleeping place. Night was fast approaching and he wanted to be sure he didn't have any dangerous bed mates while there was still some light. He collected ferns and picked up leafy branches as he climbed the hillside.

On arriving at the overhang that marked his sleeping place, a quick reconnoitre confirmed he had it to himself. He lay down the ferns to serve as his makeshift mattress then covered himself with the leafy branches he'd collected.

Snug as a witchetty grub.

Only after he was lying down did he remember the mudpack to keep mosquitos at bay. Fortunately, the pesky insects didn't seem interested in him tonight, so he decided not to bother with protection.

Before the last of the light faded, John remembered the section of the page he'd torn from the January 25, 1820 edition of the London newspaper *The Sunday Times*. He still carried it with him—in his shirt pocket. Though crumpled and torn, it had somehow remained intact despite being on his person almost daily for the past six months—even surviving immersions in a river in the past few days.

John drew the crumpled paper from his pocket and straightened it as much as he could. Then, holding it up to what little light was left, he began reading aloud a verse from John Keats' poem *Lamia* for perhaps the hundredth time. "She was a gordian shape of dazzling hue, vermilion-spotted, golden, green, and blue," he recited.

"Striped like a zebra, freckled like a pard, eyed like a peacock, and all crimson barred. And full of silver moons, that, as she breathed, dissolved, or brighter shone, or interwreathed, their lustres with the gloomier tapestries. So rainbow-sided, touched with miseries, she seemed, at once, some penanced lady elf. Some demon's mistress, or the demon's self . . ."

He drifted off into the deepest of sleeps, clasping in his hand the crumpled piece of the newspaper he'd been reading from.

29

AFTER AN EARLY BREAKFAST OF the last of his witchetty grubs, complemented by some edible roots John had uncovered, he was on his way. Having eaten well—by recent standards at least—this morning and the previous evening as well, he was feeling stronger than he had in a while. He strode out with renewed vigour, still heading north.

Always north.

The Irishman felt confident he'd soon find a ship that would take him to civilisation.

Freedom here I come.

John still wore the makeshift fern bonnet, which had served him so well the previous day. He was thankful for the shade it provided, and already he considered it a permanent part of his wardrobe—that is if the remains of his tattered clothing could be classed as a wardrobe.

The fugitive wasn't sure if it was his imagination, but it felt like the days were growing hotter the further north he ventured.

He now carried a spear he'd fashioned from a fallen branch. Using large stones—one of which had a useful cutting edge—he'd stripped the branch of twigs and had sharpened one end of it to a fearsome point. The weapon, which was almost as long as himself, gave him renewed confidence.

John also carried a shoulder bag of sorts. This he'd also fashioned from ferns, and he'd tied a vine to it and that served as a strap. Thus far, he only carried some wild berries and two of the large stones he'd found in the makeshift bag, but he was sure he'd find more uses for it as his journey progressed.

As he strode out, he reviewed his strategy. "Another day's hard walk should put enough distance between me and Moreton Bay," he told himself. "Then I'll lay low by day and walk by night." He figured it was worth risking being seen by Aborigines to further distance himself from those who would like to hang him.

Bastards.

While John was continuing his northward trek, his fellow convicts were commencing another day's hard labour in the quarry at the bay. His Irish mates, who worked together as usual, were labouring on the quarry's rock face—the same face from which John had escaped three days earlier.

Seamus O'Neill and Pat Kennedy worked side by side, wielding their pick-axes under the watchful eye of a guard.

When the guard wasn't looking, O'Neill nudged Kennedy and nodded toward the fissure their mate had used to exit the quarry. Its entrance was now sealed off by iron bars which had been inserted into holes drilled into the rock. "They don't trust us Irish, eh Pat?" O'Neill observed.

"Apparently not, Seamus," Kennedy chuckled. Referring to John, he asked, "I wonder if the tracker will bring him back?"

"Maybe, maybe not."

"If you had to bet?"

"If I had to bet . . . knowing Graham . . . I'd say he'll elude 'em all."

"Quiet you two!" the guard bellowed.

The pair returned to wielding their pick-axes without argument. They and their fellow convicts dared not argue since John's escape. Lord Cheetham had been so riled by the Irishman's actions he'd vowed to hang the next of his countrymen to step out of line.

No Irish convict had dared step out of line. This had only served to further rile Cheetham, and he'd ordered Captain Marsden to have several Irishmen flogged just the previous day—John's mates Paddy O'Donnell, Luke Donovan and Sean O'Driscoll among them. They'd each received fifty lashes from Old Bumble, and today were suffering as they toiled in the heat of the quarry.

Against his better judgement, John had left the cover of the trees and ventured out onto grassy, rolling plains. The crude spear he carried emboldened him, and he now took risks he hadn't been prepared to take earlier.

The fugitive was feeling pleased with himself for he'd successfully speared a freshwater fish he'd seen in one of several billabongs he'd encountered that morning. As it turned out, the raw fish had proven almost inedible, but merely spearing it gave him confidence for future fishing expeditions.

While he walked, he constantly surveyed his surroundings. The plains were dotted with stands of gum trees and clusters of ant hills. To the east, on his right, the blue Pacific was just visible in the distance; to the west, on his left, bush-covered hills—some quite steep—stretched to the horizon, while straight ahead of him, to the north, the plains gave way to rainforest.

The sun was directly ahead of him also, so he guessed it was mid-day give or take. He estimated the rainforest was a good five miles distant. *An hour or so away,* he thought.

Passing beneath a gum tree, he noticed a fat koala perched on one of the lower branches. It was so close he could almost spear it without even having to release the spear from his grasp. He eyed the animal, and could already envisage barbecuing it and slicing up its plump rump. The koala stared back at him as it chewed gum leaves.

John raised his spear. Closer inspection had told him he'd have to throw it after all to connect with the furry fellow. But the spear only had a yard or so to travel, so he knew he could hardly miss. Lining the koala up, he tried to ignore its cuteness.

Just kill it, man!

The koala stopped chewing and stared directly at John as if suddenly interested in the newcomer. Its big, button-shaped, brown eyes seemed to be looking into his very soul.

Stop looking at me, will you?

Still the koala stared at John. It had become a staring contest.

John finally lowered his spear. Looking up at the koala, who had now resumed chewing, he said, "I won't be so kind next time." He resumed his trek across the plains.

The sun was now high in the sky and John still hadn't reached the rainforest. He'd been delayed by the last billabong he'd come across. Its still waters had looked so tempting, and he was so hot, he'd given into temptation and stripped off and dived into it. The sensation had been so enjoyable he stayed longer than he should have.

Now, as he strode still dripping wet toward the rainforest, he became aware he had company. Not human company, but canine company—or dingoes to be more accurate. Five of the free-ranging, native dogs emerged at speed from the rainforest. They were chasing a wallaby, which John hadn't noticed until now. As it turned out, the wallaby was heading straight toward him, bringing the dingoes with it. "Don't bring them this way!" he muttered.

The wallaby finally noticed the man coming toward him and veered off toward a grove of gum trees. One by one, the dingoes gave up the chase. Their prey was just too elusive.

John, who had crouched down so as not to draw attention to himself, thought it strange to see so many dingoes together. They had a reputation for being solitary animals, and they'd nearly always been alone when he'd seen them before. He likened them to the semi-tame wolves he'd once seen on a gamekeepers' reserve in Ireland, except the dingo's coat had a distinctive yellow sheen.

The nearest of the dingoes, which John estimated was around half a mile away, suddenly looked in his direction. The Irishman debated whether to lie down, but opted not to in case the sudden movement alerted the animal. Too late. It had seen him and was now coming for him.

Realising he'd been seen, John stood up and grasped his makeshift spear tightly. He debated whether to wait and spear the dingo when it neared him or whether to flee. The decision was made for him when the other four dingoes headed for him as well.

John desperately looked for an escape route. The billabong he'd just bathed in was a good two hundred yards behind him, and the nearest trees were further away still. "Watering hole it is!" he told himself. Without further delay, he sprinted back toward the same billabong he'd not long vacated. He could tell it was going to be a close-run thing. The dingoes were closing in fast, and the billabong was still a hundred yards away. He just hoped he'd make it. He also hoped these dingoes had an aversion to water.

John pumped his legs as fast as they'd go. The sound of the dingoes' breathing as they nipped at his heels gave him added motivation. He reached the watering hole and jumped in, but not before the lead dingo managed to nip his ankle. "Ow!" he exclaimed.

When he surfaced, he was relieved to see the dingoes hadn't followed him in. They were excitedly running up and down the bank, and, to John's eyes, appeared sorely tempted to join him. Until now, he hadn't known that, unlike wolves, dingoes have an aversion to water, or an aversion to swimming at least.

The dingo that had spotted John turned out to be the pack leader. Bigger than the other members of the pack, he just looked at his quarry, growling.

"Come and get me, you dopey mutt!" John shouted.

Sensing he'd been challenged, the pack leader stood tall on all four legs and barked in that distinctive manner of his species. It was a curt sound more reminiscent of a cough than a bark.

John wondered if the dingo had a vocal defect. "What's wrong, boy?" he asked. "You got a cold or something?"

The taunting only served to anger the pack leader even more. He jumped into the water and then jumped out almost as quickly. It was obvious he'd immediately regretted his impulsiveness, and he spent the next few minutes violently shaking himself to dry off. All this to the amusement of his human quarry who hurled more insults his way.

John was up to his neck in the water. He still had his spear and his makeshift fern bonnet, and his crude shoulder bag was still hanging over his shoulder and in once piece.

The fugitive decided to locate a more shallow part of the billabong. He set off, taking care not to get too close to the bank. As he slowly pushed through the water, the dingoes followed him, obviously hoping he'd tire of this game and climb out.

John soon discovered the watering hole was deceptively deep, and several times he sank over his head.

After several minutes of exploring, he gave up and returned to his original position.

The dingoes took up their original positions on the nearest bank. Four of them lay down in the grass. Only the pack leader remained standing, ears erect and eyes alert.

John and the pack leader stared at each other. They were only a few feet apart. The Irishman tried to think of a suitable name for the big dingo. Finally, a name came to him.

Cheetham!

"How long you going to stand there, Cheetham?" he asked. "Because I'm not going anywhere until you've gone."

Cheetham the dingo seemed to realise the man in the billabong was addressing him, and he growled by way of acknowledgement.

John glanced up at the sun and realised it was still only mid-afternoon. He hoped the dingoes would give up on him soon.

The shadows were lengthening and, despite the warm daytime temperature, John was chilled to the bone. Still standing in neck-deep water, his teeth were chattering and his legs were cramping up. And still the dingoes showed no sign of leaving. "Come on, boys," John said. "Enough's enough. Give a poor Irishman a break."

The dingoes were all lying down now, and four of them at least appeared to have lost interest in him. Three of them seemed to be asleep; another vacillated between sleep and wakefulness; only Cheetham remained fully awake, his all-seeing eyes permanently fastened on the man in the water.

"Cheetham, if you and your friends don't piss off soon, I'm going to have the lot of you flogged," John warned. When the pack leader didn't respond, he added, "And I'm going to personally see you receive one hundred lashes."

The pack leader had finally heard enough, and he, too, fell asleep.

Observing the sleeping pack, John wondered if he could climb onto the bank and spear one of them—preferably Cheetham—and dive back into the water before the others got him.

There's only one way to find out.

He inched forward, his spear firmly clasped in his right hand and his eyes firmly on Cheetham, the nearest dingo. Now close to the bank, and only a few feet from the pack leader, he slowly and deliberately pulled himself up onto the grass.

So far so good.

Once on the grass, John just lay there, motionless and hardly daring to breathe.

After what seemed an age, he pushed himself upright ever so slowly then raised his spear even more slowly.

Cheetham chose that moment to open one lazy eye.

For John, time seemed to stand still. His throwing arm felt as though it was paralysed. And when Cheetham launched himself at him, the dingo seemed to be flying through the air in slow motion.

Suddenly galvanised, John flung himself backwards into the billabong, narrowly avoiding the maddened pack leader's charge. Cheetham only just pulled up short of the water, thereby avoiding another dunking.

By now, all the dingoes were running back and forth along the bank, all fully alert.

"Damnation!" John cried. Only now did he realise in the melee he'd lost his spear. Finally, it floated to the surface. The Irishman was forced to swim a few strokes to retrieve it, by which time he was colder than ever and in a very bad mood. He spent the next five minutes abusing his canine tormentors, and only ceased the abuse when he ran out of energy.

As the standoff between man and dog continued, two days' trek to the south—at the Moreton Bay penal settlement—Lord Cheetham, the commandant, and Captain Marsden, his second-in-command, observed the convicts' progress on the new building and construction projects in and around the settlement.

Dusk was falling, and the convicts were preparing to finish up for the day.

The commandant wasn't happy about the convicts' productivity, or lack of, which was impacting on the Governor's expansion plans, and he was lecturing Marsden on the need to improve efficiency levels. "More huts are needed to accommodate the increased number of inmates," Cheetham complained.

"We cannot work miracles," Marsden pointed out. "The men . . . ah . . . the convicts are ill and overworked and half starved. They can't work any—"

"Of course they can work harder!" Cheetham snapped. "They are beasts of burden after all. That is what they are bred to do for God sake."

Marsden observed his superior as he rambled on. The Governor's expansion plans and targets were clearly weighing on Cheetham's mind, and his mood and disposition weren't helped any by his continued abuse of opium. It was becoming increasingly evident the commandant was indulging his addiction more than ever, and that was impacting more and more on his ability to function.

Cheetham's mood hadn't been helped either by John Graham's recent escape, and every day that passed without any sign the fugitive had been captured only served to further agitate the older man.

The officials were standing between the settlement and the fields in front of Marsden's cottage where more gangs of convicts were tilling the ground to prepare it for planting in corn and other crops.

"Is that really necessary?" Cheetham asked, pointing to the convicts.

"If the ground isn't ready to plant come the spring, there will be even less food for the convicts, and for the rest of us, too," Marsden said.

The conversation lapsed when they noticed three Redcoats emerge from the rainforest behind the cottage.

"Who is that?" Cheetham asked, straining to identify the newcomers.

In the fading light, Marsden was only just able to make out their identities. "It is Lieutenant Hogan's party, sir," he said at length. Any hope the soldiers had found their man dissipated as he realised they'd returned empty-handed.

Cheetham smiled for the first time that day. His smile faded when Marsden informed him it appeared the party may have not have found John Graham.

"What?" the commandant asked.

Marsden repeated the bad news.

By now even Cheetham's old eyes could see the hunting party had met with misfortune. Only the two privates were on horseback. Hogan was being dragged along on a makeshift stretcher behind the younger private's horse. The stretcher had been fashioned from branches, fern fronds and vines. Barega, on foot as always, brought up the rear.

The two officials waited in silence until the men reached them. They then listened in stony silence as the older private explained how John had given them the slip and how the lieutenant had ended up breaking his leg.

⊰•———•⊱

As night arrived, the standoff continued between John and the dingoes at the billabong on the grassy plain some forty miles north of Moreton Bay.

The Irishman was beyond cold now. He was almost comatose. If it hadn't been for the leg cramps that tormented his calves and thighs, he would surely have fallen

177

asleep and possibly drowned. As it was, he had to keep moving around to ease the excruciating pain that comes with cramped muscles. That only served to tire him even more. It was a vicious circle with no end in sight.

The dingoes had varied their routine by taking turns to sleep while the others stood guard. Occasionally, one or two would disappear—presumably to hunt easier game—and leave the others to continue their guard duty.

By late afternoon, it had become clear to John they weren't going to give up easy. By nightfall, it had become very clear to him they were determined he would be their next meal and they were in it for the long haul. To add to his misery, it began to rain.

Soon, it was raining so hard it seemed he could drown just as easy above water as below.

30

THE UNSEASONAL RAIN THAT HAD arrived with the darkness continued unabated well into the early hours—by which time John had lost all track of time. If it hadn't been for the occasional flash of lightning, he wouldn't have known the dingoes were still waiting for him so dark was it and so heavy the rain.

One by one, as the hours passed, the dingoes departed until only Cheetham, the pack leader, remained. Having been surprised by his spear-wielding quarry once, he remained awake and watchful, seemingly oblivious to the rain and unbothered by the lightning.

John alternated between abusing Cheetham and pleading with him to leave. More than once, he'd been reduced to tears, imploring the dingo to leave him be.

The rain now fell with such intensity, it felt to John like he was trapped beneath a waterfall. He had to cup his hand over his mouth in order to breathe without swallowing water.

The lightning that had accompanied the torrential rain until now abated, plunging John's world into darkness. It was a darkness he'd never experienced before—so dark he couldn't see his hand in front of his face.

Close to drowning, he forced his legs to carry him to the near bank then, using the last of his reserves and not caring whether Cheetham got him or not, he hauled himself up onto the grass and lay there, gasping and totally spent. He was so exhausted it only vaguely registered that he was alone. The last of the dingoes had given up on him.

John woke with a start as his right calf cramped up. He had to extend his leg and curl his toes up toward him to ease the pain. As the spasm passed, he realised it was still raining and still pitch black, but the fact that he hadn't been eaten reconfirmed that Cheetham and company had departed before he'd pulled himself from the billabong.

Lying there in the darkness, he tried to marshal his thoughts. The overriding thought was the dingoes could return for him.

I have to get out of here.

So, with some effort, he pushed himself to his feet and prepared to head for the rainforest he'd been trying to reach earlier.

He set off then immediately retraced his steps when he remembered his spear and shoulder bag. In the darkness, they took some time to find. Finally, he struck out again to the north with spear in hand and bag over his shoulder. As he walked he remembered his fern sun bonnet, but he wasn't going back for that. He guessed it was floating somewhere in the billabong.

After reaching the shelter and comparative safety of the rainforest, John had passed what was left of the night in what could only be described as an opening in a cliff-face. Too small to be called a cave, it nevertheless shielded him from the torrential rain. Even so, he'd been unable to sleep, so cold was he and so frequent were his leg cramps.

Dawn's arrival saw no let-up in the rain. It continued unabated, as heavy as ever.

John cursed his misfortune. "As if being chased by dingoes and trapped in a billabong wasn't hard enough, now I have to put up with cramps and cold," he complained. Sitting with his back to the cliff, he wrapped his arms around his legs and held them tight to him in an effort to keep warm. That only encouraged his cramps to return, and he had to straighten his legs again.

Marsden emerged from the backdoor of his cottage and stretched in the early morning sun, as he did every morning that the sun shone, which was most mornings here at Moreton Bay. He planned to ride into Brisbane Town to check on building progress there, but first he wanted to speak to Barega. He'd discussed the unsuccessful hunt for John Graham at length with Hogan the previous evening, but he wanted to hear the tracker's side of the story.

Only as he headed for the annex adjoining the stables at the rear of his property did he notice storm clouds on the northern horizon. The sight of storm clouds surprised him somewhat for the official rainy season was long gone. Still, he thought, unseasonal rains weren't unheard of in this part of the world.

Before he reached the annex, the door opened and his maid Orana emerged. "Good morning, Orana," he said.

"Good morning, Captain," the friendly native woman smiled.

"I need to speak to Barega," Marsden informed her.

Orana hesitated. "He went walkabout last night," she said.

Marsden frowned. He knew what *walkabout* meant. In Barega's case, it signalled he could be gone a day or a month, or even longer. "Where did he go?" he asked.

Orana pointed north. "He went that way," she said.

"Did he say what he was doing?" Marsden already knew the answer, but he wanted his maid to confirm it for him.

"He say he want find the Irish's tracks before rains wash them away," Orana said.

"Good enough," Marsden said. The captain walked into the stables to saddle his horse. As he attended to this, the first of many tasks ahead of him that day, he wondered whether Barega would have any more luck this time. He hoped he would. The issue of the Irishman's continued freedom was becoming a thorn in his side. There was a very real danger John Graham would assume folk hero status amongst the convicts if he wasn't found soon.

Ten miles north of Marsden's cottage, Barega was eating up the miles as his long legs carried him ever northwards. He'd taken John's escape even harder than had Marsden and Lord Cheetham, and he was determined the Irishman would not elude him this time.

The tracker had planned to set out after John at first light, but the prospect of rain had prompted him to head off during the night: he wanted to catch up to his quarry before the rain washed his tracks away forever. As it was, he could see he was probably too late. The black clouds to the north told him the rain had arrived, and even from a distance he could tell it was heavy.

Barega was heading to where he'd last seen John. It was obvious to him the fugitive was intent on continuing up the coast, so that made the job of tracking him all the easier. Unfortunately, the route he was following would take him through the territories of people who were enemies of his tribe, but that didn't faze him. He could move like a ghost through the wilderness, and if by chance he was seen, he could outrun any pursuer. He'd yet to meet a man who could match him for speed or endurance.

Thinking of John made him run even faster. His trusty spear and nulla nulla seemed light in his hands, and as always the silver crucifix bounced against his bare chest as he ran. In addition to the weapons he held, he also carried four extra spears in a sling over his back together with the woomera that would lend extra power to his arm when he next threw one of those spears.

Looking out from his rocky shelter in the cliff-face, John couldn't see more than twenty yards through the torrential rain. He'd experienced downpours like this in the wet season, both at Moreton Bay and at Parramatta, but never during the so-called dry season.

Normally, he'd have welcomed the rain as it provided some relief from the heat here in the winterless north, but he was still cold after the hours he'd spent immersed in the billabong, and was yearning for the sun's warmth.

As it was, he was resigned to remaining in his temporary abode for to venture out into the torrent would be to invite injury or some other serious mishap.

Thinking of the time he'd spent in the billabong reminded him to check if his newspaper cutting was still in one piece. John reached into his shirt pocket and drew out the crumpled page that contained his favourite John Keats poem, *Lamia*. He was relieved to find it had survived relatively unscathed.

In the dim light of early morning, he skimmed the poem until he found a verse that appealed.

It read:

> *And so he rested, on the lonely ground,*
> *Pensive, and full of painful jealousies.*
> *Of the Wood-Gods, and even the very trees.*
> *There as he stood, he heard a mournful voice,*

Such as once heard, in gentle heart, destroys.
All pain but pity: thus the lone voice spake:
"When from this wreathed tomb shall I awake!
When move in a sweet body fit for life,
And love, and pleasure, and the ruddy strife
Of hearts and lips! Ah, miserable me!"
The God, dove-footed, glided silently
Round bush and tree, soft-brushing, in his speed,
The taller grasses and full-flowering weed.

John read the verse again and yet again, determined to memorise it as he had several others. He'd become paranoid about losing the precious piece of paper that contained Keats' poem. It was, at this point in his miserable life, his most treasured possession.

As he began reading the verse for a fourth time, the rain eased and he finally dozed off. When he eventually woke five hours later, the sun would be shining and he'd be warm and dry.

The first sensation John was aware of when he woke was the warmth of the sun on his face. There was another sensation, too, but in his sleepy state he couldn't make sense of it.

Then he felt it again. Something was moving beneath his outstretched leg. With some difficulty, he opened one eye. To his horror, he saw a black-coloured snake crawling through a small gap between the underside of his left knee and the ground. He tensed involuntarily and the reptile bit him. It bit him twice in fact, but it happened so fast he thought it had only struck once.

John leapt to his feet and scurried away in case the snake came for him again. To his relief, it slithered off into the surrounding bush.

Only after it had disappeared did he give any thought to what variety of snake it was. He had no idea whether it was venomous or not. It had happened so quickly, he hadn't identified the snake. If he had to guess, it was a harmless tree snake, but it could just as easily have been a red-bellied black snake, which he knew was highly venomous. He had observed the Quandamooka treating them with the utmost respect whenever they came across one.

Lordy, what else can go wrong?

He discovered what else could go wrong when he rolled the left leg of his breeches up and saw two distinctive sets of fang marks just above the side of his knee. "Jesus!" he cursed. "The bastard bit me twice."

John's first thought was to retrieve one of the rocks from his makeshift shoulder bag—the rock with the cutting edge—to cut the wounds and then suck the poison out. Then he remembered the natives as Parra had recommended not using that technique. "Shit, shit, shit!" he cursed again. He fought to suppress the panic that was welling up inside him. If it was a red-bellied black snake, he knew he'd be dead within the hour.

Somewhere, in the furthest recess of his mind, he recalled an account he'd heard of an early European explorer, in Van Diemen's Land, who had survived a venomous snake bite by lying down and remaining totally still for half a day or so. John never did know whether that was an old wives' tale or a true story, but he had no better ideas, so he decided to try it.

Returning to his sleeping position inside the cliff-face, he lay down and willed himself to go to sleep.

What if I never wake up?

The thought of dying in his sleep frightened him so much it kept him awake. So he just lay there, determined not to move a muscle.

Damn it, I need to piss.

He considered standing up, or at least kneeling, to urinate, but decided against it. If the story about the European explorer was true, he'd survived the snakebite only by remaining perfectly still. *Makes sense staying still,* he thought. *Slows the blood flow to the heart.*

When he could hold it in no longer, he peed where he lay.

⋯⋯⋯

The first John realised he'd survived was when he woke from a deep sleep late that afternoon. He was surprised not only that he'd survived, but that in his heightened state of fear and anxiety he'd actually managed to sleep.

Relieved, his first instinct was to laugh out loud, and so he did. Then, for the first time in ages, he knelt and murmured a prayer of thanks to God.

The smell of stale urine reached his nostrils, reminding him he needed to bathe and wash his damp breeches.

⋯⋯⋯

As the Irishman celebrated his good fortune, Barega reached his quarry's last known hiding place—the cave on the same hillside where Lieutenant Hogan had shattered his leg. Although it had taken John and his pursuers two days to reach this point, the tracker had taken less than a day.

Dusk was approaching, but there was sufficient light for Barega to quickly establish that, as he'd suspected, John had in fact holed up here. The tracker regretted that he hadn't ignored Hogan's order and continued up the hillside. It wouldn't have taken long to find and kill the man he knew as *the Irish*.

Barega studied the same Aboriginal paintings that John had admired on the cave wall. They told a story only the tracker and others of his race could understand. He soon became lost in the past as the paintings brought to life the deeds of his ancient forefathers.

Suddenly conscious of the fading light, he left the cave to search the surrounding terrain. A quick reconnoitre confirmed what he already knew: the torrential rain that had swept through the region earlier had washed away any tracks John may have left.

Barega realised the odds were now on the Irishman's side. It was a huge territory, and anyone tracking John would have to be lucky to pick up his tracks. But he'd known that before he set out after him. The odds didn't faze him. He'd always been

183

lucky.

◆〉————〈◆

John had been intending to resume his northward trek as soon as daylight faded, but he didn't want to push his luck so soon after being bitten by the snake. For all he knew, he could still have poison in his system—that is if the snake was venomous. And so he decided to rest up until the following night.

No need to take more risks than I have to.

He still didn't know if the snake had been venomous. The fact that he hadn't suffered any ill effects, despite having been bitten twice, told him it was a harmless variety. However, he determined that if he ever got to relate the story to anyone, it would be the fiercest, ugliest, most venomous snake on the continent.

And it bit me ten times, not twice!

He spent the last moments of daylight searching for witchetty grubs. His search was unsuccessful, but he did find a few wild yams and some strange-looking roots, which, if his memory hadn't failed him, he recalled seeing the Quandamooka eating.

After placing his newly sourced food supplies in his shoulder bag, he returned to the shelter that had served him so well during the rainstorm. There, with the memory of the snake incident still fresh on his mind, he had the presence of mind to barricade the opening with shrubs he'd uprooted. The theory was he'd hear a snake if it tried to slither through the barricade.

"Good in theory at least," he mumbled.

That done, he sat cross-legged on the leafy mattress he'd fashioned for himself, and fished the yams and roots from his makeshift bag. The yams were edible—just. They were like nothing else he'd tasted. He couldn't even begin to describe the aftertaste.

Like sour turnips perhaps?

However, the roots were nigh inedible. John managed to force one down, after much chewing and masticating, but couldn't bring himself to try another. He had an idea the roots should be ground to pulp before ingesting, so he promised himself he'd experiment with that come tomorrow.

As always, he yearned for cooked food. "I need to make a fire," he muttered. "I mean, how hard can it be?"

The memory of the Quandamooka making fire on the riverbank at Moreton Bay still vivid in his mind, he pulled two of the bushes from the barricade he'd erected and hauled them back inside the shelter, as far from the entrance as possible. These he proposed using to fuel the cooking fire he planned to make.

The moon hadn't yet risen, but there was sufficient light, just, to allow him to see what he was doing. He selected a sturdy, foot-long twig, which he inspected closely, and some dried leaves, bark and grass from amongst the other bushes. Then he picked out a curved piece of bark to serve as a receptacle for what he was planning. Into it, he placed the grass and dried leaves he'd gathered. "That should do it," he said with a confidence he didn't feel. He'd seen how hard three natives had worked to make fire, and he couldn't imagine how he, an insignificant white man, could achieve the same result.

Sitting down, he adopted the same cross-legged position he'd assumed earlier. He held the twig in a vertical position between his hands, ensuring one end rested on the bark receptacle on the ground in front of him. "Here we go," he muttered. He began rubbing his hands backwards and forwards with as much energy as he could muster. The twig immediately broke under the pressure. "Damn it!" he swore.

John hurried over to his bushy barricade and selected a larger twig from one of the bushes. This he stripped of twigs and leaves before returning to his work.

He quickly found the larger twig, which was as thick and round as his little finger, to be eminently more suitable for the task. It rotated between his palms as he moved his hands back and forth as fast as humanly possible in an effort to create the friction needed to create a spark.

John understood the science involved in making fire even if he didn't possess the skill required. The friction created by moving the branch's tip continuously and without let-up was sufficient to cause the bark compressed beneath it to heat to the point it began smouldering, thereby lighting the tinder surrounding it.

Good in theory.

In practice, it was something quite different. Within minutes, John found he was sweating like a pig. After five minutes, his hands felt raw and he was rapidly running out of strength in his arms and shoulders. "Bloody hell!" he cursed. He refused to give up. All the while, he wracked his brains trying to remember the technique the Quandamooka had employed. He recalled they'd used a wooden base, not bark, and he wondered if that was his mistake.

Too late now.

After another five minutes, he was close to giving up. He was nearly crying with the pain, and the palms of both hands were bleeding, yet still there was no sign of smoke let alone flames.

It finally became too much for him. "Christ almighty!" he swore, throwing the stick away in a fit of anger.

John couldn't remember when he'd last felt so frustrated. He regretted he hadn't thought to bring a tinderbox to create the spark needed to make a fire.

Even some pieces of flint and steel would have done.

Only now did he notice the moon had risen. In the moonlight, he glanced at his hands. Raw and blistered, the palms of both hands bled profusely. They hurt, too.

John promised himself he'd never attempt to try to make a fire using that method again.

31

J OHN WOKE BEFORE DAWN TO the realisation his hands felt as though they were on fire. When daylight arrived he would see the palms of both hands were still red and raw, and his blisters had filled with fluid. Again he cursed himself for having attempted to make fire.

The fugitive had decided today was to be dedicated to food gathering. He was tired of making do with grubs and yams and the like, and he wanted a decent feed. He just hoped his hands would be up to it.

Dawn arrived and he studied his palms. They were even worse than he'd imagined. Before he did anything, he intended to bathe his hands, and dress them, too, if he could find something to wrap around them. He didn't want to risk infection setting in.

And so, armed with his spear, he ventured into the surrounding bush in search of a stream he suspected was nearby. He'd heard the trickling of water in the stillness of the night, and had identified the sound as a stream. He preferred the idea of bathing his hands in the pure waters of a stream rather than in a billabong or other comparatively stagnant watering hole as he'd found they were sometimes polluted.

Kookaburras led the dawn chorus of birds. They were joined by numerous other bird varieties with rainbow lorikeets, galahs and other varieties of cockatoo to the fore. Their calls told John there was every chance birds would feature on today's menu.

In the grey light of dawn, it didn't take him long to find the stream he'd suspected was there. He knelt beside it and immersed both hands in the cool water. "Ahhh," he murmured as the water soothed his hands. He left them in the stream for some time before bending down to drink from it.

His thirst assuaged, John's thoughts turned to finding a suitable dressing for his hands. At Parramatta, he had learned that Aboriginal healers applied herbal leaves to treat open wounds and serious skin problems, but he didn't know which leaves they used. Figuring any leaf would be better than nothing, he scouted around for a suitable plant, or one that looked suitable at least. He soon found one in the form of a small tree whose leaves seemed disproportionately large for the size of the tree. A single leaf, he discovered, covered one entire palm.

Without hesitating, he selected two leaves for his left hand, and he secured them using cotton threads he pulled from his tattered breeches. He dressed his right hand in the same manner. That done, he collected handfuls of the leaves for future use, and these he stuffed into his shoulder bag.

John then set off through the bush, his eye out for a plump native pigeon or brush turkey to spear. He wasn't sure if he was imagining it, but his hands already felt better.

The first creature he came across within range of his spear was not a bird, but a goanna, one of the more predominant of Australia's monitor lizards. It was clinging to the trunk of a tree just a few yards distant. John was aware goannas had a nasty bite, so he kept his distance.

Although not the biggest goanna he had ever seen, it was all of six foot in length. He debated whether to leave it be. However, he'd heard Aborigines considered the goanna a tasty treat, so he decided to chance his arm.

Approaching as close as he dared, he aimed his spear and threw it with all his strength. His aim was true and the spear skewered the goanna to the trunk. It reacted to the violent assault by writhing and hissing, its sharp claws lashing out at the tree it had been clinging to and tearing strips of bark from the trunk.

John watched, mesmerised, as the huge lizard entered its death throes. Its long, snake-like tongue flicked out as if trying to catch imaginary flies, and its fearsome claws tore more bark from the tree. The Irishman reminded himself never to tangle with one of these dragon-like beasts.

When the reptile finally breathed its last, John cautiously reached up and tried to remove the spear that pinned its carcass to the trunk. His wounded hands made this task more difficult than it should have been, and it took several painful attempts before his weapon came free. The goanna fell to the ground with an audible *thump*.

John waited for the burning sensation in his hands to ease then bent down and hoisted the carcass onto his shoulders before heading back to his shelter. There, using the sharp cutting stone he'd retained, he sliced portions of flesh from the creature's belly. He thought the white flesh reminiscent of crayfish in appearance, but that was where the similarity ended: it was most unappetising, and what little he managed to force down his throat, he almost regurgitated.

Spitting to remove the residue from his mouth, he lamented, "The blacks call this a delicacy!" He thought the Aborigines needed their taste buds overhauled.

Logic told him the creature should be cooked first. He recalled seeing the Quandamooka cooking monitor lizards and snakes over the campfires.

How he wished he could make fire.

As the morning sun rose above the treetops, another thought came to him. He sliced generous strips of flesh from the goanna's belly and back, and then looked around for a north-facing rock to place them on. Finding one that would remain fully exposed to the sun all day, he lay the strips in rows atop the rock. He glanced up at the sun. "Medium to well done, thank you," he advised the sun as if placing an order in an eatery.

John wasn't sure if he was imagining it or not, but the sun felt extra hot today. It reminded him he needed to fashion another makeshift hat for himself. So he set off to locate some suitable ferns.

It didn't take him long to find a grove of lush ferns. They were just inside the rainforest that bordered his hiding place.

Thirty minutes was all he needed to fashion another sun bonnet. It would have taken him less time had it not been for the state of his hands. This bonnet was better fitting and more presentable than the first one he'd made, and it offered more protection from the sun, too.

Job done.

Satisfied with his latest adornment, he set off to further investigate his surrounds, and to look for more game to spear.

In the course of the morning, he experienced several near misses trying to spear brush turkeys and cockatoos in the bush, and he had no success trying to spear fish in a muddy pond he came across. He blamed his blistered hands for his poor aim.

Finally, he stumbled across a raspberry bush laden with ripe raspberries, so he topped up his bag with the delicious fruit before returning to his shelter.

On reaching the shelter, he was pleasantly surprised to find the sun had baked the strips of goanna flesh, or, more correctly, it had baked the exposed surface of the flesh. He discovered the underside was still raw, so he turned the strips over then returned to the shelter to daydream and snooze while he waited for the sun to complete its work.

While John rested up, Barega continued to follow in his quarry's footsteps, albeit by chance. Whether it was more by instinct than chance is debatable. Either way, he followed almost the exact route north that John had taken.

When tracking Man or animal, Barega tried to put himself in the mind of his quarry, constantly asking himself what his prey was likely to be thinking, where he was heading and what evasive action he would take.

In this case, he was certain John was still heading north even though he hadn't found his spoor. To double back would increase the fugitive's likelihood of running into his pursuers, so the Irishman wouldn't risk that, he thought. John did have the option of heading inland, but the tracker doubted he'd do that even though other convicts, to their peril, had. Those who had fled west and somehow evaded their pursuers had inevitably perished in the heat of the interior.

Barega sensed John was different to the others. He'd picked him as more intelligent than most convicts, and more cunning, too, and he was certain the fugitive was still heading north. He was also sure his quarry planned to try to board one of the white man's ships known to occasionally frequent these shores.

By early afternoon, the tracker had unknowingly bypassed the shelter where John was hiding out.

Since early morning, Barega had traversed the same scrubby, bush-covered hills his quarry had crossed, and had left behind the grassy, rolling plains where John had almost speared the koala and had subsequently ended up trapped in the billabong. Quite by chance, he had briefly stopped to drink from the same watering hole. If he hadn't been distracted by the sight of a wedge-tailed eagle soaring in the invisible thermals high above, he'd have seen the makeshift fern bonnet John had lost in the billabong. It floated amongst a cluster of water lilies near the far bank.

John dozed in the entrance to his shelter. He had stripped naked, even removing his boots, and had soon been lulled to sleep by the feeling of the warm sun on his body. He'd woken only spasmodically to brush a fly or beetle from his face or to confirm there were no snakes around.

His rumbling tummy reminded him to check on the progress of the goanna strips he'd left out on the rock, and so, still naked, he went to investigate. He was pleasantly surprised to find they'd been baked a golden brown all over. Unfortunately, the taste didn't match the appearance of the morsels, but they were at least edible—and they satisfied his hunger for the moment at least.

John made a mental note to employ the same food preparation technique again.

Garnish the meat with some berries next time.

A loud buzzing of flies carried to him. It was coming from beneath a bush where he'd left the goanna's carcass. He walked over to investigate and realised every fly in New South Wales—or so it seemed—had discovered the carcass. Fighting his way through the cloud of angry flies, he picked up the carcass and carried it to the nearby billabong, dropping it into the shallows for better storage. The flies hovered above the water, clearly frustrated they couldn't get to the carcass, which lay barely an inch beneath the surface. They turned their frustration on John, buzzing him until he was driven to dive into the billabong.

Surfacing, he chuckled as the flies gave up on him and buzzed off. Only then did he remember his blistered hands. He hoped he didn't pick up an infection from the water.

Against his better judgement, he remained in the billabong a while, swimming a few lengths and luxuriating in the feeling of the cool water on his hands and body before climbing out and wandering back to his shelter. There, he changed the dressings on his hands, securing new leaves to the palms of each. He then donned his tattered clothes and boots, grabbed his spear and shoulder bag, and set off for the nearby rainforest in search of more food.

Just inside the rainforest, he saw a sight that turned his stomach. A huge scrub python was in the process of devouring an adult kangaroo it had just caught and crushed.

John estimated the python was all of sixteen feet long. The roo looked sizeable, too, even though only its hind legs could be seen protruding from the python's mouth. In swallowing its prey, the reptile had distended its mouth an unbelievable distance. The Irishman guessed, correctly, that the python's jaw was rigged with ligaments, tendons and muscles, allowing it to swallow large animals.

Soon, nothing could be seen of the dead roo, although its body shape was still readily identifiable in the python's swollen belly.

John had seen at least a dozen pythons since escaping—usually when trekking through rainforests—but never one this big, and never one in the act of eating its prey. He found the sight disturbing, and promised himself to keep a closer eye out for these particular snakes in future as he didn't wish to end up as lunch for one.

His first ever encounter with a python had been up close and personal. He'd climbed into a tree to look for nuts, and had discovered he was sharing a branch with a python. It wasn't as big as the one in front of him now, but it was big enough to give him a fright. He had been so surprised, he'd released his grip on the branch and fallen to the ground.

He shuddered at the memory and continued on his way, making a wide berth around the giant python, which was now sleeping off its meal.

The Irishman was starting to realise that mid-afternoon in the rainforest wasn't the most productive time of day to hunt. Compared to dusk and dawn, when the trees and the forest floor seemed alive with birds and animals, the rainforest seemed devoid of life. Apart from the sound of his breathing, and the occasional whip-crack call of an elusive eastern whipbird, the forest slept.

He was about to return to the shelter when the familiar sound of a brush turkey carried to him. On investigating, he found a solitary turkey foraging for seeds and insects. It was so preoccupied, it hadn't noticed the intruder.

The Irishman lined up his target and let fly with his spear. His aim was faulty and the spear missed the turkey by a yard or more.

Startled, the big bird flew up into the branches of the nearest tree. It was the first time John had seen a brush turkey fly. Until now he hadn't realised how clumsy they were in the air. This one misjudged its flight and flopped back down onto the ground. Only on its second attempt did it manage to find a secure perch.

John debated whether to retrieve his spear for another try. He decided against that and reached into his bag, drawing out the largest of several stones he now kept in it.

The turkey was preparing for another short, panicked flight as John took aim. This time, his aim was true and the rock struck the bird just before it took off. The turkey fell to the ground and lay there, stunned.

John quickly wrang the bird's neck and set off back to the shelter. He walked with a spring in his step, suddenly confident in his hunting and food-gathering skills. His mouth was watering at the thought of brush turkey for dinner. In anticipation, he began plucking the bird as he walked.

Back at his shelter, John finished plucking the brush turkey. He then placed it on the same rock he'd left the goanna strips on earlier, hoping the late afternoon sun would at least warm the big bird. That done, he returned to his shelter to rest up some more before eating.

Lying there, on his bed of palm fronds and leaves, he found he was looking forward to resuming his trek north. He felt fully rested at last, and, apart from his blistered hands which still hurt a little, he was ready for whatever lay ahead.

If he was honest, the prospect of walking at night through this unfamiliar landscape was a little daunting. He was aware snakes and other creatures hunted by night, and he knew there was a very real possibility he could fall over a cliff or into some unseen crevice in the dark. However, he'd been over all that in his mind and he believed the risk of being accosted by natives while walking during the day outweighed all the other dangers combined.

A flash of yellow caught John's eye. He looked around and saw an adult dingo rush from the bushes and grab the turkey he'd left on the rock. "Hey!" he shouted. He picked up his spear, jumped to his feet and ran after the thief.

When he saw the dingo was going to get away, he let fly with his spear. This time, his aim was true, but the wild dog swerved at the last minute and the spear's sharpened tip buried itself in the earth where the canine intruder had been only a split-second earlier.

"God-damn you, dog!" the Irishman cursed as he watched the dingo disappear into the trees on the far side of the billabong, the plump brush turkey firmly clasped between its jaws.

Initially, John had thought it likely the dingo was a member of the pack that had chased him into the billabong and damned near caused him to drown. Casting his mind back to that traumatic episode, he easily recalled the descriptions of all five dingoes. After all, he'd had a lot of time to observe them.

He quickly deduced the thief he'd just seen wasn't a member of that pack. Half of one ear—its right ear—was missing, and it had a distinctive reddish-coloured mark on its back.

Resigning himself to yet another meal of yams, slugs and berries, John retrieved his spear and slowly trudged back to the shelter, cursing as he went.

He'd never know it, but the dingo that stole his raw turkey would soon come down with a bad bout of food poisoning that would see him laid low with stomach cramps and diarrhoea for the next two or three days.

⋅ε⋅———⋅3⋅

Later, as John finished his meagre evening meal and prepared to depart the shelter that had served him so well, eight miles north of his present position Barega was surveying an encampment of Aborigines. The tracker remained unaware he had bypassed John's shelter as he'd continued his trek north, his way guided by the light of a full moon. He'd stumbled across the Aboriginal encampment as he ventured down to a beach.

Putting himself in the mind of his quarry, Barega had guessed John would be resting by day and walking by night. Certainly that's what he would do in the Irishman's situation. That would lessen his chances of being seen by unfriendly natives.

The Aborigines the tracker now studied from the cover of a grove of palm trees above the beach were certainly unfriendly. He knew that for a fact. He'd immediately identified them as members of the Goenpul tribe—long-time enemies of his people, the Joondaburri.

Barega had heard the Goenpul before he'd seen them. They were participating in a corroboree, a traditional celebration of dance and song. The sound of singing and rhythm sticks had carried to the tracker when he was still a mile or so from the beach.

Now, as he observed them, he estimated there were at least a hundred gathered around a large campfire. The men, who were all naked and painted in white ochre, were the only ones dancing. Those women who were present had been relegated to

191

minding the children while watching their menfolk from the shadows beyond the fire.

Barega studied the women and other spectators, trying to see if John was among them. He imagined if the fugitive had been caught by the Goenpul he'd be dead by now. Still he looked for him in case he had been spared.

Seeing no sign of John, the tracker silently backed away from the beach and began retracing his steps toward Moreton Bay. He figured his quarry was unlikely to have come this far north anyway given he'd only escaped a few days earlier.

Barega's plan was to take his time and weave his way home in the hope he would pick up John's spoor. If that didn't work he'd start searching again at the first available opportunity. He had no intention of giving up on the Irishman.

As John resumed trekking north and Barega began his return journey south, inadvertently putting themselves on a possible collision course, Moreton Bay's convicts, soldiers and settlers alike settled in for another night. For most it would be a night like any other.

In the convicts' huts, which were now so jam-packed it was nigh impossible for the inmates to sleep, the lights were already out; in the soldiers' quarters, and in the officers' quarters, too, the King's men talked, drank and played cards; and in nearby Brisbane Town, most of the newly arrived settlers mixed with each other and with many of the original settlers in the town's sole tavern, making new friends and renewing old friendships over glasses of rum and jugs of ale.

On the edge of town, in Lord Cheetham's mansion, Cheetham indulged his opium habit in the company of his main supplier, a French importer from Sydney Town. For the importer, who was not an opium user himself, this was his first visit to Moreton Bay. He'd only come at Cheetham's insistence.

Until now, the Frenchman had used a middle man to courier opium to Moreton Bay or, indeed, to courier anything anywhere this far afield. However, the commandant was such an important client, he felt he could hardly turn his invitation down. Watching him now, indulging his habit in the privacy of his own home, the importer could see he'd have a big-paying client for life in Cheetham. The Englishman was well and truly hooked on the drug.

A quarter-of-a-mile away, in Marsden's cottage overlooking the penal settlement, the captain drained the last drops from a bottle of red wine as he read the latest letter he'd received from his daughter. He read by the light of a lantern in his den. Helen's letter was well thumbed for he'd already gone over it several times—most recently only an hour earlier when he'd read it aloud to Matthew before the boy had gone to bed.

Since his wife's death, and since Helen's departure for Sydney Town, the cottage had seemed awfully quiet to Marsden. Not even his son's boisterousness seemed to adequately fill the silence that had descended since the two women in his life had departed.

That no doubt explained why he'd started drinking more than usual in recent weeks. At least that's how Marsden justified it in his own mind. But there was more to it than that, and he knew it.

In fact, his life was starting to spiral out of control. Cheetham's cruel management style was worsening by the day, and, as head warden—in name at least—Marsden was expected to carry out the commandant's orders and even champion his harsh disciplinary methods. Unfortunately, complaints about Cheetham to Sir Ralph, the Governor, continued to fall on deaf ears.

Marsden had been left with a decision to make: either resign his commission and return to England or put aside his moral concerns and carry out Cheetham's orders. After much soul-searching, he'd decided on the latter. And now he was paying the price as his weakness—for that's how he saw it—made him feel as if he'd given away his manhood. He was only thankful his dearest Vera wasn't here to see him now.

The captain opened a second bottle of wine, filled his glass and then returned his attention to Helen's letter.

It read:

> *Dearest Papa*
>
> *I do miss you and Matthew so, and trust this finds you both well and not missing me too much. Please be assured I am enjoying my new life in Sydney Town and am making many new friends.*
>
> *The Browns have made me feel very welcome, and I do so enjoy boarding with them. I feel truly blessed that they agreed to take me on as a trainee teacher in the junior school they have established.*
>
> *I know it is early days, but I feel I have found my calling. I believe I was born to teach, and I do love it so.*
>
> *I received another letter from Lieutenant Hogan in the latest mail shipment, and he advised that he hopes to visit me when he comes to Sydney Town soon.*

That had been news to Marsden when he read it for the first time. As he considered the ramifications of the lieutenant visiting his daughter, he realised he still wasn't overly comfortable about the courtship that was evidently building. Marsden reminded himself that Helen didn't yet know about Hogan's recent accident, and the visit she spoke of wouldn't happen any time soon.

The captain yawned. It had been a long day and he was looking forward to turning in for the night. Stifling another yawn, he drained the last of the wine from his glass and resumed reading:

> *It will be the first time I have seen the lieutenant since leaving Moreton Bay, and I must admit to being slightly nervous as I still do not know how I feel toward him. From the tone of his last letter it would seem he does not harbour the same reservations.*
>
> *I do so miss mama, and I know you and Matthew do as well. It is comforting to know her final resting place is within sight of the*

cottage. Please place a flower for me on mama's grave next time you visit her . . .

Marsden fell asleep in his chair, letter still in hand and empty wine glass on the floor.

Just two hundred yards from the Marsden cottage, in the infirmary adjoining the officers' quarters, Hogan was in the process of replying to the latest letter he'd received from Helen. That was no easy task for he was writing propped up in his allotted bunk, and he was still in some considerable discomfort. His shattered leg, which was now dressed and strapped in a splint, was slightly raised thanks to three strategically placed pillows.

After the lieutenant had been hauled back to Moreton Bay following his recent mishap, Doctor Andrews had patched him up to the best of his ability, applying a temporary splint and confining him to bed. There he would remain until the army's head surgeon from the Parramatta military hospital arrived to operate on him a few days from now. Such an operation was beyond Andrews' expertise—more so since the doctor had been drinking more heavily than usual in recent weeks—and Marsden had insisted the head surgeon intervene. That hadn't gone down well with Andrews, or with Cheetham for that matter, but Marsden had gotten his way. And for that Hogan was thankful.

Initially, Hogan had been in excruciating pain. Andrews had successfully treated that by dispensing opium, which was the army's standard treatment for pain. It had worked almost immediately, and for the first time Hogan understood the appeal the drug had for Cheetham and other users. Even so, he promised himself he would not become reliant on it.

Hogan was sour about the way things had turned out. He'd been looking forward to visiting Helen soon to pursue his courtship of her, and now he was having to inform her he couldn't travel for some time. He blamed John Graham for that.

The Irish fugitive had been occupying his thoughts a lot of late. He dearly hoped the tracker would find John and kill him. That is if he wasn't already dead.

32

F OR NO GOOD REASON, JOHN deviated from his plan to follow the coast almost as soon as he set out that night. No good reason other than an inexplicable urge to head inland.

Experience had taught the Irishman to follow his instincts—and on this occasion his instincts told him to quit the coast. "Only for tonight," he told himself. And so he headed west, toward the interior.

Several times he nearly turned back.

You'll find no ships inland, you bloody fool!

Still he headed inland.

It was slow going because he had to skirt around bush-covered hillsides and dense patches of rainforest so that he could remain out in the open where the moon and stars provided sufficient light to allow him to see any crevices or other dangers.

As he walked, he felt he was being followed. Several times he doubled back to a vantage point to survey the terrain behind him, but to no avail. Other than the occasional hoot of a Boobook Owl or the gentle clucking of a kangaroo, there was no other sign of life.

The feeling persisted. John decided to check once more, and so, after summiting a small hill and descending a few steps on the other side, he quickly doubled back to the summit. Lying in the long grass, he surveyed the valley he'd just crossed. "There it is!" he whispered to himself. Something flashed in the moonlight. Two pinpoints of light.

There it is again!

Fearing he was being tracked, he gripped his spear tightly.

Whoever it is, or whatever it is, they're following my tracks.

He estimated the two pinpoints of light were seventy-five yards or so distant. As they closed to within fifty yards of his position, he relaxed.

Dingo!

In the moonlight, he could just make out the shadowy form of a dingo. Whether it was the same one that had taken off with his turkey earlier he couldn't be sure, although he suspected it could be. He debated whether to try to spear the animal if it came near him.

As the dingo neared, it suddenly froze and sniffed the air.

John, who was lying prone in the long grass, remained perfectly still. The dingo looked directly his way even though the Irishman knew he couldn't be seen.

Bastard knows I'm here.

John was ready to leap up and spear the dingo when it turned tail and disappeared into the night. He leapt to his feet and brandished his spear. "Bloody thief!" he shouted after the fleeing animal. Even though the dingo was but a shadowy shape in the dark, he was more convinced than ever it was the one that had taken his dinner.

Alone once more, he immediately regretted his outburst, realising he'd have been heard if there were any Aborigines within earshot. Anxious to distance himself from this spot, he hurried down the far side of the hill and continued inland.

As he walked, he was blissfully unaware that the dingo he'd spooked was indeed the one which had taken off with his turkey. It had devoured the raw bird in no time at all, and then tracked the man who had supplied the turkey, thinking him a good potential provider of more readymade meals.

Since setting off after John, the dingo hadn't been feeling well. Now, as it distanced itself from the angry man, it began to suffer mild stomach cramps. The cramps continued, becoming increasingly painful and forcing the dingo to rest up. It soon became nauseas and it regurgitated the raw bird it had eaten.

The dingo had an overwhelming desire to drink, so it set off to locate water, stopping every so often as the stomach cramps worsened.

On the coast, Barega continued his southward trek. He moved slower now, deviating a few hundred yards inland every now and then in the hope of intercepting John or stumbling upon his hiding place. At one point, the tracker came to within a stone's throw of the shelter the fugitive had quit earlier that very night. Had it been daylight, he'd have seen the signs left by his quarry. In the dark, however, despite the presence of a full moon, he missed the signs.

The further John pressed inland, the more barren the terrain became. Trees and shrubs gave way to tussock and scrubby bushes, and hills gave way to plains that were treeless apart from the occasional gum. He wondered whether he'd reached the place they called *the Outback*—he hadn't, but he wasn't to know that—and he began questioning why he'd decided to deviate from his plan to stick to the coast. "There was no good reason to do that," he told himself. "Doubt you'll find a berth to China out here, you bloody idiot."

John realised he hadn't sighted water in some time. Not a river nor a stream nor even a billabong.

He was reminded of Noel's summation of his experience in the interior.

Desert, he'd said. Nothing but desert. No water. Not even a drop.

Without further debate, he did an about-turn and headed back toward the coast, and, as he retraced his steps, he promised himself he wouldn't deviate from his original plan again. "So much for following my instincts!" he muttered. He wasn't to know that on this occasion those instincts had saved him from a likely rendezvous with the tracker.

A weary John reached the coast not long before dawn. He stopped just short of the actual shoreline and soon found a suitable place to rest up through the coming day—in a clearing in a patch of dense rainforest.

The fugitive set about constructing a lean-to, using fallen branches and fern fronds he'd collected from the surrounding trees. As he added the finishing touches to it, he realised he hadn't achieved much over the past night. However, his hands were feeling much improved, and that was a big relief as he had feared they would become infected.

One small victory at least.

Dawn was breaking when he finally lay down. By the time sunlight chased the dawn away, he was already fast asleep.

As the sun rose high in the morning sky, the trees surrounding the clearing John had chosen to rest up in kept the sun's rays from him, but they caught the treetops above, signalling another fine day. However, not even the Kookaburras' chatter could rouse the Irishman. He remained fast sleep.

Some five hundred miles as the crow flies south of the forest clearing John was holed up in, Helen Marsden had already been in class for an hour at the junior school she taught at—such was the time difference between Sydney Town and the winterless north.

Helen had a big day ahead of her, for today marked the first time she would teach her young pupils on her lonesome and without the guidance of one or other of her benefactors. Until now, either William Brown or his wife Thelma, or sometimes both, had sat in whilst she taught. Not today, though. She was on her own, and she was shaking like a leaf.

The trainee teacher took her new profession seriously. Her class comprised thirteen students aged between six and eight. All children of settlers wealthy enough to afford the private school's fees, they were the youngest in the school. Even so, they were bright and hungry for knowledge.

The Browns, with whom she also boarded, had noted Helen's potential from the first day she had reported for work at the school they'd established. They considered she would make an excellent teacher, and they told her father as much in the course of their frequent correspondence with him.

Helen's first lesson was devoted to spelling. The chalk she held squeaked as she wrote "Sydnee" on the blackboard, deliberately misspelling the word. Turning back to her pupils, she asked, "Who can tell me what that word is?"

Several tiny hands shot up. She pointed to the owner of one of those hands—a keen lad who reminded her of a younger Matthew. "Yes, William?" she asked.

"That's Sydney, Miss," the boy said.

"Yes, but have I spelt it correctly?" Helen asked.

No hands were raised this time, and the young woman spent the next few minutes teaching her young charges how to spell Sydney correctly.

Through the course of the day, as one lesson merged into the next, Helen became more and more confident. By the end of the school day, she was more certain than ever that teaching was her calling in life.

As Helen's first day at school ended, John was deep in the rainforest, scouting for food to take back to the clearing he'd been holed up in since dawn. Through trial and error, he was discovering new roots, shoots and fruits, and learning which were edible and which weren't. He'd even discovered a tasty grub that was to be found in large quantities around the base of certain fern varieties, and it was these he was gathering now.

Night was falling by the time he returned to the clearing. After eating the grubs he'd collected, he walked out of the rainforest and resumed his trek north.

His first destination was the nearest beach. He knew it was fairly close as he could now hear waves breaking on the shore.

John approached the beach cautiously—and for good reason: he was aware Aborigines frequented the shoreline, collecting shellfish and other seafood and often overnighting on the sand in their temporary bivouacs. For that reason, he had avoided all beaches until now. The chances of falling foul of natives were just too high.

Tonight, he was prepared to make an exception. The main reason being he desperately wanted to source more food to supplement his meagre supplies.

The beach he found himself on was thankfully deserted. Bordered by palm trees, it formed a small bay. It was separated from the next bay by a rocky abutment. Moonlight was reflected in rock pools at the base of the abutment where the rocks met the sand, and John made a beeline for these.

A quick reconnoitre of the first rock pool he came to yielded immediate results: the rocks were covered with mussels. Using his ever-useful stone—the one with the cutting edge—he prised a large mussel from the nearest rock and then, using the same sharp edge, prised the shellfish open. He fished the mussel from it with his fingers and popped it into his mouth. The fleshy mussel tasted salty and rubbery— and oh so tasty.

So enamoured was he with the taste, he attacked the rock with fervour, prising off as many mussels as it took to fill his shoulder bag. That done, he set off again, making his way around the rocky abutment to the next bay. As he walked, he selected a couple of large seashells he thought would make useful cutting tools, and these he also crammed into his bag.

I need a bigger bag.

The moon disappeared behind a cloud as John entered the next bay, limiting his depth of vision for a moment. Even so, he could see this bay was considerably bigger than the one he'd just left.

When the moon reappeared, he dropped to one knee and grasped his spear tight. In the moonlight he could see native bivouacs further along the beach.

Lots of bivouacs.

He wasn't to know he'd arrived at the same beach that had hosted the Goenpuls' corroboree the previous night. The same beach where Barega had observed the enemies of his people dancing and singing.

There was no sign of life. John hoped the bivouacs' occupants were all asleep. The nearest one was some fifty yards away, and it was impossible to gage whether it was occupied or not.

John realised he was very exposed where he was. Dropping onto his belly, he began crawling up the beach to a grove of palm trees he'd noticed. The short journey seemed to take forever, and he feared he could be clubbed or speared in the back any minute. He finally made the cover of the palms and then took stock of his situation.

Studying the bivouacs more closely, he saw they seemed abandoned. Some were in a collapsed state, as if their occupants had given up on them or had had to depart in a hurry.

Still he didn't move. He just observed the bivouacs, looking for a sign of life.

No-one home.

It finally dawned on him the encampment had been abandoned. And so, with some trepidation, he emerged from the cover of the palms and approached the nearest bivouac. He relaxed as his suspicions were confirmed: there was no-one home.

Looking around at the other bivouacs, and at the remains of the same big campfire the natives had danced around only the night before, he couldn't read the signs and therefore had no way of knowing the encampment had been deserted only that morning.

His eyes were drawn to discarded items that indicated the campsite's occupants may have departed hurriedly.

Half buried in the campfire's ashes, he noticed what looked like an axe-head. Closer inspection revealed it was a tomahawk-like weapon. Its razor-sharp adze head had been tied firmly to a wooden handle that was smooth to touch. *A very useful weapon,* John decided. Blowing the ash from it, he inserted it through his belt so that it rested against his hip. He found the feel of it comforting.

Sensing an opportunity, he embarked on a search of the entire site, starting with the nearest bivouac. Like all the bivouacs, this one had been fashioned from driftwood, branches, palm fronds, leaves and long grass. Extremely basic, it appeared to be barely large enough for two or three adults, or for a small family perhaps.

In one bivouac, the Irishman found a wooden bowl he could see would fit neatly in the palm of his hand. He guessed it was an eating or drinking bowl, or both perhaps, so he stored it on top of the mussels, shells and stones in his shoulder bag.

In another bivouac, he made his best discovery of all. He almost missed it. The lean-to was in a collapsed state—as if its owner had demolished it in a fit of anger—and at first glance he thought it contained nothing that would interest him. He'd been just about to leave when he noticed a length of fur protruding from beneath a palm frond. On investigation, he discovered it was a cloak that had been made from pelts sewn together using some kind of sinew.

Kangaroo sinew perhaps?

If he had to guess, the pelts were possum skin. Regardless, they were soft and warm to his touch.

Out in the moonlight, one glance was enough to tell him the cloak was in good condition and, more importantly, it looked about the right size. Removing his shoulder bag, he slipped the cloak over his head. Sleeveless, it came down to his knees.

So warm!

He liked it so much, he kept it on.

John was suddenly anxious to depart. After another quick look around the site, he hurried off. His discovery of the encampment had served as a timely reminder he wasn't alone in this part of the country, so he vowed to exercise extreme caution whenever he ventured anywhere near the shoreline. In fact, he decided, in future he'd steer clear of the foreshore except when he needed to fish or collect shellfish.

Thinking of shellfish reminded him of the mussels he'd stored in his bag, and he found himself looking forward to his next meal break.

33

———❦———

"I F I SEE ANOTHER BLOODY gum tree, I may slit my wrists!" John promised himself as he walked between two stands of eucalypts. He'd been doing that a lot of late—talking to himself, that is—and that had surprised him for he'd rarely talked to himself before now. Not to any great extent at least, and certainly never to the point where he argued aloud with himself. That had all changed in the past month.

It had been a month, almost to the day, since he'd escaped Moreton Bay. In fact, it had been thirty-two days. He knew that because he was keeping a calendar of sorts on his makeshift spear. Each night, using the blade of the tomahawk he'd found at the Goenpuls' abandoned campsite, he carved a notch on his spear, signifying another day of freedom. "Freedom?" he asked himself. "Ha!" If this was freedom, he wasn't sure he wanted it.

His rudimentary calendar also told him it had been twenty-nine days since he'd sighted another human being. "Twenty-nine days since the tracker and Lieutenant Hogan's search party almost caught me," he mumbled. Until now, he'd never been alone for more than a day or two. "That probably explains why I'm talkin' to myself."

The enforced solitude had rammed home how much he desired the company of others, and how much he missed talking to people. At such times, he invariably thought of home and Noel and other dear friends.

The past month had been a difficult one for the fugitive. Walking by night, sleeping and foraging for food by day and generally living rough was starting to take its toll. Two recent bouts of food poisoning—one a result of eating raw fish and one the result of eating strange berries—hadn't helped either. These had left him feeling weak and washed out, and he now hadn't an ounce of fat left on his lean frame. He knew a lesser man would have perished weeks ago.

Despite the hardship, or perhaps because of it, he was proud of his achievements. "I'm still alive," he often told himself, "and by God I'm going to stay that way!"

As well as escaping Moreton Bay and eluding his pursuers, for the time-being at least, he'd taught himself how to survive in the wilderness. He was slowly learning how to kill or capture wild game—be it fish, fowl, snakes or lizards—and he was discovering which roots and berries were edible. He was also starting to feel at one with the environment, choosing safe walking routes, avoiding hidden dangers, and finding watering holes and suitable places to rest up.

Regardless, he felt he was reaching the end of his tether. He was becoming obsessed with connecting with a ship, and even more obsessed with the thought a ship could be nearby and he'd miss it. So he had taken to venturing down to the shore more and more, even during daylight hours. And even when he wasn't by the sea, he tried to keep it in sight as much as possible.

John saw a billabong and headed for it. Kneeling beside it, he studied his reflection in its still waters. "Who is that wild man?" he asked himself. If he was hardly recognisable before, he was unrecognisable even to himself now. His unruly, matted hair was longer than ever and his beard was now full-grown; and although he still wore the same clothes, they were more tattered than ever and would, he guessed, barely see him through the remainder of winter. Fortunately, it was August now so he imagined his clothes would only have to last another month or so. Already, it seemed, the days were warming.

The Irishman bent down and drank greedily from the billabong. As he drank, he suddenly had a feeling he was being watched. He quickly looked around, but saw nothing. Nervous, he continued on his way, clutching his trusty spear. The tomahawk against his hip gave him added comfort.

John had felt he was being followed for several days now. He wondered if it was Barega. Thinking of the tracker forced him to walk faster.

He had left his latest hiding place to fulfil his daily mission and find food. Today, his heart had been set on a brush turkey or some other sizeable bird. He'd only eaten grubs and yams since his latest bout of food poisoning a few days earlier, and he needed to fill his belly soon or he feared he'd fade away.

John had holed up in a cave on the coast. He estimated he had ventured a good two miles inland from the cave, and decided he'd turn back soon if he didn't find what he was looking for.

After ten minute's fast walking, he relaxed. He had sighted no other living creature, other than birds in the trees and a harmless carpet snake, and he'd convinced himself he was alone in this little corner of the world.

That all changed in an instant when, half a mile away, to his left, he saw a column of smoke rising above the tree tops.

A campfire!

He instinctively dropped to one knee and surveyed the terrain all around him.

Nothing.

Every cell in his body told him to get the hell out of there. However, he had an overwhelming desire to find out who was at the campsite. So, using extreme caution and keeping to the trees where possible, he went to investigate.

As he neared the site, he realised he could no longer see any smoke. He wondered if he'd been seen.

Ignoring the urge to flee, he lay down and crawled forward on his belly, ensuring that he kept long grass and bushes between himself and the spot where he imagined the campsite to be.

He found himself atop a rise overlooking a bare patch of earth ringed by yet more gum trees. In the centre were the fresh remains of the fire he'd seen. Its embers still glowed red. There wasn't a soul around. Not that he could see at least.

John lay there, unmoving, for at least five minutes.

Is it a trap?

Still, he saw no sign of life.

His eyes were drawn to the fire's still smouldering embers. As before, they glowed red. They seemed to beckon him. He could imagine roasting a pigeon or turkey or some other delicious bird over the fire. His imagination worked overtime.

What I'd give for a roast pigeon.

Satisfied that whoever had lit the fire had departed, he cautiously stood up and walked down into the clearing. There, he extended one hand over the remains of the cooking fire, and withdrew it quickly when he realised the ashes were still red hot.

Looking at the embers, he reached another decision. "I need a fire," he whispered. He quickly gathered up handfuls of long grass, leaves and twigs, and placed them on top of the embers. To his delight, the fire reignited. "Praise the Lord!" he said.

Aware smoke would draw unwelcome attention, he resisted the urge to add more fuel to the flames. Instead, he reached into his shoulder bag and pulled out the wooden bowl he'd uplifted from the Goenpul campsite. John grabbed his tomahawk and used its flat edge to transfer burning embers from the fire into the bowl. He added tinder to the embers, and this quickly ignited. Then he reached back into his bag and pulled out the sun bonnet he'd fashioned from fern fronds. He wrapped it around the bowl so that it protected the flames from the elements.

The Irishman's plan was to carry the fire back to the safety of his cave, and then find, catch or kill something to cook over it. He realised he'd need a quantity of tinder for this delicate task, and so set about filling his bag with as much grass and as many twigs and leaves as it could hold. That done, he set off back to the coast, taking extreme care not to drop his precious cargo or let the fire go out.

Glancing at the early afternoon sun, he calculated he had another four hours of daylight left. "Plenty of time," he told himself.

Only now, as he walked, did he wonder about who had lit the cooking fire in the first place. Whoever they were, he hoped they were long gone.

It took John more than two hours to reach his cave. He'd almost lost the fire several times until he'd realised walking too fast created too much draft, and so he'd had to walk at a speed little faster than crawling pace. Also, the fire had consumed more tinder than he'd envisaged, forcing him to stop to collect more grass and leaves along the way.

As he neared the coast, a sea breeze threatened to extinguish the flames, forcing him to walk backwards and hold the make-do fire container close to his body. By now little remained of the sun bonnet he'd wrapped around the burning tinder. All but a couple of fronds had been burnt to a crisp.

His problems weren't over when he reached the cave. Now he had to find a way to keep the fire burning long enough to permit him to find something to cook over it. He also had to delay adding too much tinder to the flames for fear the smoke would attract attention should anyone still be in the area.

So many problems.

First, he prepared his fire well back from the cave's entrance so that any smoke would dissipate as opposed to spiralling skyward in a single column and drawing attention to his presence. "Good in theory," he muttered. Then he collected driftwood from the nearby beach and fallen branches from the surrounding trees, and he stockpiled these inside the cave.

At this point, the fire was flickering only faintly. He kept a close eye on it to ensure it didn't die out.

When he considered there was barely an hour left before nightfall, he knew he couldn't delay any longer, so he piled as much wood onto the fire as he dared. The fire immediately took, and the flames leapt toward the cave's rocky ceiling. "Yes!"

Satisfied, he grabbed his spear and headed out—his immediate destination the dense bush he'd spotted a hundred yards or so north of the cave. He hoped he'd find some wildlife there.

Outside the cave, he paused to observe the smoke and was alarmed to see it wasn't as unnoticeable as he'd hoped. Against the clear, blue sky, it was quite noticeable to him. "Damnation!" he cursed.

He debated whether to go back and douse the flames, or at least remove some of the wood he'd added to the fire. "To hell with it!" he said. His desire for a cooked meal outweighed his security concerns, so he headed toward the bush. He ran fast, aware time was against him. "Somehow, I have to spear a fish or a bird, or anything that bloody moves, and get back before the damned fire goes out!" he reminded himself.

He was puffing by the time he reached the trees.

John couldn't stop grinning as he turned a brush turkey over on the makeshift spit he'd fashioned above his cooking fire. After setting out from the cave, he'd almost immediately stumbled across not one but a pair of turkeys. They'd been engaged in some kind of mating ritual, or so it seemed to their stalker, and the bigger of the two—presumably the male—didn't even see John's spear until it was too late.

The Irishman had returned to the cave with his trophy bird shortly before dusk and, as it turned out, long before the cooking fire was in any danger of dying out. On approaching the cave, he'd been pleased to see the amount of smoke coming from it was barely detectable, to his eyes at least. Certainly it couldn't have been seen unless someone was looking for it, and then only if they were within fifty yards of the cave.

Now that it was dark, he knew he was safe. The smoke couldn't be seen in the night sky, and the fire was far enough back from the cave's entrance its flames couldn't be seen by anyone unless they were standing directly outside the cave.

John found he was almost trembling with excitement as he prepared to eat his first hot meal in a long time. "My first home-cooked meal since . . ." He tried to remember his last home-cooked meal. Then it came to him. "Since Molly," he smiled. Molly Bourke was the insatiable wife of an Irish industrialist who had taken to entertaining John when her husband was away on business. He smiled at the memory. "Ah, Molly. Where are you now?" She'd provided his last home-cooked meal before he'd been jailed for stealing from his employer.

While waiting for the turkey, he enjoyed an entrée of mussels, which he'd collected from the beach that morning. At the same time, he prepared a side dish of raspberries he'd picked after killing the turkey. He placed these in his wooden bowl. The inside of the bowl had been permanently blackened as a result of the use he'd put it to earlier, but was otherwise none the worse for wear. He guessed its original owners had crafted it from extremely hard wood.

Finally, after poking the turkey with the edge of a sharp seashell, he deemed it ready to eat. He removed it from the fire and laid it down on a palm frond. The sight of the bronzed bird, and the beautiful smell, literally made him drool.

Using the same shell as a carving knife, he carved one of the turkey's legs off. It came away with very little effort on his part. He tried to pick it up, but it was too hot. "Ouch!" He dropped the leg and blew on his burnt fingers to cool them. "Serve me right. Let it rest." And so he left the cooked turkey to rest—as he knew all the best chefs did.

Finally, when the meat had cooled sufficiently for him to touch it, he enjoyed his first mouthful.

Later, by the light of the still burning fire, John reclined on the sleeveless, fur-lined cloak he'd found at the Goenpul encampment. It had proven to be a more-than-useful find, serving as a makeshift mattress on the warmer nights and as a blanket on the cooler nights; it even served as a raincoat on those rare occasions it rained.

The Irishman couldn't remember when he'd last felt so satisfied. His turkey dinner had been cooked to perfection, even if he said so himself, and he'd savoured every mouthful. He'd resisted the urge to eat the entire bird, knowing that the uneaten portions would serve nicely as cold meals for the next day or two. Even so, having devoured almost half the turkey, his belly felt full. Pleasantly full.

Feeling another familiar urge, he reached into his shirt pocket and pulled out the crumpled page he'd so often referred to. He quickly selected a verse from Keats's *Lamia*—one of the few he hadn't yet memorised—and, by the light of the fire, began reading aloud. "She was a gordian shape of dazzling hue, vermilion-spotted, golden, green, and blue," he said. "Striped like a zebra, freckled like a pard, eyed like a peacock, and all crimson barr'd. And full of silver moons, that, as she breathed, dissolv'd, or brighter shone, or interwreathed. Their lustres with the gloomier tapestries, so rainbow-sided, touch'd with miseries." Pausing only to burp, he continued, "She seem'd, at once, some penanced lady elf, some demon's mistress, or the demon's self."

Suddenly too tired to continue reading, he folded the page and safely returned it to his pocket then returned his attention to the fire's flames. How he wished he could take the fire with him when he resumed his trek north. He found the flames so comforting, he was tempted to remain in the cave another day or two so that he could enjoy it longer, but he dismissed that thought almost as soon as he'd had it. "Need to keep moving," he reminded himself. "I have a ship to catch."

His mind made up, he added the last of the wood to the fire, so determined was he to extract every little bit of pleasure from it. He was asleep before he knew it.

In the warmth of the cave, John enjoyed his best night's sleep since leaving Ireland. It was a sleep filled with dreams—pleasant dreams—of his homeland and people he'd known.

One dream was so real that when he thought about it later, he wasn't sure if he'd really been dreaming. It had taken him back to Dundalk, in County Louth, Ireland, to the day he'd first met Molly Bourke, the industrialist's wife.

It was nearing the end of his working day, and he was delivering a cart-load of steel railings to the Bourkes' stately home on the outskirts of Dundalk. He'd expected the industrialist to take delivery of them, but was greeted by Molly who advised him her husband had been called away on business.

John had been taken with red-headed Molly from the outset. He was especially taken with her voluptuous figure. Although middle-aged, she'd retained her youthfulness—and she'd retained her passion for young men. She liked the look of John as soon as she saw him, and she made no secret of that.

It didn't take long before the young man found himself in Mister and Missus Bourke's bedroom. Molly had enticed him there by informing him she had a job she wanted him to attend to upstairs. Not that he needed much enticing. Once there, she attacked him with such passion he was momentarily taken aback, but only momentarily.

That first late afternoon interlude started on the large four-poster bed in one corner of the room and ended on a Persian rug in the hallway outside the room. Exactly what had transpired between the bed and the rug neither could clearly recall, but they'd both enjoyed the experience so much they agreed to repeat it sometime.

Sometime became once or twice a week at least. Their secret trysts were facilitated by Mister Bourke's frequent business trips, which more often than not took him away to England.

Unfortunately, it turned out their trysts weren't so secret. Nosy neighbours noticed John's comings and goings, and one duly reported her suspicions to Molly's husband. When confronted, both Molly and John denied any impropriety.

Molly feigned disgust that her husband would believe a neighbour ahead of his loving wife, while John's case was helped in no small way by the fact he regularly had to deliver supplies the industrialist had ordered from his workplace. Even so, the lusty pair had to exercise greater discretion thereafter.

John now made unofficial visits to the Bourkes' estate after dark to minimise the risk of being found out. That worked for a couple of months—until the suspicious husband cut short a business trip and returned to find John and Molly fast asleep in his four-poster bed.

Mister Bourke, a keen shot with a pistol, challenged John to a duel, and only some stern talking by the local constabulary convinced the older man that that wasn't a wise course of action for so prominent a citizen to be seen to be involved in. A merciful outcome for John who had never even fired a pistol let alone fought a duel.

The matter was settled when John promised to stay away from the Bourkes' estate and Molly promised to remain faithful. Neither promise was kept, and it was only

John's imprisonment for theft and his subsequent transportation to Australia that finally separated the two lovers.

John woke at the point in his dream that he was arrested on suspicion of theft and thrown into Dundalk's cells. The dream had been so real he had to look around to confirm he wasn't in fact in a prison cell.

Embers from the cooking fire still glowed, providing enough light for John to confirm he was indeed a long way from Dundalk. The memories of his liaisons with the sensual, red-headed Molly came flooding back, bringing a smile to his face. He drifted back to sleep, still smiling.

34

WINTER WAS RAPIDLY HEADING TO spring, and the days were predictably warming as John trekked ever northwards.

A month had passed since he had encountered the last sign of human life—the smouldering campfire he'd stumbled upon—and he had no idea how far he'd come since then. Even more depressingly, he'd yet to see a single ship. He hadn't sighted so much as a distant sail, and was beginning to wonder whether ships did venture into these waters.

In the past month, he had changed his routine, staying put in the one place for several days at a time, and, in one case, remaining at the same location for an entire week. His rationale was that he was no less likely to sight a ship if he stayed put than if he kept walking—especially if his hideout offered a good view of the shoreline. Other advantages of his new routine were it was less tiring—in theory at least—and it allowed more time to discover the best food sources in the immediate vicinity.

In the two months since he'd escaped Moreton Bay, the coastal terrain had changed little. Until now, that is. Now the scenery, here on the coast at least, could only be described as indescribably beautiful.

He didn't know it, of course, but he'd reached the region that would one day be named *the Sunshine Coast*. Miles of unbroken, white-sand beaches were separated by bays even more picturesque than those he'd encountered earlier; behind the palm trees standing guard like sentries above the beaches, stands of gum trees gave way to rainforests more lush than any he'd seen before; and inland, the hills now resembled mountains, so high and craggy were they.

If the first month hadn't been kind to John, the second month had been even less kind. Since filling his belly with the brush turkey he'd cooked on a spit a month ago, he'd eaten poorly. Wild game had unaccountably proven more elusive than ever, limiting his diet in the main to nuts, berries, yams, grubs and mussels. He was only just getting over a bad bout of the flu, and he'd been struck down by yet another bout of food poisoning—this time the consequence of eating a raw pigeon. As a result, he'd lost even more weight and was weaker than ever.

So skinny and undernourished was he now, he'd taken to wearing his fur-lined cloak day and night, and this despite the warming temperatures.

For John, one day merged with the next, and the weeks became a blur. He had given up on recording the passing of days on his spear, so he'd lost track of time. If he had to guess, it was mid-August, but it was in fact only a few days shy of September, the first official day of spring.

Today had started like any other. He'd risen early and foraged for mussels in the rock pools on the beach. Finding barely enough for his first meal of the day, he then struck off inland, intent on finding game.

By mid-morning, he hadn't sighted any game—nothing close enough to spear or catch at least—and he was beginning to lose heart. "I have to eat soon or I'm a dead man," he muttered.

Stay positive, boyo!

Despite his weariness and his inability to think straight, the Irishman was aware he was becoming more and more negative about everything. He willed himself to think positive thoughts, but it was a losing battle. Loneliness, hunger and exhaustion, along with bouts of illness, conspired to beat him down. He was losing hope and he knew it.

John entered a gully. It led him deep into a hillside. He followed it in the hope he'd find a fish in one of the freshwater pools along the way.

As he walked, he looked around, studying the terrain. That was something he did a lot these days for he hadn't been able to shake the feeling he was being followed, and, as always, he thought of Barega. "Surely the tracker's given up on me by now." He glanced behind him yet again. "I must be a hundred miles from Moreton Bay by now."

In reality, he was only seventy miles from the penal settlement, so slow had been his progress of late. That was seventy miles as the crow flies. In reality he'd walked a couple of hundred miles since his escape, heading inland on occasion and even back-tracking a few times.

A hundred yards further along the gulley, something made him look to his right. There, on a bluff overlooking the gully, not thirty yards away, stood a dingo. It was staring straight at him.

He recognised it immediately as the same dingo that stole his raw turkey a month or so back, and likely the same one that had tracked him a day or so later. Its distinctive markings were hard to miss: half its right ear was missing, and the reddish-coloured mark on its back left no doubt it was the same wild dog.

Man and beast stood and stared at each other for a long time. Finally, the dingo turned and disappeared into the rainforest that bordered the gully. Only then, as it departed, did John identify the dingo as a male. He tried to come up with a name for him, but could think of nothing that would suit. So he settled on the name *Dingo*.

John continued on his way. Rounding a corner, he encountered a large monitor lizard, half asleep and sunning itself on a rock. He approached it as close as he dared and then raised his spear.

Stay still, my beauty.

He unleashed his spear, and gave a yell of delight as the weapon found its mark. The big lizard, now fully awake, reared up on its hind legs, hissing and pawing at the air with its front claws. In no time, it lay dead at John's feet.

John removed his spear, slung the reptile's carcass over his shoulders and set off back toward his coastal campsite. As he walked, he became aware he was being followed. The Irishman glanced behind him and wasn't overly surprised to see the dingo trailing him. He stopped and the dingo stopped. "You planning to steal my food again, Dingo?" he asked.

The dingo, which was around forty yards away, tilted its head slightly to one side, as if trying to make sense of the question.

John chuckled to himself and resumed walking. The Irishman didn't need to look around again to confirm Dingo was still following him. He found the companionship, such as it was, strangely comforting. The dingo, after all, represented the first companionship of any kind that he'd had in over two months. It felt like they were almost kindred spirits.

Two solitary creatures making our way through life . . . trying to survive.

As John and his newfound companion walked along the gully in the northern half of New South Wales, Helen was being courted by Lieutenant Hogan many miles to the south, in Sydney Town.

The lieutenant, who was on sick leave whilst rehabilitating after the operation on his shattered leg, had sailed south to visit Helen as soon as he was sufficiently mobile. Now on crutches, and, according to the army's head surgeon, likely to walk with a limp for the rest of his life, he had timed his visit to coincide with a weekend to be sure his heart's desire was free to see him.

They were sitting on a blanket on a hillside overlooking the harbour, and were eating a picnic lunch Helen had prepared at the insistence of her benefactor, Thelma Brown. The kindly woman's husband had even provided a bottle of wine to go with the picnic.

Missus Brown had been so enamoured with Hogan when Helen introduced her to him, she offered to accompany them on the picnic. To the lieutenant's dismay, Helen supported the idea, and only some fast talking by him had persuaded the women that three could be a crowd.

Now, alone with Hogan, Helen found to her surprise she was happy he had talked her into a picnic. She was feeling more at ease with him than she'd have thought possible. Sensing the lieutenant's eyes on her, she looked at him squarely and asked, "What is on your mind, Desmond Hogan?"

Hogan smiled and brushed a strand of loose hair from Helen's forehead. "If you knew that, you might send me packing," he smiled.

Helen averted her face too late to avoid letting Hogan see she was blushing.

"I caught you," he chuckled.

"What?"

"I caught you blushing."

"Nonsense," she scoffed. "I always turn pink in the Australian sun." She and her companion both laughed.

Hogan took the open wine bottle from the picnic basket and topped up Helen's glass. Looking at her, he said, "I think you know what is on my mind, Helen."

"Yes," she said with a frankness that surprised him, "I think I do."

They touched glasses and drank some more.

Helen continued, "But I need to hear it from you."

Hogan was momentarily taken aback. He hadn't expected the conversation to progress to this point so early in proceedings. In planning for this long overdue visit, he'd rehearsed what he wanted to say to Helen so many times he could quote it from heart. And so he did. "Helen . . . I . . . You know how I feel about you . . ." he ventured. When Helen didn't respond, he continued, "I have thought of nothing else since . . . no-one else . . . since you left Moreton Bay. I know beyond doubt I want to spend the rest of my life with you . . ."

Helen had never been one for beating around the bush. Her father had instilled that in her. That's why she'd initiated this frank discussion with Hogan. Now that she'd taken that step, she was starting to regret it. Even though she was feeling more and more at ease in the lieutenant's company, she still wasn't totally sure how she really felt about him. She remembered how she'd felt when she kissed John Graham, and this was nothing like that. She could still feel John's lips on hers, and she could still see his mesmerising blue eyes.

With Hogan she suddenly felt everything was moving a little too fast for her liking. She had her career to think of. Teaching was her life now, and she still wasn't sure where the ardent lieutenant fitted in with her plans, or even *if* he fitted in with her plans. Besides, she wasn't at all certain she wanted to be a soldier's wife. She had observed her mother's life, and felt that she wanted more.

Sensing Helen was distracted, Hogan asked, "Helen? Are you listening?"

"Of course," she assured him. "That was very sweet."

"Sweet?" Hogan scowled. "I wasn't trying to be sweet. I was trying to be serious."

Helen could see her companion was annoyed. At the risk of further spoiling the mood, she quickly changed the subject, asking, "Did they ever find John Graham?"

"No they never found him!" Hogan snapped. "But they will." Annoyed beyond words to have been reminded of the Irish fugitive at such a time, he drained his glass, corked the wine bottle and stood up. Looking down at Helen, he said, "I think we had better go."

Without argument, Helen packed up the picnic, folded the blanket and followed her companion to the horse-drawn cart that awaited them nearby. Hogan helped her up onto the cart and then, grasping the reins, joined her atop it.

The journey back to the Browns' residence was made in silence. It was a deafening silence.

That night, after eating some raw portions of the monitor lizard he had speared earlier, John pulled his fur-lined cloak about him as he lay down to sleep in a bush clearing. He'd been feeling out of sorts these past couple of days and so had decided against trekking through the night, opting instead to stay put and catch some extra sleep.

He had no sooner laid down than he experienced another of those déjà vu moments: a deadly black snake appeared, seemingly from nowhere, and crawled over his outstretched legs. In the moonlight, he clearly identified it—beyond doubt this time—as a highly venomous red-bellied black snake.

This time, it crawled over his knees, not under his raised knee as the last one had, and this time, fortunately, John didn't jump. He lay there, frozen, holding his breath, until the snake slid on by. When it disappeared into the bushes beyond, he resumed breathing. He couldn't believe his good luck. Nor could he believe he'd nearly fallen victim to another snake.

So much for lightning never striking twice.

John also couldn't believe how calm he'd remained. He'd always hated snakes, and his time in the wilderness had done nothing to lessen his hatred, or his fear, of them.

He debated whether to relocate to a safer place. The decision was made for him when it started raining. Soft at first, it was soon pelting down. "Damn!" he cursed. "What does a man have to do to get a good night's sleep here?" He collected his spear and shoulder bag, and his trusty tomahawk, and headed out to find a cave or some other shelter.

The Irishman found himself in a gorge. It was similar to the gully he'd followed earlier, only deeper. Cliffs pressed in close on either side of him, and he felt confident he'd find a cave sooner or later. That was if he could see it. It was almost pitch dark down here, and the torrential rain further reduced what little visibility there was.

He followed a dry riverbed through the gorge. At least it had been dry before the rain started. Now it was waterlogged, and what began as a trickle soon became a small stream.

After ten minutes without sighting a cave, or anything that would provide shelter, John was starting to worry. The small stream he'd been wading through was flowing faster by the minute. He was now waist-deep in water and he had to work hard to make any progress against the current.

It wasn't long before he began to fear for his life.

I need to get to higher ground!

He searched desperately for a way out, but the cliffs on both sides of the gorge were sheer.

Should I try to go back?

John realised he couldn't fight against the current, so he turned back and began retracing his steps. He was now up to his chest in water, and in danger of being swept away.

The Irishman heard it before he saw it: a surge of water coming down the gorge. It sounded like the roar of a dozen steam engines. In the darkness, John could barely make out the white foam that accompanied the new menace. It seemed to him as high as a three-storeyed building. He wasn't to know a billabong on the cliff-top a hundred yards behind him had burst its banks, sending thousands of tons of water cascading into the already waterlogged gorge. Now it bore down on him like a tsunami.

When the cascade reached him, it enveloped him with a ferocity he could never have imagined. The next minute felt like a lifetime. He couldn't tell which way was up and which way was down. The current hurled him along the gorge, bouncing him off rocks like a rag doll. He swallowed so much water he thought he must surely die. In fact, he wasn't sure he wasn't already dead.

Mercifully, the torrent delivered him to the point where he'd entered the gorge, unceremoniously dumping him onto the open ground. The water quickly spread out over the open countryside, forming pools and small streams, but posing no further threat.

Bruised all over from the battering he'd taken, John could only lie there, gasping and coughing for a long, long time. And still the torrential rain fell.

Only now did he realise the floodwaters had stripped him of all his possessions. All but his breeches and his boots. Gone were his shirt, his cloak, his shoulder bag, spear and tomahawk. As the realisation set in, he began cursing. First, he cursed the rain and the floodwater. Then he cursed his stupidity for entering a gully during a rainstorm. Finally, he cursed his luck.

When he ran out of things to curse, he cried. He cried for the friends and family he'd lost. He cried for the God he'd never known. Most of all, he cried for the life he'd never have.

As it so often happens in the winterless north, the day following the storm dawned clear and sunny. John had somehow managed to catch some sleep after his near-death experience. He'd located a semi-dry space on high ground between two huge fallen trees, and had curled up there to see out the storm. It hadn't been long before exhaustion overtook him and he slept.

Despite having slept, John felt battle weary as he emerged from his shelter to face the new day. The realisation he'd lost his possessions bothered him much more than the bruises he'd received. "What the hell do I do now?" he asked himself. The very thought of trying to survive in this hostile wilderness without his cloak and his hunting weapons filled him with dread.

Drawing on his inner strength, or what was left of it, he forced himself to face up to his latest problems.

First things first, Graham. You need to eat.

Determined to survive, he set off in search of yams and grubs and anything else that would sustain him. As he searched, he was unaware he was being observed from the nearby cliff-top by Dingo, the wild dog that seemed to have adopted him.

PART THREE

THE
HOMECOMING

35

THE ROCKY LEDGE JOHN OCCUPIED offered uninterrupted views up and down the coast. It was situated near the top of a sheer cliff that rose several hundred feet above the sea. Behind the ledge was a sheltered crevice, which had served as the Irishman's home for the past week.

Seabirds, which roosted on the cliffs along this part of the coast, constantly dive-bombed the human trespasser, but he took no notice of them.

John was in bad shape. Since fleeing Moreton Bay, he'd never been at a lower ebb. Mentally and emotionally, he was jaded and depressed, and had all but given up; physically, he was a shadow of his old self and was hardly recognisable as the strong, fit convict who had escaped from the quarry and outwitted his pursuers three long months ago.

The fugitive hadn't recovered from the near-death experience he had in the flooded gorge a month earlier. Much time had been lost trying to replace the tools and clothes he'd been stripped of in that frightening incident—time he would normally have devoted to food-gathering and resting up. As it was, he had managed to make another spear for himself, and a shoulder bag, too, but he hadn't been able to replace his tomahawk or the shirt and cloak he'd lost. These had been replaced by a makeshift cloak he'd fashioned from palm fronds, ferns and leaves. So flimsy was it, the ferns and leaves had to be replaced every few days.

Worst of all, he'd been struck down by illness, and it was taking all his strength just to get through each day. Hence his decision to stay put for a while when he'd found the crevice he was now holed up in. He had suffered a recurrence of the flu he'd come down with, and the after-effects of that were still lingering. More alarmingly, one of the hands he'd blistered when trying to make fire had belatedly become infected, and that had put him out of action for several days. As luck would have it, it was his right hand, which made completing simple tasks more problematic than usual.

As a result of those setbacks, and a few more besides, he now looked like a man waiting to die, and that's exactly how he felt, too.

John leaned forward and looked down at the ocean waves crashing onto the rocks far below. He didn't have to lean forward far as he was right on the edge of the ledge.

Death by suicide.

The thought of ending his life had come to him quite frequently in recent days. Until now, he'd always pushed it from his mind immediately, but today for some reason it wouldn't go away.

Is this what my life has come to? Debating whether to live or die. And not a soul knows let alone cares.

A seagull, whose roost was very close by, dive-bombed the Irishman, startling him. Suddenly fearful—not of the gull, but of his suicidal thoughts—he pushed himself back from the edge of the ledge. "Get a grip, man!" he chastised himself. "Stop wallowing in self-pity."

Still on his haunches, he manoeuvred himself backwards into the sheltered crevice. Here, though it was open at the top, a large, protruding rock above his head protected him from the elements. Fortunately, it hadn't rained since he had taken up residency here.

Now that he was safely back from the ledge, he came to a decision. "Time to move on," he coaxed himself.

He'd stayed here longer than he should have. Part of that had been out of necessity, for he desperately needed to rest up, but part had been out of the malaise that had overtaken him of late, and he knew it was time to pull himself together.

That he had survived so long in the Australian wilderness was nothing short of a miracle. He should have died several times over. The fact he had survived against such overwhelming odds was a credit to his endurance, his determination and his ability to adapt to ever-changing circumstances. However, the fact he'd gotten through these past few weeks was more down to good luck than good management.

Ill, starving and near death, he had made a couple of fortuitous discoveries. Firstly, he had stumbled across new sources of food in the form of emu eggs and macadamia nuts—both highly nutritious foods. The eggs he'd discovered in an emu's nest on the plateau behind the cliffs he now occupied; the nuts he'd found on the ground beneath a grove of macadamia trees in the rainforest bordering the same plateau. These discoveries couldn't have come at a better time. Emu eggs are high in protein, calories, vitamins, minerals and fatty acids while macadamia nuts are extremely high in calories, vitamins, antioxidants, nutrients and minerals essential for peak health. For someone in John's state, he'd have been hard-pressed to have found two better food-types.

Secondly, he'd found a safe, comfortable resting place, close to a supply of fresh water. The views it offered also ensured if there was a vessel anywhere within twenty miles of the coastline, he would see it. Unfortunately, he hadn't seen a sign of a sail—a fact that had done nothing for the state of morbidity he'd spiralled into.

Now that he'd come to the decision to move on, he was feeling slightly better about himself. And so, he gathered up his few remaining possessions, quit the shelter that had served him so well and climbed to the plateau above.

A glance at the sun told him it was mid-morning. It was warm, too. Spring time brings with it summer-like temperatures in this part of the world, and for that he was thankful. If he'd had to contend with cold weather through his recent illness, he was in no doubt he'd have died. Now it was so warm he didn't need the leafy cloak he wore, and he would have dispensed with it if it hadn't been for the fact it helped prevent his shoulders and torso from becoming sunburnt.

On the plateau, he set off to the north, making his way through a maze of ant hills as he headed toward a path he'd spotted earlier. Gone was the spring in his step that he'd always been able to rely on. His legs felt heavy, and just placing one foot in front of the other was an effort. He was soon sweating.

The path he was heading for led down to a rocky bay where he hoped to find mussels and other seafood. Between him and the path stood a stand of gum trees. As he made his way through the trees, he noticed the trunk of one of them had been ring-barked. Close inspection told him that could only have been done by a human. No other animal, or natural phenomenon, could have stripped the tree of its bark so symmetrically.

Blacks!

John resumed walking, alert for more signs of human life. It wasn't long before he found them.

Not a hundred yards from the ring-barked tree, he came across a vacated Aboriginal encampment. A broken spear, a damaged boomerang and the indistinguishable bones of some animal, or animals, lay scattered in the ashes of an old campfire.

The Irishman looked around for any useful items he could commandeer. Finding none, he continued his trek, ever-watchful.

As John headed north, Barega was only fifteen miles away, nearing the entrance to the gorge where his quarry had almost drowned a month earlier. The tracker's all-seeing eyes surveyed the terrain, and he quickly ascertained the area had been flooded in recent times. What little grass there was had been flattened, while all around bushes and plants lay bent, broken and twisted.

Barega hadn't given up on finding the Irishman. At every opportunity, he'd trekked north in search of some sign that John had survived. This was the farthest north he had ventured yet in his hunt for the fugitive.

Something caught his eye amongst rocks a little way away from the gorge. He hurried over to the rocks and found the fur-lined cloak John had been stripped of in the torrent. Quick inspection of the garment confirmed it was a pelt cloak of the kind favoured by the Goenpul people.

The tracker was about to continue on his way when he noticed the remains of the spear John had lost in the floodwater. It had snapped in half. Barega picked the weapon up and studied it. He quickly deduced it was too crude a spear to have been made by any Aborigine other than a child perhaps.

Suspecting it may have been made by John, he headed into the gorge where he hoped he would either find his quarry's body or some sign that he'd survived. Preferably the latter as he wanted to find and kill the Irishman himself. This had become personal for him.

John needed to rest even though he'd only set out from his cliff-top shelter a few hours earlier. The steep climb back up to the plateau from the bay he'd trekked down to, to look for shellfish, had left him tuckered out. It hadn't been worth the effort either for the bay's rock pools had yielded no seafood of any kind.

Thirsty, he stopped at the first billabong he came to and drank his fill. When the ripples on the surface disappeared, he studied his reflection and was shocked at the gaunt, haggard, sunburnt face that stared back at him. "Jesus!" he muttered. "It's the wild man of Borneo!" The sunburn reminded him he should make another sun bonnet. He hadn't bothered to replace the one he'd lost in the gorge, but he knew he'd need protection soon as the days were rapidly heating up.

A distant movement amongst the ant hills caught his eye. It had been so quick he thought he may have imagined it.

There it is again!

This time, he recognised it as a dingo. *His* dingo. The reddish markings were readily identifiable even from a distance. He waved to the wild dog. "Dingo!" he shouted. He immediately felt silly for his canine companion was well out of earshot, and, he reminded himself, the dingo wasn't exactly a pet.

John hadn't realised how much he'd missed Dingo. He hadn't seen him since he'd holed up on the cliff-top, and he wondered if the animal had been looking for him.

Something else caught his eye—something much more sinister: above the treetops to the south, a column of smoke rose into the cloudless sky. He estimated it was about a mile away, and one look at it told him it was a cooking fire.

Suddenly energised—his weariness forgotten—he hurried off, anxious to distance himself from whoever it was who had lit the fire.

⚜

It was mid-afternoon before John dared stop. The fugitive was just about spent now, and desperately needed to rest. He was hungry, too, and thirsty.

After drinking from a gently flowing stream—the first waterway of any kind he'd come across since drinking at the billabong—he sat down in the shade of a gum tree, his back against its trunk. His thirst assuaged, he thought about dipping into his meagre food rations. He didn't have to look inside his shoulder bag to know it contained the last of the emu eggs he'd gathered along with half a dozen macadamia nuts and several yams.

Determined to leave the egg for dinner, he selected three of the nuts and two small rocks from his bag. Placing one of the nuts on top of a flat rock he used for this very task, he grasped the other rock and brought it down hard on the nut's sweet spot. That spot was a tiny white dot, which was easy to miss if his aim wasn't accurate. It wasn't accurate in this case, and the nut's hard shell remained intact. "Goddamn it!" he cursed. Lining the nut up again, he brought the rock down harder. Too hard this time, and the nut shattered into tiny pieces that flew in all directions.

When are you going to learn, Graham?

Resigned to having lost that nut, he selected another one. This time, his aim was good, and the shell split open, giving easy access to the delicious meat of the nut. He popped it into his mouth, savouring the taste as he set about cracking open another one.

John ended up eating all the remaining nuts, but they did nothing to diminish his nagging hunger, and he found he couldn't stop thinking about the emu egg. "Damn it!" He gave into his temptation and fished the egg from his bag.

Emu eggs are large, but this one was huge. It was so big it spanned the width of both John's palms when he cradled it in his hands. After removing the long grass he'd wrapped around it for safekeeping, he pulled out a large, sturdy piece of bark that he also kept in his bag. It served as a useful plate on such occasions. Using one of his rocks, he then cracked the egg's greenish shell, taking care not to spill any of its precious contents.

John had seen the Quandamooka drinking the contents of emu eggs from a hole they'd made in the top of the shell. He'd tried to emulate that, but had failed miserably, losing the entire egg. He found the alternative method, while slower, was safer. On this occasion, the egg yolk and egg white combined to fill most of the bark platter.

The Irishman was so engrossed in preparing his meal, he didn't realised he was being observed. When he finally tilted his head back and raised the platter to his mouth, he saw a solitary Aboriginal hunter standing as motionless as a statue to his left, not a stone's throw away.

The native, who appeared to be middle-aged, was staring straight at the white intruder. Wearing only a loin cloth, he held a spear and woomera in one hand while strapped to his back was a nulla nulla. As black as coal, his chest and limbs were decorated by large welts, a result of his being scarified by cutting his flesh in the tradition of his tribe. From a cord tied around his waist hung half a dozen small pelts, the result of his latest hunting expedition no doubt.

John was so surprised to see another human being—the first he'd sighted in over three months—he dropped his platter, spilling its contents onto the dry earth.

Still the hunter didn't move. Nor did he take his eyes off John.

The squawk of an eagle finally prompted the Aborigine to avert his gaze and look skyward. John followed the other's gaze and saw he'd been distracted by a wedge-tailed eagle soaring just above the treetops. It was close enough for its distinctive wedge-shaped tail and its feathered legs to be clearly seen.

John looked back only to see the hunter had disappeared. It was as if he'd never been there.

I only looked away for an instant.

He wondered if he'd been seeing things.

Suddenly spooked, he pushed himself to his feet, gathered up his spear and his meagre belongings and hurried off, keen to distance himself from where he'd seen the native.

He hadn't gone more than a few yards when he pulled up. Still not sure he hadn't imagined what he had just witnessed, he returned to where he'd seen, or thought he'd seen, the hunter standing just a few moments earlier.

Footprints on the dusty ground confirmed he hadn't imagined it. Really worried now, he took off, his weariness forgotten for the moment.

⊰────⊱

Heat, thirst and sheer exhaustion had reduced John to a slow walking pace. He'd

221

headed directly inland to distance himself from where he sighted the Aborigine, and the route had taken him through dry, scrubby country with nary a stream nor billabong in sight.

He was desperate for water, so finding the lifesaving fluid was now his first and only priority.

Another hour passed before he came across a billabong. He was so thirsty and over-heated by now that he flopped face-first into it. On surfacing, he sat there, in water up to his chin, gulping down mouthfuls to quench his thirst.

In no time, he felt revived. "Ah, true bliss," he murmured. He gulped down some more water then closed his eyes and raised his face to the sun, luxuriating in the feeling of its warmth on his face. The sun's warmth contrasted beautifully with the coolness of the water.

When he finally opened his eyes, he started when he saw the same Aboriginal hunter staring at him on the billabong's opposite bank. The hunter's spear was raised, and it was aimed at him. Then, one by one, a dozen more hunters appeared, as if by magic, from out of the surrounding scrub and joined their companion. Like him, all were scarified with raised welts covering their limbs and torsos. Bearded and naked except for their loin cloths, they were a fearsome sight. All brandished spears or other traditional weapons, and, if the startled Irishman wasn't mistaken, they looked ready to use them.

36

JOHN HAD NO WAY OF knowing the hunters confronting him were members of the Kabi, the area's predominant tribe. Nor could he know the Kabi, or Kabi Kabi as they were sometimes called, had never seen a European before. If he had known that, he'd have understood the startled expressions on the faces of those before him.

Though the Kabi had observed the white man's ships sailing past their shores for some years now, they'd yet to see any of the passengers or crew of those strange vessels as they had never ventured close to shore. Not in their territory at least.

John's heart was beating faster than ever before. Faster even than when Molly Bourke's irate husband had discovered him with his wife and challenged him to a duel. Realising his life probably depended on what he did next, he slowly stood up and raised his hands to signify his surrender.

The nearest hunter, a big, raw-boned native armed with a stone nulla nulla, took this to be an act of aggression and leapt at John. His leap brought him to within striking distance of his target, and he brought the club down savagely. The nulla nulla was aimed at John's head. If it had landed squarely, it would surely have crushed his skull. As it was, the Irishman leaned to his left just in time, and the club smashed into his right shoulder, almost breaking it. The force of the blow rendered him unconscious, and he sank beneath the water's surface. His attacker raised his club for the death strike, but a word from one of his companions—the same hunter John had seen earlier—prompted him to hold off. Instead, he reached out with his other hand, grabbed a handful of his victim's long hair and pulled him over to the bank.

Only after he'd been hauled onto the grass did John start to come round. The world around him seemed to be spinning. His shoulder hurt so much he was certain it was broken, and his head hurt, too. While his evasive action had saved his life, the club had grazed his head, leaving a nasty gash above his right ear. Blood flowed freely from the wound.

Only now did he become aware of the hunters around him. Staring down at him, their faces were pressed so close to him that he couldn't see the sky. They seemed to be highly excited and were all talking, or shouting, at once.

John couldn't make head nor tail of what they were saying, but judging by their aggressive expressions and the way they brandished their weapons, they were debating whether to kill him now or later.

Or whether to kill me quickly or slowly perhaps.

The middle-aged hunter who had given John a stay of execution motioned to the captive to stand up.

Using his good arm, John painfully pushed himself to his feet. He stood there, swaying, as the hunters began poking his white skin with their fingers as if to determine that he was real and not an apparition. This sparked more debate.

Finally, the hunters forced him to start walking back toward the coast. They followed close behind their captive, prodding him with their spears and chattering excitedly amongst themselves in the language of the Kabi.

As he stumbled along, frightened for his life and still only half conscious, John didn't notice Dingo following a couple of hundred yards behind.

The shadows were lengthening by the time the hunters and their captive arrived at the Kabis' campsite.

Even before they arrived, John could tell it was home to a fair number of people. Smoke from twenty or more cooking fires could be seen rising above the treetops, and the laughter of children carried to him.

The captive, who had been stripped of his leafy cloak and now wore only his boots and breeches, could hear a didgeridoo being played. The musical instrument's earthy, meditative sound was unmistakable. He'd heard Aborigines playing didgeridoos at Parramatta on occasion. Now, the traditional instrument's unique and constant tones were being carried through the trees on a gentle sea breeze. The sound merged with another that he couldn't quite identify. Then he realised it was the sound of waves lapping up onto an unseen beach, which he guessed was only fifty yards or so away.

John wasn't quite prepared for what he saw when he was finally marched into the encampment. It appeared to be home to around eighty natives—men, women and children. They were going about their everyday lives. At least they had been until the white stranger appeared in their midst.

The menfolk had been performing various tasks ranging from skinning animals they'd killed and repairing fishing nets to making weapons and constructing, or reconstructing, bivouacs; the womenfolk had been tending the cooking fires or looking after the younger children; and the older children had been running around, as children everywhere do, and playing games.

That all changed when they saw the white man.

For the members of this Kabi clan, life as they knew it changed at that moment in time. The children, who were all naked, screamed and ran, panic-stricken, to their mothers; the women, some of whom were also naked, seemed almost as frightened and many of them retreated into their bivouacs; and the men, who wore loincloths or animal skin coverings, appeared as nonplussed as their fellow hunters had been when they first saw John.

To the Irishman's eyes, these Aborigines looked quite different to those he'd seen at Moreton Bay and at Parramatta before that. The Kabi, especially the men, appeared wild and primitive. Yet they had a certain warrior-like nobility about them at the same time—most noticeable in the proud way they carried themselves. And, like the hunters who had captured him, they were all bearded and scarified. Even the teenage boys, it seemed, had undergone scarification. John noticed the welts on a few of them were still red and raw.

The clan members' dwellings, he observed, looked similar to those he'd seen when he stumbled upon the Goenpuls' campsite. They were a motley collection of bivouacs and lean-tos fashioned from driftwood, tree branches, ferns and palm fronds. The whole site had a temporary look to it, and he guessed these people, like others of their race, were nomadic.

John wasn't to know the encampment was home to one of the Kabi's largest clans. His estimate that it accommodated around eighty people was a bit light. It was, in fact, home to close to a hundred. At least twenty men and teenage boys were away hunting and fishing, and they would drift in over the next day or two, returning the clan to full strength.

The clan had once numbered more than two hundred, but starvation, illness and conflict with other tribes—and conflict with other Kabi clans on occasion—had reduced its numbers over the past couple of decades.

One who remembered the good old days, when the clan was at its strongest and most influential, was Mirritji, one of the senior elders, and it was he who strode forward on his impossibly bowed but still sprightly legs to greet the hunters and their captive. "Where did you find the white spirit?" he asked. Mirritji's question was directed at the hunters, but, like everyone else in the camp, he only had eyes for the white stranger.

Observing the elder with the bowed legs, John wondered if this was the man who would decide his fate. He knew enough about Aborigines to know theirs was an egalitarian society in which everyone was equal. However, he was astute enough to realise certain individuals would hold more sway than others—and if he had to bet the old man standing before him was one of those.

The middle-aged hunter who had first seen John said, "We found him in the billabong where the girl drowned." He referred to the unfortunate drowning of Mirritji's youngest granddaughter the previous summer, so the elder immediately knew which watering hole his opposite referred to.

By now a crowd was starting to gather around John and his escort of hunters. Clan members pressed forward, anxious to get a good look at the man their spokesman had referred to as the *white spirit*.

Men and teenage boys touched and prodded John, just as the hunters had done when they'd captured him. He grimaced with pain as someone prodded his injured right shoulder a little too enthusiastically.

Emboldened, some of the women emerged from their bivouacs, dragging their children with them for a closer look.

One young mother who preferred to observe from afar, for the moment at least, was Mamba who remained in her bivouac with her two young boys. Since losing her beloved husband Moilow in a skirmish with enemies of the Kabi almost a year earlier, the handsome woman with sparkling brown eyes and fine features had lost her confidence, and so kept to herself when anything out of the ordinary happened. And today's event was certainly out of the ordinary. So, from the privacy of her humble dwelling, Mamba kept a tight hold on her sons Murrowdooling and Carravanty as the menfolk decided what to do with the white spirit that had appeared in their midst.

Throughout all this, John was only just keeping it all together. If it wasn't for the two hunters now supporting him, he'd have fallen to the ground. The blow to his head had left him dazed and bloodied, and his right shoulder was now completely numb. Worse, he felt as though he was in a dream—as if he was out of his body and watching someone else being harangued, prodded and poked by savages.

This can't be happening.

The same big, raw-boned hunter who had damn near crushed John's skull with his club grabbed him by the hair and began shouting questions at him, demanding answers and becoming ever more irate when the captive remained mute. The fact that John couldn't remotely understand him did not for one moment enter his mind. Losing his patience, he cuffed John over the head, dazing him and almost causing him to black out.

If John survived this ordeal, he would learn the big native's name was Turo, a fearsome warrior who had killed more men than he could remember. He was covered in battle scars—the most prominent being a nasty welt on one shoulder, a result of his being caught up in the same skirmish that had claimed the life of his good friend Moilow.

As John's head cleared and he was able to think more clearly, he realised a fiery debate had broken out amongst the men. It seemed every man in the encampment had something to say about the white stranger in their midst. Several appeared ready to come to blows. The belligerent Turo, John noticed, was to the fore.

An impressive-looking young warrior stepped forward. The others addressed him as Gabirri. He stared at the captive through deep-set, intelligent eyes.

John returned Gabirri's stare. He'd noticed that until now, the young warrior had said little, preferring to observe what was going on and keep his own counsel.

Gabirri touched John's chest, as if to confirm he was real, and then turned to the nearest of John's captors. "Why did you bring the white spirit here?" he asked.

"Because that was our wish," the hunter, a young man, simply stated. The young hunter grinned sheepishly, revealing all but one of his front teeth were missing, a result of an altercation with another young buck.

"The white spirit brings bad luck!" Gabirri said with more than a touch of impatience.

"Gabirri speaks the truth," Turo said. Looking around at John, he added, "We must burn him."

The elderly Mirritji began to protest, but he was drowned out as Turo and the other hunters seized John and dragged him toward the nearest cooking fire.

Only now did the Irishman realise what was in store for him. Terrified, he began struggling to try to free himself from the iron grip of those holding him. The sight of women piling more driftwood onto the fire caused him to struggle even more violently. Still he couldn't shake off the men holding him. He could only watch, horrified, as the fire took and flames leapt skyward.

The hunters pushed their captive to the ground alongside the fire—so close that its heat caused John to grimace. Two of them then tied his hands and feet as they would a carcass they were about to barbecue.

Looking on, Turo nodded to the same two hunters to pick the white man up and throw him onto the fire. One of them immediately grabbed John by the wrists and the other grasped his ankles. By now, all the assembled, even the women and children, were cheering and shouting encouragement to the pair tasked with ridding the white spirit from their midst.

If the Irishman had been in any doubt about what his captors had planned for him, he was in no doubt now. As he was lifted off the ground, he began writhing and screaming. "Please!" he screamed. "Put me down!"

At the sound of John speaking in a foreign tongue, the Kabi fell silent. The pair holding him dropped him to the ground and stepped back, startled.

"See," Turo said at length. "This soul is evil."

"I mean you no harm!" John pleaded. More frightened than he'd ever been before, he was sobbing now.

Only now, from the shelter of her bivouac, did Mamba have a clear view of the white man. Like the others of her clan, she'd been mesmerised by her first sighting of a white. However, for no apparent reason, when she looked at John she thought of her beloved Moilow. Mamba stood up and led her two boys by the hand over to join the others. She wanted a closer look at the stranger.

By the time Mamba had forced her way through to the fire, she saw that Turo and Gabirri were about to throw John into the flames.

Mootemu, the clan's oldest person, chose this moment to intervene. From the front ranks of the assembled, *the Ancient One*, as he was known, raised one hand.

Only the observant Mirritji noticed the senior elder's signal. "Wait!" he ordered.

Turo and Gabirri restrained themselves from throwing John onto the fire.

"The Ancient One wishes to speak," Mirritji announced.

All eyes turned to Mootemu, and silence descended as the agitated crowd awaited his words of wisdom.

It was evident to John, who by now had been lowered back to the ground, that despite the Ancient One's wizened appearance he commanded much respect.

Mootemu swayed atop a pair of spindly shanks as he prepared to address those who were so keen to see the white stranger burn. "The white spirits are ancestors who return from the Dreaming land," he reminded his fellows. His lips quivered when he spoke, and his voice was so quiet the assembled had to strain to hear him. Pointing at John, he continued, "Perhaps this white spirit is one of ours."

Mirritji and several other elders grunted and nodded in agreement. Turo and Gabirri, and many of the others, too, clearly didn't agree, but they remained quiet for the moment.

John, who was now hyperventilating so petrified was he, looked to Mootemu as his possible saviour. He sensed the elder could somehow be his salvation.

Mootemu glanced around at his people, fixing his rheumy eyes on those closest to him. He said, "If anyone recognises this white spirit, let him speak now."

The menfolk looked from one to the other. It seemed no-one recognised John.

At length, a grave Mootemu announced, "He is not one of us." He nodded to Turo and Gabirri. "Burn him until nothing is left but his white bones."

The two hunters bent down and seized John who, having ascertained his death sentence had just been pronounced, began struggling and screaming even more than before. By now, all the assembled were cheering once more. All except Mamba that is.

The fetching young mother stepped forward, still leading her boys by the hand, and she stopped in front of Turo and Gabirri. She looked down at John and quietly declared, "He is Moilow."

Those standing closest to her quietened when they heard Mamba's declaration.

Mootemu, however, who was the closest to the young woman, hadn't heard her, such was the state of his hearing. Reaching out and touching her arm, he asked, "What say you, woman?"

"I recognise him," Mamba said, nodding toward John. "He is my husband returned."

Turo and the other hunters were highly displeased by this turn of events. Addressing Mamba, Turo said, "Woman, keep quiet!"

"He is Moilow," Mamba insisted. She pointed at John so there could be no mistaking who it was she referred to. For the first time, she smiled at John and said, "He has come back to me."

All the assembled, even Mootemu, stared at her in disbelief. John shared their confusion though he hadn't a clue exactly what it was they were confused about.

Turo, who had been Moilow's best friend, bent down, grabbed John's hair and twisted his head around so that the captive's face was close to his own. He studied John closely. Finally, he enquired, "Moilow?"

John could only stare back at the big hunter, clueless and not understanding what was being asked of him.

"This is not Moilow!" Turo said, angrily pushing John's head back hard onto the ground.

"He is Moilow," Mamba insisted yet again, but her words were lost in the arguing that had broken out again amongst the assembled.

The menfolk were ready to consign John to the fire for good this time.

Mirritji looked back to Mootemu only the see the Ancient One had wandered off, choosing to return to his bivouac. That was the old man's style: he would pass on his wisdom and then step aside to let his people decide how to resolve whatever issue they were confronted with.

And so, Mirritji realised it had befallen him, as the next senior elder, to suggest a solution for the current dilemma. This time it was his turn to hold up his hand. When he had everyone's attention, he turned to Mamba and said, "Ask if your sons recognise their father."

Silence once more descended. Now every eye was on the young mother and her two boys.

Mamba turned to Murrowdooling and Carravanty. The younger Carravanty shyly clung to his mother's leg when he realised he and his brother had become the object of everyone's attention. Mamba looked intensely into the eyes of each boy. Pointing to John, she asked, "Is he your father?"

The boys looked fearfully from their mother to the white stranger and then back to their mother.

"Well?" Mamba asked.

Murrowdooling nodded slowly. "Yes," he murmured. "He is Moilow, our father."

"Louder, boy," Mirritji ordered.

"He is our father," Murrowdooling said clearly so that all could hear.

Mamba turned back to her youngest son. "Carravanty?" she asked.

Carravanty hesitated. Finally, he nodded, indicating he agreed with his mother and with his older brother.

Mamba smiled triumphantly and turned back to Mirritji who, she noticed, was now staring more closely at the man she thought of as Moilow.

Mirritji looked around at Mamba and smiled. Turning back to John, he looked fondly into the Irishman's eyes and then, to John's everlasting surprise, roared with laughter. "Moilow, you have returned!" he shouted joyously. He rubbed his hands through John's hair, muttering to himself as he tried to make sense of the miracle he was witnessing.

Turo still wasn't convinced. "If he is Moilow, why does he not speak our language?" he asked.

The others looked to the elder for his answer.

Mirritji said, "He speaks the language of the white spirits. In dying, all is forgotten. Only his love for Mamba and his sons is remembered, and that is what has brought him back." The elder showed a stern face to Turo and the others. "He is Moilow," he added with a finality that indicated the argument was over.

On hearing this, the assembled rejoiced, cheering, chanting and singing to celebrate the return of one of their own. At least most of them did. The returned hunters and some of the other men weren't entirely convinced. A sceptical Turo and two of his fellow hunters stomped off, making their cynicism clear to one and all. Turo glared at Mamba as he and his friends pushed past the young mother and her boys.

It was with huge relief that a bewildered John realised he had been spared. He could tell he was on the brink of fainting—not surprising considering he'd been hyperventilating. The last thing that registered with him before he passed out was the assembled natives smiling at him and addressing him as "Moilow."

37

J OHN REGAINED CONSCIOUSNESS TO FIND himself still on his back, but free of his bindings and, more importantly, still alive and in one piece. All around him, Kabi clan members pressed close, jostling for a close look at the white spirit they believed had come back to them. The expressions on their normally inscrutable faces ranged from astonishment and awe to incredulity and amazement.

While the clan members looked on, a matronly woman fussed over John, cradling his head with one hand while lifting a wooden bowl of water to his lips with the other. He drank greedily from the bowl, emptying it in no time. The kindly woman handed the empty bowl to a boy and motioned to him to refill it. The boy scampered off to a nearby billabong and returned moments later with another bowl of water, which John emptied as fast as he had the first.

Throughout all this, the woman smiled and repeated a word that sounded like "Moilow" to John's ears, but he couldn't be sure. She then administered a herbal concoction to her patient's head wound before dressing it with the leaves of some plant John had never seen before.

Only now did the Irishman remember the young mother who had, if he wasn't mistaken, spoken up for him. He looked around, but couldn't sight her through all the bodies pressed around him. Children tried to touch his white skin, but the woman charged with caring for him chased them off with some stern words.

Dusk was fading to darkness by the time the woman finished her ministerings and motioned to two of the nearest men to help John to his feet. This required a couple of attempts, so weak and unsteady was the Irishman.

Now standing, he looked around to find he was surrounded still by a sea of faces. It was now too dark to read their expressions. However, going on body language and the occasional angry murmurings that reached his ears, he thought not all the menfolk seemed happy their white captive had been spared.

Mirritji came forward and, grasping John by the hand, led him through the assembled throng. At the same time, the elder shouted something to the others and, whatever it was he'd said was greeted with cheering. The stranger they now knew as Moilow was about to find out he was to be guest of honour at a feast clan members were preparing.

The elder led John to the centre of the encampment where a large cooking fire— larger than any of the others—was being prepared by some of the women. Mirritji motioned to John to sit with him amongst several other elders whose number included Mootemu. The Ancient One nodded gravely to the guest who returned the acknowledgement in kind.

Other men drifted over to take their place by the fire, and it wasn't long before every adult male and teenage boy in the encampment was seated around it. They chattered amongst themselves and periodically glanced over at John. Every now and then well-wishers would drift over, individually or in small groups, to pay their respects to the white spirit who had so honoured them by returning to the clan.

Quite what John had done to deserve such respect he couldn't imagine—just as he couldn't imagine what had transpired to convince his captors to spare his life. However, in typical Irish fashion he went along with the adulation and hospitality his Kabi hosts were extending.

The word "Moilow" seemed to be on everyone's lips, and John wondered who or what Moilow was.

It soon became obvious to the lucky Irishman that this was a men's only occasion because the women departed as soon as they had finished preparing the fire, leaving the menfolk to enjoy the occasion.

In no time, male volunteers hung the carcasses of hunters' recent kills over the fire while others laid skinned snakes and lizards along with the filleted remains of fresh fish in the fire's hot embers. The carcasses, John noted, included kangaroos, wallabies, rodents and wild pigs.

He marvelled at the array of food on offer.

These savages eat pretty well.

Little did he know for these people it was either feast or famine—as it was for all the continent's Aborigines. At certain times game, fish and fowl were plentiful. This was one of those times for the creatures of the earth, sea and sky were ever more bountiful as summer neared. At other times—especially during the winters—food became hard to come by, and the natives often starved. Hence their need to constantly relocate to new hunting grounds.

Watching the carcasses sizzle in the heat reminded John how ravished he was. His mouth watered as he observed the fat and juices drip down, causing the flames to crackle.

While the food simmered, the same women John had seen earlier reappeared, carrying bowls containing various food items. These they distributed to the menfolk. The guest of honour was delighted to discover the items included macadamia nuts— ripened and not green as his had been—mussels and other shellfish, Witchetty grubs and a variety of edible roots and herbs. These he tucked into with a fervour that impressed his hosts.

"Moilow is hungry," one man said to his companion.

"Perhaps they did not feed him in the spirit world," the man's companion said.

A woman appeared out of the darkness and draped a warm cloak over John's bare shoulders to keep him warm. He didn't see who it was as she retreated into the shadows before he could identify her, but he wondered if it was the young mother who had spoken up for him. In fact, it was. Mamba had just given John her departed husband's cloak. It was one of the last earthly possessions of Moilow's that she'd kept.

Teenage boys tasked with tending the food cooking on the fire carved off generous portions of tenderised meat and distributed them in eating bowls to the men.

John noticed the best cuts were given to himself and to the senior elders in whose company he'd found himself. He also noticed those same elders watched every move he made as he proceeded to make short work of each and every morsel of food that came his way.

Now and then, Mootemu and Mirritji shared a word. It was obvious to John that he was the subject of their private discussion.

The Irishman gulped down mouthfuls of roasted pork that had been garnished with wild berries. As he savoured each mouthful, he absentmindedly wondered where these people kept their pigs, not realising the pork he ate came from wild pigs that lived in the surrounding hinterland. He hadn't come across any sign of pigs in his travels these past three months, and he wasn't aware they could be found in the wild throughout much of the continent. If he had known his history, he would know that English explorer Captain James Cook introduced pigs to Australia half a century earlier.

When John was onto his third helping of pork, Mootemu indicated to Mirritji he wished to speak. The elder stood and helped the Ancient One slowly to his feet. Mootemu then stood behind John and placed one bony hand on the guest of honour's head, or on the leafy dressing that covered his head at least. This signalled to the others that he wished to speak, and a hush fell over the assembled.

Mootemu surveyed the men before him, his rheumy eyes watering even more than usual in the smoky atmosphere. When he finally started speaking, his trembling voice was barely louder than a whisper. "After three long seasons separated, we welcome Moilow back into our midst," he said.

The Ancient One's welcoming words were greeted by nods and murmurings of assent from most but not all the men. His hand remained on John's head, which the Irishman found both disconcerting and comforting. Disconcerting because he didn't know what the old man was saying; comforting because he sensed an influential ally in him.

Mootemu continued, "We thought this brave warrior and hunter had been taken from us forever when the Noonuccal dogs killed him." At the mention of the cannibalistic Noonuccal, angry murmurings came from many of the men, and some spat on the grass to show their contempt for their long-time enemies. "But the spirits of the rainforest saw fit to return Moilow to us."

This was greeted by more murmurings of assent.

In the darkness, a little distance away, Mamba observed proceedings with her young sons from the entrance to her bivouac. Carravanty was asleep, but Murrowdooling was wide awake. He and his mother could just make out what Mootemu was saying.

"The Ancient One speaks of your father, Murrowdooling," Mamba whispered.

The boy nodded. Cuddling close to his mother, he could sense the pride she was feeling at that moment. It made him feel proud, too.

Mootemu had more to say, but his strength was giving out and he needed to sit down. He pressed down harder on John's head to support himself for he was aware that to sit before he'd finished speaking would be a sign of weakness to the others. "When a white spirit returns to his people, he has forgotten much," he said. "So I ask you to be patient with Moilow when he learns to fight and hunt and fish with us again." With those concluding words, he motioned to Mirritji to assist him back to his shelter for the night.

As the two esteemed elders shuffled off into the darkness beyond the cooking fire, the assembled considered the wisdom the Ancient One had just shared with them. They weren't to know that Mootemu hadn't been speaking from experience when he said a white spirit has forgotten much when he returns to his people. That was pure speculation on his part as he had no prior experience of Kabi clan members, or anyone for that matter, ever returning from the dead. However, he suspected that's as it truly was, and it sounded convincing, even to his ears.

Not all the men were convinced. Turo and some of his fellow hunters remained sceptical.

Gabirri, who sat next to Turo, vacillated between scepticism and certainty that it was as the Ancient One had said. Like Turo, he'd seen nothing in the white spirit that reminded him of Moilow. However, he respected Mootemu, idolised him even—as did all the Kabi—and he knew if the great man said that's the way it was, then that's the way it was.

Interrupting his thoughts, Turo said, "You seem to be in two minds about the white imposter, Gabirri."

To the younger man, it seemed Turo had been reading his mind. "I do not recognise our friend," Gabirri said, referring to Moilow and nodding toward John, "yet the Ancient One says it is him."

Turo remained silent. He was more convinced than ever the white man was an imposter, but he hesitated to voice his opinion as to do so would be to denigrate Mootemu's wisdom, and that would be a serious breach of tribal etiquette. He'd decided to bide his time and let the white hang himself with his own actions.

John, by now, was nearly asleep. It took all his willpower to keep his eyes open and stop from drifting off. If it hadn't been for the renewed expressions of goodwill being extended to him by the men—and for the throbbing of his head wound and his injured right shoulder—there was no doubt he would now be asleep as the exhaustion he'd felt earlier had returned tenfold.

Since Mootemu's wise words, all but Turo and one or two others had accepted that the white spirit was indeed Moilow returned. This motivated them to make John feel even more welcome, and they crowded around him, patting his head, talking to him and laughing. Some felt compelled to remind the white spirit of past experiences they'd shared, oblivious to the fact he couldn't understand them.

Somewhere amongst the assembled a didgeridoo began playing, sending its haunting tones around the encampment once more. This was the signal for heightened celebrations, and men appeared out of the shadows, their near-naked bodies painted in the white markings of their tribe. They began dancing around the fire. The dancing was accompanied the sound of sticks and boomerangs being beaten together, the resulting drumming sound all but drowning out the didgeridoo.

The noise did nothing to ease the headache the Irishman had developed as a result of the blow to his head.

Most of the dancers, he noticed, worked themselves up to a frenzy. He had never seen anything like it. He'd seen the Quandamooka men dancing back at Moreton Bay, but they had been fuelled by alcohol and their dancing lacked the raw authenticity of what was taking place in front of him at this moment.

More men, both young and old, joined in the dancing, which, to John's eyes at least, appeared to involve much foot stamping and jerky movements involving body and limbs. If he wasn't mistaken—and he wasn't—some of the dancers imitated birds and animals.

There was no mistaking the animal one young man was imitating as his kangaroo-like hopping carried him right around the fire in less than thirty impressive leaps. Not to be outdone, others emulated him. One whose efforts exceeded his ability ended up on his backside in the fire's hot embers, his loincloth catching alight. To the amusement of all, the poor fellow uttered a mighty bellow, leapt to his feet and sprinted to the nearby billabong to cool his burning arse.

John missed that incident. He was fast asleep on the grass.

Loud barking woke John. At first he thought it was a dog, but it seemed to be coming from high in the surrounding trees. The foreign sound carried to him once more.

There it is again.

In the moonless night, it was too dark to see more than a few paces. Even the nearby trees were nothing more than shadows in the darkness.

John was now propped up on one elbow—his left elbow for his injured right shoulder was still too sore to put any weight on it—and staring into the night to try to spot the noisy culprit who had woken him. Silence had returned and so he lay back down. He would learn later the dog-like barking was the signature call of the barking owl, which the Kabi referred to as *Timid Girl* because its bark sometimes degenerated into a shrill scream not unlike that of a frightened girl.

After waking, it had taken John a few moments to remember where he was. It all came back to him with a rush—the memory of his capture by the hunters, his subsequent near-death experience and then the extraordinary feast that had followed. He vaguely remembered being shepherded from his place by the cooking fire to a nearby bivouac. Whose bivouac it was he had no idea. He'd seen the shadowy outline of two or three sleeping figures inside it, but from the entrance where a place had been prepared for him he had no way of knowing the dwelling was home to Mamba and her two boys.

John pulled the cloak he'd been gifted earlier tight around him to ward off the chill that came with a strong sea breeze that had sprung up. The cooler temperature was a welcome respite from the oppressive heat and humidity of late.

Lying there, he tried to raise his right hand to adjust the leafy dressing that covered his head wound, but his shoulder hurt too much, forcing him to use his left hand. That done, he realised the herbal leaves the matronly woman had used for the dressing seemed to be working. His headache had eased and the wound wasn't giving him as much pain as it had.

The overwhelming tiredness he experienced earlier returned, and he was asleep again before he knew it.

38

THE LAUGHTER OF CHILDREN CARRIED to John, waking him. Even before he opened his eyes he could tell the sun had long been up. It had risen above the treetops, and he could feel its warmth on his face.

Other sounds and sensations carried to him, too. He tried to make sense of them, relying on his sense of hearing and smell rather than his sight.

I hear the ocean.

The sound of waves on a nearby beach carried to him, louder than the previous night. He could hear the low murmur of men conversing, and the higher pitch of women's voices; rowdy boys could be heard engaging in roughhouse antics some distance away; the sounds of construction carried to him as natives assembled something—a bivouac if he had to guess; and he could smell a myriad of scents and fragrances, nearly all of which were foreign to him apart from the lingering smell of smoke from recently extinguished cooking fires; he thought he recognised the perfume of one or two spring flowers, but couldn't be sure.

Finally, he opened his eyes only to shut them immediately as the sun's glare near-blinded him. In that instance, he thought he'd seen two familiar faces. He had: Murrowdooling's and Carravanty's. Shielding his eyes this time with his hand, he opened them again and saw Mamba's two boys staring at him not three paces away.

John winked at the boys, and they ran off, startled.

Only now did he notice a smoky haze covered the sun. He recognised the phenomenon as he'd seen it several times before—during the dry season at Parramatta when the smoke from inland bushfires had been blown to the coast by hot westerly winds. Judging by the density of the smoke, he guessed today's fire, wherever it was, was a major one.

The movement of bodies all around him alerted him to the fact he was once more the object of attention for everyone—or so it seemed—in the encampment. Upon realising the white spirit was awake, clan members had descended on him, shouting greetings his way and smiling at him. He smiled back, but held his tongue—ever mindful of the consternation he'd caused when he last spoke to them.

Don't wanna give 'em another excuse to cook me.

Murrowdooling and Carravanty returned to his side, this time with their mother. Mamba smiled shyly at John and motioned to him to accompany her to the remains of a still smouldering cooking fire she'd prepared next to her bivouac. "Come, Moilow," she said with a touch of impatience when the man she thought of as her husband showed no inclination to do her bidding.

There's that word Moilow again.

As before, John wondered what the word meant. The context in which the woman had just used it told him it was probably someone's name. That was immediately confirmed when some unseen fellow greeted him as Moilow. It dawned on him they'd confused him with someone else. He wondered if that someone else was another European they'd befriended or had had dealings with. *This woman's lover perhaps?* he asked himself, looking at the fetching young mother standing before him.

Studying Mamba closely for the first time, the Irishman decided if Moilow or whoever he was had taken her as a lover, the man had good taste. *Very easy on the eye,* he decided. He also wondered if she was the result of some union between a European and an Aborigine, so fine were her features compared to any other Aboriginal woman he'd seen.

"Moilow!" Mamba said, losing patience. She and her boys walked over to the cooking fire, leaving John to join them in his own time.

Finally, he roused himself. With some difficulty, he pushed himself to his feet, but discovered he couldn't motivate his legs to move. He felt sore all over—and weary. So weary he just wanted to sleep.

The Irishman realised the results of long months spent living rough in the wilderness, not to mention two-and-a-half years' hard labour in convict settlements prior to that, had finally caught up with him. He *had* to rest. And so he lay back down and, to the annoyance of Mamba and the amusement of the others, he fell asleep almost immediately.

The same smoky haze John had observed that morning was being observed by the residents of Moreton Bay. On the front veranda of the Marsdens' cottage, Captain Marsden and Lieutenant Hogan sat overlooking the penal settlement. They'd been there for the past hour, passing the time talking.

Neither man was in uniform. Marsden wasn't scheduled to report to work until after lunch while Hogan, who was sitting in the comfortable chair the captain's late wife had favoured, was still *enjoying* enforced leave. In fact, the young lieutenant wasn't enjoying his extended break. He'd been forced to extend his sick leave because complications had meant his fractured leg had to be broken again and reset by the army's surgeon, thereby extending his rehabilitation by some months. Still on crutches, it would be another two months before he would, in the surgeon's opinion, be ready for desk duties and another four months before he'd be ready for active duty.

Marsden wasn't in the best of moods either as he was somewhat hung-over—a result of having drunk a little too much wine the previous night. It was starting to become a regular occurrence, and he reminded himself he needed to cut down on his drinking.

In the penal settlement below the cottage, gangs of convicts performed a variety of tasks, including assisting the army's carpenters with construction of new huts to accommodate the increasing convict population—a never-ending requirement. Between the settlement and the cottage, more gangs were employed tilling the fields and finishing construction of stone fences separating those same fields.

Every now and then, the crack of a whip could be heard as guards punished those convicts they considered were shirking their duties. Marsden and Hogan knew the lash wasn't exclusively used on those guilty of shirking. Bored or sadistic guards, and soldiers, too, sometimes resorted to using the whip for little more than their own amusement. It was something Marsden had tried to stamp out, but, as with a lot of things these days, he had all but given up.

A quarter of a mile downriver, toward the bay, the refurbishment of the wharf continued at an impressive pace. Impressive because settlers, not convicts, had been hired to do most of the work, and they had already proven their value. Lord Cheetham and the Governor had placed much importance on completing the wharf's upgrade as that was considered essential to the settlement's growth.

Between the wharf and the settlement, the shanty town that was home to the Quandamooka, or home to those of their tribe who had chosen to settle here at least, had grown alarmingly as more and more clan members arrived every week in the hope of trading goods and flesh for alcohol and other trappings of the white man. They had brought with them a multitude of problems, but complaints to Cheetham about the escalating problems had predictably fallen upon deaf ears. It was yet another battle Marsden had fought and given up on.

Marsden and Hogan had formed an uneasy alliance in recent months. The captain still wasn't overly enamoured by the young man's continued courtship of his daughter, but he felt he owed it to Helen to get to know him better on a personal level. It was after all a father's duty, he reminded himself.

As for Hogan, his interest in his superior was purely professional. He sensed Marsden was lukewarm about welcoming him into the family, but he paid no mind to that. He was going to marry Helen and that was that. *If* she'd have him, that is. And that still wasn't certain by any means. No, Hogan's interest in Marsden was purely professional.

The younger officer looked up to his captain and considered him a mentor of sorts. Even more than that, however, he lusted after Marsden's job. Since Cheetham had refused to countenance repeated requests that he be transferred to another post elsewhere in the colony, Hogan had decided he wouldn't settle for anything less than the top posting at Moreton Bay. And, until he eventually achieved his new goal he was determined to learn as much as he could from the man whose role he planned to usurp.

Marsden suspected Hogan had designs on the top job, but he adhered to the philosophy a man should keep his friends close and his enemies closer—and so he encouraged the lieutenant's companionship, or at least he didn't discourage it. Not that he considered Hogan an enemy, but he certainly didn't consider him a friend. The younger man would have to earn that status.

"It appears the fire season has arrived, sir," Hogan said, observing the hazy sky.

Here, closer to the source of the inland blaze, the haze had taken on an orange glow, giving every living and inanimate object on the ground a distinctly orange tinge. Even the complexions of the two officers appeared orange.

"It does appear so," Marsden agreed. Bushfires were a year-round hazard in many parts of Australia, but October marked the start of New South Wales' official fire season and, right on schedule, the first fire of the season had taken hold.

Neither spoke again for a while. Hogan would have preferred to converse, but he was aware his superior often preferred the sound of silence, and he respected that.

The sounds of boys playing interrupted their reverie. Young Matthew was playing an outdoors game he called *Soldiers* with several other boys his own age. The boys, with one exception, were the sons of new settlers in the nearby township. The exception, like Matthew, was the son of another army officer. The officer concerned resided in the soldiers' family quarters—a new recent addition to the penal settlement. Marsden and Cheetham were still the only senior officials who occupied separate, stand-alone residences at Moreton Bay.

Matthew led the boys at a fast clip around the corner of the cottage. "Catch me if you can!" he shouted, aiming a toy rifle at the others who were chasing him. The pretend gun was a gift his father had asked the smithy to make for the lad.

"No studies for Matthew today, Captain?" Hogan asked Marsden. He had to raise his voice to be heard above the noise the rowdy youngsters were making.

"No, there has been a death in his teacher's family and she is away until next week," the captain said, referring to the woman who home-schooled his son. "Until then, I have agreed to let Matthew have some friends around to play."

The boys disappeared around the back of the house, and a modicum of peace and quiet returned.

"Any word from Cheet . . . ah . . . from Lord Cheetham, sir?" Hogan asked. The commandant had been away visiting the Governor in Sydney Town for the past three weeks, and Hogan for one was enjoying the break. Cheetham was, to his mind, growing more eccentric and more impossible to deal with by the day. The lieutenant was in no doubt Marsden shared his opinion for they'd discussed this very issue only recently.

"I received a letter from him two days ago," Marsden said. The letter he referred to had been delivered by the latest vessel to visit. In addition to mail and other supplies, it had delivered another forty-four convicts—an event that was being repeated more often than ever these days. One result of this was the soldiers and settlers didn't have to wait so long for supplies; another result was the number of convicts continued to exceed the settlement's available facilities, and, as a consequence of that, they were falling ill or dying in ever-increasing numbers.

Hogan waited for Marsden to continue.

At length, Marsden added, "He says Sir Ralph has agreed to a further increase in convict numbers." He sat back and waited for his subordinate to digest that piece of sobering news.

"God help us all," Hogan muttered. He adjusted his position to make himself more comfortable. His injury required him to keep his fractured leg straight and in a raised position, so he was sitting with the leg resting on a stool his superior had placed in front of him.

"Yes. I fear God is the only one who can help us," Marsden agreed.

Both men were painfully aware that Cheetham was now truly in the grip of his opium addiction. New supplies of the drug had been arriving on every second vessel from Sydney Town, and so the commandant was kept well supplied. Apart from the modest amount required for use in the infirmary, he was the only opium user at Moreton Bay. The only one the two officers were aware of at least.

Why the Governor tolerated Cheetham's excesses they couldn't imagine. Both men were aware that Sir Ralph knew about the commandant's addiction. Marsden had confronted the Governor about it more than once—once face to face and several times in correspondence.

So far, neither officer had mentioned Helen, though she was constantly on the minds of each. It was Marsden who finally broached that delicate subject.

"Heard from Helen since we last spoke, Lieutenant?" Marsden asked, referring to Hogan by rank rather than Christian name as was his preference even when socialising with him. He was aware relations between the young couple had been strained since Hogan had visited Helen a month or two back because his daughter had informed him of that in a recent letter. But she'd been guarded in her comments, and he wanted to learn more from Hogan.

"Ah . . . No I haven't, Captain," Hogan said.

The lieutenant didn't volunteer any further information. He didn't need to. From where Marsden sat, the fact that Helen hadn't bothered to write to her suitor since his visit spoke volumes. He was about to question the younger man some more when Matthew and his mates reappeared, rowdier than before.

A stocky boy playing the role of a soldier cuffed a scruffy lad over the ear, causing the lad to cry out in genuine pain. "Do as you are told, convict!" the stocky boy ordered.

"Lash him!" another boy suggested.

The stocky boy thought that a good idea and produced a length of cord he carried with him for just such an occasion. He proceeded to lash the scruffy lad who suddenly decided he didn't like this game and took off around the back of the house with his flogger in hot pursuit.

Marsden and Hogan chuckled.

"Off with his head!" the lieutenant shouted at the self-appointed flogger as the two lads disappeared around the side of the house.

An older boy who was playing the part of yet another soldier pointed at Matthew. "You there!" he shouted. "Step forward!"

Matthew shuffled forward, convict-like, with head bowed.

"The punishment for attempted escape is death by hanging!" the older boy said. "Take him away!"

A freckled lad grabbed Matthew who immediately broke free and ran off.

"John Graham, stop right there!" the older boy demanded.

Only now did Marsden and Hogan realise that Matthew was pretending to be John.

Mayhem ensued as Matthew charged the older boy and tried to wrestle him to the ground. The other boys piled into the fray.

Neither Marsden nor Hogan were impressed. The former launched to his feet and strode down the veranda steps. "Matthew!" he shouted.

Matthew, who was now at the bottom of the pile of boys, looked up smiling. It wasn't until his now-irate father grabbed him by the arm and hauled him aside that he realised he was in trouble.

"How dare you," Marsden grumbled. He rounded on the other boys. "You think John Graham a hero?" he asked. "Go home all of you!"

Startled, the boys scurried off. None of them quite knew what they'd done to earn the captain's wrath.

Matthew wrestled in his father's iron grip. "Papa, you're hurting me!" he complained.

The captain spun the boy around so that he was facing him. "You are not to admire that fugitive," he warned. "Graham was a thief and a scoundrel!"

Matthew was shocked by his father's anger. He bit his lip to hold back the tears that threatened.

Marsden finally calmed down and released his son. "Go to your room now," he ordered.

Still unsure what he was guilty of—it was only a game after all—Matthew ran inside.

Looking on, Hogan caught Marsden's eye and shrugged. "Boys will be boys, eh Captain?"

"Aye," Marsden said sullenly, returning to his seat on the veranda.

Neither man spoke again. Each was alone with his thoughts; each thought of the Irish fugitive and wondered if he was dead; each hoped he was dead, but for different reasons—Marsden because confirmation of John's death would help deter attempted escapes by convicts who admired the Irishman; Hogan because he was embittered by Helen's obvious infatuation for him.

◆£━━◆3◆

Later that morning, as Marsden and Private Henry Askew lifted Hogan up onto the tray of a horse-drawn cart the young soldier had brought up from the settlement, Barega emerged from the bush behind the cottage. Covered in sweat and wearing only his loincloth, the tracker had just returned from his latest unfruitful search for John. He'd been running almost non-stop for the past three days. Strapped to his back was the broken spear he'd found near the gorge where John had nearly drowned.

"What luck, tracker?" Marsden asked.

Without a word, Barega unstrapped the broken spear and handed it to the captain.

"What's this?" Marsden asked.

"Spear not made by Aborigine," Barega said.

"May I?" Hogan asked from atop the cart.

Marsden handed the broken spear to his lieutenant.

241

Hogan studied it and was immediately struck by its crudeness, as Marsden had been, too. "It could only have been made by a European," the lieutenant said.

Marsden nodded and turned back to Barega. "Where did you find this?" he asked.

Barega described the gorge's location.

The captain was perturbed to learn how far it was from Moreton Bay. "Did you sight the Irishman?" he asked.

Barega shook his head. "I see . . . remains of big flood that maybe kill the Irish, Mister," he said, recalling the aftermath of the devastating floodwaters he'd seen in and around the gorge. "I also see . . . clothes . . . lost in big flood."

"White man's clothes?" the captain asked.

Barega shook his head again. "Clothes . . . like these," he said, touching his loincloth.

Marsden thought on this for a moment and then looked the tracker squarely in the eyes. "Not a word of this to anyone, understood?"

Barega nodded and ran off toward the settlement.

Marsden then turned to the private. He said, "That goes for you, too, Private Askew."

"Yes, Captain," Askew said.

"Give us a moment, will you?" Marsden asked.

"Sir." Askew walked off a little way, leaving his commanding officer alone with the lieutenant.

Looking at Hogan and at the broken spear he still held, the captain said, "There is every chance the spear and the clothes were Graham's."

"I agree, sir."

"If the tracker is right, Graham is likely dead."

Hogan didn't comment.

"Agreed?" Marsden asked.

Hogan nodded. "Most likely, sir."

Marsden looked straight at his opposite. "Officially then . . . John Graham *is* dead."

Holding his superior's gaze, a thoughtful Hogan eventually said, "Yes Captain, he is dead."

"Then that is what we shall tell the men," Marsden said decisively.

The lieutenant understood the subtext behind his superior's announcement. Just knowing it was possible that John was still alive was impacting on the soldiers' already low morale. However, it was having just the opposite effect on the convicts: every day that passed and the fugitive was not returned to the settlement either dead or alive only served to further encourage them. John was fast achieving hero status amongst them, and more and more were attempting to escape.

Both officers hoped the announcement that John Graham had died would put an end to all that once and for all.

39

TOPLESS AND BAREFOOT, JOHN WALKED along the beach near which the Kabi encampment was situated and which, until today, he hadn't seen. In fact, he hadn't seen or done much at all in the week since he'd been taken in by the people who now viewed him as one of their own.

The Irishman had spent much of the past week resting, eating and catching up on lost sleep. Three months of trekking through hostile terrain, always hungry and always at the limit of his physical reserves, had taken more out of him than he'd realised. To the bemusement of his hosts, he'd slept continuously for the first two days, and since then hadn't ventured more than a stone's throw from the bivouac he shared with Mamba and her boys, preferring instead to lie around and observe the comings and goings of clan members. That's how tired and lethargic he'd been.

Even now, he was far from his old self. His injured right shoulder, which he'd been sure was broken, had, until midway through the week, left his whole arm numb, reducing it to a useless appendage. Only some energetic massaging had restored full movement to the arm, but the shoulder remained tender. The massaging had been done courtesy of the same matronly woman who had dressed the head wound he'd also sustained when captured. She was Mamba's aunt, though John had no way of knowing that.

The Irishman still suffered the lingering effects of the bouts of flu and food poisoning he'd suffered, and this, combined with long periods of little or no food, had left him very weak. If it hadn't been for his ultimately fortuitous capture by the Kabi, he was certain he'd have died for he'd reached the end of his physical reserves and had all but lost the will to live. "Don't celebrate too soon," he often cautioned himself. "These savages may do away with me yet."

John had hoped he'd have the beach to himself, but as soon as he'd emerged from the palm trees bordering it he had counted at least thirty clan members engaged in various activities in and out of the water. In the water, fishermen cast nets; from rocks at both ends of the small bay, more men speared fish; in the pools amongst those same rocks, women collected shellfish; on the beach itself, women—some with babies strapped to their backs—collected sea shells and driftwood; and at the water's edge older children played.

The Kabi smiled and waved at John when they noticed him.

As soon as the children noticed the white man they started following him. They had been fascinated by him—the first white they'd ever seen—ever since his capture, but they remained a little fearful of him. Hence their inclination to keep some distance between themselves and the man their parents called *the white spirit*.

Wading through the shallows, John relished the feeling of wet sand beneath his toes. Every now and then, the last vestiges of a wave lapped around his knees and ankles. The pleasant sensation took him back to his boyhood days in Ireland when, once every summer, or twice if he was lucky, his mother would take him to the beach after church and he'd run barefoot through the shallows. Invariably, he would earn a scolding when he'd trip and his Sunday-best clothes would end up saturated.

John suddenly stopped walking and spun around to face the children following him, pulling a scary face and holding his hands up to impersonate an ogre. Startled, the children took off in the other direction, laughing and shrieking all at the same time.

When John resumed walking, they resumed following him only closer than before, their courage growing all the time. He repeated his ogre impersonation, receiving the same reaction.

Having studied each of the adult clan members with whom he shared the beach, he turned his attention to his surroundings. The bay was picture perfect. A cloudless blue sky merged with the blue sea, rendering the eastern horizon all but invisible; small, even waves curved onto a gently sloping white-sand beach, carrying foam to the high water mark; behind the palms fringing the beach, the tops of gum trees could be seen, and beyond them, in the distance, forest-covered hills stretched westward toward the continent's interior.

It was hot, too. So hot that John decided to go for a swim. Removing his tattered breeches, he studied his undershorts. Once white, they were now grey. That didn't surprise him. After all, he'd been wearing them day in, day out for over three months. "I best wash these one of these days," he mumbled to himself. Putting the undershorts out of his mind, he ran into the sea and dived under the waves.

When he came up for air, he noticed every clan member within sight was now watching him. At first he thought he might have offended them somehow. Then, when he noticed they were smiling more than ever in his direction, he realised it was his spontaneity that had captured their attention. Suddenly stripping off and diving into the sea was the first lively thing he'd done since arriving in their midst. *Perhaps it reminded them of Moilow,* he thought. He waved at the natives and they waved back.

John started when he noticed something white on the horizon.

A sail?

He relaxed when he identified the object as a small cloud—the only one in the sky—that had not long formed.

The false sighting reminded him his goal hadn't changed.

I need to find a ship.

He just hoped when he did find a ship it would be northbound—ideally bound for China, or better still England—but he was prepared to settle for any ship.

If it's southbound and I end up in Sydney Town or Botany Bay, or even Van Diemen's Land, I can always stow away or preferably work my passage on a northbound ship from there.

New Zealand, the new British colony twelve hundred miles to the east of Australia, was another option for him. He'd heard more and more trading vessels were crossing the Tasman Sea from Australia to New Zealand, and he had heard rumours that one or two escaped convicts had found sanctuary there. There was talk of gold in that country, too, and that interested him.

John decided to test his injured shoulder. He attempted to swim a few strokes, but pulled up when he found that hurt too much. Instead, he rolled over and floated on his back, luxuriating in the feeling of weightlessness and wellbeing that he experienced. He lost track of time, and remained like that, floating, for ages. As he did, he swore he could feel his strength returning and his worries evaporating. He reminded himself to do this every day.

Finally, he left the water, donned his discarded breeches and resumed walking along the beach. He was still trailed by a procession of children. Their numbers were growing all the time as more children joined them. They were closer, too, and growing ever more bold. No longer did they run away shrieking when he performed his ogre routine.

Only now did he notice Murrowdooling and Carravanty among the children. He guessed Mamba wouldn't be far away. She never let the boys out of her sight for long—especially not the younger Carravanty. John looked up the beach, and sure enough he spotted the boy's mother observing them, and him, from amongst the palm trees. She smiled shyly when she realised she'd been seen, and he acknowledged her with a wave.

John's relationship with Mamba hadn't changed, not that he'd noticed at least, since they had first met. It was as though neither could fathom how to bridge the gulf that existed between them. Of course, their situation wasn't helped by the fact that neither could speak the other's language, so much remained unsaid, or, more accurately, *everything* remained unsaid.

In recent days, Mamba had made tentative steps to try to converse with him, in her native tongue of course, and he had occasionally responded in his language. The only word he recognised was *Moilow,* which Mamba seemed to include in every second sentence. That no longer surprised him for he'd long since worked out he was Moilow—as far as Mamba and everyone else was concerned that is. Or almost everyone else.

Turo, the big hunter who had come close to crushing John's skull and then burning him to death, had kept his distance since that first memorable meeting. However, the pair had on occasion exchanged glances since then, and the expression in Turo's eyes had left John in no doubt he was on notice.

Though the Irishman had been inactive over the past week, until now at least, that hadn't kept him from observing the Kabi, their strange speech, customs, rituals, clothes, weapons, songs, dances, games, foods, cooking methods and, where possible, their relationships—with their children, their spouses and, occasionally, the spouses of others—and their widely differing personality traits.

The past week had opened his eyes in more ways than one. He'd been constantly reminded of the old adage his dear mother often quoted. "Never judge a man by his clothes, son," she used to say. To which he would respond: "Never judge your son by his girlfriends, máthair." For some reason she would find that response highly amusing, and reply with a witticism of her own along the lines of, "If I judged you by those trollops I'd have given up on you long ago, John Graham."

The Kabi had constantly surprised him. For all their primitiveness and savagery, they were capable of great kindness and gentleness; they were industrious, hardworking and uncomplaining in the face of hardship; they showed deep affection for each other and had great respect for their elders; theirs was a truly egalitarian society, classless and democratic, where every individual was considered as important as the next person.

Within the first few days, old stereotypes had been forever dashed. John's view of native peoples—a somewhat racist view he would now admit—was fast being overturned. No longer did he consider them all savages and cannibals. He now realised, for the first time in his life, these people were human beings with the same desires, fears and prejudices as himself or any other European.

That said, he wasn't blind to their faults. He was mindful they could turn to savagery at a moment's notice—he'd witnessed that first hand—and he abhorred the way the men treated their women. More than once he'd seen a husband beat his wife if she didn't pleasure him when he wanted it. Not only beat her, but knock her senseless if the occasion required, as it seemed to all too often. He had been amazed how resigned the women were to such treatment, and how readily friends and family turned a blind eye to such attacks.

As for Mamba, John had come to realise she was in a somewhat unique and unenviable position. She was, as far as he could tell, the only solo mother in the clan. He sensed there were other women who had been left widows, or whose husbands had deserted them, who had quickly formed relationships with other men—either single or married men for bigamist relationships were, he'd observed, not only common but encouraged.

Why Mamba hadn't married or entered into a relationship of convenience at least he couldn't imagine. He was very aware the menfolk found her attractive for they often looked at her with undisguised lust. Turo, in particular, appeared to lust after her even though, from what John could deduce, he already had several wives.

The Irishman had yet to learn that, since Moilow's death, Mamba's life had been hell. Life for an Aboriginal woman in a relationship was hard enough—for they had to perform most of the daily chores, including much of the heavy work—but for a single woman, especially if she was a mother, it was particularly difficult.

Mamba had loved Moilow so much she hadn't been able to look at another man since his passing let alone consider enter into a relationship with one. As a result, she had no man to lean on when faced with such tasks as building or repairing her bivouac, carrying her possessions to new encampments or sourcing food.

For food, she often had to rely on hand-outs from friends and relations. That was workable when food was plentiful, as it was now, but not when food was scarce—an all too common occurrence in most if not all Aboriginal communities, especially during the winter months when edible flora and fauna became scarce and fish stocks dwindled.

The young mother took comfort from the fact her people would never let her or the boys starve if they could help it, but life was difficult all the same. Not only for her, but for her sons, too. Her predicament wasn't helped by the fact that single mothers were looked down on and often ostracised in Aboriginal society. The Kabi believed all women should belong to a man, and woe betide any who didn't for that could only mean the woman had somehow earned the wrath of her ancestors' spirits.

Murrowdooling and Carravanty were uncomplaining, but Mamba knew they missed their father, and as the sons of a solo mother they also missed out on a lot compared to other children. For their sake, she had recently vowed to accept the advances of one of the many men who were showing interest in her. Not Turo, though. Even though he'd been Moilow's best friend, she despised him. An incorrigible womaniser, he already had four wives and, in her opinion, he still wasn't satisfied. He had even tried to seduce her when her husband had been alive. Moilow, trusting soul that he was, had laughed off any such suggestion when she'd relayed this to him.

John's arrival had been timely. Something about him had reminded Mamba of Moilow, and when the opportunity had arisen to speak up for the white spirit, she hadn't been able to resist. After the event, when analysing her motives for having acted as she did, she couldn't in all honesty say she believed the white spirit was Moilow. However, with every passing day, she became more and more convinced her husband may have returned to her. This despite not being able to converse with him or share anything other than a fleeting glance.

The shadows were lengthening when John returned to the bivouac he shared with Mamba and her boys. Now wearing the cloak he'd inherited, he found the young mother preparing the evening meal over a cooking fire in the company of several other women. A glance told him the meal comprised generous helpings of seafood of various varieties—a gift from one of several fishermen who, when fish supplies permitted, kept her plied with the bounty of the sea in the hope she would reward him one of these days.

Murrowdooling and Carravanty played with other boys in the grass nearby. John winked at the young brothers, and for the first time they didn't run away. They actually beamed a smile at him—a spontaneous gesture that wasn't lost on John or Mamba.

Though Mamba had been without a man for nearly a year now, she and her sons hadn't exactly been living alone. Her bivouac was one of a cluster of dwellings occupied by relatives, including aunts, uncles, cousins, an older sister, a younger brother and two grandparents—a grandfather on her mother's side and a grandmother on her father's side. Mamba's parents had both passed away some years ago.

The relatives often banded together, sharing food and sometimes eating around the same fire—as was the case tonight.

The matronly woman who had dressed John's head wound was, it turned out, one of Mamba's aunts, and she was one of the women helping Mamba now with the cooking. She smiled at John when she saw him and greeted him as Moilow.

"Evening to you, Cheeba" John said, addressing the woman by name. He'd heard Mamba and others address her as such, or so he thought. In fact, he'd misheard them. Her name was actually Jiba, which he would learn later means *the moon—*

appropriate in her case because she had a round moon face.

Jiba smiled to signal her appreciation that the white spirit she knew as Moilow had at least attempted to use her name. At the same time, she wondered why he'd pronounced it incorrectly for, like others in his extended family, she had been close to him before he died.

John noticed everyone who was within hearing distance had stopped what they were doing when he spoke. It was the same whenever he said anything. He'd spoken so little since arriving they still found his use of English a novelty. More than that, they found it magical for his use of the strange language convinced them even more that he was from the spirit world.

On the spur of the moment, and for no good reason that he could think of, John began to recite one of the verses he'd memorised from Keats's poem *Lamia*. "It seemed he had loved them a whole summer long," he intoned, looking straight at Mamba. "And soon his eyes had drunk her beauty up, leaving no drop in the bewildering cup."

The lyrical Irishman noticed he had the full attention of everyone within earshot, and others were drifting over to investigate what it was that had so captured the attention of their fellows. Drawing himself up to his full height and theatrically spreading his arms wide, he continued, "And still the cup was full, while he afraid, lest she should vanish ere his lip had paid." He still hadn't taken his eyes off Mamba, and he saw that she appeared entranced by his performance.

By now, John noticed a small crowd of perhaps twenty or more had gathered around, keen to hear more of the foreign tongue the white man spoke. Throwing his voice as if on stage, he continued, "Due adoration, thus began to adore. Her soft look growing coy, she saw his chain so sure. Leave thee alone! Look back! Ah, Goddess, see, whether my eyes can ever turn from thee!"

The look in Mamba's eyes told John that even though she couldn't understand the words he spoke, she sensed they were meant for her. They shared a smile, each signalling to the other that they understood.

More clan members had arrived, attracted by John's impromptu performance. Encouraged, he launched into another verse.

The evening meal turned out to be a festive affair. Almost half the clan members gathered around Mamba's cooking fire, sharing food they'd brought with them. Using mime to communicate, Mamba and others insisted that John recite more poetry for their entertainment—and so he did, reciting many of the twenty or so verses he'd memorised from Keats's poem.

Between verses, he half-heartedly insisted he was too tired to recite any more, but his audience was equally insistent he continue, and so he obliged to the delight of all.

Amongst those gathered around the fire, John noticed the impressive young Gabirri, senior elders Mootemu and Mirritji, and other men whose number included some of the hunters who had captured him. There was no sign of Turo, however. The belligerent one was still having nothing to do with the man he viewed as an imposter.

Many of the men had brought their wives and children with them, and they added to the air of festivity. Mirritji, despite his age, had three wives and they were all here.

John was encouraged to find that he seemed to be gaining acceptance within the clan—with its menfolk in particular. Until tonight, most of those men now gathered around the fire had had nothing to do with him. Now their attitude toward him seemed to be thawing. He wasn't to know that, for the most part, they hadn't been avoiding him as such. Rather, they were obeying the Ancient One's request that they give Moilow time to adjust after so long away from them.

When everyone had had their fill, of food and poetry, and the fire had all but burnt itself out, clan members began retiring to their shelters for the night. Soon, only Mamba and her boys—*three* boys if her Moilow was included—retired to their bivouac.

Only now did John notice the animal pelt that marked his sleeping place was no longer at the entrance to the bivouac. Mamba had moved it to just inside the narrow entrance, close to where she and her sons slept.

The Irishman gave no sign that he was surprised as he entered the dwelling. He had to bend down and crawl in on all fours, so low was the entrance.

As Mamba got Murrowdooling and Carravanty settled for the night, John lay down on the pelt and looked around the bivouac's dark interior. This was the first time he'd been invited inside. Moonlight shining through the dwelling's entrance provided sufficient light for him to determine its interior was almost as basic as the exterior. Strong branches served as the framework for the walls while overhead lengths of driftwood supported the roof. Leafy branches and fern fronds served as walls, and the roof was made up of palm fronds. The fronds, it appeared, had been laid end over end, theoretically providing a watertight roof. How watertight it was hadn't yet been tested for there had been no rain since the clan relocated here three weeks earlier.

The pelts of roos and other animals covered most of the grass underfoot, providing protection for the occupants from aggressive bull ants whose bite, John had discovered, was something to avoid if possible. More pelts lay scattered about. These served as blankets and pillows as and when required. They weren't required tonight, so hot and humid was it.

The bivouac's exterior didn't do justice to the interior for inside it was roomier than John had expected. Ceiling height aside—an adult couldn't stand upright when inside—it seemed to him it could, at a pinch, accommodate five or six people. Mamba, who was now lying next to her sons, was, John estimated, a good body's length from him.

In the dark, he couldn't tell if she was looking his way or not, or even if she was still awake.

The tiredness John had experienced earlier returned. He realised he'd probably over-exerted himself, but he felt he had somehow turned a corner—both physically and in other ways. He couldn't articulate, not even to himself, what those *other ways* were exactly, but he sensed they included his relationship with Mamba.

The Irishman soon gave into his tiredness, and drifted off.

His was a dream-filled sleep. For the first time ever, he dreamt of Mamba, and for the first time in a while he dreamt of a long forgotten Irish girlfriend. At one stage, his dreams overlapped: he dreamt he was undressing the Irish lass in her bedroom one minute, and next minute he was making love to the sultry native woman whose bivouac he shared.

40

FOR THE SECOND MORNING IN a row, John joined Mamba and her boys for breakfast. Previously, he had slept in, arising mid-morning, or even later some days. Today was different. He felt stronger—still not a hundred per cent, but definitely more robust—and was keen to venture further afield than he had yesterday.

Mamba noticed the change that had come over him. The man sitting at her cooking fire was more like the Moilow she remembered. She smiled at him as she served him a bowl of reheated meat left over from last night's meal.

The young mother had wondered when the real Moilow was going to show himself. She had seen definite signs of that the previous day, and today had started out as well if not better. Mamba was especially pleased to see that Murrowdooling and Carravanty were becoming increasingly at ease in John's company. Their initial fear, she'd observed, had disappeared, and now they were showing signs of acceptance that the white man who had appeared in their midst was indeed their father.

One change in John that had surprised her, and everyone else, too, was he'd shaved his beard soon after rising. Exactly what he'd used to achieve his now clean-shaven look she wasn't sure, but he'd obviously had some difficulty for his face was covered in small scratches. In fact, he had used a piece of flint-like rock he'd found together with the sharp edge of a broken seashell. For a mirror he'd used the still surface of the nearby billabong. It was a practice he intended to perfect and adhere to daily—if only because it felt civilised and it served to separate him from the bearded black men in whose company he'd found himself.

Mamba wasn't sure she approved of the new-look Moilow. Her Moilow had never shaved before, and she couldn't imagine what had moved him to shave now.

Watching John as he finished a second helping of the food she'd prepared, she was impressed by the easy manner he had with her sons. He hadn't tried to force things, preferring to let them get to know him again and accept him on their own terms, in their own time.

Mamba smiled when John poked a face at the boys after catching them looking at him. Both boys laughed, further demonstrating how at ease they now were in his presence.

Others had noticed the difference in the white spirit also. The change in him in the past day had been hard to miss. In whispered conversations around the encampment, more than a few commented that Moilow was back, or was on his way back at least, from the spirit world.

Moving shadows alerted John and Mamba to a group of men passing by close to their bivouac. The two looked around and saw the group numbered almost a dozen strong, and they were heading into the bush beyond the encampment.

John saw they appeared to be ready for war as each member of the group carried two or more weapons. He recognised several of them, including Turo and Gabirri and two of the other hunters who had been involved in his capture. Turo, he observed, stared lustfully at Mamba as he walked passed at the head of the group. The Irishman had observed that on several previous occasions, and for some unfathomable reason it was starting to annoy him. He noticed the young woman averted her eyes and appeared uneasy in the lecherous man's presence.

Turo switched his gaze to John, and the malice in his eyes was there for all to see.

As Turo and the others disappeared into the bush, John caught Mamba's eye and smiled at her encouragingly. Not for the first time, he wished he could communicate verbally with the young woman so that he could learn what her relationship was with Turo.

Mamba returned John's smile, equally frustrated that they couldn't speak each other's language. She whispered a silent prayer to the spirits of the forest, asking that they allow Moilow to speak in the dialect of the Kabi sooner rather than later.

When John had finished eating, he excused himself and donned his boots. He had a day's exploration planned, and he was looking forward to it. "See you later," he said.

The Irishman hadn't gone more than a few yards when Mamba called to him. He turned to see her selecting berries and fruits from a large bowl and also something that looked like smoked eel from the fire's embers. She placed these into a shoulder bag, which she handed to him. "You will need this today, Moilow," she smiled.

John thanked her with an answering smile. He then placed the bag over his shoulder and set off again, aware that Mamba was watching his departing back. The shoulder bag, he noticed, was far superior to any of the bags he'd made from ferns and palm fronds whilst on the run. It had been fashioned from the pelt of a wallaby or some similar animal, and lovingly stitched—presumably by Mamba.

As he departed, he didn't notice Mirritji, who had been observing him for some time, order a teenage boy to follow him and keep a discreet eye on him. If he had, he'd have realised the Kabi didn't entirely trust him. Not yet.

The morning sun was high in the sky when John reached the top of a steep hill he'd been climbing for the past two hours. He was sweating profusely and breathing hard as a result of the unaccustomed exertion. His lungs were heaving, and his legs felt like concrete, but he felt alive. Truly alive.

The Irishman had found himself on a grassy hilltop just above the tree line. Pleasantly tired, he flopped down onto the ground and lay there, staring up at the sky.

He soon became lost in thought.

Invariably, he thought about the incredible turn of events that had brought about such dramatic changes in his life. *A week ago I was nearly dead,* he reminded himself. *Now . . . now I'm on my way back to full health . . . and I'm living with a tribe of Aborigines!*

He laughed out loud, aware how bizarre his recent experience seemed even to himself.

John knew if he shared his recent adventures with his Irish mates, they wouldn't believe him. "Not even Noel would believe me," he murmured to himself. Having been spared after being captured by the Kabi was unbelievable in itself, but not even he could quite believe he'd ended up something of a celebrity within the clan.

Again he laughed out loud.

Having rested and recovered his breath, he sat up and, for the first time since arriving on the hilltop, took in the views.

Beautiful.

In front of him, and far below, was the Kabi encampment. Clan members looked no bigger than ants as they went about their everyday lives. From here, they were so small the adults were indistinguishable from the children.

A short distance beyond the encampment, the blue Pacific sparkled, reminding him to have another swim in the bay when he returned. Native fishermen could be seen out on the bay in their canoes.

To his left and right, or north and south, the coastline continued as far as he could see. The rainforest that bordered the beaches to the north seemed more lush than any he'd ever seen, and the hills more rugged than any he encountered on his trek from Moreton Bay.

Looking south, he could see the approximate coastal route he'd followed from the penal settlement. He looked for some sign of the settlement, but realised it was far too far away to be seen. Not even the bay was visible from here.

Swivelling around on his haunches, he saw rolling hills—some bush-covered, some not—stretching ever westward toward the dry interior. The hills were separated by deep valleys or gorges marking the likely location of streams or rivers, and by vast plains dotted with stands of ever-present gum trees and ant hills. A mob of red kangaroos could be seen grazing alongside a distant billabong.

Turning back to face the sea, he jumped to his feet when he saw the unmistakable sight of a ship. The northbound vessel was a good ten miles, perhaps more, offshore. Despite the distance, he identified her as a three-masted schooner. She was a wonderful sight. "Hey!" he shouted, waving his arms above his head. "Over here!" The excited Irishman stopped shouting and waving when he realised from that distance anyone looking his way would hardly see the hill he was on let alone see him atop it. "Bloody idiot," he chastised himself. He sat down again and watched the northbound schooner, not taking his eyes off her until she eventually disappeared from view.

Sighting the vessel had been an emotional experience for him. It reminded him of his ultimate goal—to board a ship that would carry him to freedom—and it brought back to him how much he missed civilisation.

He wondered how many other vessels had sailed by without his knowledge. Logic told him that more than a few had. That thought depressed him, and it was with a heavy heart he set off back toward the encampment.

John returned via a different route. This time, he descended the southern side of the hill he'd just climbed, heading for a stream he'd spotted from the summit. It had reminded him he was thirsty.

Reaching the stream, he drank his fill.

It suddenly struck him that he didn't have to return to the encampment. "There's nothing to stop me trekking north," he told himself. The sight of the schooner had reawakened him. He debated his options.

To flee or not to flee?

After quite some time, common sense prevailed. "A week ago I was almost dead," he reminded himself. He resumed walking toward the encampment—toward the place he currently thought of as home. "If I tried to flee, these savages would track me down within a day," he muttered. He was convinced if he gave the Kabi one good reason to put him to death, they surely would, and so he resigned himself to remaining with them for the time-being at least.

Once a prisoner always a prisoner!

As he walked, he had a feeling he was being followed. He glanced behind him, but saw nothing. He was reminded of the times Dingo had tracked him. Remembering the dingo that had temporarily adopted him, he stopped and studied the bush behind him, looking for a sign of the wild dog with the distinctive reddish markings. "Is that you, Dingo?" he called.

Seeing nothing, he put it down to his imagination and resumed walking.

41

S TRANGE SOUNDS CARRIED TO HIM from somewhere in the trees ahead. At first he couldn't make sense of the sounds. He proceeded with caution. As he drew closer to the source of the noise, he identified the sounds of combat. The grunts and curses of natives were accompanied by the clanging of clubs and spears against shields.

John's first instinct was to flee. However, he didn't detect any malice in the sounds that reached him. It sounded, to him, that whoever it was making the noise was practising or play-fighting rather than fighting for real. This was immediately confirmed when two of the combatants laughed and exchanged what could only be described as banter.

The Irishman resumed walking. He soon reached a clearing, and his earlier assessment was proven correct. There, in the clearing, were the armed clan members he'd seen earlier. They were honing their fighting skills. Their near-naked bodies glistened in sweat as they went at each other, weapons flailing.

From his hiding place in the trees, John watched as the aggressive Turo held off two men with the heavy wooden, spear-like weapon known as the nulla nulla. Similarly armed, his opponents swung their weapons at the big native, seemingly intent on taking his head off. Turo parried the blows and responded with forceful blows of his own. The first blow felled one of his opponents, and the second blow caused the other to hop away on one foot, holding his other leg after having been struck across the shin. This attracted jeers and laughter from those waiting their turn.

Nearby, Gabirri was in a spirited contest with another young native. They also used nulla nullas, but they had shields as well, and these, John observed, they used both defensively and offensively. The shields, it seemed, had been fashioned from the bark of large trees. They were quite sizeable, affording excellent protection if used by someone who knew what they were doing. And, by all accounts, Gabirri knew what he was doing, despatching his opponent with apparent ease. To the amusement of the others, the vanquished man limped away, rubbing a bruised knee.

Four others who had paired off were also going at each other, using a variety of weapons and combinations of weapons. To John's eyes they appeared more evenly matched.

Those not currently involved sat around, observing the action, chatting or, in one case, snoozing while they awaited their turn.

When one pair of combatants needed a breather, another pair would take their place—if they felt like it.

John, who had seen British soldiers honing their bayonet and hand-to-hand combat skills during training drills at Parramatta, thought the Kabis a lot less organised. There appeared to be little structure to their practice with participants stopping whenever the mood took them for a chat or to exchange banter. Some wandered off every now and then to assuage their thirst at a nearby billabong while others sat or lay down whenever they wanted a rest. Nevertheless, the Irishman couldn't help but be impressed. Despite the casual approach, there was little doubt these men were natural fighters. He guessed they were battle-hardened, too, as it was common knowledge the coastal tribes were constantly at war.

Gabirri paired off with Turo, and John watched, transfixed, as two went at each other. Both were now armed with nulla nulla and shield, and it was immediately obvious they were very evenly matched. They wielded their weapons with expertise, each reigning blows down on the other. Only expert use of their shields prevented them from serious injury or worse. The blows seemed for real, and there was little doubt the loser of this contest would be left bruised and bleeding.

Only now did John notice the presence of women in the trees beyond the clearing. He recognised Mamba and her Aunt Jiba among them. They were collecting bunya nuts from the towering bunya pine trees so common to this region, and none appeared to be taking any interest in the practice fights that had so captured the Irishman's attention.

John was so fascinated by the fighting, he left the cover of the trees and wandered into the clearing for a better view. All except Turo and Gabirri acknowledged him with a nod or a smile.

A spare nulla nulla lying nearby caught John's attention. Curious, he picked it up and copied the combatants' technique, thrusting the weapon outwards and parrying imaginary blows. Only now did Mamba and the other women notice him. They stopped to watch.

When the men noticed John trying to emulate them, they stopped what they were doing to observe him. Several laughed out loud at his amateurish efforts.

Realising he was now the centre of attention, John lowered his borrowed weapon, more than a little embarrassed.

"I see you have forgotten how to fight, Moilow!" one native shouted. Quietly, to his friends, he added, "That is not the Moilow I remember."

Most of the men were amused. Not Turo, though. Angry, he strode over to confront John, pulling up only a foot short. "Why do you mock us?" he asked.

Unable to ascertain what it was that Turo had asked, John stared back at him mutely. He noticed the belligerent native stood slightly taller than himself, which made him more than six foot—tall for an Aborigine. He was strongly built, too, and appeared ever-ready for a fight. Finally, John looked down at the weapon still in his hand. "It's heavier than it looks," he said sheepishly.

Turo observed the white man as he tried, in vain, to interpret the strange language he spoke. At length he said, "You cannot be Moilow." He leaned forward until his face was almost touching John's, forcing his opposite to take a step back.

The Irishman experienced a sinking feeling in his gut.

The bloody savage is going to challenge me!

Turo thrust his shield into John's free hand. The big man turned around and held his hand up to the others. One of them—the same one who had just moments ago accused John of forgetting how to fight—hurried over and handed Turo his own shield.

Without warning, Turo rounded on John and aimed a blow for his head. The Irishman just managed to parry the nulla nulla with his shield, but was too slow to block the next blow that Turo aimed at his shins. The painful strike drew blood and caused John to cry out.

The other men gathered around the pair as they circled each other warily.

John was now hobbling and he was already breathing hard. All his remaining strength had drained from him, and the weapons in his hands seemed heavy and unwieldy. He aimed his nulla nulla at Turo's head, but it was easily parried.

The Irishman sensed his opponent could finish him any time he wanted to.

The bastard's just playing with me!

Turo had had enough. Knocking his opponent's shield aside, he jabbed him in the stomach, winding him. John doubled over, gasping for air, at which point Turo struck him on the back, sending him face first to the ground. Fortunately for John, the big man had used his forearm to deliver the coup de grâce. If he had used his nulla nulla, the Irishman didn't doubt he would be dead.

Using his foot, Turo rolled John onto his back, then, standing astride him, raised his nulla nulla above his head and pretended to deliver a death blow. The weapon stopped just short of John's forehead. Looking down at his opponent, Turo said, "You are not Moilow." Turning to the others, he said, "He is not Moilow." With that, he turned his back on John and returned to his companions.

Gabirri was about to resume practising when he noticed John was having trouble getting back to his feet. He hurried over to the struggling white and helped him up.

"Thanks," John mumbled.

The two looked at each other for one brief moment before Gabirri returned to the others.

John realised he'd well and truly outstayed his welcome, and so he set off for the encampment. He was hobbling now and he was hurting all over as a result of the beating he'd just sustained. As he departed, he wasn't aware he was being observed by Mamba and the other women.

An elderly woman looked at Mamba and said, "Moilow is not the same."

Mamba ignored her companion and resumed collecting banya nuts. The look on her face told the elderly woman that Mamba agreed with her observation.

The route John followed to reach the encampment turned out to be problematic for he soon encountered a gully whose sides were too steep to safely descend, forcing him to walk some distance to circumvent it. This was more than a little frustrating as he was tired and in pain, and he was thirsty once more.

How do I get myself into these predicaments?

As he had so often done on his recent trek north, a resigned John just focused on putting one foot in front of the other as he walked away from the edge of the gully.

Had he been more alert, he may have noticed he was being followed. Nowra, the teenage boy whom Mirritji had ordered to follow the white spirit as he set out from the encampment, had been on his tail all day. Fit and agile, like all Kabi boys his age—all except those injured or handicapped in some way—Nowra was darker than any of his fellows. This was appropriate for his name translated as *Black Cockatoo*.

Nowra had been honoured to have been given such an important assignment, and he was enjoying himself immensely. Observing the white spirit acting strangely, waving and talking to himself had fascinated him. Watching him fight, or trying to fight, had been hilarious. He couldn't wait to relate what he'd seen to his friends.

Now, the teenager had a decision to make. He'd just arrived at the edge of the same gully John had reached moments earlier, and he had the choice of following his quarry or descending into the gully and saving time. It was obvious to him that John was returning to the encampment, so he decided to make good use of the shortcut the gully would provide and wait for the white to catch up to him. He began climbing down the steep bank, taking care to make good use of available hand and toe-holes in the rocks.

Nowra hadn't descended more than a few feet when a loose rock caused him to lose balance and fall. He let out an involuntary yell as he tumbled to the gully floor twenty feet below.

John heard the teen's shout even though he was a good fifty yards distant. Sensing it was a cry of distress, he quickly backtracked to identify who it was who had called out.

He soon arrived at the place where he'd viewed the gully not long before. It happened to be the very place Nowra had begun his descent.

Groans alerted him to the youth's plight. Still he could see nothing. Protruding rocks concealed the gully floor. "Hello?" he called out.

The groaning ceased.

"Who is there?" John called again.

No response.

John studied the rock-face below and saw loose rocks and scuff marks where Nowra had lost his balance. "Hello?"

Still no response.

Fearing whoever it was had fallen was either dead or unconscious, John threw caution to the wind and began climbing down the rock-face. He was halfway down before he sighted Nowra. The youth was hobbling away from him, apparently keen to avoid the embarrassment of being found out by the person he was meant to be tracking. It appeared he had sprained an ankle or wrenched a knee perhaps, or both.

So I was being followed.

John resumed climbing and soon reached the bottom of the gully. "Hey!" he shouted at the youth who was now a good seventy-five yards distant.

On realising he'd been seen, Nowra pulled up. He *had* sprained his ankle and was relieved he could now rest it while he waited for John to catch up to him.

The youth was too embarrassed even to turn around to face the approaching white man. He was mortified that he was now the quarry, and the man he'd been tasked with tracking was now tracking him. Nowra could already hear his friends mocking him. As for Mirritji: it didn't bear thinking what he would say.

John, who was hobbling himself, finally caught up to Nowra. "Are you alright?" he asked.

Only now did the youth look around at him. Glancing at his left ankle, which was now noticeably swollen, he mumbled something unintelligible.

John quickly checked Nowra's ankle and determined it was only a sprain. Glancing up at him, he said, "It's not broken." The youth's expression signalled he didn't understand. John added, "It's only a sprain."

Nowra tried to put his weight on his left foot, and his ankle gave way. He'd have fallen had John not supported him. Before he knew what was happening, John grabbed his arm and put it around his shoulders.

"Best get you home," John smiled as he took as much of Nowra's weight as he could manage.

They set off like that along the gully floor. It was slow going as John was battling his own injuries. Both his shins hurt like hell and his back ached as a result of his run-in with Turo. *We must look a right royal couple,* he thought.

Mirritji thought so, too. The elder had stumbled across the pair whilst out searching for a tecoma vine needed to make a new spear. Looking down from his vantage point above the gully, he had quickly established what had just transpired. Nowra had fallen and injured himself, and the man he was supposedly tracking had gone to his assistance.

Now, as Mirritji observed John helping the injured youth, he didn't see a white man. He saw a white spirit. "It is Moilow," he said to himself.

The elder retreated from the edge of the gully, anxious not to be seen or to cause Nowra any further embarrassment. Even from a distance, he'd been able to establish that the injured youth was ashamed that he'd been caught out so badly.

Down on the floor of the gully, John and Nowra were having to stop every so often to rest—the former because he was running out of energy, the latter because his ankle hurt so much.

To take their minds off their plight, John began chatting away to his dark young companion in English, and every now and then he'd ask him a question. Eventually, he received a smile from the bemused youth, and it wasn't long before Nowra was responding and chatting away in his native tongue.

Observing his young companion, John couldn't help noticing how brilliantly the youth's snow-white teeth contrasted with his coal-black skin whenever he smiled, which was frequently.

The shadows were lengthening by the time they staggered into the encampment. The unlikely pair were both exhausted—and they were best of mates.

Dusk was falling as Mamba returned to the encampment after her bunya nut-gathering excursion. She arrived at her bivouac to find Murrowdooling and Carravanty playing outside and John nursing his battle wounds just inside the entrance. The weary Irishman had removed his cloak and rolled his breeches up, and Mamba could see the incident with Turo had left him with savage welts across his shins and a badly bruised back—not to mention a bruised ego.

If John was expecting sympathy from Mamba, he was about to be disappointed. She spent a full minute berating him for having fought so badly, and another minute imploring him to try harder to revive his fighting skills—and his language skills, too, while he was at it.

"I do not know what is worse, Moilow," she said, standing over him, "watching you trying to fight or listening to you when you speak."

John realised he was receiving a tongue-lashing—though he didn't know why—but he held his own tongue.

Mamba continued to lecture him while, at the same time, tending his wounds. After fetching some mud from the nearby billabong, she smeared it over the welts on his shins, concealing them beneath a mudpack that dried as quickly as it was applied. The mud's cooling effect immediately lessened the pain.

She then motioned to him to roll over onto his front. He complied and she proceeded to massage his bruised back, using a herbal paste she kept for just such emergencies. This, too, eased his pain. Better than that, her touch felt heavenly. The sensation almost put him to sleep.

"Ahhh . . . you are a gem, Mamba," he sighed.

Mamba abruptly stopped massaging. This was the first time John had used her name, and it had caught her by surprise. It was, as far as she was concerned, a watershed moment in their relationship.

Sensing her hesitation, John looked up. He was surprised to see her eyes glistened with emotion. "What?" he asked, momentarily perplexed. When a solitary tear ran down the young woman's face, he became even more perplexed. "I'm sorry!" he said, fearing he'd upset her.

Mamba smiled, putting him at ease. "I now know it is really you, Moilow," she murmured. "You can take as long as you like to truly come back to me," she added. "I will wait."

John sat up and stared at her. He didn't know what she had just said, but somehow that didn't matter. He had a feeling he'd find out—all in good time. In the meantime, it felt good to him just being around her. It felt right, too. Surprisingly right.

42

NEXT MORNING, AS HE ENJOYED his first meal of the day in the company of Mamba and her sons, John wasn't sure if he was imagining it or not, but the menfolk—Turo and one or two others aside—seemed to be affording him even more respect than usual. Every so often, men would wander over, either singly or in pairs, to bid him good morning and wish him well. Some would even pat his head, as was the custom of these people.

The Irishman couldn't work out what he'd done to deserve such attention, but he took it all in his stride, acknowledging well-wishers with a smile and a word of thanks.

John looked at Mamba to see if she knew what was going on. She pretended to ignore him, giving no indication whether or not she knew any more than he did. The mischievous gleam in her eye told him she did. "You wouldn't tell me even if I could understand you, would you?" he asked.

Mamba *did* know what was going on. Her grandfather had relayed to her soon after rising that morning that, despite being injured himself, John had gone out of his way to assist the injured Nowra after his mishap in the gully the previous afternoon. Grandfather, apparently, had received that titbit from a neighbour who had learned it from another neighbour.

As it turned out, on returning to the encampment Nowra had confided in a trusted friend, telling him of the incredible experience he'd had with the white spirit, and swearing his friend to absolute secrecy. The friend had inadvertently let the news slip to another friend, and before the sun had set everyone in the encampment had heard the story.

As for Nowra, rather than being embarrassed, as he'd feared he would be, he found he had good reason to be proud of his new status as a major player in the drama that had played out the previous day. After all, his name would forever be associated with the white spirit in Kabi folklore.

Nowra was among the first to come and wish John well, and, to the Irishman's surprise, and Mamba's, too, the dark teenager with the dazzling smile sat down and chatted away like a long, lost friend. John responded in kind, marvelling at the same time how people who didn't remotely understand each other, somehow did. Understand each other, that is. At the same time, he saw the humour in the situation, and couldn't stop chuckling to himself every now and then.

The day's surprises weren't over. After they'd finished eating, Mamba stood and extended her hand to John. Mystified, he pushed himself to his feet and looked at her enquiringly. The fetching young woman laughed gaily and ran off into the trees, pulling the bemused Irishman after her.

Mamba led him up a steep track through the bush. They were soon sweating profusely in the early morning heat. Already it was evident another hot, humid day was on the way.

John was breathing hard by the time they reached a grassy clearing near the summit of the hill they'd been climbing for the past five minutes. The injuries he'd sustained the previous day still hurt, though they were much improved as a result of the attention they had received from Mamba.

Entering the clearing, the young mother indicated they should sit down facing each other. Only after they were seated did John notice a gap in the surrounding trees afforded an uninterrupted view of the encampment and the bay beyond it. As before, fishermen could be seen out on the bay in their canoes.

Turning his attention back to Mamba, he could see she had something on her mind.

Mamba reached out, grasped both his hands in hers and looked into his eyes. "It is time you recovered your memory of our language, Moilow," she said earnestly. "We will begin now."

John found himself looking into her dark brown eyes. He found them beguiling.

Mamba tightened her grip when she realised her man was not concentrating. "Moilow!" she snapped. "We begin now."

Momentarily startled, John wondered what she was saying and what she expected of him.

Mamba released John's hands. She then pointed, first at his eye and then at hers. "Mee-ar," she said.

"What?"

"Mee-ar," Mamba repeated

"Me . . . aha?"

What the hell is she on about?

"Mee-ar," Mamba said yet again. Trying to remain patient, she pointed once more at her eye.

Finally, John understood.

She's giving me a language lesson!

Playing along for the moment, he said, "Mee-ar."

A relieved Mamba nodded.

John pointed to his own eye and said, "Mee-ar." Without pausing, he added, "Eye."

Now it was Mamba's turn to look puzzled. "Eye-ee?"

The Irishman shook his head. "Eye," he repeated.

"Eye," Mamba said, near-perfect this time. She then pointed to her lips. "Damboor."

"Danaboor."

Mamba shook her head. "Damboor."

John found himself staring at her lips. He began to imagine all sorts of things and suddenly looked away. *What the hell am I doing?* he asked himself. *I'll be gone soon.*

"Damboor," Mamba repeated, more insistent this time. She was proving a hard taskmaster.

The Irishman stared at her blankly.

Jesus, this is crazy.

At length he said, "I'm not who you think I am."

Mamba looked at him uncomprehendingly.

John touched his chest. "John Graham," he said, formally introducing himself to her for the first time. He then pointed at her. "Mamba."

Mamba shook her head and reached out and touched John's chest. "Moilow!" she insisted.

Frustrated, John stood up and began walking back down the hill. A confused Mamba could only watch as he disappeared into the trees.

After returning to the encampment, John headed for the beach. There, he stripped off once more to his undershorts and entered the water, relishing the feeling of cool saltwater on his skin. It was a welcome respite from the heat, and it soothed his injuries also.

The saltwater also soothed the facial cuts he'd inflicted upon himself once again when he'd shaved earlier. This morning's shave had gone better than yesterday's, but it still wasn't ideal. He promised himself he'd find some better shaving tools than those he was currently using.

As soon as he was waist-deep, he tried a few cautious swimming strokes and was relieved to find his shoulder didn't hurt too much. The Irishman swam for a minute or two before rolling over and floating on his back. He didn't want to overdo it and reinjure his shoulder.

Lying there, staring up at the blue beyond, he went over what he'd just experienced with Mamba. The language lesson had caught him by surprise. It had brought home to him that she and the rest of her clan truly believed him to be one of them, and they fully expected him to master their language and embrace their way of life. The very thought horrified him. *Are these savages colour blind?* he asked himself. *Can't they see I'm white?*

He decided it would soon be time to move on.

I have a boat to catch.

He tried to swim a few strokes backstroke, but the awkward movement hurt his shoulder so he rolled over and dog-paddled a short distance. Only then did he notice Gabirri. The impressive young native was standing in the shallows, staring at him.

Gabirri beckoned to the Irishman as soon as he saw that he had his attention. "Greetings, Moilow," he said when John approached.

John grunted by way of acknowledgement.

"We hunt," Gabirri announced. With that, the native strode up the beach to collect something he'd left beneath the palms.

John quickly dressed, donning his breeches, boots and cloak, before hurrying to catch up to the native. When he reached the palms, he found Gabirri gathering up items that included three spears, each with different barbs, two woomeras and a variety of smaller weapons, including knives fashioned from shells and rocks, a tomahawk-shaped club and a shoulder bag not unlike the one Mamba had loaned him. A peek into the bag confirmed it contained edible roots, berries and nuts.

Gabirri threw the bag over his shoulder and scooped up most of the weapons. These he attached either to his back or around his waist, using cords apparently fashioned from strips of flax. The native pointed at the remaining weapons—a spear and the club—and motioned to his opposite to claim these for himself.

As he stooped to pick up the two weapons, John was starting to realise the native had an adventure of some sort planned.

Nice of him to ask if I want to join him.

The Irishman had no sooner picked up the weapons than Gabirri set off through the palms toward the encampment. As they strode through it toward the hills beyond, John noticed Mamba who had only just returned to their bivouac. She waved at him when she saw him. He pretended not to see her.

John lay prone in the long grass, trying to ignore the hot afternoon sun as it beat down on his exposed back. He'd made the mistake of removing his cloak an hour or so earlier, and now he was paying for it. He could sense a bad case of sunburn coming up.

The Irishman daren't move. His eyes were fixed on his hunting partner who was crouched behind a bush a few yards in front of him, his woomera raised and ready to release a spear at a wallaby that grazed nearby. The unsuspecting wallaby was slowly munching its way toward Gabirri, but it still wasn't close enough for the native's liking, and so the wait continued.

So far, the day had been an eye-opener for John. By morning's end, Gabirri had demonstrated how proficient a hunter he was and how inept at hunting he, John, was. How he had survived three long months living off the land, he didn't know. Before noon, Gabirri had notched up half a dozen kills, including a boar, a roo, a python, a brush turkey and two other birds the Irishman had never seen before.

John, on the other hand, had killed nothing. It hadn't been for want of trying. He'd thrown his borrowed spear at three different targets—a wallaby and two monitor lizards—without finding the mark once. Gabirri had remained extraordinarily patient, but the Irishman could sense beneath his quiet reserve he was wondering why he'd bothered to invite the man he called Moilow along with him.

Up ahead, John could see that his hunting partner was preparing to launch his spear. The wallaby, it seemed, had hopped to within range.

Still the native waited.

John felt like he was frying beneath the sun. His exposed back was burning up. He *had* to do something about it.

The cloak he'd removed lay close by.

If I can just cover my back and shoulders with it.

Aware the slightest movement could spook the wallaby, he reached out, ever so slowly, his fingers reaching for the cloak.

That's all it took. The wallaby saw or sensed the movement and bounded away. Gabirri stood and released his spear. The woomera it had been attached to ensured its flight was smooth and fast, but the wallaby was faster and it evaded the spear by a foot or more.

Gabirri rounded on John, his reserve forgotten for the moment. "Moilow, why did you move?" he asked.

"Sorry . . . I . . ."

"You know not to move when stalking!" a frustrated Gabirri grumbled. He'd resisted the urge to criticise his companion's hunting technique earlier, but this time he couldn't restrain himself. "Did you forget everything in the spirit world?" he asked.

John could only shrug his sunburnt shoulders.

The white man's ineptness was particularly galling for Gabirri because Moilow had been a hunter without peer, and they'd often hunted together.

Gabirri suddenly and unexpectedly smiled when he recalled one of a number of humorous incidents the pair had experienced whilst hunting. "Do you remember the time that big red turned on you?" he asked, referring to an event involving a red kangaroo. Not waiting for John to respond, he continued, "I thought it was going to drown you." He burst out laughing at the memory and clapped John over his sunburnt back, causing him to grimace.

The change of mood had taken John by surprise. He wasn't to know the incident Gabirri referred to related to the time Moilow had cornered a wounded roo in a shallow stream. The big red had bowled him over and then trampled him underfoot, as if trying to drown him. Only Gabirri's intervention had saved him from serious injury or worse.

Not wanting to discourage Gabirri's sudden good mood, he laughed along with him. This only served to encourage his fellow hunter who began relating every humorous experience he and Moilow had ever shared during their trek back to the encampment.

The shadows were lengthening when John and Gabirri found themselves in a bush clearing. John immediately recognised it as the same clearing he had visited with Mamba that morning. The encampment was visible through the gap in the trees. Clan members could be seen starting to prepare their evening meals, and the smoke from their cooking fires curled up into the sky. It was a scene of tranquillity.

The two hunters lay the carcasses they'd been carrying on the grass and stopped to admire the view. It felt good to be free of the heavy loads for a moment—more so for John whose sunburnt shoulders had been causing him some pain.

John had been carrying the python, and Gabirri the roo. The smaller carcasses and weapons they'd divided up between them. The Irishman was convinced the python must have recently swallowed a whole horse, so heavy was it.

From where they stood, they could recognise individual clan members. John found he was looking for Mamba, but he couldn't see her.

They were about to resume walking when Gabirri suddenly tensed.

John glanced at him. "What?"

Gabirri pointed to a stand of gum trees a hundred yards or so north of the encampment.

At first John saw nothing. Then he noticed a movement. Focussing his eyes, he saw a native stumbling, near-naked, toward the encampment. The native appeared to be alone and was likely injured, or wounded perhaps, for his movements were clumsy and he kept falling over every few yards.

43

W ITHOUT A WORD, GABIRRI BEGAN running toward the encampment. John followed. They left the carcasses where they'd dropped them.

Their arrival at the encampment coincided with the newcomer's arrival. The native, who, it was now clear, was not Kabi, staggered into the clearing and collapsed at the feet of Turo who had been amongst the first of the others to notice him. It wasn't long before other clan members came to investigate.

It was immediately obvious to John the native was in distress for he just lay there, gasping for breath and groaning in pain. He'd been badly wounded. Blood flowed freely from nasty slashes to his chest, arms and back, he was covered in scratch marks, his feet were raw and bloodied, and he appeared to be exhausted—all signs that he'd fled some distance over rugged terrain after being attacked by someone who clearly wanted him dead. Some of his wounds had been opened to the bone, and it appeared his attacker, or attackers, had used a knife or some other cutting instrument.

At Turo's bidding, a boy scurried away, returning moments later with a calabash of water, which he held to the wounded man's mouth. The native gratefully gulped down the water while yet another clan member tended to his wounds. Having drunk his fill, he then did his best to answer the questions his rescuers were firing at him.

Through the press of bodies around him, John didn't have a clear view of the native, but what little he could see indicated he was from another tribe. His physical characteristics were quite different to those of other Aborigines. Lighter skinned and slighter of build than the Kabi, with finer features, he reminded John of Mamba. The Irishman wondered if she originally had some connection with his tribe. Added to that, the scarification that covered his limbs and torso also covered his face—another feature which set him apart from the Kabi.

The Irishman would learn later the unfortunate man, whose name was Derain, was the last surviving member of a clan of the Ngadjonjii tribe, from the rainforests to the north. Appropriately, his name translated to *Of the Mountains*. Marauding raiders from another tribe had slaughtered all but him.

Mirritji's arrival prompted the clan members to make way for the elder. He pushed his way through to see what had drawn such a crowd.

On seeing Mirritji, Turo started bringing him up to date with what he'd just learned. "This man says he is of the Ngadjonjii tribe," he advised. "He calls himself Derain."

"What happened to him?" Mirritji asked.

"He says his people were attacked by the Wanjuri."

Mirritji frowned at the mention of the Wanjuri. They were a warrior-like northern tribe who had caused problems for the Kabi before.

Turo continued, "He says the Wanjuri are sweeping south along the coast, killing all in their path." He turned back to Derain. "How many of them?" he asked.

"Many," the wounded native said, struggling to remain conscious.

"How many is many?" Turo demanded.

"I counted . . . a hundred . . . before . . . I . . . lost count," the Ngadjonjii mumbled.

"How long before they reach us?" Mirritji asked.

Turo looked at Derain who, by now, was lapsing in and out of consciousness. "How long before the Wanjuri dogs arrive here?" he asked. When the wounded native didn't respond, he bent down and slapped his face to make him focus. "How long?" he asked.

Derain shook his head as if to clear the fog that was threatening to overwhelm him. "Two . . . days . . . at most," he mumbled before losing consciousness once more.

Looking up at Mirritji, Turo said, "He says—"

"I heard him," the elder said. He stared off into space. The information they'd just received was the worst possible news. The Wanjuri were battle-hardened warriors, numerically stronger than the Kabi and intent on expanding their territories. Every few years, for as long as Mirritji could remember, they went on the rampage, attacking anyone not of their tribe. His own father and two of his uncles had fallen victim to them in past raids.

All eyes were on Mirritji. The respected elder had had more dealings with the Wanjuri than any of them. He would know what to do, they hoped.

Mirritji looked westward, toward the setting sun. Finally, he said, "It is too late in the day to abandon our camp. We leave at first light."

That wasn't what Turo wanted to hear. "We should stay and fight, not run!" he said. The warrior in him wanted blood—the blood of his enemies.

"You heard what the Ngadjonjii told us," Mirritji said, glancing down at Derain. "They outnumber us."

"We Kabi are worth two of—"

"We risk sacrificing too many of our women and children if we stay to fight."

Turo considered this and finally lowered his eyes, indicating he agreed with the older man, albeit reluctantly. Pointing at Derain, who was conscious once more, he asked, "What do we do with the Ngadjonjii?"

"You know what to do with him," Mirritji said. The elder didn't want his people to be encumbered by a wounded man from another tribe. Not while they were fleeing enemies who would happily kill every last one of them. He turned and strode straight for Mootemu's bivouac, intent on advising the Ancient One of the alarming news.

Behind him, Turo raised the nulla nulla he carried and, without hesitating, brought it down savagely on Derain's skull, killing him instantly. It happened too fast for John to avert his eyes. He winced as blood and brain-matter flew from the victim's shattered skull.

Turo then motioned to two youths to remove the body. The youths jumped to it. Each grabbed one of Derain's feet and began dragging him toward the nearby trees. Obviously, there was to be no formal burial for the recently deceased.

The others hurried off to advise friends and family members of the new developments and to begin preparations for their impending departure.

Gabirri accompanied John back to Mamba's bivouac. As they walked, the native discussed the news Derain had delivered. It all went over John's head of course, but the Irishman could tell whatever it was, it was serious.

On arriving at the bivouac, Gabirri quickly relayed the news to Mamba before departing. Her reaction was further confirmation for John that something serious had happened, or was about to happen. Mamba immediately called Murrowdooling and Carravanty to her and sat them down in front of the cooking fire she had already begun preparing. She planned to feed them and get them bedded down in anticipation of the early morning start ahead.

·Ɛ·————·Ȝ·

John had just finished eating the cooked meal Mamba had prepared when Gabirri appeared out of the darkness and motioned to him to accompany him to a campfire in the centre of the encampment. They arrived to find all the clan's menfolk were assembling alongside the fire. There was a distinct air of solemnity around them.

It was immediately evident to John that a ceremony of sorts was about to commence.

The men, who wore only their loincloths, were painted white in the markings of the tribe. Those whose artwork was complete were helping others, applying ochre to faces and bodies.

Gabirri saw Nowra and called the youth over to him. Nowra, who was already painted, had been rendered near-unrecognisable by his markings. After relaying some brief instructions to the youth, Gabirri left him to ensure John was made ready for the ceremony.

Nowra solemnly led the Irishman over to a large tub around which a number of men were gathered. The tub, which was in fact the base of a hollowed-out tree-trunk, was full of mud collected from the nearby billabong, and the men were applying the mud to their bodies and faces.

The youth charged with supervising the white spirit motioned to him to remove his clothes. John obliged, removing his cloak, boots and breeches, but leaving his undershorts on. Nowra then commenced applying the mud to John's face.

Feeling slightly silly, John smiled, but his smile was not returned. A further reminder for him that this was serious business. The ceremony he had been roped into was in fact a result of what had transpired earlier. It was a ritual intended to appease the spirits of war—to ensure they would watch over the Kabi and keep them safe from the bloodthirsty Wanjuri who were sweeping down the coast.

By now most of the men were seated around the fire. They were chanting to the accompaniment of the drumming sound made by the clan's musicians who beat sticks together to produce the cacophony. Two clan members played didgeridoos, adding to the unique atmosphere.

Nowra led John over to where a place had been left for him between Gabirri and Mirritji. They nodded to the new arrival as he sat down. John noted the respect with which they greeted him, and he returned the gesture.

No sooner had he sat down than the men rose, as one, to their feet. John remained seated, unsure what, if anything, was expected of him. A stern glance from Gabirri told him he was expected to join in, and so he stood up.

Standing on the spot, the men began chanting louder and stamping their feet on the ground. It wasn't long before they appeared to fall into a trance. Still the chanting and stamping continued.

John looked around at the others and then down at his own bare skin. In the flickering light of the campfire, he realised that notwithstanding his white skin and his permanently grey undershorts—or what was left of them at least—he was hardly distinguishable from the natives around him. That was unless they looked at his sunburnt back. It was causing him so much pain, he was sure his skin was glowing red like the fire's embers.

Without warning, or even any noticeable signal, the men dropped, as one, onto all fours and began circling the fire, mimicking the sounds and actions of dingoes. John, who was standing close to the fire, watched, bemused and transfixed, as the men scampered in a circle around him, growling and barking like the wild dogs they were emulating.

For one crazy moment, it seemed they were honouring him. He put that idea out of his mind immediately.

⊷⋲•————•⋺⊷

John was ready for sleep when the ceremony finally ended and he was able to return to Mamba's bivouac. It had been another long and strenuous day—and dramatic, too. He arrived at the bivouac to find the cooking fire Mamba had prepared still burning, and she was sitting beside it. She had been waiting for him, though he didn't know that.

Mamba had watched the ceremony from the shadows, and had been overcome with pride when she saw her Moilow participating. She was aware a great honour had been accorded him, even if he wasn't aware of that, for to be invited to participate in such a ceremony showed that he had finally gained full acceptance by the clan.

Now, as she studied the man before her, the pride she experienced earlier returned. John was still adorned in his ochre markings, and was still wearing only his undershorts. "Moilow," she smiled as she began to rub the markings from his face and body with a damp sponge she used for this very purpose.

As the young mother rubbed the last of the ochre from John's face, he studied her face by the light of the cooking fire. The flickering light accentuated her refined features, reminding him how naturally beautiful she really was. She caught him looking at her, and her eyes sparkled. John thought he saw something in her eyes he hadn't seen before. Something more than the genuine affection he was already aware she had for him.

The Irishman's eyes strayed down to the young woman's slender body. Her arms and legs—or what he could see of them at least beneath the cloak she wore—looked toned to perfection, as to be expected of someone like her who lived so active a life.

John had found Mamba attractive the first time he'd seen her. Nothing had changed since that first memorable meeting when he had almost ended up as a burnt offering to whichever gods it was that they worshiped, and he'd openly admired her natural beauty at every available opportunity ever since.

Tonight was different, however. Standing close to her like this, by the firelight, he found her incredibly attractive, and he suddenly realised he lusted after her. This was confirmed when he felt his manhood hardening. She noticed it, too. His undershorts did little to hide his sudden hankering.

John switched his gaze back to Mamba's eyes and was surprised to see no sign of shock or even embarrassment. She seemed to understand, and, if he wasn't mistaken, she even seemed to welcome the interest *the Colonel,* as he called it, was showing toward her.

Mamba dropped her hands to John's hips and let them rest there for a few tantalising moments before grasping his upright member. "Come with me, Moilow," she murmured huskily. Without taking her eyes from his, and without releasing her grip, she walked backwards toward the entrance of her bivouac, pulling him gently but firmly after her.

Inside the bivouac, John was pleasantly surprised to find they had it to themselves. He wasn't aware that Mamba had anticipated, or hoped for, a romantic liaison with her beloved Moilow this night, and had arranged for her sons to stay with one of her aunts. The young mother hadn't intended to rush things with her returned husband, but when she had heard about the raiding Wanjuri and the risk they posed to the Kabi, she'd decided to bring forward her plans. After all, as Mootemu had confided in her a short time earlier, there may be no tomorrow. It was the Ancient One who suggested she consummate her relationship with the white spirit sooner rather than later.

John didn't object as the sensual young woman pulled him down on top of her on a pile of cloaks she'd had the foresight to spread out on the floor of the bivouac. Mamba still held him, tighter than ever, and didn't release her grip on him even as he removed his undershorts.

"Damn it!" John cursed as his fumbling attempts to remove Mamba's cloak failed.

Only now did Mamba release his grip on him. With one deft movement, she unhooked her cloak and threw it away.

Now both naked, they urgently explored each other's body. For each, this was their first sexual experience in nearly a year—for it was almost that long since Mamba had lost Moilow, and since John had departed Parramatta and its ladies of the night who gave themselves to the convicts, or to those convicts who could afford their services at least.

Past experiences were forgotten as John gave in to his lust and buried himself deep inside Mamba. So enraptured was he, he'd forgotten all about his sunburn.

Mamba murmured his name, or the name she knew him by at least, over and over as their lovemaking reached a crescendo. They climaxed quickly and simultaneously in a tangled mass of arms and legs, and for a long time afterwards they just lay there, without speaking, savouring the utter and absolute contentment each felt.

After a long silence, Mamba whispered, "Moilow, I am so grateful you have returned to warm my heart again."

John didn't hear her. He was asleep.

They made love twice more that night, each time better than the last. The urgency that had accompanied their first effort was replaced by a mutual desire to explore each other's bodies and prolong their enjoyment.

From Mamba's perspective, making love to her Moilow was even more enjoyable than she remembered.

From John's perspective, making love to Mamba was like nothing he'd ever experienced before. Any thoughts he may have had about returning to civilization were shelved for the moment; he couldn't think about anything else besides the nubile woman lying on his chest right now.

44

THE FIRST HINT OF DAWN had yet to materialise when the Kabi quit the encampment that had served them so well.

Mirritji's decree that they should depart at first light had been brought forward when trackers reported the Wanjuri raiders were closer than Derain had indicated. Two trackers had run through the night until they came across the Wanjuris' advance guard. After running non-stop back to the encampment, they had reported that the raiders were little more than a day's trek away, not two days as they'd been advised.

There was a very real fear the Wanjuri would chase after them when they inevitably came across their disbanded encampment. It would be immediately evident the sizeable site had only recently been disbanded, and the raiders would soon work out the encampment had been occupied by the Kabi. It was feared this would provide too big a temptation for the Wanjuri to resist. They hated the Kabi as much as the Kabi hated them, and they would know a clan of this size would include a number of women. For the younger Wanjuri raiders especially, that fact alone would give them all the incentive they needed to pursue their enemies.

The Wanjuris' reputation for wholesale rape—and for taking women as slaves on occasion—was well known. In the past, they had been known to resort to cannibalism, too, though it wasn't known if they still practised it.

And so, there had been no debate when the two Kabi trackers had returned with the bad news shortly before dawn. The encampment had been vacated immediately. Clan members fled inland, their rationale being the Wanjuri were sweeping down the coast and wouldn't want to deviate from the route they followed. Some of the older and wiser heads weren't so sure, though they didn't share that with the women and children for fear of unduly alarming them.

Eighteen men—half the clan's able-bodied men—trailed behind the main group to provide some sort of rear-guard action should the raiders come after them. Working in pairs, they formed a chain that stretched all the way back to the site they'd not long vacated. The strategy was when any pair came into contact with the Wanjuri, they would alert the others and join forces to try to repel or at least delay their enemies.

That left eighteen able-bodied men, including John, with the main party. The Irishman noticed the men carried only their weapons. Food, garments and other essentials—not to mention babies and young children—were carried by the women. He had yet to learn that was always the way with these people: the men preferred to be left unencumbered by anything other than their weapons so that they could respond speedily to any sudden threat, or to the unexpected appearance of wild game in the immediate vicinity.

John had opted to remain close to Mamba and her sons. Armed with a spear and the tomahawk-like club Gabirri had insisted he keep, he carried most of Mamba's meagre possessions. These included cloaks, wooden eating and drinking bowls, and items crafted from seashells, bark and plant fibres whose uses he could only guess at. As for Mamba, she carried a sleeping Carravanty and the remainder of her possessions while a drowsy Murrowdooling trailed along behind her, holding onto the cloak she wore so as not to become separated.

When dawn finally broke, John immediately knew where they were: they were near the same billabong he'd been sitting in when Turo and his fellow hunters had appeared out of nowhere. The memory of that painful encounter came flooding back to him. Such a short amount of time had passed since then yet so much had happened.

Was that a lifetime ago?

He surveyed the familiar terrain. Nothing had changed. The grassy plains were still dotted with ant hills and stands of gum trees. A mob of roos could be seen drinking at a distant billabong. They bounded away when they realised they had company.

If he had been in any doubt where they were heading, he was in no doubt now. They were trekking toward the interior. He wondered if he was finally going to see the Outback he'd heard so much about.

John caught Mamba's eye and they shared a fleeting smile.

The relationship between the pair had completely changed overnight. Their lovemaking had brought them together—closer than he'd have thought possible and as close as she had hoped. As far as she was concerned, they were husband and wife once more.

It no longer mattered to either so much that they couldn't speak the other's language. Each was developing an understanding of what the other meant, or even what the other was thinking, and they were now able to communicate surprisingly well via a simple smile, a nod or even a look.

Analysing his feelings toward Mamba, the Irishman instinctively felt there was more to it than lust. He was under no illusions the lovemaking had much to do with his sudden interest in the beguiling young woman, but he sensed there was more to it than that. He'd enjoyed regular sex with the comfort ladies of Parramatta, and with many women in Ireland before that, but had never felt this way before. He could feel himself falling for her.

As a result of these unexpected feelings, he felt something approaching a proprietary interest in the young mother and her children. He found himself worrying about their welfare.

You're getting soft, Graham.

Looking at Mamba struggling to support her sleeping child as well as her material possessions, he wondered how she'd coped without a man. He knew enough about Aborigines to know they were always on the move, relocating from one site to another, and he realised it was hard enough for the women with partners given the heavy loads they had to carry. Quite apart from food-gathering, cooking and other onerous tasks that befell them. For a single mother to have to cope on her own it would be, he was certain, doubly hard.

Mamba tripped on a rock and fell to the ground, dropping Carravanty before John could reach the pair. The boy woke with a start. To his credit, he didn't cry or utter a word of complaint.

John picked up the sleepy lad while Murrowdooling helped his mother to her feet.

"I will carry him," John said, cradling Carravanty on his hip.

Mamba gave a smile of appreciation, gathered up her scattered possessions and resumed walking.

The Irishman looked at Carravanty and saw that he was now wide awake. The boy grinned as the realisation set in that the man he knew as Moilow was carrying him.

John turned his attention to the other clan members. Only now did he notice many of the able-bodied men, including Gabirri and Turo, were absent. A quick headcount confirmed only seventeen of the men had stayed with the main group. Two days earlier, when it appeared all the clan's able-bodied men were in the encampment, he'd counted thirty-five. He guessed this morning's absentees were protecting the group's flank. At least he hoped they were for he'd worked out that he and his adopted kin were fleeing others who wished them grievous harm.

The Irishman saw that other males in his group included half a dozen elderly men too old and frail to fight even if most did carry a weapon, and ten or so boys, including Murrowdooling and Carravanty, who were too young to fight.

One of the elders was Mootemu who, John noticed, was lying on a makeshift stretcher that was being pulled along by two youths. Trekking was obviously beyond the Ancient One's present capabilities. The Irishman identified Nowra as one of the youths pulling the stretcher, which, he could see, comprised two long poles connected by uniform lengths of vines and flax to support Mootemu's weight. Nowra was still limping slightly as a result of his tumble in the gully two days earlier.

John was faintly amused to see that despite the elderly Mootemu's incapacitation, he held a spear in his bony hands and appeared ready to skewer anyone brave enough to try and take it from him.

Less amusing was the sight of some of the women, mothers included, carrying weapons as well as their everyday possessions. Two of them were noticeably pregnant. It brought home to John just how serious the situation he'd found himself in really was.

⊰⊱————⊰⊱

Two miles behind the fleeing clan members, Gabirri and Turo watched over the abandoned encampment from the hillside above it. They had chosen to stay behind to establish beyond doubt whether the Wanjuri raiders did venture this far south.

From their hiding place in the bush, the pair had an uninterrupted view of the vacated site and coastline beyond. If the raiders approached via the sandy shoreline or the palm groves fringing it, their approach would be noticed whilst they were still some distance away; if they kept to the rainforest that hugged the coast, they'd remain unseen almost until they arrived at the site.

The Kabi warriors didn't expect the Wanjuri to appear en masse. Their enemies' modus operandi was to send scouts, or trackers, out ahead to ascertain the whereabouts of their quarry and to ensure their main force didn't walk into an ambush. Once contact was made, the scouts would report back to the others, or, if their numbers allowed, they would harry their enemies until the main force arrived.

Both Gabirri and Turo knew how the game was played. They'd experienced it before. They were very aware that scouts could cover long distances in a short amount of time, and if they opted to keep to the exposed shoreline, they could arrive at any moment—and so the pair remained on high alert.

It was late morning when Gabirri and Turo realised they were about to have company. A large flock of black cockatoos suddenly rose, as one, from a palm grove at the far end of the bay they overlooked. Squawking, the birds flew off. The commotion they made, and the suddenness with which they departed, signalled to the pair that something had disturbed them.

Sure enough, a spear-wielding native emerged from the palm trees, heading straight for the abandoned encampment. Even from two miles distant, Gabirri and Turo couldn't help but be impressed by the native's effortless running style. He covered the ground with seemingly effortless ease despite the sand underfoot. Spear and woomera in one hand, he carried three more spears on his back. The extra spears were held fast by a line that extended diagonally over his chest and one shoulder. They bounced on his back as he ran, and they were attached in a way that allowed for quick release should they be required.

"Wanjuri," Gabirri said.

Turo nodded.

Shorter and more heavily muscled than any of the other coastal people, the Wanjuri were physically quite different to other tribes. They also favoured the spear over all other weapons, using it as a stabbing weapon as well as for throwing. While the Kabi and other tribes used nulla nullas, knives and other weapons as well as the spear, the Wanjuri used the spear almost exclusively both for fighting and hunting. As a result, they were extremely proficient with the weapon.

"Is he alone?" Turo asked as the native continued toward them.

His question was answered immediately when two more spear-wielding warriors appeared, also running fast. More still appeared, and they didn't stop until they reached the vacated encampment.

"I count ten in all," Gabirri whispered. He looked gravely at his companion before returning his gaze to their enemies. Each was aware of the significance of such a large advance guard. They were obviously intent on finding and delaying the fleeing clan members until the main force caught up to them. That was the only logical conclusion to draw from the presence of so many.

The two Kabi watched as the raiders began a reconnoitre of the site, studying the remains of old cooking fires and discarded possessions, and searching the abandoned bivouacs as they tried to ascertain how many clan members had occupied the site.

They also searched for, and quickly found, signs showing whether the Kabi had fled south along the coast or west toward the interior. Every now and then they came together to report their findings.

Gabirri and Turo had seen enough. They looked at each other and then silently retraced their steps. As soon as they were confident they were out of earshot of their enemies, they began running hard through the bush to inform the others what they'd just seen.

Behind them, the Wanjuri continued their reconnoitre of the site. After conferring once more, they fanned out and headed inland at a steady trot. They were able to make good speed for the Kabi clan members had left many signs to follow.

It took an hour for the Kabi pair to find and alert the others who made up the rear-guard. Thirteen of them—Gabirri and Turo included—remained behind to deal with the immediate threat posed by their enemies while the other five hurried to catch up to the main group. The latter would be needed should any of the Wanjuri warriors break through the trap that was being set for them.

The remaining warriors chose a gully as their killing ground. An ideal site for an ambush, it was the same ravine John and the injured Nowra had followed to return to the encampment a couple of days earlier. The fleeing clan members had ventured into the gully as it offered the quickest route to the interior, so it was likely their enemies would use the same route.

The warriors didn't have long to wait. A signal from Turo, who was hiding in a cluster of bunya pine trees on the cliff-top above the gully entrance, alerted them to the approach of the Wanjuri.

Turo was one of six Kabi hiding near the ravine's entrance. Gabirri had led the others toward the far end of the gully where they hid amongst the rocks.

They planned a pincer manoeuvre, though they called it by another name of course. The strategy, used so successfully by the ancient Greeks during the first Persian invasion and by successive armies ever since, had been perfected over many decades by the Kabi who found it a useful tactic against larger forces. They'd had many opportunities to perfect it for their enemies usually outnumbered them. The Kabi, incidentally, were convinced the manoeuvre had been first devised by their forefathers and was unique to their tribe. They called it *the eel trap*—named after the wooden trap they used to snare the long-finned eels that abounded in the streams and rivers throughout their territory.

From his bird's eye view amongst the trees, Turo counted only seven raiders. They had assembled near the entrance to the gully and showed understandable reluctance to enter it as it was an obvious site for an ambush.

Finally, the raiders entered the gully, their spears at the ready and their eyes scanning the rocks and cliffs on either side of them.

The sun was at its zenith now, and friend and foe alike were conscious of its burning heat. In the gully, the heat was intense as the sun's rays reflected off the rock walls—as John had discovered for himself.

From the far end of the ravine, Gabirri and the others couldn't yet see the approaching Wanjuri, but they could see one of their own perched atop a tree above a point where the ravine veered away from them. The lookout was relaying to them signals that he, in turn, was receiving from Turo. Those signals told Gabirri that seven raiders were approaching along the gully floor.

Gabirri and his companions tensed when their enemies came into view. They saw at once the raiders were breathing hard. They had obviously been pushing themselves in their haste to close with the fleeing Kabi, and their muscular bodies glistened with sweat.

Four of Gabirri's companions had hidden themselves in clefts and gaps in the cliffs on both sides of the gully. He and the others were waiting behind rocks and fallen trees on the gully floor. Those who occupied the higher ground were charged with making the first move. They would release spears from their woomeras simultaneously, and that would be the signal for the others to attack.

From his hiding place behind a large boulder, Gabirri saw the four Kabi warriors above rise as one and release their spears. Three found their mark and three Wanjuri went down—two dead and one wounded.

The wounded raider had been speared through the thigh, and he screamed in agony as he struggled to pull the weapon's vicious barb from his thigh. His suffering ended almost immediately when a large rock smashed his skull. The rock had been thrown by the warrior whose spear had missed its intended target. His companions followed suit, and soon all four were throwing rocks down on their enemies.

As soon as the first spears had been thrown, Gabirri and his companions had left their hiding places and charged the four surviving raiders, their nulla nullas and shields flailing. Their charge predictably coincided with an attack by Turo and his companions from the rear. The Wanjuri didn't have a chance, and they were quickly dealt with, although two Kabi—one of Gabirri's companions and one of Turo's—suffered minor flesh wounds.

In the brief but bloody confrontation, the Kabi had observed the spears thrown by their enemies made a strange whistling sound as they flew through the air. They'd never noticed such a phenomenon before. A quick inspection of the spears revealed they were not dissimilar to their own. Around nine foot long, each had been fashioned from the tecoma vine, and sharp wooden barbs had been secured to the tip using kangaroo sinew, and, in one instance, emu sinew. However, that's where the similarities ended. The Wanjuris' spears featured a new configuration of barbs—both at the tip of the weapon and a few inches below the tip.

Intrigued by the discovery, several Kabi warriors gathered up the fallen spears under the watchful eye of Gabirri and Turo. The pair were mindful that three of the original ten raiders hadn't been accounted for. They realised it was likely that, for whatever reason, the trio had bypassed the gully in their pursuit of the fleeing clan members. Anxious to catch up to the clan, the warriors quickly quit the gully and followed the route they knew would take them to their kith and kin.

45

THE SHADOWS WERE LENGTHENING, AND still the Kabi hadn't received word from Turo and the others. Mirritji, whose bandy legs had carried him to the head of the column of clan members who walked ever westward, hoped the warriors hadn't been overrun.

Apart from the occasional pause at a stream or billabong to quench their thirst, the fleeing clan members hadn't stopped to eat or even to rest. Those who were hungry had eaten while they walked, and those mothers with infants had breastfeed them without stopping either. Such was their desperation to distance themselves from their enemies.

Looking ahead, Mirritji tried to measure the distance to the bush-covered hills that marked the western horizon. Reaching them before nightfall was the immediate goal, for the valleys and rainforests in those hills offered a relatively safe haven for the tiring clan members. It would not do, he knew, to spend the night out here on the plains. Here, they would be far too exposed if the Wanjuri caught up to them.

The elder thought it would be a close run thing. By his estimation, the hills were around six miles away and dusk was fast approaching. Normally, all but the most infirm would easily reach the hills before darkness fell. Today was different, however. Clan members were labouring in the heat, laden down as they were by their weapons, their food provisions and all their earthly possessions such as they were.

Looking around, Mirritji saw the column now stretched back more than half a mile. He signalled furiously to the tail-enders to close the gap. Stragglers, he knew, would pay the price if the raiders caught up with them.

John and Mamba and the boys were about halfway back in the column. The Irishman was now carrying Murrowdooling, who had finally succumbed to his weariness, while Mamba was carrying Carravanty. Both boys were fast asleep.

Since their early morning departure, John and the young mother had conversed more than they had in all their time together. Most of what was said wasn't understood, but, more often than not, the sentiment and meaning behind it was. Each was slowly learning the meaning of words, which, until now, had been foreign to them.

Mamba was currently singing to herself—something John had observed her do often, especially whilst walking. He found the melody enchanting, captivating even, and though he could understand little of what she sang about, it nevertheless strangely resonated with him. For reasons he couldn't explain, it made him feel at one with nature.

"What do you sing about, Mamba?" he enquired, speaking slowly so that she would get the gist of what he was asking.

The young woman smiled patiently and then rolled her eyes in mock exasperation—as if to say this was something John should know. "Why you ask . . . such thing . . . Moilow?" she asked in pigeon English. "Surely remember . . . the Songlines."

John just shrugged. He had heard her and others often talk about something they called *the Songlines,* but still he didn't know what they were.

When Mamba saw that her man looked genuinely bemused, she reverted to her native tongue. "You know we sing to the land and its sacred landmarks because it is alive," she said. "Our ancestors have told us it is so, remember? The Songlines allow us to follow the paths left by our spirit ancestors from the Dreamtime." She paused to assess whether John understood.

The Irishman had heard Mirritji speak of *the Dreamtime.* He understood it no more than he did the Songlines, but he knew better than to dismiss it as twaddle, so he nodded to indicate he was following her so far.

Encouraged, Mamba continued, "By following the . . . Dreaming Tracks . . . we walk in footprints of those . . . who went before us . . . and so we journey safely . . . and never get lost."

That bit John did understand. He had long observed the Kabi never seemed to lose their way, not even when venturing into foreign territories never before visited. He'd learned that for their initiation, the clan's boys *went bush,* as they called it, armed only with a spear and often trekking hundreds of miles into the interior—an age-old ritual which, if they survived, formally ushered them into manhood. On occasion, they didn't return. Not because they'd become lost, he'd been assured, but because some other catastrophe had befallen them. More often than not, that catastrophe was a failure to find food or water, or falling foul of enemies of the Kabi. Whatever the reason, the end result was usually death.

Mamba suddenly pointed to a roo bounding across the plain some distance away, its powerful hind legs leaving small puffs of dust in their wake. "Kangaroo," she said.

John nodded. "Same in my language," he said.

Mamba didn't understand, but she wasn't bothered. Noticing a solitary sulphur-crested cockatoo flying past, she pointed to it and said, "Garrawi."

"Garrawi," John said. "Cockatoo," he added by way of translation.

"Cockatoo," Mamba repeated.

In the course of the day, John had learned and memorised the Aboriginal names of a variety of birdlife and game that Mamba pointed out along the way, and, in turn, Mamba had learned the English translations. Progress was slow, but they both had plenty of time.

"Daning!" Mamba shouted, referring to a death adder she'd spotted sunning itself just a few feet in front of John.

"Shit!" John leapt backwards, waking Murrodwdooling, when he saw the deadly snake. He'd been so busy studying the cockatoo, he hadn't noticed the reptile. The Irishman immediately identified it as a death adder, having first been introduced to one in the quarry at Moreton Bay, and having seen several more since fleeing the penal settlement. He looked at Mamba and realised she was smiling at his near-misfortune.

"Daning," she repeated, pointing to the snake as it slithered away into long grass.

"Daning," John said. That was one word he was confident he wouldn't forget. Only now did he realise Murrowdooling was amused by his reaction to the death adder. The boy had been brought up around snakes, and couldn't understand why the man he knew as Moilow was suddenly fearful of them.

Looking around, John noticed stragglers were falling further behind. At the tail end of the column some three hundred yards distant, he saw that a family of five—a couple and their three young children—were struggling to maintain contact with the main group. He wasn't aware that the man was ill, having contracted a respiratory illness, which caused him breathing difficulties, and his wife, who was pregnant, was having a time of it just coping with her children. They were all dropping further and further behind.

John, who had been watching the family's progress for a while, turned to Mamba. "I will be back soon," he said. The Irishman placed the possessions he'd been carrying on the ground and began striding back toward the rear of the column, clutching the spear he'd inherited.

He hadn't gone more than a few yards when he saw three Wanjuri warriors emerge from bush not far behind the struggling family. "Hey!" he shouted. He began waving his arms to warn the family and other clan members close by.

Before the couple and their young children even recognised the threat, they were overrun. The couple and their eldest child were fatally speared by their attackers who, ignoring the two surviving children, retrieved their spears and hurried to catch up to the other stragglers who only now had realised they were in danger.

A horrified John was sprinting toward the end of the column, which was in a state of chaos. The stragglers were screaming in terror, and women and children were fleeing in all directions.

John wasn't alone in rushing to lend his support. Other armed men, and one of the women, too, were racing to intercept the Wanjuri.

All three raiders released their spears, felling another three Kabi. The latest victims included the female warrior. She died slower than the others, a spear through her stomach. The weapon had been thrown with such force, its barbed tip had gone right through her and had buried itself in the ground, pinning her where she'd fallen.

John was tempted to stop and put the dying woman out of her misery, but there was no time for that. He noticed that the nearest attacker, who had already unhooked one of the extra spears he carried on his back, had him lined up in his sites. As the raider released his spear, John threw himself to the ground and the weapon flew over his head, missing him by a good yard. Even so, he heard its distinctive *whistle* as it flew by.

Before the Irishman could regain his feet, his muscular assailant was onto him. A well-aimed kick to the ribs knocked the wind from John's lungs and sent him rolling over the ground. As he rolled, he noticed the Wanjuri was reaching for another of his spears—a stabbing spear, shorter than the others. Rather than continuing to roll away from him, John quickly reversed his roll, bringing himself close to his attacker. As the Wanjuri raised his spear, the Irishman drew his knees to his chest and thrust his feet out as fast and as hard as he could. He was aiming at the native's nearest leg, and the heels of both boots landed on target—just above and just below the knee. He heard the leg break an instant before his assailant emitted an agonising scream and fell to the ground, writhing in pain.

John scrambled to his feet, ready to defend himself from other attackers. A glance told him reinforcements had arrived, and the two surviving raiders had been forced to flee. They were in full flight, running for the nearby bush from which they'd emerged a short time earlier. Before they reached the trees, Gabirri and Turo emerged, spears raised. The new arrivals were breathing hard, having run hard since departing the gully.

One by one, the other returning Kabi warriors appeared. They surrounded the two Wanjuri who immediately fell to their knees and prostrated themselves on the ground—a traditional sign of submission and a plea for mercy.

Clan members dragged the other raider—the one John had incapacitated—into the circle and dumped him alongside the other two. He was still whimpering in pain and clutching his broken leg.

John didn't wait to see how the Kabi treated their prisoners, or even if they bothered to take prisoners. He'd seen enough bloodshed for one day.

As the Irishman traipsed back to re-join the others, he learned the Kabi didn't keep prisoners. They didn't kill their captives quickly either.

The Wanjuri captives' cries of pain rang out until well after the Irishman caught up to Mamba and the boys.

The clan members reached the bush-covered hills without further incident and before darkness set in—just in time to find a suitable campsite alongside a stream in a well hidden valley before night finally fell.

Although they were confident the marauding Wanjuri no longer posed a risk, they opted not to light cooking fires for fear of giving away their position should their enemies still be in the vicinity—a precaution they would adopt for the next few days.

Clan members combined to share their cold food rations, to care for the wounded, to chant whispered prayers to the spirits of war, and to lament the violent deaths of six of their own this bloody day.

As families erected temporary shelters for the night, Mamba showed John how to make a bivouac using available branches, vines, ferns, grass and leaves. He was surprised how quick and easy it was for someone who knew what he or she was doing. Fortunately, Mamba knew what she was doing. She'd had plenty of practice after all.

It was with some excitement the couple prepared to retire for the night. The memory of their previous night's lovemaking was still vivid in the minds of each. In fact, John had thought of little else since then.

Ironically, when they finally bedded down, they and the boys—like everyone else in the camp—were so tired they fell asleep almost immediately.

On a bluff overlooking the campsite, a pair of yellow eyes surveyed the site's sleeping occupants. Dingo had been following the clan members since he'd spotted the white man amongst them earlier in the day. The presence of so many people made the native dog with the distinctive reddish marking on his coat nervous, so he'd kept his distance, remaining unseen. Now, under the cover of darkness, the dingo stared at the place where the white man and the three people with him had bedded down. Even with his excellent night vision, Dingo couldn't see the white from here, but he knew exactly where he was.

Next morning, as clan members deserted their temporary camp site and headed deeper into the hills that had given them sanctuary, ninety Wanjuri warriors inspected the abandoned Kabi encampment on the coast. They were studying the spoor left by the site's former occupants and, more importantly, they were looking for some sign of the members of their advance guard who had so mysteriously disappeared.

As the Wanjuri searched the site, they didn't realise that they themselves were under observation. Barega, the tracker, was observing them from the cover of trees on a nearby hill. He'd arrived shortly after sunup to find the Wanjuri blocking the northbound route he followed in his search for the elusive John Graham.

Barega hadn't given up looking for the Irishman. Even though his masters at the Moreton Bay penal settlement had deemed that John was officially dead, the tracker wasn't convinced. Until he found a body, the Irishman was still alive as far as he was concerned.

After Barega had reported to Captain Marsden and Lieutenant Hogan that he'd found signs that John had possibly died after being caught up in a flood, the officers had announced to one and all that the escapee was dead. Not only that, but Marsden had ordered the tracker to stop searching for the Irishman.

That hadn't stopped Barega from going walkabout from time to time, and when he did he always headed north for that's where John had headed.

A commotion in the encampment below drew Barega's attention. He saw several trackers entering the site on the run. They were pointing toward the interior, and they seemed excited about something. Barega wasn't to know they had found the bodies of their fellow warriors in the gully and on the plains beyond. They'd also found signs confirming the Kabi had fled en masse toward the interior.

After some discussion, the Wanjuri warriors headed back the way they'd come—northwards along the coast. They realised their quarry had too big a start on them, and the inland hills provided too many hiding places for people who didn't want to be found. Besides, the Wanjuris had ventured far enough, and their latest campaign had been a great success. It was time to return home to boast of their conquests.

Barega waited until the last of the raiders had disappeared—and then he waited some more. The tracker was patient if nothing else. While he waited, he absentmindedly fingered the silver crucifix that hung from his neck. When he was finally convinced the Wanjuris weren't returning, he ventured cautiously into the empty encampment, his spear and nulla nulla at the ready.

It didn't take him long to determine what had transpired at the site. The more recent broad footprints of the short, muscular Wanjuri were easily distinguishable from the narrower footprints left by the Kabi. Barega estimated a hundred or more of the latter had hurriedly quit the encampment a day or so earlier, and they'd headed inland.

One set of prints stood out more than any other. They were the distinctive boot prints John had left. They could be seen throughout the site, and, furthermore, they could be seen amongst the many footprints heading west. Barega realised they could have been left by any white man, or by any man wearing boots for that matter, but logic told him they were the Irishman's.

Without further delay, the tracker began following the tracks inland at a fast trot. He could already picture John Graham's head skewered to the end of his spear as he made his triumphant return to Moreton Bay.

PART FOUR

A LIFE
TRANSFORMED

46

J OHN PULLED HIS CLOAK TIGHT around him to provide some protection against the rain squalls that swept in from the sea. Black clouds scudded across the sky, signalling to all the occupants of the land below that the wet season wasn't yet over.

From his vantage point on a hillside overlooking the Kabi's latest encampment—a sheltered site adjacent to a pebble beach—the Irishman could normally see for many miles up and down the coast. Not today, however. The rain limited visibility to a few hundred yards at best.

In the months since the clan had fled the marauding Wanjuri, John had lost track of the days. He had ceased his recording of each passing day some time ago. However, his internal clock, together with nature's unmistakable signs, told him he had been with the Kabi all of six months. Nature's signs included the autumn leaves, which had now all but fallen, and the arrival of the wet season some months earlier, and so, if he had to bet, it was April.

A later-than-usual end to the wet season had threatened to upset John's internal clock. Even so, his estimate was spot on: it was April and he had been with the Kabi a little more than six months.

In that time, little had changed *and* a lot had changed. The nomadic lifestyle of the Kabi clan members continued as it had since the Irishman first arrived in their midst, and much as it had for millennia. They still hunted and captured game, speared and netted fish, collected shellfish from the seaside and gathered berries, roots, grubs, nuts and other edibles from the surrounding countryside; they still moved on to greener pastures when their food sources ran out or when threatened by numerically stronger enemies; and they still lived and loved and fought and laughed as they always had.

Their way of life had been an eye-opener for John. If there were grubs or berries to be found, fish to net, game or birds to spear, or snakes and lizards to catch, they ate; if there weren't, they starved. It was as simple as that. All too often, the Irishman had experienced the inconvenience of relocating to a new campsite only to have to quit it a few days later because food was scarce, or, on occasion, nowhere to be found. Consequently, he and the others had gone hungry from time to time.

Predictably, the man the clan members knew and, in the main, accepted as Moilow was becoming more like them every day—both in appearance and manner. His once-pale skin had been darkened by the sun, and any fat he may have had, had been burnt off by the physical demands of daily life. When he wasn't trekking between campsites, he was fishing and hunting with the men, or helping Mamba and the other women gather berries and shellfish, or playing boisterous games with Murrowdooling and Carravanty and their friends.

Even his garments were Kabi-like. Throughout the summer he'd gone topless, wearing only his breeches and boots. Now, as the days cooled, he'd once more taken to wearing the cloak Mamba had given him.

These days, his breeches resembled shorts. They'd become so torn and ragged, Mamba had cut them off at the knees and had reinforced the remaining material with pieces of kangaroo pelt. The resulting garment, in John's opinion, now more resembled a traditional loincloth than the breeches they'd once been, but he kept that opinion to himself. "I'm not looking to win any fashion awards," he oft reminded himself.

His last remaining visible link to his European origins—besides his white skin— was his boots. Even these were hardly recognisable for he had worn the front of each boot away so that his toes were exposed. This had proven problematic because the holes allowed stones and other objects to enter his boots from time to time. He'd gotten around that by gluing dried moss to the front lip of each boot's sole, thereby keeping foreign objects at bay and, as it turned out, making each boot decidedly cooler and more comfortable.

Apart from that and the laces, which he had long replaced with threads Mamba fashioned from emu sinew, the boots remained as sturdy as the day they'd been issued to him by the army's stores master at Moreton Bay. He viewed this as one of life's miracles given the abuse his boots had been subjected to—first in the penal settlement's quarry and then in the months since his hurried departure from that accursed place.

John's relationship with Mamba, her sons and most of the other clan members had changed, too. His connection with Mamba had gone from strength to strength since they'd first made love that memorable night in the seaside encampment they'd had to flee. The time they spent in each other's company had given each a rudimentary understanding of the other's language, and so they could now communicate verbally.

To be fair, Mamba had a better understanding of the English language than John had of the Kabi dialect. She now spoke pigeon English whereas his mastery of Kabi amounted to knowing what individual words meant without always being able to put those words together to make an intelligible sentence.

The Irishman's mastery of other skills, however, was a little more impressive. His acceptance by the menfolk–Turo aside—had seen him become increasingly involved in their hunting and fishing expeditions, and, as a result, he was fast becoming proficient in each of those endeavours.

Gabirri, who was now a firm friend, had taken him under his wing and taught him how to use traditional weapons, in particular the spear. To Gabirri's disgust, John had never mastered use of the woomera—that vital instrument all good hunters used to propel their spears further than was otherwise possible—and the native was never slow to criticise him for his lack of skill with that tool. His disgust was due in no small part to the fact that the Moilow of old had been an expert with the woomera.

Gabirri had to soften his criticism a little when John proved he had a good eye and a strong throwing arm, hitting his target considerably more often than he missed. Without the aid of the woomera, he couldn't throw a spear as far as the others, but he was already very accurate, sometimes felling a kangaroo or wallaby even as it bounded away, or, on occasion, skewering a low-flying bird as it flew by.

John's fighting skills were even more impressive. Since embarrassing himself when first attempting to master the use of the Kabis' weapons, he had watched and learned. To Turo's annoyance, he had been invited to practice regularly with the clan's warriors. The white's natural ability and perseverance had impressed all—even the belligerent Turo.

John was now adept with the nulla nulla and other traditional weapons as well as the spear. It hadn't been easy for him, and he'd received many blows, cuts and bruises along with the odd concussion en route to learning how to use the weapons well enough to defend himself at least.

The woomera aside, one instrument he hadn't been able to master was the boomerang. That hadn't been for want of trying. Gabirri and others had tried ad nauseam to teach him how to throw the unusual wooden hunting weapon that was unique to the Aboriginal people. They'd all but given up on him. Only the knowledge the old Moilow had been a dab hand with the boomerang had encouraged them to persevere as long as they had.

Activity in the encampment below caught John's eye. A game involving most of the clan's youths had just begun. It was an impromptu game, invented by the Kabi, in which two teams compete for possession of a buroinjin, or ball, stuffed full of grass and encased in kangaroo hide. In this case the ball was well worn for it had been used many times. Neither John nor the participants could know the game would one day be known as *buroinjin* and would be played throughout the continent.

The Irishman had watched the game often enough, but he still didn't understand the rules. From what he could deduce, participants had to carry the buroinjin over an imaginary line behind the opposing team. In theory, holding and tackling weren't permitted, but in practice, it seemed, anything was permissible. It reminded John of an Irish game called *Last Man Standing*. Participants approached it as if their lives depended on winning. Injuries were common, as were disputes and arguments. It was all in good fun, Mamba had assured him, but he wasn't so sure. On this occasion, the relentless rain had turned the encampment into a quagmire, and it wasn't long before the youths were covered in mud.

The Irishman noticed several younger boys had joined in. He frowned when he recognised Murrowdooling and Carravanty amongst them. "Little buggers will be thrashed if they don't look out," he muttered. He was tempted to rush down the hill and intervene before they were injured, but he relaxed when he saw Mamba hurry over to them and order them away. "There's a good mum," he murmured. He looked at the fetching young woman lovingly as she shepherded her sons from danger.

A big native approached Mamba and appeared to confront her. John recognised him immediately as Turo. Even from a distance, it was apparent the two were arguing.

Mamba had mentioned to John recently that Turo had begun pestering her to leave the man she believed was Moilow and to move in with him. The Irishman had stated he would remonstrate with the persistent Turo, but Mamba had made him promise to keep his distance. He'd agreed, but he sensed the time was fast approaching he would need to intervene.

John stood up when he saw Turo begin throwing his arms about. It was obvious the native was shouting at Mamba who motioned to her sons to leave her and return to the bivouac. Yet again the Irishman was about to rush down the hillside when Turo stormed off, leaving Mamba to herself. Relieved, John sat down, determined to enjoy his solitary vigil a little longer.

Much as he liked Mamba's company, and the boys' company, too, he did enjoy his "quiet time" as he called it. He tried to get away by himself every day if circumstances allowed. This was the only time he could think clearly and order, or re-order, his priorities. While he had come to love Mamba and her sons, and had grown fond of the other clan members—making good friends with more than a few—he never forgot who he was or where he came from. More importantly, he never forgot his goal: to catch a ship and return to civilization.

The lack of opportunity to escape his current situation was both frustrating and disappointing. Since his first sighting of a ship six months earlier, there had been several other sightings, but, like the first one, the vessels had all been well out to sea and had shown no inclination to approach shore let alone anchor close by. He was starting to think this section of the continent's eastern seaboard was avoided by ships. *Dangerous offshore reefs?* he wondered. *Or the risk of attack by unfriendly natives perhaps?* He didn't know—and that was the frustrating part.

If I knew for sure, I could plan accordingly.

Exactly what his options were, he wasn't sure. The thought of striking out again, on foot and alone, in this inhospitable country didn't appeal. Memories of his overland trek from Moreton Bay were still vivid.

All I can do is wait. Wait and see.

And so, as he'd done so often in recent times, he resigned himself to waiting until either an opportunity presented itself or he received inspiration from somewhere.

John wasn't even sure where he was exactly. All he knew was that he had ventured further north than he'd ever been before—and by quite some distance if he wasn't mistaken. After quitting the hills that had provided sanctuary from the marauding Wanjuri, he and the clan members had returned to the coast and trekked north via a circuitous route that saw them return inland several times. If someone had told him they were now a hundred-and-fifteen miles as the crow flies from Moreton Bay, he wouldn't have been surprised.

The wind freshened, bringing more rain with it, and prompting him to pull his cloak around him tighter still.

Observing the clan members going about their everyday business below—be it repairing their shelters or making new ones, fixing fishing nets, talking, playing or whatever—he noticed they seemed oblivious to the rain. It was no different during heatwaves, floods, droughts, cyclones or, indeed, any conditions. Their ability to endure and to accept whatever nature threw at them never ceased to amaze him.

John now knew many of the clan members by name. From where he sat he could see Jiba, Mamba's moon-faced, matronly aunt. She was returning from the beach with several other women, their baskets near-full of shellfish and shells they'd been gathering and, as usual, Jiba was smiling away.

The Irishman recognised Mamba's grandmother Umina and older sister Tirranna among the women. Neither, in his opinion, bore much resemblance to Mamba. Physically, they were quite different, being darker of skin and not at all pleasing to the eye. Not to his eye at least. Tirranna, according to Mamba, was her older sister, and Umina was their paternal grandmother.

John found it strange neither woman had a lot to do with Mamba. When questioned, she'd shrugged her shoulders and made light of it, but he suspected it saddened her. He felt it had something to do with her association with him. Not everyone was convinced he was the white spirit she said he was. He wasn't to know that Turo had been lobbying against his continued presence, forcefully arguing that the white spirit was an imposter, and, it seemed, one or two believed him.

Mamba's only other sibling—her younger brother Kulan—had been similarly distant since she'd taken the man they knew as Moilow into her bivouac. Mamba had recently confided in John that she and Kulan had been close. She didn't say so, but he sensed she missed the closeness she once shared with him. He vowed to take it up with her at the first opportunity.

Only now did John notice that Kulan was one of the mud-covered youths participating in the buroinjin game. He and the others were hard to recognise beneath their mudpacks.

The Irishman saw the bandy Mirritji start remonstrating with another of the youths whom he identified as Nowra. By all accounts, Nowra had hurt one of the younger boys. From here, John couldn't tell whether it had been deliberate or accidental. Regardless, the youth was receiving a real tongue-lashing from the elder.

A middle-aged man watched on, amused, as the tongue-lashing continued. When he turned around, John recognised him as Banjora, the middle-aged hunter who had first sighted the white when he ventured into the Kabi's territory—an event both men would remember forever. For one it was the first human he'd seen in three months; for the other it was the first white man he'd ever seen.

Banjora's name translated to *a Koala*, which John thought very appropriate for the hunter was as furry as a koala bear beneath his shock of wild hair and his long, tangled beard.

It never ceased to intrigue John how fitting the names of many clan members were. Mamba's brother's name, for example, translated to *Possum*, which he thought fitting—not because Kulan remotely resembled one, but because he was a possum hunter renowned for his ability to scale trees and catch the furry animals with his bare hands. He'd seen him do it numerous times.

Beneath the overhang of a shelter, he could see the Ancient One, Mootemu, sitting cross-legged, observing the activity around him. The Irishman had become close to the old man in recent weeks, seeking him out for companionship whenever he felt a bit low. Though neither could really follow the other, they nevertheless had lengthy discussions, which left each feeling strangely content. John viewed his sessions with Mootemu as therapy.

Next to the Ancient One's shelter, he noticed Yileen, the clan's nungkari, or traditional healer, kneeling over a young girl beneath the overhang of his bivouac. Yileen, whose name translated to *a Dream,* was in the process of administering his healing know-how to the girl who, John had learned, was dying of some mysterious ailment. Looking on was the girl's mother whom the Irishman recognised as Myndee, a friend of Mamba's, and even from this distance he could see she was worried.

John had first-hand experience of Yileen's healing powers—once shortly after his capture when he was near death, and again after being bitten by a poisonous red-back spider a couple of months ago. At first, he'd thought Yileen well named for he considered him a dreamer, but as time passed he'd come to respect the healer. Certainly the Kabi respected him; they believed he worked miracles, and they claimed he could send his healing powers to others over great distances.

Alongside a bivouac far removed from the others, John could just make out the figure of Karadji who was perhaps the most revered clan member despite the fact he was still only a teenager. Karadji was the Kabi's shaman and, as such, was believed to possess magical powers. The elders regularly consulted him whenever they needed guidance, which, the Irishman had noted, was frequently. They sought his advice, so he'd been told, on virtually everything that affected the clan, be it hunting, fishing, climate, marriage, tribal disputes or war.

As he did so often, Karadji was currently shaking wooden rattles in the direction of the other bivouacs, and chanting to himself. Just what the teenage shaman was trying to achieve, John hadn't a clue. However, he'd learned enough in his time with these people to know that he shouldn't dismiss Karadji's supposed powers out of hand. He had seen some things he couldn't explain, not even to himself, over the duration.

John was distracted by the sight of Turo approaching a bivouac located not far from his own. The big native was greeted at the entrance by the shelter's sole occupant whom the Irishman recognised as Warrah, a teenage girl notorious for providing sexual favours for any man, or boy, prepared to give her food or pelts or anything else she considered worthwhile. John considered her name especially apt for Warrah translated to *Honeysuckle.* Although too ugly for his liking, she did have a nubile body that was not yet ravaged by age and, in his expert opinion, was not at all undesirable. He watched with interest as the girl accepted a pelt Turo had brought with him, and then led him by the hand into the privacy of her bivouac.

Turo, he noted, appeared totally unconcerned by the fact that three of his five wives—he'd taken on another wife in the last month—were observing his visitation. Although John couldn't see their faces, their body language told him that they, too, were unconcerned. Sexual freedom, he'd long observed, was the norm amongst all Aboriginal people. He silently thanked his lucky stars that Mamba wasn't like the other women for he wouldn't be prepared to share her. Not unless his life depended on it, which, in hindsight he realised it probably would.

Thinking of Mamba reminded him he needed to return to his bivouac. His rumbling tummy told him it was almost time for a mid-day bite, and his woman—for that's how he thought of her—would be preparing something to eat soon if she wasn't already.

Two things happened as John descended the hill. One he saw; the other he didn't.

Firstly, the rain stopped and the sun peeped out from behind the clouds. That event was impossible to miss.

Secondly, behind a bivouac on the far side of the encampment, a clan member not so tolerant of sexual freedom found his wife with another man and, enraged, clubbed him to death with his nulla nulla.

47

THE FIRST JOHN BECAME AWARE of the sudden violence that had just occurred in the encampment was when the victim's wife and children began screaming. Those who ran to assist the distressed family members quickly discovered the cause of their distress. The dead man, whose skull had been crushed, was covered in blood.

Although the Irishman couldn't see what had happened, he could certainly hear the screaming and the arguing that had broken out behind the bivouac. He hurried to investigate. Moments later, the killer, who was splattered in his victim's blood, was dragged into the centre of the encampment by angry clan members.

What followed was a lesson in Kabi justice. The accused was subjected to an immediate and impromptu trial. This Aboriginal-style court hearing was chaired by Mootemu, the jury comprised all the clan's menfolk—or all those not away hunting at least—and the public gallery accommodated all the women and children. Attendance at such trials was not deemed compulsory, but it seemed to John that everyone was present—even Murrowdooling and Carravanty whom, he noticed, were with their mother. He wondered at the wisdom of exposing children to such things, but he knew better than to intervene.

It seemed to John that the accused had been found guilty even before his trial began for the men were hurling insults and waving their spears at him.

Only now did John realise he knew the offender. Jarra was one of Turo's friends and, like Turo, was known for his hot temper and his belligerence. The Irishman had occasionally been paired with Jarra when practising to fight with the nulla nulla. He'd found him a tough nut, and had received many a bruise from him.

Mootemu raised his hand, and a hush fell over the assembled. "Jarra has admitted to killing one of our own," the Ancient One said.

The old man spoke so quietly, clan members had to strain to hear him. Even so, they hung on his every word for they were aware a man's life hung in the balance. In the background, the crying and weeping of grieving family members continued unabated. John couldn't work out exactly who was grieving for who. It wasn't clear to him whether the unfaithful wife was crying over her dead lover or her jealous husband.

Mootemu continued, "The accused says the assault was a matter of honour because the deceased was with his wife."

"That does not justify murder!" one irate man yelled out.

John recognised the man as a brother of the deceased.

Others added their voice. They sounded equally irate.

"Quiet!" Mootemu shouted, raising his voice for the first time. Turning to the accused, and lowering his voice once more, he asked, "What say you, Jarra?"

After what seemed an age, Jarra lowered his head and mumbled, "I have nothing to say, Ancient One."

The assembled took this as an admission of guilt, and, as one, they cheered mightily.

Mootemu, whose hearing was as frail as the rest of his body, turned to Mirritji who was standing close by and asked, "What did he say?"

"He said he is guilty," Mirritji said, applying his own interpretation to what the accused had just said.

Mootemu looked back at Jarra and waited for the cheering to subside. Finally, he said, "By your own admission you are guilty." After another pause, he asked, "How do you wish to die, by spear or nulla nulla?'

Without hesitating, Jarra answered, "By spear, Ancient One."

With that, the assembled clan members erupted, cheering and baying for blood. The men beat their spears against their shields, all but drowning out the cheering.

If the trial was quick, what followed was as quick or quicker. Jarra was marched to the foot of a large bunya pine tree and was left standing, alone, in front of its trunk, facing the clan members. Men then laid stones out in a tight circle around the condemned man. These, John would later learn, marked the area Jarra was confined to. To flee, or even to step outside the designated circle, would be construed as an act of cowardice, thereby condemning him to eternal damnation in the Afterlife.

That done, the menfolk assembled, spears at the ready, in a row some thirty yards from the condemned man who had now also been armed with a spear and shield. Jarra was to be given a warrior's death, the theory being if he went bravely all would be forgiven and he would be well remembered. Well remembered by everyone except his wife and the deceased's loved-ones perhaps.

Even though John had never witnessed or even heard of such a thing before, he could see what was coming. He wanted to walk away, but he found he couldn't. He was gripped by the drama taking place before his eyes.

As the clan's oldest able-bodied elder, Mirritji had the honour of throwing the first spear. In past years, the honour would have gone to Mootemu, but the Ancient One was now too feeble for so strenuous a task.

A hush fell over the assembled once more as Mirritji raised his spear and prepared to release it.

Thirty yards away, Jarra faced the elder, spear in one hand and shield in the other. The spear, in his case, was a token only for he would not use it. To die with a weapon in hand was considered a warrior's greatest honour.

Mirritji threw his spear with surprising power for one so old. It was dead on target, too, and Jarra was only just able to deflect it with his shield, slipping and sliding in the mud underfoot as he did so. The spear's barbed tip skidded off the shield and buried itself in the tree trunk behind the condemned man. Onlookers acknowledged Mirritji's accuracy and Jarra's skill with murmurings of respect.

Turo stepped forward, indicating he'd be next. Friend or no friend, he wanted the honour of being the warrior to deliver the death strike. The two acknowledged each other with a respectful nod. Facing his old friend, the big warrior released his spear with awesome power. The weapon flew straight. Jarra managed to block it with his shield, but the spear's force was so great its tip pierced the shield, stopping only an inch or two short of his nose, and forcing him backwards. He'd have fallen had the trunk not stopped him.

That was the signal for the other men to act. One after another, they released their spears with barely a moment's pause between throws. To his credit, Jarra managed to block or parry the first dozen spears, but one got through—and then another and another—and the condemned man slumped to the muddy ground. Even then, the spears kept coming until his body was hidden beneath them.

The suddenness with which the accused had been deemed guilty, and the savagery with which he'd been despatched, shocked John. Still he was unable to tear his eyes away from the body. If there was such a thing as a human pincushion, he decided, he was looking at it now.

What shocked him even more was the reaction of the assembled clan members. They were cheering as if they were at a major sporting event.

Even the women and children for God's sake!

When he noticed Mamba and her boys cheering along with the others he decided he had seen enough.

His earlier hunger forgotten, he headed back up the hill. He needed to be alone once more.

As he departed, he didn't notice he was being observed by Mamba. She thought it strange that her Moilow wasn't participating in the celebration. The Moilow of old would have been to the fore.

⋅€⋅——⋅3⋅

Sobs and cries of grief carried to John's bivouac, waking him. They were a woman's cries, and they came from a nearby shelter.

The Irishman reached for Mamba, and was surprised to find she wasn't there. In the darkness, he could just make out the sleeping forms of Murrowdooling and Carravanty.

Outside, the wailing grew louder. It was now accompanied by chanting.

John crawled through the bivouac's low entrance and saw a group of women in front of another bivouac some thirty yards away. He recognised the shelter as one occupied by Mamba's friend Myndee whose young daughter, he knew, had succumbed to a mystery ailment, and he thought he recognised Mamba amongst the women. Closer inspection revealed it was her. She and the other women were comforting Myndee. Among them were Mamba's grandmother Umina and older sister Tirranna.

When John joined the group he saw that the clan's nungkari, Yileen, was in their midst, chanting and administering his traditional healing powers. It was the healer's chanting, the Irishman realised, that he'd heard. Yileen was kneeling before the prone figure of a young girl whom John guessed was Myndee's daughter. Even from where he stood it was apparent the girl had died.

Mamba and her sister Tirranna each held one of the bereaved woman's hands, and the elderly Umina stroked her hair as she wailed, her tormented face turned to the moon, which had just emerged from behind clouds.

Yileen held a wooden bowl over the dead girl's face. It contained tinder, which he'd lit, and smoke billowed from it, stinging the eyes of those closest. The nungkari blew the smoke so that it passed over the face of the dead girl whose open eyes, John noticed, seemed to be staring straight at him. Suddenly uneasy, he returned to his bivouac, content to leave the grieving to those who were closest to her.

When John next opened his eyes, he wasn't sure if it was the early morning sun streaming through the bivouac's entrance or the sound of a woman chanting somewhere in the distance that had woken him. The sound could only just be heard above the waves lapping the nearby shore.

The fluttering of an eyelash on his chest told him that Mamba was awake, too. "Can you hear that?" John asked in the Kabi tongue.

"Hear what?" Mamba asked, yawning.

"Chanting."

Mamba listened. "Yes," she said at length. "It is Myndee."

The events of the night just gone came back to John. He realised he should have guessed it was the dead girl's mother. "Is she alone?" he asked.

Mamba nodded. "She needs to be alone to do what she is doing," she said.

John's interest was suddenly piqued. "What is she doing?" he asked. When Mamba didn't answer, he gently shook her shoulder. "What is she doing?" he asked again, insistent.

"That is of concern only to the women, Moilow," Mamba assured him.

"But—"

She shushed him by placing her forefinger over his lips, indicating he should remain quiet. Turning to Murrowdooling and Carravanty who stirred nearby, she asked, "Are you awake, boys?"

"Yes," they murmured drowsily and in unison.

"Go and collect driftwood for the cooking fire," she ordered.

Grumbling, the boys pushed themselves to their feet and, crouching low, filed from the shelter to do their mother's bidding.

"And take your time!" Mamba called out after them.

Only now did John realise what she was planning. One look at the mischievous gleam in her eye told him he was about to get lucky.

Mamba threw her cloak off and rolled astride him. To her surprise, John threw her off him.

"I need to pee," he mumbled in English. He quickly crawled from the bivouac to relieve his full bladder behind the shelter. Looking around, he noted several other men were doing the same. It was an early morning ritual for the menfolk. The women, he'd noticed, were a little more circumspect and sought more privacy for their ablutions. On this occasion, he took a lot longer than usual. His little soldier had become greatly enlarged as a result of Mamba's advances, and consequently he was finding it difficult to urinate.

"Moilow!" an impatient Mamba called from inside.

"Coming," John replied. Looking down at his uncooperative old fellow, he muttered, "C'mon you tardy bastard!" Finally, he managed to relieve himself, and he hurried back to Mamba.

"What kept you?" Mamba asked.

The urgency in her voice signalled to John that she needed him as much as he needed her.

You're a lucky man, John Graham.

"Later," he said, tearing his breeches off and mounting her.

This time, it was Mamba's turn to throw him off. Laughing, she sat astride him and, with no further foreplay, lowered herself onto his now fully cooperative old fellow. "Mmmmm!" she purred as she began rocking gently above him.

Now it was John's turn to purr except in his case it was more of a groan. Somewhere in the back of his brain he heard the waves lapping on the shore and the woman chanting, but he paid no mind to either.

Though John's morning had started exceptionally well, the morning meal and the day that followed were a sombre affair for it was a time of grieving.

The first hint he had that this was going to be different to any other day he'd experienced was when he joined Mamba and the boys for breakfast. His arrival at the cooking fire had coincided with the return of Myndee from the waterfront. The grieving mother was hurrying back to sit with her daughter's body, which lay in state outside her bivouac and which was currently surrounded by other family members. Clan members were coming and going as well to pay their respects.

It was only when Myndee reached her daughter's side that John noticed blood masked her face and covered her shawl. She was clearly in pain, and she groaned and wailed continually. No-one else seemed to notice her distress.

"What the . . ." John jumped up and hurried toward her.

"Wait, Moilow!" Mamba called after him.

As John neared the distressed woman he was alarmed to see she'd lost an eye. Before he could reach her, Mamba grabbed his arm.

"Leave her, Moilow!" she said.

"She's lost an eye!" John said, pointing at Myndee's bloodied face.

Mamba didn't relinquish her grip on John. When she finally had his attention, she said, "It is our way."

Only now did John notice Myndee held a blood-covered stick in one hand. Horrified, he looked from the stick to Mamba and back at the stick. "You mean . . ." He turned back to Mamba.

She nodded. "It is the way of our people, Moilow. You know that," she added, firm in her belief that her returned husband had witnessed this ritual more than a few times over the years.

John could only shake his head in disbelief.

"When a woman loses a daughter, it is her right to remove an eye if she so chooses," Mamba said, "to appease her ancestors' spirits."

"And if she loses a son?" a disbelieving John asked.

"It is the same, but it must be the other eye." Mamba pointed to her right eye.

John looked back to Myndee and saw that she'd gouged out her left eye in accordance with the brutal custom.

Mamba gently but firmly pushed John back toward the cooking fire he'd just vacated, and then she walked over to join with the others and to lend support to her grieving friend.

The remainder of the day was devoted to performing ritualistic burial rites, mourning the loss of Myndee's daughter. Those rites, led by none other than the young shaman, Karadji, took the form of chanting, singing and dancing. Men and boys adorned themselves in ochre, while male relatives of the deceased went one step further: using sharp shells and the barbs of spears, they cut themselves all over until they bled.

A column of mourners carried the body of the deceased, which was now dressed in a fine cloak adorned with eagle feathers, to a site that had been prepared in the middle of the encampment. There, it was laid out on a bed of shells. The dancers then prostrated themselves before the body, and began running around it on all fours, barking like dogs.

A number of Kabi—young and old—had died since John joined the clan, but this was the first time he had remained in camp to observe the grieving and the rituals that invariably followed. He preferred to make himself scarce at such times for fear of inadvertently offending clan members or upsetting grieving relatives. On this occasion however, he chose to stay close and observe the activities from a small rise overlooking the encampment.

It was at times like this the Irishman felt like the foreigner he truly was amongst these people. He still couldn't reconcile those he'd come to know—Mamba, Gabirri, Mirritji and Mootemu included—with the barbarity of many of their customs. Today's incident involving Myndee being a case in point.

No-one was even surprised let alone concerned that poor woman gouged her eye out!

As the rituals and chanting continued, John noticed a number of men were busy constructing what looked like scaffolding on the far side of the encampment. They topped it off with a platform fashioned from long branches, which they tied together using vines.

A movement from one of the bivouacs distracted John. He could just make out the familiar figure of Mootemu sitting, cross-legged, beneath its overhang. Like John, the Ancient One had chosen to observe the day's activities from afar.

The Irishman realised Mootemu was waving to him to come to him. He stood and walked over to join the old man.

"I greet you, Moilow," Mootemu said in his own tongue as John neared.

"And I . . . greet you . . . Ancient One," John replied hesitantly in the other's language.

Mootemu patted the bare earth next to him, indicating the white man should sit beside him. John did as he was asked, and the two sat in silence, observing the activity around them.

At length, Mootemu turned to John and asked, "You no longer approve of our customs, Moilow?"

"I . . ."

The elder held up one hand, indicating he hadn't finished. "It is of no matter," he said. "It will be different when your full memory returns."

Most of what Mootemu said was over John's head. He caught only a few words, and yet it kind of made sense.

Mootemu continued, pointing to the dancers who had now worked themselves into a frenzy. "They are guiding the girl's spirit home," he said.

John nodded, though he didn't totally understand.

Encouraged, the Ancient one said, "When the spirit is home, she will be born again . . . as you were, Moilow."

Daylight was drawing to a close when half a dozen agile young men picked up the body and, between them, carried it to the top of the platform that had been erected earlier. There, some twenty feet above the ground, they lay the body out so that the dead girl was facing the sky, and they covered her with leaves and plants women had collected from the surrounding bush.

Mootemu, who hadn't spoken in the last hour, turned to John. "The body will stay there until we next return," he said.

John wondered if he may have misheard for he was aware they would not return to this site for many months. "Until . . . we next . . . return?" he asked.

Mootemu nodded. "Then the girl's loved-ones will scatter her bleached bones so that Mother Earth can reclaim her," he advised.

This time, John couldn't understand what the Ancient One was saying. He would learn later that the bones of the deceased were eventually scattered in a cave or placed in a cavity in the trunk of a tree.

The two unlikely companions watched as the clan members gathered around the platform. All the men chanted while the women sang praises to the Sky Beings, and prayed for a safe and speedy journey home for the dead girl's spirit.

Amidst all the grief, John saw one ray of sunshine. Amongst the women, he observed Mamba embracing her grandmother and her older sister as they sang. The three looked close—closer than they'd been since he'd known them. He prayed, for Mamba's sake, that today's sad event may be the start of a reconciliation for the three of them for he sensed he was the root cause of their estrangement.

48

SIX MONTHS HAD DONE NOTHING to dim Helen's memories of John Graham. She often thought of him. There was no doubting the roguish Irishman had made quite an impression on her in the short time she'd known him.

Helen occasionally thought of John at the most inappropriate of times—this being one of them.

The young beauty, now twenty-one, was dining as a guest of Lieutenant Hogan in the officers' mess at the army's headquarters in Sydney Town. *Mess* was not an appropriate term for the officers' dining room as it wouldn't have looked out of place in a respectable hotel in London or New York. Diners, who included officers and wives, sat at candlelit tables and were served by staff who could easily be confused for civilian waiters were it not for their nametags, which denoted the military rank and number of each.

The diners wouldn't have looked out of place in London or New York either. Officers were all in uniform, and, like Hogan, their red tunics were adorned with proudly polished service medals that glinted in the candlelight; the women wore their finest fashionable garments, but none looked more beautiful than Helen. She was the envy of the other women, attracting admiring glances from them, and from their dining partners, too.

Entertainment was provided by a string quartet whose members played quietly in one corner of the large room. On occasion they would play a waltz, as they were doing now, and some diners would take the opportunity to twirl their partners on the dance floor.

Hogan, who had recently been declared fit to resume light duties at the Moreton Bay penal settlement, still walked with the aid of a walking stick as a result of his accident some six months earlier. The army's head surgeon had successfully reset the lieutenant's shattered leg, but he'd warned him it would likely be another twelve months before he could resume active duty. Until then, he'd resigned himself to performing admin duties.

In the months since Hogan's last visit, he and Helen had corresponded frequently, or as frequently as the postal services and shipping schedules between Sydney Town and Moreton Bay allowed. Neither had forgotten the tension of their last meeting or the awkward manner in which they'd parted company. A chivalrous Hogan had since apologised for his "ungentlemanly conduct" by letter even though they both knew it was more Helen's fault than his. Her mentioning John Graham to the man who had more reason than most to dislike him had been insensitive at best.

Despite Helen's efforts to deter Hogan's interest in her, he'd remained as desirous of her as ever, and he'd made no secret of that desire in his letters. She, on the other hand, was still uncertain about what she most wanted from life—her teaching career or marriage—and more importantly she was still uncertain of her feelings for her suitor.

Looking at him now, so handsome and so dashing in his uniform, she knew he'd be considered a great catch by any other woman in the room. However, the same misgivings she'd had all those months before persisted. She wasn't as convinced as he apparently was that they would make a good match, she wasn't sure she wanted to be a soldier's wife, and she didn't even know if she wanted to marry him, or anyone for that matter, just yet. Furthermore, she had thrown herself into her teaching, and she wasn't confident there was room for anything else, or anyone else, in her hectic life.

As if he'd been reading her thoughts, Hogan asked, "Have you given any further thought to my proposal, Helen?"

Both knew what proposal he referred to. It was a marriage proposal he had warned her to expect when he next visited Sydney Town. The *warning* had been delivered in the last letter he'd sent to her—a letter she had received less than a week before he'd arrived. And he'd only arrived yesterday, so she hadn't had long to think about it.

A wine waiter approached, open wine bottle in hand, before Helen could answer. Hovering at Hogan's side, he asked, "More wine for you and the lady, sir?"

"Yes," Hogan said, motioning to the waiter to refill the two near-empty glasses.

The young couple looked at each other as the waiter topped up their wine.

Helen was grateful she had been given a moment to respond. She'd rehearsed her answer more than once, but now that the time had come she found she was becoming increasingly flustered, which wasn't like her at all. She was normally in charge of her emotions. She had intended to say something along the lines of, "Thank you my dear Desmond, I would love to marry you, but first I must ask for my father's blessing as I could not proceed if he were opposed to our union." That, she thought, would be the death knell for any marriage plans because she knew, and Hogan knew, that her father had reservations about any such union.

The waiter finally departed.

Helen took a deep breath and said, "I would love to marry you, Desmond,"—Hogan smiled when he heard that opening gambit—"but only if you are prepared to wait the two years it will take me to complete my teacher training here." She had decided to soften her answer to give the lieutenant some hope at least. Her thinking was that if he was prepared to wait, at least she would have some time to come up with a better reason for him not to marry her. That is *if* she wanted to give him such a reason.

Hogan's smile had been replaced by a frown as he considered Helen's answer. He'd been expecting a *Yes* because her recent letters had given him no cause to think she would reject him should he propose. In fact, her letters had given him just cause to expect a positive answer. Suspecting she may be hedging her bets, he tersely asked, "Are you toying with me, Helen?"

"Not at all," Helen said. As she spoke, she realised her words sounded hollow even to her ears. "I—"

Hogan raised one hand, indicating she should remain quiet. It had just occurred to him that Helen still held a torch for John. He thought she'd have gotten over her infatuation for the Irishman long ago, but, if his suspicions were correct, he was wrong about that. Suddenly angry, he asked, "Did you hear about John Graham?"

Surprised by the unexpected change of topic, Helen said, "No."

"Oh . . . I thought your father would have said something." He waited for a response. When there was none, he added, "Graham drowned in a big flood up north."

Helen nearly dropped the glass she was now holding. Hiding her shock as best she could, she asked, "When?"

"About six months ago. Maybe a little more."

"How do you know?"

"The tracker told us." Hogan smiled at Helen. He could tell she was shocked, and the sadistic side of him was enjoying being the bearer of bad news on this occasion.

"Did he see the body?" Helen hated Hogan at this moment. His smile told her that he was enjoying himself.

"No . . ." He hesitated for a moment, and that wasn't lost on Helen. "But the tracker found the convict's things, and he said there's no doubt Graham drowned."

Helen ignored the lieutenant's penetrating gaze as she absorbed what she'd just been told. She held onto the faint hope that John had somehow survived. Logic told her if no body had been found then he could still be alive. Her keen mind also told her that her father and Hogan would consider it in the army's best interests if Moreton Bay's soldiers and convicts believed John to be dead even if he wasn't. Equally, they would consider it in her best interests if she believed that, too. Shrugging, as if to say *who cares*, she said, "Anyway, that is no concern of mine."

Hogan knew she cared more than she was letting on. He also knew that he was at another crossroads in his rocky relationship with the young beauty sitting opposite him. If it had been any other woman, the decision would have been easy. However, Helen was so beguiling and so damned beautiful he couldn't bring himself to walk away. For better or for worse, he decided to persevere, for a while longer at least. He noticed the quartet had just begun playing another waltz. Smiling, he stood up and asked, "Shall we dance?"

Taken aback by his sudden change of mood, Helen accepted the other's invitation before she even realised it. Next minute, she found herself out on the dance floor, which, she realised, they shared with only two other couples at that moment. Aware that all eyes were on her, she was thankful her mother had insisted she take dance lessons in London. As a result of those lessons, she was a good dancer. If she was good, the lieutenant was very good—even though he was somewhat handicapped by his injury. That came as no surprise to her for she'd seen his dancing prowess close up at the Governor's dinner at Moreton Bay.

"Did I tell you, you look beautiful tonight?" Hogan whispered as he held her close to him.

"Three times if I recall," Helen smiled. Her smile hid the mixed feelings the news of John's rumoured death had left her with. It also hid her concerns over the obvious pleasure Hogan had experienced delivering the bad news. She'd had glimpses of the lieutenant's sadistic side before. Regardless, she allowed herself to meld into her partner's tight embrace as he expertly led her around the dance floor.

Despite her reservations about Hogan, not to mention his suitability as a husband, there was no doubting she found him physically attractive. If his proposal had been to make love as opposed to marriage, she wasn't at all confident her answer would have been no. She found herself blushing at the thought.

The waltz ended, the quartet adjourned for a drinks break, and the dancers returned to their tables.

Seated once more, Helen and the lieutenant finished their main course and then enjoyed another glass of wine while they awaited the arrival of dessert. Throughout, they made light conversation, taking care not to revisit the touchy subjects of marriage and John Graham.

As they consumed their second bottle of wine, Hogan outlined the activities he had planned for them over the next couple of days. The weekend was about to commence, and he wasn't returning to Moreton Bay until Monday morning.

Helen surprised herself by agreeing to go along with Hogan's plans. After all, she reasoned, school was out until Monday and she had nothing better to do.

Over the next two days, the couple saw a lot of each other. They spent Saturday shopping in town, walking around the waterfront, visiting the local sights and picnicking in one of the parks. Sunday was spent sailing on the harbour aboard a skiff owned by a close friend of William and Thelma Brown, Helen's benefactors and owners of the private school she taught at.

Helen and Hogan had reached an unspoken agreement that neither would broach the subject of marriage again at this point in time, and neither would mention John Graham's name ever again. It was an agreement that suited each for it allowed them to enjoy each other's company for the remainder of the short time they had together.

From the lieutenant's perspective, Helen would eventually end up as Missus Hogan whether she realised it or not. If he was nothing else, he was a confident chap, and, even if he said so himself, he was a bloody good catch for any woman.

From Helen's viewpoint, the jury was still out on whether she would agree to marry her suitor. That aside, she was enjoying his company and was fairly certain she would agree to see him again.

Hogan had surprised her in many ways during this visit—not the least because he hadn't tried to bed her. If he had, she suspected she may have acquiesced. The fact he hadn't, earned him some points as a gentleman in her mind and raised him up slightly in her estimation.

49

J OHN SHARED A JOKE WITH Murrowdooling and Carravanty as they accompanied Mamba and the other clan members to yet another encampment.

In the last eighteen months, the boys had gotten close to the man they believed to be their father—every bit as close as their mother had hoped they would. They were growing up fast, too. Murrowdooling was now eleven and Carravanty seven, and like all Kabi boys they were full of energy and cheek.

"Moilow walks like a turtle in those silly boots!" Murrowdooling advised his younger brother. He spoke in the tongue of his people, but used the English word for *boots* as there was no Kabi equivalent for that word.

"He walks more like a crab," Carravanty countered, giggling like a girl for his voice had yet to break.

"Hey, I heard that!" John said, feigning annoyance. He dropped his spear and the other items he'd been carrying, and took after the boys who shrieked as they tried to evade him. They were too slow, and he picked one up under each arm and threatened to drown them both at the next stream or billabong they came to. This sparked more laughter.

"Behave you three!" Mamba cautioned. The antics of her three *boys,* as she referred to them, never failed to amuse her, but as was often the case their timing wasn't always good. On this occasion, she'd been observing the Songlines tradition of her people, and singing to sacred landmarks along the way.

"Best be quiet, boys," John said, lowering the brothers to the ground and gathering up his possessions, all the while trying not to look guilty.

Mamba flashed a glance John's way to let him know her censure applied equally to him. She knew he knew that she wasn't fooled when he played the role of the innocent party at such times. Her Moilow was a big boy at heart, oftentimes every bit as boisterous as her sons. She resumed singing while behind her, her boys followed a little more sedately than before.

As they walked, John observed his little family—for that's how he now thought of them—with pride. They'd become a tight unit in the two years he'd been with them, and he couldn't imagine life without them.

Watching Mamba walking at the head of their little group, uncomplaining beneath the weight of half their possessions and singing so hauntingly to the spirits of her ancestors, his heart went out to her—as it inevitably did whenever he looked at her. Their relationship had only strengthened in the past eighteen months. He didn't doubt that had been helped by their ability to better communicate. Her pigeon English had much improved while his understanding of the Kabi dialect was now passable. Passable to the extent he could usually make himself understood to clan members, and more often than not he got the gist of what they were saying when they spoke.

As for Murrowdooling and Carravanty, their English was every bit as good as their mother's, which made both Mamba and John proud. The family now had a language of their own, slipping in and out of English and Kabi as and when the mood took them. Often, one or other would start a sentence in one language and end it in another, or they would ask a question in Kabi only for it to be answered in English. It was confusing to all but them.

It was still only mid-morning, yet it was already hot—unseasonably hot considering summer was not yet here. John was really feeling it, too, and he was perspiring heavily. Relocating to yet another encampment was the last thing he'd felt like doing. For the life of him, he couldn't think what was wrong with the previous site. It was next to a freshwater lake, which offered excellent fishing, and it was surrounded by fertile hills and valleys, which offered plenty of berries, grubs and game.

Earlier that same morning, John had asked Mamba, "Why do we move again?" She had answered, "You forget this . . . as well . . . Moilow? It time . . . to meet all our brothers . . . and sisters." The exchange had reminded him that Mamba still thought of him as her husband-returned—not that he needed reminding as he lived with it every day—and she never ceased to be surprised when he queried something she thought he should remember, which happened quite often.

John noticed Mamba's eyes were now fixed on a craggy, bush-covered hill to their left, and she began singing louder and with more feeling. He remembered seeing the hill once before—this time last year to be precise—and he recalled Mamba had told him it was the place where her father had died. He could see tears now rolled down her face, and he wanted to comfort her, but he resisted because he had learned she didn't appreciate being distracted at such times.

Since Mamba had first told him about the Songlines, John had imagined more than once he could hear them singing back to him. It only happened when he was alone, and then only very occasionally. Once, quite recently, it had seemed so real he'd mentioned it to Mirritji. John had half expected the elder to laugh at him, but Mirritji had assured him it was the Songlines he'd heard. He remembered advising the old man that he couldn't understand the words of the song. Mirritji had smiled and said, "The language of the Songlines is in the rhythm of the song, not the words, Moilow. The rhythm is an echo of the sky and of the land below. Listening to it, or singing it, guarantees you always have a path to follow."

"I can make no sense of the sound I hear," John had complained.

"You must clear your mind and listen harder, Moilow," Mirritji had patiently advised. "The Songlines guided you back to us. They will guide you again."

The next time John thought he heard the Songlines, he took the elder's advice and listened harder, but still he could make no sense of the sound. Yet he found it comforting.

Looking around, he noticed the ranks of the Kabi were swelling almost by the minute as members of other clans began to join them on their trek to the coast. They appeared out of the trees and valleys and gullies—individuals and family groups laden down with their possessions. Women shepherded groups of small children while some of the men carried fresh carcasses of roos and other creatures they'd killed along the way.

John had experienced this phenomenon the same time last year when all the tribe's clans converged on the same site—a coastal encampment, which he adjudged to be close to the halfway point in the Kabi's territory. They were gathering for a corroboree, a celebration of sorts. It was one of two such gatherings every year during which the clans interacted with each other and with the Dreamtime through various rituals and celebrations.

Last year's corroboree, he recalled, had involved three days of feasting, singing, dancing and copulating. Husbands swapped wives—for one, two or three days at least and sometimes for keeps—and youths pursued single women and sometimes married women, too. Little wonder, he thought, Kabi women of child-bearing age seemed to be permanently pregnant. Needless to say, the odd fight broke out, but generally everyone was surprisingly well behaved. John couldn't help wondering how convivial they would be if alcohol were added to the mix.

These occasions were also an opportunity for fathers to exchange eligible daughters to would-be husbands in return for pelts, weapons, or, if they were lucky, something more substantial like a canoe. Fathers of sought-after daughters were always pleased when these events came around.

Before they reached the coast, the column's numbers had swelled to several hundred. Gay chatter and laughter could be heard as long-time friends greeted each other up and down the column, which now stretched over a mile.

Newcomers studied John with interest. For a few, it was their first sighting of him or, indeed, of a white man. Most, however, had seen him at least once or twice before, but even they were intrigued and they stared openly at him.

The sound of waves crashing onto a beach carried to them. Mamba stopped singing and looked around at her boys. "Not long to go now," she said.

John was thankful for that. They'd been walking since dawn, and he was about ready to rest. He could tell the boys were tired, too, though, like their mother, they never complained. Turning to them, he said, "I think it's time for a song. What do you think, boys?"

The brothers beamed at John.

"Old Ireland Free!" Murrowdooling insisted in perfect English.

Carravanty echoed his older brother, leaving John with no option but to sing the popular request. Normally, he wouldn't mind, but he'd already sung that same song ten times that day. It was a firm favourite of the brothers.

"Old Ireland Free it is then," the Irishman said resignedly. He broke into song. "It was early, early in the spring . . . The birds did whistle and sweetly sing . . . changing their notes from tree to tree . . . And the song they sang was Old Ireland free!" Looking at the boys, and at Mamba, too, he said, "Your turn now." The three of them burst into song, singing the same verse over and over, in near-perfect English, while John whistled along to provide the accompaniment.

None of them minded that they'd now become the centre of attention. Smiling clan members gathered around them, anxious not to miss out on the entertainment on offer. A few hummed along, and one enterprising songster—an affable youth—even sang along in the Kabi dialect, making up the words as he went.

The Kabi arrived at their destination to find an advance party from a local clan had already begun preparing the large site, which overlooked a long stretch of beach that extended a good two miles to the north and south. Their preparations included the construction of a hundred bivouacs or more for themselves and for the new arrivals. They had also collected driftwood from the beach and fallen branches from the surrounding bush, and had stockpiled these at intervals throughout the encampment. The timber would serve as communal cooking fires. The biggest pile of wood was situated in the middle of the site, and that's where the main feast and dancing and singing would take place.

John and Mamba quickly secured one of the smaller bivouacs for themselves while all around them others settled in and generally made themselves comfortable. One of the first stops for all-comers was the nearby freshwater stream that flowed down from the mountains for it was brutally hot—a harbinger of even hotter days ahead perhaps as it was still only late spring. After assuaging their thirst, many found the stream too tempting to resist, and they flopped into it, letting the cool water wash over them.

It was mid-day and there was no time to waste as there was much to do before the evening's festivities got underway. The womenfolk fed the children and lay the toddlers down to sleep in the shade of their shelters while the menfolk busied themselves either hunting, fishing or trading.

Boys adjourned to a grassy area of open space for a game of buroinjin, that traditional ball game that was unique to the Kabi. This was noted by Murrowdooling and Carravanty who immediately approached John.

"Can we play buroinjin, Moilow?" Murrowdooling asked hopefully. Past requests had been rejected as John considered the game too rough for boys so young.

"Not yet, Murrow—" John stopped when he noticed Mamba flash a warning frown in his direction. "One moment," he said to the boy. He wandered over to Mamba. "What?" he asked.

"You cannot . . . protect sons . . . forever . . . Moilow," Mamba murmured in hesitant English.

"But—"

"You said . . . you played . . . when old as Murrowdooling," she reminded him.

John didn't remember saying any such thing, but he knew she was right about his not being able to protect the boys forever. Returning to Murrowdooling, he said, "You can play, but be careful."

Murrowdooling ran off, grinning from ear to ear, to join the other boys.

Before Carravanty could ask to join his brother, John turned to him and said, "But not you, young man. Not until you are older."

The disappointment in the younger boy's eyes was there for all to see, but he didn't argue and John didn't weaken. John's proprietary interest in the boys meant he wasn't intending to expose them to injury or danger any sooner than he had to—something Mamba had long noticed, but until now had never commented on.

Two boys Carravanty's age approached the lad and asked if he wanted to go hunt for grubs. Needing no second invitation, he ran off with them, his disappointment of a moment or two earlier already forgotten.

John chuckled as he watched the boys scamper away. He suddenly became aware Mamba had snuck up behind him when her arms encircled his waist. She stood up on her tiptoes and whispered an invitation in his ear.

John wasn't sure he'd heard her right. "What?" he asked.

She repeated her invitation, and this time John heard her. Smiling, and suddenly aroused, he turned around and kissed her.

Arm in arm, they retreated into their new bivouac. Once inside, Mamba pulled two leafy branches across the opening to give them complete privacy.

50

A SHORT TIME LATER, JOHN and Mamba strolled hand in hand through the encampment, taking in all the sights. There was much to look at.

It appeared all the Kabi clans had finally arrived for the corroboree for the encampment was overflowing with people. Latecomers were preparing their cooking fires and adding finishing touches to the shelters they'd erected while the others were engaged in a whole range of activities. Many just stood around talking, renewing old acquaintances and reminiscing amidst much laughter and gaiety.

Trading was now underway, and it was every bit as rowdy as the nearby buroinjin game, which continued still and showed no sign of ending anytime soon. John spotted Murrowdooling amongst the boys involved, and he was relieved to see that the lad was still in one piece with no obvious signs of injury.

Mamba saw the Murrowdooling, too, and laughed. "See, Moilow!" she said. "I told you."

"Told me what?" John asked even though he knew the answer.

"I told you . . . you . . . worry too much . . . about our sons."

The Irishman inclined his head, acknowledging that as usual she was right.

Mamba added, "Mother know . . ." Pretending that she'd forgotten how to say it in English, she looked to him to finish the popular refrain he had taught her.

"Mother knows best," John said, prompting her.

"I agree!" Mamba smiled triumphantly. "Mother know best." It was a catchphrase she liked, and she often used it around all her boys.

John chuckled as it dawned on him he'd walked into that one.

The couple were drawn by the sounds of energetic bargaining. They stopped to observe four men from their own clan bidding for time alone with the wife of a man from another clan. It was immediately obvious to John they considered the woman desirable for they were desperately trying to out-do each other. Their trade offerings, which lay in a mounting pile on the ground in front of the woman's husband, included a live python, shellfish, roo pelts, a shield, spears, fishing nets and several boomerangs.

John studied the woman and decided that, if looks alone counted, she wasn't worth any one of the offered items. *Beauty's in the eye of the beholder*, he reminded himself.

It was the older of the competing traders who finally prevailed. He'd already offered the python and the fishing net, but his trump card came in the form of a possum-fur cloak, which he presented with a flourish, draping it around the shoulders of the woman.

The woman, who, John had observed, seemed to have eyes only for the youngest of the traders, immediately fell in love with the cloak and flashed a toothless smile at her longsuffering husband. At this obviously pre-arranged signal, he nodded to the older trader, indicating he'd won the right to have his way with his wife.

An argument erupted when the husband advised the successful trader he must return his wife to him before sundown. It only ended when the dissatisfied man withdrew his offer and stormed off with his fur cloak and fishing net in hand and his pet python draped over his shoulders.

Two other traders departed, similarly dissatisfied, taking their trade items with them, leaving only the youngest trader and his solitary offering, a boomerang. Another toothless smile from wife to disgruntled husband sealed the deal, and the excited young trader hurriedly escorted the woman away, determined to make the most of the remaining daylight.

John and Mamba thought the whole episode amusing, and spent the next short while speculating on exactly how the young trader and the toothless woman would entertain each other—and whether the disgruntled hubby would ever see his wayward wife again.

Through the trees, John observed a number of men from the various clans throwing boomerangs in a large clearing. He saw Gabirri, Mirritji, Turo and a number of other familiar faces among them.

Mamba noticed John's interest in them. "Go and join them, Moilow," she said in her native tongue.

"You are sure?" John responded in kind.

Mamba nodded.

They shared a quick kiss and John hurried off to join Gabirri and the others.

Thirty or more men were testing their boomerang-throwing skills against each other. It was always the same when the clans came together: the menfolk invariably used the occasion to show they were stronger, faster and more skilled hunters and fighters than anyone else. Earlier, they'd held mock fights with spear and shield, and with the nulla nulla, too, and consequently many of them now sported cuts and bruises, which, John noticed, they wore like badges of honour.

Gabirri, who was about to throw his boomerang, observed John approaching and waved him over. The Irishman acknowledged his friend with a smile and hurried to join him.

The interchange was noted by Turo. "Why do you always invite the white spirit imposter to join us?" he asked Gabirri.

"Why do you not see that he is Moilow?" Gabirri retorted.

A surly Turo didn't respond, but he spat on the ground to show what he thought of the white man. Turo was more cranky than usual because a big fellow from another clan had gotten the better of him in combat, and now Gabirri was showing him up with the boomerang. In fact, Gabirri was showing everyone up for there was no-one in the entire tribe more skilled than him with this particular hunting weapon.

John arrived as Gabirri was about to release his boomerang in the direction of a target contest organisers had placed at the far end of the clearing some sixty or so yards distant. It was a buroinjin, which, at a glance, John could see was well past its use-by date. The roo pelt encasing had been struck by boomerangs so many times today the grass stuffing protruded from it. The buroinjin was attached to the top of a spear that had been driven into the ground. Each time a contestant struck the target, it was moved ten paces further away. Now, at the longer distance, contestants had yet to achieve a successful strike.

Gabirri released his boomerang, and John and the others watched as it travelled in a graceful arc, curving from right to left and barely rising higher than the intended target. He let out a triumphant yell as the weapon struck the buroinjin with such force it knocked the buroinjin and the spear that supported it to the ground. Cheering broke out and Gabirri basked in the accolades his fellow contestants bestowed upon him.

To John's amusement, the young man then proceeded to inform all his fellows how great he was with the boomerang. Turo, who had had enough of Gabirri's boasting and who had missed the target by a good five yards on his last throw, walked off in disgust.

"Why do you leave us?" Gabirri asked, laughing, when he noticed his fellow contestant depart.

Turo didn't deign to respond, but he did raise one hand and flash a sign, which John imagined conveyed something rude. This only served to make Gabirri laugh all the more.

Mirritji, who had only just noticed John, approached the new arrival. "Moilow, it is your turn," he said, pointing to a small pile of boomerangs lying nearby.

Gabirri supported the elder's suggestion. "Yes, Moilow," he said, picking up one of the boomerangs, "see if you can beat me now." He added, "You never could before."

As John took the boomerang from his friend, he realised every eye was upon him. He'd have declined the offer if it wasn't for the fact he would lose face as he already knew the outcome.

You're about to make an almighty fool of yourself Graham.

The assembled looked on with interest—especially those who had never been this close to the white man before—as he aimed at the target. To his eyes it seemed to be more like a hundred long paces away than sixty, and he found he had to squint as he was looking directly into the late afternoon sun.

John let fly. The release felt surprisingly good. The boomerang soared higher than any of the others had travelled—and higher than warranted for a target so low to the ground—and he lost sight of it in the glare of the sun. That was the last time he saw it. Until it hit him. And even then he didn't see it, but he certainly felt it.

Gabirri and the others saw the whole thing. John's throw had been powerful enough, but it had been far too high. The boomerang had begun its return journey at point high above the intended target and directly in front of the sun. For the entirety of its return flight, it had remained hidden from the Irishman in the sun's glare.

The boomerang struck John a glancing blow on the forehead. Although it was nearing the end of its flight, and therefore had lost much of its momentum, the force of the blow was nevertheless sufficient to knock him out.

When he came to, and when the mist cleared and he was finally able to focus, he realised he was still the centre of attention, although this time he was lying on his back and his fellow contestants were gathered around him, looking highly amused by what they'd just witnessed. It took him a moment or two to realise where he was and what had just happened.

I must've knocked myself out!

Gabirri and the others laughed amongst themselves as they relived what they'd just witnessed. No-one seemed concerned that John could be concussed or, worse, that he could have been killed.

The Irishman found his companions' light-hearted response to his plight disturbing. He'd long observed that for all their fine traits, the Kabi delighted in the misfortunes of others—even, or especially, when those misfortunes befell a friend. It was an aspect of their humour he couldn't fathom let alone relate to. Right now, for example, no-one was laughing louder than Gabirri.

"Were you trying to hit the sun, Moilow?" Gabirri asked, prompting yet more laughter.

Still dizzy, and more than a little embarrassed, John pushed himself to his feet. Only now did he notice his mishap had left him with a nasty cut above one eye, and his head hurt, too. Blood trickled from the wound. "I . . . try to stop boomerang . . . with my head," he muttered self-depreciatingly in an attempt to deflect the embarrassment he felt.

Those men from other clans who had never heard John speak before observed him, more intrigued than ever, as he spoke. They understood most of what he said as he spoke haltingly in their dialect.

John continued, "Next time . . . I use a . . . different . . . method."

This prompted still more laughter.

As the laughter faded, the men began dispersing. The sun had now dropped behind the trees, and dusk was fast approaching. Nightfall would signify the start of a whole new round of festivities, which the men were looking forward to.

Gabirri assisted John back to the encampment, still chuckling at his friend's misfortune.

⊷∈•————•Ɛ⊷

John and Mamba watched the evening's festivities from beneath the overhang of their bivouac. The bivouac was one of a cluster of shelters that occupied a small rise close to the centre of the encampment, so they and their immediate neighbours had a good view of the festivities.

Festivities were of a ceremonial nature, and they involved only the men and youths of the assembled clans. Painted in white ochre and wearing only their loincloths, the participants danced around the huge campfire that had been built for just this purpose. As usual, they danced to the beat of drumming sticks and to the

313

unique vibrations of didgeridoos.

John had opted out of joining in the ceremony because his mishap with the boomerang had left him with a bad headache and a lump on his head the size of an egg. Mamba's Aunty Jiba had wrapped his head in a herbal leaf dressing, and Mamba herself had dispensed a herbal drink, which had done much to reduce his pain, but still he felt a little fragile.

The Irishman was still smarting over the amusement his misfortune had caused his companions—in particular his friend Gabirri. His mood hadn't been helped, either, by Mamba's reaction to his plight. Upon seeing the blood pouring from his wound, and on learning how he'd done that to himself, she had been every bit as amused as Gabirri. That had been the last straw for John and he'd withdrawn from her and sulked. His sulking had, unfortunately, only served to further encourage Mamba who took every opportunity to remind him the Moilow of old would never have knocked himself out with his own boomerang.

Only now, hours later, was he beginning to see the funny side.

They noticed Murrowdooling and Carravanty meandering up from the campfire. The brothers had been watching the festivities up close, dreaming of the day they would be old enough to participate. For Murrowdooling, that day wasn't far off.

"It appears the boys . . . have had enough . . . for the night," John observed in the Kabi tongue.

"They will be tired," Mamba said.

When the brothers arrived at the bivouac, Murrowdooling appeared surly, not looking at John and Mamba, and answering questions with monosyllables. He retired to his bed mat inside the bivouac without even saying goodnight.

"What is wrong with your brother?" John asked Carravanty.

The younger boy just shrugged.

"He is tired, Moilow," Mamba said. "That is all."

"That is no excuse for . . ." John struggled for the right word. Switching to English, he said, "That is no excuse for rudeness." Both he and Mamba had noticed the older boy had appeared surly of late. They put it down to his age, but John sensed something was troubling him. "Murrowdooling!" he called out.

A moment later, Murrowdooling emerged from the bivouac. "What?" he asked, looking at the ground.

"Look at me when I speak to you," John insisted.

Murrowdooling looked up, and only then, by the light of the moon, did John and Mamba notice that his face was covered in fresh cuts and bruises.

"Who did that to you?" John asked, alarmed.

The boy mumbled something incoherent.

"Speak up, lad," John said.

"I got hurt playing buroinjin," Murrowdooling mumbled.

"That game is so rough," a sympathetic Mamba said. "Come here, son." She held out her arms, and Murrowdooling reluctantly went to her and allowed her to give him a big hug.

John chuckled, recalling how he responded to his own mother hugging him in front of others when he was Murrowdooling's age. "Alright, you two," he addressed the brothers in English. "Time to turn in."

The brothers disappeared inside the bivouac, leaving John and Mamba alone once more.

At length, Mamba said, "Perhaps we should ban Murrowdooling from playing that game . . . It is so rough."

Surprised by her change of heart, John said, "No. Buroinjin will toughen him up."

God knows he will need to be tough to survive what lies ahead of him.

"But he is so young," Mamba protested.

"Murrowdooling is growing up faster than you realise, Mamba." John said. He added, "He will be a man before you know it."

51

A S THE CAMPFIRE IN THE centre of the encampment died, and the menfolk began returning to their bivouacs, John prepared to retire and join Mamba and the boys inside their own bivouac. Mamba had retired earlier, leaving him to witness the remainder of the festivities on his own.

He had only just stood up when he noticed a shadowy male figure approach. As the figure neared, he saw it was Gabirri.

"I bring you goodwill, Moilow," the young native said, extending one of several traditional greetings the Kabi used, depending on the circumstances.

"I accept your goodwill, Gabirri," John responded, using the accepted response for this particular greeting. "What brings you to my bivouac?"

"Karadji has requested our company," Gabirri informed him.

John knew he referred to the young shaman, the clan's most revered member and one whom he'd had little to do with to date. Karadgi, he'd learned, was a private person who generally only met with those who requested a meeting or who needed his supposed magical powers. He'd have been surprised to learn that the shaman often thought of him and often conferred with his ancestors' spirits regarding the white spirit. "What does Karadgi want with me?" he asked, somewhat mystified.

"The shaman will tell us that when we see him," Gabirri said.

"Where is he?" John asked.

His friend pointed to the top of a hill that overlooked the encampment and the bay whose shores it hugged. In the moonlight, the hill's summit appeared barren and foreboding.

John had been ready to turn in, but he sensed something important was in store for him. Besides, his headache had all but gone, and he was feeling much improved. Without another word, he fell in beside Gabirri, and together they struck off toward the hill, a full moon lighting their way.

The two were breathing hard by the time they reached the hill's summit. They hadn't wasted any time, and the hill had proven to be deceptively steep.

On the summit, as Gabirri had indicated, they found Karadji. The young shaman didn't acknowledge them. He was sitting alone and cross-legged, chanting to himself while looking out over the moonlit bay.

In the moonlight, they could see Karadji's eyes were open, but he appeared to be in a trance.

John went to say something, but Gabirri held up one hand, indicating they should not speak until spoken to.

While Karadji continued chanting, the two friends studied the large encampment below. The glow of embers of two hundred cooking fires gave the site an ethereal effect, which, to John's eyes, looked almost magical.

Finally, the shaman stopped chanting and looked at them. "I welcome you," he said, speaking in the tongue of the Kabi people.

The voice sounded deep to John's ears, deceptively deep for one apparently not yet out of his teens.

"We accept your welcome, Karadji," Gabirri said respectfully.

The shaman motioned to them to sit down facing him. They did as asked, sitting cross-legged like their host.

John returned the other's stare as Karadji studied him through hooded eyes. Clean-shaven like himself, the shaman wore a full-length cloak that extended down to his ankles. It was a cloak of many colours, unlike any other John had seen. Four eagle feathers hung from his long hair, a large shell hung from each pierced ear, and a stick the length of a man's hand protruded through his nose.

However, it was the face that captured John's attention.

The face and the eyes.

His was a face full of character and wisdom, and his eyes, John decided, were those of an old soul. When Karadji looked at him, it felt as though he was looking into his own soul.

At length, the shaman said, "It is good you came, Moilow." Before John could respond, Karadji motioned to a small pile of wood and grass next to him and said, "You should make a fire."

John hadn't noticed the pile until now. The shaman had evidently placed it there to serve as tinder for the fire he'd referred to. Next to it, he saw, were two fire sticks, dry grass and other essentials needed for starting a fire. He wondered if Karadji was setting him some sort of test.

After John's failed efforts to make fire during his months alone in the wilderness, he'd sworn never to attempt that again. That experience had left him with bloodied hands, which had subsequently become infected and had impacted upon his ability to hunt and gather food so markedly he'd almost starved to death. However, since then, Gabirri and others had painstakingly taught him how to make fire, and, even if he said so himself, he'd become quite adept.

The Irishman reached over and picked up the fire sticks and other necessities. Those necessities included a square piece of wood upon which he lay some of the dry grass. He then grasped the sticks between the palms of both hands, and placed the bottom end of the sticks through the tinder so they were hard up against the wood. That done, he began moving his hands rapidly back and forth.

Karadji watched with interest, and Gabirri watched with some pride for he'd invested more time than anyone else in teaching John this art, as he toiled. It was hard going, and John had worked up a real sweat before the first signs of smoke appeared. He paused only long enough to blow softly on the smoking tinder. It wasn't long before small tongues of flames appeared.

John transferred the burning tinder to the pile of wood, and the fire took almost immediately. Flames leapt high, creating dancing shadows on the faces of the three men.

Karadji resumed chanting. From beneath his cloak he produced a wad of pitjuri, a tobacco-like plant with unique properties. Tearing a piece from it, he rolled it into a ball and popped it into his mouth before tearing the remaining wad in half and handing a piece to John and another to Gabirri. The two friends followed the shaman's lead, each rolling their wad into a ball and popping it into their mouths.

John noticed his companions were now chewing, and Gabirri motioned to him to do the same. He began chewing.

"Pitjuri," Gabirri explained. "Magic powers."

It wasn't long before the plant's hallucinogenic powers became apparent. John could feel himself being transported into another dimension where every object seemed bright and vivid. The moon and stars looked twice their normal size, and ten times brighter than normal, and he felt joyful, almost euphoric.

Evidently, his companions were feeling the same way for they were now lying back, their eyes on the heavens above. John lay back, too, and studied the starry night sky.

Karadji pointed to the distinctive Southern Cross constellation. "That is the Stingray in the Sky," he said.

John sensed the shaman was addressing him, though his eyes remained fastened on the constellation. This was immediately confirmed when Karadji added, "Gabirri will explain."

Taking his cue, Gabirri sat up and picked up one of the fire sticks John had used. He noticed John was still lying down, so he reached over and tapped him sharply on the forehead with the stick.

John got the message and slowly sat up. As he did, it felt as though he was in someone else's body. Everything he did and everything he saw seemed to be happening in slow motion.

Ever so slowly, the Irishman looked down and saw that Gabirri was drawing something in the dirt. In the flickering firelight, the outline of a stingray took shape. John looked back up at the Southern Cross and nodded to himself as the Stingray in the Sky gradually, and in its own time, revealed itself to him. The constellation's two pointers, Alpha Centuri and Beta Centuri unmistakably resembled the stingray's tail.

Still speaking in his own tongue, Gabirri began explaining the significance of the stingray. He quickly realised John was not following him. Reverting to pigeon English, he started again. "Stingray . . . is my . . . totem," he said. "My name—"

"No!" Karadji interjected fiercely, surprising them both. The shaman sat bolt upright and looked at Gabirri. "The story of the stingray must be told in the Kabi tongue. The Sky Beings have decreed it." Karadji then knelt before John, placed one hand on top of the Irishman's head and whispered a prayer to the beings he'd just referred to. Then he lay back down and nodded to Gabirri to resume.

Speaking in his native tongue once more, Gabirri said, "The stingray is my totem animal. My name, Gabirri, means stingray . . ." He paused to see if John was following him. To his surprise, he appeared to be, and so he continued. "Many rainy seasons ago, our Kabi ancestors saw the stingray jump out of the sea into the sky,"—he pointed at the constellation—"and there it is."

John looked up once more and smiled. For some reason the stingray was even more recognisable now that Gabirri had so clearly explained the reason for its existence. In his drug-induced state, he wasn't remotely surprised that he'd understood Gabirri perfectly. Nor was he surprised when the stingray came to life and began to swim east-west across the night sky.

The Irishman succumbed to the effects of the pitjuri long before the stingray completed its mystical journey.

When he woke, hours from now, he would remember the stingray's incredible journey, or what he'd seen of it at least, and he'd recall word for word the story Gabirri had related. However, he would have no memory of the magic Karadji had performed in giving him total comprehension, if only for a short time, of the Kabi tongue.

Two days later, only the hundred or so members of Mootemu's clan remained at the encampment. They, too, would have moved on if it hadn't been for the fact that the clan's menfolk had drawn a short straw of sorts, for this year, as John was about to learn, it was their turn to clear the scrub and prickly vegetation that surrounded the site.

If left unchecked, the unwanted vegetation made access to the encampment difficult, so each year it fell to the menfolk of one of the clans to clear it away to ensure the Kabi had easy access to the site for next year's corroboree. They achieved this through clever use of fire—a practice their forefathers had refined over tens of thousands of years.

In his time with the Kabi, John had witnessed the menfolk do some amazing things with fire, or with *karl* as they called it, and often at great risk to life and limb. Armed only with leafy branches, they cleverly controlled fires by diverting and channelling them so that the flames destroyed unwanted vegetation.

The Irishman had learned the Kabi used fire for compelling environmental reasons as well as for improving access to important campsites or hunting grounds. As Mirritji had explained to him, fires allowed regeneration of the bush, encouraging new growth and attracting more animals as well as plants the clan needed for warmth and for cooking.

Sometimes, John had observed, the Kabi made use of natural fires caused by lightning strikes and the like—a frequent occurrence in this part of the world, especially during the hot summers when bushfires were a constant menace. On this occasion, however, the men planned to light the fire themselves.

The plan was to clear the lower slopes of a hill—the same hill John and Gabirri had climbed to see the shaman—of unwanted vegetation.

As had been the case the previous summer, John was recruited to assist. However, unlike the previous summer, he was tasked with patrolling the upper slopes to ensure sparks or embers did not start fires there. He rightly assumed he had been delegated this straightforward task because his fire-fighting efforts the previous summer had been so amateurish he'd put himself and others at risk of being burned alive.

Carrying two large, leafy branches, the Irishman headed off up the hill alone while some forty men and youths set fires at regular intervals on the lower slopes. Even though it was still early in the day, it was already hot and a light westerly was blowing—ideal for what was planned.

John followed the same route up the hill that he and Gabirri had taken. This time, he stopped in a bush clearing some fifty yards from the summit. From here, he had a clear view of the others working below, and of the encampment beyond. In the encampment, he could see the women and children gathering up their possessions in readiness for the clan's impending departure.

The encampment and the men at the foot of the hill were soon concealed behind billowing smoke. Fortunately, the westerly ensured any sparks and embers were blown out to sea. Even so, John knew to remain alert as wind direction could change at a moment's notice.

Every now and then, the smoke cleared long enough to allow him to observe the men at work below. To his eyes, they seemed to be dicing with death. Working either in pairs or in small groups, they thrashed the burning grass and vegetation with their branches, diverting the flames so that healthy stands of trees were spared while unwanted vegetation was destroyed.

Mirritji appeared to be directing proceedings, frequently ordering one group or other to relocate or to assist others working elsewhere on the hillside.

To the uninitiated, like John, it looked like chaos in motion—and yet it worked. The lower slopes were rapidly cleared of unwanted vegetation, and not a man was burnt let alone lost.

The fires quickly burnt themselves out, and the soot-blackened men meandered back toward the encampment. John could hear them laughing and joking as they walked away, obviously happy about a job well done. They stopped at a freshwater pool on the way to bathe the soot and ash from their hair and their bodies. Behind them, green belts of trees miraculously lay untouched while between those belts the blackened earth lay bare, stripped of vegetation by the fire that had raged only a short time before.

Mirritji looked up the hill, spotted the Irishman in the clearing and waved to him. That was the prearranged signal for the latter to return.

John was so close to the top of the hill, he decided to climb to the summit before descending. He'd never seen the view from the top during the day. Besides, he thought, he had plenty of time. It was still only mid-morning.

Moments later, as he crested the hill, he nearly jumped out of his skin when he saw a sailing ship at anchor close to shore.

Holy Mother of God!

52

THE THREE-MASTED VESSEL WAS IN a bay some two miles to the north. Even from this distance, John identified her as a barque. He hadn't seen the ship earlier because the bay had been hidden from view in the bush clearing he'd occupied.

Riggers could be seen in the rigging of two of her masts while crewmen were engaged in various tasks on deck. From here, they were ant-like figures. They and the flag that fluttered above her stern were too distant to recognise.

Before he even thought about what he was doing, he began running headlong down the hill, determined to reach the barque before she sailed off.

The Irishman was near-exhausted by the time he neared the bay. He hadn't run so hard since dingoes had chased him during his trek north from Moreton Bay.

When he finally reached the bay, he was relieved to see the barque was still at anchor. The nameplate on her hull identified her as *Northern Travails,* and the Union Jack fluttering above her stern marked her as a British vessel.

John noticed a skiff had been pulled up onto the sand. It was resting close to the mouth of a stream. Whoever had rowed the skiff ashore was nowhere in sight, although the oars remained in the craft. He resisted the urge to rush over to the skiff and row out to the barque, which, he estimated, was fifty yards at most offshore. "It could be a military vessel," he muttered to himself.

It wouldn't do to board her and discover she's bound for Moreton Bay!

Erring on the side of caution, he remained hidden in the trees, preferring to study the barque and her crew before committing himself to their mercy.

He quickly deduced the ship was no military vessel. Her crew, who were currently engaged in a variety of maintenance duties on deck, wore civilian dress and didn't look or act remotely military. "Where are you headed?" he wondered aloud. "North or south?" Unfortunately for him, a ship at anchor gave no clue as to which direction she was headed.

Just who had brought the skiff ashore was answered when two sailors emerged from the trees. Each man was rolling a water barrel along the stream's near bank, so it was immediately obvious they'd come ashore to replenish their supplies of freshwater.

The sailors were so close he could hear them talking, and, judging by their grumbling, he could tell they weren't happy.

"How come we always get the short bloody straw, Moffett?" the older man asked, his accent revealing he was a Cockney.

"Fecked if I know," the man called Moffett answered in a lilting Irish accent. "Perhaps it has something to do with us calling the chief mate a faggot!"

"*You* called 'im a fuckin' faggot, not me!" the Cockney grumbled.

"Yeah, but you agreed wi' me, Gerald," Moffett reminded his companion.

Listening to the sailors, it took all John's self-control not to rush out and hug them. They and their crewmates aboard the barque were the first whites he'd seen in over two years. Two years and three months to be exact. That's how long it had been since he fled Moreton Bay.

What was holding him back, he wasn't sure. He'd already established the vessel and her crew looked innocent enough. He had no way of knowing whether the barque was heading north or south, but he had long-since decided a southbound vessel wouldn't be a deal-breaker—provided said vessel wasn't planning to visit Moreton Bay. And he wouldn't know that, of course, until he'd boarded her. Unless . . .

I could just ask these two.

Throwing caution to the wind, he stepped out from the trees and onto the beach. He'd almost reached the two sailors before his countryman saw him.

"Lookout Gerald!" Moffett shouted. "Bloody Abo!"

The Cockney spun around, thinking he and his mate were under attack.

By now, John had realised the pair thought he was an Aborigine. He was aware that his sun-darkened skin and long, unruly, black hair could give that impression, not to mention his shorts, which he knew could easily be mistaken for a loincloth.

Only now did John notice the Cockney was armed with a pistol. He'd drawn it as he'd spun around, and was now aiming it his way. John raised both his hands in the air to show that he was unarmed. Staring at the Irish sailor, he uttered a greeting only he would understand. "Maidin mhaith," he said.

Both sailors looked surprised—in particular the sailor known as Moffett.

"What'd 'e say?" the sailor known as Gerald asked his mate.

"He said 'good morning' in Irish!" Moffett advised him.

"Or should that be good afternoon?" John asked, looking up at the sun.

"Who in God's name are you?" the Cockney asked, looking the wild Irishman up and down.

"Finbar Harte," John advised the astonished pair. He extended his right hand, but the sailors were as yet too wary to allow the stranger to come too close. Undeterred, he continued, "I'm an Irish traveller who is down on his luck. I was aboard a vessel not unlike yours when savages attacked us some forty miles to the south, and I was the only one spared."

"Holy Virgin Mary," Moffett said, crossing himself.

"Why'd they spare you?" a suspicious Gerald asked.

"To this day, I do not know," John said with all the innocence he could muster.

"What vessel were you aboard?" Gerald asked, still suspicious.

"An American schooner called 'The Good Hope,'" John said without missing a beat. "She was England bound, and I was returning home to see my dear máthair in

Dublin."

Gerald turned to Moffett. "Máthair?"

"Mother," Moffett explained.

The sailors listened spellbound as John related his well-rehearsed tale of woe. By the time he'd finished, he had them convinced he was who he said he was. Only now did they allow John close enough to shake hands. Not satisfied with that, he picked each man up in a bear hug, and he had to be restrained from kissing them.

"I guess yer 'appy to see us," Gerald said.

"Happy?" John asked, grinning. "You wouldn't believe how happy I am to see you!" After fielding more questions, he asked, "Where would the Northern Travails be heading?"

"We're bound for Sydney Town," Moffett said.

This news came as a disappointment for John as he'd hoped they were sailing north.

"Via Moreton Bay," Gerald added, "to deliver urgent supplies."

John's heart sank at that news. "Moreton Bay?" he asked. "Are you sure?"

"Of course we're sure," Gerald said. "Why wouldn't we be sure?" The Cockney's eyes narrowed as he studied John afresh. His eyes dropped to John's unconventional footwear. Not even the cut-out toes of his convict-issue boots could hide that they were boots—unlikely footwear for a ship's passenger. Suspicions renewed, he raised his pistol at John and said, "Yer a fuckin' escaped convict, aren't ya."

"C'mon, Gerald," Moffett complained. "He's one o' us."

'He might be one o' your lot, but 'e sure as hell ain't one o' mine," the Cockney said.

John realised he'd put himself in a bit of strife. His worst fears had been confirmed: he had been identified as an escapee, and the boat he'd enquired about was heading straight for Moreton Bay. "Well, I best be on me way," he said with a forced grin.

"You stay right there Finbar Harte or whatever yer name is," Gerald said, waving his pistol under John's nose.

John swapped his grin for a cold glare. Stepping toward the Cockney so that the barrel of the man's pistol was now hard against his chest, he said, "I'm going now, and I'll leave it to you whether you shoot me or not." Without further delay, he turned and began walking slowly but purposefully up the beach.

"Stop or I'll shoot!" Gerald said, cocking his pistol.

John continued walking.

Behind John, Gerald prepared to shoot. As he pulled the trigger, Moffett knocked the pistol upwards so that the shot was high.

"What the fuck did ya do that fer?" Gerald asked.

"What harm did he do us?" Moffett asked, looking at the departing figure of his fellow Irishman.

The two sailors watched John until he disappeared into the trees. Then it was as if he'd never been there. All that remained were the unconventional prints his modified boots had left in the sand.

53

CAPTAIN MARSDEN'S UNTETHERED HORSE GRAZED nearby as the widower paid his respects beside his wife's grave. It was a weekly ritual for the good captain who was nearing the end of his recital of *The Lord's Prayer*. " . . . Forever and ever, Amen," he murmured, placing a bunch of fresh-cut flowers he'd brought next to his late wife's headstone.

Regardless of whether or not he was on duty, Marsden always wore his officer's uniform for this weekly occasion. Today, he happened to be on duty, and he looked splendid as always in his red tunic, adorned as it was with well-deserved medals that glinted in the early morning sunlight.

And, as always, he had a final word for his dearest before departing. "I miss you, old girl," he said. "And Helen and Matthew miss you, too . . . Rest in peace, my darling." He wiped a tear from his eye, mounted his waiting horse and trotted off down the hill toward the penal settlement.

For Marsden, the past couple of years had passed painfully slowly. Since his wife's death, over two years ago now, and since Helen's departure for Sydney Town, he'd been desperately lonely. Consequently, he was drinking more than ever these days. Not enough to impact on his duties, but enough to cause him some concern. He was aware it was an unwise indulgence, and he promised himself he'd quit tomorrow. Always tomorrow.

The captain's loneliness had been compounded when he sent Matthew to join his sister in Sydney Town at the start of the school year. Home-schooling the boy hadn't worked out, unfortunately. Not because of any lack of application by Matthew or because of any failing on the part of his private tutor, but because the tutor had taken ill and spent more time away sick than she did teaching.

In the end, it had been an easy decision. He had sent Matthew to board with his sister at the Browns' residence and to attend junior school with Helen at the private school she taught at. He sent him on condition that Helen wasn't one of his teachers for he knew the boy would consider that a punishment, as most brothers surely would. The Browns had readily agreed to that condition, and Helen certainly hadn't objected.

Marsden visited his children once every three months, but only for a few days at a time as that was the only free time he could arrange.

Lord Cheetham had sunk to new depths in pandering to his opium addiction, and he was now absent in almost every sense of the word. When he wasn't smoking opium or recovering from his latest binge, he was trying to manage the penal settlement's affairs from home, rarely venturing outside his mansion. As a result, more and more of those affairs were being left to Marsden.

This arrangement would have suited the captain if it hadn't been for the fact that Cheetham insisted the strict rules governing the treatment of convicts—rules that the commandant had imposed—be followed to the letter. Marsden had always considered those rules too harsh—*inhumane* was the word he'd used in formal complaints—but his complaints had been ignored. They'd been ignored by the commandant *and* by the Governor, so he had no-one else to turn to. He was on his own.

Marsden suspected Lieutenant Hogan acted as Cheetham's eyes and ears in the settlement, keeping the commandant appraised of any easing of the treatment or punishment of the convicts, but he couldn't prove it. It irked him that his daughter's suitor could be Cheetham's spy.

The captain saw his lieutenant at that very moment—just as he was thinking of him. Hogan, whose leg had healed, was now back on active duty. He was walking toward the officers' quarters as Marsden approached. As always, the lieutenant walked with a limp. His surgeon, he'd been told, had advised him it would be a permanent impediment.

"Lieutenant Hogan," Marsden called out.

Hogan stopped walking as soon as he saw Marsden. "Captain," he said, returning his superior's salute.

"Everything in order?" Marsden enquired.

"Yes, sir. I am getting through my rounds."

"I notice you are walking more these days."

"Doctor's orders."

"How is the leg today?"

"As well as can be expected thank you."

"Very well. Carry on, Lieutenant."

The two saluted and parted company.

As he rode away, Marsden couldn't help thinking how strained relations remained between the lieutenant and himself. They were so strained he couldn't imagine ever accepting Desmond Hogan as a son-in-law. He turned his mind to other things.

Despite the early hour, the settlement was buzzing. Convict gangs were engaged in a multitude of tasks, and the curses of their guards and the crack of whips could be heard everywhere.

The settlement had changed out of sight since John's escape. Convicts now numbered one thousand nine hundred and twenty-three with more arriving by the month. The convict population had fallen short of the Governor's two-year projection, but not by much. Marsden considered the shortfall, such as it was, a blessing because the construction of new facilities was not keeping pace with the increased numbers of convicts. As a result, the convicts' quality of life had further deteriorated, and death and illness remained their ever-present companions.

Escape attempts were increasing once more, too. After a brief lull, more and more convicts were now opting to risk the hangman's noose rather than wait for the Grim

Reaper to visit them in his own time.

Marsden observed convicts felling trees in the distance. Others stripped fallen trees of branches and secured chains and ropes to the trunks; still more convicts lined up to haul the logs to the riverbank just upstream from the wharf—between that facility and the penal settlement. There, the army's carpenters together with labourers from the nearby township were busy building a wooden bridge, which would eventually span the river. It would be the first of many such bridges.

The familiar caravan of horse-drawn carts travelled to and from the quarry, transporting rocks the convicts extracted for never-ending roading and construction projects, which, in turn, required still more convict labour. The road connecting Brisbane Town with the penal settlement and wharf had long been completed, and now new roads were being built connecting the settlement with the coast and with the interior.

Renovation of the wharf had also been completed. It could now accommodate up to three medium-sized ships at a time, and these days it was rare not to see at least one vessel in port. Even now, Marsden noticed, there were two ships alongside the wharf—the latest being a three-masted barque that had not long arrived. He'd heard she was en route to Sydney Town.

Work continued in the fields where teams of convicts were engaged year-round tilling, planting, pruning or picking, depending on the season, and building barns, storage sheds and fences regardless of the season. The work was not weather-dependent either. There was always heavy work for the convicts to do, and they worked in all weather—even in the fiercest storms.

Perhaps the most obvious change in and around the settlement was the Quandamookas' shanty town that had once lined the riverbank was no more. The native squatters had been chased off as a result of complaints by the settlers. That development had been welcomed by all except those soldiers who had availed themselves of the comforts provided by some of the Quandamooka girls.

It was rumoured that a dozen or so female residents in the nearby township were now meeting the needs of the soldiers, and those of some of the male residents, too, although to the captain's knowledge that was only conjecture.

Marsden was aware at least half Moreton Bay's convict population was employed on construction projects in the township. That's where he was heading now. He had a scheduled meeting with Cheetham.

Like the penal settlement, Brisbane Town was expanding rapidly. Its expansion was even more impressive with new settlers arriving weekly, and new buildings—commercial and residential—popping up almost as frequently. The riverside town that would one day be known as Brisbane City now had a permanent population of two hundred and eighteen, and new arrivals showed no sign of slowing.

As Marsden approached Cheetham's mansion, he psyched himself up for another challenging one-on-one. Dealing with the commandant was never easy—especially not when under the influence as the old man was more often than not.

Sure enough, Cheetham was under the influence when he finally shuffled into his den. The commandant had already kept Marsden waiting ten minutes, but he made no apology for that. "Good morning, Captain," he mumbled as he flopped into his armchair.

"Good morning, Lord Cheetham," Marsden said, not bothering to rise from the chair he occupied. It was immediately clear to him that Cheetham had been smoking opium—and probably not that long ago. He'd come to recognise the signs. The older man's eyes looked red and unfocussed, he was unshaven and he moved as if moving in slow motion. Even his speech was slow.

A knock on the door alerted them to the arrival of Cheetham's Aboriginal maid, Lucy.

"Come!" Cheetham called.

The door opened and Lucy entered, carrying a tray. On it were two cups full of piping hot, black tea. She set the tray down on Cheetham's desk and hurried from the den, evidently keen to remove herself from the presence of the man who had long considered her one of his chattels.

Not for the first time, Marsden wondered what the relationship was between Cheetham and the maid. He wasn't to know that sexual relations between them had ceased a good year earlier, around the time the commandant had stepped up his use of opium, and these days Lucy was engaged more as a servant and caregiver than anything else.

"Help yourself," Cheetham said to Marsden as he reached for one of the cups.

Marsden didn't feel like tea, but he picked up the other cup to appear sociable.

Cheetham drank from his cup and then turned his glassy eyes on his subordinate. "Let's get straight to it, Captain. I have some pressing business to attend to," he mumbled.

"Yes, my Lord," Marsden said. He had a fair idea what that pressing business entailed, but he didn't mention that. Instead, he said, "You will recall I mentioned my daughter plans to relocate to Moreton Bay from Sydney Town to establish a junior school in the settlement . . ."

"Yes, yes," Cheetham said dismissively. It was apparent he was already growing impatient. "When is she coming?"

"At the end of the current school year."

"Your daughter . . . Helen . . . right?"

"Yes." Marsden was surprised Cheetham remembered his daughter's name, but then he reminded himself the old man had a thing for younger women. "She is being sponsored by old family friends who operate the school she teaches at." When Cheetham offered no further comment, Marsden added, "As a junior school will benefit the soldiers' children as well as the settlers' children, she and the friends I mentioned wondered if the army may consider financing construction of the planned school room?"

Cheetham's furrowed brow wrinkled even more as he tried to focus his scattered brain on the proposal that had been put to him.

Marsden could see his opposite was battling. Cheetham was deathly pale, he was sweating like a pig and he seemed very fidgety. The captain was surprised that in his state he'd even made it down the stairs.

"How many children will the new school accommodate?" Cheetham asked at length.

"Twenty to start with. And the estimate is at least half of those will be soldiers' children." Marsden was tempted to remind Cheetham that the number of married soldiers and wives based at Moreton Bay was increasing, and already there were thirteen children living in the family quarters. However, he remained silent. He didn't wish to load more information on the commandant in his present befuddled state.

To Marsden's surprise, Cheetham said, "I think that proposal has merit, Captain. I will seek the Governor's approval and let you know."

"Thank you—"

Before Marsden could finish, there was another knock on the door. This time, Lucy entered without waiting to be invited. She looked at Cheetham. "Two visitors from big ship to see you, Master," she said in broken English.

"Who?" Cheetham demanded.

"Not say," Lucy said. "One is captain."

"Show them in," Cheetham said, angry that unexpected visitors were about to take up more of his valuable time.

Two seamen entered the den. The senior of the two introduced himself to the commandant. "Lord Cheetham, allow me to introduce myself," he said, extending his hand to Cheetham. "I am Captain Clive Tindall, master of the Northern Travails, and this is Ordinary Seaman Sean Moffett, from the same vessel." The man's strong Devonshire accent left no doubt as to his origins.

Observing Tindall, Marsden recalled *Northern Travails* was the name of the barque he'd seen alongside the settlement's wharf earlier. He and Cheetham were about to learn Tindall's subordinate was one of the two seamen who had the recent encounter with John.

Cheetham rallied himself long enough to complete the formalities, introducing Tindall to Marsden. The commandant then asked, "How can I help you, Captain Tindall?"

"My Lord, this man"—he nodded toward his subordinate—"had an interesting encounter with a stranger two days ago, and I suspect it may interest you."

"Go on," Cheetham said.

"I will leave it to Ordinary Seaman Moffett to relate in his own words exactly what happened." Turning to the Irish seaman, he nodded.

Moffett then advised Cheetham and Marsden of his and his mate's unexpected encounter with the Irishman who called himself Finbar Harte.

"When was this again?" Marsden asked.

"Two days ago, sir," Moffett said.

"And to the north of here, you say?" Marsden asked.

Tindall nodded. "In a bay some one hundred miles to the north," he said.

"You have a map," Marsden observed, nodding to a folded document the

328

barque's master carried.

Without waiting to be asked, Tindall unfolded the map on Cheetham's desktop, and then pointed to the bay where the encounter with the mysterious white man had occurred. "It is exactly one hundred and three miles from Moreton Bay," Tindall said, having previously calculated the distance.

"Can I keep this, Captain Tindall?" Marsden asked.

"Certainly, Captain Marsden."

Turning back to Moffett, Marsden enquired, "Can you describe this Irishman again, Mister Moffett?"

Moffett quickly described the stranger—in more detail this time.

"And he was definitely Irish?" Marsden asked.

"No doubt about it, sir. He had the lingo and the blarney off pat."

"I guess it takes an Irishman to know an Irishman," Marsden smiled.

"Feckin' right, sir."

Tindall nudged his subordinate.

"I mean . . . you're right about that, sir," Moffett said apologetically.

Marsden was in no doubt the stranger the two seaman had encountered was John Graham, and he could tell by the look on Cheetham's face that he was in no doubt either.

Cheetham looked straight at the seamen. "Can I ask that you keep this to yourselves, gentlemen?" he asked.

"News of the encounter travelled around my ship as soon as Moffett and his friend returned from shore," Tindall said.

"I am sure it did," Cheetham replied, "but I would ask they do not mention a word of it to anyone ashore."

"I can put your mind at rest there, my Lord," Tindall said. "No-one else is coming ashore. We only berthed here to deliver an urgent package on our way to Sydney Town, so we will be departing immediately."

The commandant breathed a sigh of relief—not only because no-one else would be coming ashore, but because he knew what the likely contents of that package were. He'd ordered an extra shipment of raw opium direct from the Orient, and had been eagerly awaiting its arrival. "Thank you, Captain," he said. "And where may I ask where did Northern Travails journey from last."

"From Manila and before that from Shanghai, my Lord," Tindall said.

"Ah," Cheetham smiled.

Tindall excused Moffett and himself, and the pair hurried off, leaving Cheetham and Marsden alone once more.

"What do you think, Captain?" Cheetham asked.

"It is obviously John Graham, sir."

"I cannot believe Graham survived."

"It does beggar belief."

"The men must not hear of this." Cheetham was adamant. "The convicts will rebel if they get one sniff of this."

"There is no reason they should hear anything."

"Good." Cheetham added, "However, I would like the tracker to start looking for Graham again."

"I have a feeling . . . the tracker has been looking for him . . . for some time," Marsden said hesitantly. He'd never before shared his suspicions with his superior.

"What do you mean?"

"Well, Barega often goes walkabout as you know. And when he does, he inevitably heads north along the coast. I suspect he's hunting Graham."

"Haven't you asked him?"

"I have, but Barega is a closed book. He discloses nothing."

Cheetham closed his eyes and rubbed them with the knuckles of both hands. He was feeling strung out, and he desperately needed to savour the feeling of opium flowing through his veins. Determined to wrap the meeting up, he forced himself to focus. "Very well," he said. "Order Barega to keep hunting, but ensure he understands he is *not* to mention this to anyone else besides you and Lieutenant Hogan. Understood?"

"Yes, my Lord," Marsden said. The captain couldn't escape the feeling the past was repeating itself. How he longed to hear the last of John Graham.

"Now," Cheetham said, "if you will excuse me I must attend to some urgent business." He was almost running by the time he reached the door.

Marsden noted the *pressing business* the commandant had referred to earlier had, in the space of fifteen minutes, become *urgent business*. Not for the first time, he wondered how on earth Cheetham managed to retain his title and remain commandant of Moreton Bay.

54

BAREGA STUDIED THE DISTINCTIVE PRINTS he instinctively knew had been left by John. Part boot, part toe, they stood out amongst the hundreds of footprints left by the Kabi clan members who had attended the annual seaside corroboree.

The prints told the tracker the large encampment had been vacated five days earlier at most. Although dated, the signs had been preserved in the dry earth thanks to the continuing spell of fine weather, which had resulted in a total lack of rain along the entire coastal strip. A quick scout around confirmed several hundred Kabi—there was no doubt in his mind they were Kabi—had occupied the site, and the most recent footprints signalled the various clans had headed off in a dozen different directions.

A further search confirmed John and perhaps a hundred clan members had headed directly inland, toward the heavily forested hills that lined the western horizon.

When Marsden had produced a map that showed the bay where the suspected sighting of John had occurred some two days earlier, Barega had identified it immediately. Three days hard running had brought him to the encampment two miles south of the bay. Now he had the choice of reporting his findings back to Marsden or continuing to follow the Irishman's tracks. He opted for the latter.

Barega's luck ran out after he'd run some ten or so miles inland. Localised thunderstorms had washed away his quarry's spoor, leaving no tracks to follow.

The tracker was very aware the Kabis' territory encompassed a large area—too large for one man to effectively cover. He decided he would have to return another day. Sooner or later, he knew, he would be lucky.

And so he headed back to Moreton Bay. It hadn't been a wasted trip, he told himself as he jogged south. After all, he had confirmed that as recently as five days ago the Irishman was still alive.

Helen was having difficulty keeping her good news to herself. She was trying her best to appear appreciative of the excellent roast dinner Missus Brown, the lady of the house, had lovingly prepared, but all she could think of was the contents of a letter she'd received from her father that afternoon. Her dining companions, who included her brother Matthew and Mister and Missus Brown, did their best to include her in the dinnertime conversation, but they could clearly see her mind was elsewhere.

Finally, Missus Brown said, "Oh, for goodness sake Helen, put us out of our misery and tell us what occupies you so."

"Thelma," William Brown cautioned, "if our Helen has something to tell us, I am sure she will do so in her own good time." Turning to Helen, Mister Brown added, "Isn't that so, young lady?"

"Yes, of course, Mister Brown," Helen said, embarrassed. Realising she'd been caught out, she admitted, "I do have some good news to share with you, but I did not want to be so rude as to mention it before we finished this fine meal."

"Tell us now, sis!" Matthew insisted.

"Matthew, shush!" Helen said.

"No, your brother is right, Helen," Missus Marsden said. "You must share your good news now."

"Very well," Helen said, conceding defeat. "If you will excuse me just one minute." She stood and left the room, returning a minute later holding the letter that was the cause of her excitement.

"Oh how deliciously mysterious," Missus Brown said, eying the folded letter. "Is it a proposal from that lovely young lieutenant?"

"It is not," Helen assured her as she took her seat at the table once more. Opening the letter, she said, "I received this from my father this afternoon, but I only read it a short time before joining you for dinner." She hastily added, "Otherwise I would have shared the news with you earlier."

"Go on, go on," Missus Brown urged her, barely able to contain her impatience.

Helen was about to start reading when she handed the letter to William Brown who sat opposite her. She said, "I feel it would be appropriate if you read the passage concerned, Mister Brown." Before he could respond, she leaned across the table and pointed to the passage she referred to. "From here to . . . here," she said.

"Very good," Mister Brown said. Donning a pair of reading glasses he carried in his shirt pocket, he began reading. "You will be pleased to know I redecorated your room—"

"No," Helen interjected. She pointed once more to the passage she wanted Mister Brown to read.

"Ah, yes." The man of the house began reading, this time from the correct place. "You will also be pleased to hear, my dear Helen, that today I learned the Governor has approved your request that the army finance construction of the schoolroom . . ." Mister Brown looked up, amazed. He resumed reading, "That the army finance construction of the schoolroom the Browns are planning for Brisbane Town."

"Oh, William!" Missus Brown gasped. "Isn't that wonderful?" Before she knew it, her husband planted a sloppy kiss on her cheek. "Not in front of our guests, William!" she said unconvincingly.

Helen and Matthew shared a smile.

"What else does Tom have to say?" Missus Brown asked, urging her husband to continue reading Marsden's letter.

Mister Brown said, "He says . . . I only put your request to Lord Cheetham two weeks ago and—"

"When was Tom's letter dated?" Missus Brown asked.

"He sent it one week ago," Helen said.

When Mister Brown saw he had everyone's attention, he resumed reading once more. "I only put your request to Lord Cheetham two weeks ago and did not expect that he would hear back from Sir Ralph so quickly. The good news does not end there, however."

Missus Brown gasped yet again.

Mister Brown continued reading. "The Governor appreciates that the presence of qualified teachers in Moreton Bay will greatly benefit children of both the settlers and the soldiers. Therefore, he has agreed to finance the construction of not one but two schoolrooms, and he has ordered Lord Cheetham to ensure that the army's carpenters have the rooms ready for the new school year." Mister Brown looked up. "Praise the Lord!" he shouted, handing the letter back to Helen.

Before Missus Brown could recover her surprise, her husband stood and prised her from her chair, and then danced her around the dining room to the encouragement of Helen and Matthew who had become caught up in the couple's joy.

When some normality returned to the room, the Browns resumed sitting and they discussed with Helen their plans for the new school year, which was now only three months away. Having already established private junior schools in Melbourne and in Hobart, Van Diemen's Land, as well as here in Sydney Town, Brisbane Town was to be the next stage in their plans to establish schools nationwide. They had intended to set Helen up as a sole charge teacher in Brisbane Town regardless of whether any support from the army was forthcoming.

Helen, who had now all but completed her teacher training, would be returning to Moreton Bay next month when the present school year ended—in plenty of time to take up her new position. Although she was still only twenty-two, the Browns were in no doubt she was ready for the responsibility that came with a sole charge teaching position.

The plan had been to build one schoolroom in Moreton Bay before the start of the new school year. News that the army was financing construction of not one but two schoolrooms opened up the possibility an assistant teacher could be appointed to help Helen.

Mister and Missus Brown were still deep in discussion when Helen and Matthew excused themselves and retired for the night to their bedrooms.

Matthew, who was now fourteen, would be returning to Moreton Bay with Helen next month, but only for the holidays. He would then return to Sydney Town to continue his schooling, and he would continue boarding with the Browns whom he'd come to think of as an uncle and aunt, or second parents even, just as Helen had. It was an arrangement that suited all parties for the Browns had never had children of their own. As for the siblings, they were enjoying the freedom that came with boarding away from home even if they did miss their father.

Now in the privacy of her room, Helen lay down on her bed and re-read her father's letter. She was interrupted by a knock on the door.

"Helen, it's me," Missus Marsden called. "May I come in?"

"Come in," Helen said.

Missus Marsden entered, closed the door behind her and, without waiting to be asked, sat down on a bedside chair. Smiling mischievously at Helen, she said, "I didn't wish to broach the subject in front of the men, but I had to ask . . . Is your imminent relocation to Moreton Bay good news for a certain lieutenant?"

Blushing, Helen knew her benefactor referred to Lieutenant Hogan whom the older woman had made no secret of the fact she considered a good match for her. Had the question been posed by anyone else, she'd have told them to mind their own business. Not Thelma Brown, though. She considered her more a friend and confidant than a benefactor or a landlady. The kindly woman had been an inspiration to her, encouraging her love of teaching and, more importantly, filling a gap that had been left by the passing of her mother. "Missus Brown, I—"

Missus Brown shushed her. "Call me Thelma, my dear," she said. "We know each other well enough now."

Helen continued, "Well, Thelma . . . I can say that Lieutenant Hogan is looking forward to my relocating to Moreton Bay."

"I am sure he is."

Ignoring the twinkle in the older woman's eye, Helen continued, "And in his latest letter he warned me to expect a marriage proposal when he next sees me."

"Oh that is grand." Missus Brown reined in her enthusiasm when she observed Helen didn't appear overly excited. "But?"

"*But* . . . I am not sure my father will approve," Helen confided. "Relations between him and the lieutenant are somewhat strained."

"Nonsense. You, young lady, are the apple of your father's eye, and not even the King of England would be considered good enough to call you his wife."

Helen giggled at the very thought. She suspected her benefactor may be right, but still she had her reservations—not about Hogan's suitability as a husband, for she'd already come round to the idea that he was suitable, but about her father accepting him as a son-in-law. That, she feared, may be a bridge too far.

55

J OHN PUSHED HIS WAY THROUGH dense rainforest, his progress not helped by the boar he carried across his shoulders. He'd speared the boar—a big adult male pig referred to locally as a *tusker*—a short time earlier at the bottom of a steep gully as luck would have it. Now, having expended quite some energy carrying it out of the gully, he was faced with a lengthy walk back to the encampment.

In the weeks since the Kabis' corroboree had ended and John's clan had quit their coastal encampment, they had ventured deeper into the rainforest than he'd ever been before. It had opened up a whole new world to him—a world of indescribable beauty.

Now, for example, as he emerged from the gully, he was confronted by a vista that took his breath away. Craggy, heavily forested hills—their peaks hidden by wispy cloud—bordered a wide valley, which resembled a veritable garden of Eden. A fast-flowing stream ran the length of the valley, its course interrupted by a large lake whose sparkling waters were disturbed only by the ripples left by a brace of native ducks, which had evidently made it their summer home.

The valley floor was carpeted year-round by lush, green grass, which provided excellent grazing for mobs of roos, although not a solitary roo was in sight at this point in time. Not surprising given it was around mid-day and the roos normally only come out to drink or graze beside the lake at dawn and dusk. Small stands of trees dotted the valley floor, and between them the ground cover included bushes laden with berries—raspberries in particular.

In addition, the birdsong was almost deafening. From within the surrounding rainforest, the calls of a dozen or more varieties of birds provided a heavenly chorus befitting the splendid surroundings.

John had to drop the carcass he carried and rest up half a dozen times before he reached the end of the valley. Fit though he was, the tusker was a heavy brute, and the heat and humidity conspired to sap his strength. Fortunately, there was no shortage of water to assuage his thirst, so he was able to drink as often as he liked.

The Irishman's thoughts turned to Mamba. She had promised a reward if he returned with a reasonable kill. The tusker he carried was, in his opinion, reasonable by any hunter's standards. He quickened his pace at the thought of the reward that awaited him.

As John headed back to the encampment, Mamba was beating cloaks and pelts she'd hung up on a line that stretched from her bivouac to a neighbour's bivouac.

She beat them with a paddle-shaped length of wood to remove the dust from them—a regular housekeeping chore through the summer months.

The neighbour on this occasion was her older sister Tirranna with whom she had enjoyed a happier relationship of late. Tirrana, who lived in an extended family that included eleven children, including four of her own, was helping Mamba. The sisters toiled side by side, taking turns to whack the cloaks and pelts, and doing their best to ignore the clouds of dust each blow caused.

Throughout the encampment, other women attended to their daily tasks while their children played. The menfolk were noticeably scarce. Most, like John, were away hunting. They would drift back in dribs and drabs over the next day or two.

"What is Moilow like now?" Tirrana suddenly asked.

"What do you mean?" Mamba asked, pretending she hadn't noticed the twinkle in her sister's eye.

"You know what I mean, little sister."

Both women had stopped toiling now.

Mamba smiled slyly. "He is even better than I remember," she confided.

Both women burst into fits of giggling.

Tirrana suddenly grew serious.

"What?" Mamba asked. Only now did she realise her sister had seen Turo approaching.

Tirrana quickly excused herself and retired to her bivouac. Like Mamba, she had no time for Turo.

The belligerent Turo was always on the lookout for an opportunity to accost Mamba. She and John were so close it wasn't often the young woman was alone, or so it seemed to Turo, and so, when the white wasn't around he wasn't slow to confront her. Her relationship with the man he considered an imposter continued to gnaw away at him. It also made him desire her all the more.

Mamba wasn't going to let Turo see she was frightened of him, so, rather than retreat to her bivouac, she remained right where she was, beating the pelts.

"It is good you do woman's work," Turo said by way of opening the conversation.

Only now did Mamba look directly at him.

The look on the young mother's face left Turo in no doubt his company wasn't welcome. Undeterred, and intent on getting straight to the point, he said, "We both know the white spirit is not Moilow." When Mamba didn't respond, he said, "He is an imposter."

"*We both know* you are consumed by jealousy, Turo," Mamba said, "and few others share your opinion of my husband." She resumed beating the pelt nearest Turo with an intensity that conveyed the anger she felt. A cloud of dust rose from it.

"Your husband!" Turo said, raising his voice. "He is no more your husband than I . . . than I . . ."

As Turo struggled manfully to find the right words, Mamba ceased working. She looked straight at Turo and said, "From the Dream World he knew you asked the elders for permission to make me your wife."

Turo was shocked to hear this from her. Such approaches to the clan's elders were always made in the strictest of confidence, so Mamba should not be aware he had made any such request.

As if reading Turo's mind, Mamba added, "From the other side, my husband heard what you asked."

"That is not possible!" Turo blustered.

Undeterred, Mamba added, "So Moilow returned to spare me such a fate."

Turo was so angered by this he took a step toward Mamba. The young woman thought he was about to strike her, but she held her ground and showed no fear.

Neither knew that John had observed their exchange. He'd just arrived back at the encampment as Turo had approached Mamba and her sister. Anticipating trouble, he dropped the carcass he'd been carrying and hurried toward the pair. He was still some distance from them, so he couldn't hear what they were discussing. However, the body language of each told him they were arguing.

Turo had come close to striking Mamba. He'd struck many women—his own five wives included—many times for far lesser *offences*. On this occasion, something made him hold off. "We will discuss this again," he promised, turning and striding away. Only then did he notice John approaching. The two adversaries glared at each other as they passed by within striking distance of each other.

John walked straight up to Mamba. "Did he touch you?" he asked.

Mamba shook her head. "No, Moilow."

"What did he want?"

"He . . . He was only asking me about my sister," Mamba lied. She wanted to defuse the situation, and she wanted to avoid violence.

John didn't believe her. He pulled away and turned to go after Turo, but Mamba reached out and restrained him.

"No, Moilow!" she said. "Leave it."

"But—"

"It was nothing, my husband." Smiling, she changed tack and said, "It is a shame you came back empty-handed from your hunting."

His anger suddenly forgotten, John said, "Wait here." He hurried away to retrieve the carcass he'd left behind, returning moments later with his kill across his shoulders and a smile on his face. "You mentioned a reward," he said, dropping the carcass at Mamba's feet.

Mamba smiled knowingly and led him into their bivouac.

Later that day, John and Mamba sat facing each other, naked, on a moss-covered rock near the bottom of a waterfall. From high above, a narrow plume of water cascaded down the red-coloured rock face, the force of the water sending up clouds of fine spray that settled on the pair, keeping them cool. The spray filtered the sunlight, creating a perfect rainbow effect.

Since Mamba had discovered *the sanctuary,* as they called it, whilst out collecting berries ten days earlier, they'd visited it as often as they could. So far, they'd had the place to themselves, and they hoped it would stay that way. They hadn't even brought the boys here, such was their desire to keep it to themselves.

Usually, their visits culminated in lovemaking. This time, however, having made love not so long ago, they were content to talk. Today, theirs was a meaningful discussion, touching on subjects they'd not broached before. They had to speak up to make themselves heard above the sound of the falls.

"That day the men caught me," John asked in English, "why didn't they kill me?"

Mamba reached out and took both his hands in hers. Smiling, she said, "Because . . . you are Moilow."

John shook his head, indicating that he disagreed.

"You *are* Moilow . . . my husband," a patient Mamba insisted. Reverting to her native tongue, she said, "You remember when you were killed by our Noonuccal enemies . . ."

"Killed?" John asked, sticking to English.

"Yes." Only now did Mamba show signs of impatience. "Noonuccal warriors killed you when you were away hunting with Turo and the others."

This was the first that John had heard exactly how Mamba's husband had died. She and others had avoided mentioning the specifics until now, believing that to do so would invite bad luck. Gabirri had explained that much to him.

John squeezed both Mamba's hands and looked into her eyes. Switching to Kabi, he said, "Mamba . . . I am not who you think I am. I am white—"

"Moilow," Mamba sighed. "We are all white underneath. When we are burned over a fire, our flesh turns white . . . and our bones are white." Ignoring John's bemused expression, she continued, "White spirits are our ancestors returned to us." She pulled one hand free and gently squeezed the skin on John's forearm. Reverting to English, she said, "You Moilow . . . my husband . . . returned to me."

John considered arguing the point, but he realised that was a waste of time.

She really believes I am Moilow.

Smiling, he leaned forward and kissed her. Before he knew it, Mamba was sitting on his lap, her slender legs wrapped around his waist.

Giggling, she wriggled her hips seductively until John's aroused member slipped inside her. They remained like that for a long time, losing themselves in each other, enjoying the moment and oblivious to the fine clouds of spray that drifted over them from the nearby waterfall.

The shadows were lengthening when John and Mamba returned to the encampment. Their arrival coincided with the return of Murrowdooling and Carravanty who, it appeared, had been playing in the surrounding bush.

"Hello boys, what have you been up t—" John stopped when he noticed Murrowdooling's face was cut and bruised. "Who did this to you?" he asked, tilting the boy's face up to his.

"I got it playing buroinjin," Murrowdooling mumbled.

"Tell me the truth, boy," John said.

"I told you," a defiant Murrowdooling said, pulling himself free of John's grip and running off.

"You stay right here!" John ordered.

The boy ignored him, and disappeared into the bush.

John and Mamba looked at each other. They sensed something was wrong. Murrowdooling had been acting surly and withdrawn of late, and this wasn't the first time he'd turned up cut and bruised.

Mamba turned to Carravanty. "What happened to your brother?" she asked.

"He was playing—"

"And do not tell me he was playing buroinjin, Carravanty!" Mamba cautioned.

A guilty Carravanty mumbled, "Orad beat him."

Mamba knew at once whom her younger son referred to. Orad was one of the youths who played buroinjin. He was also Turo's oldest son, and, like his father, he had a reputation for being a bully.

"Who is Orad?" John asked.

Before Carravanty could answer, Mamba said, "He is one of the older boys who Murrowdooling plays buroinjin with." She withheld from John the fact that the youth was Turo's son.

"He beats him a lot," Carravanty volunteered without waiting to be asked.

John and Mamba looked at each other. A lot made sense to them now. Murrowdooling had been acting withdrawn for some time, and the frequent cuts and bruises he suffered went beyond the norm even for the most active of boys.

The Irishman came to a decision. He looked down at Carravanty. "Go find your brother," he said. "Tell him I want to see him . . . now."

Carravanty scampered away to do as asked. As he ran off, John yelled, "And tell him he is *not* in trouble."

John and Mamba resumed walking toward their bivouac. As they walked, Mamba asked, "What do you have in mind, Moilow?"

"You will see," John grinned.

56

EARLY NEXT MORNING, IN A bush clearing some distance from the encampment, John gave Murrowdooling his first bareknuckle boxing lesson. Although not a trained pugilist, the Irishman had been involved in enough street fights—more than enough if truth be known—to know how to defend himself, and he considered it was time Murrowdooling learnt.

John hadn't told Mamba what he was up to for he knew she wouldn't approve. However, he'd confided in Carravanty, and had given him permission to sit in on the lessons. He'd even promised the younger boy he would teach him to box in the not-too-distant future.

En route to the bush clearing, Carravanty had pointed out Orad to John. Turo's oldest son was among a group of youths heading out to hunt. A tall, strong looking boy, he was older than Murrowdooling by some years.

John spent the first short while teaching Murrowdooling the fighter's stance. "Keep your guard up!" he ordered as the boy tried to emulate his instructor.

Murrowdooling raised his right hand higher so that it was close to his jaw, ready to fend off any punches John may throw his way. The results of the beating he'd received yesterday were even more obvious this morning. His bruises had turned an ugly purple, and the cuts were red and raw. Both his eyes were puffy—one so much so he couldn't see out of it.

"Now throw your left straight . . . like this," John said, throwing left jabs in the boy's direction.

Murrowdooling did as asked, and his instructor was impressed by the boy's speed and natural ability.

John turned and winked at Carravanty who, he noticed, was watching spellbound. The Irishman turned back too late to stop a crisp left jab landing flush on his nose. "Ouch!" he grunted.

Both boys laughed.

As Murrowdooling's first boxing lesson continued, Barega was trekking inland from the coast in search of the Irishman's spoor. The sighting of John's tracks at the Kabis' last coastal encampment had been the last indication the tracker had that his quarry was still alive.

None knew better than Barega how tenuous life was in the Australian wilderness, but he'd been following the elusive Irishman long enough to know how hardy and tenacious he was—and how lucky he was, too. He'd lost count of the number of times John had cheated death.

The tracker's mission to find John had received a recent boost when Marsden had ordered him to resume his search for the escaped convict. Not that he'd ever stopped searching for him, but now that it was official he was almost fulltime on the case. His latest meanderings had brought him to within ten miles of the Irishman's present location. He sensed he was close, but he needed a lucky break. A single footprint, or boot print, would be sufficient.

Barega continued inland. The rainforest was dense now, and by his standards progress was slow. Still he kept walking and searching for signs.

Captain Marsden and Lieutenant Hogan tried their best to hide their excitement from each other as they awaited the arrival of the schooner that was slowly closing with the Moreton Bay penal settlement's wharf.

The officers, who sat astride their horses, were resplendent in their red tunics and ceremonial uniforms. Behind them, two horse-drawn carts waited, one manned by Corporal Davies and the other by Private Askew. The officers and non-commissioned soldiers alike were already feeling the heat even though it was still only mid-morning. To add to their woes, the flies were out in force, and men and horses twitched and swatted at the pests in their futile attempts to keep them at bay.

Although still some distance away, Marsden and Hogan could just make out the familiar figures of Helen and Matthew by the schooner's starboard rail. The siblings were flanked by their benefactors, William and Thelma Brown. All four had seen the two officers awaiting them, and were now waving enthusiastically. The officers returned their waves.

For the captain, this would be the first time he had seen his children in two months. That's how long it had been since he'd last visited Sydney Town. Today was special for him because it not only marked the arrival of his children for Christmas, which was fast approaching, but it marked the start of Helen's new life as sole charge teacher at Brisbane Town's soon-to-be-opened school.

As for the lieutenant, this would be the first time he'd seen his beloved Helen in five months for that's how long it had been since he'd been able to arrange leave. He suspected his superior had gone out of his way to delay authorisation of his most recent leave applications, but he couldn't be sure.

Hogan had been putting off asking an important question of Marsden. Now that the captain's daughter was almost here, he couldn't put it off any longer. Turning to his superior, he said, "Ah . . . Captain, I have something to ask of you."

"Yes, Lieutenant?" Marsden responded. He had a feeling he knew what was coming, and he wasn't sure his subordinate would like his answer.

"I . . . ah . . . I love your daughter, sir, and I would like your permission to ask her for her hand in marriage," Hogan said.

"I will think on that and let you know my answer, Lieutenant Hogan," Marsden said without a moment's hesitation.

Hogan had been hoping for something a little more positive, but he hid his disappointment. "Yes, sir," he said.

"Papa!"

Marsden looked up and saw Matthew was now jumping up and down on the schooner's deck. "Hello, Matthew and Helen!" he shouted. The vessel was now so close he could see his children, and the Browns, clearly. "And hello William and Thelma!" He smiled at the Browns, and they returned his greeting.

A soldier's face at one of the portholes below deck reminded Marsden that the schooner was bringing yet another shipment of convicts to the bay. His clerk had advised him earlier there would be forty-four convicts on board. The captain had hesitated to allow his children to travel aboard a convict ship, but disrupted shipping schedules over the holiday period meant they would have had to wait ten days for the next ship.

Switching his gaze to Helen, Marsden noticed she only had eyes for Hogan. He scowled at his subordinate who immediately looked away.

It wasn't long before the paying passengers were filing down the gangplank. The two officers dismounted and tethered their horses before walking onto the wharf.

Helen and Matthew were among the first to disembark. They were met at the foot of the gangplank by Marsden who embraced each.

As soon as he could extricate himself from his children's embrace, he greeted the Browns. "William and Thelma, how good it is to see you again," he said.

"And you, too, old boy," William Brown said, pumping his opposite's hand.

"Hello, darling Tom." Missus Brown said, effusively planting a kiss on Marsden's cheek.

Behind them, Marsden was vaguely aware that Hogan was greeting Helen, but he was too preoccupied with the Browns to take much notice. If he had been able to turn around, he'd have seen that Helen allowed Hogan to give her a restrained peck on the cheek.

When the greetings were over, Marsden and Hogan led the new arrivals to the waiting carts while sailors hurried to collect their bags from below deck. The captain explained to the Browns that one of the carts would transport them and their luggage to their hotel in the township while the other cart would transport his children up to the cottage.

It was left that they would all meet up that evening for dinner in the officers' mess at the penal settlement.

Before they went their separate ways, Hogan managed to have a private word with Helen. "So, you are really here to stay this time, Miss Marsden?" he asked. It was more a statement than a question.

"Yes I am, Lieutenant Hogan," Helen smiled.

"And not before time, if I may so."

"Why thank you, Lieutenant." After a moment's hesitation, Helen added, "I saw you having a word with Papa . . ."

"Ah . . . yes," Hogan admitted. "I forewarned him that I plan to ask for your hand in marriage, and I asked for his blessing."

"Oh . . . and did he give it?"

"He said he would think on it," Hogan answered glumly.

Helen touched his arm. "I did warn you, didn't I?" she asked. When Hogan nodded, she added, "Don't worry, I will have a word with him later."

The lieutenant was encouraged by Helen's positivity. As for Helen, she was very aware it wasn't that long ago she wasn't at all certain whether she wanted to marry Hogan. Exactly what it was that had brought about her a change of heart, she wasn't sure. Perhaps it was his persistence, she told herself. If that really was the reason, she hoped she was doing the right thing.

While Marsden was reacquainting himself with his children, John was giving Murrowdooling another boxing lesson under the watchful eye of the ever-present Carravanty. The student was proving a quick learner, and though the Irishman had never taught anyone to box before, he considered Mamba's oldest son a natural in every sense of the word. "Stick and move," he said in English, "stick and move."

Murrowdooling lowered his fists and stopped moving around. "What you mean . . . stick and move, Moilow?" he asked, mystified.

"I mean . . . keep doing what you're doing," John said, shuffling his feet and flicking out left jabs toward the boy. "Flick out your jab . . . like this." He threw another jab Murrowdooling's way. "And shuffle your feet . . . like this." He shuffled backwards and forwards and side to side."

"Why shuff . . ."

"Shuffle," John said, helping the boy out.

"Why shuffle my feet . . . like this?" Moilow parodied his instructor's foot movements in exaggerated fashion, causing Carravanty to burst out laughing.

"Not like that!" John chuckled. He realised the lad was trying to wind him up. "Like this." He shuffled some more and urged Murrowdooling to do the same.

The boy did as he was asked, and he did it perfectly.

John had long considered Aborigines well suited to the pugilistic arts. Quick and lithe, with hard heads, they were, in his opinion, born to box. He considered Murrowdooling to be living proof of that. In the space of a few lessons, the boy was holding his own in their sparring sessions, and, on occasion, was landing the odd surprise blow. John had the bruises to prove it.

Marsden and his children arrived at the cottage in time for a home-cooked lunch prepared by the family's faithful maid Orana. After lunch, the Marsdens walked to Missus Marsden's nearby gravesite to pay their respects.

Observing his children as they laid flowers at the foot of the headstone, Marsden said, "Your mother would be very proud of you two, you know that, don't you?"

"Thank you, papa," Helen said, brushing a tear from her eye.

"Yeah, I know, pop," Matthew grinned.

"*Yes*, I know, *father*," Marsden corrected the boy. Matthew had picked up some slang since he'd last seen him, and he'd recently taken to addressing him as *pop* in his letters, and, as always, Marsden wasn't slow to let him know he disapproved.

"Yes, I know, father," Matthew mumbled.

Marsden ruffled the boy's hair affectionately then draped a loving arm around both his children, and together they bowed their heads and recited the Lord's Prayer, all the while looking down at the headstone.

A short time later, as they turned to walk back to the cottage, Helen placed a restraining hand on her father's arm. "Papa, may we talk for a moment."

"Certainly, my dear."

"In private," Helen said, looking pointedly at her brother.

"It's alright," Matthew said, walking off. "I know when I'm not wanted."

"If only that were true!" Helen said, laughing as the boy headed toward the cottage. Alone now, she and her father wandered arm in arm in the opposite direction. They walked in silence for some time, admiring the hilltop view of Moreton Bay and its surrounds.

Finally, Marsden said, "I assume this has something to do with Lieutenant Hogan."

A surprised Helen said, "Yes, papa. How did you know?"

"Fathers know these things," Marsden assured her.

Helen was momentarily speechless. She had a speech prepared, but her father's comment required a change of tack. "Um . . . then you know Desmond intends to ask you for my hand in marriage," she ventured.

"Yes, my dear. The good lieutenant informed me of that just this morning." He added, "I would have appreciated a little more notice."

Father and daughter stopped walking and faced each other.

"Papa, he only recently informed *me* of his intention." Helen knew she sounded defensive. She also knew her father did not approve of Hogan as a future son-in-law. He was about to reconfirm that.

"Helen, you know I want more for you than the life of a soldier's wife," Marsden said.

"Mama did not object to being a soldier's wife," Helen responded. She met her father's level gaze. "There is more to it than that, isn't there, father?" she asked.

Marsden knew when his daughter used *father* instead of *papa* he wasn't in her good books. "We both know . . . I think you can do better than the lieutenant," he said at length. When Helen didn't respond, he asked, "What's more important is . . . what do *you* think, my dear?"

"Papa, Desmond loves me—"

"He may love you, at least he may say he does, but do you love him?"

Helen hesitated. After a long pause, she said, "He is a good man . . . and I do admire him so. She hurried on before her father could interrupt again. "And I am sure I will grow to love him."

They resumed walking, slowly retracing their steps to the cottage.

"At least you are honest," he said.

Helen had more to say, but she could see her father was deep in thought, so she remained quiet.

Finally, Marsden stopped walking and took both Helen's hands in his. "Well, your mother did say Lieutenant Hogan was the one for you," he smiled.

"So you approve?" a hopeful Helen asked.

"I approve."

"Oh thank you, papa!" Helen threw her arms around him and kissed his cheek.

When Marsden was finally able to come up for air, he announced, "I will convey my blessing to the good lieutenant at dinner this evening." He quickly added, "But rest assured I will also convey to him that if he does not treat you well he will receive my wrath."

"Yes, papa," Helen said dutifully.

In another bush clearing not far from yet another temporary encampment, John gave Murrowdooling another boxing lesson. This time, Carravanty wasn't the only spectator. Gabirri and Mirritji had stumbled across the trio whilst returning from a hunt, and, having never witnessed boxing before, they stopped to watch.

Murrowdooling had improved out of sight, and John had to remain on top of his game to avoid being hurt. The boy was firing out left jabs like a professional streetfighter, and he was moving like one, too. However, his best attribute, in John's opinion, was his right hand. Like most of the top boxers, he threw his right sparingly, but when he did, there was some weight behind it. Not enough weight to drop John—not yet at least—but enough to make him think twice about dropping his guard.

"Body, head," John said. "Body, head."

Murrowdooling alternately targeted John's head and body, switching effortlessly from one to the other.

"Good!" John said, grunting as a hard body blow landed.

Looking on, Gabirri and Mirritji couldn't make head nor tail about what they were witnessing.

"Moilow teaches his son to fight like a kangaroo," Gabirri observed.

"Let us hope Murrowdooling can hop away like a kangaroo if his enemy decides to fight back," Mirritji chuckled.

The spectators didn't realise the sparring they witnessed wasn't boxing in its purest form. It was Irish-style boxing that John had learned in the bars and back alleys of his hometown, and it included more than a few dirty tactics. The Irishman was teaching his charge some of those tactics now. "Use your elbows!" he ordered.

Murrowdooling threw a straight right hand, but at the last second he bent his arm so that his elbow connected with John's face—at least it would have had the Irishman not been expecting it and hadn't blocked the blow with his left hand. Unfortunately for him, Murrowdooling followed up with a kidney punch that caused him to grimace and back up.

"Time to rest!" John announced before the boy could do any more damage. That last blow had stung, and he needed to buy some time to regain his breath. Breathing hard, he glanced at Gabirri and Mirritji. Their bemused expressions told him they didn't have a clue what was going on.

"What is this?" Gabirri asked, giving a somewhat hilarious imitation of a boxer shadow boxing.

Murrowdooling and Carravanty burst out laughing at Gabirri's antics.

"It is called boxing," John explained.

"No matter what it is called, my friend," Gabirri responded. "It looks like the mating dance of an emu on heat." With that, he and Mirritji wandered off, chuckling at what they'd just witnessed.

"Don't mind them," John said to Murrowdooling.

"We box more?" the boy asked hopefully. He was keen to continue.

"Can I box?" Carravanty piped up.

"Certainly, young fellow," John grinned. He motioned to Murrowdooling to shadow box while he gave Carravanty a lesson.

The Irishman quickly discovered the younger brother was also a natural. As he proceeded to teach Carravanty to spar, he kept a fatherly eye on Murrowdooling who was now shadow boxing on the far side of the clearing. The boy looked like he'd been boxing for years, and John almost pitied the next bully who picked on him.

Murrowdooling was unaware his instructor was observing him as he boxed an imaginary opponent. So, he didn't notice him smile when he threw a left-right combination, and then followed up with a well-aimed kick to his imaginary opponent's unprotected groin—another tactic John had taught him—before following up with a kidney punch.

Not seven miles from where John and the boys were training, Barega was inspecting moss-covered rocks at the foot of a waterfall whose spray created a beautiful rainbow in the late afternoon sun. It was the same private place that John and Mamba had frequented before the clan quit their previous encampment a few days earlier.

Close to the waterfall, where the spray was the heaviest, any tracks that may have been left in the moss had long since been washed away. However, on several moss-covered rocks further away, the tracker found what he was looking for: the Irishman's distinctive boot prints.

Barega followed the spoor back to the Kabis' deserted encampment. There, he found still more boot prints among the myriad of bare footprints, confirming beyond doubt that John was still living with the Kabi.

The tracker sniffed the air. Although there was scarcely a cloud in the sky, he knew it would rain soon. He could smell it. So, without further delay, he set off at a fast trot, following the tracks in the hope they would lead him to the Irishman before rain washed them away, and, ideally, before night set in.

57

BAREGA HADN'T VENTURED MORE THAN a mile when the first drops of rain fell. Since he'd sensed rain was coming, storm clouds had quickly rolled in, hiding the sun and turning day into something resembling night, it was so dark. He was having trouble seeing the spoor he followed even before the rain began pelting down.

The tracker wasn't helped, either, by the rainforest, which was now so dense he'd been reduced to walking pace. Added to that, the raindrops had devolved into steady rain.

Nevertheless, he could still see the tracks—just—and he followed them doggedly. Fortunately, the overhead canopy of trees kept the worst of the rain at bay.

Barega's efforts came to nought when the steady rain gave way to a torrential downpour; the rain fell in such volume it battered its way through the forest canopy and washed away all tracks on the forest floor below.

Barega pressed on, but night fell quickly, forcing him to start looking for a dry place to overnight. In the morning, he would resume his search for John, but he wasn't hopeful. Without tracks to follow, finding anyone in this vast territory was a real longshot. If there was one consolation, he told himself, he was looking in the right corner of that vast territory.

The tracker soon found a small cave in the side of a hill, and, after eating half a dozen big, juicy witchetty grubs he'd found earlier, he quickly made himself comfortable inside it. As he did most nights, he went to sleep fondling the silver crucifix that rested on his chest.

As Barega slept, his master hosted an informal dinner in the officers' mess at the Moreton Bay penal settlement. Captain Marsden had opted for the officer's mess ahead of the nearby township's only eatery because the former offered finer dining and more salubrious surroundings. The civilian eating house was in the township's only hotel, an establishment which left much to be desired—and not just because half its rooms at any one time were let to the town's growing number of prostitutes. It was also poorly managed, and the eatery's food and service were below par.

The officers' mess at Moreton Bay was a far cry from the officers' mess at Sydney Town. Smaller and more reminiscent of a church hall than a classy restaurant, it nevertheless offered reasonable standards of food and service for the officers and wives. And so, it had been an easy decision for Marsden when it came to choosing a venue for tonight's celebratory dinner.

As was the case at Sydney Town, and, indeed, in every British Army officers' mess throughout the Empire, official dress was compulsory for the officers, and so Marsden and Hogan, and all their brother officers, were dressed in their finest—red tunics, shiny medals, polished boots and all.

The women, too, wore their most fashionable garments, and, as usual, Helen was the most beautiful woman in the room, and, indeed, in Moreton Bay.

Marsden was hosting his children, their benefactors the Browns and Lieutenant Hogan. Theirs was one of forty tables of which perhaps half were occupied— primarily by groups of officers and, in a few cases, by officers and their wives. Married couples had the option of dining in their own quarters, and many took advantage of that. It was an unwritten rule that young children were not permitted to dine in the mess.

Tonight, Marsden was celebrating the return of Helen and Matthew, the promotion of his daughter to sole-charge teacher at Brisbane Town's new school, and the company of his dear friends the Browns. And, thanks to his recent change of heart, he was celebrating, or acknowledging at least, the engagement of his daughter to Hogan. Before sitting down, he had privately informed the lieutenant that he and Helen had his blessing to marry after all.

As an army waiter cleared the first course dishes from the table, Marsden rose and clinked a teaspoon against his empty wine glass, indicating to his fellow diners that he wished to speak. When he saw he had their attention, he said, "I will keep this short."

"That is good to hear, father," a cheeky Matthew said.

"Thank you, son," Marsden said, trying his best to appear unamused, but failing miserably when a smile touched the corner of his mouth. "This is a special occasion for a number of reasons, not the least being it marks the first time we Marsdens"— he glanced at his children—"have all been together here at Moreton Bay for a long time."

Helen and Matthew smiled lovingly at their father.

"Of course," the captain continued, "our little family has been made smaller by the loss of my dear wife, and so in many ways this reunion is bitter-sweet."

"Hear, hear," William Brown agreed. He added, "We all miss sweet Vera."

Thelma Brown nodded, biting her lip to stop herself from shedding a tear.

Marsden quickly filled his empty wine glass then said, "We are also celebrating Helen's promotion to the position of sole charge teacher at Brisbane Town's first junior school."

"And well deserved her promotion is, too," Missus Brown said. Her husband nodded in agreement.

Helen smiled at her benefactors who sat opposite her, and then glanced at Hogan who sat next to her. The lieutenant winked at her, letting her know he was proud of her.

Marsden raised his wine glass. "A toast to Helen!" he said.

"To Helen!" the adults said, raising their wine glasses in unison.

"To *Lady* Helen!" Matthew said, raising his glass of fruit juice and emphasising the title he'd spontaneously bestowed upon his sister.

"To *Lady* Helen!" the others said, laughing, as they toasted the young beauty.

Helen blushed. "Stop it, please," she protested half-heartedly. "I am no lady."

This only served to encourage more humorous remarks from Helen's fellow diners—in particular from Matthew who was on form tonight.

When the chatter died, Marsden continued, "A toast also to my dearest friends, William and Thelma Brown."

"Hear, hear," Helen and Hogan said.

"The manner in which you have opened your home, and your hearts, to Helen and Matthew puts me in your eternal debt," Marsden said.

"That has been no hardship, I can assure you, old chap," Mister Brown insisted. His wife echoed her husband's sentiments.

"Nevertheless," Marsden said, "your kindness has been noted . . . as has the way you have fostered Helen's talent as a teacher."

"If I may," Missus Brown interjected, indicating she wished to speak. "Helen has proven to be an excellent teacher," she said, "and her promotion is well deserved."

Helen basked in the accolades her benefactor and mentor bestowed upon her.

Missus Brown continued, "I can assure you teaching comes easy to her, and she would succeed in her chosen profession with or without our help." She smiled at Helen and nodded to Marsden, indicating she'd had her say.

"Thank you, my dear Thelma," Marsden said. Turning Helen and Hogan, he said, "And last, but not least, I have a special announcement."

Only Matthew appeared not to know what was coming, but the Browns feigned excitement as they awaited the captain's announcement.

"It is with pleasure I announce the engagement and forthcoming nuptials of Helen and Lieutenant Hogan," Marsden said. He watched as the Browns and Matthew congratulated the couple and plied them with questions.

Helen caught her father's eye and smiled a big *thank you* his way. He returned her smile. At the same time he told himself the deed was done. His beautiful daughter's future wellbeing would soon be in the hands of another man. It felt strange, and he wasn't sure he'd ever get used to that.

Missus Brown cornered the young couple. "When is the big day?" she asked.

Hogan said "As soon as we can arrange—"

"The wedding date has yet to be discussed," Helen said, jumping in before her new fiancé could complete his sentence.

Hogan looked sideways at Helen, but she didn't appear to notice as she was now fielding more questions from the Browns.

Murrowdooling walked alone beside a small lake. The boy was a study in concentration as he observed the lake's still waters, looking for the tell-tale bubbles that more often than not signalled the presence of a freshwater eel. In his right hand he carried a net John had attached to the end of a long branch for just this purpose.

The net, made from emu gut, had been cut from an obliging fisherman's net.

From where Murrowdooling was, he could just make out the clan's latest encampment at the far end of the lake some half a mile distant. The clan had relocated there from its last encampment in the rainforest a week earlier.

The boy was so engrossed in his search for eels, he wasn't aware he was being stalked. A small group of the clan's youths had spotted him a short while earlier, and they were using the cover of ant hills and gum trees to sneak up on him. Their ringleader was the bully Orad, Turo's oldest son.

Murrowdooling hadn't had a confrontation with Orad since John had begun teaching him to box. That wasn't on account of any kindness or consideration on the aggressive youth's part. It was simply that their paths hadn't crossed—until now.

The first Murrowdooling became aware that he had company was when Orad rushed up behind him and pushed him into the lake. He surfaced, coughing and spluttering, to see five youths looking down at him and laughing. The first face he saw was Orad's.

"What do we have here?" Orad asked. "Is it the elusive freshwater eel?"

The other youths laughed.

"Perhaps it is the rare platypus," another youth said.

More laughter.

Still spluttering, Murrowdooling pulled himself from the water. He went to retrieve the net he'd dropped, but Orad beat him to it.

Studying the net and the branch it was attached to, the big youth observed, "This must be a special net to catch the rare platypus." As his friends egged him on, he snapped the branch in half and threw both ends as far as he could out into the lake.

Speaking for the first time, Murrowdooling calmly said "You had better fetch that for me, Orad." He had to look up at his nemesis who towered over him.

There was a moment's silence then the other youths roared with laughter.

"The spindly spider wants you to swim out and fetch his net, Orad!" the youngest of the youths exclaimed.

Orad wasn't amused. He rounded on Murrowdooling and threw a wild punch.

The young boy anticipated the punch—John had taught him to anticipate—and he easily evaded it. "Is that the best you can do, Orad?" he asked tauntingly. His instructor had taught him that, too. "Make your opponent as mad as hell," John had said, "then he will be blind with rage and easy to pick off." His taunt had the desired effect, and Orad charged him blindly, flailing at him as he came.

Murrowdooling expertly slipped the first punch, parried the second and then, before the third punch could be thrown, delivered a punch of his own to his opponent's kidney. Staggered by the blow, Orad fell to one knee, holding his side and grimacing in pain.

The other youths were so stunned, they could only stand and watch.

Before Orad could recover, Murrowdooling put all his weight behind his right elbow and slammed it into the side of his opponent's head. The blow flattened the youth, sending him crashing face-first to the ground.

Murrowdooling thought the fight was over because Orad showed no signs of standing up any time soon. That was his first mistake. His second mistake was moving too close to his opponent to see if he had any fight left in him.

Orad was tough if nothing else. Shaken though he was, he recovered quickly from the latest blow he'd received. He grabbed Murrowdooling's leg as soon as the boy approached. One violent twist of the leg saw Murrowdooling upended. Orad was onto him in a flash, raining kicks and punches down on him—all to the cheers of his mates.

As the blows rained down, John's words kept coming to the boy. "Stay calm and protect yourself at all times," John always said.

58

CURLED UP IN THE FOETAL position, Murrowdooling cradled his head in his hands as the assault continued. Consequently, he took most of the blows on his hands, arms and shoulders. All the while, he looked for an opening.

The opening came when Orad began to tire. As soon as the bully paused to catch his breath, Murrowdooling sprang to his feet and snapped out a series of stiff left jabs. Again his instructor's words came to him. "Body, head, body, head," John always said. And so, the boy switched his attack, alternating between Orad's head and body.

It wasn't long before the battered youth's face was a bloody mask. The two facial bruises Murrowdooling had received were nothing by comparison.

Orad's mates looked on in disbelief as their ringleader got what was coming to him.

Murrowdooling was now gasping for breath. Fighting for real, he'd discovered, was a lot harder than friendly sparring—even if John had worked him hard during their sessions. He sensed he needed to finish Orad soon before the bully got his second wind.

Another stiff jab to Orad's face caused the big youth to take a step backwards. This left him open to a kick in the testicles, which Murrowdooling promptly delivered with all the force he could muster. The kick resulted in a grunt of agony from Orad who doubled over in pain. As the bully's head came down, Murrowdooling lifted his knee hard into Orad's face, knocking him out.

The triumphant boy couldn't relax. He spun around, half expecting Orad's mates to attack. One look at their faces told him they would present no threat to him today, so shocked were they by what they'd witnessed. Even so, Murrowdooling wanted to ensure he retained the advantage. He eyed each of them then drew himself up to his full height and asked, "Who is next?"

No-one took up the challenge.

Relieved, Murrowdooling calmly turned his back on the youths and set off for the encampment. He suddenly stopped and turned around. Pointing at Orad, who was only now starting to come round, he said, "Tell him I want my net back in one piece, or the same thing will happen to him again."

Two of the youths nodded, indicating they would do as asked, but Murrowdooling didn't notice because he was already walking away from them. As he did, he walked with a straight back and his chin held high. He was fair bursting with pride.

As Murrowdooling walked back into the encampment a short while later, he came across John who was helping Mootemu skin a wallaby the Irishman had speared earlier that day. John acknowledged the boy with a nod then did a double-take when he noticed the two fresh bruises on his face. Excusing himself, he hurried over to Murrowdooling. "You alright?" he asked.

Murrowdooling nodded, unable to hide his proud grin.

The boy's grin told John everything he needed to know. Winking at Murrowdooling, he said, "We'll talk later." He hurried to re-join Mootemu while the boy walked off to share his latest news with friends.

That night, by the embers of their cooking fire, John and Mamba sat talking with their two boys. They had much to talk about for Murrowdooling had described—several times and in some detail—his earlier encounter with Orad.

This was Murrowdooling's night, and John was content to let him have his moment of glory. As the boy related yet again how he'd delivered the coup de grâce to the unfortunate bully, the Irishman made a mental note to teach him the importance of humility. *But that can wait,* he thought. *Let him enjoy the moment.*

The only dampener on the night from Murrowdooling's viewpoint was his brother didn't believe he'd defeated Orad. Carravanty insisted the bully was too old and too big for Murrowdooling.

That all changed when, out of the darkness, none other than Orad approached. The youth, whose face was so bruised he was almost unrecognisable, was carrying something. As he neared, it became evident the object he carried was Murrowdooling's net, which he'd evidently retrieved from the lake. "This is for you," Orad mumbled through swollen, cut lips as he handed the net to his conqueror.

John noticed the big youth kept his eyes averted. Or one of them at least. The other one was swollen shut.

A grim-faced Murrowdooling accepted the net without a word. He was delighted to see it had been repaired, but he took care to maintain his grim expression.

Orad walked away without another word. Gone was his usual swagger.

John nudged Murrowdooling. "You should say something to him," he whispered.

Murrowdooling evidently agreed. He looked at the retreating youth and opened his mouth to call out to him. John was expecting him to say a simple thank you. Murrowdooling surprised him by shouting, "I will be happy to show you how to fight when you are fit enough, Orad!"

Carravanty burst out laughing, while Orad gave no sign that he'd heard the taunt and kept walking.

John scowled at Murrowdooling. "That wasn't what I had in mind," he muttered.

Murrowdooling flashed a cheeky grin.

John made another mental note—to teach the boy the importance of humility sooner rather than later.

Mamba had remained silent throughout all of this. She was happy that her oldest son had taken an important step on his journey toward manhood, but she worried that the recipient of today's beating was none other than Turo's son. The belligerent Turo already had it in for her little family, and she feared today's incident would only stir up more ill feeling.

John sensed Mamba's unease. He leaned over and whispered, "It will all be alright."

Mamba smiled. Her Moilow always knew when something bothered her. His strength and confidence also helped dispel any fears she may have.

The young woman tensed when yet another big shape emerged out of the darkness. She relaxed when she identified the new arrival.

Gabirri smiled at the family members when he was close enough to see their faces. Looking at John, he said, "I bring you . . . goodwill, Moilow." The traditional greeting was delivered in English. Pigeon English, but clear and easily understood.

"I accept your goodwill, Gabirri," John replied in kind. He and Gabirri had spent so much time together, hunting and socialising, the young native was picking up the English language at an impressive speed. Not as impressive as Mamba and her sons, but impressive nevertheless. Consequently, many of their discussions were in English these days.

"Come," Gabirri said, motioning to the Irishman to accompany him.

John looked at Mamba and shrugged. Both knew better than to ask where Gabirri intended to take him. On any given day, such an invitation could result in a fireside chat outside another clan member's bivouac or a three-day hunting trip away in the hills.

"Do I need overnight supplies this time?" John asked, switching to the Kabi dialect.

"No," Gabirri replied in kind. "Only bring yourself." Looking at Mamba, he added, "Your husband will be back to warm you long before dawn."

Mamba was happy about that.

"Back later," John said to Mamba and the boys. The Irishman climbed to his feet and followed Gabirri who led him toward a bivouac close to the lake. He recognised it as Mootemu's shelter. The Ancient One, he knew, always liked to be close to water.

It was a moonless night, but the stars guided their way. John couldn't remember ever seeing more stars in the night sky. They lit up the heavens.

As the two friends neared the bivouac, they saw Mootemu sitting alongside Mirritji in front of a roaring cooking fire. The respected elders, who evidently had not long finished eating, hadn't yet noticed the younger men approaching. They were talking about the stars and pointing to celestial bodies they recognised.

When the elders finally noticed the younger men, Mirritji motioned to them to join them by the fire. Greetings were exchanged as the newcomers made themselves comfortable.

After a long silence, Mootemu looked at John. "Do you remember the story of the whale, the koala and the starfish, Moilow?" he asked.

John shook his head, indicating he didn't remember any such story. Gabirri and Mirritji glanced at each other, and smiled in anticipation of the tale.

Mootemu reached for a pile of branches stacked nearby. His gnarled fingers closed around the nearest branch. The old man threw it onto the fire, and he stared into the crackling flames as the branch ignited. Clearly, he wasn't going to be rushed.

Finally, Gabirri said, "Why don't you tell Moilow the story, Ancient One?"

Mootemu nodded. Turning to John, he said, "The story starts with three warriors who lived on a little island. They were called Whale, Koala and Starfish." The elder could see that John was struggling to follow the story. He turned to Gabirri. "You speak his tongue," he said. "You finish the story."

Gabirri willingly took over from Mootemu. Looking at John, he switched to English and said, "Three warriors . . . Whale, Koala and Starfish." He held up three fingers so there could be no misunderstanding. When he saw that John understood, he said, "Whale was only one who had canoe . . . and as food on island run out . . . Koala and Starfish ask if they can . . . borrow Whale's canoe.

Mootemu and Mirritji listened keenly even though neither understood what the young native was saying.

Gabirri continued, "They say they . . . they will catch fish and bring back . . . to share . . . with Whale." He eyed John. "Understand?"

John nodded.

Gabirri continued, "Now . . . Whale think about this and decide . . . if they leave . . . they not come back and he starve. So . . . Whale say no."

"Tell him what Whale says," Mirritji ordered.

"I did!" an annoyed Gabirri said in his own tongue. Switching back to English, he said, "Koala was . . . sneaky one. He go to Starfish and . . . they decide steal canoe . . . When Whale fall sleep they . . . drag canoe to the water. Starfish get in first . . . but before Koala can join him . . . Whale wake up."

Mootemu and Mirritji constantly looked from the storyteller to John to satisfy themselves he was following the story.

Gabirri continued, "So . . . Whale and Koala start . . ." He looked to John for help. "Start fight?"

"Fighting," John prompted.

"Start fighting," Gabirri said. "Whale winning so . . . Koala stab him . . . in back of neck with sharp stick . . . and climb into canoe."

"Don't forget the fight," Mootemu interjected.

Gabirri nodded impatiently then continued. "They start rowing away . . . but Whale pull stick out. Being good swimmer . . . he catch up with them . . . jump out water and land on canoe . . . Smash canoe into five pieces . . . Whale see that Koala swim to beach . . . so he catch up to him . . . and punch him in face . . . and flatten his nose . . . and stretch his ears out."

Gabirri's three listeners laugh as he pulled an authentic-looking koala face.

"Koala get away . . . by running up tree," Gabirri said. "So . . . Whale then look around for Starfish . . . who he find hiding in rock pool. He pound him flat . . . stretch him this way and that. . . . It was around this time . . . they took on the shapes they are now."

Mirritji and Mootemu nodded solemnly, prompting John to do the same.

Gabirri continued, "Koala stay in tree . . . Starfish stay in rock pool . . . and Big Whale stay in the water . . . that wound in his neck letting him breathe." He paused theatrically. "So . . . every year . . . when we see Big Whale swim up coast . . . he not going anywhere special . . . he just looking for Koala and Starfish . . . to give them another beating." The young native smiled, signalling the story was over.

John clapped appreciatively and exchanged smiles with his companions.

Mootemu fixed John with a long stare. The Irishman wasn't sure what was coming. Finally, the Ancient One smiled and said, "Maybe Turo thinks you are a koala?"

The men laughed.

John and Gabirri stayed long into the night, talking with the two elders. Finally, when it became clear Mootemu was ready for sleep, the younger men excused themselves and meandered back to their own bivouacs.

Before the pair separated, Gabirri confided something to his friend. "When you first returned . . . I not sure you were Moilow," he said in hesitant English. Reverting to Kabi, he touched John's shoulder and said, "Now I know it is you."

John went to respond, but Gabirri placed the palm of his hand on John's chest, indicating the discussion was over. He smiled quickly then walked off into the darkness.

News of the beating Murrowdooling had given Orad quickly spread throughout the clan, and it wasn't long before everyone knew that John had taught his boy to box.

Within a week, in an unexpected development, Murrowdooling and Orad were good mates, and the younger boy was now popular with the clan's youths as well as with those his own age. And, as Murrowdooling himself was quick to point out to anyone who cared to listen, he was popular with many of the girls, too.

It was John's observation the boy was fast becoming a man—and he was developing into quite a character. The Irishman often discussed Murrowdooling, and Carravanty, too, with Mamba. She was understandably proud of both her sons, and, John realised, he was proud of them as well. For some time now, he'd thought of them as his sons.

The Irishman couldn't help wondering if his increasing attachment to Mamba and the boys was the reason he dreamed less these days about returning to his old life in Ireland.

The Marsdens' dining room was full of revellers as the Marsden family and friends celebrated Christmas. Those *friends* included none other than Lord Cheetham who was there courtesy of the fact he had basically invited himself.

Captain Marsden hadn't been thrilled when he learned Cheetham would be attending, but he could hardly say no—especially not when the commandant had offered the free use of one of the army's chefs and two waiters to cook and serve the

Christmas dinner.

Prominent amongst the guests who sat around the Marsden's dining table were Mister and Missus Brown, Lieutenant Hogan, two junior officers and last but not least Lord Cheetham. Also in attendance, seated between Helen and Matthew, was Orana. Marsden had insisted she have Christmas Day off, and that she join the family for dinner that night as reward for being so loyal a housemaid over so long a period.

There was much merriment around the table for the wine and spirits were in plentiful supply, and the officers in particular were letting their hair down after what had been a long and trying year for all army personnel stationed at the bay.

The commandant, who had apparently abstained from smoking opium for a day or two, was in good form, proposing toasts and reciting poetry as and when the mood took him.

Since arriving at Moreton Bay, Helen and her benefactors, the Browns, had spent nearly every spare minute overseeing construction of the two new schoolrooms and finalising the curriculum for the coming school year. In the space of one week, they had achieved much. Construction of the rooms would be completed in plenty of time, and Helen had so familiarised herself with the curriculum she could quote it by heart—a trick neither of the Browns had ever mastered in all their years' teaching.

The Browns had decided that the school's second classroom would, for the first year at least, serve as a bedsit for Helen, and the army's carpenters had designed it with that purpose in mind. In the second year, or as soon as new enrolments dictated, Helen would find alternative accommodation and the room would be converted to a classroom.

Cheetham, who had also provided the wine from his own cellar for tonight's dinner, stood up to propose yet another toast. Swaying slightly on his feet—a result of one wine too many—and holding his overflowing glass toward Helen and Hogan, he said, "To the bride and groom—"

"*Future* bride and groom," Marsden corrected him amidst fresh laughter.

"To the *future* bride and groom," Cheetham said. "May you have many children and may they be happy and healthy."

"Hear, hear," the menfolk agreed. All except Marsden who was a little more subdued than usual.

Missus Brown buttonholed Helen and her fiancé, and questioned them about their forthcoming marriage. "Have you two set the date yet?" she asked mischievously.

The young couple glanced at each other, then Helen said, "Not yet Missus Brown." She never could get used to calling the older woman *Thelma,* and so had reverted to addressing her by her more formal title.

"Well don't leave it too long," Missus Brown said. She added, "And don't forget to invite Mister Brown and I."

"We certainly won't," Helen smiled. She looked at her fiancé and noticed he was studying the bottom of his wine glass.

As soon as Missus Brown turned away to talk to someone else, Hogan leaned over and reminded Helen she had been home a full week and they'd yet to even discuss their wedding let alone finalise a wedding date.

"All in good time, Desmond," Helen said. "I cannot even think about wedding dates before the new school year starts."

"Wedding *date,*" Hogan said somewhat unnecessarily, "not wedding *dates.*"

A loud knock at the back door interrupted proceedings. Marsden excused himself and left the room to answer the door. Moments later, the captain reappeared at the dining room's door. He caught Helen's eye and indicated to her that he wished to speak to Hogan. Helen alerted her fiancé who quickly left the table and joined his superior.

The two officers walked down the dimly lit passageway toward the back door, which Hogan saw was open. When they stepped outside, Hogan found Barega waiting for them. The tracker wore only his loincloth, and he carried a spear and a club. His body glistened in sweat, and he was breathing quite hard—a result of having run non-stop through the day and into the night.

Hogan turned to his superior for an explanation.

"He claims to have found signs that John Graham is still alive," Marsden said. Turning to Barega, he said, "Isn't that so, tracker?"

"Yeah, Mister," Barega said. "The Irish is alive."

"How do you know?" Hogan asked.

"Tracks, Mister," Barega said simply. Pointing at Hogan's polished boots, he said, "Boot tracks . . . with toes."

"With toes?" Marsden asked.

The tracker quickly explained how for some time now John had been wearing his worn boots with holes in the toes. As he talked, he fingered the silver crucifix that hung from his neck.

Marsden turned to Hogan. "That makes sense," he said. "Even the strongest boots in the world don't last forever in the wilderness." The captain turned back to Barega. "Where did you find his tracks?"

The tracker pointed north. "Three days hard running that way," he said.

"On the coast?" Hogan asked.

Barega shook his head. "Half day trek from sea," he said.

Marsden asked, "Who else knows this?"

"No-one else, Mister," the tracker said.

"Good," Marsden said. "Make sure it stays that way."

Barega prepared to leave. He hesitated. "You see Orana?" he asked hopefully.

"She is inside," Marsden said. "I will tell her you have returned."

The tracker grinned and walked off to the nearby annex he and the maid shared. Tired though he was, he evidently still had some energy left.

As soon as Barega was out of earshot, Hogan said, "That is the third time the tracker has found proof that Graham is still alive, sir."

Marsden nodded.

Hogan continued, "I request permission to lead a hunting party to find the

Irishman, sir."

Marsden shook his head. "Not before we have a firm fix on his current location, Lieutenant. He added, "And when we have that firm fix, I will be leading the hunting party, not you."

"But sir—"

"That is all for now, Lieutenant."

"Yes, Captain."

As the two officers prepared to join the others inside, they noticed Helen standing at the backdoor. The look on her face told them she had heard everything.

Looking at the two most important men in her life, she said, "You told me John Graham was dead . . ."

Neither man responded. They could think of nothing they could say that would satisfy Helen at that moment or that would make them look better in her eyes. After all, they had lied to her about the Irishman. And so they continued through to the dining room without comment.

59

SIX MONTHS AFTER MURROWDOOLING TAUGHT the bully Orad a lesson neither of them would forget, Mamba's oldest son was once more the centre of attention. Now thirteen, Murrowdooling was one of six boys—three from his clan and three from neighbouring clans—who were undergoing the same initiation rites all Kabi boys their age experience. The boys, who were naked, had been oiled from head to foot and plastered in white ochre. Cockatoo feathers had been attached by gum to the hair of each.

Murrowdooling stood out from his companions as he was a full head taller than the next tallest boy even though he was the youngest of the boys by several months.

More than two hundred Kabi looked on beneath a full moon on as the boys huddled together in the middle of a circle while thirty or more men crawled around the circle's perimeter, scratching at the earth like dingoes and howling like wild dogs. The clan's numbers had been swelled to twice its normal size by the presence of members of other clans. They watched, transfixed, as the ceremony continued.

John, Mamba and Carravanty were among the onlookers. Carravanty was so engrossed, it was clear to all that he couldn't wait until it was his turn to undergo the rites.

For John, this was the second time he'd witnessed these particular initiation rites. Mamba had previously explained the men were imitating dingoes to give the boys power over the dingo. On this occasion, John noticed two of the men carried grass models of kangaroos. He pointed them out to Mamba.

"The kangaroos will give the boys good fortune when hunting," Mamba said, a touch of impatience creeping into her voice. She added, "You know that, Moilow."

John nodded. He knew better than to advise her he didn't know that and he wasn't Moilow.

Mamba, along with the mothers of the other five boys, was justifiably tense for tonight marked the start of a ritual that would see her oldest son pass from boyhood into manhood. That is *if* he survived what lay ahead of him.

John was aware that what awaited Murrowdooling and the other boys was a month-long test of their survival skills. Before the night was over, the boys would be cast out—alone, naked and without weapons or supplies—into the wilderness. As well as surviving off the land, they each had to return with a clump of Spinifex, a hardy, drought-resistant grass found only in the interior. From the clan's present coastal encampment, the boys were faced with a trek of around two weeks before they were likely to encounter that unique plant, so it was unlikely they'd return before the next full moon.

The Irishman shared Mamba's tension. He'd long considered Murrowdooling, and Carravanty, too, his son, and he genuinely feared for the boy's survival. Only the previous year, seven boys had set out for the interior and only six returned. Of those who returned, two had failed to reach the interior, several suffered symptoms of malnutrition and dehydration, and all reported near-death experiences.

Gabirri had mentored Murrowdooling, teaching him to hunt and to survive off the land, and he'd assured John the boy was ready. But that didn't stop the Irishman from worrying.

As the evening's rituals came to an end, relatives of the boys surrounded them and wished them well for the ordeal ahead.

John hung back, leaving Mamba and Carravanty to share some last words with Murrowdooling. The Irishman had said all he needed to say to the boy in a private discussion earlier.

Mirritji, who had taken it upon himself to officiate, called the six boys to him. After relaying final instructions to them, he sent them out, one at a time, into the night.

John and Mamba watched as Murrowdooling, who was the last to leave, headed out. Before he took his first step, the boy glanced back at John. The two shared a knowing look before Murrowdooling ran off and disappeared into the darkness.

Later, in the privacy of their bivouac, John and Mamba couldn't sleep. A full moon often had that effect on them. Their thoughts, naturally enough, were with Murrowdooling.

Having survived three months alone in the wilderness, John could well imagine what the boy was going through. He recalled he'd never felt so small, or so lonely, as he had when trekking north alone from Moreton Bay. In some ways, the experience had been worse than in the first few days when he was pursued by Barega and the soldiers. At least then he had some sort of human company—even if they were trying to kill him.

John had instilled in Murrowdooling the need to look after his physical requirements first and worry about reaching the interior last. "If you die of thirst or hunger," he'd told him, "you will never reach your destination." Gabirri, he knew, had given the boy the same advice, so he hoped it had sunk in.

"What are you thinking, Moilow?" Mamba asked, rolling over to face him.

"You know what I am thinking," John said. Somewhat unnecessarily, he added, "I am thinking of Murrowdooling."

Mamba smiled. In the moonlight her teeth gleamed white. "You worry more than you used to," she said. "Sometimes I think you worry more than me."

Any thoughts of sleep were quickly forgotten as the couple discussed their hopes and fears for Murrowdooling.

John noticed that Mamba seemed more relaxed than before, and he commented on that very fact.

"I spoke to my ancestors' spirits," she confided.

"And . . . what did they say?"

"They said they will protect Murrowdooling."

Not convinced, John said, "I hope he doesn't get lost."

Mamba propped herself up on one elbow and smiled patiently. "You forget the Songlines, Moilow. He cannot get lost."

Before John could argue, Mamba threw her cloak off and pulled him over on top of her. Giggling, she caressed him until she was ready to enter her.

Later, as Mamba slept on his chest, John relived in his mind the events of the past six months. It had been a dramatic period marked by skirmishes with other tribes—and, in one case, with another Kabi clan—and bushfires, floods, births, deaths and starvation.

The winters, John had discovered, were the worst, and this present winter—it was June, although John had no way of knowing that—was the worst yet. Food had proven harder than usual to come by. Kangaroos, possums, emus and other wild game were scarcer than usual, fishing stocks were down, shellfish were scarce, too, and all the clan members had gone hungry. The signs of malnutrition were everywhere—especially amongst the children whose swollen bellies attested to their constant hunger. More than a few deaths could be attributed to the ongoing shortage of food.

One result of the shortage was the clan had to relocate more often than usual. Food sources at any one campsite were invariably exhausted within a day or two, forcing the clan members to seek new hunting and fishing grounds. For people already weakened by hunger, the constant moving was too much for some.

In the past week alone, two sickly, old people had simply walked off into the bush and laid down to die—as was the custom of these people. John had been horrified when he'd first observed this. Experience had taught him it was the best way. For nomadic hunters and gatherers like the Kabi, the elderly and the infirm were liabilities. No-one knew this better than the elderly and the infirm themselves, and they inevitably took their leave with a minimum of fuss. For the Irishman, it was yet another example of how resolute and unselfish the Kabi were.

John crawled as quietly as possible through the long grass, his spear firmly clasped in his right hand and his eyes on the solitary big red kangaroo that grazed alongside a billabong. His heart was beating fast. This was the first big red he had seen in weeks, and the first roo of any kind he'd seen in days. He could imagine how many hungry mouths this animal would feed.

The Irishman had been stalking the roo for the past hour, crawling between the ant hills that surrounded the watering hole. As he reached the ant hill closest to his quarry, he tried to estimate the distance.

Thirty yards at least. Maybe more.

Without the benefit of the woomera, or spear-thrower, that Aboriginal hunters used, thirty yards was about as far as he could throw the spear with any accuracy.

And that was if the target was stationary. If the target was moving, his accuracy dropped to ten or fifteen yards at best, which probably explained why he hadn't killed more than a dozen roos in all his time with the Kabi. Not for the first time, he reminded himself he must learn to master use of the woomera.

That would increase the range to fifty yards give or take.

From behind the ant hill, he couldn't see the big red. He risked a peek around the side of the hill and was relieved to see the roo was still there. Its big ears constantly twitched, reminding John not to make a sound.

John's belly rumbled.

Damned hunger pains!

To his ears, the rumbling sounded like rolling thunder. He was convinced the roo had heard him, but another quick peek confirmed the animal was still there.

As he prepared to act, he reviewed the steps he needed to follow to achieve a successful kill.

Jump up, raise spear, plant feet, raise left hand, sight target, throw spear.

Experience told him he could do all that in one second flat. Experience also told him that nine times out of ten he would miss his target if that target was a roo.

These roos are so damned quick.

The Irishman slowed his breathing. He took a deep breath, held it and sprang to his feet. He released the spear in less than a second, but the roo was already on its way, bounding toward distant trees. "Feck!" John cursed as the spear missed its target by a yard or more and disappeared into the billabong. When he realised he'd lost his spear, he shook his fist at the retreating roo. "Go hIfreann leat!" he cursed. In case the roo didn't understand Gaelic, he shouted, "To hell with you!"

Still smarting, he dived into the billabong to locate his spear. The watering hole proved to be a lot deeper than most, and it took a good ten minutes to retrieve the weapon.

After scrambling from the billabong, drying off and recovering his composure, he commenced the long trek back to the encampment. With every mile, his mood deteriorated. He'd spent the best part of the day hunting, and, as was the case yesterday and the day before, he'd be arriving home without anything to show for it.

John didn't doubt that other hunters would also return empty-handed, but that was little compensation. He and he alone was responsible for feeding his family, and without a kill he would have to rely on the generosity of neighbours if he and Mamba and Carravanty were to eat. It wouldn't be the first time of late they'd had to rely on the generosity of others to survive. He was reminded yet again of the need to learn to master use of the woomera.

Gabirri may be prepared to attempt to teach me again.

His thoughts turned to Murrowdooling. For perhaps the twentieth time that day, he wondered how the boy was faring. "He's fine," he told himself. "He hasn't even been gone a day." He tried not to imagine how worried he'd be a month from now if the boy hadn't returned by then.

John was walking across hinterland—open plains between the coast and a range of bush-covered hills. The clan had made camp on the eastern edge of the plains, overlooking the sea. Smoke from clan members' cooking fires could just be seen in the distance.

A clump of bushes caught his eye. They were of a variety he wasn't familiar with, and they were flush with black berries he'd never seen before. Sighting berries in mid-winter struck him as unusual for they were generally only available in spring or summer.

John was pleasantly surprised the berries were edible. A little sour, but definitely edible. After gulping down several handfuls of the mysterious berries, he removed his cloak and fashioned it into a carry-bag of sorts. Then he filled the makeshift bag with berries and resumed walking homeward.

In the thirty minutes it took him to reach the encampment, he'd come down with severe stomach cramps. Mamba took one look at the berries he'd collected, and she ran off to fetch Yileen, the clan's nungkari, or healer. She didn't need to tell John not to go anywhere; he was lying prone on the ground, frothing at the mouth and almost unconscious.

The Irishman didn't know that he'd eaten poisonous berries—the same berries the Kabi occasionally used for baits they left out to poison possums and other creatures.

Mamba returned almost immediately with Yileen, that mystical figure of indeterminate age whom the clan held in high regard. He brought with him some of the tools of his trade, and these he laid out neatly alongside his patient who was now unconscious, but still frothing at the mouth. His tools included a calabash of smouldering embers, leafy fire sticks and a bowl of some herbal concoction.

Chanting, Yileen held the fire sticks against the embers until their leaves caught alight, sending plumes of smoke skywards. These he waved over John's upper torso for quite some time.

By now, John had stopped frothing, but his complexion was now an awful grey-green, and his breathing sounded laboured.

Mamba went to stroke John's forehead, but Yileen motioned her away. The healer then cradled John's head in one arm, and with his other hand he poured the herbal concoction he'd brought with him into his patient's mouth. John simultaneously came round and threw up where he lay. This process was repeated several times as the Irishman disgorged the contents of his stomach.

John wasn't out of the woods yet. The poison was still in his system, and lesser amounts of the deadly berries had killed others. He groaned and mumbled incoherently.

Yileen placed his hands on John's chest. Still chanting, he soon fell into a trance. The healer then raised his hands. None of those watching—not Mamba nor any of the friends and family who had gathered around her—could know that Yileen was now able to see inside his patient. His supernatural powers included extraordinary vision, which not even he could explain, and he could see the black poison that circulated through John's veins.

Clenching and unclenching his fists, the healer seemingly mimed the action of pulling the poison from John's body. This strange ritual continued for almost an hour during which time John lapsed in and out of consciousness.

Finally, during a brief period of lucidity, John sat bolt upright and threw up once more. This time, he disgorged a large amount of bile from his gut, and he remained conscious. His breathing quickly normalised, and the colour returned to his face. Only now did he notice Yileen. The mysterious healer was studying him closely.

"What happened?" John asked.

Yileen simply shook his head before gathering up the tools of his trade and walking off.

The next face John saw was Mamba's. Mistaking the angry look on her face for concern, he reached out for her. She slapped his hand away.

"How could you eat those berries, Moilow?" she asked. "You know they are poisonous." She stomped off and disappeared inside her bivouac.

Only now did John remember the berries. The Irishman realised they must have been poisonous, and he cursed himself for his carelessness. He also realised that Mamba's frustration was not only because of the berries; she was frustrated that he'd returned home empty-handed, forcing them, once again, to rely on the generosity of neighbours if they were to eat any time soon. Neighbours who could ill afford to share their meagre food stocks.

60

IT WAS TWO DAYS BEFORE John was well enough to venture from his bivouac. The deadly poison had robbed him of his energy, and it took what little strength he had to just wander about the encampment. To his frustration, and Mamba's, too, he was too weak to resume hunting, and it would likely be another day or two before he was strong enough.

Mamba was no company for she was still annoyed with him, and, as he'd learned over time, her way of dealing with that was to give him the cold shoulder. That never lasted more than a day or two, and the making up was always pleasurable. He knew she'd come round eventually.

On the second day, after a small meal of witchetty grubs and smoked eel, provided courtesy of the husband of Mamba's one-eyed friend Myndee, John ventured out to find Yileen. He wanted to thank the healer for likely saving his life.

As he walked through the encampment, he couldn't help noticing the menfolk were conspicuous by their absence. The Irishman was aware most of the clan's men would be away hunting or fishing to find food for their families, and he was reminded he should be doing his bit, too, for his family. His carelessness of two days earlier still nagged at him, and he could understand Mamba's frustration.

On arriving at the healer's bivouac, he was greeted by one Alba, a haggard, toothless woman who resided with Yileen. The healer referred to her as his assistant, but clan members suspected she was something else altogether as they'd yet to see her ever assist Yileen with anything other than preparing his meals and generally acting as a beast of burden—like all the clan's women.

"Yileen is not here," Alba said when she saw John.

"Where is he?" John asked.

Alba pointed to a small, tree-covered hill beyond the encampment. It was the only hill here on the seaward side of the plains, so it was impossible to miss. "He is with the shaman," she said.

John thanked the woman and debated whether to bother with Yileen today. The hill wasn't far away, but it would mean a climb, and he wasn't sure he was up to it. Finally, he set off for the hill, telling himself he could always turn back if he ran out of puff.

The nearer he got to the hill, the steeper it looked. He was about to turn back when Yileen emerged from the trees at the foot of the hill. "I bring you goodwill, Yileen," the Irishman said as soon as he was close enough to be heard.

"I accept your goodwill, Moilow," Yileen said. "We were expecting you."

John wondered who else he referred to, and why they were expecting him. He reached out to touch his opposite then thought better of it. "I came to thank you," he said.

The healer waved a dismissive hand. He never looked for thanks.

Only now did John notice a faint column of smoke rising above the treetops about halfway up the hill behind Yileen.

Observing what had caught John's attention, the healer said, "You must go up there." He added, "Karadji said you would come." Without further ado, Yileen resumed walking back to the encampment, leaving a bemused John alone.

The Irishman shrugged his shoulders and set off up the hill, his curiosity piqued.

How could the shaman know I was coming?

He was breathing hard before he reached the source of the smoke. It was coming from a cave carved into the side of the hill. As he neared it, he could see Karadji sitting in front of a fire just inside the entrance, his back toward him.

Only now did John notice the young Shaman wasn't alone. The Irishman could just make out half a dozen figures sitting beyond the fire, their identities distorted by the flames. He eventually recognised the nearest of those figures as Mirritji. Only now did the elder notice John, and he waved the new arrival over to join him and the others.

John quickly entered the cave and sat down next to Mirritji. Common courtesies were put aside as the shaman was working himself into a trance, and he didn't wish to be disturbed.

A quick look around confirmed that Mirritji's companions included Mootemu, Banjora, Turo and three other elders. Behind them, in the gloom, he could just recognise Nowra and Orad. He guessed the two youths had carried Mootemu up the hill, and would no doubt carry him back down when it was time.

John turned his attention back to Karadji as the shaman began chanting, his surprisingly deep voice echoing throughout the chamber that apparently served as his temporary workplace. Still adorned in his full-length cloak of many colours, and still wearing eagle feathers in his long hair, the shaman was no longer clean-shaven. He now wore a wispy beard that reminded John of a Chinaman's beard.

Eyes closed, Karadji extended his arms and opened both his clenched fists to reveal he was holding crystals. They sparkled in the firelight, capturing the attention of all.

The shaman's hooded eyes suddenly flew open. He stared into the crystals for what seemed an age before looking at his audience. "I see changes coming for our people," he said ominously. "I see white spirits coming. A few at first. Then many thousands until they cover the land like ants."

John alone knew that Karadji referred to Europeans.

Looking back at the crystals, the shaman continued, "They bring with them fire sticks"—the Irishman guessed he referred to firearms—"that belch smoke and bring death and destruction."

John wondered if his companions were thinking about him at that moment. He glanced around at them and was relieved to see their full attention was on Karadji—except for Turo. He was glaring at him malevolently.

"Who are these white spirits?" Mirritji asked, barely able to contain his curiosity.

The shaman lifted his eyes from the crystals to Mirritji. "The crystals do not tell me that," he said. "They only tell me the white spirits come from across the sea." He waved an arm behind him, motioning toward the ocean he knew was at his back. "They will be carried here beneath white clouds"—the Irishman imagined he referred to ships' sails—"and they will be carried overland astride four-legged beasts that snort and run like the wind."

John knew that Karadji referred to soldiers' horses. Just as the Kabi hadn't seen Europeans—before his arrival at least—they hadn't seen horses or firearms either. And they'd only ever seen ships on distant horizons, too far away to clearly identify except for their billowing, cloud-like sails. John wondered how Karadji could know all this, and he marvelled at the accuracy of his prophesy for there was no doubt in his mind the young shaman was right about everything.

Karadji suddenly fell backwards, releasing the crystals, which scattered everywhere. The shaman appeared to be unconscious. John went to assist him, but Mirritji motioned to him to remain seated. The elder turned and nodded to the two youths sitting in the shadows. They jumped to their feet and half carried Karadji to a grassy ledge just outside the cave's entrance. There, they made him comfortable and waited patiently for him to come round. It was evident they'd done this before.

Mirritji glanced back at John. Noting his concern, he said, "The crystals take all Karadji's strength from him." He added, "He will recover soon."

Silence settled over the men. The shaman had given them much to ponder.

It was Turo who finally broke the silence. Pointing at John, he hissed, "I warned you the white imposter would bring us back luck!"

John wasn't surprised that Turo chose to turn Karadji's prophesy back on him. However, he was surprised that it was Banjora, the middle-aged hunter who had discovered him, who came to his defence.

"The white spirit has proven many times that he is Moilow," Banjora said.

Turo rounded on Banjora. "I thought you were my ally!" he snapped. "The white spirit is not Moilow." He switched his glare back to John. "More like him will come. The shaman has said as much."

The belligerent Turo's prediction hung over the men like a heavy blanket, effectively quashing further discussion.

Outside the entrance, Karadji pushed himself to his feet and set off alone down the hillside. He appeared to have fully recovered. One by one, the others left the cave until only John and Mirritji remained. The two hung back just inside the cave's entrance.

Finally, Mirritji placed a friendly hand on the Irishman's shoulder. "Come with me," he said. The elder walked off, his bandy legs carrying him deeper into the cave.

Mystified, John followed. The cave was a lot deeper than he'd imagined. As he and Mirritji turned a sharp corner, a flickering light carried to them. They continued walking until they reached the source of the light. There, at the end of the cave, they found a young native painting an image on the cave's rear wall. John recognised the man as Warrane, an artist known up and down the coast for his artistic talent.

Warrane was painting by the light of flaming torches he had jammed into cracks in the rock face. So involved was he in his work, he didn't even appear to notice the two men at first. He acknowledged them with a brief nod when he did finally realise he had company.

John watched spellbound as the artist drew an as-yet-unidentifiable image on the rock. Warrane dipped the fingers of his right hand into a bowl of charcoal he carried in his left hand, and then used his charcoal-coated fingers to complete the outline. Then he wandered over to a nearby rock pool, washed his blackened fingers in the water before dipping them into yet another bowl. This bowl contained ochre of various colours. Selecting red ochre and still using his fingers, he then applied the ochre to sections of the image. As still more colours were applied—all of them bright and vibrant—John realised the artist was painting a mystical scene.

As if reading his younger companion's mind, Mirritji said, "He paints the Dreamtime."

John nodded, but he was none the wiser. He'd often heard the Kabi talk about the mystical *Dreamtime*—or *the Dreaming* as some referred to it—but to this day no-one had satisfactorily explained to him exactly what it was. The Irishman had often discussed it with Mamba and Gabirri, and with Mootemu, too, but never with Mirritji. He hoped the elder would explain it clearly to him.

Mirritji said, "You know about the Dreaming Tracks, Moilow."

John nodded. He knew *the Dreaming Tracks* the elder referred to was another name for the Songlines that Mamba had taught him about.

Mirritji continued, "The blood of our ancestors"—he pointed to the red ochre that Warrane had just applied to the latest image—"flows along those tracks, linking us to the land and to the totems that roam that land."

"Totems?" John asked.

"The great Animal Spirits," Mirritji explained. Pointing at himself, he said, "My totem is the emu."

"What is my totem?" John asked.

The elder looked at John as if he should not have to ask that question. "Your totem is the dingo, Moilow," he said at length. Returning to his explanation, he said, "The migration of the great Animal Spirits created our world during the Dreamtime. To understand the Dreamtime, you must understand that we do not own the land. The land is our mother and she owns and nurtures us."

John nodded. Mirritji was making sense so far.

When the elder was sure John was following him, he continued, "The land is where everything starts and ends. It is our lifeblood. In the Dreamtime, the great animal spirits became part of our landscape,"—the Irishman knew he referred to the sacred landmarks Mamba had told him about—"and these can only be seen by the chosen ones."

John had previously been told that only certain men could see or experience the Dreamtime, and he assumed it was they who Mirritji referred to.

The elder continued, "We are the descendants of our totems, our Dreamtime ancestors. And they have charged us with caring for our mother, the land." He could see John was confused. "Ah, Moilow," he said. Placing both his hands on the white's shoulders, and talking to him as if he was a child, he asked, "Do you forget everything?" When John didn't respond, he said, "The Dreamtime is the creation . . . the beginning of everything. Look,"—he pointed at the image Warrane had now all but completed—"the Dreamtime is where all knowledge comes from."

John looked at the image that now dominated the cave's back wall, and he was rendered speechless by its beauty. White clouds formed the top border of the image. Golden rays of sunlight pierced the clouds, highlighting creatures on the earth below. Dingoes, snakes, eagles and whales were among the creatures represented. Stick-like figures representing hunters walked among the animals, spears raised. Rivers and other waterways had been coloured blood red. "It's beautiful," John murmured in English.

Mirritji studied his companion and nodded. "Moilow remembers the Dreamtime now," he smiled. He turned and walked back along the cave floor, leaving John to study the colourful artwork.

The Irishman felt he had a better understanding of the Dreamtime now. He was under no illusions. He knew even if his life depended on it, he couldn't remotely begin to explain it to anyone else, and yet, thanks to Mirritji, he had an awareness of the phenomenon that he hadn't had before. The Dreamtime was, he decided, more a feeling than anything. Something that words could never adequately describe, and something only an Aborigine could ever fully understand.

Suddenly tired, John turned and followed Mirritji out of the cave. Squinting as he emerged into the bright sunlight outside, he found the elder waiting for him.

The pair descended the hill together, closer now than they'd ever been before.

As John and Mirritji retraced their steps to their encampment on the plains, some twenty miles to the south Barega was talking to a Kabi hunter he'd fortuitously come across from another clan. The chance meeting occurred in a bush clearing Mirritji's clan had recently camped in.

The hunter Barega had encountered advised him the clan members had vacated the site only a week earlier and had been heading for the hinterland further to the north. He also confirmed the white spirit was with them.

The tracker already knew that John had been here recently. He had seen his quarry's distinctive boot prints as soon as he'd arrived. They had been well preserved until the next downpour in soft ground next to a billabong conveniently located in the centre of the clearing.

Barega thanked the hunter. In appreciation of his assistance, he removed the silver crucifix from around his neck and held it out to his opposite to accept. As the grateful hunter reached for the crucifix, the tracker dropped it. The hunter bent down to retrieve it. That was the last thing he ever did. Barega quickly drew out his nulla nulla and clubbed his unsuspecting victim over the head. The single blow was delivered with such force a second blow was not required to ensure the hunter would never mention their conversation to anyone else.

Barega returned the nulla nulla to the twine noose he wore around his waist before retrieving his treasured crucifix and heading into the surrounding bush. His destination: the hinterland the hunter had referred to.

61

THE NEXT FULL MOON CAME and went, and still there was no sign of Murrowdooling or any of the other five boys who had headed into the wilderness a month earlier. Mamba and the other mothers involved were beside themselves, but they kept their concerns to themselves for custom dictated they not burden the menfolk with additional worries—the theory being the men had enough to worry about what with ensuring there was sufficient food to eat and remaining ever-alert for attacks by the clan's numerous enemies.

However, John wasn't fooled. He knew Mamba was worried. God knows *he* was worried. He frequently assured Mamba that Murrowdooling was okay, but she wasn't convinced. She and all the mothers were aware that most if not all the boys should have returned by now.

John was concerned the boys wouldn't be able to find the clan. Clan members had relocated at least ten times in the past month, and the Irishman estimated the present encampment was a good thirty miles from where the boys had originally departed. Then he remembered the Songlines, and he relaxed, a little.

He and Mamba needn't have worried. Three days after the full moon, the boys began drifting into the clan's present encampment.

Murrowdooling was the first to arrive. He beat the next boy home by a full day. Within a week, all six boys had safely returned. All but one had returned with a clump of Spinifex grass, which proved that five at least had reached the interior. It was deemed a good result.

Mamba was so thrilled to see Murrowdooling she wouldn't let him out of her sight, and she plied him non-stop with questions. Questions he answered with all the enthusiasm of a teenage boy being questioned by his mother. Most of his answers were monosyllabic.

John was the first to notice a change in the boy. He seemed to have matured far beyond his years, and the look in his eyes told the Irishman he'd seen and experienced much in his time alone in the wilderness.

Physically, the boy was in good shape. Better than any of the other boys—some of whom displayed signs of malnutrition and exhaustion. In a quiet moment, he advised John that he'd taken his advice, and Gabirri's, and had initially focused on his wellbeing. "I made a spear and I killed a wallaby with it the first day," he said in his own tongue. "Then I skinned the wallaby and made this loincloth"—he pointed proudly to the loincloth he still wore—"and then I made fire and cooked the wallaby. Its meat fed me for three days."

John could hardly contain his pride. He ruffled the boy's hair and motioned to him to continue.

"The rivers were still swollen after the late end to the wet season, and that slowed me down," Murrowdooling said. "Some were too treacherous to cross so I had to walk a long way to bypass them."

"That explains why you were all late getting back," John said.

Murrowdooling nodded. "And once I was chased by the Noonuccal dogs," he said, referring to the tribe that had been responsible for his own father's death.

"Don't tell your mother that," John cautioned. He knew Mamba would have nightmares if she found out the cannibals who had killed her husband had almost killed her son.

"No, I will not," the boy assured him.

"What was the interior like?" John asked.

Murrowdooling thought for a while. He pointed to the plains that stretched all the way to distant hills in the west. "As flat as that," he said. "No hills. No ocean. Hardly a tree or bush in sight." He then looked at the dry earth beneath his feet. Picking up a handful of dust, he let it slip through his fingers. "And the earth is as dry as that . . . with little water to be found . . . Sometimes I could not find water for days."

"How did you survive?"

"Emu eggs," Murrowdooling grinned.

John recalled his own experience, drinking the fluid in raw emu eggs to survive when water was scarce.

"I nearly caught an emu chick, too," the boy said. "But its mother kicked me"—he pointed to a new scar on his left knee—"and the chick escaped."

They both had a chuckle about that.

After a long silence, Murrowdooling looked at John. "Can I hunt with you tomorrow, Moilow?" he asked.

"You'll want to rest, surely?" John said.

Smiling, Murrowdooling shook his head. Switching to English, he said, "No, Moilow . . . I wish to hunt . . . with you."

The Irishman looked fondly at Murrowdooling. When he looked at him, he no longer saw an Aborigine boy. He saw his oldest son.

❦

Helen dipped her feather quill into an open ink bottle and prepared to draft an overdue letter to Matthew. In the six months since her young brother had returned to Sydney Town to resume his schooling there, she'd only written twice while he had sent her a letter every month at least.

The young woman got as far as writing the date—*July 15th, 1830*—when the sound of horses' hooves distracted her. She looked up and saw a troop of Redcoats entering Brisbane Town on horseback. From her vantage point atop a small rise outside the new schoolhouse, she had a commanding view of the township and the road that connected it to the penal settlement downriver.

The school day had not long ended, and Helen was sitting on the front doorstep of the schoolhouse, determined to take advantage of the late afternoon sun. It was a

373

cool mid-winter's day—unusually cool for the bay—and she wore a heavy cardigan over her work smock to keep warm.

Now halfway through Moreton Bay Junior School's inaugural year, and halfway through her first year as sole-charge teacher, Helen was loving the experience. If there had ever been any doubt about her calling to be a teacher, there was none now.

The school's role was growing rapidly—a reflection of the township's growth as more and more settlers continued to pour in. Opening day's attendance of nine young children had quickly been eclipsed, the role growing to eighteen with more children on the waiting list. This growth in pupil numbers had required Helen to vacate the school's second room, which she'd been using as a bedsit, so that it could be converted to the classroom it was always intended to be. Consequently, she now resided in town—in a cottage she rented from an absentee owner. Her father had suggested she live with him, but she'd successfully argued that she wished to remain independent.

As the Redcoats neared, Helen saw the troop was being led by Lieutenant Hogan. He waved as soon as he saw her, but she pretended she hadn't noticed him and returned her attention to the blank page in front of her.

Even now, six months or so after she'd learned that Hogan and her father had lied to her about John Graham, the lieutenant was the last person she wanted to see. As soon as she'd learned that John was still alive, and not dead as the two most important men in her life had insisted he was, she'd called off her engagement, and since then she had refused to speak to Hogan or even acknowledge him.

Helen was still angry at her father, too, but somehow she felt more let down by Hogan. The young woman felt he'd deceived her. She didn't believe that was any sort of foundation for a marriage—and she had advised him as much. Subsequent attempts by the lieutenant to reconcile had been met with stony silence.

In many ways, the situation suited Helen. Her teaching job had proven extremely demanding, and while she'd met the challenge head on and had thrived on the heavy workload that came with it, she was aware married life would have been an added complication. A complication she wasn't sure she was ready for.

Even if she hadn't been teaching, she wasn't sure she was ready for marriage. During the wee small hours, when she tossed and turned alone in her bed, unable to sleep, she often wondered if she would ever be ready to marry; she asked herself if she would think differently if she met the right man; she also asked herself if Hogan was the right man. That would invariably lead to another question: If circumstances had been different, would John Graham have been the right man?

Helen often thought of the cheeky Irishman with the startling blue eyes—even more so since she'd learned he was still alive. She wondered if she hadn't met him if she may be Missus Helen Hogan by now.

The young woman returned her attention to the blank page and began writing. *Dear Matthew . . .*

Distracted once more—this time by the sound of a solitary horse approaching— she looked up to see that Hogan was galloping toward her, and it was clear he intended to speak to her.

Helen quickly ran inside the schoolroom, shut the door and locked it. She stood with her back against the door, willing Hogan to depart.

After a minute or so, she relaxed when she heard the sound of the horse galloping away. She unlocked and then opened the door, and gasped when she saw the lieutenant standing on the bottom step. He'd obviously sent his horse on its way without him.

"Helen, I just want to talk to you," Hogan said.

Resisting the urge to slam the door in his face a second time, Helen said, "We have nothing to say, Lieutenant Hogan."

"But I—"

"And I am not sure we will *ever* have anything to say to each other," Helen said.

A chastened Hogan turned to go. He hesitated then turned back, suddenly resentful. Helen took a step backwards when she saw the anger on his face in his eyes.

"It's John Graham, isn't it!" Hogan said accusingly. "We would be married now if it wasn't for him."

This time, Helen did slam the door on Hogan. After a short while, she looked out the window and watched Hogan's retreating back as he stomped off to recover his horse and re-join his troop.

As she stood there, Hogan's words kept coming back to her. *It's John Graham, isn't it!* Without thinking, she clamped her hands over her ears, as if to block the lieutenant's words out.

PART FIVE

DAYS OF
DARKNESS

62

IN THEIR NEVER-ENDING SEARCH FOR new hunting grounds, the Kabi followed a track that opened out onto a beach overlooking their journey's end—a large island a few miles off shore.

Great Sandy Island, the world's largest sand island, was usually an annual destination for all the Kabi clans. For John, this would be his third consecutive visit to the island. For some reason that had never been explained, his clan hadn't visited the island during his first year with them. They had visited it every year since, however, and in that time he'd gotten to know it pretty well.

Although distinguished by its mighty, ever-changing dunes, which rose as much as seven hundred and fifty feet above sea level, the island that would one day be known as Fraser Island had woodlands, coastal heaths, mangroves, swamps and scores of freshwater lakes surrounded by dense rainforests and vast stands of gum trees. The land and its waterways were home to a great variety of wildlife—a fact not lost on the Kabi whose ancestors had been visiting the island for the past five thousand years or more.

Clan members waited patiently as Mirritji spoke to several Kabi from another clan who, it appeared, had just paddled over from the island in small a dugout canoe. The men were in deep discussion at the water's edge.

John, who, as always, was with Mamba, Murrowdooling and Carravanty, took the opportunity to drop his spear and lower the cloaks and other possessions he'd been carrying to the ground. They'd been walking non-stop for several hours, and he was grateful for the rest.

"Can I go for a swim?" young Carravanty asked.

Mamba shook her head. "No, son," she said. "We will be on our way soon."

Not one to take no for an answer, the boy turned to John and tugged on his loincloth. "Can I swim, Moilow?" he asked.

"Now what did you mother just say, Carravanty?" John asked.

The boy grinned at his older brother as if to say it was worth a shot. John pretended not to notice. He couldn't help thinking how like Murrowdooling the younger boy was shaping up to be.

Two cheeky imps to watch out for!

He smiled to himself. It seemed like only yesterday that he was a boy, too.

John and Murrowdooling exchanged some good-humoured banter. These days, Mamba's older boy usually gave as good as he got during the frequent ribbing sessions he and the Irishman engaged in. Since Murrowdooling's initiation into manhood the previous year, the boy had matured into a young man to be reckoned with. He had real leadership qualities, and he often demonstrated a superior intelligence. Physically, he'd changed, too. Tall and lithe, his physique was enhanced by the scarification he'd undergone after his successful initiation. That had left him with permanent welts over his limbs and torso.

These days also, when John spoke, it was usually in the Kabi tongue. As his familiarity with the language increased, he and his adopted family spoke less and less English. After four years, he was almost as comfortable speaking Kabi as he was speaking his native language.

Although he no longer kept track of the passing of each month, he was vaguely aware he'd been with the Kabi around four years as he had kept a track of the seasons. He was just going into his fifth summer with the clan, and that's how he knew the four-year milestone would be passed soon if it hadn't been passed already.

In fact, it was October 1831, which made it four years to the month since Turo and his fellow hunters had captured him.

John didn't know where the years had gone. In some ways, it seemed like yesterday that he was dragged into the clan's seaside encampment and almost burnt alive. It also felt like it had happened to someone else. He could hardly remember who the real John Graham was. He was Moilow in almost every sense. After all, that was the name he answered to day in, day out. And though he'd never met the man, it felt almost as though Moilow had taken him over. Even his thinking seemed different.

For a long time, that had scared him. He feared he could be losing his mind. Slowly, he'd adapted. He learned to accept the new life that had been forced upon him. More recently, he'd learned to embrace that new life. "You're only here once, Moilow, or whatever your name is," he often told himself, "so you best make the feckin' most of it."

Since Murrowdooling's initiation, John had up-skilled, mastering the use of the woomera so that he could throw a spear much further, and with far greater accuracy, than before. This was a tribute to the patience of Gabirri who had invested many long hours teaching his friend how to use the all-important spear-thrower. One immediate result of this was that John rarely returned empty-handed from a hunt these days. Not when game was available at least. This further endeared him to Mamba, and to other clan members, too.

Added to that, John looked more Aboriginal than ever. Although still uniquely clean-shaven, his skin was even darker—if that was possible—and he now wore a loincloth like all the other men. His only concession to his former life, apart from his daily shave, was he still wore his boots, or what remained of them. The cut-out toe space was bigger than ever, and little remained of the original boots. He'd had to reinforce them with sturdy fig leaves to hold them together, and he wasn't confident they would last much longer. The thought of being without his boots didn't faze him as he often walked about barefoot.

Not all approved of the white spirit who had become part of their clan. Turo remained bitter about John's acceptance as did several of his closest allies. Of late, they'd kept their distance, but the Irishman sensed they were always waiting for him to falter.

"What can they be talking about?" Mamba asked, looking at Mirritji and the other men who were still deep in discussion down at the water's edge. She and others were starting to become impatient even if it was still only mid-morning. There was plenty of time to cross to the island.

"I will check," John said. He picked up his spear and wandered over to join Mirritji who was now talking to the oldest man in the group. The group's members were from one of the Kabi's smaller clans. They'd been joined by Gabirri, Turo and several others.

"He says the Gureng are on our island," Mirritji said to John as soon as he noticed him. "A thirty-strong war party."

The Irishman knew the elder referred to long-time enemies of his people. The Gurengs' visits to the island the Kabi thought of as their own had coincided once before in John's time with the clan—two years earlier—and that had resulted in bloodshed and the loss of life on both sides.

"Thirty warriors, you say?" John asked, looking at the stranger.

The man, an elder, nodded. "At least thirty," he said.

"We can match that," Turo said.

Ignoring Turo, John asked, "Where are they camped?"

The stranger pointed to the northern end of the island. "At the northern end," he said, confirming the fact.

"We will make camp at the southern end." Gabirri said. "The Gureng will not even know we are there." He spoke with the knowledge that nearly eighty miles separated Great Sandy Island's northern end from its southern end. Tribes could easily live at opposite ends of the island for many months and likely believe they had the place to themselves.

Mirritji pondered this for a moment. Finally, he nodded. "We should cross over without delay," he said. "The longer we are here, or out there on the water"—he pointed out to sea—"the more chance there is for us to be seen."

The members of the two clans separated, and Turo and Gabirri took charge of the launching of canoes the clan kept nearby for just this purpose.

"John, come!" Gabirri said, motioning to the Irishman to follow Turo and himself along the beach. They were quickly joined by other male clan members.

Behind them, the last of the stragglers reached the beach. The very last to arrive was the elderly Mootemu who had been poorly of late, and who had had to be carried between two men from the inland encampment they'd vacated earlier that morning. Walking was now beyond the Ancient One who had come down with some mystery ailment, and whose recovery had defied even the best efforts of Yileen, the healer. Not even the intervention of Karadji had helped the ailing Mootemu who was now lying on the sand, resting. Clan members feared they would soon lose him to the Sky Spirits.

John and the other men ran toward an inlet, which they soon reached. They followed the inlet a good quarter-mile inland until they reached a rocky peninsula that jutted out into the water.

John knew exactly where they were heading. He'd accompanied the men here twice before—most recently the previous summer.

Half way along the peninsula, they found what they were looking for: a cave effectively screened from prying eyes by mangroves and other vegetation. They quickly pulled the vegetation aside to reveal three canoes resting on the cave's sandy floor—exactly where they'd left them. The paddles for each lay alongside the craft. Two of the wooden dugouts could seat around twenty paddlers and one could seat ten, so at least two trips would be required to transport all the clan members and their possessions to the island. It was a time-consuming process, but one they were well used to.

The men half-carried the dugouts from the cave. Fortunately, the water was close by. Even so, it required some effort to launch the three craft. The Irishman and two others scrambled into the smaller canoe while five jumped into the other two craft.

With an incoming tide to contend with, and with so few paddlers aboard each canoe, the journey back to the beach was a lot slower, and the men were breathing hard by the time they finally beached the canoes. They were greeted by clan members who immediately loaded their possessions into the craft. Those who couldn't be accommodated in the first crossing, sat patiently in the sand, resigned to waiting for the canoes to return to take them to the island.

Mootemu and the two men charged with assisting him boarded the smaller of the three dugouts. The Ancient One, who had fallen asleep on the beach, fell asleep again almost as soon as he sat down, his back supported by the knees of the man behind him.

John and his family found themselves amongst those in the first crossing. They were seated toward the prow of one of the larger canoes. All able-bodied men and women were expected to paddle, and Mamba showed once again she could paddle with the best of them. Ignoring the salt spray that flew into their faces, they observed Great Sandy Island as they paddled.

Slowly, the island drew ever closer, its towering sand-dunes reaching for the sky like mighty pyramids.

As always, John admired the island's beauty. He marvelled at its dunes and its lush green vegetation. Apart from the aforementioned skirmish with the Gureng, Great Sandy Island held fond memories for him. In his experience, the hunting was always good and the food plentiful at this time of year, and there was free time in which to relax and allow the body to recover from the demands of the winter just gone. This would be his first visit to the southern end of the island, and he was looking forward to it.

Clan members kept their eyes peeled for signs of their enemies. They knew they were most vulnerable when their strength was divided, as it was now. With half the clan still waiting on the mainland behind them, that left them exposed—more so those in the advance party. Their tension rubbed off on John. As the shoreline neared, he found he was looking closely at every rock and every tree, and imagining an enemy warrior behind each.

Only the children seemed oblivious to the potential danger. Sitting on the floor of the canoe, quashed between the adults, they turned their faces to the spray and squealed with delight as waves broke over the prow, drenching them. Several older children were charged with bailing water from the bottom of the canoe. They did this using large, wooden calabashes. It was the same in all the dugouts.

The three canoes were heading for a sandy beach in a horseshoe-curved bay. It was an idyllic setting, but the paddlers weren't interested in the scenery at that moment. They were focused on keeping their canoes upright in the surf, and ensuring they weren't heading into an ambush.

John's canoe was the first to beach. A reasonable wave delivered the craft well up onto the sand so that only those sitting in the stern got their feet wet when they jumped out.

The men immediately formed a circle around the women and children, their spears pointed outward in readiness for a surprise attack.

Fortunately, they didn't have long to wait for the next two canoes to arrive. Within a minute or two, they beached close by, and the men in each adopted an identical defensive formation to that of those in the first canoe.

They relaxed when no attack eventuated. Logic dictated that if an attack was coming, it would have happened straight away, before the men could organise their defences.

Without having to be asked, two men split from each of the three defensive formations and ran up the mountainous dunes that bordered the beach, intent on rooting out any natives who may be lying in wait.

·€·————·3·

After a short while, the men returned, still in pairs, and reported that the area was clear of any enemies. That was the signal to make camp, and this was done with the usual minimum of fuss, although some extra care was taken to select a site that could be easily defended.

The site selected after some scouting around was a hilltop not far from the beach. It afforded uninterrupted views of the surrounding terrain and it offered easy access to the shore.

As an extra safeguard, Mirritji suggested a roster system be established to ensure three or four armed lookouts were on duty at any one time during daylight hours and half a dozen during the night. This was readily agreed to, and four youths were immediately despatched to patrol the camp's perimeter to reduce the chance of a surprise attack by the Gureng. As an afterthought, two more youths—Nowra and Orad—were ordered to guard the canoes.

The two men charged with caring for Mootemu lay the Ancient One down in the shade of a bush, and immediately set about making a shelter for him. He'd slept the entire journey from the mainland, and he appeared to still be sleeping. Other clan members kept their distance. They knew if he'd died, they'd be told soon enough. Several whispered prayers to their ancestors' spirits, asking that they watch over Mootemu.

63

⊸⊱————⊰⊷

OOKING AROUND, JOHN COULD SEE the encampment had been well chosen. The hill was largely bare and devoid of dense vegetation, so anyone approaching could be seen some distance away. Its crater-like summit contained a sky-blue lake, which would provide the clan members with all the freshwater they needed. The lake was unusual in that it had a small, bush-covered island in the middle of it, and its crater-like summit, in turn, contained a tiny lake. Adding to the uniqueness of the scene, the tiny crater lake was dark green, contrasting with the blue of the larger lake. The lakes had long been referred to by the Kabi *as the Green and Blue Lakes.*

John busied himself making a bivouac. For this task he recruited the services of Murrowdooling and Carravanty who had become quite adept at building shelters, while Mamba prepared a cooking fire for the evening's meal. All around them, other clan members performed similar tasks. It was still only mid-afternoon, so there was plenty of time.

When their bivouac was completed, John and the boys wandered down to the beach for a well-deserved swim.

"Last one in is a galah!" Murrowdooling shouted as he sprinted toward the water.

Laughing John and Carravanty took after him, diving in as soon as the water was up to their knees. The saltwater was delightfully cooling, and the Irishman felt rejuvenated almost instantly.

A water fight followed, as it invariably did whenever the three went swimming. The two boys ganged up on John, and he was soon gasping for breath as they jumped on him and pushed his head beneath the waves.

John looked up to see Mamba walking down onto the beach. She was laughing at her three boys' antics.

Finally, John managed to extricate himself from the brothers' clutches and wandered up to join Mamba who was now sitting on the sand. "Those boys of yours are getting too strong," he gasped as he sat down beside Mamba, luxuriating in the feel of sand and saltwater on his skin.

"Those boys of *ours*," she said, reminding her Moilow they were his boys too.

John grinned and returned his attention to the brothers who were still wrestling in the water. "Go easy on your brother!" he shouted as Murrowdooling got a bit too rough for his liking with Carravanty.

A shadow on the sand alerted John and Mamba to the fact they had company. They looked up and saw it was Mirritji.

The elder didn't sit. He stood looking around, taking in the scenery and observing clan members who were busy familiarising themselves with their new encampment and its surrounds. Fishermen were already spearing fish from nearby rocks while others were preparing to cast nets; women were collecting shellfish and others were watching over small groups of young children as they played in the shallows. It was idyllic.

The contentment on Mirritji's face was there for all to see. Certainly, John didn't miss it. "You have chosen our new campsite well, Mirritji," he said.

The elder nodded. "Yes," he said. "It is a fine place."

Mirritji's attention was drawn to two large crabs engaged in deadly combat at the water's edge. Intrigued, he wandered over atop his bandy legs to watch the violent spectacle. John pushed himself to his feet and walked down to join him.

The elder was now bending down, hands on knees, studying the two crabs. He frowned when one crab overpowered and then devoured the other. With a sudden flash of intuition, he looked up at John. "We must move to a new encampment," he said.

"Why?" John asked. "We have just arrived here." He looked around as Mamba joined them.

Mirritji shrugged. Without explanation, he walked along the beach, calling out to other clan members, and motioning to them to follow him back up to the encampment. They sensed his urgency and quickly followed the respected elder.

John looked quizzically at Mamba.

"Mirritji wise," she said, speaking English. "He know what best . . . for his people." She called Murrowdooling and Carravanty to her, and then led them up toward the encampment.

A bemused John followed, annoyed by the prospect of having to go to the trouble of relocating to another site all because an old man had seen two crabs fighting.

Vacating the encampment began as soon as the last of the clan members had been ferried over from the mainland. It required manhandling all the clan's possessions over the sand-dunes and loading them, along with clan members, back into the canoes. Even so, it was done with a minimum of fuss, and, John noticed, with nary a grumble from anyone other than himself.

The others had obviously learned to trust Mirritji's instincts. Those instincts had saved them more than once.

On this occasion, Mirritji had advised clan members he received a sign they should relocate to another coastal site a few miles to the north. Even though the move would take them closer to their enemies, he told them, it would be safer.

The lateness of the hour was considered a minor inconvenience only. The afternoon sun was dipping fast, and it was obvious to all it would be dusk before the first of the clan members reached the new campsite; it would be well and truly dark before all the clan members arrived and the site could be made ready. Not ideal, but not the end of the world either.

It was only as John was about to depart the encampment that he noticed Mootemu. The Ancient One was now sitting up, his back resting against the trunk of a gum tree—the only tree on the hill's summit. It was apparent someone had left him there.

From where John stood, he couldn't tell whether Mootemu was awake or asleep, or dead for that matter. He went to check on him when Mamba intervened.

"Leave him, Moilow," she said.

"But we can't leave him here," John protested. He strode toward Mootemu, but he was stopped in his tracks when strong fingers closed around his arm. He looked around to see Gabirri standing there, looking staunch.

"The Ancient One is too ill to move," Gabirri said.

"Mootemu needs our help," John said. A feeling of helplessness came over the Irishman as it dawned on him the fate that awaited Mootemu. He looked back at the Ancient One and saw that he was now lying down. His face was turned toward him, and John imagined he saw his eyes move. The Irishman looked at Gabirri.

The young native just shook his head, indicating it was what it was.

Mamba stepped between the two. "Gabirri is right, Moilow," she said, looking over at Mootemu. Her voice barely a whisper, she said, "It is Mootemu's time to go to the Dreaming Land." She took John by the hand and led him down the hill.

Before they disappeared over the crest of the hill, John looked back at Mootemu. He nearly stumbled when the old man smiled at him, and then he disappeared from view.

As the last of the clan members quit the hilltop, the Ancient One observed them sadly through rheumy eyes. His blurry vision meant he could no longer identify individuals, but he was comforted just knowing they were there.

A short time later, Mootemu thought he saw the three canoes heading north along the island's coast. Then he heard his ancestors' spirits calling to him from the Dreamtime, and everything went black.

The relocation took longer than envisaged, and it was dark before the first of the clan members even reached the new campsite Mirritji had directed them to. Fortunately, a return journey was not required as those men not needed to paddle the three canoes travelled along the shoreline on foot.

John was among those tasked with paddling, and for that he was thankful as he was aware those on foot were more exposed to the threat of attack. Besides, he preferred to stay close to Mamba and the boys whenever there was danger in the air.

Mirritji had insisted those in the dugouts keep the menfolk on shore in sight at all times, so the paddlers had to frequently slow their paddling, or even cease paddling on occasion, so as not to get too far ahead. It wouldn't do, he'd advised, for one party to be attacked without the other party knowing.

John considered the new campsite inferior to the one they'd vacated. It was a beachside clearing in the dense rainforest that hugged the shoreline along this section of the island. While it offered good access to fishing and hunting grounds, and there was no shortage of freshwater, the encroaching rainforest offered excellent cover for their enemies should they decide to mount a surprise attack. For this reason, the clan's elders decided the clan would relocate yet again the following morning. Until then, all fires were banned, and a dozen men and youths were appointed to patrol the surrounds and also to guard the canoes. The lookouts would be relieved every few hours, so everyone would get some sleep at least.

That night, after a meal of shellfish, berries and yams that Mamba and the boys had somehow managed to collect in the dark, they bedded down in a makeshift shelter they'd fashioned from branches and ferns. The Irishman had been rostered for lookout duties on the first shift, so he took his spear and reported to the beachfront. There, he found he was one of three lookouts tasked with guarding the dugouts. His companions were Mamba's younger brother Kulan and the artist Warrane.

The hours passed quickly enough, and John estimated it was around midnight when he and his two companions were relieved by three others.

The Irishman wasn't surprised to find Mamba and the boys fast asleep when he returned to his bivouac. He lay down on a cloak next to Mamba, but found he couldn't get to sleep. It was hot and humid, and there was no breeze to ease the stifling conditions, so he took his cloak and crawled outside. There, alongside the bivouac, he lay down beneath the stars.

Moments later, he was joined by Mamba. "I thought you were asleep," he murmured.

"I was," Mamba said sleepily. "You woke me." She nestled into John's arms and they soon drifted off.

⋆⊱━━⊰⋆

Later, John awoke with a start. He thought he'd heard something. Exactly what, he wasn't sure. He stared into the blackness of the surrounding rainforest.

Realising he'd left his spear inside the bivouac, he retrieved it and then walked around the encampment, looking out for anything unusual.

One shadow appeared darker than the rest. John tensed when he saw the shadow move. "Who is there?" he asked.

"It is me, Moilow," the answering call came.

John relaxed when he recognised Gabirri's voice. The shadowy figure approached, spear in hand, and John saw it was indeed Gabirri.

"Is something wrong, Moilow?" the young native asked.

"I thought I heard something."

"I heard it, too," Gabirri smiled. "And there it is." He pointed across the clearing.

John looked to the far side of the encampment. At first he didn't see it. Only when it moved did he identify it as a wallaby. He felt a little foolish when the wallaby hopped away into the trees.

Gabirri chuckled at John's obvious embarrassment. The two went their separate ways without another word.

John returned to Mamba's side to find she was awake.

"What is the matter?" she asked.

"Wallaby," John said, lying down beside her. In the dark, he couldn't know that Mamba was smiling to herself, and thinking the Moilow of old wouldn't have mistaken the sound of a grazing wallaby for an intruder. Before he knew it, Mamba was naked and she was pulling him over on top of her. At the same time, she removed his loincloth. "What are you up to?" he asked.

"No, Moilow," she giggled, grasping his suddenly upright member. "What are *you* up to?"

John responded by kissing her passionately. He quickly realised Mamba was in no mood for foreplay. She pulled him into her and locked her ankles together behind his back, pulling him even deeper inside.

It had been several days since they'd last made love, and they both came almost immediately. Sleep came almost immediately, too, and they drifted off into the deepest of slumbers, each totally satisfied.

64

❦————❧

I N THE DIM LIGHT OF the predawn, the only sounds around the Kabi encampment were those of the rainforest. It was too early for the kookaburras' dawn chorus, but other birds were beginning to let others of their kind know they were awake. The birdcalls, faint at first, gradually increased in both frequency and volume, and it wasn't long before they were coming thick and fast. Finally, the kookaburras added their chatter to the noise.

That was the sound the Kabi clan members usually woke to whenever they camped in or close to the rainforest.

This particular morning, they were so tired after their voyage to the island and their last minute relocation to the new campsite that most slept through the dawn chorus. John and Mamba were among those who slept on. They were still lying outside their bivouac, oblivious to the world.

One of the first to arise was Banjora, the hunter who had the distinction of being the first clan member ever to see John. He emerged from his bivouac and wandered off into the trees to urinate.

Just inside the treeline, he closed his eyes as he prepared to relieve himself. The ageing Banjora resigned himself to a wait. For some reason he couldn't explain, it was taking him longer these days to begin urinating and even longer to finish, and he was having to pee two or three times a night—an annoyance he was slowly learning to live with. As he stood there, contemplating, he opened his eyes and looked around. Only now did he realise he hadn't seen any sign of the lookouts he knew had been posted around the encampment. The thought crossed his mind that should have seen at least one by now.

Finally, the urine stream began to flow, and he closed his eyes once more, enjoying the feeling of relieving the pressure on his full bladder.

The next sensation he felt was that of a spear entering his throat, its wickedly barbed tip exiting the back of his neck and pinning him to the trunk of the tree just behind him. It had been thrown with such force, after tearing through Banjora's larynx it had cut through the top of his spinal cord and buried itself deep in the trunk. He died quickly—too quick to make a noise other than a brief gurgling sound.

The spear had been thrown by one of twenty-seven Gureng raiders who had surrounded the encampment during the night. They'd been alerted by hunters who had sighted smoke from cooking fires the Kabi had lit after making landfall at their first campsite the previous afternoon. The Gureng had observed their enemies making their way by land and sea to this, their latest encampment, and they'd immediately planned a dawn attack.

The Gureng were not unlike their Moreton Bay cousins the Quandamooka in appearance except they looked even more primitive—and considerably more primitive-looking than the Kabi. All the raiders wore wooden and bone adornments inserted through their ears, and some wore them through their noses, too. And, like the Wanjuri and the Ngadjonjii, their faces were scarified as well as their bodies. While most were armed with spears and woomeras, they all carried heavy nulla nullas fashioned from bone or stone, and it was these they favoured in combat. They were painted for war, too, their usual white ochre markings replaced by the red ochre that symbolised violence amongst the coastal tribes.

Although outnumbered by the Kabi, they had the advantage of surprise for their presence hadn't yet been noticed. They would have attacked earlier if it hadn't been for the larger-than-expected number of lookouts they'd encountered. Besides the three guarding the canoes, they'd stumbled across four others patrolling the camp perimeter and the surrounding rainforest, and it had taken some time to quietly deal with them. They had avoided those guarding the canoes for fear they'd give themselves away.

In the end, it was not a lookout who gave their presence away. It was a young teenage girl who emerged from her family's bivouac and entered the rainforest in search of roots and berries that would complement the morning meal she and her mother had planned. The girl, who was naked, thought she was seeing things when she saw Banjora. At first, her mind wouldn't believe what her eyes were telling her. Then, as it registered the dead man was supported only by the spear that pinned him to the tree, she let out a bone-chilling scream that reverberated throughout the encampment. Her scream was cut short when a raider stepped out from behind a bush and viciously clubbed her over the head, killing her. For good measure, he reversed his nulla nulla and stabbed her with its sharp end. However, the alarm had already been raised.

The encampment came alive as Kabi clan members emerged from their bivouacs with weapons and shields in hand.

The first John knew anything was wrong was when he woke to find Mamba shaking him violently. Still half asleep, he looked around and thought he must be dreaming. Alarmed clan members were shouting and screaming, armed men were running in all directions while terrified women fled with children in hand and, in some cases, with babies in their arms. Several clan members were felled by spears hurled from within the surrounding trees.

John was on his feet now, his own spear in hand. He had brought it with him when he'd decided to bed down outside the bivouac—a habit he'd gotten into long ago. His first thought was for Murrowdooling and Carravanty, and he was relieved to see they were sheltering inside the bivouac.

Murrowdooling emerged from the shelter, his own spear in one hand and John's nulla nulla in the other. He handed the nulla nulla to the Irishman.

"You take your mother and brother," John ordered the boy. "Find a place to hide."

Murrowdooling nodded. He grabbed Carravanty's hand. Mamba grabbed the younger boy's other hand and the three of them ran off toward the nearby beach.

They and other fleeing clan members had to thread their way between the men who were now fighting for their lives.

Surveying the violence around him, John saw the Kabi were in danger of being overwhelmed. Even though they outnumbered their Gureng enemies, they'd been disadvantaged by the element of surprise the raiders had so effectively employed. Four Kabi warriors had already been killed—and that wasn't counting the four lookouts killed earlier or the deaths of Banjora and the teenage girl.

Nearby, Gabirri was holding off two club-wielding Gureng warriors with his spear. Using it as a club, he struck one over the head with the sharp end and jabbed the other in the stomach with the blunt end. The former fell down, dazed, and the latter doubled over, winded. Gabirri promptly drew out his nulla nulla and savagely clubbed both until they stopped moving.

A little further away, Turo had his hands full trying to hold off three raiders. The big warrior was armed only with a nulla nulla, but he used it with devastating effect as he dropped one and then another attacker with two mighty blows. The third attacker, a young native with only one eye, looked as though he'd prefer to run away, but he held his ground and swung his own nulla nulla toward his bigger opponent. Turo easily parried it, and then he jabbed the sharp end of his weapon in the young native's good eye, blinding him. The wounded raider fell to his knees, wailing in agony. Turo left him to his misery, and looked around for his next victim.

The Irishman observed also that three of the Kabi women had joined the fighting. He noted their ferocity matched that of the men. Two of them had armed themselves with shields and spears, and one—Turo's youngest wife—was wielding a nulla nulla. All three handled their weapons with considerable expertise.

Until now, John felt as though he was still in a dream. The whole scene was so surreal. Everything seemed to be happening in slow motion. Things sped up real quick when a raider threw his spear at him. The Irishman threw himself to the ground. The spear flew by where he'd been standing a split-second earlier, but the warrior was onto him in a flash. Surprise registered on the man's face when he realised his opponent was white.

John's attacker flailed at him with two tomahawk-like weapons fashioned from bone. Still on the ground, the Irishman managed to avoid the first blow by rolling to his right. He rolled quickly back to his left in a desperate attempt to avoid the second blow, but was a fraction too slow and the weapon's blade grazed his shoulder. Not enough to immobilise the shoulder, but it drew blood and it hurt like hell. The raider was now standing astride him, ready to deliver the coup de grâce.

The Irishman was in no position to use either his spear or his nulla nulla to defend himself as he'd dropped one weapon, and the other had somehow ended up pinned beneath him. Instinctively, he brought one foot up as hard as he could. He was aiming for his attacker's testicles, and his aim was spot on. The raider fell down, writhing in agony.

John jumped to his feet, intent on finishing the warrior off. He grabbed the two nearest weapons—his attacker's makeshift tomahawks—and brought one of them hard down on the back of the warrior's head, damn near decapitating him.

391

Glancing around, he saw natives everywhere locked in combat. He had to look closely to determine who was who. The death toll was rapidly rising on both sides. John could see a dozen or so bodies, and at least half of them appeared to be Kabi.

Though the Gureng had gotten the better of the conflict at the outset, it was John's assessment that the tide seemed to be turning. He thought despite the rude awakening the Kabi had received they seemed better organised, and they fought with more desperation. That didn't surprise him. After all, they were fighting for their families' lives as well as their own.

Amidst all the shouting, the cries of the wounded and the general sounds of combat, one voice could be heard above all the others. Mirritji, who was in the thick of the action, was constantly shouting orders, directing defenders to fill any gaps that opened up in their defences. The plucky elder was drawing on a lifetime's experience, directing the clan's warriors with guile and deception, and the raiders were beginning to wilt.

The defenders' stocks were boosted by the return of the three lookouts who had been guarding the canoes. They'd been debating whether to stay with the dugouts or join the fray, and they'd opted to join the fray—their rationale being they could always make, borrow or steal canoes later if their own craft were taken or destroyed.

The Kabi received a further boost when three more lookouts arrived to lend a hand. The latest arrivals had been amongst those charged with patrolling the rainforest, and they'd been a mile or two from the encampment when the Gureng attacked. It had taken them until now to make their way back. Resigned to receiving an ear-bashing from Mirritji for allowing their enemies sneak past them in the night, they threw themselves into the battle.

John found himself fighting alongside Mirritji. The elder, who was armed with a nulla nulla and shield, was fighting with the strength and ferocity of a young man. Using his shield as a weapon, Mirritji forced one raider to the ground with it, and then bashed another to the ground with his nulla nulla. John despatched the first of the fallen warriors with one of the two makeshift tomahawks he still carried while Mirritji despatched the other. The pair looked at each other briefly, respect registering in the eyes of each. Then they became separated as the fighting swirled around them.

Out of the corner of his eye, John saw two more raiders coming for him. One was a huge warrior—bigger even than Turo and, for that matter, bigger than any Aborigine he'd ever seen—and he had murder in his eyes. The Irishman wasn't to know the raider was Jirra, the Gurengs' leader and a warrior with a fearsome reputation. The huge warrior wielded a stone club that was so big John doubted he could even raise it above his head.

Holy Mother of God!

Jirra's smaller companion carried a knife and a shield, his eyes only just visible above the top of the shield.

John backed away as the two raiders came for him. Fortunately for him, their number was reduced to one when a spear felled one of them. Unfortunately, the victim was the smaller of the two natives.

Jirra didn't even appear to notice his companion had been felled. He swung his club in a circular motion above his head as he closed in on the Irishman. He, too, couldn't hide his surprise at being confronted by a white.

John, who was back-peddling furiously now, could hear the sound of the club as it *swished* through the air just inches away from his head. He tried to parry the first serious blow using one of his tomahawks, but his weapon disintegrated beneath the force of the mighty blow. Its force jarred every bone and ligament in his right hand and arm, leaving the whole arm numb and temporarily useless. At least he hoped it was temporary.

Jirra was grinning now. He swung his club yet again at John's head, and the Irishman only just managed to duck beneath it. The big warrior swung again, but this time he changed the angle, aiming for his opponent's knee. John avoided it only by diving away. Jirra was onto him before he could regain his feet, and he was sure he was done for.

I didn't think it would end like this.

Mamba and the boys flashed before his eyes as he waited for his opponent to deliver the death blow.

The blow never landed. Jirra's swing was cut short when a Kabi warrior struck the raider from behind. Only when the huge native hit the ground did John see his saviour was Gabirri. His friend glanced at him before delivering another savage blow to the side of his enemy's head with one of two nulla nullas he held. Even then it appeared the big man wasn't dead. His eyelids fluttered and he was groaning.

Gabirri ran off to help Turo who was struggling to hold off two more raiders, leaving John to finish the fallen Jirra.

Using his good arm, John struggled to his feet, reached down and, with his good hand, picked up one of the tomahawks he'd dropped. He was about to put Jirra out of his misery when Mirritji called out to him.

"Leave him, Moilow!" the elder shouted.

Mystified, John looked around at Mirritji.

A breathless Mirritji explained, "He is the Gurengs' leader." He added, "We need him alive."

The sight of their fallen leader was too much for the surviving raiders who turned tail and fled, their numbers now greatly reduced. Even though the conflict had barely lasted five minutes, it appeared they'd lost at least half their men.

Mirritji quickly rounded up a dozen defenders who had received minor wounds at worst, and he sent them after the fleeing Gureng. Their orders were to kill every last one of them if they could. The chosen ones took after their fleeing enemies, vengeance in their hearts.

John thought it likely they would have some success for several of the Gureng survivors seemed to have been badly wounded, and he thought it doubtful they could outrun their fleet-footed pursuers.

Those clan members, like John, who had families and loved-ones, hurried down to the beach to look for them. Mamba and her boys, and indeed most of the women and children, had headed for the beach to escape the raiders.

It was with great relief all the women and children were found to be safe and sound. They'd escaped unscathed. Some had stayed by the canoes. Others had fled along the shoreline and hidden in the rainforest or in one of the many caves to be found along this part of the island.

Murrowdooling had led Mamba and Carravanty to one of those caves. He'd hidden them at the back of the cave, and had stood guard with his spear just inside the entrance in case their enemies came looking for them. Their reunion with John was an emotional one. They had feared he may be dead, and he'd feared they may have been killed as well.

John and his little family returned to the encampment to find the other clan members in a state of grief. The Kabi's death toll was thirteen with as many again suffering wounds of varying severity. All the survivors had lost friends and loved-ones, and, in the space of one bloody skirmish, the clan's fighting force of able-bodied men had been almost halved.

Mamba immediately hurried to comfort bereft clan members and to help care for the wounded. John and Murrowdooling followed her lead, dispensing help wherever they could.

Few of the clan's warriors had escaped unscathed, and most needed attention of some kind. John's injuries were fairly typical. He still had little feeling in his right arm, and he was covered in bruises and abrasions.

Yileen, the healer, scurried from one wounded warrior to another, employing his healing powers and overseeing a small army of female helpers who had volunteered to help him tend the wounded. Under his tutelage, they'd become highly proficient in dressing wounds and injuries.

Able-bodied clan members carried the bodies of loved-ones down to the beach and lay them to rest in one of the caves. There, the bodies would remain until disposed of by way of a mass burial or cremation in the coming days, depending on circumstances. If the threat of attack remained, or, for any other reason a hurried departure was required, then the bodies would be cremated.

Other clan members unceremoniously hauled the bodies of their enemies to one side of the encampment and left them there in a heap. Several warriors took the opportunity to spit or piss on the bodies. One badly wounded warrior even defecated on the upturned face of a raider he'd identified as having caused his injuries. Then he and the others covered the bodies with branches and driftwood before setting them alight.

Men, women and children cheered as the raiders' bodies were reduced to ashes. None except John seemed to notice the sickly smell of burnt human flesh that hung over the site.

Jirra, the raiders' wounded leader, was forced to watch this gruesome ritual. As soon as the huge warrior had regained consciousness, he'd been tied to a stake in the middle of the encampment. Children threw stones at him, and youths spat at him and pissed on him, too, signalling their contempt for the leader of their enemies.

Observing Jirra, John wondered what was in store for the huge man. He had no doubt whatever it was it wouldn't be pleasant.

Jirra's face was a bloody mask as a result of the clubbing he'd received from

Gabirri, and the blood still flowed freely from large gashes the nulla nulla had left in his skull. That he was still alive was a miracle. John was doubtful any other man could have survived such savage blows.

The Irishman didn't have long to wait to see what was in store for the Gureng warrior.

Clan members formed a circle around Jirra as Mirritji and several other elders and warriors began interrogating him. One or two prodded him with the tips of their spears to encourage him to speak the truth.

"Where is your encampment, Jirra?" Mirritji asked. He knew the warrior by name, such was his reputation.

"At the northern end of the island," Jirra mumbled through bleeding lips.

Mirritji looked around at the assembled and nodded, indicating their captive had spoken the truth thus far. Turning back to Jirra, he asked, "How many Gureng dogs are left?"

When Jirra didn't answer, Turo prodded him in the chest with his spear. "How many?" Turo asked, repeating the question Mirritji had put to him.

"There *were* forty of us," the raider said.

Again, Mirritji nodded. That tallied with what other Kabi had told him on the mainland. "Why do you come to the Kabi's land and attack us?" he asked.

Jirra didn't immediately answer. When Turo prodded him again with his spear, the raider spat a mouthful of blood and phlegm at him. It landed flush on Turo's face. Furious, the warrior raised his spear in readiness to skewer his enemy to the stake he was tied to.

"No!" Mirritji ordered. "Not yet."

Turo glared at Jirra as he reluctantly lowered his spear.

Mirritji looked back at the captive. "Why do you come to the Kabi's land and attack us?" he asked again.

"The white man has invaded our land," Jirra said at length. "They kill our people and force us to find new hunting grounds."

That rang true with John who was aware the Gureng's homeland was south of the Kabi's and thus closer to Moreton Bay, which, he knew, was the nearest European settlement. Thus, he thought, it was likely the Gureng would have had contact with whites.

The Kabi, on the other hand, were mystified by the raider's announcement as they had yet to see a European—not knowingly at least.

"Who is this . . . white man . . . you refer to?" Karadji, the shaman, asked.

Ignoring Karadji, Jirra looked around for John. When he saw him, he pointed his jaw toward him. "The Kabi fight beside the white man," he said accusingly.

"He is the white spirit of Moilow," Mirritji said when he realised who the captive referred to.

"He is not a white spirit, and he is not of your blood," Jirra said. "I have seen many like him. He is the white man I speak of. He and his kind come from a land far away."

All eyes turned to John.

"He is a white spirit," Gabirri insisted, echoing Mirritji.

Jirra shook his head. "We Gureng thought the same as you," he said. "But we soon paid for our mistake."

Gabirri stepped forward, his nulla nulla held high. "Liar!" he shouted. "Pointing at John, he said, "He is Moilow!"

Jirra shook his head again. More adamant this time, he said, "No, he is one of the white men I told you about."

Again, the clan members looked at John.

Mirritji walked up to the Irishman. "Is this true?" he asked.

John didn't answer. He knew he was damned if he answered and damned if he didn't.

Talk about being between a rock and a hard place.

He knew he was only alive because the Kabi truly believed he was the white spirit of Moilow, or most of them did at least.

Jirra's declaration was like music to Turo's ears. He stared hard at John, the shaman's recent prophesy that the Kabi's land would be overrun by white spirits still fresh on his mind—and on the minds of a few others as well.

I see white spirits coming. A few at first. Then many thousands until they cover the land like ants.

Recalling the words of Karadji, Turo marched over to John, his nulla nulla raised. Mirritji made no attempt to calm him. Instead, the elder stepped aside and waited to see what transpired.

Turo sensed he'd taken the initiative from Mirritji. Emboldened, he turned to the other clan members. "Remember the words of the shaman," he said. "He warned there would be many thousands of white spirits coming"—he pointed an accusing finger at John—"like him."

Clan members nodded and a number murmured their support for Turo's pronouncement.

None of them noticed Karadji hurry off to his bivouac. The captive's declaration had given the shaman much to ponder. He needed to consult his crystals.

"I have said all along the white spirit is not Moilow," Turo said. He then rounded on John. "You are an imposter!"

Before John could respond, Turo brought his nulla nulla down hard on his head. The Irishman was unconscious before he hit the ground, so he didn't hear Mamba's screams, nor did he hear her boys' cries of distress.

65

BAREGA DISMOUNTED HIS HORSE AT the top of a rise overlooking the same beach the Kabi had launched their canoes from only the previous day. Even from a distance, he could see the tracks the prows of their dugouts had left just above the high water mark in the sand. He lifted his gaze to Great Sandy Island and wondered if John Graham was there.

The tracker had learned to ride a horse in the past eighteen months. The decision to learn hadn't been his. Rather, it had been Marsden's. The captain had insisted that Barega learn to ride, his rationale being that the tracker was spending so much time searching for the Irish fugitive it made sense that he expedite the process by traveling on horseback.

At first, Barega had resisted. He and his ancestors had always travelled overland on foot and had tracked their prey on foot. He'd argued that he could sight spoor and read signs more quickly and more accurately on foot than on horseback. His arguments had fallen on deaf ears. Marsden had insisted, and that was that. If Barega wished to retain his job as the army's head tracker, he had to toe the line.

It had taken Barega half a year to realise tracking on horseback had its advantages. Riding enabled him to reach almost any destination far quicker than he ever could on foot, and when his quarry's tracks were faint or hard to find, there was nothing to stop him dismounting his steed and traveling on foot for a while.

It was another six months before the tracker could claim any level of proficiency astride a horse. Riding wasn't in his blood, and it went against every instinct he had. At first, he had to resist the urge to dismount so that he could feel the earth beneath his feet. Then, ever so slowly, his confidence grew. Now, after another six months, he felt at home in the saddle, and he could ride as well as most of Moreton Bay's soldiers.

On this occasion, his silver crucifix aside, the horse was his only concession to the ways of the white man. Both Marsden and Hogan had tried to convince him to master the use of firearms, but he'd resisted that. He was content to stick with the spear, the nulla nulla and the knife, which he carried with him now. And he still travelled barefoot and wore only his loincloth whenever he ventured away from home.

His brief, to find the Irishman, remained unchanged. Capturing John Graham was now an obsession of Moreton Bay's senior officers, and it was an obsession of his, too. When not pursuing other escapees, he spent the bulk of his time tracking John. He came across his tell-tale boot prints from time to time, but had yet to find him or the clan that sheltered him.

Barega's black, deep-set eyes studied the Kabi family he'd been observing for some time. The five of them—a young couple and their three small children—were eating their mid-day meal next to a cooking fire on the beach. The tracker had no doubt they were Kabi, and he hoped they'd have some news of John. Mounting his horse again, he headed slowly down toward the beach.

It wasn't until Barega arrived on the beach that the couple noticed him or his mount. They leapt to their feet, weapons in hand. The man held a spear in the throwing position while the woman held a nulla nulla threateningly. Neither could take their eyes off the tracker's horse, and Barega realised they'd never seen such an animal before. The couple's children innocently studied the creature and the man astride it, and continued eating, oblivious to any potential threat either may pose.

Barega smiled and dismounted his horse a little distance from the adults so as not to further alarm them. "I bring you goodwill," he said, shrewdly using the Kabi greeting he'd learned.

The Kabi couple hesitantly lowered their weapons. "I accept your goodwill," the young man said still unable to take his eyes off the horse. He and his wife took a backward step when the animal snorted and stamped the sand with one hoof.

Barega settled his horse down then pointed to the marks the canoes had left in the sand. "Is your clan on the island?" he asked, looking at the island behind the couple.

"It is not our clan," the young man said, still suspicious of the stranger and the creature he'd ridden in upon.

Barega switched his gaze to the man's young wife. He eyed her lustfully. Looking back at the man, he asked, "Are the Kabi there?"

The young man nodded. Pointing to the southern end of the island, but still not taking his eyes off Barega or the horse, he said, "The Kabi are at the southern end." He knew with certainty for he was one of those whom Mirritji and the others of his clan had spoken to on the beach only the previous day. "Other tribes are also on the island," he added.

"What tribes?" Barega asked, concerned to learn the Kabi didn't have the island to themselves.

The young man shrugged. He wasn't going to mention the Gureng in case the stranger was of that tribe. He somehow doubted that he was, but if he was wrong he knew that would make them mortal enemies.

"Who are your people?" Barega asked, knowing full well he was Kabi.

"We are Kabi," the man said, annoyed that the stranger was once more eyeing his wife with undisguised lust.

"Do you know if a white man is with the Kabi on the island?" the tracker asked.

The young man nodded. "He is a white spirit," he said. "They called him Moilow."

As Barega digested this, he debated whether to kill the young man and have his way with the woman. He'd been attracted to the woman from the outset, and he felt he had to have her. He also wanted to kill or capture John Graham, and that over-rode all other considerations for the moment. Reluctantly, he nodded to the couple, mounted his horse and galloped off.

Behind him, the couple watched him ride away, still not quite able to believe their eyes. "What is that creature?" the woman asked.

Her husband shrugged. He and his wife immediately put the rider and his mount out of their minds. It was the way of these people. Anything they couldn't explain, they quickly dismissed. All would be explained, they believed, in the Dreaming. Until then, they needed to focus on surviving and meeting the demands of daily life—no easy task.

The tracker galloped south, intent on reporting the Irishman's whereabouts to his masters. He knew time was of the essence. John Graham's clan was on the island, but they could leave at any time. If the soldiers returned before the clan members quit the island, the Irishman would be theirs for the taking.

That thought made him ride harder—that and the knowledge that the Marsdens' maid Orana eagerly awaited his return to Moreton Bay. The young mother on the beach had aroused his desires, and he needed to satisfy those desires urgently.

John regained consciousness to find himself lying, hogtied like a captive pig, on his stomach. Blood flowed into his eyes and mouth from the blow he'd received, blurring his vision and making breathing difficult. There seemed to be a lot of noise and activity around him, but he couldn't make sense of it.

As his senses slowly returned, he saw the clan members were kicking and punching Jirra who, like himself, had also been hogtied. In both cases, their hands had been tied behind their backs, and their ankles tied to their hands so that their backs were arched and the back of their heads pointed toward their heels. It was extremely uncomfortable.

John looked around to see if he could see Mamba or the boys. They were nowhere in sight. Relief flooded through him. He didn't want them to witness this.

The Irishman wasn't to know his family had been confined to the beach. Mirritji had had the foresight to order the lookouts guarding the canoes to keep Mamba and her boys with them. Like John, he didn't want them to see what was happening in the encampment.

Only now did John notice freshly-dug dirt alongside a hole in the ground nearby. He assumed it was a grave.

Not for me, I hope.

Although shallower than most graves, it was certainly long enough and wide enough to accommodate a big man.

Jirra, who was close to the hole—so close he could see down into it—began struggling as two men tried to pick him up. They obviously intended to drop him into the hole. When it became clear they couldn't lift the huge warrior, two youths came to their aid.

Before they dropped Jirra into the hold, Turo stopped them. He'd just noticed John had come round.

"The white imposter should see what is in store for him," Turo said.

Two other men—men John had previously considered allies—ran over to him and carried him over to the hole, laying him down alongside Jirra.

The Irishman recoiled when he saw what awaited the Gureng captive in the bottom of the hole. There, curled up in an ominous coil, was a snake. John identified it immediately as a coastal Taipan, one of the deadliest snakes on the continent. Clearly agitated, the reptile hissed at the clan members and would have struck out at them if it hadn't been contained. Its dark brown colouring, its deep, rectangular block-like head, its unusually large eyes and incredible fangs—the longest of any Australian snake—left John in no doubt it was a Taipan.

Jirra had identified it, too, and he was struggling mightily to escape his bonds. To no avail. The bonds held fast.

Every now and then, the snake tried to crawl out of the hole, but clan members prevented it by pushing it down with pieces of driftwood.

At a nod from Mirritji, the four men standing over Jirra began lowering him into the hole using vines they'd tied around him. They were straining to hold the big man. At the same time, they took care to ensure they didn't over-balance and end up in the hole with him. Clan members crowded around, cheering as their enemy was lowered ever closer to the angry reptile.

John found the whole spectacle too awful to watch, and yet, try as he may, he couldn't take his eyes off the snake. Still hissing, it had retreated to one end of the hole where it awaited its victim.

By now, Jirra had ceased struggling. Credit to him, he didn't plead for mercy or even cry out. John just hoped he could be half as brave if it turned out that it was his turn next.

The Gureng's leader finally reached the bottom of the hole. He'd been lowered so that he faced the end that was occupied by the Taipan. Less than two feet separated one from the other. Still the snake hadn't struck. It was as if it feared a trap.

John and the clan members watched in silence as the snake eyed its fellow captive. The two stared at each other for several long, drawn out moments. All the while, the Taipan's tongue flicked out toward the man who had invaded its space.

Finally, it struck. Uncoiling most of its eight-foot length, it struck three times. It struck so fast, the onlookers only saw one strike. However, the three sets of fang marks on Jirra's face—one on his forehead and one on each cheek—left no doubt how many times the snake had struck.

Still Jirra didn't cry out. Those watching were disappointed their enemy didn't give them the satisfaction of screaming or pleading for mercy.

The Taipan reverted to its coiled-up, defensive attitude, its rectangular head still visible and its eyes still moving about. It was as if it knew the damage had been done, and it only needed to wait a while for its venom to work.

John was aware the bite of this particular variety of snake was always fatal. At Moreton Bay, in a rare moment of sobriety, Doctor Andrews had told him and another convict he'd never heard of a human ever surviving the bite of a Taipan. The Scotsman had advised them that the snake's venom affected the victim's nervous system and prevented the blood from clotting. Andrews said victims inevitably died a quick but painful death.

And so it turned out for Jirra. The big man began vomiting, his face contorted in pain. Onlookers weren't to know his pain had as much to do with muscle cramps, which his bonds had caused, as it had to do with the venom that now coursed through his body. Convulsions followed, and Jirra's whole body twitched and convulsed so violently it seemed his bonds may break after all.

Finally, after what seemed an eternity to John, and no doubt to Jirra, too, the captive lay still.

Even from several feet away, the Irishman could see the big man was dead.

The Taipan struck its victim again—on Jirra's neck this time—for good measure. It was as if it had been biding its time. Now, it seemed, it just wanted to make doubly sure its victim was dead.

As before, John and the others had only seen one strike. However, two sets of fang marks on the victim's neck signalled that it had struck twice this time.

The same four men who had lowered Jirra into the hole pulled him from it. They had to work harder to achieve this, and they were sweating by the time the huge body was hauled up onto the grass.

Clan members converged on their enemy's body and kicked it and stomped on it, stopping only when they'd reduced the carcass to a bloody, unrecognisable pulp.

One by one, they turned their attention back to John.

It was Mirritji who spoke first. "Is there any reason this man"—he looked at John—"should not meet the same fate as Jirra?"

"No!" said Turo. "Glaring at John, he added, "I have said all along he is not Moilow. He is a white devil, and he will weaken the Kabi just as the Gureng have become weak." He added, "He must die."

Clan members murmured their agreement, and several elders nodded.

Gabirri stepped forward. Looking down at John, he said, "It might be, as you say, that he is not Moilow. But he has shown the same courage. When the Gureng attacked, it was Moilow who fought alongside us."

The elders and other clan members listened intently to the respected young warrior. Blood still flowed from a head wound he'd received earlier—a reminder to all that he had earned the right to speak.

Gabirri asked, "Has he not hunted with us? Fished with us?" He eyed the elders. "Has he not been a husband to Mamba, a father to her children, a brother to us all?"

Several elders nodded.

Turo couldn't restrain himself. "He is not Moilow!" he shouted. "He is an imposter!"

Arguing broke out between those who leaned toward Turo's viewpoint and those who leaned toward Gabirri's.

Mirritji held his hand up for silence. When he had the attention of all, he quietly said, "Both Turo and Gabirri speak truth from the heart."

Clan members could see the wisdom in the elder's words.

Mirritji looked at John, and John instinctively knew what was coming. "However," the elder said, "the shaman's prophesy has been proven correct. Jirra"—he glanced at what was left of the raider's body—"said the white man has invaded his land. The Gureng dog said his kind"—he pointed to the Irishman—"killed members of his tribe and forced them to find new hunting grounds." Mirritji took a deep breath. He declared, "And so . . . the white man who calls himself Moilow must die."

All but a few clan members cheered wildly. Gabirri, Nowra, Warrane, Yileen and a handful of others—notably those related by blood to Mamba—remained silent.

Turo and another man picked John up and held him over the hole. As Jirra had done, the Irishman struggled for all he was worth. Unlike Jirra, the Irishman cried out and pleaded for his life. His pleas were ignored.

John was now hanging just a few feet above the Taipan, suspended from vines that had been tied around him earlier. "Jesus, no!" he screamed. "For God's sake, stop them someone!" His cries intensified as he found himself being lowered toward the snake, which was now hissing in anticipation. Its eyes locked onto John's, and the Irishman felt as though he was falling into a hypnotic state.

When he was only a couple of feet above the Taipan's swaying head, he heard a commotion above him. He thought he heard the shaman's voice, but he couldn't be sure. To his relief, he felt himself being pulled up out of the hole. Below him, the snake struck out at him in frustration, but it was well short and the Irishman was safely out of the hole before it could try again.

John once more found himself lying face-down on the grass. The Irishman looked around and saw Karadji in earnest conversation with Mirritji and the other elders. He could see the shaman referred constantly to something he was holding in one hand, but from where he lay he couldn't see what it was he held. Nor could he hear what was being said. He noticed Turo had also joined the elders, and he could tell he wasn't at all happy about what he was hearing.

"The crystals have spoken," Karadji informed the elders. "They told me bad luck will befall the clan if we kill the white spirit. Many, many seasons of bad luck."

"But—" Turo began to object. He held his tongue when the shaman and the elders glared at him. Not even the belligerent Turo dare argue with Karadji.

Mirritji looked over to where John lay. Turning back to the shaman, he asked, "What do the crystals say we do with him?"

Karadji stared at John for a long time. Returning his gaze to the crystals, he said, "They tell me the white spirit must be forever banished, alone, into the wilderness." He stressed the word *alone*.

Mirritji and the others considered this in silence.

The shaman continued, "That is not all the crystals tell me."

The others looked at him expectantly.

"They tell me the Gureng will soon be reinforced by others of their tribe," Karadji said. "Our enemies will return soon in even greater numbers. And so we must return to the mainland at first light tomorrow." He added, "It is then, and not before, that the white spirit must be cast out into the wilderness." The shaman didn't wait to be questioned. Returning his precious crystals to a hidden pocket in his cloak of many colours, he turned and walked back to his bivouac.

The men looked to Mirritji.

After a moment's thought, the elder said, "You heard the shaman. We must prepare to return to the mainland at first light. Until then"—he pointed to John—"keep him in a cage." Mirritji walked off, leaving Turo and the others to carry out his orders.

66

·ε·——·з·

JOHN REACHED THROUGH THE NARROW gap between the bars of the small bamboo cage that was now his prison and stroked Mamba's face. "It will be alright," he assured her, putting on a brave face for her sake and for the sake of Murrowdooling and Carravanty.

"How can you say that, Moilow?" Mamba sobbed. "Soon you will be out of our lives," she said, dissolving into tears. She'd been beside herself since learning of the fate that awaited her beloved Moilow.

John looked at the boys and shrugged as if to say there was nothing he could do about the predicament he'd found himself in. In the moonlight, he could see both boys were upset. Carravanty was close to tears. Murrowdooling remained stoic, but the Irishman could tell he was worried.

Since the onset of darkness a short while earlier, John had been imprisoned in a bamboo cage the clan's fishermen normally used for trapping eels. Too low and too narrow to either stand up or lie down, he could only sit with his back bowed, his arms wrapped around his shins and his chin resting on his knees; and naked apart from his boots, he was cold, sore, tired and miserable. He was also relieved. Relieved to be alive. Twice that day—once during the morning's conflict and again when he had been condemned to share Jirra's fate—he'd nearly died. Whatever strife he may be in now, he told himself, was preferable to being skewered by an enemy's spear or sharing a hole in the ground with a deadly snake.

John's heart went out to Mamba and the boys. Much as he loved them, he was upset that Mirritji had given in to Mamba's pleas that she and the boys be allowed to be with him.

They shouldn't have to see me like this.

Like him, they were at a loss to make sense of everything that had happened since the attack on the clan that morning. Events had moved so fast they were all in shock.

All around them, the wailing and chanting of grieving loved-ones filled the night as clan members mourned the loss of friends and family members. For the younger clan members, the day just gone had been the bloodiest and saddest in their short lives.

John forced himself to think about the challenges now facing Mamba and the boys. Worried though he was for his own welfare, he was more worried about theirs. He suddenly reached out and gripped Murrowdooling's arm. "In case I don't get a chance to talk to you tomorrow . . . you take care of your mother and your brother," he said. "Understand?"

Murrowdooling nodded. "Yes, Moilow," he said.

404

"Good." John could see the boy understood, and he was in no doubt he would do as he'd been asked.

He's a good lad is my boy.

Looking at Carravanty, he reached out and ruffled the lad's hair. "And you do what your brother says, young man," he said.

Carravanty nodded with all the seriousness of his older brother. He was growing up fast, and John regretted he wouldn't be around to see how he turned out.

The Irishman looked at Mamba. "Take the boys back to the bivouac now," he said.

Mamba shook her head. Turning to the boys, she said, "Go back to the shelter . . . and stay there."

Murrowdooling immediately led his younger brother back to their bivouac.

"You should go, too," John said to Mamba. The look on her face told him she wasn't going anywhere.

Mamba sat down, her back resting against the bamboo bars of the cage. She sighed as John gently caressed her neck and shoulders. "What will become of us, Moilow?" she asked.

John didn't answer her. He'd been asking himself the same question.

As John and Mamba settled in for a long, uncomfortable night in the open, leading members of Moreton Bay's community—military and civilian—were arriving at the Moreton Bay Junior School for an official function. The occasion was to celebrate milestones the school had achieved—not the least being Helen's recent promotion to the position of head mistress.

Since the school opened early the previous year, it had gone from strength to strength—something Helen's benefactors, the Browns, insisted was a reflection of their young colleague's teaching prowess and youthful energy. In a little less than two years, the school's role had expanded to thirty-nine, necessitating the construction of a third classroom and the hiring of two more teachers. The new teachers—one male and one female—were both recent arrivals from England and were both older than Helen. In the case of the new female teacher, she was older by some years.

The school's expansion reflected the impressive growth of Brisbane Town and the penal settlement. More new settlers, soldiers and convicts were now flooding into the area, and with them, or with the settlers and soldiers at least, came more children. Almost half the school's role was made up of children of the settlement's married soldiers whose number was increasing all the time. For this reason, Lord Cheetham had received the Governor's agreement that the army should finance the cost of the school's extensions.

The latest of those extensions—the third classroom—was the venue for tonight's function, and it quickly filled to capacity. Attendees were here to listen to Helen's benefactor, William Brown, who had arrived from Sydney Town with his wife earlier in the day to talk about plans in the pipeline to open a school for older children. Currently, there was no schooling for Moreton Bay's older children, and the Browns wished to rectify that quickly. They had the full blessing of the townspeople, the army and, most importantly, the elected members of the newly-formed Moreton Bay District Council. All six of those elected members were here tonight, and for that the Browns and Helen were grateful. They were grateful because they realised the army's generosity couldn't be relied on forever, and future expansion of the area's educational services and facilities would need to be financed by civic means.

The front row seats were occupied by the councillors, the Browns, the two new teachers, and Helen and her father.

When Captain Marsden considered all who were intending to attend the function were present, he stood and called the meeting to order. The decision that he chair it had been forced on him after Cheetham had advised him he couldn't do the honours. Marsden was well aware why his superior had opted out. The commandant was increasingly incapacitated these days as a result of his opium addiction. So much so that if the rumour mill could be believed even the Governor was becoming concerned. Cheetham's demotion was considered by many to be only a matter of time. For the past year or so, he had been commandant in name only. Marsden, to all intents and purposes, was now the commandant—something all except Cheetham recognised.

"Ladies and gentlemen, if I can have your attention," Marsden said. When the assembled quietened, he announced, "It is my pleasure to welcome tonight's guest speaker"—he motioned toward Mister Brown—"my good friend William Brown."

Mister Brown thanked Marsden. After sharing with his audience an amusing tale of a night spent drinking with the captain in London in their single days, he succinctly outlined his plans to expand Moreton Bay's educational services to accommodate older children. He didn't need to remind his audience that, as things stood, once pupils of the junior school turned fourteen their parents had to send them to Sydney Town if they were to continue their schooling. Nor did he need to remind them few parents could afford that.

The guest speaker then announced that he had a purchase option on a vacant two-acre property across the road from the junior school, which he considered a very suitable site for the new school he and his wife were proposing. Looking directly at the councillors in the first row not five feet away from him, he said all that was preventing the new facility from proceeding was finance. The councillors fidgeted before his gaze, aware the pressure was on them.

Mister Brown went on to summarise the impressive growth of Moreton Bay's Junior School. Before he was through, no-one in the audience was in doubt that Helen was the main reason for the school's growth and success. Captain Marsden glowed with pride as the speaker praised Helen's abilities as a teacher and as an organiser.

Helen found her benefactor's effusive praise more than a little embarrassing, but she smiled graciously.

At the end of the address, none applauded more enthusiastically than Missus Brown and Helen's teaching colleagues. They alone—other than Captain Marsden himself perhaps—knew how tirelessly Helen had worked to progress the school and help its young pupils better themselves.

Joining in the applause was Lieutenant Hogan. Unknown to Helen, the officer had snuck into the crowded room and occupied the last remaining seat at the back.

Hogan still carried a torch for the young woman. Even though they'd hardly shared more than a dozen words since he had tried to speak to her outside the schoolhouse over a year ago, relations between them had thawed to the extent they now acknowledged each other on the odd occasion they came across each other.

In recent weeks, Hogan had gone out of his way to *accidentally* bump into Helen—sometimes when she shopped after school, twice after the Sunday church service at the army chapel and once when she was riding along the riverbank. So far, he thought, she would think their meetings innocent, and, he hoped, she'd think he was at tonight's function in an official capacity as a representative of the army. That was why he was in uniform now. He knew her father wouldn't be fooled—the captain had already scowled his way when he noticed him from the front of the room—but Hogan wasn't going to be deterred.

Well-wishers stayed behind to congratulate Helen and the Browns on the school's progress. Hogan hung back, hoping to have a word with Helen, as the crowd thinned.

Only now did Helen notice her former fiancé. Their eyes locked for the briefest of moments, and she felt herself blushing. The young woman wasn't altogether surprised to see Hogan. She had noticed their paths crossed quite frequently of late, and she suspected it wasn't always accidental. She'd come to realise she still had feelings for the dashing lieutenant. She just hoped her feelings didn't show.

Since calling off her engagement, Helen hadn't exactly been living the life of a nun. She'd had no shortage of suitors and she had enjoyed the company of several eligible young men. She still saw two of them on a regular basis. One was a junior army officer, the other the son of the town's seed merchant. And during occasional visits to Sydney Town, she socialised with a good looking young doctor Missus Brown had introduced her to. However, none matched up to Hogan, and she considered none of them a serious prospect for marriage.

Soon, only Helen, the Browns, the two new teachers, and Marsden and Hogan remained.

Missus Brown spotted the lieutenant and hurried over to him. Before Helen knew it, the woman was dragging Hogan over to her.

"Look who I found," a beaming Missus Brown enthused.

Hogan smiled at the others, but he had eyes only for Helen.

"Good evening, Lieutenant Hogan," Helen said.

"Good evening, Miss Marsden," Hogan said, gallantly kissing Helen's hand. "May I congratulate you"—he turned to the others—"and all of you for the wonderful progress you are making here."

"Isn't it grand!" Missus Brown said before anyone else could answer. Ever a fan of the good lieutenant, the matchmaking side of her brain was working overtime. "This deserves a celebration," she announced. "Let us all meet at our hotel for a drink." The establishment she referred to was the newer and better of the township's two hotels—the one she and Mister Brown always stayed at when they visited.

Everyone but Helen and her father thought that a good idea. The captain made his apologies and excused himself, advising all that he had an early start in the morning. On his way out, he had a quiet word to Helen. "Remember, you have school in the morning, young lady," he said.

"Papa," Helen smiled. "You make it sound as if I am still a school pupil."

"A father never wants to admit his daughter has grown up," Marsden whispered, kissing Helen's cheek. Before stepping outside, he added, "Your mother would be very proud of you tonight . . . I know I am."

"Thank you, Papa." Before Helen could excuse herself from the late-night drinks Missus Brown had suggested, she found herself being steered out the door between the Browns and her fellow teachers.

Outside, they found a horse-drawn cart and its driver awaiting them. They headed for it. As they walked, Helen avoided looking behind her to see if Hogan was following. Somehow she sensed he was—and she wasn't at all sure how she felt about that.

The conversation in the hotel's bar was somewhat forced. Despite the Browns' best efforts to keep the mood gay and light, Helen and Hogan weren't sure what to say or how to act in each other's company. It was an unusual situation and neither understood the required protocol.

Finally, Mister and Missus Brown gave their apologies and retired for the night. One by one, Helen's teaching colleagues excused themselves until only she and the lieutenant remained.

After a strained silence, Hogan said, "Your father looked very proud of you tonight, Helen."

The young woman nodded, but offered no comment.

After two more failed attempts to start a discussion, Hogan once more lapsed into silence.

Finally, Helen smiled at the lieutenant who, she could see, was starting to think he was wasting his time. "I haven't made it easy for you tonight, have I Desmond," she said.

Hogan was taken aback. Before he could respond, Helen added, "In fact, I haven't made it easy for you this past year or two, have I?"

"No, you haven't," the lieutenant said when he found his voice at last. He returned her smile and wondered what had prompted her change of heart. It was, after all, the first sign of any affection he'd had from her in nearly two years.

Hogan would have been surprised to learn that Helen suspected their impromptu meetings of late were anything but accidental. That she'd said nothing to deter him was a reflection of the feelings she still harboured for him. She was mature enough to admit that much to herself. Where those feelings would lead, she wasn't sure. Only now, sitting here with him, did she acknowledge to herself that she was willing to find out.

They both spoke at once.

"You first," Hogan said, motioning to Helen to take the lead.

"I . . . It was good to see you this evening," she said.

Hogan smiled and, for the second time that night, his eyes locked with hers.

Suddenly flustered, and fearing things were moving too quickly, Helen stood up. "I really must go," she said.

"Allow me to walk you home," Hogan said.

Helen declined the invitation, but her unexpected escort insisted.

Stepping out onto the street, Helen allowed Hogan to lead her toward the nearby cottage she rented. They hadn't gone more than a few steps when she stopped and turned to him. "How do you know where I live, Lieutenant Hogan?" she asked. Helen already knew the answer. She had spotted him following her home after she'd been out shopping the previous week.

"I . . . um . . . it was just an educated guess."

"I'm sure," Helen smiled.

They resumed walking. After a few more steps, Helen put her arm through Hogan's. It seemed the most natural thing in the world—to both of them.

One block later, they stopped outside Helen's cottage. They turned and looked at each other.

Helen said, "I would invite you in, but . . ."

Hogan smiled. "I understand." He added, "Thank you for this evening." He leaned forward to kiss Helen's cheek, but she turned so that her lips met his.

Their kiss was brief, but passionate.

Helen pulled away, embarrassed by her brazenness.

"I would like to do this again sometime, Helen" an earnest Hogan said.

"So would I, Desmond," Helen replied. She hurried inside, closing the front door behind her and leaving a flabbergasted Hogan on the doorstep. Standing inside, her back against, the door, she smiled to herself as she listened to the lieutenant whistling to himself as he walked away. It was, she thought, a contented whistle.

67

J OHN'S TRANSFER BACK TO THE mainland next morning was left until the canoes'
second crossing. Mamba, Murrowdooling and Carravanty were among those in
the first. Mirritji had thought it best they be kept apart. The compassionate elder
didn't want the day ahead to be any more difficult for them or for John than it
already was.

Departing Great Sandy Island had been delayed by the need to farewell those clan
members who had died in the violence of yesterday. In the interests of safety, the
traditional observation of complex and lengthy burial rites had been sacrificed for a
hasty departure. The bodies had been removed from the cave in which they had been
left overnight, and they'd been cremated on the beach. Loved-ones had then
scattered the ashes in the sea.

It was mid-morning before the clan's three canoes brought John and the
remaining clan members over from the island. The prisoner, who was still naked
apart from his boots, was seated in the middle of the smallest dugout. He was stiff
and sore after the events of yesterday. A cramped night spent in the bamboo cage
had done nothing for his physical state. He was hungry and desperately thirsty, too,
as he'd been allowed no food or water.

John climbed out of the canoe and looked around for Mamba. It didn't take long
to spot her and the boys. They were waving at him. He went to go to them, but was
prevented by Turo who brandished his spear threateningly. It was then he realised
that Mamba and the boys were also being kept away from him. Two youths had been
tasked with guarding them.

The Irishman noticed the other clan members were talking excitedly. Those who
had arrived on the beach first had immediately seen the hoof tracks Barega's horse
had left in the sand above the high tide mark, and they were discussing them with
those who had just arrived.

It was a little while before John realised the tracks had been left by a horse. He
guessed its rider was a soldier, or a new settler perhaps, and he wondered if the rider
had been looking for him.

Arguments broke out as some clan members claimed the tracks had been left by a
giant lizard, and some swore they'd been left by a demon from the Dreamtime.
Clearly, none of them had ever seen a horse. The Kabi couple who had spoken to
Barega the previous day could have enlightened them, but they were long gone.

John looked back to check on his family and noticed that Murrowdooling had
joined a group of hunters who were heading for the plateau above the beach. All
carried spears, and it was obvious they were heading out to hunt. The dramatic

events of the last day or two meant there had been no time for hunting, so food was in short supply.

Murrowdooling walked purposefully, two spears and woomera in hand, and, if John wasn't mistaken, he was wearing his cloak—the one Mamba said had belonged to Moilow. He watched the boy until he disappeared from view, and he feared that would be the last time he'd ever see him.

A short while later, on the plateau, Murrowdooling stopped to look back at the beach. It was so far away, he couldn't recognise John or any of the clan members. Two other hunters nearby motioned to him to join them. Murrowdooling shook his head, indicating he wished to hunt alone. They ran off into the rainforest that bordered the plateau, leaving him alone.

Mamba's oldest boy headed directly inland. He ran fast now, aware the success of what he was planning depended on his returning to the beach in time to speak to John before he was cast out into the wilderness.

Beneath the cloak that until yesterday had been John's, or Moilow's, he wore John's loincloth over his own, and he carried on his hip one of the makeshift tomahawks the Irishman had used in battle the previous morning. He also carried a bag Mamba had filled with fruit, nuts and smoked fish and eel that she'd hastily prepared.

The boy had realised food, weapons and clothes would greatly improve John's odds of survival. Hence the urgency he was giving this, his most important mission ever. He was intending to leave the provisions for John to find at a place they were both familiar with—alongside the lake the clan had camped beside only three nights earlier.

Murrowdooling recalled the trek from the lake to the beach had taken clan members several hours. However, traveling alone the fleet-footed boy had no doubt he could reach it and return to the beach in a fraction of that time. Whether that would be soon enough to intercept John before he disappeared forever into the wilderness, only time would tell. He pushed himself harder, his feet flying over the grassy plain.

On the beach, clan members watched in silence as John was formally cast out of the clan. The procedure, which the Kabi had followed since time began, was a simple one: the banished clan member—in this case the man they'd known as Moilow— walked a gauntlet between two lines of youths and men who prodded him with their spears as he passed by. The prods were none too gentle either, and his naked torso was covered in fresh bruises and cuts before he reached the far end of the gauntlet. And that was on top of those injuries he'd suffered the previous day.

As a final indignity, the outcast had been stripped of his boots, too. So he now had to venture into the wilderness completely naked. He wasn't too concerned about having to go barefoot for he'd done without his boots a lot in recent times.

It was beholden upon every able-bodied man in the clan to contribute to the outcast's suffering as he departed, so Gabirri and others John considered friends were among those prodding and jabbing him with their spears. Turo made sure he got in two heavy jabs—one in each buttock.

The only sound that could be heard, apart from the occasional grunt of pain from John, was the sobbing of Mamba and Carravanty who watched from afar as the man they loved was banished from their lives. The Irishman looked back and smiled grimly at the pair as he walked resolutely up the beach toward the nearby plateau. His heart was heavy at the thought he would likely never see them again, and he resisted the urge to look back a second time for fear he would break down.

"Moilow!" a plaintive Mamba cried.

Still John didn't look back. If he had he'd have seen clan members prevent Mamba from running to him. She was distraught and her cries carried to him, causing him to miss a step and almost stumble as he reached the track leading up to the nearby plateau.

On arriving at the plateau, he debated which way to head. Only now did he realise he'd given no thought to what he would do or where he would go. He'd been hoping for a miracle—a miracle that never came.

North or south . . . or west?

He looked inland, and thought of heat and blowflies, droughts and bushfires, flash floods and lack of wild game; he looked south and thought of Moreton Bay and soldiers and the hangman's noose: he looked north and thought of sailing ships and freedom. "North it is," he said to himself, and so he struck off to his right, intent on following the coast north.

As he walked, he tried to ignore his hunger and his thirst, and he tried to ignore the pain his wounds and injuries caused him.

He also tried to ignore the pain he already felt from his enforced separation from Mamba and the boys. That pain was the worst of all. What really hurt was he hadn't been able to properly say goodbye.

A small billabong near-hidden amongst ant hills caught his eye. He hurried over to it, knelt down and drank his fill before resuming his trek northwards. A goanna, which had been sunning itself on a rock, scurried away, startled by the Irishman. John was equally startled. He hadn't seen it until the last moment. It was a reminder he needed to stay alert in case of snakes. His near-death experience with the coastal Taipan remained with him.

Ahead of him was dense rainforest. He debated whether to skirt around it, but he stayed on course and it wasn't long before he found himself in the darkness of the forest.

Only moments before he'd disappeared from view, Murrowdooling had caught sight of him. The boy had sprinted all the way back from the lake—such was his desperation to intercept John. Now wearing only his own loincloth, and armed with only one spear, he was breathing hard and covered in sweat. "Moilow!" he shouted, determined to attract John's attention.

In the rainforest, John hesitated.

What was that?

"Moilow!" It was louder this time.

Murrowdooling!

John recognised the boy's voice. He retraced his steps and almost literally bumped into Murrowdooling as he emerged from the trees.

"Murrowdooling!" John said, embracing the boy. "What are you doing here?"

When the boy was able to extricate himself from John's embrace, he quickly relayed what he'd been up to.

The Irishman listened with growing pride as Murrowdooling explained he'd hidden provisions for him alongside the lake they'd camped next to. "A spear you say, and a woomera?" he asked.

"And your cloak and loincloth." The boy added, "Also food supplies."

"Next to the lake, you say?"

"Yes. Remember Mootemu's bivouac?"

John cast his mind back. He nodded. It was the closest bivouac to the lake. He remembered it well.

"I left them hidden there, in the remains of his bivouac." Murrowdooling looked around nervously. He and the other boys were under strict orders not to speak to or interact with John, and he was aware he'd be severely punished if they were seen together.

John picked up on the boy's nervousness. "You had better go," he said. In case of prying eyes, he stepped back into the trees so that he couldn't be seen by anyone else. Now he could only see the boy's face through the foliage. "Look after your mother and brother, boy," he said.

Murrowdooling nodded.

There was so much more John wanted to say to him, but the boy had already gone. Looking at where he'd been a moment earlier, he murmured, "I love you, son."

Within an hour, John had reached the lake and found the lifesaving provisions Murrowdooling left for him. They were exactly where he'd said they'd be—hidden in Mootemu's vacated bivouac.

Now, wearing his loincloth and cloak, and armed with his tomahawk, spear and woomera, he felt better prepared to face the world—even if he no longer had his boots. Surviving alone in the wilderness without clothes or weapons would have been a tough ask, of that he was sure.

He checked the contents of the flax bag Murrowdooling had left, and was delighted to find the boy hadn't been exaggerating. It was full of all the foods he'd mentioned, and a few more treats besides.

John sat down and enjoyed his first meal in quite some time. He hadn't eaten in a day-and-a-half, and he was famished.

While he ate, he thought about the turn of events that had brought him to this new crossroads in his life. He also analysed his short and long-term goals.

Short-term goal's easy. Survive.

It was his long-term goal that wasn't so clear. His first thought had been to connect with a ship. Now, as the reality of being separated from Mamba and the boys set in, he wasn't so sure. Truth be known, he was missing them badly.

68

THAT NIGHT, AS JOHN SPENT his first night alone in the wilderness in four years, Hogan wined and dined Helen in the same hotel they'd socialised in with the Browns only twenty-four hours earlier.

After separating the previous evening, both had experienced a near-sleepless night. And both were excited by the realisation a spark may have been lit.

A large bunch of fresh-picked red roses had greeted Helen on her arrival at school that morning. One of her early-bird pupils advised her that the gentleman hadn't left his name, but the description left no doubt who the bearer of gifts was. Not that there was ever any doubt.

Hogan had left Helen the previous evening determined to remain a little aloof. After all, he reasoned, he'd been doing all the chasing and it was high time she chased him. Come morning, all such intentions had evaporated. He *had* to see her again— and soon. And so he'd arisen early, intent on delivering a bouquet of flowers to the schoolhouse before Helen reported to work. The town's florist, whose shop doubled as a tobacco and gun shop, wasn't yet open, and so Hogan had raided a homeowner's flower garden to pick the roses he desired. He promised himself he would recompense the unsuspecting homeowner.

Later, during Helen's lunch break, he had engineered yet another of his spontaneous meetings, inviting her to join him that evening for dinner, and, to his surprise, and hers, she'd accepted.

Although secretly delighted she was being pursued once more by the dashing lieutenant, Helen had surprised herself by being such a pushover. It had always been her plan, *if* there was ever to be a reconciliation with her former fiancé, she would make him work hard to regain her affections.

Looking at him now, after two glasses of wine and a romantic dinner by candlelight, she could feel her inhibitions evaporating.

Hogan raised his glass. "I would like to propose a toast," he smiled.

Helen raised her own glass.

Hogan continued, "To the most beautiful woman in all of New South Wales."

They clinked glasses.

Blushing, Helen tried to think of a witty response to hide her embarrassment. She thought of saying something like, "So you are saying there is someone outside New South Wales more beautiful." Instead, she said, "Thank you, Desmond."

Hogan reached out and brushed a strand of blonde hair from her eyes. He was about to lean forward and kiss her, but he stopped himself when he realised other diners were watching.

The restaurant was three-quarters full. Around half the patrons were guests of the hotel. The remainder were a mix of local settlers and married soldiers. In most cases, the latter were in the company of their wives—the exception being an officer who was in the company of another soldier's wife. The absentee soldier was on an overnight patrol in the hinterland behind Moreton Bay, but that's another story.

A waiter approached Hogan. "More wine, sir?" he asked.

The lieutenant looked at Helen. She shook her head. Hogan said to the waiter, "No thanks, just the bill."

The waiter bowed and hurried off. The couple smiled at each other. Behind the pleasantries, each wondered what the other was thinking.

Helen hoped her escort couldn't read her mind. She was wondering whether she should invite Hogan in for a nightcap when he walked her home.

Hogan was thinking he would accept her invitation if she invited him in for a nightcap. For that matter, he was thinking he'd accept her invitation if she invited him in for anything.

The waiter soon returned. After Hogan settled the account, he offered his arm to Helen. She linked her arm through his, and allowed him to escort her from the premises. He'd left his horse in the stables behind the hotel, and he hoped he'd have no further use for his steed that night.

Outside, they walked slowly along the near-deserted street. It was a moonless night, but they were guided by the dim light of lanterns hanging from shop billboards. The only sounds were the croaking of frogs in a nearby creek and the occasional *whoosh* of bats flying to or from their hidden roost. The bats were normally only ever seen at dusk, and then only as sinister black shapes against the dark sky.

Neither spoke until they arrived outside Helen's cottage. Then they both spoke at once—something they'd done once already that night and once the previous night. They laughed.

"You go first this time," Helen said.

"No," Hogan insisted. "Ladies first."

Helen could feel her heart rate rising. She could also feel herself blushing, and she was thankful there were no lanterns near her cottage. If there had been, she was in no doubt her escort would have guessed what she was thinking just by looking at her face. Finally, she asked, "I . . . I wondered if you would like to come in . . . for a nightcap?"

"Yes . . . thank you." Hogan hoped his own nervousness didn't show. He could tell Helen was nervous.

Helen was shaking by the time she opened the front door. She'd left a lantern on in the drawing room, and she led Hogan along the passageway toward it. In the drawing room, she turned to her guest. "Make yourself at home while I prepare drinks," she said. She disappeared into the adjoining kitchen, leaving her companion alone for the moment.

Hogan filled in time observing his surroundings. The drawing room was neat and unpretentious. Portrait paintings of the cottage's absentee owner and his family hung from the walls.

The clinking of glasses in the adjoining room was followed by the sound of breaking glass, prompting Hogan to hurry through to investigate. He entered the kitchen to see Helen had dropped a glass on the floor, and she was now picking up the pieces. "Here, let me," he said, hurrying over to assist her.

"I am so clumsy!" Helen admonished herself.

"Nonsense. It can happen to anyone," Hogan assured her. He quickly collected the remaining glass fragments and dropped them into a rubbish bin. That done, he turned to find Helen selecting a replacement glass from a cupboard. Without thinking, he walked up behind her, placed his arms around her waist and kissed her neck. He immediately regretted his hastiness. "I . . . I'm sorry," he said.

Helen didn't respond. Not trusting herself to speak, she placed her hands over Hogan's. They were still resting lightly against her tummy, and they felt hot to her touch. The heat spread rapidly, and she gasped as she felt a delicious fluttering in her very core. Before she knew what she was doing, she turned so that she was facing him. She pressed her hips hard against his and she kissed him passionately.

Hogan literally swept Helen off her feet. Picking her up, he asked, "Where's your bedroom?"

"Along the hallway!" a breathless Helen gasped.

Hogan carried her into the dimly lit hallway, lightly bumping her head on the door frame in his haste. "Sorry!" he muttered.

Helen was too distracted even to notice. "Hurry!" she ordered. She could feel her ardour rising.

Hogan needed no extra encouragement. "Which room?" he asked as he stumbled along the hallway.

"Next one," Helen said.

Reaching the door to Helen's bedroom, Hogan resisted the temptation to kick it down. He freed one hand and opened the door. In the faint light coming from the lantern in the drawing room, he could just make out a four-poster bed against the far wall.

"Over there!" Helen pointed at the bed. She couldn't wait much longer.

Hogan reached the bed in two long strides and unceremoniously dropped Helen on top of it. He then found himself on top of her. They began tearing at each other's clothes, desperate to have each other.

After much panting and fumbling, they were both naked. Technically, Hogan wasn't quite naked: his trousers and undershorts were still around his ankles because he'd yet to remove his boots. He reached down to pull them off, but Helen restrained him.

"Later!" she ordered, guiding Hogan into her.

Their lovemaking lasted all of thirty seconds, so desperate were they to have each other and to satisfy their lust. They came to together in a glorious explosion of pent-up passion. So exhausted were they, they fell asleep almost immediately.

Theirs was a deep, contented sleep.

Helen woke with a start, thinking she'd slept in and was late for work. She relaxed when she realised it was still dark, and she remembered it was the weekend so there was no school until Monday.

Then she remembered she wasn't alone.

Hogan's warm breath on her back reminded her that she shared her bed with another. His deep, steady breathing told her that he was sleeping.

Recollections of their night of lovemaking came back to her in vivid flashes. After that first time, they'd made love two or possibly three times more. She'd lost count. Each time, she recalled, had been even better than the previous one. The young woman smiled at the memory of their recent lovemaking, and she was very tempted to wake Hogan for a repeat. She resisted the urge, reminding herself it would be even more pleasurable if she made herself wait a while.

It occurred to her that her feelings for Hogan had changed. Whilst it hadn't been a case of love at first sight—in fact, even now she wasn't certain she truly loved him—he did excite her, and she enjoyed his company.

As the early morning light filtered through the bedroom curtains, Helen turned over to face her lover, waking him in the process.

"Good morning, beautiful," Hogan mumbled sleepily.

"Good morning, Lieutenant," Helen smiled.

Hogan looked lovingly at her. Kissing her gently, he whispered, "I love you." To his surprise, Helen suddenly burst out laughing. "What?" he asked.

"I've just realised you still have your boots on," Helen giggled.

"Oh . . ." He reached down to remove them, but Helen stopped him.

"Later," she said. Pushing him over onto his back, she sat astride him and was pleased to find he was ready for her. This time their lovemaking reached even greater heights.

The depth of Helen's passion surprised the lieutenant. It surprised her, too. She'd always been aware of her innate sensuality, but Hogan had tapped into something deep inside her. Something she never knew existed. Something she couldn't even describe. All she knew was it made her feel good—very good.

Hogan had one more surprise in store for her. He waited until they'd dressed and breakfasted together. Then, as he was preparing to depart, he dropped down onto one knee and looked up at her. "Helen, will you do me the honour of being my wife?" he asked.

Only now did Helen realise he was holding an engagement ring. "Yes," she said without a moment's hesitation.

"Yes?" a disbelieving Hogan enquired.

Smiling, Helen nodded. "Yes, Desmond. I will marry you."

Hogan stood up and slid the ring onto her finger.

Helen admired the ring's solitary diamond. "It's beautiful," she murmured. The diamond sparkled in the light shining through a stained glass window, momentarily enrapturing her. She took that as a good omen.

They kissed. It was a long, passionate kiss—and before they knew it they were back in bed. This time, Hogan remembered to remove his boots first.

69

CAPTAIN MARSDEN SAT OILING THE barrel of his rifle on the veranda of his cottage. He looked up every now and then to admire the panoramic view of Moreton Bay and its surrounds.

It was already hot even though it was still only mid-morning, and Marsden perspired freely. It wasn't so much the heat that affected him; it was the high humidity. But, like all the bay's residents, he'd learned to live with it. It was a case of having to.

From Marsden's veranda, the world seemed to be at peace. It was a picture of tranquillity. The captain knew better. If he looked closer, he could see gangs of convicts toiling in the heat. From here, he couldn't hear the grumbles of the convicts or the threats and curses of their guards, but he could hear the faint crack of the guards' whips as they exhorted their charges to work harder. Based on the meticulous record-keeping of the army's clerks, he knew there was every chance that, by day's end, another convict would be dead and two or three more would be laid low by any one of a number of illnesses that plagued the settlement.

Dysentery remained the biggest curse. Even the soldiers regularly fell victim to it.

The captain was in civilian dress for he had a rare day off. Rare because free time was becoming an increasingly scarce commodity these days, and the reason for that lay squarely at the feet of Lord Cheetham. Cheetham's spiralling addiction meant Marsden was having to take over more and more of the commandant's duties. Consequently, he'd been working around the clock.

It wasn't all bad. Cheetham's increasing absenteeism meant Marsden had more freedom to run the penal settlement his way, and one result of that was the settlement was operating more smoothly than it had in a long time. That hadn't seen an end to escape attempts—convicts were still prepared to chance their arm and risk the hangman's noose—but more and more work projects were being completed and the settlement was growing.

Marsden's private life had improved, too. For the past six months, he'd been in a relationship with a Welsh woman who had lost her husband in an unfortunate accident the previous year. The woman, Mildred Jones, was the town's librarian. Their relationship was on the slow-burner for neither had been looking for a partner, but Marsden was sure Missus Jones could be the one to replace his beloved Vera, and his children thought so, too. They'd been encouraging him to pop the question in recent weeks.

One positive result of his new love interest was he'd quit turning to the wine bottle at the drop of a hat. These days, his drinking was limited to social occasions, and he felt better for it.

Two approaching riders caught his eye. He identified the closer of the two as Helen. Her companion was partly hidden on the horse behind her, but Marsden could see flashes of a red tunic and realised the man was a soldier. It wasn't until the riders neared that he saw it was Hogan.

The expressions on their faces signalled to him that they came bearing news. He could guess what that news was. Helen waved and he waved back.

Marsden stood and awaited them on the veranda's top step. He'd always thought it only a question of time before his lieutenant's pursuit of Helen paid dividends. He was aware Hogan had been following his daughter around, even if she hadn't realised it. And he suspected she still held a candle for him. He didn't blame her. Eligible marriage prospects in Moreton Bay were rather limited for a beautiful young woman, and Hogan was, he conceded, the best of what he could only describe as a pretty ordinary bunch. Certainly, some people—like Missus Brown and, for that matter, like his dear, departed Vera—considered Hogan a fine catch.

The animosity Marsden had felt toward Hogan had largely melted with time. The lieutenant had proven himself worthy of his rank, and he'd demonstrated the same determination in his pursuit of Helen as he had in his career. For that, he'd begrudgingly given the man full marks.

Helen reined in her horse close by, and leaned forward so that her father could kiss her cheek. He obliged. "Good morning, papa," she said.

"Good morning my dear," Marsden smiled. Looking at Hogan, who had just reined in behind Helen, he executed a smart salute. "Lieutenant."

"Good morning, Captain," Hogan said, returning his superior's salute.

Marsden asked, "What brings you two here?" He already knew the answer. He'd spotted the new engagement ring on his daughter's finger.

Helen dismounted her steed and stood before her father, looking up at him expectantly. "Papa, we have some news to share with you," she said, "and we wanted you to be the first to know."

Before she could say any more, Marsden reached forward, grabbed her left hand and held it up so that the new ring on her third finger was visible. Smiling at Helen, he asked, "May I be the first to congratulate you, my dear?" He bent down and kissed the back of her hand.

"Oh, papa! You guessed." Helen threw her arms around Marsden and hugged him.

"It wasn't difficult, young lady." Looking at the ring, he said, "I could see it glinting in the sunlight a mile away." The captain glanced at Hogan who had just dismounted his horse. His lieutenant was looking relieved. It was obvious he'd been expecting a similar reaction to the last time he'd proposed to Helen. "Congratulations to you, too, Desmond," Marsden said, using his subordinate's Christian name for the first time ever.

"Thank you, Captain," Hogan said, extending his hand. To his surprise, Marsden brushed his hand aside and hugged him.

"A handshake is too formal for my future son-in-law, don't you think?" Marsden asked.

"Yes, sir," Hogan laughed. Next to him, Helen mouthed *Thank you* to her father.

The young woman mounted her horse. Looking down at the two men, she said, "Now, I am going to leave you two to bond." Before they could object, she galloped off.

Marsden turned to his subordinate. "Are you on duty at present?"

"Not until this afternoon, Captain."

"Well, I know it's early, but I think this deserves a celebratory drink." Motioning to Hogan to take a seat, he headed inside. As he departed, he said, "It's Tom when we are off duty . . . as long as it's not in front of the men."

"Yes, sir . . . ah . . . Tom," a surprised Hogan said.

Marsden returned moments later with two small glasses of sherry. He sat down next to his son-in-law-to-be on the veranda's top step, and handed him a glass. "To the future," he said, raising his own glass.

"To the future," Hogan said.

They downed the contents of their glasses in one gulp.

Later that morning, Marsden and Hogan were just about talked out. They'd covered almost every topic under the sun—from tales of their boyhood to the state of the world—and had really gotten to know each other. The lieutenant had come to see there was a softer side to his superior, and the captain had realised there was more to his subordinate than met the eye.

Hogan glanced through the doorway behind him at the grandfather clock whose loud ticking could be heard out on the veranda. The clock told him it was almost noon. He was about to excuse himself when he and Marsden noticed a rider approaching from the north.

Even before they could see the rider clearly enough to recognise him, they identified him as Barega because of the spears he carried across his back. The sunlight glinted on their shiny barbs. Barega was the only Aborigine, in these parts at least, who rode a horse.

The two officers were standing in front of the cottage when the tracker pulled up before them. They could see he was sweating profusely, and he'd been driving his horse hard.

"I found the Irish," Barega said, grinning.

Marsden and Hogan knew he referred to John Graham.

"Where?" Marsden asked.

"On Great Sandy Island, Mister," Barega said.

The officers knew of the island—it figured on the latest maps—though neither had ever seen it in person.

"When did you see him?" Hogan asked.

"Not see Irish," Barega said. "I see tracks." The tracker explained how he'd seen John's distinctive boot prints amongst those of the Kabi clan members, and how members of another clan had confirmed that John was among those who paddled over to the island.

"How long ago?" Marsden asked. He noticed the tracker had become distracted. Barega was smiling at someone on the veranda. The captain didn't need to turn around to know it was Orana he was looking at. "How long ago?" he repeated, his annoyance showing.

"Two days, Mister," Barega said, dragging his eyes away from his woman. "Three days maybe . . . since Irish go to island." He added that he'd learned the Kabi usually remained on the island for several weeks at a time.

"So we have him," a triumphant Hogan said, glancing at Marsden.

"*If* he's still on the island," Marsden said. Looking back at the tracker, he said, "See to your horse, and don't stray too far." He expected he'd have need of Barega's services in the near future.

Barega walked his horse around behind the cottage where, he hoped, Orana would be waiting for him. He wasn't disappointed.

Out front, the captain and his lieutenant began making plans. Their immediate problem, they agreed, was they needed a boat.

Marsden and Hogan fidgeted impatiently as they awaited Lord Cheetham's arrival. They were aware time was slipping by, and they needed to act fast if they were to capture John Graham while he was still on Great Sandy Island.

The two officers were sitting in the study of Cheetham's mansion. They'd been waiting ten minutes, and still the commandant hadn't showed.

Neither commented on the untidy state of the study. Used teacups, old newspapers, overflowing ashtrays and various documents lay scattered about, and the place looked like it hadn't been cleaned in weeks.

Every instinct in Marsden's being had told him to proceed with John's capture without consulting his superior. He was very aware Cheetham's state of mind was such he may not appreciate the opportunity that had dropped into their laps. However, his commitment to duty was such that proceeding independent of Cheetham was never an option. Especially considering they would need to commandeer a boat if they were to complete their mission.

The loud ticking of a grandfather clock coming from the hallway outside the study was doing nothing for the officers' patience. Marsden had taken to pacing up and down the study while Hogan had resorted to silently counting the patterns on the wallpaper. They relaxed a little when they heard the commandant descending the stairs.

Neither officer was prepared for what he saw when Cheetham entered the study. Unshaven, dishevelled and red-eyed, the commandant was wearing pyjamas beneath an ill-fitting dressing-gown, and had obviously just hauled himself out of bed. He mumbled an apology of sorts as he weaved his way between the two visitors and headed for his desk.

Marsden and Hogan glanced at each other as Cheetham manoeuvred himself unsteadily around the side of his desk and sat behind it. As he did, he lost one of his slippers, but he didn't appear to notice.

The two officers had long known about Cheetham's opium addiction, but this was something else altogether. The commandant looked as though he'd completely lost it.

"I have been feeling out of sorts of late," Cheetham said by way of further apology. When his subordinates offered no comment, he asked, "Now what is it that's so urgent I had to arise from my sick bed?"

Both officers observed he slurred his words and his hands trembled as he spoke.

"We believe we know where John Graham is," Marsden said without preamble.

That got the commandant's attention. Capturing the Irish upstart had long been an obsession of his—as it had for the officers before him. "Tell me more," he ordered.

Marsden quickly brought his superior up to date, stressing the need to act quickly if they were to have any chance of capturing John.

"Great Sandy Island you say?" Cheetham asked.

"Yes, my Lord," Marsden said. He motioned to Hogan to show the commandant the map he'd brought with him.

The lieutenant quickly spread the map out on the desk and pointed to the island. "We have it on good authority he is there, my Lord," he said. "The tracker informed us he is still with the Kabi."

Cheetham looked up at Marsden. "What do you propose, Captain?"

"Sir, if we are to capture John Graham while he is contained on the island, we will need to act quickly," Marsden said.

Cheetham nodded. His eyes were now closed, but it seemed he was still listening.

Marsden continued, "For that we will need a boat."

The commandant's eyes flew open. "Do we have a boat?"

Marsden shook his head. He was tempted to respond, "The commandant of Moreton Bay should know the army does not have a boat." However, he said, "No, my Lord."

Cheetham closed his eyes again. Although he'd been smoking opium since early morning, the commandant was sufficiently lucid to know he'd been handed an opportunity to capture John. He was also aware he needed to show leadership at this time. Aware his hands were trembling, he placed them below the desktop. "What do you suggest, Captain?" he asked at length, his eyes still closed.

Marsden looked at Hogan and actually shook his head to signal his frustration with his superior. Taking a deep breath, he said, "We need to commandeer the next vessel that berths here, sir."

"When is the next ship scheduled?" Cheetham asked, suddenly anxious to end the meeting.

Marsden nodded to Hogan.

"The East Sunrise is scheduled to dock tomorrow at noon I believe," the lieutenant said, referring to a schooner that occasionally delivered supplies to Moreton Bay. She would do admirably for what he and Marsden were planning.

"Do it," Cheetham said. He stood up, signalling that the meeting was over. His withdrawal symptoms were worsening. As an afterthought, he asked, "How many soldiers will you need?"

Not wanting to push his luck, Marsden said, "At least six, sir."

"Take ten," Cheetham said, more anxious than ever that the meeting end. He was no longer trying to hide his trembling hands or his desire to terminate the meeting.

"Thank you, sir," Marsden and Hogan said in unison. Pleasantly surprised, they glanced knowingly at each other as the commandant stumbled toward the door.

Before leaving the study, Cheetham turned back to the officers. "Bring that Irish sod back to Moreton Bay," he said. "I want to see him swinging from the gallows."

John was making good progress on his trek north. He was still surviving on the food rations Murrowdooling had brought for him the previous day, and he felt fit and strong despite the wounds and injuries he'd received. The marks the clan members' spears had left on his back and buttocks had turned an angry red, but none had festered, and he was hopeful they would fade before they had a chance to. In the tropics and sub-tropics he was mindful that even minor abrasions could easily fester.

After starting out in the rainforest, he'd headed for the coast as he found the going too slow. Now, as he walked along a rocky beach, he could see the northern end of Great Sandy Island some distance behind him. The dramas of his short stay on the island were still vivid in his mind.

John's plan was still to liaise with a ship. Although he'd only seen one ship close to shore in all his time with the Kabi, he thought there may be a good reason for that. The best reason he could come up with was there may be so many offshore reefs along this stretch of the shoreline that ships' masters were reluctant to venture too close to land. He hoped that would change further up the coast.

The Irishman wasn't overly bothered by the thought of having to fend for himself alone in the wilderness. Armed as he was with tomahawk, spear and woomera—thanks to Murrowdooling—he felt considerably more confident than he had when fleeing Moreton Bay. Since then, he'd learned to track and to hunt and make fire. In short, he'd learned how to survive.

What did bother him was the thought that he'd never see Mamba and the boys again. He tried to put them out of his mind, but he couldn't. It ate away at him.

70

HELEN ROSE EARLY, AS SHE always did on a Sunday, to attend the early morning service at the army's chapel. It was a weekly ritual she enjoyed. Usually, she walked the quarter-mile from the township to the penal settlement. Today was no exception. She enjoyed the walk along the riverbank. It made her feel at one with nature and close to God, and it always put her in the right frame of mind for the chaplain's service.

On this occasion, she stepped out the front door of her cottage to find Hogan waiting for her. He'd just arrived on horseback and hadn't yet dismounted.

"Desmond!" Helen smiled. "I wasn't expecting to see you." She noticed he wasn't in formal dress. In place of his red tunic he wore a casual, long-sleeved, khaki shirt, his rifle was slung over one shoulder and he wore his hunting knife on his hip. It dawned on her he was heading out on army business. "Escapees?" she asked.

Hogan quickly dismounted. "Afraid so, my darling," he said, kissing her.

"Who is it this time?" she asked.

"It . . . it's John Graham," a grim-faced Hogan said.

"Oh." That was the first time she'd heard John's name mentioned in over a year. For all she'd known, he could have died in that time.

"The tracker confirmed he found his tracks." Hogan studied his fiancé's face and realised the news had shaken her. "Your father and I are leaving by boat early this afternoon."

"By boat?"

Hogan nodded. "Graham is believed to be on an island to the north," he explained.

As Helen digested this, she wasn't sure how she felt. She realised she was annoyed John's name had come up again—especially at this time. At a time she should be happy and excited about the future.

"Will you come to wave me off?" Hogan asked hopefully.

"Of course," Helen said, recovering from her surprise. "Early afternoon you say?"

Hogan nodded. He promised, "I will get word to you as soon as I know the exact time." He hesitated. "I would accompany you to the chapel, but your father needs me."

"I understand," Helen said. "You go."

They kissed again, and Helen watched as her fiancé galloped back toward the penal settlement. Instead of following him, she returned inside her cottage. She was no longer in the mood for a Sunday service.

The master of *The East Sunrise* looked on as Marsden and Hogan supervised the loading of soldiers, horses and supplies onto his schooner, his anger barely contained. Marsden had advised the gruff Scotsman the moment the vessel had docked alongside the wharf that the army was commandeering her and her crew, and he'd posted an armed guard on board to ensure there was no resistance.

A short time earlier, Captain William McDowell had been marched off the schooner at gunpoint when he refused to allow soldiers on board. And he'd refused to sail the ship north to Great Sandy Island until Marsden had threatened him with jail. Requests that Marsden produce paperwork from his superiors to show he had permission to commandeer the vessel had been ignored, alerting McDowell to the fact it was likely the army's actions had not been officially sanctioned and therefore were probably illegal.

Since then, ten soldiers had boarded the schooner, and thirteen horses had been loaded into her hold. And now workers from the township were helping soldiers load the supplies, weapons and ammunition.

Helen, who had not long arrived on horseback, watched proceedings from the riverbank nearby. The young woman observed her father, who had already said his goodbyes, and Hogan in a heated discussion with the schooner's master. It was obvious even to her the captain's vessel had been commandeered.

Hogan noticed Helen. He excused himself from the debate, and hurried over to her. "You came," he said, relieved.

"Of course," Helen smiled. Her gaiety felt forced, but she wanted to keep their parting light. "How long will you be gone?" she asked.

"That depends how long it takes to find . . ." Not wanting to mention John by name, he didn't finish the sentence. "That depends," he added lamely.

After an awkward silence, the two made small talk. It was as if they each sensed the shadow of John Graham hanging over them. Hogan knew then that that wouldn't change until the Irishman was dead. He promised himself he would see to it personally that John didn't return to Moreton Bay alive.

"Lieutenant!" Marsden called out.

Hogan looked around and saw the schooner was ready to depart. Turning back to Helen, he said, "I must go."

"Of course," Helen said.

They kissed somewhat awkwardly then Hogan turned and hurried back to the schooner.

"Good luck!" Helen called after him. Watching him board, she debated whether to stay and wave the vessel off. Her mind was made up for her when she noticed Barega staring at her. The tracker was standing by the schooner's near rail. He grinned when he saw the young woman looking his way.

Suddenly unnerved, Helen mounted her horse and trotted back toward the settlement. As she rode, she tried not to think of the fate that awaited John.

On board, Hogan looked to the riverbank and saw that Helen was already departing. Disappointed, he watched her for a while and noted she never looked back. He could guess what was on her mind. It only hardened his resolve to deal with John Graham once and for all.

John's progress had slowed to a slow shuffle. Feeling lethargic, he looked behind him and was disappointed to find he could still see the northern end of Great Sandy Island. He'd hoped to have left it far behind by now.

At first he'd feared he may be ill. Then it slowly dawned on him his lethargy was more mental than physical. The very thought of fleeing north, alone, was making him feel ill. Depressed even.

Pull yerself together, man!

He dropped his spear, sat down on a rock and stared out to sea. Mamba's smiling face kept coming to him. "How I miss you," he said to himself. He missed the boys, too.

It finally dawned on him. "I can't live without them!" he murmured. Wrestling with his emotions, he considered going back for them. He thought of a dozen reasons he shouldn't go back—not the least being the clan members would probably kill him if they saw him again.

Then he stood up. His decision made, he turned around and headed back.

Don't despair, Mamba. Moilow is coming home.

71

LIEUTENANT HOGAN AND SIX SOLDIERS waited in The East Sunrise's longboat as Barega studied tracks left by the Kabi and their canoes on the beach at the southern end of Great Sandy Island. Among the soldiers were the Devonshire veteran Sergeant Charlie Benson, Corporal Angus Davies and the young Private Henry Askew.

While they waited, four oarsmen from the schooner kept the longboat steady in the shallows. Behind them, barely fifty yards offshore, *The East Sunrise* stood at anchor. The neighing of horses could be heard coming from their temporary quarters below deck.

The schooner had delivered the soldiers to the island soon after dawn, having sailed through the night from Moreton Bay. Rather than accompanying Hogan and the other soldiers ashore, Captain Marsden had opted to remain on board the schooner with the remaining four soldiers to keep Captain McDowell and his crew in line. Master and crew were not happy their vessel had been commandeered, and there had been talk of rebellion, so Marsden had deemed it wise to maintain a military presence on board.

Among the soldiers who remained behind was the Birmingham veteran Sergeant Christopher Rogers, and Marsden was relying heavily on him to ensure order was maintained. The abrasive Rogers hadn't disappointed him so far.

Barega had suggested to Hogan that he go ashore first—before the soldiers and oarsmen could despoil the tracks the Kabi and their dugouts had left above the high tide mark in the sand. Now, as the tracker studied those tracks, he could see the Kabi had been here and John's boot prints were clearly visible amongst them; he could also see they'd departed in some haste. All the signs pointed to that.

The tracker, armed as always with his spear, nulla nulla and hunting knife, ran up the beach to reconnoitre the Kabis' vacated encampment. There, he found the reason for their hurried departure. The signs of battle were everywhere, and the ashes of the cremated bodies were there for all to see.

The faint sound of a woman wailing and chanting carried to Barega. It was coming from somewhere inside the surrounding rainforest. The tracker went to investigate.

It didn't take him long to discover the source of the noise. It came from a clearing just a short distance away.

A bereaved Gureng woman was grieving the loss of her husband whose bloated, flyblown body lay at her feet. She alone had come to investigate when the raiders hadn't immediately returned from their raid. Her fellow clan members had told her she was worrying about nothing, insisting her husband and the other raiders would return soon enough. Not convinced, she had trekked to the Kabis' encampment to see for herself. Her husband's body was the only one she'd found. All the others had been burnt to ash.

The woman didn't appear to have seen Barega even though he was standing right in front of her. The tracker saw that she'd gouged one eye out as a demonstration of her grief. Blood flowed from the nasty, self-inflicted wound.

Only when he touched her shoulder did she stop wailing and look at him through her remaining eye. "Did you see the Kabi dogs who did this to your men?" Barega asked.

The woman shook her head.

"Did you see where they went?"

The woman pointed toward the mainland. "To the mainland," she murmured. "They always go back to the mainland."

Barega had all the information he needed. He turned to go then he looked back at the woman. She wasn't the prettiest woman he'd ever seen, especially not with her missing eye and bloodied face, but he suddenly desired her. Throwing his weapons aside, and casting off his loincloth, he jumped on the woman before she even realised what was happening. She screamed, but the scream was cut short when the tracker punched her. Now barely conscious, the woman could only groan as Barega had his way with her.

A short time later, a satisfied Barega returned to the abandoned encampment to find Hogan and two of his soldiers inspecting the site.

"What do you say, tracker?" the lieutenant asked when he saw Barega.

"The Kabi were here, Mister," the tracker said. "Kabi leave after attack by Gureng."

"They left? Left to go where?"

"Back to mainland."

Hogan cursed. That wasn't the news he'd hoped for. Here on the island, John Graham's capture would have been a certainty as he and his Kabi friends would have been contained within a confined area. The mainland was a different proposition. There, they had hundreds of miles to range over. Looking at Barega, he asked, "When did they leave?"

"Maybe . . . two days."

"Damn!" Hogan cursed yet again. He was aware John could be anywhere by now. "Was John Graham with them?" he asked.

Barega nodded. "Irish with them," he said. He led the lieutenant back down to the beach, and pointed out the boot prints their quarry had left in the sand. They stood out from the soldiers' boot prints because the indents left by John's toes were there for all to see. The tracker was very familiar with John's boot prints by now, and, indeed, he was familiar with the footprints of many of the Kabi clan members. He had an eye for such things, and, once seen, he never forgot them. That's something else that set him apart from most other trackers.

A short while later, Hogan reported the tracker's findings to Marsden aboard the schooner. The decision was made to sail to the mainland. Barega had insisted he could show them the beach the Kabi had departed from for the island. He had assured them they'd have returned to the same beach.

John was making good time on his trek south. The previous day, after deciding he needed to be with Mamba and her boys, he'd run at a slow but steady pace down the coast until nightfall. Now, having had a good night's sleep and having eaten the last of the rations Mamba had supplied, he was veering slightly away from the coast on a heading he hoped would bring him into contact with the clan—or with their spoor at least.

The Irishman was aware the odds were against his finding the clan members. They had a two-day start on him, and, he knew, they could have headed in any direction.

Where did you go?

Since embarking on his return journey yesterday, he'd been wracking his brains trying to remember the path, or paths, the clan members had followed after returning from Great Sandy Island in previous years. While the Kabi were, to an extent, creatures of routine, they often deviated from the norm—usually for no reason he could make sense of—and that meant tracking them was no straightforward task.

John seemed to recall they'd headed directly inland after returning from the island two years ago, but for the life of him he couldn't remember which way they'd gone last year.

Was it south along the shoreline?

He cursed his short-term memory.

Recalling the individual paths the nomadic Kabi followed, and matching those paths with seasons or events was, for John, tantamount to finding a needle in the proverbial haystack. The clan members were constantly on the move, relocating from one hunting ground to another so often and so frequently he honestly couldn't remember half the places he'd been.

Focussing on the problem at hand, he willed himself to remember where the clan had headed after returning from the island last year. The route he currently followed left open the two options he considered most likely: either the clan headed inland or south along the coast.

Make a decision, man!

He mentally tossed a coin. One side of the imaginary coin was *south*, the other side was *inland*. The imaginary coin came up *inland*. "Inland it is!" he muttered, changing course slightly so that he was now veering further away from the coast and following a south westerly course.

John was alarmed to see dark clouds building to the west. Aware that a storm or flash flood would forever hide the clan members' tracks, he quickened his pace.

Marsden and the same soldiers and oarsmen waited in the longboat while Barega scouted the beach the Kabi had returned to on the mainland. Hogan had remained on the schooner this time to ensure the remaining soldiers kept an eye on the vessel's master and crew.

The tracker signalled to the oarsmen to come ashore. He'd seen enough. While there were no signs of the Kabis' canoes having returned, fresh footprints showed the clan members had most definitely returned. That indicated their dugouts had remained in the shallows while they'd unloaded their provisions. Barega guessed the canoes were hidden nearby.

Marsden was the first to disembark from the longboat. He hurried over to Barega. "What news?" he asked.

The tracker quickly brought Marsden up to date. In a conversation that barely differed from the one he'd had earlier with Hogan on the island, he pointed out John's distinctive boot prints in amongst the scores of bare footprints.

Marsden and Barega followed the tracks. The tracker was first to notice their quarry's boot prints ended halfway up the beach. Pointing this out to Marsden, he said, "The Irish now barefoot, Mister."

"How do you know the Kabi didn't kill him?" the captain asked.

Barega pointed to a set of footprints that had obviously been left by an adult. "Those belong to Irish," he said. The tracker was in no doubt the tracks were John's. He recognised the familiar marks the Irishman's toes had left in the sand.

"How do you know they are John Graham's?" Marsden asked.

Barega explained what he'd observed. He also pointed out that while John's feet and toes were as long as those of the Kabi men, they were more slender and European-like. And, he said, the length of John's stride was longer than that of most Aborigine males, indicating the prints had been left by a tall man—a man of John's height.

Marsden nodded. He was satisfied the prints were John's. He and Barega studied the tracks left by the Irishman and the Kabi. They were leading up toward the hinterland behind the beach, and it appeared the clan was heading west. "They are heading inland," Marsden observed. He looked to his tracker for confirmation.

Barega thought it likely the captain's assumption was correct, but he'd learned it was dangerous to assume. "I go see, Mister," he said. Without waiting for permission, he ran off, leaving Marsden and the soldiers alone.

Marsden didn't have long to wait. The tracker soon returned. He was sweating after his exertions. "They go inland," Barega confirmed. He explained he'd followed the Kabis' spoor some distance across a plain that couldn't be seen from down here on the beach, and the signs indicated their next destination was indeed to the west.

The captain had heard enough. "You wait here," he ordered the tracker. He then hurried back to the beached longboat, ordering the oarsmen to launch it and motioning to his soldiers to board it.

Within moments, they were heading back to the waiting schooner.

On board *The East Sunrise,* Marsden advised Hogan what he'd found ashore. The captain then ordered his subordinate to ready the soldiers and horses for disembarkation.

"All of them?" Hogan asked.

"All of them." Marsden had a feeling all available men and horses would be needed for what lay ahead. As the lieutenant hurried to carry out his orders, Marsden took Captain McDowell aside. He was aware the co-operation of The East Sunrise's master was essential if the mission was to succeed.

Marsden's dilemma was, if he took all available soldiers ashore that would leave no-one to guard the schooner's master and crew, and there would be nothing to stop them sailing off and leaving their unwelcome passengers with a long overland trek home. Eyeballing the surly Scotsman, he said, "Captain McDowell, I know you are unhappy with the way the army has treated you and your men—"

"Unhappy?" McDowell grumbled. "Unhappy does not remotely do justice to how I feel, Captain Marsden . . ."

Marsden allowed his opposite to rant until he got everything off his chest. In the two minutes it took for McDowell to do that, he threatened everything from suing the army to challenging Marsden to a duel.

When the ship's master finally quietened, Marsden said, "Captain, I can only apologise for the way you have been treated." He then explained, quickly and clearly, how the army had been hunting John Graham for more than four years, and how the Irishman's success had motivated other convicts to try to escape.

McDowell listened intently, his anger slowly dissipating as Marsden explained why he'd commandeered his vessel.

"As a result, more convicts are trying to escape, more soldiers are being endangered, and more and more men are dying," Marsden continued. "I fear still more will die if John Graham is not caught soon and brought to justice. We have now picked up his tracks, and there is a good chance we can capture him." He looked into McDowell's eyes. "But for this we need your co-operation."

McDowell pondered what he'd been told. "You want a guarantee we will not sail off and leave you stranded," he said.

"Exactly." Marsden nodded.

McDowell studied his opposite. Despite the circumstances, he couldn't help but like the army captain who had commandeered his vessel and whom he adjudged to be a straight-shooter. He saw something of himself in Marsden. Under other circumstances, he suspected, the two could be friends. At length, he extended his hand, and said, "You have my word, Captain. We will be here when you get back."

A relieved Marsden shook the other's hand. "Thank you, Captain." He added, "I will ensure you are fully recompensed when we return to Moreton Bay . . . and I will be the first to buy you a drink."

"You had best make that two drinks, Captain!" McDowell said.

The two men laughed, and each clapped the other on the shoulder in a sign of gruff affection.

72

T HE AFTERNOON SHADOWS WERE LENGTHENING when John had his first
stroke of good luck. He found the first sign of the Kabi. The sighting had
little to do with his tracking skills. Rather, it was a shawl that Murrowdooling
had left fluttering, like a flag, atop the trunk of a dead tree. The trunk was on the
summit of a hill whose upper slopes were devoid of vegetation, so it was hard to
miss.

John recognised the shawl as Mamba's. Moilow—the *real* Moilow—had made it
for her from the pelt of a wallaby, and she'd often worn it.

Murrowdooling must have left it there to catch my attention.

He couldn't imagine Mamba or Carravanty being able to climb the trunk, so tall
was it and largely devoid of branches.

John scouted around the bottom of the hill and soon located the clan members'
tracks. Like Barega, he was sufficiently familiar with the clan to know whether the
tracks and other signs were theirs. The shawl Murrowdooling had left confirmed that
beyond doubt, and the tracks reconfirmed they were heading inland. He remembered
now that clan had come this way last year.

The Irishman hurried on his way, keen to catch up with Mamba and the boys. As
he proceeded, he noticed the clouds he'd observed earlier had disappeared. He
thought that a good omen, and he thanked God his luck was holding.

Two miles further inland, the Kabi clan members followed a familiar path. It was
the same route they'd followed after returning from the island the previous two years.

The mood amongst the clan was still solemn. Clan members grieved the recent
violent deaths of loved-ones, children cried, and bereaved women wailed and chanted
as they walked.

None grieved more than Mamba. Although John hadn't died, it felt as though he
had. Her Moilow was gone from her life once more, and this time she believed it was
forever.

Mamba and Carravanty walked at the rear of the long column of clan members.
Their progress was slow as they were carrying all their possessions between them.
The grieving woman was aware that tail-enders were at risk of being attacked should
there be enemies in the vicinity, but she was beyond caring. In some ways, she
wanted to die. If it hadn't been for her sons, she would have killed herself, or at least
gouged an eye out.

Murrowdooling was nowhere to be seen. Mamba wasn't worried. The boy was old
enough to fend for himself. Besides, she knew what he was up to. She had told him it

was a waste of time looking out for the unfortunate outcast, but the boy wouldn't listen.

At that moment, Murrowdooling was scouting the countryside a mile or so behind the column, looking for some sign of John. For some reason he couldn't explain, he felt sure the white spirit he knew as Moilow would return.

In fact, John had returned and he had, at that moment, made visual contact with the clan members. After sighting the shawl, he had made an educated guess which way the clan was heading, and he'd taken a shortcut to intercept them. The shortcut had delivered him to a stand of trees that afforded excellent cover. From here, he was able to observe the clan file past him without fear of being seen.

Now that he was here, he wasn't at all sure what his next step would be. He suspected clan members would kill him if they saw him. Certainly Turo wouldn't hesitate. So he took care to remain hidden.

It took the clan thirty minutes or more to file past, so spread out was the caravan. Still John hadn't sighted Mamba or the boys. All sorts of thoughts flashed through his mind. He feared something may have happened to them.

Then he spotted Mamba and Carravanty. They trailed the others by fifty yards or more.

There you are!

Resisting the urge to call out, he picked up a stone and threw it so that it landed just behind the pair. Mamba stopped walking when she heard the stone strike the bare earth. She looked around. At first, she didn't see anything. Then she saw John. He'd just stepped out from behind a tree. Mamba smiled and was about to run to him when she noticed he was motioning to her to keep walking. She did as he suggested, pulling the unsuspecting Carravanty along by the hand.

Only now did Mamba notice Mirritji. The elder was a hundred yards ahead, and he was motioning to her and others bringing up the rear to walk faster and close ranks. Not wanting to give away John's presence, she hurried to oblige.

John was considering whether to approach Mamba when he noticed Mirritji. He melted back into the trees.

As Mamba and Carravanty quickened their pace to catch up to the others, Murrowdooling appeared some distance behind his mother and brother. John watched as the boy caught up to them. He observed Mamba talking to him, and he guessed she was advising him his father had returned. Sure enough, he saw Murrowdooling glance toward his hiding place. John showed himself long enough to catch the boy's eye and smile at him.

Captain McDowell watched from The East Sunrise's starboard rail as the last of the soldiers climbed down into the longboat that would take them ashore. Marsden was among them. Hogan and the other soldiers were already ashore.

As the longboat pushed off from the schooner's side, Marsden looked up and caught McDowell's eye. The vessel's master nodded to him, and Marsden responded in kind. They had sealed their agreement with a handshake, and Marsden was confident his opposite wouldn't let him down.

Looking toward the shore, Marsden saw that all thirteen horses were safely on the beach. They'd been tethered together and forced to jump into the sea. The three soldiers who had shepherded them to shore were now drying themselves off and preparing to don their uniforms.

Marsden's arrival on the beach coincided with the tracker's return. Barega had used his time ashore to follow the Kabis' tracks some distance on foot. The tracker confirmed the Kabi were still heading inland.

Hogan was keen to make use of what little daylight was left. "We have a good two hours before dark," he said.

Marsden agreed with his lieutenant's assessment, and he was equally keen to set off after their quarry. The captain nodded, "Prepare the men, Lieutenant," he ordered. "And tell them to remain alert."

"Yes, sir." Hogan relayed his superior's orders to the soldiers. They quickly checked their weapons and mounted their horses, the excitement of the hunt showing in their faces.

Barega was already heading out on his horse.

John waited until after dark to make contact with Mamba and the boys. The Kabi had chosen a clearing alongside a billabong in a valley in which to overnight. The valley, which was sandwiched between bush-covered hills, was covered in scrubby bush and the occasional stand of gum trees. It afforded John plenty of hiding places.

Mamba had erected her bivouac some distance from the other shelters. She would have erected it even further away if she'd thought it wouldn't look suspicious. As it was, it was around thirty yards from her Aunt Jiba who happened to be her nearest neighbour.

As the flames of twenty or more cooking fires died, and the remaining embers began to die, Mamba emerged from her bivouac and wandered into the nearby bush. She walked normally so that any onlookers would assume she was going to pee. If anyone did challenge her, she was aware she'd be at pains to explain the bundle of food she carried.

John, who had been watching out for her and the boys, didn't show himself immediately. First, he did a quick reconnoitre of the bush in the immediate vicinity to ensure no-one else was around. Satisfied, he mimicked the hoot of an owl—a call he'd mastered and a call he and Mamba had agreed to use if ever they needed to attract the other's attention.

It did the trick, and within moments Mamba found herself in John's arms. "Moilow!" she gasped as John kissed her. "Murrowdooling said you would come."

"Shhh!" John cautioned. He led her deeper into the bush, anxious his presence remain hidden from the other clan members.

They walked without talking for five minutes or so, stopping only to kiss each other every so often. It was as if they couldn't believe they'd been reunited.

John was heading for a cave he'd found before darkness fell. Now, guided only by faint moonlight, it took him a while to locate the entrance. Finally, he found it. "In here," he said, leading Mamba by the hand.

Inside the cave's entrance, they sat down on a bed of ferns and leaves that John had laid down earlier. It was so dark, they could only see the whites of each other's eyes.

"I have some food for you," Mamba said, handing over the bundle she'd brought with her.

John, who hadn't noticed the bundle in the dark, accepted it gratefully and placed it on the ground. The Irishman then reached out and touched Mamba's face. He withdrew his hand quickly when he realised she was silently crying. "Mamba, what is it?" he asked, alarmed. She smiled, and he saw the whites of her teeth.

"I am so happy to see you, Moilow," Mamba quietly sobbed.

The Irishman kissed her tenderly. She responded. Their kisses quickly became more passionate, and before they knew it they'd both stripped naked. Mamba pulled John over on top of her. She suddenly needed him more than she'd ever needed him before.

The lovemaking that followed was the most meaningful either had ever experienced. Afterwards, they lay side by side, contentedly holding each other's hand and not speaking for a long time.

Finally, Mamba murmured, "I love you Moilow."

"I love you, too my darling," John replied.

They both could have slept then, but they knew sleep would have to wait. There were things to discuss. Things like how they could truly be together again.

John had been thinking on this ever since he'd decided to return for Mamba. He quickly outlined his plan, explaining that it would require her and the boys to separate themselves from the clan the following day. He added, "Then we can meet up and head back to the coast."

Mamba thought a night-time escape would make more sense, but John explained they wouldn't get far at night, and clan members would immediately suspect they'd fled if she and the boys were found to be missing at daybreak. "If you quietly separate from the others during the day, your absence may not even be noticed until nightfall," he said. "We can be halfway back to the coast by then."

And so it was agreed.

As soon as they'd finalised their plans, John escorted Mamba back to the encampment. There, they kissed and reluctantly went their separate ways.

While John and the Kabi slept, Marsden's men were still in the process of bedding down. The soldiers had made good use of the last hours of daylight, pushing their horses hard and closing in on the Kabi. They hadn't made camp until after dark, so the evening meal had been a late affair.

The decision to push hard before nightfall looked like it would pay dividends, however. Barega had advised they should catch up with their quarry the following day.

73

JOHN OBSERVED THE KABI ENCAMPMENT from the upper branches of one of the tallest trees near his overnight hiding place. It was already mid-morning, and the clan members were showing no sign of relocating anytime soon. In fact, everything pointed to their staying put for the time-being.

A disillusioned John descended the tree. He hadn't factored into his planning that the clan could stay put for a while. If they did, he was aware that would make it more difficult for Mamba and the boys to slip away without being noticed.

The Irishman returned to the cave he'd overnighted in. He arrived to find a worried-looking Mamba awaiting him just inside the entrance. They kissed.

"Mirritji and the other elders have decided the clan will stay here for a few more days," Mamba said.

"I guessed that," John said. "That makes things more difficult."

"What will we do, Moilow?"

Hiding his frustration behind a smile, John said, "We remain patient. The time will pass soon enough." He noticed Mamba was holding something wrapped in a pelt, which he guessed was for him. "Is that for me?"

The young woman knelt down on the leafy bed that had served John so well, and she unravelled the small bundle she'd brought to reveal it contained more fresh food, including the cooked hind quarters of a wallaby Murrowdooling had killed. "For you," she smiled.

They kissed again. John was about to suggest they do more than kiss when a movement outside the cave entrance caught his eye. "Shhh!" he whispered.

Mirritji came into view. He was walking straight toward the cave entrance, and he, too, carried a small bundle.

John and Mamba backed up as far as they could into the cave. It was far enough that they couldn't be seen from the entrance, but not far enough to remain hidden should Mirritji come much closer. They held their breath as the elder entered the cave.

Mirritji stood looking down at the food Mamba had brought and the leaves that John had gathered. The old man placed his bundle on top of the leaves and then looked into the blackness of the cave. He couldn't see the couple, but it was evident to them he knew they were there. This was confirmed a moment later when he murmured, "I have brought some pine nuts for you, Moilow." He turned to go then hesitated. Looking back, he said, "It is best the others do not know the white spirit has returned, Mamba." His bandy legs carried him from the cave, and the couple were alone again.

"He must have seen you when you came to me last night," John whispered.

"I took care that I was not followed," Mamba said.

John chuckled. "He is a cunning one that Mirritji."

They cautiously returned to the entrance. There, on the cave floor, they saw that the elder was true to his word: he had brought some pine nuts.

John's first thought was whether other clan members knew of his hiding place.

Mamba appeared to have been reading his mind. She said, "It is not safe for you here, Moilow."

John nodded. "I will hide up in the hills," he said.

"How will I find you?"

"I will find you," John smiled. "When the clan next moves, that is when you and the boys will do what we discussed."

They kissed and then held each other tight.

The more miles that flew by, the more worried Barega was becoming. The tracker had been riding hard since leaving the soldiers at dawn, and still he hadn't been able to distinguish John's tracks from those of the Kabi whose spoor he followed.

Every hundred yards or so, Barega left a square of white cloth for the trailing soldiers to follow. He carried the cloth in a bag attached to his saddle, and he was careful to leave the cloth squares where they could be easily seen.

A good hour had passed before Barega realised John's tracks were no more to be seen. In his haste, he hadn't noticed that the Irishman had headed north soon after setting out from the coast. The oversight was understandable given John was now barefoot, and his footprints could easily be missed or overlooked amongst those of the clan members. Nevertheless, the tracker cursed himself for his lack of vigilance.

Since realising his oversight, Barega had been dismounting his steed every mile or so to study the Kabis' tracks more closely. He thought it possible that John had headed out, alone or with others, to hunt. And, if that was the case, then the Irishman would soon catch up to the clan members—if he hadn't already.

An unusual sight caught Barega's eye. Tied to the top of a tree trunk on the summit of a hill was the shawl that Murrowdooling had left for John. The tracker galloped to the foot of the hill and there he was relieved to find the Irishman's tracks.

A scout around soon revealed that John had approached the hill alone and from the north, or from the northeast to be precise. Barega assumed he'd rendezvoused with the clan members at this point. He couldn't know, of course, that his quarry hadn't caught up to the clan at that point.

A relieved Barega urged his horse forward. He could sense he was close now.

The tracker had a near-unobstructed view of the Kabis' encampment. He was in a clearing high in the hills above the valley the clan members occupied.

Standing upright in his stirrups atop his patient horse for an even better view, he observed men throwing spears. They appeared to be competing to see who could throw their spears the furthest. Nearby, youths participated in a high-spirited game of burinjoin while the younger children played or slept. The womenfolk gathered firewood and pine nuts, and attended to other chores.

It was evident the clan was here for a day or two at least. To the tracker's eyes, the encampment had a semi-permanent look about it. That would suit his purposes admirably.

One fetching young mother caught his eye. She was collecting berries with a small boy. Barega wasn't aware he was looking at Mamba and Carravanty. He noticed the woman stood out from the other females. Her features were finer and her skin fairer. The tracker decided he would look out for her when he returned.

Barega glanced at the sun. It was already mid-afternoon—too late for the soldiers to mount any sort of attack before dark. He calculated it would take them until after dark to reach the encampment. So, he thought, it was looking like a dawn raid. At least, that's what he would advise Marsden.

Before departing, Barega looked for some sign of the Irishman. The tracker absentmindedly fingered his silver crucifix as he scanned the encampment. He was disappointed his quarry was nowhere to be seen, but he found solace in the knowledge he would see him soon enough.

The shadows were lengthening by the time the tracker made contact with the soldiers. Although they had maintained a reasonable pace since departing the coast, they were still several hours' hard riding from the Kabi encampment. Barega immediately reported to Marsden, and the captain agreed a dawn raid was the most suitable course of action.

74

ASNORTING SOUND WOKE JOHN. At first he thought he may have been
dreaming. Then he heard it again. He wondered if it was a kangaroo.

Or a dingo perhaps?

He'd seen roos and dingoes in recent days, so he wasn't unduly alarmed.

The Irishman had relocated to another cave he'd found in the hills a mile or so to
the east of the Kabis' encampment. He figured he'd be safe there as long as he didn't
venture far during daylight hours. Mamba and Mirritji had provided sufficient food
for him to last another day or two, and he hoped by then the clan members would
quit their present site.

It was still dark outside, and he estimated dawn was a little way off. He debated
whether to go back to sleep.

The sound of another *snort* carried to him. Louder than before.

Sounds like a horse!

He jumped to his feet and quickly walked to the cave's entrance. The cave was
located in the side of a hill overlooking the floor of the same valley the clan members
occupied. From the entrance, he peered out into the darkness.

Shadows on the valley floor caught his eye.

Are they trees? Or ant hills perhaps?

He wracked his brains, trying to remember the layout of the terrain below.

A moment later, one of the shadows moved. And then another.

And then another snort carried to him.

Holy Mother of God! Those are horses!

The Irishman grabbed his spear and his tomahawk, and crept down the hillside to
investigate.

He didn't have to go far before he could make out a dozen or so horses and
riders.

Feck! Soldiers!

It was too dark to recognise any of the riders, but their uniforms and weapons
signalled that they were soldiers. He could hear their murmured conversations,
although from where he was he couldn't decipher what they were saying.

There was no doubt in John's mind they'd come for him. This was confirmed
when he observed a lone Aborigine approaching the soldiers on foot from the
direction of the Kabi encampment. The native was running hard. Even before he
reached the soldiers, John knew who it was. The tracker's unusually long legs and his

effortless running style left him in no doubt it was Barega.

Bastard!

John watched as Barega reported to two soldiers whose bearing indicated they were officers.

They must really want me if they sent two officers!

He wondered whether he was looking at Marsden and Hogan. It was still too dark to tell.

The Irishman had worked out by now that the soldiers had learned he was with the Kabi, and they evidently believed he was still with them. It was evident they were planning a dawn raid on the encampment. The very thought sent chills down his spine. He knew the British Army well enough to know that they'd attack the sleeping clan with all guns blazing, and they wouldn't stop shooting until they'd caught or killed their quarry. That had been their modus operandi for nearly two hundred years, and, he believed, that wasn't likely to change any time soon.

The British consider these natives to be little better than animals. They'll kill every last one of them to get at me.

John realised he had a decision to make: to flee or to sound the alarm.

It was an easy decision. The lives of Mamba and the boys, and, indeed, all the clan members, were in his hands.

The Irishman took a closer look at the shadowy figures below. Dawn was coming, and the men and horses were a little easier to see now. He counted thirteen horses. Their hooves, he noted, had been swathed in rags to minimise the noise they made.

Turning his attention to the soldiers, he finally recognised Marsden and Hogan among them. He recognised some of the others, too, and even after all this time he was able to put names to Sergeant Benson, Sergeant Rogers, Corporal Davies and Private Askew.

John had seen enough. He quietly pulled back, keen to reach the Kabi encampment ahead of the soldiers.

When he was a safe distance from the raiding party, he began running headlong through the bush. He was very aware dawn wasn't far off—and that's when he expected the soldiers would attack.

The Irishman estimated he was still a good half mile from the encampment when the sound of muffled hooves carried to him. He looked behind him and saw the soldiers were following Barega who was now on horseback. They were riding along the valley floor at a slow canter so as not to create too much noise and wake their quarry.

Desperate to reach the encampment first, John began sprinting. He hoped the soldiers would rein in their mounts soon and make the final approach on foot. That would allow a more stealthy final approach. More to the point, it would give him more time to sound the alarm before the shooting began.

Sure enough, the soldiers soon reined in their horses. John pulled up and observed them through the trees. He estimated they were just a few hundred yards short of the encampment, and he watched as they began to disperse on foot. Leading their horses by the reins, it was immediately evident they planned to surround the encampment before launching their raid. They proceeded with the utmost caution so as not to give their presence away.

John realised he had to act now and he had to act fast. Throwing caution to the wind, he resumed running toward the encampment. He remained alert to the possibility he would stumble upon one of the raiders. If he did, he hoped it would be Barega. He'd enjoy skewering the tracker with his spear—and then chopping his head off for good measure.

The Irishman reached the encampment without incident. Just inside the trees that bordered the camp's eastern perimeter, he took stock of his situation. There was no sign of life in the encampment, but he knew it wouldn't be long before clan members began emerging from their bivouacs. Dawn was breaking and the kookaburras were already chattering away.

As he considered his next move, a noise alerted him to the presence of someone nearby. He peered through the trees and saw a soldier trying to pacify his horse. The steed had been startled by something—a snake or lizard perhaps—and it was trying to rear up. Its rider finally managed to calm it.

John realised he could delay no longer. It wouldn't be long before all the soldiers were in place, and then, he knew, it would be too late. Putting his fate in the lap of the gods, he ran into the middle of the encampment, shouting, "Ambush! Ambush! Ambush!" He shouted in the Kabi dialect. Switching to English, he screamed, "Soldiers are coming!" He'd belatedly realised the Kabi had no word for *soldiers*. Not surprising given they'd never heard of them.

Sleepy clan members stumbled from their bivouacs. Startled, they looked at the white spirit who had unaccountably reappeared in their midst. Turo was to the fore. He was glaring at John. Turo's oldest son, Orad, emerged from an adjoining shelter in the company of two younger brothers. Like their father, all three carried weapons, and, John could see, they appeared ready to use them.

Still the soldiers hadn't shown themselves.

"Ambush!" John repeated in Kabi. "White men are coming!"

"That's John Graham!" a soldier shouted from inside the trees to the Irishman's left.

John thought he recognised Hogan's voice, but he couldn't be sure.

"I want him alive!" another man shouted.

John recognised that voice.

That's Marsden!

John was still some fifty yards from Mamba's shelter when a rifle shot rang out. Thinking it was meant for him, he dropped to the ground. Only when he looked up did he realise he hadn't been the target. The bullet had struck Orad who was now rolling around on the ground, mortally wounded. Blood flowed from a nasty hole in his chest. A woman screamed. John guessed it was Orad's mother.

The rifle shot was the signal for the soldiers to attack. They attacked as one from out of the trees. Charging astride their mounts with their rifles held high, they shouted the battle cries of the British Army as they spurred their horses and converged on the clan members.

Hogan and Barega were to the fore. The tracker, John noted, was the only one who didn't have a rifle. He wielded a spear, and he carried his nulla nulla and hunting knife on his hip.

Chaos ensued as more startled clan members emerged from their shelters, and more shots rang out. Another two clan members—a man and a woman—fell as bullets found their mark.

Women and children screamed, and ran for their lives, and so, too, did some of the men. Their reactions, John thought, were totally predictable. After all, this was the first time any of them had ever seen soldiers or horses, and it was the first time they'd heard gunfire.

Many of the clan members froze, unable to believe or make sense of what they were hearing and seeing. Survivors—if there were any—would later inform disbelieving kin they were attacked by fierce white spirits who rode huge, snorting dragons.

Three more clan members were shot. The Irishman saw that Warrane, the artist, and Mamba's brother Kulan were among the victims. Neither was moving, and the third victim, a young girl, was clutching her stomach and moaning in pain. Even from some distance away, John could see her wound was fatal.

Only now did he see Mamba and the boys. They were running toward the trees, but they were herded back by Private Askew who had obviously been tasked with ensuring no-one escaped the cordon that had been established around the site. The Irishman tried to intervene, but found his path blocked by other soldiers. He identified the nearest of them as Sergeant Rogers. The Birmingham veteran had just bowled Turo over with his horse, and was about to shoot him where he lay. Without thinking, John hurled his spear at the sergeant. His aim was true, and Rogers slumped forward in his saddle and then fell to the ground, the spear protruding from his back.

Turo nodded his thanks to the Irishman. They were joined by Mirritji and Gabirri. The looks on their faces told John they and the other clan members had been shocked into a stupor—almost as if they'd fallen into a state of inertia. He realised he must take charge before it was too late. "Rally the others," he shouted, "otherwise it will be a slaughter!"

John's companions responded immediately. All three began shouting and signalling to the other clan members to form a defensive huddle in the centre of the encampment. Many responded quickly, some not so quickly. Those who were too slow were shot dead or ridden over by the soldiers' horses.

Throughout all this, Barega was causing mayhem. Riding hands-free so that he could use both his spear and nulla nulla, he was using both weapons to good effect. He used his spear as a lance to skewer any clan member he came across, and then employed his nulla nulla to finish them off.

The soldiers were equally ruthless, using rifle, pistol or cutlass to deal with any threat real or imagined.

John was horrified by the mayhem unfolding around him. The air was filled with the sounds of battle and the smell of gun smoke; the groans and cries of the wounded provided background noise to the gunfire and the shouts of the soldiers and the screams of the clan members.

Marsden was equally horrified. His last orders to his men had been to capture John Graham without harming the natives if at all possible. That had all gone out the window when a nervous soldier had fired prematurely, killing Turo's son. The shot was all it had taken to spark the soldiers' bloodlust. From that moment on, there was no controlling them.

The captain was particularly concerned by his lieutenant's actions. After that first shot, Hogan had disregarded orders and was acting no better than the men under him. At that moment, the lieutenant was desperately trying to get to John, but he was hindered by fleeing clan members. He dealt with them by shooting them or riding over the top of them.

Marsden was also concerned the Kabi were now starting to fight back. The captain saw they'd formed a tight circle within the cordon he'd established, and the men were now hurling their spears at his soldiers. He noticed a few women fighting amongst them, too. To his eyes, they were as savage and fearless as the men.

In the first volley of spears, three soldiers were hit. Two died immediately. The third, Corporal Davies, was pulled from his horse and clubbed to death.

Every now and then, when a soldier ventured too close, a native would race out and attempt to club him from his horse.

Marsden noticed that John was in the thick of the action. The Irishman, who stood shoulder to shoulder with the clan's males, was wielding his tomahawk with a savage ferocity.

Realising the carnage would only end when John was either killed or captured, the captain spurred his horse, intent on getting closer to his quarry.

If Marsden could have known what was going through the Irishman's mind at that time, he'd have been surprised.

John blamed himself entirely for what was happening. It was, he thought, like the Gureng raid all over again—only a hundred times worse—and he regretted he hadn't turned himself in before the soldiers attacked.

This could've been avoided, you feckin' idiot!

The dead and dying—men, women and children—were everywhere; the wounded—soldiers and natives alike—groaned and cried out in pain.

John looked around for Mamba and the boys, and was concerned he couldn't see any of them.

Please God, let them be alright!

Then he saw them. Murrowdooling, who was holding a spear, was trying to shepherd his younger brother and their mother to the relative safety of a nearby bivouac. It was, John noticed, one of the few bivouacs still standing. Most of the others had been levelled by the horses.

Disregarding his own safety, John sprinted toward the trio. When he reached them he was relieved to find they were unharmed. "Come with me!" he ordered, herding them toward a large clump of ferns a short distance away. After pulling them into the ferns, John hugged them tight. He could feel their fear. "Stay here until I come for you," he said.

"I am coming with you to fight," Murrowdooling said.

"No!" John said. "You will stay here to protect your mother and your brother." When he was satisfied Murrowdooling would do as he was told, he smiled at Mamba and Carravanty. He could see they were terrified, and his heart went out to them. "Don't worry," he smiled. He reached out and touched Mamba's face lovingly then hurried off to re-join the fighting.

"Take care, Moilow," Mamba murmured as she watched her man depart.

John ran to re-join the other clan members, unaware three riders were coming for him. Marsden, Hogan and Barega had all seen their quarry separate from the clan's main fighting force, and they were now closing fast with him.

The Irishman was relieved to see the clan members now appeared to be holding their own. More spears had found their mark, more soldiers had died and more still had been wounded. He was so anxious to re-join the fray, he didn't notice the three riders coming for him. Murrowdooling did, however, and he ran out to intercept them.

Barega, who was the closest of the three riders, turned his horse slightly so that it was on a collision course with the boy.

"Murrowdooling!" Mamba cried out.

John pulled up when he heard Mamba's cry. He turned just in time to see the tracker's spear enter Murrowdooling's chest. It had entered with such force, its barbed tip protruded from the boy's back. At the same time, as he fell face-down on the bare earth, a large volume of blood shot out from his open mouth. "Noooo!" the Irishman shouted as he sprinted back to assist. Even then, he knew the boy was dead.

It felt, to John, as though he was running in quicksand. Everything around him was happening so fast, and he felt powerless to intervene. Only now did he notice Marsden and Hogan coming for him.

Mamba, who was closer to Murrowdooling than John, left her hiding place and ran toward her dead son. In her haste, she ran directly into the path of a wild-eyed Hogan who, John noticed, showed no intention of slowing down.

John shouted, "Mamba! No!"

Mamba didn't hear him. She just wanted to get to her boy.

Hogan saw the young mother, but he made no effort to avoid her, running his horse right over top of her, so desperate was he to reach the Irishman. Mamba was trampled beneath the pounding hooves of the lieutenant's horse.

John threw himself to one side as Hogan shot at him. He thought he felt the wind of the bullet fly past his head, but he couldn't be sure.

Hogan pulled his steed around in a tight circle, and came at the Irishman again. This time, he didn't bother with his pistol. It was clear he intended to run his quarry down as he had Mamba. Behind the lieutenant, John saw that Marsden was bringing his rifle up toward him.

John leapt to his left a split-second before Hogan's horse could bowl him over. As the horse sped past, he slashed out with his tomahawk, and had the satisfaction of feeling its sharp blade connect with the lieutenant's right knee. Hogan cried out and fell from his horse. Landing hard, he lay on his back, clutching his wounded knee and groaning in agony.

A rifle shot rang out. It was so close John initially thought he'd been shot. Remembering the threat Marsden posed, he spun around and saw the captain had dropped his rifle and was clutching his upper leg. A spear protruded from his thigh, its tip buried in the saddle beneath him. John realised the spear had been thrown by Gabirri. The native had intervened just in time to spoil Marsden's aim. The Irishman saw that his friend had now turned his attention to Hogan. Gabirri finished the wounded lieutenant off with one savage blow of his nulla nulla.

John glanced over at Mamba and Murrowdooling, and was alarmed to see neither was moving. He looked back at Marsden and saw the captain was now being led away to safer ground by Barega. Somehow, Marsden had managed to remain upright in his saddle. The spear still protruded from his thigh, and his face was creased in pain.

The tracker looked over at John as he and Marsden rode away. Grinning, he held up the silver crucifix that still hung from his neck. It glinted in the sunlight.

John was tempted for one brief moment to chase after him. Instead, he ran over to check on Mamba and Murrowdooling.

One look at the boy was enough to tell him he was dead. He'd known it from the outset.

A groan from Mamba, who was lying close by, told him she was still alive. Hurrying to her, he knelt down beside her.

John physically recoiled when he saw the extent of Mamba's injuries. Her front teeth had been knocked out, her face was bruised and bloodied, both her arms and one of her legs had been fractured, and he guessed one or more ribs had been broken. Blood trickled from her mouth, which made John suspect a rib may have punctured her lung. She was having trouble breathing, too, and was barely conscious.

"My darling Mamba," John murmured, ignoring the carnage around him. "What have I done to you?" He could see she was dying, and he blamed himself.

Mamba reached up and touched John's face. "It is not your fault," she murmured in the dialect of the Kabi. Looking over at Murrowdooling, she asked, "Is my boy alive?"

John nodded. "He will be fine," he lied.

Mamba smiled. John cradled her head in his arms and tenderly kissed her bloodied face. Unable to hold back his tears any longer, he wept uncontrollably.

Mamba whispered something John didn't catch. He bent down so that his ear was close to her lips.

Switching to English, Mamba whispered, "I always knew . . . you not Moilow." She smiled once more as the light slowly faded from her eyes.

John held her against his chest. Raising his head to the heavens, he screamed. It was a tormented scream full of anger and pain.

Only now did John remember Carravanty. He looked around and was relieved to see the boy hadn't witnessed the death of his mother and brother. At least he hoped he hadn't. Carravanty was still hiding in the ferns. A movement within the foliage confirmed he was safe.

John was relieved to see the conflict was ending and the surviving soldiers were withdrawing. The death of their lieutenant and the withdrawal of their wounded captain had been the last straw for them. They had already lost nearly two thirds their number. Most of the survivors had been wounded and they clearly had no stomach left for the fight. As it was, they were having to employ a fighting withdrawal as the surviving Kabi men harassed them every step of the way. Another soldier fell, a spear through his chest, bringing the number of dead soldiers to eight.

As for the Kabis' casualties, there were too many to count. Dead and wounded clan members lay strewn around the entire encampment. In some cases entire families had been wiped out. The sounds of battle had been replaced by the groans and cries of the wounded.

John closed his eyes and placed his hands over his ears as the ghastly sights and sounds threatened to overwhelm him.

God forgive me.

75

NEXT MORNING, A PALL OF smoke covered the sun, turning it red and casting an eerie glow on everything below. The smoke came from the Kabis' encampment, which had been turned into one huge cremation site.

The clan's elders—or those who had survived the previous day's massacre at least—had made the decision to quit the encampment in case the soldiers returned with reinforcements. That had necessitated burning dead clan members in one mass ceremony, dispensing with traditional burial rites.

It was Great Sandy Island all over again—only worse, much worse.

The chanting and wailing of loved-ones filled the air as surviving clan members paid their last respects to the fallen. Even though they lived in a world where death was their constant companion, nothing had equipped them for this. Yesterday's slaughter was like nothing they or their forefathers had ever experienced, and nothing could have prepared them for the carnage that unfolded.

Survivors wandered about, zombie-like, barely able to comprehend what had happened. The inescapable smell of burning flesh pervaded the atmosphere, serving as a constant reminder of the recent horror.

No official count had been conducted of the dead and wounded. However, John did a quick count, and reckoned fifty clan members had been killed.

Damn near half the clan!

In addition to the dead, many clan members had been wounded—some gravely—and it was evident some of them would not survive.

Yileen, who had himself been wounded, was working tirelessly to administer his healing powers to the wounded. For once, his powers had little effect. He'd never before seen or treated people with bullet wounds. John had to show him how to remove bullets from gunshot victims, using a knife he'd recovered from one of the dead soldiers.

John knew all the dead and wounded by sight and many of them by name, and he blamed himself for their misfortune.

The words of Karadji echoed over and over in his head.

I see white spirits coming. A few at first. Then many thousands until they cover the land like ants.

John was in his own private hell. As well as blaming himself, he was grieving the loss of Mamba and Murrowdooling. Only now that they were gone was it that he fully realised how much he loved them. He couldn't imagine life without them.

The Irishman was now wearing the undershorts, shirt and breeches he'd removed from one of the dead soldiers, and the socks and boots he'd removed from another. He'd also salvaged the bayonet from one of the rifles the soldiers had left behind. Any hopes he could arm himself with a rifle had been dashed when Mirritji had ordered all the firearms be destroyed. The order had been prompted by the actions of a boy who almost killed his grandmother after playing with one of the rifles. The bullet had grazed his grandmother's forehead, and had left her so traumatised she hadn't uttered a word since.

"What will happen to us now, Moilow?"

It was Carravanty.

John turned around to see the boy looking up at him, his face full of bewilderment. Still only twelve, he hadn't been able to make sense of the catastrophe that had befallen the clan. The Irishman knelt down and hugged the boy. Speaking in the Kabi tongue, he murmured, "We will be fine, you and I." He wasn't sure he believed it, but he knew he must stay strong for Carravanty.

"Where are they now?" Carravanty asked.

John realised Carravanty was referring to Mamba and Murrowdooling. The boy had seen their bodies and had witnessed their cremation, but still he couldn't believe they were gone. The Irishman held him out at arm's length and looked into his eyes. "They are on their way to the Dreaming," he said.

Carravanty nodded. He'd heard much about the Dreaming, or the Dreamtime as some called it, but, like John, he still didn't fully understand it. Still, it brought him comfort.

The clan members were now preparing to move out. They'd decided to head further inland, so anxious were they to distance themselves from the soldiers.

The Irishman returned his attention to the task at hand. He was busy securing a wooden sledge to one of the horses the soldiers had left behind, while Carravanty was loading supplies onto it. The horse had wandered into the encampment during the night, putting the fear of God into the clan members. John had quickly secured it, assuring doubters it meant them no harm. They weren't convinced. However, they softened their stance when the Irishman explained he'd use the animal as a packhorse to carry his and other clan members' possessions.

John moved as though he was in a trance. He was stiff and sore, and he had a cut on his forehead that wouldn't stop bleeding. Added to that, he'd barely slept overnight, and what little sleep he managed to grab was punctuated with dreams of Mamba being crushed beneath the hooves of Hogan's horse, and Murrowdooling being skewered by Barega's spear. His hatred for those two men knew no bounds. He was only sorry the tracker's body wasn't amongst those of the fallen raiders.

As he tied a second vine connecting the sledge to the horse's saddle, John noticed a group of natives on the far side of the encampment. They were hard to see through the smoke. Even so, it was obvious they were talking about him as they looked his way every so often. A closer look revealed that Mirritji, Turo and Gabirri were among them. They appeared to be arguing.

Mirritji noticed John looking their way, and he motioned to him to approach.

Leaving Carravanty to finish loading supplies onto the sledge, John walked over to join the men who still appeared to be arguing. He could well imagine what they were arguing about.

The men quietened as the white approached.

"I bring you goodwill," John said.

"I accept your goodwill," Mirritji and Gabirri said in unison.

The others did not return the greeting.

John knew what was coming. He had been banished from the clan, and now he was back—and clearly not everyone was happy. He studied their expressions, trying to determine who was an ally and who wasn't.

An elder pointed an accusing finger at John. "The banished one led the white men and their beasts to us!" he said.

"He alerted us to their arrival!" Gabirri countered.

"The white spirit is to blame for the death and destruction!" another elder shouted.

"He fought with us against the white men," Mirritji reminded them.

"He was banished and he defied the spirits by returning to us!" yet another elder said.

The exchange continued. Throughout it all John tried to assess the prevailing mood. It seemed, to him, to be evenly split between those who supported him and those who would see him dead. He was in no doubt if the latter prevailed, he would be put to death. Despite this, he felt extremely calm. Part of him hoped his detractors would prevail.

Throughout the exchange, Turo remained strangely silent. Finally, when the arguing subsided, the big native stepped forward, stopping barely one pace from John. Looking at his long-time nemesis gravely, he said, "It is as Mirritji said. The white spirit fought alongside us." He pointed to the wound on the white's forehead, saying "He risked death and he bled as we all did."

Turo didn't remind the assembled that John had also saved his life during the attack, but he didn't need to. They were all aware of it.

The big native reached out and placed the palm of his right hand against John's chest. "He *is* Moilow," he said. Withdrawing his hand, he nodded to John and stepped back.

The two former enemies studied each other. Respect registered in the eyes of each.

After a short silence, Gabirri held up his spear. "He *is* Moilow!" he said, repeating Turo's assertion.

It wasn't long before all the assembled took up the refrain, chanting, "He *is* Moilow! He is Moilow!" The chant was taken up by all the clan members.

John accepted their endorsement with humility then slowly walked back to join Carravanty. Behind him, as the chanting faded, all except Mirritji dispersed. The elder watched John for a few moments before hurrying atop his bandy legs to catch up to him. "Moilow!" he called.

The Irishman stopped and waited. He could see something was bothering the old man.

Mirritji placed a caring hand on John's arm. "Something troubles you, Moilow."

It was a statement, not a question, and John knew the elder wasn't just referring to the loss of Mamba and Murrowdooling.

John looked away. "As long as I am here, the Kabi are in danger," he said.

"Will the white men return?" Mirritji asked.

John wondered how best to answer him. He thought the soldiers would return for him, but not any time soon. Not until they'd taken time to lick their wounds. However, he wanted the elder to understand the risk his continued presence posed the clan. He also wanted him to appreciate that more and more British would be coming, and there was nothing the Kabi could do to stop them. Turning back to him, he said, "It is as Karadji predicted. A few whites will come at first, and then many thousands will come until they cover the land like ants."

Mirritji looked long and hard at John. Finally, he said, "You are Kabi. I am Kabi. We face all dangers together, as one." With that, the old man walked off.

It was early afternoon before the clan members filed out of the encampment that had turned out to be the final resting place for so many of their number. The smoke from the earlier mass cremation still lingered as did the smell of burnt flesh.

John and Carravanty brought up the rear of the Kabi caravan. Their horse, which John had named *Noel,* in memory of his friend Noel Thomas, hauled the sledge he'd made. The sledge was laden with their meagre possessions and those of a number of their fellow clan members. A youth who couldn't walk as a result of having been shot in the knee sat astride the horse. He'd taken some convincing, but now that he realised Noel wasn't about to buck him off or eat him he was quite happy.

Other wounded clan members who were incapable of walking were carried on makeshift stretchers behind the few remaining able-bodied men and youths.

The clan members filed past the dead soldiers who they'd left hanging upside down from the lower branches of two gum trees on the edge of the encampment. All eight corpses had been stripped naked and mutilated before being strung up by their ankles as a warning to any soldiers who may return. Hawks and other birds of prey had already begun tearing the flesh from the bodies.

John didn't look at the corpses as he filed past, but he glimpsed Hogan's body— or what was left of it—out of the corner of his eye. The once-dashing lieutenant had been reduced to a mutilated cadaver.

The Irishman experienced a stab of guilt. He felt he was indirectly responsible for Hogan's death, and for the other soldiers, too. Then he had a flashback to Hogan callously riding his horse over Mamba, killing her, and his guilt subsided.

For the first time in a while, he thought of Helen. He could imagine what the young woman would think of him when she learned from her father what had happened to Hogan and the other soldiers.

At that moment, Captain Marsden was lying, alone with his thoughts, in Captain

McDowell's quarters aboard *The East Sunrise,* which was now plying its way south back to Moreton Bay. The schooner's master had kindly made his bunk and cabin available for the wounded captain.

Marsden was in a foul mood. He'd had plenty of time to consider the events of the last couple of days, but even now he wasn't sure exactly where it had all gone wrong.

By any measure, the raid on the Kabi's encampment had been a disaster. The plan had been to remain hidden until a confirmed sighting was made of John Graham. Then Marsden himself was to lead a quick grab-and-snatch raid that would result in the capture of the fugitive and, hopefully, no loss of life on either side. Instead, he'd lost nine men—another soldier had died during the fighting retreat back to the coast—and he couldn't guess how many clan members had been killed.

Marsden's first instinct had been to blame Hogan for the disaster. While the lieutenant hadn't fired the first shot—that is the pre-emptive shot that had sparked the slaughter—he had certainly disobeyed orders, and his actions had encouraged the soldiers to engage in what could only be described as a bloodbath. However, the captain had been a professional soldier long enough to know that as the senior officer, the responsibility for what happened was his and his alone.

The retreat to the coast had been a continuation of the nightmare. Marsden, Barega and the other two survivors had been harried much of the way by angry clan members who seemed intent on killing every last one of them. Only sharp shooting had kept the natives at bay, wounding two of them in the process.

Marsden had been lucky to survive. The spear had just missed a major artery. Even so, when the weapon was pulled from his thigh, he lost a large amount of blood and would likely have died had it not been for the first aid skills of Private Askew, one of the survivors.

On reaching the coast, all except Barega had been rowed out to the waiting schooner where they received immediate first aid for their wounds. The tracker was the only man to escape unscathed. He was tasked with leading the soldiers' horses back to Moreton Bay overland. That had always been the plan as there was no way to load horses onto a vessel anchored offshore. Only five horses were making the trek. The remainder—apart from the one that John captured and another that had to be put down—were now running wild in the wilderness.

Marsden feared his career could be finished as a result of the failed expedition. He could just imagine the headlines in the Sydney and London daily newspapers: *Nine British soldiers killed by Stone Age savages in doomed raid.* The repercussions didn't bear thinking about.

Marsden's mood wasn't helped any by the conditions *The East Sunrise* had encountered since she weighed anchor the previous afternoon. The schooner was pitching and rolling quite violently in high seas, and every movement caused the captain pain. A three-quarter full bottle of rum McDowell had thoughtfully left out for him eased the pain a little. However, Marsden's over-riding concern was not for himself, his wound or his career; it was for his daughter. She was only hours away from learning her fiancé had been killed.

One of the captain's biggest regrets was that there hadn't been the opportunity to recover his lieutenant's body, or any of the soldiers' bodies for that matter. He didn't want to think about what the natives had done with them.

Helen was conducting her afternoon rounds of the junior school when a soldier alerted her that *The East Sunrise* was about to berth at the wharf. Hogan had left orders with the soldier to alert her as soon as the schooner returned.

When questioned whether John Graham had been captured, the soldier—a private—assured her he didn't know. He'd come to the school as soon as he'd sighted the vessel.

Helen hurried to her nearby cottage and saddled her horse. She was under the assumption both the lieutenant and the Irishman were on board.

It was with mixed feelings that she set off for the wharf. On the one hand, she was looking forward to seeing Hogan again; on the other hand, she wasn't sure she wanted to see John. She had been able to put the Irishman out of her mind—most of the time at least—and she was afraid seeing him again may complicate things. At present, she'd gotten used to thinking of herself as the future Missus Hogan, and she didn't want anything to upset that.

Approaching the schooner, she was bemused to see so few soldiers disembarking. She counted only two, and there was no sign of Hogan or her father—or John for that matter.

Helen galloped over to one of the two soldiers she'd sighted. Reining in beside him, she noticed he'd been wounded and was looking downcast. She asked, "Where are the others?"

The soldier mumbled something incoherent and wouldn't look at her.

"Where is my father?" Helen asked.

The soldier walked off without answering.

Mystified, Helen approached the second soldier. She recognised him immediately. It was Private Askew. "Where is my father, Private Askew?" she asked.

"He'll be on deck soon, Miss," Askew said. "He was wounded." Noting the alarm on the young woman's face, he quickly added, "But he will be fine." The private hurried off before he had to field any more uncomfortable questions.

"Where is Lieutenant Hogan?" Helen called out.

Askew didn't respond.

Helen's concern was growing. She'd observed Askew seemed as downcast as the other soldier, and she suspected he had also been wounded as he was limping badly and there were bloodstains on his uniform. And still there was no sign of any of the other soldiers.

Then she saw her father, and her concerns momentarily faded. She waved to him, and he waved back.

Marsden was being stretchered off the schooner by two burly sailors. They were accompanied by Captain McDowell who by now was a firm friend of the wounded captain.

Still on horseback, Helen watched as her father was lifted onto the tray of a horse-drawn cart. She waited while the sailors ensured her father was made comfortable and McDowell shared some parting words with him. Still there was no sign of Hogan and the others, and her alarm was growing.

As soon as the seamen returned to the schooner, Helen dismounted her horse and hurried over to see her father. One look at his face told her the news could only be bad.

"Papa, are you alright?" she asked, kissing Marsden's cheek.

Marsden, who was never one for sugar-coating bad news, said, "I am fine, my dear, but you will not like what I have to tell you."

Helen felt a cold shiver go right through her. She suspected she was about to learn either John or Hogan had been killed—or both perhaps. It didn't escape her that the first person she'd thought of was John. "Was John Graham killed?" she asked.

Marsden shook his head. "I am sorry to advise that Desmond was killed," he murmured. The captain was surprised his daughter had enquired after the Irishman's wellbeing first, but he hid his surprise.

Helen experienced two extreme emotions in quick succession. The first was relief to learn that John hadn't been killed; the second was sadness to hear that Hogan was dead. Fighting back tears, she said, "I will accompany you to the settlement, papa."

Marsden tried to object, but Helen insisted. She hitched her horse to the back of the cart and then climbed onto the tray and sat alongside her father. The captain then ordered the soldier manning the cart to drive them back to the settlement. En route, he told Helen, in detail, what had transpired over the past two days. He made no mention of Hogan disobeying orders. Nor did he say he saw John strike the lieutenant with his tomahawk.

As her father talked, Helen tried to make sense of everything she was feeling. To her great consternation, she realised she was possibly more relieved that John was still alive than she was sad that Hogan wasn't returning.

That realisation brought her no comfort at all. In fact, it only added to the guilt she already felt over harbouring feelings for the Irish fugitive.

PART SIX

THE
SONGLINES

76

THE YEAR FOLLOWING THE SOLDIERS' raid was one of the worst in the Kabi clan's history. Losing half their number in the slaughter was bad enough, but what made it worse was the clan's fighting force had been decimated. Many of those killed were warriors who had borne the brunt of the bloody raid, and, one result of that was it left the clan exposed to attacks by other tribes.

And other tribes had been quick to take advantage of that.

In the first six months, which saw off the end of that summer and the start of the winter just gone, the clan was attacked no less than four times. The Gureng, Wanjuri and Noonuccal all mounted raids during that period—the Wanjuri returning for a second crack at their weakened enemy—further reducing the clan's numbers.

Only drastic action had saved it from likely extinction. As a last resort, it merged with another Kabi clan. *Merged* is perhaps not the right word: it was more a takeover than a merger because Mirritji's clan was effectively swallowed up when it became part of a clan known as *the Noosa clan*—the Kabi's northernmost clan and one of the strongest in the tribe. The merger boosted the clan's population to nigh on one hundred and eighty, making it the tribe's largest.

Not everyone supported the merger. Some of those with long memories opposed it because they remembered past skirmishes with the Noosa clan. A number of those skirmishes had resulted in bloodshed. However, the loss of more fighting men dictated that there was no other choice. It was either blend in with the Noosa clan or risk being wiped out. And so common sense prevailed.

The last six months hadn't been easy either. All the clans had endured a wet season like no other in living memory. Unrelenting, heavy rain had brought floods, which had restricted travel between hunting grounds and had resulted in starvation for many. The arrival of the dry season had brought little relief. Constant rain had been replaced by soaring temperatures, bushfires and a severe drought that showed no sign of easing any time soon.

The harsh conditions had resulted in widespread malnutrition amongst clan members, and half a dozen had died from starvation in the past month alone. Children and the elderly were worst affected. Those elderly who were too hungry and frail to fend for themselves more often than not wandered out into the bush where they remained, by choice, until they died—just as Mootemu had.

John's pack horse Noel had been sacrificed early on to feed starving clan members. Its meat had fed the clan well for a couple of days. Since the onset of summer, the clan members' diet consisted of whatever they could scavenge. Roo numbers had been reduced by the drought and by the bushfires that accompanied it, so clan members had to content themselves with the meat of snakes, lizards and rodents along with the occasional possum or wallaby.

For John and Carravanty, and for the others of Mirritji's clan, it was doubly hard. They remained traumatised by the violent events of twelve months earlier, and they all grieved the loss of loved-ones.

Since losing Mamba and Murrowdooling, the Irishman felt he was just going through the motions. Life no longer held the same appeal. He saw the ghosts of Mamba and her oldest son everywhere. If it hadn't been for Carravanty, he may well have killed himself. He often thought about how he'd do it. John doubted he'd have the courage to do what the old people did. His preference would be to throw himself off a cliff or perhaps eat a piece of the poisoned bait clan members left out for the possums.

Mirritji had long been concerned about the white spirit's state of mind. The elder approached John when he saw him sitting alone, atop a sand hill, staring out to sea. John, who still wore the soldiers' clothes and boots that he'd commandeered, had been sitting there, not moving, for the past hour or more. The Irishman's body language told Mirritji he wanted to be alone, but he didn't let that deter him. Sitting down alongside him, the elder said, "I bring you goodwill, Moilow."

John just grunted. He wasn't in the mood to accept anyone's goodwill, and he certainly wasn't about to extend any goodwill of his own.

Just leave me be, old man.

Mirritji got the message. He said nothing more, but still he stayed put.

Below them, along the beach, clan members foraged for food. Women and children gathered shellfish from the rocks while fishermen stalked the shallows, spears at the ready, looking for the tell-tale shadows of fish lurking beneath the surface. Offshore, more fishermen cast nets from their canoes.

The usual banter and laughter that accompanied such activity was noticeably absent. It was serious business. Even the children seemed to realise if insufficient food was caught or gathered on any given day, more clan members would starve.

Amongst those spearing fish in the shallows was Turo. The big native saw John and waved at him. John returned the other's acknowledgement with a nod of his head. The two unlikely allies had become friends since John had saved Turo's life. It was, to the Irishman, one of life's strange twists and turns. To his new friend, however, their friendship seemed entirely natural. Moilow was, after all, Turo's best friend in his former life.

An hour later, atop the same sand hill, the silence between John and Mirritji prevailed.

The elder surreptitiously studied his younger companion. John had been especially morose of late. It was evident he was missing Mamba badly, but many others were missing their loved-ones and, unlike John, they were making an effort to get on with their lives. Finally, Mirritji spoke. "Moilow," he murmured.

Still John didn't acknowledge him.

"Look at me, Moilow," Mirritji commanded.

"Leave me be," John grumbled. When he realised the elder wasn't budging, he slowly turned to him.

"You need to find yourself," Mirritji said.

John really wasn't in the mood for a philosophical discussion. However, good manners demanded that he humour the old man. "And where would I find myself?" he asked.

"In the interior," Mirritji said. "In the place we call the Dry Lands."

John knew of the place the elder referred to. It was the place Europeans referred to as *the Outback,* and it was where the clan's boys went to when it was their time to pass into manhood. "What is there for me . . . in the Dry Lands?" he asked.

"There you will find your ancestors' spirits. They will talk to you . . . from the Dreaming."

"How will I find this place?" John enquired.

Mirritji pointed inland—to the west. He said, "You only need follow the setting sun, and you will find it."

John considered the elder's advice. He was suddenly interested, but not necessarily for any reason Mirritji would approve of.

The Dry Lands would be a good place to die.

"How will I find my way back to the clan?" John asked on the off-chance he wanted to find his way back.

Mirritji smiled for the first time. "You know the answer to that, Moilow," he said.

John nodded. He did know the answer.

The Songlines. They will guide me.

A month passed before John finally decided to act on Mirritji's advice. Now that the time had come, he found he was looking forward to seeing this place they called the Dry Lands.

If he hadn't realised before what a big deal heading out alone into the interior was, he was beginning to realise it now. Almost the entire clan had turned out to see him off, and it wasn't yet dawn.

That surprised him. Although he was now fully accepted by the surviving members of the original clan—even by Turo—the Noosa clan members remained wary of him. He thought that understandable given none had known the real Moilow. Not to mention they'd never seen a white spirit before. *Come to that, I never knew the real Moilow,* he reminded himself. *And I've certainly never seen a white spirit.* Yet despite the Noosa clan members' wariness, they turned out in force to see him off.

For the coming journey, John had forsaken the clothes and boots he'd acquired, and now wore only his cloak and loincloth. He carried two spears and a woomera, and in place of his makeshift tomahawk he now carried a knife he had fashioned from the bayonet he'd removed from one of the soldier's rifles.

Over his shoulder, he carried a water bottle one of the soldiers had left behind.

He also carried a flax bag Turo's second wife, Ekala, had filled with food supplies—enough to last him two or three days. Ekala had also agreed to care for Carravanty for as long as John was absent.

Parting with Carravanty hadn't been easy. John had said his goodbyes before the boy had bedded down in Ekala's bivouac the previous night. He had promised him he'd return, and so, for that reason alone, he knew he would.

If I can survive . . . and if I can find my way back.

As dawn arrived, John recognised individual clan members who had come to see him off. Among those to the fore were Mirritji, Gabirri and Turo. Alongside them was none other than Yarran, the senior elder of the Nootka clan. Until now, he'd never given John the time of day. Now, as the white spirit prepared to set off, Yarran seemed to have had a change of heart—a further reminder to John what a big deal heading into the Dry Lands was to these people.

The Irishman suddenly felt nervous as the enormity of what he was about to take on hit him. Before he could change his mind, he turned and walked off into the rainforest that bordered the narrow coastal strip that was currently home to the clan.

As he departed, clan members called out to him, wishing him good fortune.

The last voice he heard before entering the rainforest was Mirritji's. The elder said, "Let the Songlines guide you, Moilow."

By mid-day, John had left the rainforest behind. He was now trekking through scrubby bush country that had been turned brown by the continuing drought. The long, hot months without rain had converted rivers into dry riverbeds, and billabongs and other watering holes were little more than muddy basins. Shimmering heat waves distorted the hills that lined the western horizon, and the hinterland that extended to the foot of those same hills was devoid of grass: the heat and successive fires had burnt the grass off, leaving only red earth in its place.

John nearly stood on a sleeping death adder, but he saw it just in time and gave it a wide berth. He recalled what a Moreton Bay convict had told him about death adders.

One bite from one o' those and yer dead in thirty minutes.

He momentarily pondered the wisdom of setting out minus his boots, but only momentarily. In fact, he was pleased he'd forsaken his boots and other items of European clothing. The loincloth and cloak he now wore allowed him to sweat freely, and they allowed him to move freely, too. It was so hot he'd have liked to dispense with his cloak, but he was aware it would help shield him from the sun, which beat down mercilessly. And it kept him warm during the nights, which were surprisingly cool considering the daytime temperatures.

As for his boots, he wasn't missing them one iota. Having gone barefoot for long periods over the past five years, his feet had been sufficiently toughened to allow him to walk all day without too much discomfort.

Perhaps I really am Moilow.

Despite the heat and the dangers ahead, he was feeling strangely cheerful. He put it down to a change of routine, a new challenge.

John was under no illusions concerning what awaited him. He was very aware it was a big ask for anyone to head into Australia's interior at the best of times, but to do it alone, in the middle of summer and during the worst drought in living memory, would be considered by many to be a suicide mission.

And yet he felt confident—unaccountably confident. Mirritji had assured him he needed to go to the Dry Lands, and he trusted the old man's insight.

As John trekked into the interior, Marsden was sitting down for a Sunday lunch with his new wife Mildred and with Helen and Matthew in the family cottage at Moreton Bay. The captain had finally married the former Missus Mildred Jones, at the urging of his children who considered her a fine match for their father, just three months earlier. Since then, the Sunday lunch had become part of the family's weekly routine.

Matthew was once more living at home, having relocated from Sydney Town to attend the local school at the start of the current school year. Moreton Bay Junior School was no more. Expanding the school to accommodate older children had necessitated a name change; it was now simply called *Moreton Bay School*.

Helen was still teaching at the school, but her duties went beyond teaching. As head mistress, she was responsible for the running of the school whose expanded roll now totalled sixty pupils and five teachers—four fulltime and one part-time. She still lived in the same rented cottage in town, and she was still married to her career.

Since her fiancé's death just over a year ago, Helen had immersed herself in her role as head mistress. One upshot of that was the school was going from strength to strength, and its pupils were achieving higher average results than the longer established schools in Sydney Town and Melbourne. As a result, Moreton Bay School was being upheld as a beacon for the colony's fledgling education services—and its head mistress could take much of the credit for that.

Throwing herself into her work had been Helen's way of dealing with the loss of Hogan. The downside of that was she had little time, and even less inclination, to enjoy any semblance of a social life. Her father, and her new stepmother, too, often encouraged her to branch out and socialise, but to no avail.

If she was honest with herself, she had never really grieved the loss of her fiancé. Early on, she'd come to the realisation she never truly loved Hogan. Exactly why she had finally agreed to marry him, she wasn't sure. Perhaps, deep down, she suspected it was because she feared being left on the shelf. Nowadays, she had no such fear. She was quite content being married to her job.

Helen still thought about John Graham on occasion. Even though she'd hardly known him, she had to admit—to herself at least—the cheeky Irishman with the startling blue eyes had made quite an impression on her.

As for her father, he often thought of the Irishman, albeit for entirely different reasons. Since the failed raid on the Kabi encampment, Marsden had become consumed by the desire to capture John. The memory of that dawn raid, and the resulting loss of lives, haunted him to this very day. He still had nightmares about it.

The captain had returned from that disastrous expedition fully expecting to be demoted or worse. He'd seen other officers permanently relieved of their duties and, on occasion, discharged and publicly disgraced for lesser failures.

To his surprise, there were no such repercussions. The captain put that down to one thing: timing.

The failed raid coincided with a worsening of Lord Cheetham's opium addiction. Within days of Marsden's return to Moreton Bay, Cheetham had been shipped off to Sydney Town on the orders of the Governor. Sir Ralph's patience with the addicted commandant had finally run out, and, on the advice of the army's doctors, Cheetham was temporarily relieved of his duties so that he could dry out and undergo treatment at Sydney Town's new sanatorium.

Sir Ralph was horrified that word of the commandant's addiction had been leaked to the newspapers, and several articles had already appeared in the main Australian daily newspapers, and even in one of the leading London newspapers. The publicity didn't reflect at all well on him or the British Army.

Just as Cheetham's addiction was common knowledge, it was widely known that the reason the Governor didn't permanently relieve the commandant of his duties was he valued the prestige of having a titled individual in charge of the Moreton Bay penal settlement. Such titles as *Lord* weren't to be sniffed at in the colonies, and the presence of someone so titled reflected well on the army and on Sir Ralph, too.

As for Marsden. He was in no doubt he had personally benefited from Cheetham's fall from grace. The army couldn't handle any more bad publicity, so news of the failed attempt to capture John was handled internally and kept well away from the newspapers.

By all accounts—and against all predictions—Cheetham was slowly getting on top of his addiction. However, there was still no word when he was likely to resume his duties at Moreton Bay. Until then, the running of the settlement was being left to Marsden.

After lunch, Helen and Matthew sat talking in the shade of the veranda while Marsden and Mildred enjoyed a snooze inside—another Sunday routine they'd fallen into.

"Have you heard the latest, Sis?" Matthew asked.

"No, but I have a feeling you are about to tell me," Helen said.

"They say John Graham has been living with the blacks all this time."

"I do not wish to talk about John Graham thank you, Matthew," Helen said. "Anyway, that's old news."

Lowering his voice so as not to wake his father, Matthew said, "Well here's something you don't know . . . Archie Dempsey's father . . . you know . . . Sergeant Dempsey . . . well he told us that John Graham's gone native . . . and after he killed one of the soldiers, he ate his heart."

"Nonsense!" Helen snapped. "And disgusting."

Matthew grinned. He loved winding his big sister up—even if she was headmistress at his school—and he had the bit between his teeth now. "I hear the tracker's still full time on the Irishman's trail," he said.

Helen looked up. "How do you know that?" she asked.

Matthew said, "I hear things . . . you know . . . from the other boys . . . at school."

Helen nodded. She was aware her brother mixed with the children of some of the soldiers, so it was natural he would pick up titbits of news from them. How much of that news was reliable, she had her doubts.

Matthew added, "And I use my eyes."

Yawning, Helen feigned disinterest.

Undeterred, Matthew said, "I see Barega riding north most weeks, and I see him return every other week."

"So?"

"So who else would he be looking for up north?"

Helen didn't respond, but she suspected her brother was right. She was aware how badly her father wanted to capture John Graham.

77

⊰•————•⊱

J OHN DIDN'T KNOW HOW FAR he'd come, but he knew to the day how long it was since he set out from the Kabi encampment: he'd carved a notch into his woomera at the end of each day's trek, and there were twenty-nine notches in it. *Day thirty today.*

He reckoned he must have ventured six hundred miles inland in that time. It certainly felt like that. In fact, he'd come less than half that distance.

The Irishman had started out well. Full of energy, he'd averaged twenty miles a day in the first week. Then, as the heat and shortage of water and food took their toll, he struggled to walk ten miles a day. These past few days he'd barely managed to walk more than five or six miles a day before being forced to rest up in what little shade he could find. Some days, it was just too hot for him to walk and so he stayed put. He often did that on the rare occasion he found a waterhole—especially if there was shade nearby.

Water and shade were two essentials in rare supply, he'd discovered. And the further west he ventured, the scarcer they became. If it hadn't been for his commandeered water bottle, he reckoned, he'd have died of thirst several times over. The bottle's lifesaving contents had enabled him to last between waterholes thus far, but the distances between those holes were steadily increasing.

John knew he was pushing his luck. Several times in the past week, he'd come close to quitting. Each time, he told himself *just another day.*

Some days were brutal—and this particular day was no exception. The relentless sun beat down on a desert-like landscape, threatening to fry every living thing. The only living things around that John was aware of, besides himself, were the flies that constantly plagued him. It was too hot even for the snakes and lizards, and there wasn't a tree in sight. The only visible vegetation was a few gnarled shrubs, which appeared to be dead.

The red earth contrasted with the blue sky above, and the sun's glare was so bright he had trouble focussing on anything for more than a few seconds at a time. Any longer than that and he had to close his eyes or the pain became unbearable.

Underfoot, the bare earth was often so hot that travel for the barefoot Irishman was restricted to early morning and late afternoon or early evening. It was just too hot to walk in the middle of the day.

The journey thus far had certainly taken its toll. His already darkened skin had been blackened further by the sun, and the heat and exertion had depleted his reserves of fat to the point he resembled little more than a walking skeleton. No longer clean-shaven, his beard was hanging on his chest, and he was sure if anyone saw him they would surely mistake him for a native.

Now, as the late afternoon sun dipped toward the horizon, John pushed himself as hard as he could. Desperate for water, he was heading for a solitary bush whose leaves, he'd just noticed, were tinged green. Experience told him the greenery could mean its roots were immersed in water.

John's water bottle was near-empty. He'd had his last swig from it at mid-day, and he estimated there was only another mouthful of water left at most. His throat was parched and his lips cracked, and he feared he'd die of thirst if he didn't drink soon. Not for the first time, he wondered what had possessed him to venture inland alone.

Stupid feckin' Irishman!

As he neared the bush, his hopes evaporated like the sweat on his brow when he realised its leaves were dead. The greenish tinge he thought he'd seen had been nothing more than a cruel trick of the light. Even so, he used his bayonet to dig a hole beneath the bush to make sure.

After five minutes digging, he gave up. The earth was bone dry.

John was resigned to dying. Now that the time had come, he realised he couldn't embrace it as he'd once thought he could. He still had Carravanty to live for.

He looked around, more desperate than ever to find a way out of his predicament. "Nothing," he murmured. "Nothing at all." He wondered what Gabirri and Turo would do in his situation.

They'd know what to do.

He shook his water bottle. The remaining water scarcely made a sound. Reluctantly, he removed the top and raised the bottle to his lips, savouring every last drop.

Then he lay down beneath the bush. Mercifully, it had sufficient foliage to offer some shade. Thirsty, hungry and exhausted, he wanted to sleep, but the heat and the flies wouldn't allow that. Besides, he sensed if he fell asleep he'd never wake. So he lay there, willing the time to pass and hoping for a miracle.

As the shadows lengthened, John could feel himself becoming delirious. He'd sensed all was not well when he began seeing things that weren't there. It had started the previous day when he was convinced he'd seen a billabong overflowing with water. As he approached it, it faded from sight. At the time, he thought it was a mirage, but when he saw Mamba and Murrowdooling running toward him a short while later he realised he was hallucinating.

The hallucinations had become more frequent, and earlier today he'd been certain he was walking through the green countryside of his home county in Ireland.

Now, as he fought against the overwhelming tiredness that threatened to put him to sleep for all of eternity, he was taken back in time to when he and Mirritji observed the artist Warrane paint the Dreamtime on the back wall of a cave. Even though his eyes were closed, he could see the golden rays of sunlight that pierced the clouds, highlighting creatures on the earth below. He opened his eyes, and the image remained, clearer than ever. Stick-like figures representing hunters walked among the animals, spears raised.

Snippets of his discussion with Mirritji came to him. He could hear the elder saying, "The blood of our ancestors flows along those tracks, linking us to the land and to the totems that roam that land."

"What is my totem?" John had asked.

"Your totem is the dingo, Moilow."

When John next opened his eyes, dusk had fallen. He thought he may have dropped off to asleep for he couldn't account for the past hour or two.

In the fading light he caught a movement at the edge of his peripheral vision. A flash of yellow. He thought he may still be hallucinating. Then he saw it again.

An emu?

John sat up and shook his head to clear his vision.

Nothing.

Convinced he'd imagined it, he was about to lie back down when he glanced behind him. There, not twenty yards away, was a dingo.

At first he thought it was Dingo, the wild dog that had kind of adopted him on his trek north from Moreton Bay. A closer look revealed this dingo was female, and she didn't have the distinctive reddish markings that Dingo had.

"What do you want girl?" John asked. He fully expected the dingo to take off, but, at the sound of his voice, she approached him, stopping only when she was about ten yards short. More convinced than ever that he was delirious, John picked up a stone and threw it toward the dingo. She tensed, but still she didn't run off.

Again, Mirritji's words came to him. "In the Dreamtime, the great animal spirits became part of our landscape, and these can only be seen by the chosen ones."

Finally, the dingo turned and began walking away. She stopped and looked back at John every few yards until it became obvious to him she wanted him to follow her.

The Irishman debated whether to stay or go. Every cell in his body yearned for sleep, but Mirritji's words kept coming to him.

Your totem is the dingo, Moilow. Your totem is the dingo. Your totem is . . .

"Damn it." Almost against his better judgement, John pushed himself slowly to his feet. Gathering up his spears and other possessions, he struck out after the dingo, which was now fifty yards away and barely visible in the darkness. If it wasn't for the moonlight on her yellow coat, she'd have been invisible to him.

The dingo set a steady pace—not so fast John couldn't keep up, but fast enough that he had to stride out to keep her in sight. She was heading west.

"I hope you know what you're doing, old girl," he grumbled. His thirst was killing him, literally, and he sensed he couldn't walk far—not at the pace his canine guide was setting.

Fortunately, he didn't have to travel far. The dingo pulled up not three hundred yards from where John had stopped to rest. Only as he approached did he notice she'd stopped before a crevice he hadn't noticed earlier. The reason he hadn't previously seen it was only clear now: the opening was so narrow it was hidden from sight unless you were almost upon it.

The sound of trickling water carried to him. "Water!" he gasped. He ran the last few yards to the edge of the crevice.

Only now did the dingo take off. She didn't stop to look back.

John was too consumed by his need for water to think about the dingo. He didn't even spare her a backward glance as he peered down into the darkness of the crevice. Here, the sound of water was loud—so loud he was tempted to jump in.

Common-sense prevailed. In the darkness, he had no way of knowing how deep the crevice was. *Even if I survived the jump, I may not be able to climb out,* he told himself. *Best wait for daylight.* Reluctantly, he retreated a few steps from the edge of the opening and lay down to sleep.

As before, sleep wouldn't come. His throat was so dry, he couldn't even swallow, and the sound of trickling water seemed to grow louder with every passing minute. It wasn't long before it sounded like a thundering waterfall. More than once he had to consciously restrain himself from jumping up and diving headlong into the crevice.

Eventually, sleep came. It was a restless, dream-filled sleep. He dreamed he'd been reunited in the Dreamtime with Mamba and Murrowdooling.

The squawk of a wedge-tailed eagle carried to John as he woke. He opened his eyes and saw the bird of prey circling directly above him, apparently waiting to establish whether he was alive or dead. "I'm alive, you bastard!" he croaked. He'd intended to shout at the eagle, but his throat was so parched it was little more than a rasping murmur.

The rays of the morning sun had already broached the eastern horizon, and the cloudless sky heralded the beginning of another brutally hot day.

John tried to swallow, but couldn't. Parched, he tried to cry out, but his throat was now so sore and his tongue so swollen he could make no sound other than grunt.

It took all his energy just to lie there. So delirious was he, he was convinced Mamba was lying beside him. He tried to talk to her, but no words would come.

In his confusion, he swore he could hear the sound of waves crashing onto a beach. The sound faded only to be replaced by the sound of a waterfall. In turn, that was replaced by the sound of trickling water. It came from close by. He crawled a few paces until he was at the edge of the crevice. There, twenty feet below was a spring, bubbling up from the earth. In the early morning light, it was only faintly visible.

At first, John thought he may still be hallucinating.

It can't be!

When he realised he wasn't imagining things, he looked for a way down to the bottom of the crevice. It didn't take him long to spot a track that had been carved out by generations of dingoes, and humans, too, probably, that led directly to the spring.

Retrieving his water bottle, he clambered down the track and plunged into the water. It was only a foot or so deep, but it was pure and, in the permanent shade of the crevice, it was cool. John gulped down mouthfuls of water, stopping only when he remembered he shouldn't drink too much at once.

Before he knew what he was doing, he was laughing out loud. He couldn't believe his good fortune. Nor could he believe how quickly the water had revived him. He could feel his strength returning—and so, too, his desire to live.

Only now did he think of the dingo that had led him to this place. After drinking some more and filling his water bottle, he scrambled from the crevice in the hope of seeing the animal. She was long gone.

78

JOHN REMAINED CLOSE TO THE crevice and its life-giving spring for several days before resuming his journey. When he wasn't out hunting for food, he rested inside the fissure, luxuriating in the protection it provided from the sun and the heat, while, at the same time, recovering his strength.

Food came in the form of snakes, lizards and witchetty grubs. It wasn't his favourite tucker, but it kept him alive and he wasn't complaining.

When he felt refreshed and fit enough to resume his journey, he considered returning to the coast to re-join the clan. However, he eventually dismissed that option, deciding in favour of venturing even further into the interior.

As the miles passed, he slowly came to realise a change had come over him. He felt unaccountably confident in his ability to survive in the wilderness, and he felt at one with nature. Here in the interior, the terrain was more hostile and more barren than ever, and yet, to his eyes, it had taken on a beauty of its own. Colours constantly changed with the changing light—from the subtle pink and mauve hues of the early morning, to the spectacular bright colours when the sun was at its height, and back to the subtle hues of the late afternoon. The sunrises were invariably spectacular, and the sunsets even more so.

To pass the time, John recalled past discussions he'd had with Mootemu. The Ancient One had often talked about the Dreamtime, or *the Dreaming,* as he preferred to call it, and now it was beginning to make sense to him.

He recalled one of the last times he'd spoken to Mootemu. He'd asked him how much land the Kabi owned. He could hear the old man's response. It was as if he was standing beside him now.

"Our mother is the land," Mootemu had proclaimed. "How can we own her?" The Ancient One had picked up a handful of dirt. "This is our mother. She is the earth. We cannot own her." He'd let the dirt trickle between his fingers onto the ground. "We come from the earth. And we will return to her." He'd cast his hand around from horizon to horizon. "She feeds us and nurtures us. She is who we are."

John could now relate to that. The stone fences that marked the boundaries of properties in his homeland, and elsewhere throughout the so-called civilised world, had no place here.

That discussion with Mootemu had led to his asking what role Mother Earth played, if any, in the Dreaming. The Ancient One had reminded him he'd previously explained that. Then he'd gone over it again for John's benefit.

"The land was dark and silent and without life," Mootemu had said. "And then there was the Creation when unearthly beings arose with the sun from out of the ground." The Ancient One had explained these beings resembled creatures, which would become the Kabis' totemic ancestors. "They went out into the world and created the land we see today. The sand-dunes, the billabongs, the hills, the plains, the streams, the shrubs and trees." He'd pointed to the sky. "They even made the sun and the moon and all the heavenly bodies. And finally they made the animals and people before sinking back into the land and returning to their slumber."

Most of it John had understood. Sort of. It was the last part of the story he couldn't get his head around—until now.

Mootemu had explained that, on occasion, the spirits of those unearthly beings transformed into trees or hills or rocks deemed sacred. "These sacred landmarks were connected by the Songlines," he'd said, "and could only be seen by the chosen ones."

John wondered if the spring the dingo had led him to was one such landmark. He also wondered if he'd ever make sense of the Songlines. He somehow doubted it.

The Irishman lost track of how long he'd been wandering through the wilderness. He had stopped recording the passing of the days after his near-death experience at the spring, preferring to enjoy the experience as much as he could and not worry about such trivials as time and distance.

The decision to return to the coast and reunite with the clan was made more or less on a whim. It was the sight of storm clouds building far to the east that finally tempted him to turn around and head back. He'd been gone almost three months, and in that time there hadn't been a drop of rain in the interior. He had been fantasizing about rain for weeks, so when he saw the storm clouds the temptation was too much.

His trek back to the coast only took him a month for he took the direct route, always heading due east as opposed to the rambling path he'd followed out from the coast. He didn't dally or stay put in any one place longer than he had to. Now that he had made the decision to return, he just wanted to get back. He missed Carravanty.

Finding the coast wasn't a problem. Finding the clan was.

As he neared the coast, the magnitude of the problem confronting him was clear. The Kabis' territory was huge, and the clan could be anywhere.

When he finally sighted the coast, the pull of the ocean was hard to resist, but resist it he did. A small voice in his head told him the clan was currently some distance from the coast.

North or south?

The same small voice told him it was north, and so he struck out in that direction.

Days of mindless meandering passed, and still he never found his clan.

Days became weeks, and John's frustration grew. He had not sighted the faintest sign of the clan. He'd come across two other Kabi clans, but they hadn't seen his clan since the annual corroboree on Great Sandy Island months earlier.

On this particular day, he traversed an area he'd never ventured into before. Even though the landmarks were new to him, they seemed familiar somehow.

Out of nowhere, Mirritji's parting words came to him. "Let the Songlines guide you, Moilow."

John immediately dismissed the elder's advice. He had only ever heard the Songlines once before, while with Mamba, and then they hadn't made any sense to him.

Try as he may, he couldn't get Mirritji's voice out of his head.

It was later in the day, while crossing a plain between two hilly ranges, that he heard a woman singing. He thought he recognised the voice.

Mamba?

He looked around, and was startled to see he had the plain to himself. "What the feck?" he muttered. He felt frightened as the singing grew louder. "It is Mamba!" His fear passed when he realised it was Mamba's voice he heard. And he recognised the song. It was one of the lullabies she used to chant when trekking between campsites.

A calmness came over him. He felt something brush against his arm—something invisible—but even that didn't alarm him.

Almost without thinking, he followed the singing. It led him toward a high, pyramid-shaped hill several miles to the north. He instinctively knew it was a sacred site. What he didn't know was it was Moilow's birthplace.

⋅⟨⋅——⋅⟩⋅

As John neared the mountain, he was disappointed the singing stopped. "Mamba!" he called. No answer. His heart jumped when he thought he caught sight of her. She was looking at him, smiling. She vanished almost as quickly as she appeared, and John thought he may have imagined it.

He was distracted when he heard the sound of children laughing. At the same time, he saw the smoke of cooking fires rising from a hidden campsite amongst the trees at the foot of the mountain.

Closer inspection revealed it was his clan.

Home at last.

He didn't reveal himself immediately, preferring to observe the clan members from the cover of the trees. The men were skinning animals they'd snared while the women were tending the cooking fires in preparation for the evening meal.

Nearby, young boys were playing tag, or their version of it. Their version entailed a lot of rough and tumble, and most of the participants had skin missing from elbows and knees along with the odd black eye.

John smiled when he saw Carravanty. The boy was in the thick of the action, and, once again, he reminded him of a younger Murrowdooling.

The Irishman started when Mamba's face flashed before his eyes a second time. She was still smiling, and this time he knew he hadn't imagined it.

PART SEVEN

DESPAIR AND SOLITUDE

79

T HE MOOD IN MARSDEN'S OFFICE was grim as the three officials reviewed recent developments that had negatively impacted on the running of the Moreton Bay penal settlement. These developments revolved around bad publicity the settlement had received, and was continuing to receive, over reports of the harsh treatment of convicts—in particular the army's use of the death penalty for the most trivial offences. The publicity had raised the ire of the general public, and mounting opposition had resulted in the British Government introducing a moratorium, effective immediately, on hangings at Moreton Bay.

The Governor, Sir Ralph, had been so incensed by the negative publicity he'd ordered an internal enquiry to establish who had been talking to the newspapers. He was convinced someone from Moreton Bay was feeding information to journalists.

For Sir Ralph, the moratorium on hangings had been the last straw, and he'd sailed to the bay to meet with a rehabilitated Lord Cheetham at the first available opportunity. Those two gentlemen, together with Captain Marsden, had been closeted in Marsden's office for two hours, and, from where Marsden sat, little had been achieved in that time.

The captain surreptitiously surveyed his superiors as they thumbed through back copies of daily newspapers from London and Sydney Town. They were both muttering to themselves as they read the damning reports—one of which compared Moreton Bay with the notorious Norfolk Island penal settlement.

"Look at these distortions," Cheetham grumbled, pointing to a front-page article in *The Sydney Gazette* edition of October 15, 1833. A week old, the newspaper was the most recent to arrive at the bay.

Sir Ralph and Marsden glanced at the headline, which read, *Record number of hangings prompts moratorium at Moreton Bay,* and then skimmed the first couple of paragraphs.

"Damned lies," Sir Ralph agreed.

Marsden knew better. Most of the hangings had occurred on his watch on the express orders of the Governor no less. In his capacity as acting commandant at Moreton Bay, whilst Cheetham had been away, Marsden had been forced to carry out Sir Ralph's orders, which had required that convicts be hung for even the most trivial offences. That didn't sit well with him, and he'd had many a sleepless night as a result.

The number of convict hangings had risen even more since Cheetham's return to the bay—until the commencement of the moratorium the previous week that is.

Looking at Cheetham, Marsden couldn't get over the change in him. The commandant's treatment for his opium addiction had, by all accounts, been successful. Two months had passed since he'd been discharged from the Sydney Town sanatorium, and, against all odds, he had shown no inclination to return to his old habits. Not his opium habit at least. However, he hadn't changed one bit in other respects. Marsden observed he was as cruel as ever—and the Governor wasn't about to discourage that.

"This moratorium is a knee-jerk reaction to these inflammatory newspaper reports," Sir Ralph complained.

Cheetham mumbled his agreement. "It will be lifted as soon as the Review Committee reports its findings," he said. The commandant referred to a pending visit by the Penal Settlement Review Committee whose members resided in Melbourne and Sydney Town.

"When will they arrive?" Marsden asked.

"As soon as they can be assembled," the Governor said. "I have been assured they will be here by the end of the month at the latest."

Both the Governor and the commandant were reasonably relaxed about the pending visit. The committee members were all government appointees, and their support for methods employed by officials in charge of penal settlements throughout the colony was well known, as was their unflinching support of the death penalty. Therefore, the eventual lifting of the moratorium on hangings at Moreton Bay was a foregone conclusion. Even so, the indignity of being subjected to an inspection by the committee rankled with both officials.

The Governor stared at Cheetham. "I want you to find out who is feeding the newspapers with these lies, Berty,"—he scowled as if to reinforce his anger—"and I *don't* want you to ease up on discipline in the slightest." He added, "We need to keep these convict scum under the thumb or there will be hell to pay."

Cheetham nodded.

Marsden could tell the commandant had no intention on easing discipline, regardless of what Sir Ralph said.

The Governor switched his gaze to Marsden. "I assume we have your full support in this matter, Captain."

Both senior officials eyed Marsden critically. They were mindful that he had opposed some of the disciplinary methods employed at Moreton Bay in the past.

"Of course, Sir Ralph," Marsden said at length. He hated himself at that moment. There was a time, not that long ago, when he'd have strongly resisted any suggestion the settlement's already cruel disciplinary methods be made any harsher. However, the combined efforts of the two officials in whose company he'd found himself had conspired to wear him down. In his own defence, he reminded himself they had the full backing of the British Army and Government. However, he knew that would be no defence when he finally got to stand before his Maker.

"I would remind you it is six years since John Graham escaped," Sir Ralph said. The Governor was no longer looking at Marsden, but it was obvious his comments were meant for him.

Marsden knew that Sir Ralph and Cheetham both blamed him for the disastrous raid on the Kabi clan two years earlier. He didn't condemn them for that. God knows, he blamed himself for that debacle, and not a day went by when he didn't think about it and ask himself what he could have done differently. For whatever reason, some good men had died that day—Lieutenant Hogan among them. "Six years and three months, to be precise, Sir Ralph," the captain said. He knew to the day how long it was since the Irishman had escaped.

"No matter," the Governor said, waving one hand dismissively. "The point is his legend continues to grow and his freedom continues to inspire the convicts . . . Especially those Irish bastards."

"Especially the Irish," Cheetham agreed. He quickly added, "Our tracker is on Graham's trail. He says it is only a matter of time."

Sir Ralph looked sceptical. He'd heard that before.

Marsden glanced at the grandfather clock against the far wall of his office. "Gentlemen, it is almost noon," he announced. "May I suggest we adjourn to the mess for lunch before our tour of the settlement?"

His superiors concurred, and they left for the officers' mess.

On their way out, Sir Ralph turned to his companions. "Oh . . . and gentlemen, I want a full investigation into these damned leaks," he grumbled.

"Yes, Sir Ralph," Cheetham and Marsden said in unison.

The Governor added, "Someone here is feeding information to the newspapers, and if it's one of ours I want him hung, drawn and quartered."

"We will look into it immediately," Cheetham said. The commandant looked at Marsden as he said it, leaving the captain in no doubt he was to look into the leaks personally.

•€———3•

The tour of the settlement was conducted on horseback. Marsden had organised a horse-drawn wagon for the tour, but the Governor had insisted they ride—a decision welcomed by the captain, but not by Cheetham who abhorred riding.

It was in fact an inspection of both settlements—the penal settlement, first, and the nearby township, second.

The tour of the penal settlement was an eye-opener for Sir Ralph. This was his first visit to the bay in more than two years, and much had happened in that time. The settlement's convict population was now at full capacity at two thousand five hundred men, give or take ten or so depending on fluctuations in new arrivals and deaths.

In reality, the convict population was over capacity as the original projection had only been for two thousand men. Not only that, but the army's building programme hadn't been able to keep pace with the new arrivals. There were still insufficient huts to cope with existing convict numbers let alone newcomers. As a result, men still slept two to a bunk or on the floor, and the incidence of illness and death was as high as ever. In this respect, the recent newspaper reports hadn't been remotely exaggerated—and all three officials knew it.

Chain gangs could be seen working at all manner of back-breaking tasks in and

479

around the settlement, and the results of their labour were everywhere. The cobbled road connecting the settlement to the wharf and the seashore beyond had long been completed, as had the road to Brisbane Town.

All the fields between the settlement and Marsden's cottage had been fenced and all were planted in a variety of crops, most of which failed because of the hot, dry summers. Gangs of convicts were currently digging channels from the nearby river to provide the year-round irrigation necessary to water those same crops. Some convicts were helping the army's carpenters to build a pump station, which would accommodate the steam pump needed to convey the water uphill.

A new facility caught Sir Ralph's eye. "Is that what I think it is?" he asked, pointing to a converted windmill that housed a waterwheel, or treadmill, which some forty convicts were operating. He had seen such an innovation at the Parramatta penal settlement, but it hadn't been operating at the time.

"Yes, that's our new treadmill," Cheetham announced proudly. "The convicts provide the muscle power needed to grind our grain into flour."

The explanation was unnecessary as Sir Ralph already knew that. He had signed off on the treadmill at Parra, and on this one, too.

The three officials rode over for a closer look. They pulled up in time to see the forty convicts who had been operating the treadmill climb down to the ground as another forty took their place.

"They can only last thirty minutes at a time," Cheetham explained.

The three watched as the new batch of convicts took their places on a narrow wooden tread at the top of the waterwheel. Like the men they'd replaced, they were all bare-chested and shackled with leg-irons. Many bore the signs of recent floggings, and the backs of a few were raw where the lash had torn strips from them. The convicts gripped a horizontal bar, which, for most, was at chin height. Several short men had to reach up to grip the bar, and for them the next thirty minutes would be especially exhausting.

Sir Ralph observed those who had just been relieved were, to a man, spent. Most lay on their backs on the bare earth, their chests heaving as they tried to recover their breath. They were drenched in sweat. A waterboy wandered amongst them, dispensing water from one of two water buckets he carried.

"Alright you lot!" an overseer yelled. "Ready . . ." His comments were directed at the convicts who had taken their place on the wheel. As soon as he saw everyone was in position, he withdrew a steel bolt and the wheel began to move. Woe betide any man who wasn't ready.

To avoid slipping, the convicts had to walk as if climbing stairs as the revolving wheel waited for no-one. To slip or miss a step could easily result in immediate mutilation of one or both legs by the sharp blades beneath them—a fate than had befallen more than a few unfortunate convicts. In the heat and humidity of Moreton Bay, it was a tough assignment even for the fittest of men. For convicts weakened by illness and malnutrition, and weighed down by leg-irons, it was a torture straight out of hell. It wasn't uncommon to see grown men cry at the end of a shift on the wheel. Some had even been known to plead to be shot or hung.

"I assume they do this all day," Sir Ralph said.

"Yes, sir," Marsden confirmed. "Thirty minutes on, thirty minutes off, ten hours a day."

"Make it forty-five minutes on the wheel from now on," Sir Ralph ordered. "You are losing too much time in the change-over."

Marsden didn't like the sound of that. "I wouldn't—"

"Certainly," Cheetham interjected, over-riding his subordinate.

Marsden was sure the convicts couldn't handle any more than thirty minutes at a time on *the torture machine,* as the men called it, but he remained silent—something he'd been doing more and more since Cheetham's return.

The shortest of the convicts suddenly slipped, and he screamed as a blade sliced the toe of his left boot off. He continued to scream for a few moments until he realised the blade had missed his toe, the damage being limited to the front of his boot. Fortunately for him, he was wearing oversized boots. When his companions and the watching guards realised what had happened, they laughed uproariously. The short convict failed to see the funny side, but he couldn't hide his relief at having escaped with all his toes intact.

Sir Ralph had seen enough. "Shall we continue into town now?" he asked. He was clearly anxious to get on with it—and to get out of the sun. It was a hot October day even by Moreton Bay standards.

His companions readily agreed, and they cantered off toward the nearby township.

80

FROM HER MORETON BAY SCHOOL office, Helen observed her father escort Sir Ralph and Lord Cheetham into the township. The captain had forewarned her a week ago that she could expect a visit by the Governor. Now that the time had arrived she was feeling nervous, and for good reason for she intended to give Sir Ralph, and Cheetham, too, an earful regarding the treatment of Moreton Bay's convicts.

Helen's office was actually a prefabricated, stand-alone hut that overlooked the school's classrooms and grounds, and the township, too. As headmistress of an ever-expanding school, she spent much of her time these days on administration duties as opposed to indulging her first love, teaching. That didn't sit well with her for she loved the challenge of the classroom and the interaction teaching involved. However, she was also a realist and knew that admin was an inescapable part of the job.

In the two years since her fiancé died, the twenty-five-year-old had blossomed into a sophisticated woman—more beautiful than ever. Although she had more suitors, or would-be suitors, than ever, she paid them no mind. Teaching was her life, and she made it clear to one and all she was married to her job. Her commitment to her profession and to her school had paid dividends as Moreton Bay School was now a flagship for education in the fledgling colony, and she was the education system's shining star. So much so that her name was often quoted in Australian newspapers these days.

Helen was relieved when she saw her father and his two VIP companions dismount outside one of Brisbane Town's three hotels. The young headmistress wasn't quite ready for them yet. She watched as they entered the hotel, clearly intent on escaping the heat and quenching their thirst.

There was another reason Helen was nervous about the pending visit of the Governor. She was the informant who had been feeding information about the ill treatment of Moreton Bay's convicts to the newspapers. In fact, that's what she was working on at this very moment.

It had started eighteen months ago when she realised complaints to her father, and to the Governor on occasion, about the treatment of convicts hadn't been taken seriously. Her father had told her his hands were tied—and he'd told her in no uncertain terms to keep out of the army's affairs; and, on the two occasions she'd written to Sir Ralph, he had nicely but condescendingly told her the bay's convicts were well treated compared to those at other penal settlements.

Helen's strong social conscience demanded that she act, and so she had contacted a senior *Sydney Gazette* reporter known for his critical views on the treatment of convicts throughout the colony and for his opposition to the death penalty. Her contact was none other than Deputy Editor Timothy Hershaw whom she'd first met when he visited Moreton Bay as part of the Governor's entourage six years earlier. An editorial highlighting the hanging of convicts for the most trivial offence had caught her eye, and she'd contacted Hershaw who immediately saw an opportunity. He recruited Helen long distance to clandestinely submit reports on hangings and other such events at Moreton Bay. Her first-hand, eyewitness reports, which were published in their entirety under a nom de plume, were well received by readers not only in Sydney Town but in Britain as Hershaw invariably forwarded her submissions to the major London dailies.

Helen's following had grown steadily in the past year or so, and Hershaw had assured her that her reports were instrumental in the government deciding to impose the recent moratorium on hangings at Moreton Bay.

Helen had gone to great lengths to keep her involvement with Hershaw and *The Sydney Gazette* secret. She was very aware of the damage it would cause her father's career if it became known she was the informant. Relations were already strained between them, and Marsden had often warned her to curb her *humanitarian bent,* as he put it. She was also aware the army would withdraw its ongoing financial support for her school if the truth came out, and that would be devastating for her and her pupils, and for her loyal benefactors the Browns.

Hershaw had set up a courier system that required Helen to write and address letters to a middle-aged florist who happened to be a neighbour of the deputy editor in Sydney Town—and to write her reports in Latin within the text. The florist, of course, immediately forwarded the letters to her neighbour. Helen, who was fluent in Latin, introduced the text as a poem, but in fact it was a report on the latest events at the penal settlement. Latin was chosen in the hope it would not be understood by a censor should the army decide to check the contents of outgoing mail from the bay. They gambled on the likelihood that censorship would fall to a humble clerk as opposed to an officer. Few army clerks, Hershaw advised, would understand Latin.

Any guilt Helen may have felt over this subterfuge was overcome by the knowledge she was helping in no small way to draw attention to the cruelty being imposed on Moreton Bay's convicts. The announcement of the hanging moratorium had removed any lingering doubt that she may not be doing the right thing.

Helen was working on her latest report at that very moment. She ran her eye over the Latin text.

Translated, it read:

> *The government's moratorium on hangings at the Moreton Bay penal settlement has not come a moment too soon. Hangings have escalated in recent years to the point where as many as ten convicts may be hung in the space of one week. Often for no crime greater than swearing at an officer.*
>
> *Some convicts still knowingly break rules the Army advertises as "punishable by death" – such is their desire to escape the cruelties of their incarceration. It is especially tragic when you consider the*

*triviality of their original crime. So many suffered deportation for
little more than stealing a loaf of bread.*

Why the Army . . .

Helen stopped reading when she heard the sound of horses approaching. A glance out the window confirmed her father and his superiors were riding up from the township. She quickly concealed her latest musings in a drawer and walked to the open door to await the three officials.

Marsden couldn't bring himself to smile when he saw her. He was still smarting after the latest heated discussion they'd had on the treatment of convicts in his charge.

It was the Governor himself who uttered the first greeting on sighting the beautiful headmistress. "Good afternoon, my dear," he said as he dismounted his steed. "You look as fetching as ever."

"Good afternoon, Sir Ralph," Helen smiled. She'd have liked to have told him that how she looked really had nothing to do with anything, but she liked the Governor so she held her tongue. "How lovely to see you," she said.

Sir Ralph gallantly kissed the back of Helen's hand, and so, too, did Cheetham who was now so smitten by the young headmistress he became quite flustered whenever he found himself in her presence.

"My dear," the commandant mumbled.

"Lord Cheetham," Helen said. Turning to Marsden, she said, "Father."

Marsden gave a curt nod and suggested the tour of the school begin. The school day would end soon, and he was anxious the tour be completed before classes disbanded.

Helen proceeded to give the officials a guided tour of the school, which now boasted ten classrooms, two hundred and three pupils, ten full-time teachers and three part-timers.

Sir Ralph was mightily impressed, and he wasn't slow to congratulate Helen. "This is quite a setup, young lady," he said. "It is a credit to you." He quickly added, "I imagine administrative duties prevent you from doing much teaching these days?"

"Unfortunately," Helen concurred. "I am what's called a floater. I teach when my admin duties allow or when staff shortages demand."

The school bell heralded the end of the school day, and pupils streamed from the classrooms, happy to be heading home or out to play. Marsden used this as the opportunity to suggest he and the two VIPs depart.

As the three officials untethered their horses, Helen placed her hand on the Governor's arm. She asked, "Sir Ralph, has the moratorium on hangings prompted you to give further consideration to the treatment of Moreton Bay's convicts?" Ignoring the glares coming from Cheetham and her father, she added, "I imagine your masters in Government will now be turning their attention to the treatment of those convicts who have not yet been hung."

Hiding his surprise at Helen's forwardness, Sir Ralph said, "Now don't you concern yourself with such things, young lady. You have enough to worry your pretty head about caring for your school." Before Helen could respond, he asked, "I assume you are finding the army's financial assistance helpful?"

The question was loaded, and the point the Governor was making wasn't lost on Helen. "I . . . ah . . . yes it is, thank you Governor," she said.

Sir Ralph, who was now astride his horse, smiled at Helen and rode off. It was a smile, she noticed, that a patient grandfather would give a naughty grandchild.

Cheetham rode off after Sir Ralph, leaving Marsden momentarily alone with his outspoken daughter.

The captain glared at Helen. "It is not wise to bite the hand that feeds you, young lady," he said.

"We have been over this, father," Helen bristled.

A grim-faced Marsden rode off before he or his daughter said something they would both regret.

Helen retreated into her office, determined to finish her latest submission for *The Sydney Gazette*.

A hundred miles north of Moreton Bay, as Helen worked on her latest report, John was busy showing Carravanty how to make fire the time-honoured way. They were sitting in a bush clearing several miles from the clan's current encampment, and they were planning to cook a wallaby the boy had speared a short time earlier. The carcass lay on the grass nearby.

The kill was Carravanty's first, and John was as proud as any father could be. The fifteen-year-old was the joy of his life. He was, after all, his closest living link to Mamba and Murrowdooling.

"I want to kill a big red next," Carravanty announced.

John chuckled and ruffled the boy's unruly hair. "You'll need to grow a few inches before you do that," he smiled.

"Murrowdooling was ten when he killed his first big red," Carravanty protested.

John pondered that. He nodded. "You are right," he said at length.

"Can we hunt a big red?" Carravanty asked, suddenly excited.

"As soon as you master this fire-making," John promised, "then we will find a big red for you."

Satisfied, Carravanty turned his attention to learning how to make fire using nothing more than two dry sticks, a wooden bowl and a piece of tinder. In this case, a discarded bird's nest John had found served as tinder. He'd discovered old nests burnt even better than dry grass.

John watched as his young charge furiously rubbed the sticks together, trying to create the required spark. The serious way he applied himself reminded him so much of Murrowdooling.

Since returning from his journey into the interior six months earlier, John had fitted right back into life with the Kabi. He sensed he'd returned from that journey a changed man. The clan members had sensed it, too, and more than one had commented on it. They unanimously referred to him as *Moilow* now, and they accepted him as a white spirit without reservation.

These days, he rarely spoke English—except in his thoughts and dreams—and he'd permanently discarded his European clothes and footwear in favour of the loincloth of the Kabi men. The only concession he made to his former self was he shaved daily as he preferred the feeling of being clean-shaven. His bayonette, he'd found, was the perfect instrument for shaving, and he guarded it jealously for some of the younger men had made it known they'd like to own it. Like John, they were aware it made a very useful weapon.

"Look!" Carravanty said, snapping John out of his reverie.

The Irishman saw that the boy had created his first spark. "Keep it going!" he urged.

Carravanty grimaced as he strove to create the required friction.

The pair were so engrossed, they didn't notice the shadowy figure that loomed up behind them.

John didn't even feel the nulla nulla that smashed into his skull. He was out to it before he hit the ground, and it would be a good hour before he regained consciousness.

81

JOHN WOKE TO FIND HIMSELF hog-tied over the back of a horse. It would be some moments before he could make sense of his situation. Right now he didn't know where he was or how he'd ended up in this predicament. All he knew was he had a splitting headache and he was tied to a horse.

As the fog cleared from his brain, he became aware his steed was following another horse. The two animals were attached by a length of rope. Some ten yards separated them, and he could just make out the hazy outline of a rider astride the front horse.

Who is that?

His vision was so fuzzy he couldn't tell whether the rider was male or female. He shook his head to clear his vision, and realised he was looking at the back of a man.

An Aborigine.

The native looked vaguely familiar. John shook his head again. He finally recognised him.

Barega!

As if on cue, the tracker looked back at his captive. He grinned when he saw the Irishman was awake.

John tried to say something, but no words would come. He wanted to know if Carravanty was alright. Finally, he managed to get the words out. "What about the boy?" he asked.

Barega looked back a second time. He grinned yet again and ran his forefinger across his throat, giving the cut-throat sign and leaving his captive in no doubt what had happened to Carravanty—or what Barega wanted him to believe at least.

John groaned and lost consciousness again.

When he came to, he noticed blood over his horse's flanks, leading him to think the animal had been wounded. It took him a moment or two to realise the blood was his own. It was dripping from the nasty head wound he'd been left with after Barega had struck him with his nulla nulla.

Thinking of the tracker prompted him to turn his head to look at him.

Barega seemed at ease in the saddle as he guided the two horses along a dry riverbed. Wearing only a loincloth, he carried three spears and a woomera diagonally over his back. On one hip rested his nulla nulla and on the other his trusty hunting knife. His head continually swivelled from side to side as he checked his surroundings, ever-ready for what Man or nature threw at him. So focussed was he, he paid no heed to a small flock of screeching white cockatoos that flew by barely six feet overhead. Every now and then, the sunlight caught the silver necklace that was attached to the crucifix he wore, reminding John he needed to reclaim it at the first opportunity.

Studying the tracker's back, John was consumed by hate for the native who had killed Murrowdooling and who, as far as he knew, had killed Carravanty, too. He also blamed him for the deaths of Mamba and other clan members for he knew the soldiers wouldn't have found them without Barega's help.

Sensing his captive's eyes upon him, the tracker glanced back at John. He couldn't hide his delight at having captured Moreton Bay's most wanted man. Already, he could imagine the looks on the faces of Captain Marsden and the other soldiers when he delivered the Irishman to them.

When Barega wasn't looking, John tested the bonds that held him by straining to break free of them. They held fast. His wrists and ankles were bound by rope, and it appeared the same rope had been tied beneath the horse's belly to ensure he couldn't fall or dismount. It didn't take him long to reach the conclusion he was at his captor's mercy for the moment.

Up ahead, the riverbed opened out onto a grassy plain. Barega stopped at the first billabong they came to. Like the riverbed, it was bone dry.

Another hour passed before they came across a billabong that contained water.

John could only watch as the tracker dismounted and retrieved an army water bottle from his saddle bag. After drinking his fill at the watering hole, Barega filled his bottle then walked over to his captive. He put the bottle's open nozzle to John's mouth, but before the Irishman could drink from it he walked back to his horse, chuckling to himself.

John didn't utter a word. Thirsty though he was, he wasn't going to give his captor the satisfaction of hearing him plead for water.

As they resumed their journey across the plain, John had more to contend with than just his thirst. His head hurt and he had a blinding headache as a consequence of the blow he'd received, the rope that bound him was so tight it was cutting into his wrists and ankles, and his aching body was starting to cramp up. Added to that, the sun beating down on his bare back was burning his skin.

Resigned to suffering in silence, he closed his eyes and willed himself to go to sleep.

John opened his eyes. Unsure whether he'd been asleep or whether he'd blacked out again, he looked around. Lengthening shadows told him it was late afternoon.

The Irishman was in a bad way. Thirstier than ever, his headache was worse than before, and it felt as though every muscle and every joint in his body was on fire. His sunburnt back was spasming, his legs were cramping and his head wound still bled. Every step his steed took jolted him and sent shafts of pain through his limbs.

John looked around at the horse in front and saw that the tracker was showing no sign of stopping any time soon.

For the first time, the Irishman took note of his surroundings. It seemed they'd crossed the plain and were now traversing gently undulating country that was dotted with stands of gum trees. The spasmodic shade they provided was a welcome relief. The late afternoon sun was to their right, which told him they were heading directly south, toward Moreton Bay. That came as no surprise.

John noticed something seemed to have caught Barega's eye. Squinting into the sun, he saw what it was that had caught his captor's attention. Not fifty yards away, two adult dingoes had stopped to observe the strange pair of humans passing through their territory.

John looked closer and saw they had a litter of pups. However, it was the bigger of the two adult dingoes that most interested him.

Is that Dingo?

His blurred vision wasn't helped by the watery mix of blood, sweat and salt that stung his eyes. He blinked several times to clear his vision, and immediately saw that he hadn't been imagining things.

It is Dingo!

The big dingo with the distinctive reddish marking on his coat seemed to recognise the Irishman. Ears erect and eyes fasted on John, he left his mate and their pups, and slowly ran toward the familiar figure tied to the back of the horse.

John was distracted when he noticed Barega pulling a spear from the bundle slung over his back. Only now did he realise what the tracker planned to do.

Bugger off, dog!

Dingo stopped running and sat down only thirty yards from the two men. He looked directly at John, his head on one side as if trying to determine how his unfortunate friend had ended up in such a predicament.

John watched with increasing alarm as the tracker fitted the spear to his woomera. Barega stood up ever so slowly in his stirrups, avoiding jerky movements so as not to alarm his quarry. Still Dingo didn't move.

As the tracker prepared to release his spear, John shouted, "Run, Dingo!" At the same time, he pulled hard on the rope that tethered him to his captor's horse, causing the horse to take a step back.

At the sound of John's voice, Dingo took off back to his mate and their brood. Barega's spear whistled by harmlessly overhead.

Barega glared at John before dismounting his horse and retrieving his spear. The Irishman couldn't resist laughing out loud at the tracker's bad luck. That wasn't the brightest thing he'd ever done for the tracker walked back to John and scraped his fingernails down the length of his captive's sunburnt back before mounting his own horse and resuming the journey.

A short while later, John looked around and saw that Dingo was observing their departure from a safe distance. The wild dog continued to watch them until they entered a gully and disappeared from view.

John found it somewhat comforting to know that Dingo was still alive and, by all accounts, thriving.

He's better off than me right now.

That evening, John looked on as Barega carved a juicy leg from the fat brush turkey he'd speared and not long finishing cooking over a campfire.

The captive's situation had only marginally improved since the tracker had stopped to make camp. No longer hog-tied to the back of a horse, he was now tied to the trunk of a gum tree.

On stopping at the campsite, Barega had hauled John from the horse and dragged him over to the tree. The Irishman had been made to sit, his back against the trunk, and Barega had encircled both the trunk and his captive's neck with a length of rope. Behind the trunk, the rope was tied to a stick, which, when turned, either tightened or loosened the rope depending on whether it was turned clockwise or anti-clockwise. The tracker took delight in periodically tightening it, cutting off John's air supply. It was a technique he'd learned watching soldiers torture unfriendly tribesmen they'd captured.

At first, John had cursed his tormenter, but he'd quickly learned there was no profit to be had from that. The second time he'd cursed him, Barega had tightened the rope until he'd almost passed out.

Only now, as the Irishman watched Barega carve off morsels of the brush turkey for himself did he realise how hungry he was. In a rare moment of pity, the tracker had allowed him to drink from his water bottle, so he was no longer quite as thirsty as before. However, he hadn't eaten since early morning and he was famished. His captor delighted in tormenting him further by holding the morsels up to his mouth and then slowly devouring them himself.

Finally, Barega tired of this little game. The tracker carved another leg from the big bird and tossed it over to John. He watched, disinterestedly, as his captive wolfed down the offering.

If it was up to Barega, he'd have killed the Irishman. However, he was under strict orders to bring John Graham back alive. Marsden had threatened not only would he be dismissed if he disobeyed orders, but his access to the Marsdens' maid Orana would be curtailed once and for all. The thought of dismissal didn't faze him; the thought of no longer being able to pleasure Orana did. And so he refrained from killing the captive.

Meanwhile, John finished eating and resigned himself to a long night beneath the gum tree. The rope around his neck was tight. Not so tight he couldn't breathe, but tight enough to prevent him from moving around. He knew better than to ask his captor to loosen it. The last time he'd asked that, Barega had actually tightened it even more.

The darkness brought with it a cool change, and John wished he'd thought to don his pelt cloak before setting out to hunt with Carravanty that morning. Thinking of the boy caused him to choke back tears. He believed Carravanty dead, and he yearned for revenge.

Observing Barega, who was now stretching out alongside the fire in readiness for sleep, he promised himself he'd make him pay for the grief he'd brought him over the past two years especially.

You are a dead man, tracker.

He observed Barega until the native fell asleep. Then he turned his face skyward. Through the leaves, and between the branches of the tree above him, he identified the Southern Cross constellation, and he recognised the outline of the stingray in the starry night sky.

82

FATHER AND DAUGHTER BICKERED AS Orana cleared the Sunday lunch dishes from the Marsdens' dining table. Matthew and his stepmother Mildred could only look and listen as Marsden and Helen went at each other.

"You know I am right, father," Helen insisted. "The treatment of convicts in *your* care is abysmal"—Marsden bristled at the way his daughter blamed him personally for Moreton Bay's convict problems—"and it is only getting worse."

"Civilians know nothing of the problems of running a penal settlement," the captain said, pointing an accusing finger at Helen. "And you of all people should know that."

"How can you say that?" Helen protested. "Just look at the condition of the men. Most of them are so ill and underfed they shouldn't even be working. The suicide rates are testimony to that."

Marsden brooded on that comment. The bay's suicide rates amongst the convicts were a bone of contention, and he'd often brought it to the attention of the commandant, and the Governor, too, on occasion.

Sensing she was winning the argument, Helen added, "And I won't even mention the number of men you've hung!"

"There is a moratorium on hanging at present," Marsden reminded her.

"Ha! We all know how long that will last," Helen scoffed.

Marsden rounded on his daughter. "Young lady—"

"Now, Tom," a concerned Mildred interjected. "Let us not spoil a nice lunch." The new Missus Marsden disapproved of the bickering that was becoming all too common between her husband and her stepdaughter. Like the Sunday lunch itself, it was fast becoming a tradition where the pair debated the treatment of convicts, and all too often the debates didn't end well. As a result, the relationship between the pair was becoming ever more tense.

Ignoring his wife, Marsden said, "You are entitled to your opinions, Helen, but where those opinions reflect badly on your father, that is where I must draw the line."

Helen refrained from responding. It always came down to this, she thought. Her social conscience needed to be tempered out of consideration for her father who, after all, was the head warden at Moreton Bay—in name at least. She was under no illusions that Cheetham had long since unofficially assumed the head warden's duties, but she would never say as much to her father. That would shatter whatever dignity and self-respect he'd retained.

In an effort to lighten the mood, Matthew suggested, "Shall we go riding, sis?"

"Is that any way to address your school's headmistress?" Mildred asked, light-heartedly.

"Sorry," Matthew grinned. Re-phrasing the question, he asked, "Shall we go riding, Miss Marsden?"

Helen laughed and clipped her brother over the ear. "Alright, after we help Orana wash up," she said. She and Matthew excused themselves from the table, and disappeared through to the kitchen to assist the maid with the lunch dishes.

Mildred turned to Marsden. "She means no disrespect, my dear," she whispered.

"I'm not so sure," Marsden scowled. "She considers me the enemy where the convicts are concerned."

"Nonsense. She knows you are only following orders."

Marsden lapsed into silence. Sensing he wanted to be alone, Mildred withdrew to assist in the kitchen.

Alone now, the captain lit his pipe and retired to his favourite spot on the front verandah where he brooded on his wife's last words. He *was* only following orders, but was he following them a little too diligently where treatment of the convicts was concerned? That was the question his conscience had long ruminated over.

Helen and Matthew, now on horseback, raced each other over the hills behind Moreton Bay. As usual, she was winning, but the gap between brother and sister was narrowing with each outing. On this occasion, Matthew was only a few yards behind her.

Both slowed their steeds when they saw a native emerge from the bush on horseback some distance away to the north. It took them a few moments before they identified him as Barega.

As the tracker neared, it became obvious he was pulling something behind his steed.

"He has a prisoner!" Matthew announced excitedly as he reined in alongside his sister.

Only now did Helen see the tracker was pulling a man along behind him. Neither she nor Matthew realised the man they were looking at was John. From here, he looked like another Aborigine.

The Irishman was now on foot. His horse had been released into the wild two days earlier after it had gone lame on the trek to Moreton Bay. The week-long journey had taken its toll. John was covered in bruises and scratches—most of them having been sustained since he'd been reduced to traveling on foot. His captor had set a relentless pace, causing him to stumble frequently. At such times Barega, had amused himself by dragging the Irishman over rocks and through bushes and thorns until he managed to get back to his feet.

Both Helen and Matthew remained convinced the prisoner was a native. Totally understandable given he wore only a loincloth, his skin was blackened by the sun and he sported a week-old beard. He was gaunt, too—more gaunt than usual—as he'd hardly eaten in days.

The tracker grinned at the siblings as he pulled up in front of them. "Barega has present for captain," he said proudly, glancing at his captive.

Only now did the siblings notice the captive wasn't an Aborigine.

Looking up at the pair, John recognised them straight away. Their expressions told him they hadn't recognised him yet.

Little wonder. I must look like a savage to them.

He quickly averted his eyes as he didn't want them to recognise him in this state.

Too late. Helen had just noticed his startling blue eyes. "John?" she asked. "Is that you?"

John didn't respond. He kept his eyes averted and he willed his captor to move on.

Barega finally nudged his horse, and the siblings watched in silence as the tracker hauled his captive toward the distant penal settlement.

It was Matthew who spoke first. "That was John Graham, wasn't it?" he asked.

Helen could only nod. She was still in shock.

"Will they hang him?" Matthew asked.

"No!" Helen snapped. "There's a moratorium on hanging, in case you hadn't heard."

"Alright, no need to get snippy, Miss Marsden," Matthew grinned. Whipping his horse around, he took off toward the river. "Last one to the river gets a hundred lines for homework!" he shouted over his shoulder.

Normally, Helen would have risen to the challenge. She had other things on her mind, however. Namely, John Graham. Her emotions were in turmoil.

Watching John as Barega dragged him along behind his horse, she couldn't believe how different the Irishman looked. Nor could she believe the effect he still had on her after so many years.

❦———❧

The route Barega and his captive took, took them near the entrance to the quarry where, to this day, convict gangs still toiled. John studied the quarry as they passed it. It looked much the same, he observed, as it had the day he'd escaped from it a little more than six years ago.

The convicts had stopped for a water break. John thought he recognised two or three of the closest men. They were looking his way, and were clearly taking a keen interest in the tracker's latest prisoner.

Those closest to John included Seamus O'Neill and Pat Kennedy, two of his former Irish mates, and young Billy Morris, the one-time water boy who was now a twenty-one-year-old man with muscles and a bushy beard.

Billy wasn't the only one who had physically changed in the past six years. The two Irishmen with him were barely recognisable as the same men who had once toiled alongside John. Both victims of illness and physical abuse, like most of the convicts, they were mere shells of their former selves. Stooped, malnourished and scarred, they looked like dead men walking.

◆·ϵ·———·Ͽ·◆

From where they were standing, some thirty yards distant, the three convicts initially mistook John for a native—just as Helen and Matthew had.

"Looks like the tracker has brought in one of his own this time," Kennedy said.

"Aye," O'Neill agreed. He added, "I don't mind him hunting his own feckin' kind."

Billy was the first to recognise the captive. "He ain't no bloody black," he said. "That's yer countryman."

The two Irishmen looked harder at the captive.

"Holy mother of God!" O'Neill muttered. "That is Graham!" He waved at his old friend, but John was no longer looking their way.

The three watched in disbelief as the captive was dragged past them. He stumbled and only just managed to avoid falling.

"Poor bugger," Kennedy said. "He's out on his feckin' feet."

◆·ϵ·———·Ͽ·◆

As Barega neared the penal settlement, John stumbled for the last time. He no longer had the energy needed to regain his feet. The tracker was in no mood to stop, so he literally dragged his captive the last fifty yards.

The final stages of their journey took them past the treadmill that Cheetham had so proudly shown off to the Governor before his departure a week earlier. Forty convicts currently laboured on the mill's waterwheel while another forty awaited their turn.

Amongst those waiting their turn were more who were known to John. They included Irishman Luke Donovan, the Welsh homosexual Rhys Jones and the one-eyed Englishman William Harrison. They and their comrades looked in no better shape than the convicts in the quarry. Donovan was severely malnourished as a result of a medical condition that rendered him unable to keep food down; Jones had a wicked scar on his face and bore the faded bruises of the continual beatings he'd suffered; and Harrison was near-blind, having almost lost the sight in his remaining eye. But that wasn't the Englishman's worst problem: he had an interminable, hacking cough and looked unlikely to see out the summer.

"Will you look at that," Jones said, nodding toward John who was now being pulled along on his back behind Barega's horse.

The others looked over to what had caught the Welshman's attention.

"Well I'll be . . ." Donovan muttered.

"What is it?" the near-blind Harrison asked.

"Looks like the tracker has finally caught up with Graham," Donovan said.

"John Graham?" Harrison asked.

"Aye," Jones said.

Some of the convicts toiling on the treadmill also noticed John, although they were too preoccupied to identify him. One, who thought the captive looked familiar,

495

missed a step and only just avoided the revolving blade that would have reduced his feet to mincemeat had he not recovered in time.

They watched John and his captor until the pair disappeared from view around behind the cell block.

The cell block had more than doubled in size since John was last in Moreton Bay. It was in fact two adjoining blocks, which now accommodated up to thirty prisoners at a time—a necessary development given the growth of the settlement and the increase in convict numbers. Only the worst-behaved of the convicts were sent to the cells.

A recent add-on was the addition of a small solitary confinement block, and it was reserved for the worst of the worst. It was to this block that John was bound. Comprising three small, fully enclosed cells, it was an extension to one of the existing blocks. Each cell was barely large enough to accommodate one prisoner.

John, who was now shackled in leg-irons, was frog-marched between two guards to the farthest of the three single cells. Along the way, he and his escorts passed three large, barred cells each containing half a dozen prisoners. The prisoners, who invariably heckled the guards whenever they walked by, could only gawk in astonishment at the new inmate who had appeared in their midst. To their eyes, he looked like a wild savage.

Moments later, John found himself in a tiny cell, which, for the moment at least, was his new home. Barely long enough to lie down in, it was devoid of furnishings apart from a dirty mattress and a bucket that evidently served as a toilet. Judging by the smell and the number of flies buzzing around it, the bucket hadn't been emptied since the last occupant left.

The only light in the cell came from a small, barred window. It was close to the ceiling—too high to enable an inmate to see anything outside other than the sky. Later, John would discover it was facing south, so it would admit no rays of sunshine—not even for a few minutes.

Exhausted, he lay down on the mattress. Only now did he notice a blanket rolled up alongside it. It was even dirtier than the mattress, but he was too tired to worry about that. He pulled it under his head to serve as a pillow.

Sleep came quickly.

Marsden was awoken by the sound of horses' hooves approaching from the penal settlement. The captain had been sleeping off his lunch in a hammock he'd strung up between the lower branches of the giant fig tree on his front lawn. Wiping the sleep from his eyes, he looked around and recognised James Whitelock, the former guard who was now second-in-command of the convicts' cell block. The Northerner was riding hard. It was evident he had important news.

Marsden climbed out of the hammock and awaited Whitelock's arrival.

Reining in close to Marsden, Whitelock saluted the captain even though his non-military status didn't require him to do so.

Marsden returned the other's salute. "What news do you bring, Mister Whitelock?" he asked.

"The tracker has brought the Irishman in, Captain," Whitelock said in the strongest of Northern accents.

"John Graham?" Marsden asked, suddenly interested.

Whitelock nodded. "Yes, sir."

"Is he well secured?"

"Yes, sir. Shackled and manacled."

"Has Lord Cheetham been alerted?"

"Not yet, sir."

"Alert him immediately, and have Graham brought to my office in one hour."

"Yes, sir."

Marsden strode off to his cottage, leaving Whitelock to carry out his orders.

83

J OHN FELT LIKE HE'D HARDLY slept at all when the cell's steel door opened with a *clang*.

"On yer feet, Graham!" a surly voice ordered.

John opened his eyes and saw standing over him the same two guards who had delivered him to his cell. They hauled him to his feet and marched him, still shackled, from the cell block, across an open courtyard and into the settlement's administration block. The guards stopped outside the door of Marsden's office. One of them knocked on the door.

"Come," a voice called from inside. John recognised it as Marsden's.

The same guard opened the door, and the other guard pushed the prisoner inside.

John found Marsden and Cheetham waiting for him along with former junior clerk Corporal Cedric Dunstan. The corporal, who was now the army's head clerk, sat at a desk adjoining Marsden's, his quill poised above a note pad, ready to record for posterity the details of this historic occasion.

Dunstan and the two officials, who were also seated, were speechless for a few moments. None could quite reconcile the dirty, wild-looking, barefoot man in the loincloth standing before them with the convict they remembered.

Marsden was slightly less perplexed than his companions, having seen John up close during the raid on the Kabi encampment in more recent times.

Cheetham was first to react. Red-faced with anger, he jumped to his feet and glared at the two guards. "How dare you bring this . . . this . . . man here"—he looked disdainfully at John—"looking like a bloody cannibal!" He rounded on the nearest guard. "Get him cleaned up and dressed, and then bring him straight back!" he ordered.

"Yes, sir," the guard said.

As the two guards jumped to and escorted John from the office, Cheetham shouted, "And burn that damn loincloth!"

"Yes, sir!" the guards said in unison.

The two officials looked at each other as the guards departed with their prisoner.

"Words fail me," Cheetham grumbled.

"Yes, sir," Marsden agreed. "Graham really has gone native."

Nearby, Dunstan felt he should be doing something so he dipped the end of his quill into an open ink bottle.

Marsden glanced at his subordinate. "Do not record that, Corporal," he ordered.

"No, sir," Dunstan said, placing his quill on the desktop.

Little more was said while the men waited. Although Cheetham was uncharacteristically quiet, Marsden could tell he was secretly delighted the rebellious Irishman had been recaptured. So, too, was he. Since the failed raid on the Kabi encampment, and the subsequent loss of life, he'd become obsessed with recapturing John Graham. He and the commandant had been living for the day the man was hung for his transgressions. Now that they finally had him, they were faced with the problem of what to do with him. They couldn't hang him. Not while the moratorium on hangings prevailed at least. And for both men, that was a major frustration.

Although Marsden remained opposed to indiscriminate use of the death penalty for trivial cases, he approved of hanging the worst offenders. And given the angst John had caused the army, he certainly considered him up there with the very worst.

Cheetham seemed to sense what was on Marsden's mind. "The Review Committee will recommend an immediate end to this damned moratorium," he said confidently. "And then we can hang our troublesome Irishman."

Before Marsden could respond, there was another knock on the door. "Come," he said.

The door opened and the same two guards escorted John back into the office. As the commandant had ordered, the prisoner was now showered and clean-shaven, and, most importantly, no longer resembled an Aborigine. Gone was his tattered loincloth. In its place, he wore the garb of a convict—namely, breeches and a long-sleeved shirt minus the boots.

Cheetham, for one, was satisfied. "Good," he mumbled. "That's better." Addressing John, he said, "You almost look human once again, Graham."

The Irishman ignored Cheetham, preferring to look over the top of his head at a spot on the wall. His guards, who had remained in the office, stood to attention, staring at the same wall.

John despised the officials in whose company he'd found himself. He blamed them personally for all that had happened since he'd first arrived at the settlement a lifetime ago. In particular, he blamed Marsden for the grief he'd caused him and his Kabi loved-ones. He had an image of the captain directing his troops as they slaughtered clan members. It was so clear it was as if it was only yesterday. He could still hear the screams, smell the gun smoke and taste the blood. His hatred for Marsden was so strong he didn't trust himself to look at the man for if he did he felt he would surely rip his throat out.

Cheetham continued, "You face a litany of charges, Graham." He glanced at Dunstan. "Read them out, Corporal."

"Yes, sir," Dunstan said. Referring to a document he held, he began reading aloud. "On July fifteen, in the year of our Lord eighteen hundred and twenty seven—"

"We don't need to recall the dates at this point," an impatient Cheetham interjected. "Just read the charges, man."

"Yes, my Lord," a nervous Dunstan said. He continued, "Irish convict John Graham did escape from the Moreton Bay penal settlement, subsequently leading army searchers on a fruitless chase, which resulted in a serious injury being incurred by the party's senior officer, Lieutenant Desmond Hogan, since deceased."

Cheetham and Marsden both scowled in John's direction at the mention of the now-deceased lieutenant. They squarely blamed the Irishman for Hogan's death even though he did not personally deliver the killer blow.

Dunstan continued, "For six years, John Graham caused the British Army garrison based at Moreton Bay considerable time and expense in its pursuit of this most elusive of convicts. The most graphic example of this occurred on October . . ." The corporal skipped the date. "Occurred approximately two years ago," he improvised, "when Captain Marsden led an unsuccessful raid on the encampment of the native clan that sheltered Graham. That raid resulted in the deaths of nine soldiers, including Lieutenant Hogan."

Silence prevailed as those in attendance pondered the severity of the charges. The hanging moratorium aside, under existing military regulations each charge warranted the death sentence.

It was Marsden who spoke first. Glaring at John, he asked, "Anything to say, Graham?"

John remained mute, his eyes steadfastly fixed on the same spot on the same wall.

Marsden turned to Cheetham who was visibly stewing. "Over to you, sir," he said.

Unable to control his temper any longer, the commandant spent the next few minutes berating John. The prisoner's refusal to acknowledge him only served to anger him further. Finally, when his anger was spent, he said, "You will hang for this, Graham. I can promise you that." Turning to the guards, he said, "Get him out of my sight."

The guards quickly escorted John from the office.

Marsden looked at Dunstan. "Thank you, Corporal," he said. "You are dismissed."

"Yes, Captain," Dunstan said. He quickly gathered up his documents and left the officials to themselves.

Alone now, Marsden turned to his superior. "The Review Committee can't arrive too soon," he said, referring to the pending visit of the committee members tasked with investigating the treatment of convicts at Moreton Bay.

"Amen to that," Cheetham said. He wanted to see John hang even more than Marsden did. The commandant looked at his subordinate shrewdly. "I have a punishment in mind that may circumvent the current moratorium on hanging," he confided.

"Oh?"

"Yes. I propose putting Graham in the hole for a while."

Marsden knew Cheetham was referring to a new punishment facility the commandant had ordered be installed in the penal settlement. Based on a similar facility trialled in British prisons, it had a benign technical name few people understood and even fewer used. Most simply referred to it as *the hole* for that's what it was. "How long is *a while?*" he enquired.

"Overnight, tonight," Cheetham smiled. "From dusk to dawn."

"But that's nine hours, my Lord," the captain protested.

It was, the commandant noted, only a half-hearted protest. Cheetham's smile broadened. "Exactly," he agreed.

Marsden digested this. The longest a prisoner had survived in the hole, according to reports from the British prisons, was five hours. Any longer than that, according to those same reports, was tantamount to a death sentence. As the implications of what Cheetham was proposing took shape, Marsden considered the potential ramifications if John was to die in the hole. "There would be an enquiry," he said at length.

"I have considered that," Cheetham nodded. Choosing his words carefully, he said, "It is quite possible the paperwork received from the British Prisons Authority has been mislaid." He studied his subordinate, gauging his reaction.

"That happens all the time," Marsden agreed somewhat cautiously.

Encouraged, Cheetham continued, "In all innocence, we could argue that we did not consider it unreasonable that a convict be condemned . . . or . . . rather . . . *placed* . . . in the hole overnight. And if we had known the recommended time limit is . . . five hours?" He looked to Marsden for clarification.

"Maximum three to four hours, depending on the fitness of the prisoner," Marsden said.

Cheetham nodded. He continued, "Say, four hours . . . we would certainly not have left Graham in the hole overnight." He looked squarely at Marsden as if seeking his blessing for what they both believed would be a death sentence for the Irishman.

Marsden met the commandant's gaze. He was very aware what Cheetham was suggesting, and it was evident the commandant needed an ally for what he planned. The captain knew the decision rested with him. If he officially opposed it, Cheetham could not proceed with the planned punishment because his subordinate's opposition would show up in the paperwork. Marsden weighed the pros and cons. Condemning John to die in the hole would get around the hanging moratorium. And they both wanted him dead—of that there was no doubt.

"Well?" a fidgety Cheetham asked.

"One moment, sir," Marsden murmured. He realised he'd reached a crossroads in his career. In his life even. If he supported Cheetham on this matter, he'd be crossing a line—both in his professional and in his personal life. And once crossed, there'd be no turning back. Then he thought of Helen. He suspected she still held a candle for the Irishman, and that was one complication too many as far as he was concerned. He looked back at Cheetham and simply nodded.

That was all Cheetham needed. "Very well," he said, "I will leave it to you to organise the punishment."

Yes, sir," a subdued Marsden said.

Standing up to depart, Cheetham added, "We cannot be held to blame if a convict is not strong enough to survive the punishment for his crimes."

Marsden disagreed, but he remained silent as the commandant left the office. He resigned himself to learning to live with the decision they had both made.

84

DUSK WAS FALLING WHEN TWO guards John had never seen before came for him. The pair had just begun the night shift.

"So, this is the Irishman they're all talking about," the younger of the two guards commented.

"Aye, this is the sod," the other agreed.

Although John had never laid eyes on either guard before, already he knew the younger man was a Cockney and the other one a Scotsman. Their thick accents immediately gave their heritage away. To his surprise, the Scotsman unshackled him.

"Ye won't need these where you're goin,' laddie," the Scotsman chuckled as he threw the leg-irons onto the mattress. "And if I had to bet," he added, "you'll never need 'em again."

John didn't like the sound of that. He'd overheard the guards on the afternoon shift talking about the moratorium on hangings now in place, and he had momentarily rejoiced at the news. Any joy he felt had been tempered by the fact he was aware Marsden would have something else planned for him. The Scotsman had just confirmed that for him.

Since his unproductive meeting with Marsden and Cheetham, the Irishman had enjoyed his first meal in over a week. *Enjoyed* is perhaps not the right word. The food was little more than slops, and barely edible. Even so, it had helped alleviate the hunger pangs he'd been experiencing over the past few days. Turning to his guards, he asked, "Where are you taking me?"

"You'll see soon enough," the Scotsman replied as he and his fellow guard escorted the prisoner from his cell. They marched him down the long corridor, past the occupied cells. Bored prisoners heckled them as they walked by.

Outside, it was almost dark as they led John across a grassy courtyard and around behind the army's admin block. Here, they found Marsden waiting for them. As they drew closer, John saw the captain was standing alongside a circular hole that was barely three foot in diameter.

"Welcome to your new home for the next little while," the Scottish guard whispered in John's ear.

"All set, you men?" Marsden asked the guards.

"Yes, Captain," the Cockney replied.

"Good." Looking down at the hole, Marsden said, "He stays here until first light. Is that clear?"

"Yes, Captain," the Scotsman said.

Turning to John, Marsden said, "You can think about your crimes while you are down there, Graham."

John ignored the captain. He couldn't take his eyes off the hole, and he wondered what was down there.

Marsden strode off. As he departed, he looked back at the guards and said, "Ensure one of you is on duty here at all times."

"Yes, Captain," the guards said.

The Scotsman turned to John. "I hope ye can swim, Graham," he said. When his prisoner didn't respond, he picked up a stone, held it above the hole and dropped it. The faint splash that followed almost immediately confirmed for the Irishman that the hole was near full of water.

The Cockney said, "You can leave your clothes here, if you prefer."

John declined the offer.

"Remove your shirt anyway," the Cockney ordered.

John did as he was told. As he unbuttoned his shirt, he noticed the guards pull their bayonets from their scabbards and fix them to the end of their rifles. They then pointed their weapons his way so that the tips of the bayonets were only inches from his torso. He glanced down at the hole. It looked deep and forbidding. In the darkness, he couldn't tell how deep it was or how deep the water was. Nor did he know how long he'd be down there. The fear of the unknown made him suddenly fearful for his life.

"Now we can do this one of two ways," the Scotsman said. He explained, "Ye can voluntarily lower yerself into the hole, or we help ye on yer way." He and his colleague both made stabbing gestures with their weapons to further encourage their prisoner.

John needed no further encouragement. He lowered himself into the hole until he was hanging, full stretch, by his fingertips. Even then, his feet were still clear of the water.

"Let go," the Scotsman ordered.

When John didn't let go, one of the guards—John didn't know which one, but he guessed it was the Scotsman—brought his boot down hard on his right hand, forcing him to release his grip. Only when another boot, or perhaps it was the same boot, came down hard on his left hand did he let go altogether.

A moment later, he found himself over his head in the water. He kicked hard and was relieved when his head broke the surface and he could breathe again. At the same time, a sharp pain in his side told him that he'd hit an object of some kind protruding from one side of the hole's interior when he fell. He looked up, but it was too dark to discern what it was he'd struck. Whatever it was it hurt like hell.

Because he was out of his depth, he was forced to tread water to stop from sinking. He immediately began exploring the sides of the hole with his hands, and with his bare feet, and was disappointed to find nothing to hold onto or to support his weight.

It took a few moments before his eyes adjusted to his new environment. Above him, he could just make out the shadowy outlines of the faces of the two guards who were looking down at him. They were silhouetted against the night sky. A solitary star could be seen twinkling above them—between their heads.

"You alive down there, laddie?" the Scotsman asked.

"Do you care?" John asked.

"Nay," the Scotsman chuckled.

John listened as the pair discussed who would do the first shift guarding the hole. After a brief debate, it became evident that duty would fall to the Cockney. Moments later, all was quiet, and the prisoner realised it was just him and the remaining guard in the immediate vicinity.

That was confirmed when the Cockney said, "It's just you an' me now, me ol' sunshine."

By now, John was aware he was in a steel or wrought-iron pipe. If he had to guess, it was wrought-iron—not dissimilar to those pipes used for the conveyance of water and sewerage in Britain. The Irishman was familiar with such pipes as he'd been briefly involved in their manufacture while working at the smithy's in County Louth.

Even though he'd barely been in the hole two minutes, he found that to keep his head above water, he had to simultaneously kick with his legs and paddle with his arms. He was already tiring.

The relentlessness of it was, he quickly learned, exhausting. If he eased off, even for a moment, he invariably sank beneath the surface. And to make matters worse, the blow he had suffered to the side of his chest during his fall hurt so bad he wondered if he'd broken a rib.

"Hey!" he shouted. No answer. "Hey!" he shouted, louder this time.

"What?" came the reply.

"How long am I down here for?"

"Until first light."

John thought he was hearing things. "What?"

"Until first light."

"Holy mother of God!" John said, suddenly alarmed. "That's hours away."

"A little under nine hours."

John's heart sank. He sank, too, as he'd momentarily stopped treading water, so distressed was he. On surfacing, he looked skyward and shouted, "I won't survive down here!"

There was no reply.

They mean to kill me. They couldn't hang me, so the bastards decided to drown me.

As the reality of his predicament set in, John panicked. He began screaming and thrashing around. The metal pipe around him felt claustrophobic and coffin-like. It was as if he'd been buried alive. Sheer terror filled every pore in his body. He was reminded of the time he thought he was going to be burnt alive by his Kabi captors; and he was reminded of the time they were about to consign him a hole occupied by an angry coastal Taipan. This was every bit as bad. He thought he was going mad as he screamed and thrashed about and tried to claw his way up to the surface.

The more he panicked, the closer he came to drowning. Finally, it was his survival instinct that kept him alive. Coughing and spluttering, he forced himself to calm down and focus on conserving energy.

He strived to find the easiest way to stay afloat and keep his head above water. Unfortunately, there was no easy way. The slower he kicked, the harder he had to paddle his arms—and vice versa.

He experimented by placing his back against the pipe and trying to brace himself by placing the soles of his feet against the opposite side. No go. The designers had removed that possibility by ensuring the pipe's diameter was too narrow to permit any such *cheating* by prisoners.

John cursed the pipe's designers. "Bastards!" he shouted. He knew if he had another twelve inches to play with, he could brace himself and, with a bit of luck, survive the night. As it was, he realised he was on borrowed time. Even though he was a strong swimmer, he was aware that wouldn't help in his present predicament. All that would help was his innate fitness and his will to survive.

He had the will to survive, but he doubted he was fit enough to last. The past week, thanks to Barega, had taken a lot out of him and had left him exhausted and aching all over.

Even when fully fit I doubt I could survive this.

He looked up at the night sky, and he suddenly realised he needed assurance that he wasn't alone. "You still there?" he asked.

"Yeah," came the reply. "You still alive?"

"Yeah . . . I think so."

The conversation lapsed.

I guess there's not much more to say.

John continued treading water and focussing on staying alive.

In her rented cottage not a quarter of a mile from the penal settlement, Helen couldn't sleep. She blamed the full moon whose glow pierced her bedroom curtains, bathing the room in light, but she knew better. John Graham was the reason she couldn't sleep.

Seeing John that afternoon had shaken her. The unexpected meeting had brought back so many memories and had revived so many feelings—feelings she'd all but forgotten. A myriad of emotions coursed through her. Relief, anger, sorrow, guilt. Especially guilt because she knew she shouldn't feel this way. "Damn you, John Graham!" she cursed into her pillow.

Helen wondered what was in store for the Irishman now that there was a moratorium on hangings at Moreton Bay. She imagined, whatever it was, it wouldn't be pleasant.

As Helen tossed and turned, wondering what would become of John, the

Irishman was close to drowning. His left foot was cramping, forcing him to kick harder with his right foot to stay afloat. This enforced reliance on one foot was taking its toll. He kept sinking below the surface, and only a mighty effort allowed him to lift his body high enough to suck in another lungful of air.

"Help me . . . please . . . help me!" he called. No response. He called out again, louder this time, and he received another mouthful of water for his trouble. Still no response.

John didn't know how long he'd been down the hole. It felt like he'd been here all night. In fact, he'd *only* been here four hours. He was cold, too, and his teeth were chattering. The water down in the hole was considerably cooler than the air outside, and the cold was going right through him, adding to his discomfort and contributing to the cramp, which was now spreading through all his limbs.

Chimes from the grandfather clock in Marsden's dining room told the captain it was one in the morning. The chimes hadn't woken him. He'd been awake all night, thinking. Thinking mainly about John Graham, who, if still alive, would now be over half way through his time in the hole.

Tossing and turning, Marsden tried to make sense of his feelings at that moment. One minute he wanted the Irishman dead, next minute he hoped he survived. But mainly he wanted him dead. The captain gave up on any thoughts of sleep. He climbed out of bed and donned his uniform.

85

J OHN WAS SLOWLY DROWNING. ANOTHER hour had passed, meaning he'd now spent five hours in the hole, and he was barely able to keep his head above water. He was colder than he thought possible, both his legs were now cramping badly and he was having to rely almost entirely on his hands and arms to remain buoyant—and then only if he thrashed them about furiously.

For the past thirty minutes, he'd been calling out for help. Now, even that was too much for him. Every time he called out, he ended up swallowing water. Besides, the guard never responded.

John wasn't sure if it was his imagination or not, but he thought the night was becoming lighter. He hoped that signalled the approach of dawn.

I have to hold on till sunrise.

Moments later, his hopes were dashed when the full moon appeared directly above him. The celestial orb occupied the entire night sky from John's perspective, its light illuminating the hole for the first time since his incarceration.

Damn!

He resigned himself to drowning, and allowed himself to sink below the surface.

His lungs were bursting. He knew all he needed to do to achieve eternal peace was to open his mouth and breathe in one lungful of water.

Just do it!

Mirritji's voice came to him. *You will know when it is your turn to go to the Dreamtime, Moilow,* the elder said. *You will hear the spirits of your ancestors calling.*

John listened, but he heard nothing other than the pounding of his blood in his ears. He realised he wanted to live, and he thrashed about underwater, desperate to reach the surface.

When his head finally broke the surface, he managed to gulp in some air before sinking again. It took several furious efforts to remain above water long enough to take several deep breaths.

Only now did he realise he was being watched. Marsden's head was silhouetted against the moon, making him immediately identifiable. "Help me!" John managed to call out.

The captain didn't respond. He withdrew from the edge of the hole, and moonlight once more illuminated John's claustrophobic prison.

Paddling for his life, John listened as Marsden spoke briefly to the duty guard before departing. He thought the guard was the Scotsman, but he couldn't be certain. It didn't matter anyway. Neither guard had thus far shown any interest in helping him.

A protrusion from the side of the pipe that encased him caught his attention. It was a steel bracket, which had obviously been welded to the pipe's interior, and it protruded two or three inches and an upward angle of some forty-five degrees. The bracket, which was four or five feet above him, had remained unseen until the moonlight illuminated it. John realised it must be the object that had grazed his ribs when he'd fallen into the hole. He wasn't to know its purpose was to support a canvass hose used to convey water from the nearby river whenever the water level in the hole dropped.

The prisoner was now just going through the motions. His entire being was solely focused on his next breath—and he was losing the battle.

Looking up at the steel bracket, he had an idea.

My breeches!

Calling on the last of his physical reserves, he took a deep breath and allowed himself to sink below the surface. He then tried to remove his breeches, but he was only able to unbutton them and remove one leg from them before he had to surface for air. After two more attempts, he managed to remove his breeches. He needed a couple of minutes to try to normalise his breathing. It was a losing battle. He was taking in more water than air. Working as fast as possible, he tied a large loop in one leg of his breeches and attempted to throw the loop over the protruding bracket.

Three failed attempts later, he was ready to call it quits. A mighty effort was required to propel himself far enough out of the water to successfully lasso the bracket, and so far it was just too much for him. The looped breeches kept missing the bracket by an inch or two.

Once more.

He psyched himself for one last effort. Sinking below the surface as deep as he dare, he kicked with all his might and reached up as high as possible. The loop encircled the bracket and held fast.

John was so relieved, he would have laughed out loud had he not been so busy trying to recover his breath. He coughed and spewed up a large volume of water from his lungs, and immediately felt better. His next instinct was to cry. And cry he did, so relieved was he to still be alive.

As his breathing normalised and his cramps and shivering subsided, he tied one end of his breeches around his left wrist. That enabled him to dangle from the bracket with little effort on his part even though his torso was all but completely out of the water. The combination of the water's buoyancy and his makeshift lifeline proved a lifesaving solution, and he was starting to warm up a little, too. He reckoned he could even catch up on some sleep if he wanted to.

Looking up, he saw the moon's trek across the sky had removed it from view, or from his view at least, and his temporary prison had once more been consigned to darkness. For once, he welcomed the darkness because he didn't want the guards to see what he was up to. The arrival of daylight, he realised, would present a problem, but he'd deal with that when the time came. Until then, he was content to rest up and recover his strength.

Slowly, he could feel his defiant spirit returning. He looked skyward once more. "I am John Graham from Dundalk, Ireland!" he shouted. "I can handle whatever punishment you bastards throw at me!"

Above him, the Scottish guard could be heard chuckling to himself.

Exhausted, John closed his eyes and willed himself to sleep.

John missed dawn's arrival because he was asleep. It was laughter, not the sun's rays, that finally woke him. The laughter was coming from the two guards above.

"Will ye look what this crafty bugger did to survive!" the Scotsman said.

John looked up and saw the Scotsman and his Cockney associate staring down at him. Their expressions reflected amusement and amazement.

"Talk about Irish cunning!" the Scotsman exclaimed. Calling down to John, he said, "Ye must've used up all ye nine lives by now, laddie."

John didn't join in the merriment. He cursed himself for having slept through the dawn. He'd intended to removed his breeches from the bracket before first light, and before his guards could see how he'd cheated death. Now, he feared, they would leave him in the hole permanently—and without his breeches to support him.

The two guards disappeared from view. John could hear them talking. He couldn't hear what they were saying, but the tone of the discussion sounded serious. He wasn't to know the guards had seen Marsden approaching on horseback, and they were discussing their options.

"The captain will keep him in the hole if he sees him like this," the Cockney said.

"Aye, he will," the Scotsman agreed.

"So what should we do?"

"You tell me."

The Cockney looked around and saw that Marsden was now less than a hundred yards away. "Well, the captain did say Graham should be kept in the hole till first light . . . and it is first light."

"Aye, it is," the Scotsman agreed.

The two looked solemnly at each other.

It was the Scotsman who acted first. He grabbed a rope they'd brought with them for this very purpose, and he lowered it into the hole. "Hook this around ye, laddie," he called down to the prisoner.

An elated John couldn't believe his luck when he saw the rope. He noticed the end had been tied into a loop. Releasing his drip on his breeches, he inserted his head and shoulders through the loop. "Haul away!" he shouted.

As the guards began hauling on the rope, he quickly unlooped his breeches from the bracket and dropped them into the water. He considered that a fruitless gesture, but at least, he thought, it would hide his subterfuge from prying eyes should his miraculous survival be investigated.

A moment later he lay sprawled on the grass next to the hole, quivering with exhaustion and sobbing with relief. His arrival above ground coincided with

Marsden's arrival.

Looking down at John from astride his horse, the captain couldn't believe his eyes. Nor could he hide his anger. He glared at the bedraggled, trouserless prisoner and then switched his glare at the guards. "Get him back to solitary," he snarled before riding off.

If John wasn't certain before, he was now: Marsden wanted him dead. That much was clear.

"Alright, Graham," the Scotsman said. "Ye heard the captain. On yer feet."

Twice John tried to stand up, but both times he collapsed. He was so spent. Before he could try again, the guards lifted him to his feet and half-dragged him back toward the cell block.

During the short trek back to the block, John realised a strange kind of camaraderie now existed between the three men. The guards evidently admired him for his fighting spirit and his tenacity while he was grateful they hadn't informed Marsden how he'd managed to survive.

The Irishman looked into the eyes of both men. Nothing was said, but in this brief moment in time they were all brothers.

86

L ATER THAT DAY, AS JOHN recovered from his overnight ordeal as best he could in the confines of his cell, Marsden was deep in discussion with Cheetham in the commandant's mansion. As to be expected, Cheetham hadn't greeted the news of the Irishman's survival with any more enthusiasm than the captain had.

"Perhaps I should have returned him to the hole," Marsden lamented.

"No, you did the right thing," Cheetham assured him. "We were pushing our luck as it was. With the Review Committee members due any day, we cannot afford to lose any more convicts, no matter how deserving they may be of the death penalty. And God knows Graham is deserving of it."

Marsden only partially agreed with his superior. He felt the Irishman should be dealt with, one way or another, permanently.

Cheetham busied himself searching his desk drawer. He finally found what he was looking for and pulled out a box of cigars. Without offering his subordinate one, he selected a cigar for himself and lit it. He closed his eyes and inhaled before blowing out a plume of smoke. "Ahhh," he murmured. Opening his eyes, he looked at Marsden. "These things saved my life you know," he said, glancing at the cigar.

Marsden assumed he was referring to his opium addiction, which, by all accounts, he'd somehow managed to lick.

In case the captain had missed his point, Cheetham added, "They help keep me off the hard stuff."

Marsden nodded understandingly, pretending he hadn't noticed the pungent smell now circulating throughout the den. He'd first encountered marijuana's distinctive aroma as a young soldier when participating in raids of the barracks of fellow soldiers suspected of smoking the drug, and he strongly suspected the commandant's cigars were laced with marijuana. In fact they were. His doctor at the sanatorium in Sydney Town had recommended it. He apparently held to the belief it was impossible for an opium addict to kick the habit cold turkey, and so he had wisely recommended marijuana as the lesser of two evils. So far, the ploy was working.

The captain suspected it would only be a matter of time before his superior fell back into his old habits. Nevertheless, he couldn't help but marvel how the man had gotten on top of his addiction. His eyes were clear—or as clear as they could be for someone smoking marijuana all day long—and he was comparatively lucid and on-the-ball.

After a moment's reflection, Cheetham leaned back in his chair and enjoyed another puff of his cigar. "You know," he ventured, "there may be a higher hand at work here."

"Oh?"

"Yes. Perhaps it is just as well Graham survived. We would have made a martyr of him in the eyes of the other convicts if he had died." Cheetham eyed Marsden shrewdly. He added, "Better to leave him to die slowly in solitary confinement."

Marsden considered the wisdom in that. He saw the commandant's point, but he so wanted the Irishman dead and out of his life—and out of his daughter's life, too. At length, he nodded. "Very well, my Lord," he said resignedly. "However, I want him to pay dearly for his actions."

"You don't think solitary confinement is payment enough?" Cheetham asked.

Marsden shook his head.

"Very well. What do you propose?"

"The treadmill, sir. Starting tomorrow, I want to see him worked until he drops on the waterwheel."

Cheetham smiled. He liked the sound of that. However, he had other plans. "I feel you underestimate the impact solitary confinement has on a man's soul, Captain," he said. "Separate a man from his fellows for long enough, and he will wish he were dead."

Marsden pondered that. Finally, he had to agree with the commandant. "Solitary it is then." He asked, "For how long?"

"For as long as it takes."

A short while later, Marsden found himself in yet another meeting, this time in his own office at the penal settlement. He was meeting with the two senior personnel responsible for the operation of the settlement's prison block.

In all, there were eight men staffing the prison. Overseeing them was Sergeant Charlie Benson, one of the survivors of the raid on the Kabi encampment, and he was assisted by his second-in-command James Whitelock. It was them the captain was currently meeting with. They were the only personnel employed full-time in the prison block. The other six were guards who were rotated week about.

For Whitelock, this was his dream job. The brutal Northerner relished the opportunities the prison environment gave him to bully the prisoners.

Benson, on the other hand, resented his present role. The transfer from active duty to overseeing the prison block had been dressed as a promotion, but he knew otherwise. It was, in fact, payback for what his superiors considered a very mediocre performance in the field. Benson had a reputation for being derelict in his duties, and he hadn't done himself any favours during the failed raid on the Kabi. There was some talk that he'd left his fellow survivors to their own resources during their hasty retreat to the coast, preferring to save his own skin, though that had never been proven. Consequently, he resented his present duties, and he was never slow to demonstrate his resentment.

It was Benson who Marsden was addressing now. "Sergeant, I want you to ensure that John Graham receives no visitors," he said. "No-one apart from myself or approved army personnel. Is that clear?"

"Yes, Captain," Benson mumbled.

"And by *approved* personnel I mean yourself and your subordinates, myself and my fellow officers," Marsden added. "I don't want other ranks paying social visits. And the same goes for civilians. *Especially* civilians. Clear?"

"Yes, Captain."

"Alright. Any questions Sergeant?"

"No, sir."

Marsden looked at Whitelock. "Any questions, Mister Whitelock?"

The Northerner shook his head. "No, sir."

"Alright," Marsden said. "Dismissed." He watched as the two men departed.

Alone now, he looked around his office and tried to imagine being confined within such a small space for years on end. Then he tried to imagine coping in solitary. Compared to this office, John Graham's cell not a stone's throw away was claustrophobic. "Like a rat hole," he said to himself.

The commandant's parting words came to him.

Separate a man from his fellows for long enough, and he will wish he were dead.

Marsden headed out to begin his daily rounds of the settlement. As he walked to the stables to collect his horse, he found that he was whistling to himself. It was another fine day at the bay, and all was well with the world.

John was far from wishing he was dead. He'd slept non-stop since the guards returned him to his cell, and since waking refreshed he'd spent every minute celebrating the fact that he'd survived his night in the hole. Clean-shaven once more, he was now fully dressed, having been issued with new breeches to replace the ones he'd left in the hole.

The Irishman didn't know it, but word of his miraculous survival was spreading fast around the settlement. His legend was growing amongst the convicts and soldiers, and even amongst the settlers in the nearby township.

By mid-afternoon that same day, few residents hadn't heard about John's latest exploits.

Helen learned about those exploits when she overheard her pupils talking before they departed for home at the end of the school day. The pupil who seemed most up to date was Sergeant Benson's son. A classmate of Matthew's, he was proudly relating to his friends what his father had told him over breakfast that morning when Helen happened by. She called the boy aside and he quickly brought her up to date. His account was accurate, albeit dramatized slightly for the sake of his audience. Helen sent the boy on his way as soon as she had all the information she needed. Already, she was thinking of her next report for *The Sydney Gazette*.

On arriving home, Helen drafted a letter for the Gazette's sub-editor. As always, she disguised the relevant information as a poem written in Latin, and as always she signed off with her nom de plume, *The Insider*. Tomorrow, on her way to school, she would post it at Brisbane Town's postal depot, a brand new facility which saved residents having to leave their mail at the penal settlement's depot.

After eating a home-cooked meal, Helen turned in as she had an early start planned for the morning. Unfortunately, sleep eluded her. Every time she closed her eyes, an image of John came to her. She still couldn't believe how wild he looked as he was being dragged back to the bay. "Like a native," she murmured to herself.

Try as she may, she couldn't banish the image from her mind's eye.

It was midnight when she finally gave up on trying to sleep. She came to a decision she'd been ruminating over since going to bed.

John couldn't sleep either. Having slept most of the day following his latest near-death experience, he was now wide awake, and hungry, too. He'd slept through the mid-day meal, which the guards had delivered to him on a tray. They later retrieved the tray and the untouched food when they found their prisoner still asleep.

Fortunately, he was awake when the evening meal was delivered, and he'd made short work of it even if it did resemble slops. He hadn't been able to decide whether the main course was stew or soup, so watery was it. It was accompanied by a side-serving of stale bread, a sour apple and a cup of lukewarm tea. Regardless, he'd devoured it quickly and was disappointed when his request for a second serving was refused. "No second servings here," he'd been told by yet another guard he'd never seen before.

Now, reclining on the grubby mattress that served as his bed, the prisoner looked around his tiny cell as if seeing it for the first time. Moonlight shining through the small, barred window high above illuminated his new living quarters. It also illuminated the ablutions bucket, which, although still smelly, had at least been emptied whilst he'd slept.

Charming!

Fortunately, the flies that buzzed the bucket by day were sleeping, but he knew they'd return with renewed vigour come dawn.

John estimated his cell was, at most, nine feet long and six feet wide. The walls and floor were constructed of stone. Unlike the adjoining community cells whose occupants were separated from the guards only by bars, this cell was totally enclosed. A steel door separated him from the corridor beyond it. At head height, a sliding panel covered an opening that enabled guards to visually check on him, and a narrow opening at the bottom of the door allowed them to push trays of food and other necessities through to him.

By day, the cell was so gloomy available light was barely more adequate than the moonlight at night because the south-facing window was so small. So gloomy was it, John doubted he could read anything—not even during daylight hours and not even if he had something to read.

For the first time since his incarceration, he pondered his future. He was still blithely unaware what his jailers had planned for him. "They'll either hang me or leave me to rot here," he told himself.

They'll hang me for sure.

He tried to put himself in the shoes of those who had the power of life and death over him, and he began to have second thoughts. *Maybe they'll leave me in here to rot,* he wondered. *But for how long?* Looking around, he hoped it wouldn't be for too long. He already had cabin fever. After six years in the wilderness, this place felt like the interior of a coffin.

Little better than the hole.

Thinking of his time in the hole reminded him how well off he was by comparison. "Just be grateful for small mercies, Graham," he told himself.

The faint sound of voices carried to him—so faint he thought he may have imagined it. He stood up and placed his ear against the steel door. The voices were clearer now though still too faint to hear what was being said. However, one thing was clear: one of the two people talking was a woman. He guessed the discussion was taking place in the guards' office, which he knew was located nearby. The discussion sounded heated.

A minute later, he tired of listening and lay back down on the mattress.

In the guards' office at that moment, Helen was endeavouring to convince the duty guard to allow her to visit John. The guard happened to be one Jessie Farrow, the young Cockney who had been on duty the previous night whilst the Irishman was in the hole. He was having a hard time trying to convince his late night visitor she couldn't see the prisoner.

"Captain Marsden made it very clear—"

"What is your name?" a snippy Helen demanded, cutting him off.

"Ah . . . Farrow, Miss," the Cockney stammered. "Jessie Farrow."

"Very well, Mister Farrow," Helen said, drawing herself up to her full height so that her eyes were level with his. "Do you know who I am?" she asked.

"Of course, Miss." Farrow was very aware who the beautiful young woman was standing before him at that moment. Every soldier in the settlement knew who Helen Marsden was. "You are—"

"I am Captain Marsden's daughter," Helen announced rather unnecessarily, "and I demand that you take me straight to the prisoner." Before Farrow could object further, she added, "If you don't, I will report your obstinence to my father at first light." She glared at the young guard, daring him to resist her.

A chastened Farrow wilted before the young beauty's gaze. Fumbling for a set of keys hanging from a peg on the near wall, he mumbled, "Follow me, Miss."

Helen followed the Cockney the few steps along the corridor to John's cell. Her heart was already racing, and for one moment she was tempted to run from the cell block.

Farrow slid the door's top panel across, looked inside the cell and said, "You have a visitor, Graham."

Inside the cell, a wide awake John scrambled back to his feet. Full of anticipation, he wondered who would be visiting him in the dead of night. He thought it could be a woman for he was convinced he'd heard a woman's voice only a minute earlier, and he wondered if it could be Helen. He couldn't think of any other woman who would be visiting him—now or at any hour of the night or day. Even so, when the door finally opened and he saw Helen standing there, he could hardly believe his eyes.

Without waiting to be asked, Helen strode into the cell. She turned back to the guard. "That will be all, thank you Mister Farrow," she said, leaving the Cockney in no doubt she wished to be left alone.

"Ah . . . I will be right outside the door, Miss," Farrow said.

"Close the door, thank you Mister Farrow," Helen ordered.

Farrow should have refused the order, but he was now so far under Helen's spell that didn't even occur to him. He closed the door as instructed.

The prisoner and his unexpected visitor stood there, staring at each other in the silence, less than four feet separating them.

As her eyes adjusted to the gloomy interior, Helen looked around. Her gaze fastened for a brief moment on the ablutions bucket then she studied the stone walls, the barred window, the dirty mattress and the equally dirty blanket that partially covered it. Finally, she looked back at the Irishman.

It was John who spoke first. "What brings you here, Helen?"

"I . . . I needed to see you again," she said. In John's presence, her voice lacked the confidence of a minute or two earlier.

Silence descended once again. As the quiet stretched out, Helen studied the man before her. He looked far more civilised and presentable than the bearded, wild-looking, semi-clad captive she'd seen the previous day. More like the man she remembered—except that he seemed different. Older, wiser and . . . sadder perhaps. "What happened to you, John?" she asked.

"Where do you want me to start?" John enquired. "What do you want to hear?" When Helen didn't respond, he asked, "Do you want to hear how I nearly died a dozen times when I fled Moreton Bay?" He suddenly realised he was angry. Angry that Helen had seen him like this—looking like a caged animal; angry that she was the daughter of the man who had caused him so much sorrow; angry that she represented the system that had brought him so much grief. On a roll now, he asked, "Do you want to hear how I was almost burned alive by Aborigines? Or how I was hunted down like an animal by your father's men? Or how they murdered my wife and son, and slaughtered many of our friends and loved-ones?"

"Your wife and son?" a shocked Helen asked.

"Yes, my wife and son," John said. He had no intention of making this easy on her. The meeting had been her idea, and he didn't want to encourage her. Much as he desired human companionship—female companionship especially—he sensed no good could come of encouraging Marsden's daughter. It wouldn't be fair on her, or on himself for that matter. He added, "I loved them dearly, and your father's men took them from me."

John could see his harsh words were having the desired effect on his visitor. Helen looked truly shocked. For a moment, his heart went out to her. Part of him wanted to take her in his arms and hold her, but part of him wanted to hurt her and frighten her off forever.

Helen made an effort to take control of the conversation. Thrusting out her jaw, she said, "You will be aware no doubt my fiancé was killed by those savages when my father's men tried to capture you." The way she said it left John in no doubt she blamed him for Hogan's death.

"If you refer to Lieutenant Hogan, you should be aware that he was the man who killed my wife."

Helen was rendered speechless.

John continued, his anger barely concealed. "In his haste to kill me, your fiancé rode over the top of my wife without a care in the world for her welfare."

"How . . . what happened to her?" a pale-faced Helen asked.

"She died of her injuries." John looked away. Just talking about Mamba's death made him emotional.

Helen suddenly needed to get away. She turned and looked in vain for the door handle. Realising there was no handle on the inside, she began banging on the cell door. "Guard!" she called. "Let me out!"

The door swung open to reveal an alert Farrow waiting, pistol in hand, clearly expecting trouble.

Before Helen could leave, John reached out, grabbed her arm and spun her around so that she was facing him. Their faces now only inches apart, he said, "You should also be aware of something else."

"Unhand her, Graham!" Farrow ordered, raising his pistol.

Ignoring the guard, John said, "It was me who killed your lieutenant. And I pray that he rots in hell." He released his grip on Helen and watched as she ran off down the corridor. Switching to Kabi, he shouted after her, "I am Moilow. I am Kabi. I am a stranger to you and your people. Go away and forget you ever knew me!"

Farrow glared at the prisoner then slammed the door shut, leaving John staring into space.

John lay down and replayed the conversation he'd just had over in his mind. He knew he'd been hard on Helen. Deliberately so. It had been immediately obvious to him she still held a candle for him, and out of fairness to her he wanted to snuff that flame out once and for all. That brought him little comfort. She was even more of a beauty than he'd remembered, and he'd have loved to have spent more time with her.

As the realisation set in that it was unlikely he'd ever see her again, he was suddenly angry with himself for having lied about killing Hogan.

She will think ill of me forever more.

He put that thought out of his mind almost as soon as it had come to him.

It will help her forget about me if she believes that.

John stared up at what little of the night sky he could see through the window's bars, and he thought about how things could have been between Helen and himself in another life.

For the first time in a long time, he cried himself to sleep.

87

TWO WEEKS AFTER JOHN'S INCARCERATION, members of the all-male Penal Settlement Review Committee arrived from Sydney Town to conduct their investigation into the treatment of convicts at Moreton Bay. The five-strong delegation was led by one Nate Prendergast, a retired army colonel formerly from Oxford.

Prendergast struck up an immediate rapport with Marsden who was charged with chaperoning the delegation over the two days they were at the bay.

Cheetham accommodated the committee members in his mansion, and between himself and Marsden no stone was left unturned in creating a good impression for the visitors. Soldiers and guards alike had been given firm orders that whips were not to be used whilst the delegation was here, and the convicts were to be treated humanely—or, as Cheetham unabashedly put it, "The convicts were to be treated even more humanely than usual."

For the same reasons, the treadmill was also deemed out of bounds to convicts for the duration, an *Out of order* notice being hung from both ends of the torture machine.

Committee members were transported by coach to all parts of the settlement where convict gangs were employed. That included the quarry and even the roadworks underway along the coast some miles distant.

Before the first day was over, it was evident the members were impressed by the settlement's operation and, more importantly, by the treatment of its convict population; before the second and final day was over, Prendergast had let it be known his committee would be recommending an immediate end to the present moratorium on hangings.

The last item on the delegation's agenda was an inspection of the two prison blocks, including the solitary confinement cells, or John's cell at least for he was currently the only prisoner in solitary. Inspection of the prison blocks was left to the delegation's most junior member, a young shopkeeper by trade who was barely out of his teens.

The first John realised he had visitors was when his cell door opened and Marsden led the young man into the cell. It was immediately evident the captain had previously briefed his guest on the Irishman who had been confined to solitary for little was said and the visit was over almost before it started. The young committee member took one look at the fly-blown ablutions bucket, screwed his nose up and backed out of the cell.

Marsden followed his guest out, pausing only in the doorway to glare at the prisoner before a guard slammed the door shut and locked it.

John wondered whether the captain had learned of his daughter's recent unannounced visit. He somehow doubted it because he imagined there'd have been all hell to pay if he had, and he'd have heard the commotion even from his cell.

Ten days after the delegation's visit, Cheetham received a letter from the Governor advising that the Review Committee had given the Moreton Bay penal settlement a pass mark for its treatment of convicts, and that it would be recommending an immediate end to the moratorium on hangings.

Cheetham wasted no time in riding into the penal settlement to advise Marsden of the good news.

Marsden met the commandant at the entrance to his office. "Come in, sir," he said, standing aside to allow his superior to enter.

"Thank you, Tom," Cheetham said cheerily.

It was rare the commandant addressed Marsden by his Christian name during working hours, so the captain guessed he was the bearer of good tidings.

"The Review Committee gave us the thumbs up," Cheetham announced before he'd even sat down. Handing a folded letter over to Marsden, he said, "And they are recommending the moratorium be lifted."

Unfolding the letter, Marsden read it quickly. The result came as no surprise. Nate Prendergast had left them in no doubt the settlement would receive a clean bill of health, and he'd seemed very pro the death penalty.

Deep down, on one level, the captain was disappointed by the committee's findings. He knew their report amounted to nothing more than a whitewash because the treatment of convicts at the bay was abysmal by any standard. He also knew the Marsden of old would have greeted the committee's findings with open disdain. However, to his eternal regret, he no longer knew that Marsden. The present-day Marsden had learned to live with the settlement's shortcomings, and with his own shortcomings, too. Feigning a smile, he looked at his superior and said, "That is excellent news, sir."

"It is indeed, my good man," Cheetham enthused. "I feel it calls for a drink." He eyed the three-quarter full sherry decanter on Marsden's shelf in case his subordinate hadn't gotten the message.

Marsden dutifully poured sherry into two glasses and handed a glass to Cheetham.

"A toast," Cheetham said, raising his glass, "to the resumption of normal duties."

"Hear, hear," Marsden said with as much enthusiasm as he could muster.

The pair clinked glasses and downed the contents of their glasses in one swig.

After a short silence, Cheetham asked, "So, Tom. Where does this leave us with John Graham?"

"In what respect?" Marsden asked, knowing full well what his superior meant.

"Well, when this damned moratorium is lifted, we can hang the Irish bastard." He looked hard at the captain. "If that's what we want," he added.

"I understood we had decided on solitary confinement in Graham's case."

"We had, but things change."

Marsden realised Cheetham was putting John Graham's life in his hands. "Are you saying the decision is mine regarding whether we hang him or not?" he asked.

"That is exactly what I am saying, Tom," the older man confirmed.

Marsden pondered Cheetham's words. He'd come to accept that John would remain in solitary. Now he was being offered the chance to end his life. Tempting though it was, he had come around to the idea that the Irishman who had caused him so much trouble would languish in solitary. He looked back at his opposite. "Leave him where he is, I say," he said.

Cheetham nodded. "So be it," he muttered. Pausing to light one of his specially tailored cigars, he said, "All that remains is to decide on his length of sentence."

"Twenty years in solitary," Marsden said without hesitation. He added, "Two years for every soldier who died in my command during the raid on the Kabi." The memory of the failed raid still left a bitter taste in his mouth.

"Only nine soldiers died in that raid," Cheetham reminded him. "That equals eighteen years."

"Correct, my Lord," Marsden said. "I added two years for good measure."

"Very well," Cheetham chuckled. "Twenty years has a ring to it. Bring the prisoner in and allow me to deliver the bad news in person," he said smugly. "I shall enjoy the experience."

Marsden left the office to arrange for a guard to escort John to his office. He also ordered a junior clerk to be in attendance.

Ten minutes later, a newly-shackled John found himself standing before Cheetham and Marsden in the latter's office. Nearby, a junior clerk sat at a small desk, his quill poised and ready to begin recording what was to follow.

As before, John fastened his gaze on a spot on the wall above Cheetham's head. He would not even give them the satisfaction of being acknowledged.

Marsden motioned to the two guards who had brought the prisoner from his cell to wait outside the open door. They quickly stepped out into the corridor.

Cheetham had no intention of dragging out proceedings. Looking directly at the prisoner, he said, "John Graham, you are guilty of escaping from Moreton Bay." He spoke slowly and deliberately so that the junior clerk could accurately transcribe his comments. "You are guilty of either directly or indirectly causing the deaths of nine soldiers, good men all." He glanced at the clerk. Satisfied the young man was keeping up, he added, "And you are guilty of causing the army considerable time, expense and effort in trying to locate and detain you." Pausing theatrically, he asked, "How do you plead?"

John remained mute.

Only now did Cheetham and Marsden show any signs of anger.

"Speak to the commandant when he addresses you, Graham!" Marsden snarled.

Still John remained mute.

A now irate Marsden stood up, sending his chair toppling over.

Cheetham put out a restraining hand. "Easy, Captain," he cautioned. After Marsden retrieved his chair and resumed sitting, the commandant looked at the prisoner. Summonsing as much gravity as possible, he said, "John Graham, you are hereby sentenced to twenty years' solitary confinement. For the duration of your sentence you will receive three square meals a day." He paused so that the clerk could keep up. "You will receive one hour's exercise in the prison yard every second day, and you will receive no unauthorised visitors for the duration of your sentence." Glaring at John, he said, "Speak up now or forever be damned."

Only now did John shift his gaze. Ignoring Cheetham, he fastened his eyes on Marsden. The undisguised hatred was there for all to see. "I'm forever damned anyway, so nothing you people do to me will change a thing," he said.

Now it was Cheetham's turn to fire up. Angered by the prisoner's refusal to acknowledge him, he barked, "You will address me when I address you, Graham!"

John just smiled.

The commandant turned several shades of crimson and for a moment John imagined he saw steam coming out of his ears.

Finally, Cheetham turned to Marsden, and said, "He's all yours captain. Do with him what you will." With that, he glared once more at John and strode from the office.

Throughout the exchange, the prisoner noted Marsden hadn't taken his eyes off him.

"You know," Marsden said at length, "there is a great irony to your predicament, Graham. Had you served your time as sentenced, you would be standing here in front of me today a free man."

John looked coldly at Marsden, but didn't respond.

The captain continued, "Your escape and your continued evasion have become the stuff of legends amongst the men here. I almost hesitate to make a martyr of you, but the law is the law, and I must uphold it."

"What law is written that permits one man to kill the wife of another?" John asked. "To kill women and children and elderly people? What law is that?"

"You run, we must chase," Marsden responded. "It was your escape that brought us to the Kabi. If there is blame to lay, it must be shared by you."

John was silent. The captain had struck a nerve.

Marsden continued, "For your crimes you deserve to be hung. However, we think that would be too easy on you. Hence the decision to sentence you to solitary." When John didn't respond, he added, "Give it a year and you will be wishing we had hung you."

An impassive John watched as Marsden opened a desk drawer and rummaged through it. The captain eventually found what he was looking for and withdrew a pocket-sized Bible, which he handed to John. "You will be permitted to read, and I recommend you start with the good book. Maybe it will teach you something."

John pretended to take the Bible then, using both hands, he reached up and grabbed Marsden by the lapels of his shirt. Then, pulling down with all his strength, he smashed the captain's face onto the desktop, breaking his nose and knocking him near-senseless. "I'll share no God with you!" he cursed, transferring his grip so that his hands were now around Marsden's neck. The captain's face turned blue as John began throttling him. Blood flowed from Marsden's broken nose.

Only the intervention of the guards prevented Marsden from being throttled to death. The junior clerk had been rendered stock-still by the suddenness and savagery of the attack on his superior. One guard struck John hard over the head with his baton, rendering the prisoner unconscious.

The other guard ordered the clerk to fetch the doctor to attend to Marsden while he hurried to help the captain to his feet. Behind him, the clerk ran down the corridor to do as he'd been asked.

Marsden, who was spitting blood and still struggling to regain his breath, waved the guard away. "Get him back to his cell!" he ordered, pointing at the unconscious prisoner.

"Yes, Captain," the guard said. He and his companion hurriedly grabbed John by his arms and dragged him from the office.

The Irishman had no idea how long he'd been out to it when he came round. He woke with a splitting headache to find himself lying prone on the mattress in his cell with no memory of how he'd ended up here with a lump on his head the size of an egg. An emu egg at that, or so it felt.

Gradually, as he regained his senses, he recalled the events that had transpired in the build-up to this, his latest incarceration. Cheetham's sinister words came back to him.

John Graham, you are hereby sentenced to twenty years' solitary confinement.

"Twenty feckin' years," John mumbled. Marsden's words came back to him, too.

It was your escape that brought us to the Kabi. If there is blame to lay, it must be shared by you.

The prisoner knew there was more than a bit of truth to that.

Determined not to mope or feel sorry for himself, he forced himself to consider the practicalities of his current predicament. He was realistic enough to know he'd never survive twenty years' solitary confinement. "I won't last two years!" he mumbled.

Already his thoughts were turning to escape.

88

THE SMALL BARRED WINDOW IN John's cell was too high to see out—unless he jumped up, grabbed hold of the bars and lifted himself up so that his chin rested on the windowsill. That's what he was doing now. The effort required meant he could only support his body weight for perhaps half a minute at a time.

The view from the south-facing opening was hardly worth the effort. It looked into the rear wall of the stables, which were only separated from the cell block John occupied by the width of a narrow footpath the soldiers used as a shortcut from their quarters. The wall was so close he could almost touch it if he reached out with one hand.

Not having a worthwhile view was annoying enough, but for the prisoner the worst part about it was the stable wall was so close and so high it allowed very little daylight into his cell. And being on the south side of the block meant the sun's rays would never enter the cell anyway. This had been a blessing in summer. However, it was particularly irksome in winter, as he was discovering, for it meant he lived in eternal shade and was often cold—especially at night.

The Irishman released his grip and fell back down onto his mattress. He considered jumping up for another look, but decided against it. There was certainly nothing to look at—and nothing to gain other than some exercise for his arms and upper body.

John was enduring his first winter in solitary confinement. He'd been keeping track of the days, and he estimated he'd been in solitary for six months. "That makes it June," he told himself. "June eighteen hundred and thirty-four." He was right, too.

In that time, the opportunities to escape had been depressingly few. That's what he told himself at least. In fact, he was putting a positive spin on his situation; the opportunities to escape had been non-existent.

Escape from his fully enclosed nine foot by six foot cell was impossible, so sturdy was its construction; escape from the prison block John occupied was just an unlikely given the armed guards and round-the-clock security in place.

For one hour every alternate day, as per the terms of his sentence, he was escorted to an outside courtyard at one end of the block to exercise. The courtyard was totally enclosed on all four sides, and two armed guards watched over him for the full hour, so escape from there was also out of the question.

John looked forward to these fleeting outdoor sessions. They were the only times he escaped the confines of his cell and felt the warmth of the sun or the caress of a breeze on his pale face and body. After so long in lockdown, he was now pasty white. The dark brown suntan of old was long gone.

The Irishman usually spent the full hour shirtless, running around the courtyard's perimeter. It was part of a keep-fit programme he'd adopted in the first week of his incarceration. Although the courtyard was small, it was a veritable paddock compared to his cramped cell, and it was certainly big enough to allow him to stretch out and even to sprint a short distance. Invariably, he ended these sessions with a good sweat-up.

The forty-eight hours between his courtyard visits always seemed more like three or four days. In some ways, the time spent outside only served to increase the extreme frustration he felt at being so confined. He had never been one to spend much time indoors, and he feared he'd go mad if he remained in solitary much longer.

John's daily routine consisted of eating, sleeping, reading and looking after himself as best he could. He had established something of a rapport with a couple of the guards—the two who had watched over him whilst he'd been down the hole—and they kept him supplied with reading material. This material comprised namely the bible Marsden had given him, poetry books and backdated copies of newspapers, and it helped keep him sane. The Cockney guard, Jessie Farrow, had also smuggled in a lantern, which enabled John to read any time day or night.

Meals were delivered three times a day to the prisoner on a tray, which a guard slid through the opening in the bottom of the door. The food amounted to little better than starvation rations, and it was sometimes so gross it was inedible. It was rare that John didn't find some foreign matter in his food. That foreign matter ranged from dead rodents to insects and beetles of all varieties. As a result, he had lost even more weight, and was now skinnier than ever.

From the outset, he had determined he would try to remain as fit and healthy as his circumstances allowed. He'd established a daily exercise routine, which included stretches, press-ups, situps, jumping up and down, and running on the spot. He even performed chin-ups, holding onto the bars of his window for support, and he would spend hours pacing his cell even though he could only take three long paces before having to turn around.

John insisted on being clean-shaven, and he was permitted the use of a blunt razor, which he used to shave each morning. He also showered as often as possible. Unfortunately, he was only allowed to use the cell block's shower facility once a week, and then only when it wasn't being used by the other prisoners in his block. Marsden was insistent on that. He wanted the Irishman to have as little human contact as possible.

It was this lack of human contact that was getting to John. Now, as he lay on his mattress gazing up through the bars of his window, he yearned for companionship. He went over and over in his mind past discussions with Mamba and Murrowdooling and Carravanty, and with the friends he'd made within the Kabi clan. Sometimes, he articulated the more memorable discussions aloud. In fact, he'd been talking to himself more and more of late. It was another habit he'd gotten into since his incarceration.

If there had been one moment of genuine joy in the past six months, it was the discovery of John Keats' poem *Lamia* in one of the poetry books the guards had supplied. The Irishman had been overjoyed to find the poem that he'd fallen in love with years earlier, and he read it at every opportunity.

John reached out and retrieved the book from a temporary bookshelf he'd rigged up using a short plank Farrow had supplied. He debated whether to light the lamp before opting to face the other way on the mattress so that what little daylight there was fell on the open page.

Running his finger down the page, he stopped at a verse that caught his eye and began reading aloud. "Love in a palace is perhaps at last," he said. "More grievous torment than a hermit's fast that is a doubtful tale from faery land, hard for the non-elect to understand. Had Lycius lived to hand his story down, he might have given the moral a fresh frown, or clench'd it quite: but too short was their bliss."

John discovered he was feeling emotional. He wasn't surprised. Keats' poetry often moved him so. He resumed reading. "To breed distrust and hate, that make the soft voice hiss. Besides, there, nightly, with terrific glare. Love, jealous grown of so complete a pair. Hovered and buzzed his wings, with fearful roar, above the lintel of their chamber door, and down the passage cast a glow upon the floor."

The prisoner read the verse over and over. Soon, he'd fully memorised it.

Not a hundred yards from John's cell block, Marsden was in the middle of his daily rounds of the penal settlement. This afternoon, he was accompanied by Cheetham. They were both on horseback. It was only the third time the commandant had ever accompanied his subordinate on his rounds, but as far as Marsden was concerned it was three times too many.

Relations between the two officials remained civil, but strained. Marsden resented the cigar-smoking commandant usurping what little authority he'd retained since his superior's return from his rehabilitation in Sydney Town, and Cheetham still considered the captain too soft with the convicts. However, each had learned to tolerate the other, and, as a result, arguments between the two were rare these days.

They reined in beside the treadmill where convicts were in the process of relieving forty of their fellows who had been turning the water wheel for the past forty-five minutes. The new men took their places on the top plank and, at a signal from a foreman, began walking on the spot, their shackles clinking with every step. The water wheel began to turn, slowly at first, and then more steadily. It wasn't long before the convicts were sweating profusely. Meanwhile, the men they'd relieved lay prone on the ground, trying to recover their breath and regain their strength before it was their turn once more.

Since setting off from Marsden's office an hour earlier, Cheetham had regaled the captain about the unknown informant whose scathing reports on the treatment of Moreton Bay's convicts were garnering a wide following amongst readers of *The Sydney Gazette*. Clutching a recent copy of the newspaper, the commandant opened it up and held it under Marsden's nose. "This bastard continues to hide behind the nom de plume The Insider," he cursed.

Marsden glanced at the open page. The Insider's latest column had pride of place in the top right corner of page three.

"Listen to this," Cheetham fumed in between puffs on an ever-present cigar. Reading from the column, he said, "Since the moratorium on hangings ended at Moreton Bay, the army chiefs have resumed hanging convicts at the rate of one a week, sometimes two. Often for no greater crime than looking sideways at an officer." Cheetham snorted then continued, "Meanwhile, floggings and beatings continue unabated, and the incidence of death and disease amongst convicts continues to rise at an alarming level."

Cheetham threw the newspaper to the ground and rounded on Marsden. "I want this informant found, Captain, and when he is, I want him to feel our wrath!" he said.

"Aye, sir," Marsden said.

Both were convinced *The Insider* was a man.

"His column is being picked up by the London papers, and his comments are fuelling the liberals' opposition to penal settlements," Cheetham grumbled. He eyed Marsden. "I want you to arrange for the immediate random censorship of all outgoing mail from the bay," he ordered.

"Does that include civilian mail, sir?" the captain asked.

"Damn right it does, but I'll wager this Insider fellow is one of ours. He knows more than any civilian could possibly know, so it *has* to be one of ours." Cheetham added, "And when we know who it is, I'll have him crucified."

"I will organise the clerks to censor the mail prior to each outgoing shipment, sir," Marsden promised.

"Good," Cheetham said.

They continued on their way. Their next stop was the quarry. As they rode toward it, Marsden tried not to think of the repercussions if settlers discovered their private mail was being censored.

While Cheetham and Marsden were discussing the informant's recent dissertations, *The Insider* was finishing her latest column for *The Gazette* in her office at the Moreton Bay School. As always, it was written in Latin in the guise of a poem. With a flourish, Helen signed off the critique using her established nom de plume—also in Latin—then slipped it into an addressed envelope, which she then deposited into her satchel.

The routine was well established by now, and Helen took no small amount of pride from the fact her now monthly column was gaining quite a following, not only in Sydney Town but throughout Australia and even in the home country. Her contact at *The Gazette*, Deputy Editor Timothy Hershaw, had informed her more than once that her column was increasingly being followed by members of the civil rights movement in both countries. She was especially pleased to learn that opponents of the death penalty were liberally quoting her column during protest marches and the like.

Nowhere was the column debated and discussed more than it was in Moreton Bay. Most residents—settlers and soldiers alike—despised the column and the informant who wrote it. It was very evident to all that the informant was one of their own, a fellow resident of the bay, because his, or her, local knowledge discounted the possibility it could be an outsider. The level of dislike for *The Insider* ranged from annoyance to downright hatred. Moreton Bay was, after all, a penal settlement; the rationale was its soldiers were only doing their job, and the settlers largely relied on those same soldiers for their livelihood.

Despite this opposition, there was a growing civil rights movement amongst the settlers, and every month more of them were opposing the hangings and the ill treatment of convicts.

In fact, there was a meeting of civil rights campaigners planned for that very night in town, and Helen planned to be there. She would keep a low profile for she was aware it was not a good look for the daughter of the penal settlement's head warden to be publically opposed to the army's policies. For the same reason, none of her fellow campaigners knew she was The Insider, and she planned to keep it that way.

Helen was preparing to head home. The school day had ended an hour earlier, and she was attending to some last minute paperwork. An unopened letter in the in-tray on her desk caught her eye. The letter was addressed to her personally, and its postmark signalled it had been posted in Edinburgh, Scotland, some three months earlier.

On opening the letter, she discovered it had been written by one Eliza Fraser, a Scottish woman who, she learned, was a mother of three and husband to the master of a ship that transported free emigrants to New South Wales. Intrigued, Helen began reading.

The letter, which was inscribed in beautiful italics, read:

Dear Miss Marsden

I write to express my utmost admiration for the excellent work you are doing in the field of education in New South Wales. I am not sure if you are aware, but you have a reputation in Britain for being a champion of the education of school-age children in the colony.

That was news to Helen. Her benefactors the Browns, in Sydney Town, had advised her that her reputation was spreading, but she had no idea anyone had ever heard of her beyond Australia's borders. She kept reading.

As the mother of three young children, and a firm believer in education, I do appreciate the leadership you are showing for one so young and, dare I say, for a woman. It is no secret that even in this modern age, women are not encouraged to excel in the workplace. That you have so excelled is a credit to you.

My husband James has visited Australia in his capacity as a sea captain charged with the responsibility for the delivery of free emigrants to the colony. I do hope to accompany him on a future visit, in which case I would consider it an honour to meet you if you are so inclined.

Sincerely
Eliza Anne Fraser

Helen folded the letter. Adding it to the pile of papers in her satchel, she vowed to respond to her new penfriend as soon as possible.

That night's meeting of the Moreton Bay Civil Rights Campaigners was the fledgling group's third meeting in its short history, and was, by far, the best attended yet. In addition to the group's six committee members, Helen counted twenty-six others, including herself. Most she had seen before, but one was new—to her at least. A young man, he introduced himself as an armourer who repaired and supplied firearms. Helen thought his bearing suspiciously military, so she remained wary of him. She would not put it past Cheetham, or her father for that matter, to plant an observer in these meetings.

The meeting had barely begun before the subject of The Insider was broached by one of the committee members. This sparked a rowdy discussion with almost everyone present having their say on the informant's likely identity. No-one thought to ask Helen for her opinion, and she was quite content to remain quiet on the topic. She was amused, and more than a little relieved, that everyone, without exception, thought the informant was a male.

"Without a doubt he's a settler," one member of the audience said.

"Yes he's one of us for certain," said another.

"Oh, yes," said yet another. "And I suspect he's here tonight."

This latest comment prompted everyone present, including Helen, to look around, trying to spot the informant.

Unable to resist, Helen asked, "What makes everyone think The Insider is a man?"

The attendees were silent for a moment. Their expressions indicated they were either bemused or amused by the very suggestion the informant could be female.

First to speak was the group's acting chairman. A pompous chap who also chaired the men's only Moreton Bay Club, he said, "I believe we can safely assume our informant is a man, my dear." He added, "I think you would agree The Insider has balls, and on that basis I do not believe any of the settlement's female population would qualify."

This prompted loud guffaws from the menfolk and twitters from all the womenfolk present except for Helen and a few members of the local Church Committee who were not amused by the gentleman's choice of words. Helen only just managed to resist the urge to giggle.

Next day, Marsden and head clerk Corporal Dunstan observed as a nervous junior clerk randomly checked the contents of outgoing mail in the army's mail office. He was barely a tenth the way through a pile of letters that had accumulated since the last vessel had departed the bay a week earlier. At a guess, three-quarters of the letters were from the civilian population, the balance being from army personnel.

The junior clerk used steam from a pot of boiling water he'd brought through from an adjoining kitchen to steam open the envelopes. Hesitant at first, he was quickly becoming more proficient and the pile of vetted letters grew steadily.

"Do you know what you are looking for, Private?" Marsden asked the junior clerk.

"Yes, Captain," the young man said. "Corporal Dunstan explained earlier."

"I am not asking Corporal Dunstan," Marsden snapped. "I am asking you, soldier."

"Yes, Captain. Sorry, Captain," the junior clerk stammered. "I am looking for any critical reference to hangings and ill treatment of convicts at Moreton Bay, sir."

Satisfied, Marsden turned to the head clerk. "Ensure your clerks give priority to army correspondence, Corporal Dunstan," he said.

"Yes, Captain," Dunstan said.

The clerks Marsden referred to were the two junior clerks under the corporal's command, including the one currently checking the mail.

Looking at the junior clerk, Dunstan said, "Remember to check one in three army documents and one in six civilian documents, Private." He said it more for Marsden's benefit than for his subordinate's.

"Yes, Corporal," the junior clerk said.

Marsden had seen enough. "Carry on, men," he said, striding from the office before anyone had time to salute him.

Dunstan observed the junior clerk a while longer before he, too, left.

Alone now, the junior clerk continued randomly checking the mail. He came to an envelope addressed to a woman in Sydney Town. He was about to move on to the next envelope, when he noticed the sender's name on the back of it was the captain's daughter. Curious, he opened the envelope and read the letter. The junior clerk quickly ascertained it was an innocent letter to an obvious friend. Not being a student of Latin, he couldn't make head nor tail of the passage written in that language of ancient Rome. Bored, he returned the letter to its envelope and moved onto the next one.

Marsden was still in the corridor outside the mail office. Halfway along the corridor, a window overlooked the courtyard where John and the other prisoners exercised, and the captain had noticed the Irishman was using it now. He stopped to watch as a shirtless John jogged around the courtyard's perimeter. Every now and then, the prisoner would sprint, and even from a distance Marsden could see he was sweating profusely. It was a warm winter's day even by Moreton Bay's standards.

John wasn't constrained by shackles. Security in the courtyard, and in the adjoining cell block, was so tight that shackles weren't considered necessary for the prisoners unless they were transferred or escorted to any other part of the settlement. In John's case, his entire world was confined to the courtyard and the cell block, so he remained thankfully free of shackles or restraints of any kind.

Watching his nemesis, Marsden couldn't help question his decision to let the Irishman live. Cheetham had left the final decision to him, after all, and, perhaps foolishly, he'd opted to put John in solitary rather than order his execution. He wondered if that decision would come back to haunt him.

◆€•——•3◆

John was unaware he was being observed by anyone other than the two guards charged with guarding him as he went through his paces in the courtyard. Sunlight reflected off the admin block's windows, concealing the presence of Marsden and anyone else who happened to be watching.

The guards never let him forget they were there for they mercilessly heckled their prisoner as he went through his paces. John enjoyed the good-hearted banter and gave it back to them with interest. It was, after all, the only real communication he had with other people.

After completing yet another series of sprints, he dropped to the ground and peeled off a dozen press-ups. That done, he looked over to the nearest guard. "How long to go?" he asked.

"Five minutes," the guard said.

Normally, John used the last five minutes of his hourly sessions to work himself hard. Today, however, he was enjoying the feeling of the warm winter sun on his bare skin so much that he rolled over onto his back and lay there, soaking up the sun's rays and imagining he was lying on a beach a hundred miles or so to the north.

89

EIGHTEEN MONTHS LATER, JOHN HAD given up on any thought of escape. He'd given up on himself, too, and was now little more than a shadow of his former self. Dirty, bearded and unkempt, he was skinnier than ever, and his pasty, white skin was now mottled and covered in unsightly rashes and festering sores—some of them the result of untreated insect bites.

The rot had begun a year earlier—almost one year to the day since his incarceration in solitary. Virtually overnight, he had lost his desire to keep fit and he'd lost any aspiration to look after himself. He'd stopped exercising, shaving, showering and reading, and spent his days sleeping or talking to himself and chanting in the Kabi tongue. His guards feared he was starting to lose his mind, and they had long since lost interest in trying to exchange banter, or even insults, with him because he never responded to them these days.

Though physically inactive, when he wasn't sleeping the prisoner had remained active in his imagination, almost to the point of being hyperactive. He relived past events and replayed discussions he'd had with old friends, relatives and workmates in his mind. And he talked to himself constantly, switching between English and Kabi, depending on his mood or the memory he was reliving at the time.

John was talking to himself in Kabi now. Sitting on the edge of his mattress, which remained unchanged and unwashed to this day, he was chatting away to Mamba as if she was here in the cell with him. In fact, he was convinced she was here. He could see her clearly in his mind's eye. So engrossed was he, he didn't notice the sound of carollers outside his cell. From the township, they were singing Christmas carols en route to attending the Sunday morning church service at the army's chapel.

The Irishman was so out of it, it hadn't even registered with him that it was the week before Christmas. As for what year it was, he'd long since stopped recording each passing day and didn't know it was 1835.

John was completely unaware he was being observed at that moment. Sergeant Benson was watching him through the eye-level opening in the cell's steel door. The sergeant was talking to his second-in-command James Whitelock at the same time, sharing his observations with the Northerner.

"He's talkin' Abo again," Benson said.

"He's always talkin' Abo," Whitelock said.

Neither man attempted to lower their voice. They knew from experience the prisoner was in his own little world and was usually oblivious to all going on around him.

"We always suspected Graham went native," Whitelock said.

"Aye, well, there's the proof," Benson said, indicating that his subordinate should take a look at the prisoner.

Whitelock peered through the opening and shook his head. John was now chanting in Kabi. "Poor bloody fool," Whitelock mumbled. Turning to his superior, he asked, "He ain't gonna last another eighteen years here, is he?"

Benson shook his head and walked off. "I'd give 'im another fuckin' year at most," he said over his shoulder.

After attending the morning carol service, the Marsden clan gathered for their Sunday lunch at the cottage. Orana had cooked a roast and, with some help from Helen and her step-mother Mildred, served up a mouth-watering hot meal.

"Smells good," Matthew said as the women fussed about to ensure everyone received their fair share.

"It does at that," Marsden agreed from the head of the table.

As soon as the maid departed the dining room, Helen turned to her father. "Why don't we ask Orana to join us at meal time, father?" she asked.

Marsden scowled at the very idea. "She has always eaten alone in the kitchen," he mumbled.

"Exactly," Helen responded. "I think it is high time she joined us."

"Nonsense," Marsden snorted.

"I think it is a splendid idea, Tom," Mildred Marsden said in support of her step-daughter. "At least for the Sunday lunch."

Annoyed, the captain reminded the women that maids never dined or socialised with their employers.

"In the home country maybe," Helen agreed, "but there are different rules out here in the colonies."

Sensing he was in danger of losing this argument, Marsden grumbled, "Maybe next Sunday."

"Very well," Mildred said. She smiled and winked at Helen who returned her smile.

The exchange wasn't lost on the man of the house. Marsden leaned over to Matthew, who sat next to him, and whispered, "A man has little chance in this world when two women gang up on him, son."

Matthew nodded. "You can say that again," he said.

"We heard that!" Mildred and Helen said in unison.

Changing the subject, Marsden looked at Matthew again and reminded him it was his turn to say grace.

Matthew obliged, saying grace, and then everyone tucked in.

Marsden enjoyed these family get-togethers. Sunday lunch was the only time the whole family generally sat around the same table, and it was a time he cherished for he realised it wouldn't last forever.

His children were a never-ending source of pride. Matthew, now nineteen, was a strapping six-footer and a real chip off the old block. After shaky beginnings, the boy had excelled at school, and, after the Christmas break, he would be going to Sydney Town to pursue a law career.

Helen, now twenty-seven, was as beautiful as ever and was maturing into a woman to be reckoned with—as her father always knew she would. In her capacity as headmistress of the local school she was now responsible for more than one hundred and sixty pupils, and twelve full-time and part-time teachers.

If there was one regret Marsden had it was that Helen seemed more married to her career than ever, and he feared she may never marry. Not that she didn't still have suitors. There was no shortage of marriageable men pursuing her, but none had captured her heart since Lieutenant Hogan's death. For that matter, he suspected even Hogan hadn't truly captured her heart.

Despite the abiding love and admiration father and daughter had for each other, there was still an undercurrent of tension between the two over the treatment of convicts and the army's insistence on hanging those who broke the settlement's draconian rules. Generally, the captain and Helen tried to avoid such touchy topics—especially during these family get-togethers—but occasionally one of them would get in a dig and a fiery debate would inevitably follow.

After the main course and dessert had been polished off, the family traditionally adjourned to the front veranda to read and talk, and it was no different today. As the man of the house always did, Marsden took the opportunity to catch up on the world's news courtesy of recent back-copies of London and Sydney Town newspapers, while Mildred read a book and the siblings discussed their respective highlights of the week just gone.

"Mister Scully said to wish you well with your law studies next year," Helen advised her brother.

"Thanks," a nonchalant Matthew said. Mister Scully was his head teacher at school.

"He believes you will do well in your chosen field," Helen added, barely able to conceal her pride. She took pleasure from her brother's scholastic achievements for she'd invested a lot of time in him, exhorting him to study and helping with his homework. Turning to her father, who was hiding behind a copy of *The Sydney Gazette* at that moment, she asked, "Did you hear that, papa?"

"Mmmm," Marsden grunted.

"Father!" Helen flicked the newspaper, startling Marsden.

"What? Oh . . . yes," the captain said. "Well done, Matthew." He returned to his reading. The Insider's latest column had caught his eye. Without realising it, he began muttering to himself.

"Tom, what on earth are you mumbling about?" an amused Mildred asked.

Marsden looked up. "That damned Insider chap is spreading more gossip about treatment of convicts here at the bay!" he growled. "Listen to this." He began reading from the column. "In the first week of November, no less than two convicts were hung, one died of pneumonia and a further twenty-three were deemed too ill to work. Rumoured floggings totalled thirteen though that cannot be confirmed because the army never releases information on the number of convicts flogged. Such blatant abuse of humanity's laws of decency can surely be ignored no longer. It is to the British Army's eternal shame this abuse is allowed to continue . . ." The captain threw the newspaper to the floor in a fit of anger.

"Who do you think this Insider person is?" Mildred asked.

"We haven't a clue," Marsden said, "and that's the frustrating part."

"It wouldn't be one of the soldiers would it?" Matthew asked.

"Quite likely it is," Marsden said. "Whoever it is, they know the ins and outs of our operation, so it probably is a soldier."

Helen feigned disinterest in the conversation, but she hung on every word.

Quite matter-of-factly, Marsden said, "But I believe we will know who it is soon."

"How?" a somewhat startled Helen asked.

"The clerks are randomly checking the outgoing mail before every shipment," Marsden explained. "We'll catch him soon enough."

That was news to Helen. Her first thought was the latest letter she'd delivered to the mail depot only two days ago. It wouldn't have left the depot yet as the first departure for Sydney Town wasn't scheduled until tomorrow. Helen was suddenly thankful she wrote her columns in Latin. She doubted a lowly army clerk would understand that seldom used language of the ancients.

"Oh, that reminds me," Marsden said to his daughter. "I have a letter for you." He added, "It ended up at the Army's mail depot by mistake."

Helen tensed when her father pulled an envelope out from his jacket pocket. The young woman feared she'd been found out, and it was with some trepidation she accepted the envelope. She relaxed when she recognised the handwriting. Opening the letter, she announced, "It is from my friend Eliza Fraser."

"How nice," Mildred said. "How is Missus Fraser?"

Helen quickly scanned the letter. "She is well by all accounts," she said. "Gosh!"

"What is it, sis?" Matthew asked, suddenly interested.

Helen looked up. "Eliza says she will be accompanying her husband on his next voyage to Australia, and she wants to meet me when she arrives in Sydney Town."

"Oh how exciting," Mildred said. "You must see if she can come to Moreton Bay. We would all love to meet her."

Helen was delighted to learn she would soon meet her dear penfriend. She and Eliza had exchanged half a dozen letters over the past eighteen months, and in that time had formed a genuine long distance friendship.

In the clerks' office next morning, Corporal Dunstan checked on the junior clerk currently tasked with randomly censoring outgoing mail. The younger clerk was selecting and opening envelopes from a pile of documents on his desk. A ship was departing for Sydney Town that afternoon, so it was likely he'd be fully occupied checking mail all morning.

"Anything, Private?" Dunstan asked.

"Not yet, Corporal."

Dunstan watched for a while longer as his clerk quickly checked the contents of various envelopes. He was about to leave when an open letter caught his eye. "What's that?" he asked, pointing to foreign text on the page.

"Don't know, sir." Joking, the junior clerk added, "It's Latin to me." Little did he know, the text he and his superior were looking at *was* Latin.

"Let me have that," Dunstan said, taking the letter and the envelope from his subordinate. Glancing at the back of the envelope, the head clerk saw that the sender was none other than the captain's daughter. He knew he shouldn't read Helen's private mail, but he'd been secretly in love with the young beauty ever since he first saw her, and he couldn't resist reading the letter. "Carry on, Private," he said, quickly departing the office with the letter in hand.

Dunstan entered an adjoining office and, after closing the door, he sat down and began reading. When he reached the Latin text half way down the second page, he saw that Helen introduced it as *My poem of the month*. That much was in English. What followed was all in Latin. The head clerk had no difficulty translating it. He was the only enlisted soldier at Moreton Bay who had studied Latin, and he'd excelled at it at school.

Before he'd completed translating the first paragraph, he knew who The Insider was. He couldn't believe it. His first instinct was to report his discovery to Marsden. Then he realised that could only hurt the captain's daughter, and he couldn't bear to think that he would be responsible for causing her pain.

For the remainder of the morning, the head clerk waged a private war with himself. Dunstan the soldier was in no doubt what he should do; Dunstan the man didn't want to hurt the woman he loved.

In the end, Dunstan the man won. It wasn't just because of his deep feelings for the woman who called herself *The Insider;* it was because he sympathised with the contents of her column and with her campaign to rectify the wrongs at Moreton Bay. He had long been a critic of the army's treatment of convicts, and he'd quietly celebrated when The Insider's column had first appeared. So, in the end, it had been an easy decision.

Returning the letter to its envelope, he then returned it to the growing pile of checked envelopes in the clerks' office next door. "Everything in order, Private?" he asked.

"Yes, Corporal," the junior clerk confirmed.

Dunstan departed the office even more in love with Helen Marsden than he had been five minutes earlier.

<hr/>

As the clerks went about their business, in the courtyard outside the admin block John endured his one-hour exercise session. As always, two guards looked on as their charge walked, zombie-like, around the courtyard's perimeter. For them, and for him, the times when he used to exercise to the point of exhaustion were but a distant memory.

"Dead man walking," one of the guards commented to his colleague as the prisoner shuffled past.

"Aye," the guard's colleague agreed.

The pair missed the days when they exchanged banter with John. For them, the job dragged at the best of times. Heckling the once cheeky Irishman had made the time go just that bit faster. Now there was no more point heckling him than there would be heckling a stray dog. "How long to go?" the same guard asked his companion.

"About ten minutes."

"Let's call it a day." His companion agreed. Looking at John, he shouted, "Alright, Graham . . . Time's up!"

A docile John dutifully walked over to the guards and allowed them to escort him back to his cell.

90

THAT NIGHT, ALONE IN HIS cell, John lay staring up into the darkness. Outside, rain clouds hid the moon, reducing Moreton Bay to total blackness.

Thoughts scattered through his brain, like leaves being blown about by the wind. Wide awake, he tried to make sense of the thoughts. They came to him in brief flashes, too quick to digest.

Faces came to him, too. Some familiar, some not. They seemed to be talking to him, but he couldn't make sense of the words.

John was no stranger to such weird sensations. He had been experiencing them a lot lately, and always at night. Days and nights had become one and the same. Often, he slept by day and remained awake by night.

Tonight, the sensations were more vivid than usual. Thoughts and visions and sounds collided so dramatically he feared he was going mad.

Amidst the chaos, he saw the spirits of Kabi clan members who had died. He recognised them immediately. He saw Mamba, Murrowdooling, Mootemu, Orad, Jarra, Kulan and others. They were smiling at him. Despite the darkness, he could see them as clear as day, and he could see his totem, the dingo, as well. Somewhere, someone was playing a didgeridoo. He wondered for a moment if he was in the Dreamtime.

No sooner had he had that thought than Mootemu, the most respected of elders, left the others and approached him. "I bring you goodwill, Moilow," the elder smiled.

"I accept your goodwill, Ancient One," John said, astonished to be communicating with Mootemu's spirit.

No longer smiling, the Ancient One looked John up and down, and made no effort to hide the fact that he didn't like what he saw. He then asked, "What has become of the Moilow we knew?"

John couldn't answer Mootemu. He was too ashamed. Finally, he asked, "Am I in the Dreaming?"

Ignoring the question, Mootemu said, "You must hold onto hope, Moilow." The elder's image began to fade and his voice became more distant.

"Don't go!" John implored, suddenly afraid he'd be left alone.

Mootemu didn't oblige. His image faded until it was nothing more than a faint glow in the darkness, and his voice was now so quiet it was a mere whisper. The Ancient One murmured, "You must prepare for the new life that awaits you, Moilow." And then he was gone.

Alone once more, John cried out, "Mootemu!" Panic filled him. The darkness frightened him; the very thought of being alone frightened him even more.

John tensed when he felt something touch his hand. "Who's there?" he asked. He gasped when he felt someone's hand in his.

Then, unaccountably, a calmness came over him. He knew whose hand it was he was holding. It was a feminine hand, small but firm and hot to his touch. "Mamba," he whispered.

His companion's identity was confirmed a moment later when Mamba appeared beside him. Holding tight to her hand, he allowed her to lead him toward the cell's near wall. Miraculously, they passed through the wall as if it wasn't there. Before he knew what was happening, he found himself sitting alongside Mamba on a moss-covered rock near the base of a waterfall. It was a familiar place. John recalled they'd made love there in another lifetime. He looked up and saw a perfect rainbow form in the spray from the falls.

Mamba reached out and touched his face. Smiling, she said, "You must heed the Ancient One, Moilow. He speaks words of wisdom."

Before John could respond, Mamba's image began to fade. The Irishman didn't panic this time. He was learning the spirits from the Dreamtime kept to their own schedule, not his. "How is Murrowdooling?" he asked.

"He is in good heart," Mamba said, her image faint now.

"And Carravanty?"

By now, Mamba had all but disappeared. After a moment's hesitation, she said, "Carravanty still lives beyond the Dreaming."

John wondered what she meant by that. "Wait!" he said.

Too late. She was gone.

A moment later, John found himself back in his cell. It was no longer dark. The clouds had parted and moonlight flooded the tiny space that was his home.

He lay back on the mattress. The experience he'd just undergone made no sense to him, but he knew it was real nevertheless.

John stared up at the night sky through his barred window. He could make out the Southern Cross constellation and the once-seen-never-forgotten outline of the stingray.

Suddenly tired, he closed his eyes and felt himself drifting off. Just before he fell asleep, Mamba's words came back to him.

Carravanty still lives beyond the Dreaming.

He wondered whether that meant the boy was still alive. He could think of no other meaning.

And then, in his dreams, Mootemu's words came back to him.

You must hold onto hope . . . You must prepare for the new life that awaits you, Moilow.

Cockney Jessie Farrow couldn't believe his eyes. Having just delivered breakfast to John on a tray, which he'd slid through the opening at the bottom of the door, he had heard strange noises coming from inside the cell. He'd immediately peeked through the eye-level opening, and had been amazed to see the Irishman frantically exercising.

Having just completed a dozen press-ups, a now clean-shaven John was running on the spot. He stopped every so often to perform some more press-ups or do some situps. This was his first exercise of any note in more than a year, so the prisoner didn't last long. He finally collapsed onto his mattress and lay there, his chest rising and falling rapidly as he tried to regain his breath.

Farrow, who was still watching, could restrain himself no longer. "Who are you trying to impress, Graham?" he asked. "If it's me, yer wastin' yer time."

John smiled when he realised who it was. He'd had a soft spot for the Cockney ever since he had helped him survive his night in the hole. "It ain't you I'm trying to impress, I can assure you of that," he shot back.

"So you've decided to come back to the land o' the living, have ya?" Farrow asked.

"If you call this living, you're one misguided Cockney," John retorted.

Farrow slid the panel across and walked off, chuckling to himself. He was looking forward to informing his fellow guards the Irishman they knew and loved was back.

91

A MUCH FITTER AND STILL clean-shaven John sprinted up and down the exercise courtyard adjoining his cell block. Two guards watched him as he stopped every now and then to perform some star jumps and press-ups. They directed some good-natured banter his way, but, to their disappointment, he was now too breathless to respond. Up until five minutes ago, he'd been giving as good as he got by way of banter.

It was a hot, humid February day, and guards and prisoner alike were sweating profusely. The only sounds were the buzzing of flies, the chirping of cicadas and grunts of exertion coming from the prisoner. Each competed with the other to disturb the silence. Somewhere, away in the distance, the faint crack of a guard's whip could occasionally be heard, reminding one and all that this was a penal settlement.

Now into his third year in solitary, and some two months since his unexpected visits from Mamba and Mootemu—visits John remained more convinced than ever actually happened—he was still as skinny as ever and as pasty white. Given his indoor confinement and his meagre food rations that was inevitable. But gone were the unsightly rashes and festering sores, not to mention the sorry-arsed look of the defeated man he once was. He was now better groomed and less dishevelled, when he wasn't working out at least, and he had a gleam in his eye once more.

"That's it for today, Graham!" the nearer of the two guards yelled.

"Another ten minutes," John replied breathlessly.

"Nope yer time's up," the guard insisted. He'd already incurred Marsden's wrath for showing leniency with the Irishman, and he didn't wish to put that to the test again.

"Five minutes and that's my final offer," John said, grinning, as he resumed sprinting up and down the courtyard.

The guard looked at his companion and noted he was also grinning. "Not fuckin' funny!" he grumbled.

"Relax," the other guard said. "The captain's in town meeting with ol' Bertie"— *Bertie* being the moniker guards and soldiers alike gave Cheetham when no-one else was around—"so he'll never know."

And so John was given the extra minutes he'd negotiated plus one extra for good measure.

When his time was up and he'd recovered his breath, he exchanged constant banter with the guards as they escorted him back to his cell.

In the course of his two-and-a-bit years in solitary—not counting the year he spent in a near-comatose state—John had gained the grudging respect of his jailers. All the guards admired his fortitude and some had even gotten to like, or tolerate at least, his keen Irish wit. He'd proven he could exchange verbal barbs with the best of them, and they delighted in provoking arguments with him—even though nine times out of ten they came out on the wrong side of any debate.

Now, as the guards locked John inside his cell once more, they marvelled at the turnaround they'd witnessed in recent months. "I wouldn't believe it if I hadn't seen it with me own eyes," one guard said.

"Aye, he's a new man, that's fer bloody sure," the other agreed.

Inside his cell, John enjoyed a well-earned drink from his water bucket. He then stripped off and splashed the remaining water over his sweaty face and body. Aside from the weekly shower he was permitted, this was the nearest he got to bathing on the other six days. It meant he had to keep asking a guard to refill his bucket, but he'd trained the guards pretty well by now and they usually obliged.

That done, he donned his breeches and lay down on his mattress, poetry book in hand. He opened it at the page of his favourite Keats' poem, and began reading another verse from *Lamia*.

It read:

Why this fair creature chose so fairily by the wayside to linger, we shall see;

But first 'tis fit to tell how she could muse, and dream, when in the serpent prison-house, of all she list, strange or magnificent:

How, ever, where she will'd, her spirit went; Whether to faint Elysium, or where down through tress-lifting waves the Nereids fair.

Wind into Thetis' bower by many a pearly stair; Or where God Bacchus drains his cups divine. Stretch'd out, at ease, beneath a glutinous pine;

Or where in Pluto's gardens palatine. Mulciber's columns gleam in far piazzian line. And sometimes into cities she would send her dream, with feast and rioting to blend.

John felt as though the verse could have been written for him. Moved, he began reading it again. Sooner or later he would memorise it—as he had the others before it.

While John was reading *Lamia,* Helen was teaching a class of senior pupils at the school. She had been pulled away from her headmistress duties to fill in for a teacher who was away sick. Helen didn't mind at all. Teaching was her first love after all, and she welcomed any chance to extricate herself from her all-consuming admin workload.

The lesson had not long started when she noticed a young postal worker approaching the school. He was holding a letter. Helen hoped it had nothing to do with The Insider's column, which she still wrote religiously every month. Since her father had informed her that the army's clerks were randomly checking outgoing mail in the hopes of learning the informant's identity, she had become paranoid that she'd be found out.

"Excuse me, class," she told her pupils as she hurried away to intercept the postal worker.

Outside, she waved to the young man to attract his attention, and he came to her when he saw her. "Hello," she said. She had seen him around, but didn't know his name.

"Morning, Miss," he said in a cheerful Welsh accent. "A letter arrived at the depot for you from Edinburgh. I thought it might be important so I—"

"Oh, that is very kind of you," a relieved Helen interjected. She took the letter from him and sent him on his way with a smile that made his otherwise uneventful day. A glance at the handwriting on the envelope confirmed it was from her dear friend Eliza Fraser. She was sorely tempted to read it then and there, but she put her pupils first and hurried back to class to resume the interrupted lesson.

As the lesson continued, Helen's curiosity got the better of her and she gave her pupils a brief assignment she knew would fully occupy them for the next few minutes—long enough for her to take a peek at Eliza's letter. She opened the letter and began reading.

The opening paragraphs read:

> *My Dearest Helen*
>
> *I should be half way to Australia aboard my husband's brig the Stirling Castle by the time you receive this.*
>
> *I would love to meet up with you in Sydney Town and I will get word to you as soon as we arrive in late April, God willing. If it is not possible for you to get away, you will be pleased to know I have talked James into calling at Moreton Bay on our return voyage to Britain.*
>
> *With this in mind, I would ask that you give serious consideration to returning to Britain with us, if only for a holiday. You would be welcome to stay at our family home in Edinburgh for as long as you like. It would be marvellous company for me as James is away at sea most of the time . . .*

Helen smiled to herself as she digested Eliza's invitation. For years now, she had been promising herself she would visit her homeland. It had always been a case of *maybe next year.* And when next year rolled around, she put it off again. Now, here was an opportunity she felt she couldn't resist.

By the time she had finished reading the letter, she'd made up her mind: she would accompany the Frasers back to Britain aboard *the Stirling Castle*. She vowed to inform her father and step-mother, and then hand in her notice at the school immediately.

That afternoon, Marsden checked on the junior clerk tasked with checking outgoing mail. The head clerk and the other junior clerk were both away—the former on holiday leave while the latter was on sick leave—and the remaining clerk was barely coping in their absence. "How is it going, Private?" the captain asked. Before the clerk could answer, Marsden asked, "Have you completed the figures for the stores sergeant yet?"

"Ah . . . not yet, Captain," the flustered clerk said.

"Well you attend to that and I will take over here for a while," Marsden said, pulling out a chair for himself.

"Yes, sir. Thank you, sir." The grateful clerk hurried off to complete the figures his superior referred to.

Marsden turned his attention to the mountain of unchecked envelopes on his left. He began selecting envelopes and checking their contents at random before adding them to the pile on his right.

After thirty laborious minutes, his eyes were drawn to familiar handwriting on the front of an envelope. It was addressed to a woman in Sydney Town. The sender's address on the reverse side confirmed it had been written by Helen. He tossed it aside and was about to pick up another envelope when he was drawn back to his daughter's letter. Something made him open it. He felt more than a little guilty as he began reading the enclosed letter.

Marsden skim read the letter and was about to return it to its envelope when he noticed the poem written in Latin. A former student of Latin, he had retained a working knowledge of the language even though he'd rarely used it since leaving school. The words *The Insider,* at the end of the poem, jumped out at him.

As soon as the school day ended, Helen hurried home and changed into her riding clothes. She couldn't wait to inform her father of her decision to accompany the Frasers back to Britain. Once changed, she hurried to the stables behind her rented cottage, saddled her horse and set off for the penal settlement with Eliza's letter in her shoulder bag.

Lo and behold, on the outskirts of town she came across her father who was riding out from the penal settlement. Little did she know he was coming to see her. She waved to him and thought it strange he didn't return her wave.

It wasn't until Marsden reined in, in front of Helen that she realised he was angry. Her eyes dropped to something he was holding in his left hand. She saw at once it was a letter, and she knew immediately what it was. Her heart dropped and she looked shame-faced into her father's eyes.

"You . . . How could you do this?" he asked, brandishing the letter in front of Helen's face. "My own daughter . . . the informant we have been searching high and low for!"

"Papa . . ."

"Don't Papa me, girl!" Marsden raised his right hand as if to hit her.

Helen shrank back. Her father had never raised his hand in anger before. Not to her at least.

Marsden tried to compose himself. "What do you have to say for yourself, young lady?" he asked.

Helen forced the little girl in her to one side as she faced up to her father. "I did not do it lightly, father," she said with sudden determination. "I am privy to information the general public should know about, and I chose to share that information in the interests of humanity and human decency."

Marsden could feel his blood boiling. For one moment he wished his daughter was a man so that he could thrash her to within an inch of her life. "Your actions are thoughtless!" he shouted.

"And your actions are criminal!" Helen shouted back. "How many convicts have died under your command?"

Marsden flinched as his daughter's comments struck home. "You never stopped to consider how your column reflects on me or the regiment I serve!" he shouted, even louder than before. "That is unforgiveable!" His anger slowly gave way to disillusionment. He still couldn't believe Helen of all people had done this behind his back. "Helen . . ." He was lost for words.

"Father," Helen said as something else occurred to her—something she couldn't resist adding. "Most of these convicts were born into a life of abject poverty. Most were just trying to survive, and—"

"Survive by committing crimes!" Marsden interjected, almost spitting as he did so.

"Many did nothing more than steal a pittance for themselves," an undeterred Helen continued, "in order to feed their starving families." She asked, "Wouldn't you or I or anybody in those circumstances do exactly the same for their loved ones?"

Marsden didn't reply.

"There will come a time, father, when those running this Godforsaken penal colony, as well as the scoundrels in charge of the British Empire, will be remembered as the real criminals!"

Father and daughter sat there, facing each other astride their horses, just a few feet apart.

Finally, Marsden reached a decision. Fastening a steely gaze on Helen, he said, "I will inform Lord Cheetham of your actions unless you desist from writing this . . . this . . . this disgusting column immediately." He brandished the incriminating letter once again. "And you know what that would mean for your school," he added.

Helen didn't need to be told what that would mean. Cheetham would withdraw the army's ongoing financial support for the school, and that would cause it all sorts of hardship. It would likely force a reduction of school numbers and may even force the school to close.

Defeated, Helen murmured, "I won't write any more columns."

"Speak up," Marsden demanded.

"I said I won't write any more columns." Helen could see her father was satisfied by that. She guessed he was no doubt relieved, too, for to disclose that his daughter was The Insider would be disastrous for his career. For that reason, she was also relieved.

"Very well," Marsden said. He looked at her gravely. "To say I feel let down is an understatement, Helen. In fact, I can hardly bring myself to look at you at present."

"Well you won't have to look at me much longer, father," Helen said. "Missus

Fraser has invited me to sail with her back to Britain, and I have decided to accept the invitation."

Marsden was too surprised to respond.

Helen added, "I will depart Moreton Bay aboard the Stirling Castle in May."

Momentarily speechless, Marsden could only watch as his daughter turned her horse around and rode back the way she'd come. He couldn't see the tears that streamed down her face just as Helen couldn't see the emotion that welled in her father's eyes.

PART EIGHT

THE RECKONING

92

⟶

*T*HE *STIRLING CASTLE* ARRIVED AT Moreton Bay in May of that year as Eliza Fraser had promised. Lord Cheetham and the Marsdens were at the wharf to greet the brig as she berthed. Matthew was also here. He'd interrupted his law studies in Sydney Town, arriving a few days earlier to spend time with his sister before she departed for Britain.

Helen had visited Sydney Town to spend a week with the Frasers soon after their arrival the previous month. In that time, she had formed an even stronger bond with Eliza, who, she discovered, was seven months pregnant. The Scotswoman hadn't mentioned her pregnancy in her last letter.

The week Helen spent with the Frasers had more than ever convinced her she'd made the right decision to quit her job and return to Britain. She could not remember ever being so excited, and she couldn't wait to experience new sights and adventures. "There's Eliza!" she said, pointing out the Scotswoman whom she'd just seen emerge from below deck. She waved furiously to attract her attention.

Eliza saw Helen and returned the wave. Her radiant smile signalled she was delighted to see her newfound friend once again. Eliza was a youthful-looking woman with a pleasant face framed by flaming red hair. Despite her obvious pregnant state, her youthfulness belied the fact she already had three young children. "Hello!" she called out as the brig berthed alongside the wharf.

"Hello!" Helen replied. She glanced at her father and noticed he was in discussion with Cheetham. Helen thought it strange the commandant had interrupted his schedule to join with her family in greeting the Frasers. What she didn't know was the Governor had ordered him to personally greet all vessels charged with bringing free settlers to New South Wales. Such was his desire to help foster the influx of free settlers to balance the colony's convict population. This wasn't the first such vessel Cheetham had greeted, and it wouldn't be the last. Consequently, as Helen would discover, the commandant would be spending a lot of time with the Frasers—with Captain James Fraser in particular—until they departed two days hence.

As the Stirling Castle's gangplank was lowered, Helen hurried forward to welcome the Frasers who were the first to disembark. She was closely followed by Cheetham. After greeting Eliza and her husband with warm hugs, she introduced them to the commandant.

"Welcome to Moreton Bay, Captain Fraser," Cheetham said, grasping the captain's hand, "and you, too, Missus Fraser." He effusively kissed the back of Eliza's hand.

"It's James and Eliza," Captain Fraser insisted.

549

Helen then introduced the Frasers to her family, and they took an immediate shine to the couple. Captain Marsden hit it off with Eliza's husband, sensing the seaman was a man of substance, and Mildred Marsden struck up a rapport with Eliza, finding her company most stimulating.

Captain Fraser excused himself, explaining he must attend to duties aboard the brig. He promised to catch up with the others later. He and his wife were, after all, staying at the commandant's mansion for the next couple of days. The brig's master patted Eliza's swollen tummy affectionately and hurried back on board.

Cheetham then led Eliza to a horse-drawn coach that would take her and the Marsdens into Brisbane Town. The Frasers' luggage would follow later.

During the short ride to the township, the friendly Scotswoman entertained her audience with tales of the adventures she'd shared with her husband on their voyage out from the home country and during their time in Sydney Town and Melbourne.

Eliza promised Helen more adventures on the return journey to Britain. She couldn't know that would turn out to be quite an understatement.

That night, Cheetham hosted the Marsdens and their Scottish guests at a formal dinner in the commandant's mansion. An army chef had been seconded to prepare the meal, and two waiters from the officers' mess were present to serve the diners. The end result was a dinner and service that would do justice to the finest restaurant.

Everyone except Eliza was drinking the fine wine on offer. In the interests of her unborn child, she drank fruit juice.

As always, Cheetham puffed his marijuana-laced cigars, and a cloud of smoke enveloped himself and those closest to him. Those closest to him included Captain Fraser, who sat on his left, and Captain Marsden, who sat on his right.

Early in the dinner, Fraser winked at Marsden when he identified the drug's distinctive aroma. Marsden grinned and debated whether to share with his opposite some time that the commandant was a recovered opium addict. He suspected he wouldn't, but he'd have liked to see the other's reaction to that bit of news.

Cheetham looked at Eliza who was sitting next to her husband—just close enough to be affected by the cigar smoke. The smoke was starting to wreak havoc with her sinusitis though she was too polite to complain. "What do you have planned for Helen in Edinburgh, Eliza?" he asked.

Eliza sneezed and had to blow her nose before she could answer. Sniffing, she said, "Well, she has agreed to be a nanny to our three children." Rubbing her tummy, she quickly added, "And a nanny to Number Four."

"That's his temporary name," Captain Fraser joked.

"I should hope so, James," Mildred smiled.

"Have you decided what you will call *her?*" Helen asked with a twinkle in her eye.

Before her husband could respond, Eliza jumped in and said, "I would like to call her Helen." Smiling, she turned to Helen, who sat next to her, and squeezed her hand.

Helen was momentarily overcome.

"A splendid idea!" Captain Fraser said. Raising his glass, he said, "To our daughter, Helen." He mischievously added, "*If* it's a girl."

This prompted more laughter and merriment.

Not one to be left out of the conversation for long, Cheetham said, "It sounds like your new nanny will have her work cut out."

"She will have plenty of time to see the sights," Eliza said. "I will make sure of that." The Scotswoman started sneezing again.

"My dear woman, is my cigar bothering you?" Cheetham asked, knowing full well it was while hoping his guest would be too polite to blame the cigar smoke.

"Not at all, Lord Cheetham—"

"Bertie," Cheetham insisted.

"Bertie." She blew her nose again. "It is my jolly hay fever."

Cheetham was relieved he could keep smoking. He was lost without his special cigars. Looking at Helen, he asked, "Do you think you will get down to London, my dear girl?"

Helen bristled at being referred to as such, but she hid her annoyance. "Certainly, Lord Cheetham," she smiled sweetly. "I plan to visit my Aunt and cousins in London at the first opportunity."

Turning to Captain Marsden, Cheetham said, "You will miss her, Tom." Glancing at Marsden's wife, he added, "And you, too, Mildred."

Mildred smiled and looked loving at the young woman she considered her own.

"That we will," Marsden confirmed. He looked at Helen and smiled. In the two months since he'd uncovered her treachery—for that was how he still viewed it—their relationship had understandably been more strained than ever. However, he loved her dearly and that became ever more evident to him as her departure date neared. Neither knew when she'd return or even if she'd return.

Captain Fraser looked at Matthew who sat opposite him. "And what about you, young man?" he asked. "Will you miss your sister?"

"Maybe . . . a little bit, sir," Matthew grinned. He grimaced when Helen kicked his shin beneath the table. He hastily added, "On second thoughts, yes I will miss her a lot."

The belated admission provoked laughter around the table. Brother and sister shared a moment. Each knew they would miss the other more than either would admit.

Later in the evening, Helen managed to get a moment alone with her father. She had been wanting to talk to him privately all day, and only now, while the others were preoccupied, did she have the chance. "Papa, I have a favour to ask," she said.

"Certainly," Marsden said. "Why don't we step out onto the back porch?" He led her out of the dining room.

Now outside, he asked, "What is it, my dear?" He was intrigued to know what Helen wanted. She hadn't asked any favours of him since their falling out over *The Insider* debacle, and he could only guess at what she wanted now.

Helen hesitated. The young woman had a big favour to ask of her father. She could predict he wouldn't agree to what she wanted, but she had to ask anyway. "Papa"—Marsden knew this was important to Helen because she always referred to him as *Papa* instead of *Father* when she wanted something these days—"I would like your permission to see John Graham before I leave Moreton Bay."

Marsden couldn't believe his ears. His daughter knew what he thought of the Irishman and here she was asking to see him again. He thought she'd gotten over Graham, but obviously not. "What makes you think I would ever agree to that?" he asked. "And why on earth would you want to see the man who killed your fiancé?"

Helen tried to control her temper. She quietly counted to ten then said, "We both know that is not true, don't we, Papa?"

Now it was the captain's turn to count to ten. "He as good as killed him," he finally said.

"But he didn't personally kill him," an indignant Helen said. "And yet you were happy to let me go on thinking he did." Her tone was highly accusatory. She had overheard Sergeant Benson and Private Askew—the two enlisted men who survived the raid on the Kabi—discussing that failed expedition, and she'd heard that John had only knocked Hogan from his horse. One of the Kabi had actually finished him off.

"We argue over semantics," Marsden grumbled. "The point is, Graham defied us and fought against us, and many good men died as a result."

"So your answer is no?"

"My answer is no," a defiant Marsden confirmed.

An equally defiant Helen turned and, without another word, returned inside, leaving her father stewing on the back porch.

Although Helen had expected no different from her father, she was nevertheless disappointed. Since learning that John hadn't actually killed her fiancé, she'd found herself thinking more and more about the Irishman—and, for reasons even she couldn't explain, she felt she needed to see him again.

The day before Helen's departure from Moreton Bay was one round of farewells and last-minute packing. The school's pupils and teachers gave her a rowdy send-off at morning tea time—an event that drove home just how popular she was at the school, and that left her feeling quite emotional.

As much as possible, she avoided contact with her father because she knew he would still be brooding over last night's heated discussion.

That night, alone in her bed after another dinner engagement with her family, Cheetham and the Frasers, she tried in vain to sleep. She had hoped for a good night's sleep because *the Stirling Castle* was departing early in the morning, and she wanted to be well rested for the journey ahead.

John's face kept coming to her. She could feel his startling blue eyes boring into her.

Helen suddenly sat up. She knew had to see the Irishman one last time.

93

J AMES WHITELOCK, SECOND IN COMMAND in the prison block, couldn't believe it when Helen marched into his office a little before midnight. Normally, he didn't work the night shift. That task was left to his subordinates—except when there was a shortage of guards as was the case tonight. Dysentery had resulted in three prison guards being laid low, and so he'd drawn the short straw.

Helen cursed to herself when she saw she'd have to deal with the surly Northerner. She had hoped one of the junior guards would be on duty. She'd crossed paths with Whitelock before, and hadn't been impressed. He struck her as belligerent and uncouth, and she didn't like the way he openly leered at her—as he was doing now.

"How can I help you, Miss?" Whitelock asked his unexpected visitor.

"I have come to see John Graham," Helen announced with as much authority as she could muster.

"Graham's off limits to all except the officers and guards, Miss . . . As I'm sure you're aware," Whitelock said. He looked Helen up and down appreciatively as he spoke. She looked fetching in her riding gear. It clung to the contours of her body, and showed off her curves to good effect. The Northerner guessed she'd dressed to impress the prisoner, not him, but that didn't for one moment stop him admiring her physical attributes.

Ignoring the other's obvious interest in her, Helen said, "I am sure you are aware I am Captain Marsden's daughter, sir?" It was more a statement than a question.

"All the more reason to refuse your request, Miss," Whitelock said. He hurriedly added, "Captain Marsden has made it very clear who can and can't see Graham."

Helen felt defeated. In former times, she'd have pulled her *high and mighty routine,* but she sensed that would be wasted on the uncompromising Northerner. She managed one indignant snort, and started to walk away.

"Ah . . . I have an idea, Miss," Whitelock said.

A hopeful Helen stopped and turned back. "Yes?"

"Well, Miss, if you repeat what I'm about to say to anyone I shall deny it, but if you are prepared to extend me certain favours, I'd consider letting you see the prisoner," he said, grinning.

Helen knew immediately what he was getting at, but she needed to hear it from him. "What did you have in mind?" she asked.

Whitlock's grin widened and ran his tongue over his lips, leaving no confusion over what he wanted. "We can do it in the storeroom down the corridor," he suggested hopefully.

Helen's skin crawled at the very thought of this uncouth man running his hands and tongue over her. However, a thought came to her. "When did you have in mind?" she asked.

"Right now, Miss." Whitlock was hardly able to believe his luck. He hadn't for a moment thought that she'd even consider his invitation. He could feel himself getting excited already.

"You must be joking, sir!" Helen said. She softened her tone and added, "However, if you care to come to my cottage tomorrow night I shall accommodate you." As she said it, she silently prayed the Stirling Castle's departure wasn't delayed a day.

That was good enough for Whitelock. He had all tomorrow off in lieu of the overtime he'd put in. "Tomorrow night it is," he said, grabbing a set of keys from a desk drawer. "You can see Graham now." He hesitated. "But first, a down-payment," he said.

Helen didn't like the sound of that. She asked, "What did you have in mind?"

"One kiss, Miss. That's all."

"Out of the question," Helen snapped.

Whitelock returned the keys to the desk drawer. "Over to you, Miss," he said, indicating negotiations were at an end.

Helen was tempted to leave, but she *had* to see John. "Very well," she demurred. Closing her eyes, she waited for the big oaf before her to plant his lips on hers. Plant them he did, and she literally held her breath until he finally came up for air.

Whitelock looked like he wasn't going to settle for one kiss, so Helen quickly reminded him of their arrangement. "One kiss you said." Faking a smile she hoped was sexy, she added, "That was a taste of what you can expect tomorrow night."

The Northerner liked the sound of that. Fumbling with excitement, he retrieved the keys and picked up one of two lanterns that lit the office before leading his visitor down a corridor to John's cell. Sliding open the eye-level panel in the cell door, he looked in and said, "Visitor for you, Graham." He unlocked the door and handed the lantern to Helen. Before departing, he winked at her and mumbled, "Until tomorrow night, Miss."

Helen ignored Whitelock. She had eyes only for John. He was already on his feet even though he'd been asleep moments earlier. Helen was pleasantly surprised to see he looked considerably more presentable than when she'd last seen him. Clean-shaven and well groomed, he looked a new man. And those eyes! She felt herself melting as the Irishman appraised her.

John couldn't believe Helen had visited him. He wondered if he was dreaming.

Neither spoke for some time. The Irishman was well used to long silences, but they unnerved Helen, so she spoke first. "I . . . I wanted to see you one more time . . . before . . ."

"Before what?" John asked. He still couldn't believe Helen was standing in front of him. She was the first woman he'd seen since she last visited him. That was more than two years ago, and it felt surreal. But one thing was certain, he thought. She looked more beautiful than ever.

I must surely be dreaming.

"Before what?" he asked again.

"Before I leave for Britain," Helen said. When John didn't comment, she added, "I leave tomorrow." She whispered that last titbit in case Whitelock was still outside the door.

After another long silence, John asked, "Why did you come, Helen?"

"I learned that you lied to me when you said you killed my . . . Lieutenant Hogan," she said. "When I found out what really happened I realised I couldn't blame you. You weren't at fault for what happened. Not entirely anyway."

As John digested this, he could feel his old feelings for Helen returning. He had no intention of revealing that to her, for he was wise enough to know they had no future together. However, he was pleased she'd learned that he hadn't killed Hogan. He wanted them to depart as friends, and so he talked to her. She listened, entranced, as he related to her his adventures since fleeing Moreton Bay. He told her of his incredible experiences whilst alone in the wilderness, his time with the Kabi and how he'd passed his long, long years in solitary.

Helen then told him what she'd been up to in Moreton Bay and in Sydney Town before that. She even told him, in strictest confidence, about her former newspaper column and how she'd been found out. She went up in John's estimation when she disclosed that.

After ten minutes, they were both smiling; after fifteen minutes they were laughing aloud; after twenty minutes it felt like they'd been lifelong friends.

Only the sound of approaching footsteps brought them back to reality. Moments later the cell door opened and Whitelock stuck his head in. "Time's up, Miss," he said.

Helen stared at Whitelock until he withdrew into the corridor. Then, turning back to John, she said, "I must go now." Try as she may, she couldn't hide the feelings of regret she felt. Regret that theirs was a relationship that could never be.

The feelings were reciprocated. John found he still had a deep, abiding affection for the young beauty before him.

Helen turned to go, but John put a restraining hand on her arm. He then placed the palm of his hand on her cheek and whispered, "This is a traditional Kabi blessing." He left his palm against her cheek.

Helen could feel some sort of a warm current flowing from John's hand. It warmed her face and it quickly spread through her whole body, and the sensation almost moved her to tears.

John finally removed his hand and said, "Good fortune will follow you in your travels." He added, "The spirits of the Dreaming say it will be so."

"Thank you," Helen stammered. She hurried from the cell before John could see she was about to cry.

Whitelock slammed the cell door and locked it before hurrying after his late night visitor. "See you tomorrow night, Miss," he called as Helen ran out into the darkness.

Outside, Helen quickly mounted her horse and rode off. She was so emotional after her parting with John, she didn't immediately notice her father. The captain hadn't been able to sleep either, and, knowing the prison block was short-staffed he had decided to check on Whitelock.

The first Helen noticed her father was when he rode up beside her. She was so surprised she nearly fell off her horse. "Father!" she gasped as she reined in her steed.

Marsden didn't need to ask what she was up to. It was obvious. But he asked nevertheless. "What on earth are you doing here at this hour?"

Helen didn't want to lie to her father. Not on the eve of her departure. So she didn't. "I saw John Graham," she said with a frankness that surprised Marsden.

"And Mister Whitelock allowed that?" Marsden asked.

Much as Helen despised Whitelock, she didn't want to get him into trouble. "I blackmailed him," she lied. She quickly added, "I warned him I would report him to you if he did not allow me to visit John . . . ah . . . John Graham."

Marsden saw through that. He knew the Northerner was well aware of prison rules and wouldn't be blackmailed so easily. The captain also bristled at the very thought of his daughter visiting the Irishman.

Helen felt she owed her father an explanation, but she could think of nothing that would satisfy him. At length, she said, "I decided to see him after I learned he hadn't personally killed Desmond."

Glaring at Helen, Marsden said, "We have been over that. He may not have delivered the coup de grâce, but he was right there in the thick of things, my girl. Believe me, I was there." Before Helen could respond, he added, "What you need to understand is John Graham didn't just steal from his employer in Ireland." The captain fixed her with his steely gaze. He said, "Graham also killed him . . . stabbed him to death." Marsden had only recently learned this courtesy of a letter received from the Irish Courts. Apparently, two credible witnesses to the murder had belatedly come forward, testifying that they saw John stab his employer. The court registrar had advised the relevant British authorities that if John Graham ever returned to Ireland he would be tried for murder.

A shocked Helen didn't know whether to believe her father or not. Previously, he'd been happy to let her think that John had drowned, and that he'd killed her fiancé. Why wouldn't he lie about John killing his employer?

As if anticipating this, Marsden said, "There was unfortunately insufficient evidence at the time to convict Graham of the gruesome murder he committed in Ireland. A crime for which he most assuredly would have been hung. The original court records even refer to the murder rumours." The captain added, "I can show you the records if you don't believe me." His tone was challenging. He wanted to put this matter to bed once and for all.

"That won't be necessary, father," Helen murmured. She believed him.

Satisfied he'd made his point, Marsden said, "Let us discuss this no more." He said, "You should get some sleep now."

"Yes," Helen murmured. "Goodnight, father."

Marsden watched as his beloved daughter rode off into the night. "Good night, my dear," he said to himself.

Moments later, the captain dismounted his horse and strode into the prison block. He was on his way to see Whitelock. Angry beyond words, he intended to demote the man and deduct a week's pay to boot. By the time he reached Whitelock's office, he'd decided to deduct two weeks' pay. And if the Northerner lied to him, he'd deduct three weeks' pay.

Next morning, almost half Moreton Bay's residents turned out to wave Helen off from the wharf. They included past pupils, teachers, neighbours and friends the popular young woman had touched in some way during her time in the settlement.

To the fore, of course, was Helen's family. She had already undergone tearful farewells with her stepmother Mildred and with Matthew, and now it was time to say goodbye to her father. She and the captain had barely spoken since he'd intercepted her leaving the prison block last night. Since then, Marsden had learned from Whitelock that Helen had spent at least twenty minutes alone with John Graham, and he was fuming. He couldn't bring himself to think what had happened between his daughter and the prisoner in that time.

Now, facing her father, Helen said, "Father, I know you are disappointed in me, but I have done nothing I am ashamed of."

"Well, you alone must live with your conscience, Helen," Marsden said gravely. "So I trust your conscience is clear."

"My conscience is *very* clear, father," Helen said.

Three bells signalled that *the Stirling Castle* was ready to depart. Helen was the only passenger still to board her, so she prepared to head off up the gangplank.

Looking into her father's eyes, Helen said, "Goodbye, papa." She kissed Marsden affectionately on the cheek.

"Goodbye, my dear," Marsden said.

Holding back her tears, Helen turned and walked up the gangplank where Eliza awaited her. The two women embraced and stood by the near rail, looking down at the assembled as crewmen hauled in the gangplank and made final preparations for departure.

"Behave yourself abroad, sis!" Matthew called out.

Helen smiled down at her brother. She looked for her father and was disappointed to see he'd mounted his horse and was preparing to ride off. He had mentioned he had a busy day ahead, but she'd have liked it if he had stayed at least until the brig cast off from the wharf.

Nearly three months later, on an overcast Wednesday morning, Marsden was attending to some paperwork in his office before heading out on his daily rounds of the settlement. A commotion outside the office attracted his attention. He looked out into the corridor and saw two soldiers—a lieutenant and an enlisted man—approaching. Between them, they supported a dishevelled, bearded man whose clothes were torn and tattered, and who appeared to be totally exhausted. The soldiers were struggling to support the man's weight.

Marsden thought the man looked familiar. Only as he and his escorts came closer did the captain recall he'd seen him aboard *the Stirling Castle*. He suddenly experienced an ice cold feeling in his gut. At first, he didn't recognise the feeling. It was so long since he'd felt this way. Then he knew it for what it was.

It was fear—pure unadulterated fear.

94

ARSDEN USHERED THE THREE MEN into his office. As the soldiers made the exhausted crewman as comfortable as they could on a chair, the captain ordered a clerk to fetch the doctor to see to the unfortunate fellow. He then looked to his lieutenant for an explanation.

Lieutenant Charles Otter, an English career soldier who had effectively replaced Lieutenant Hogan, quickly brought his superior up to date, explaining that he'd come across the exhausted seaman whilst on a hunting expedition some eighty miles or so to the north. He introduced the seaman as Neil Sayers, a Cornish rigger from *the Stirling Castle*. "He says the brig foundered on a reef north of Great Sandy Island late on the same day she departed Moreton Bay," Otter reported.

"On the same day?" Marsden asked. He looked down at the rigger. "That's almost three months ago."

The rigger nodded, confirming the fact.

Marsden's heart was racing so fast he thought he might have a heart attack. All he could think of was whether his beloved Helen had survived, but he couldn't bring himself to ask the question for fear he wouldn't like the answer.

"It was a nightmare," Sayers said.

"What happened exactly?" Marsden asked, his fears growing by the second.

"The bloody natives captured us!" Sayers cursed. "They—"

"From the beginning," the captain demanded, struggling to remain calm.

"The brig foundered on Swains Reef, north of Great Sandy Island," the rigger said. "At first light we could see she was doomed so we launched the boats . . . or what boats we could salvage at least. We managed to save the pinnace and the longboat . . . The other boats were washed away."

Marsden could feel his impatience growing. He badly wanted to know about Helen, but still he couldn't bring himself to ask.

Sayers continued, "Some crew members started to rebel against Captain Fraser and they wouldn't pull their weight. Seven of 'em boarded the pinnace and the rest of us piled into the longboat with the captain and his Missus."

"Go on," Marsden urged.

"We began rowing southwest, and . . . we watched as the brig sank before our very eyes." Sayers visibly struggled to contain his emotions. "Four days later, Missus Fraser gave birth right there in the boat." He added, "Her lady friend helped her."

"Lady friend?" Marsden asked, now on high alert.

The rigger nodded. "Aye, a real beauty she was, too," he said. Even now he wasn't aware Helen was the daughter of the officer who was questioning him.

Marsden's heart sank at Sayers' use of the past tense. He wondered whether the rigger referred to Helen, and he could contain himself no longer. "Who was she, do you recall?" he asked.

"It was your daughter," Otter interjected.

Marsden looked sharply at his lieutenant.

"He assured me there was only one other lady aboard," Otter explained, "and he recalled her name was Helen."

The captain turned slowly back to Sayers and prepared himself for the moment of truth. "Did the womenfolk survive?" he asked.

It seemed an eternity before the rigger answered. In fact, it was only a couple of seconds. Finally, Sayers said, "Aye, Captain. Last I saw 'em, they were being taken to Great Sandy Island by the natives."

Marsden inwardly rejoiced. He wanted to jump around and shout *Hallelujah!* Instead, he excused himself, stepped out into the corridor and headed outside. He needed to be alone for a moment to quietly celebrate the good news he'd just received. Besides, he didn't want to risk displaying any emotion in front of the men.

After composing himself, Marsden returned to his office to find Doctor Andrews checking the rigger's physical condition. The two nodded to each other, and Andrews continued his examination. Marsden was pleased to see the Scottish doctor appeared to be sober today.

Andrews muttered away to himself as he checked his patient. "No broken bones," he mumbled. "No signs of permanent damage." He pushed his fingers against Sayers' stomach. "Does that hurt?" he asked.

Sayers shook his head, but he grimaced all the same.

Andrews looked around at Marsden. "Have him brought to the infirmary when you are finished with him, Tom"—the two men had long since dispensed with formal titles—"as I will need to check him for any internal injuries. And he should be confined to bed for a day or two because he's physically exhausted." The doctor picked up his medical bag and left the office.

"Thanks, Phillip," Marsden said as Andrews departed. Returning his attention to Sayers, he asked the question that had been gnawing at him since he'd learned Helen was still alive, or most likely still alive at least. "What condition were the women in, Mister Sayers?"

"Not good, Captain," the rigger said. "Missus Fraser especially was in poor shape, having given birth and all, and the bloody natives gave us all a hard time."

"And the baby?"

Sayers shook his head. "She didn't last more'n a minute or two, and we committed her to the sea."

"She?"

"Aye, a wee girl."

Once more, Marsden had to struggle to contain his emotions. Eliza, he recalled, said she'd call her daughter Helen, after his own daughter.

Over the next half hour, Sayers related everything of importance that had happened since the passengers and crew of the brig had begun their struggle for survival. It transpired they spent many days beating backwards and forwards against headwinds, trying to reach the mainland, and all the while their reserves of food and water were running perilously low. After finishing the last of their water, they made landfall on a desolate island where they did find some water at least. There, an open mutiny broke out. The seven crewmen in the pinnace went their own way, taking with them most of the remaining provisions.

Captain Fraser, by this time, had fallen ill and was unable to intervene. Most of the crew in the longboat also mutinied, and they threatened to throw the Frasers overboard along with Helen and the rigger who had both continued to support the captain and his wife. After finally making landfall on the mainland, they found themselves surrounded by Aborigines who kept their distance because they could see the whites had firearms.

Fortunately, the starving survivors were able to trade compasses, sextants and clothing for fresh fish. Their brief good fortune was undone when five crewmembers set out for Moreton Bay, taking with them all the firearms. Those left behind were defenceless, and they were immediately besieged by the natives who took everything from them except the clothes on their backs.

Marsden could see the rigger was struggling to stay awake. The captain realised the man needed to get to the infirmary, but still he pressed him for more information. "How did the natives treat you, Mister Sayers?" he asked.

"The damned savages didn't do us no favours, that's for certain!" the rigger said. "They ran a spear through Captain Fraser because he was too ill to work, and he died of his wounds a few days later. They also killed the brig's first mate and second mate, leaving only me and the two women alive." He became distressed as he relived the nightmare. "They dragged us from camp to camp."

"And where are the women now?" Marsden asked.

"Last I saw they were being taken out to the island . . . Great Sandy Island . . . in canoes . . . and I was taken south on foot to another campsite on the mainland. I managed to escape. And two days later"—Sayers looked at Otter—"I stumbled across the good lieutenant here . . . and here I am."

Marsden thought it likely the natives who held the women were Kabi. He'd heard the tribe's clans converged on the island once or twice every year for a big corroboree, and the thought occurred that Helen and Eliza could be with the same clan John Graham ended up with. "Do you know what tribe is holding the women?" he asked.

The rigger shook his head. "They all look the same to me," he mumbled.

Otter said, "I can advise they are Kabi, Captain." He added, "Our tracker confirmed that."

Marsden had heard enough. "See that Mister Sayers gets to the infirmary at once, Lieutenant," he ordered.

"Yes, Captain." Otter hurried to do Marsden's bidding.

Turning back to the rigger as he was assisted out of the office, the captain said,

"Thank you, Mister Sayers."

Now alone, Marsden looked at a map of the New South Wales coastline he left permanently spread out on his desktop. His eyes were drawn to Great Sandy Island, and he whispered a silent prayer, asking God to keep his little girl safe.

Folding the map up and tucking it under one arm, he strode from the office. He needed to organise a rescue mission to save Helen and Eliza, but first he had to acquaint Cheetham with the latest turn of events.

Helen and Eliza had to put their aches and pains and their overwhelming tiredness aside as they toiled alongside the Kabi women, collecting food provisions, pelts and other possessions. The various clans were preparing to relocate to other sites on Great Sandy Island and, as usual, most of the work was being done by the womenfolk.

In the long months since *the Stirling Gate* foundered, Helen and Eliza had all but lost the will to live. And since their capture, they'd been reduced to little better than human packhorses by the Kabi. Eliza in particular was struggling just to get through each day. After having lost her baby and endured weeks at sea with little food and water, she was already in a bad way physically when the brig's survivors were captured. In the two months since then, the unrelenting hard labour and constant trekking to new encampments had taken their toll.

Helen was suffering, too, even though she was younger and fitter than her Scottish friend. Like Eliza, she was tired and hungry.

Neither woman could adapt to a diet which included grubs, snakes, lizards and similar unappealing fare. And, in the oppressive humidity, they were constantly thirsty despite the proliferation of freshwater streams and lakes on the island. To add to their worries, both women were afraid of the spiders and other creepy-crawlies that abounded, and the mosquitoes and sand-flies harassed them continuously, day and night.

Even though the official start of summer was still some weeks away, both women were badly sunburnt, having lost most of their clothes during the tumultuous days in the longboat when storms and ocean conspired to take everything they had, including their lives. Helen's wardrobe had been reduced to a bodice and petticoat while Eliza had lost all her clothing except for her petticoat. What little clothing remained hung from them in tatters. And it hadn't taken them long to learn that spring time in these parts was hot—hotter than Moreton Bay and, in the fair-skinned Scotswoman's case, far hotter than Scotland ever experienced even in mid-summer. As a result, their exposed skin was red and raw, and constantly blistered.

That wasn't the full extent of their problems by any means. Their care had been entrusted to the Kabi women who expected their uninvited guests to work as hard as they themselves did.

Helen and Eliza had no way of knowing they'd ended up with the same clan that took John in. If ever the possibility had existed that the clan members would have welcomed whites into their world, that had been forever dashed when the soldiers raided their encampment and decimated their numbers three years earlier. To them—

the womenfolk in particular—the two whites were an awful reminder of the terrible day ghosts mounted astride dragon-like creatures rode amongst them with weapons that belched smoke and fire, indiscriminately killing and maiming until they were finally driven off.

The last straw for the captives was they had been separated early on in their captivity. Helen had been put in the care of Mirritji's extended family while Eliza was under the protection of Turo's family. Since arriving on the island, the two family groups had often ended up at different camp sites, so the two whites sometimes didn't see each other for days on end.

Today was another of those times when the family members concerned went their separate ways. Mirritji's group was heading east, overland to the far side of the island with Helen, while Turo's group was heading along the coast by canoe to the northern end of the island with Eliza. The two women barely managed to exchange a quick wave before they and their escorts went their separate ways.

95

THE MEETING ROOM IN THE army's admin block at Moreton Bay was a large room that had rarely, if ever, been full. This afternoon it was full to overflowing. Marsden had demanded the attendance of every available officer, every soldier of senior non-commissioned rank and all three clerks—such was the importance of the hastily arranged meeting. Even Barega, the tracker, was present.

The captain's earlier meeting with Cheetham had gone as well as could be expected. As Marsden had hoped, the commandant agreed to ascribe absolute urgency to rescuing Helen and Eliza, though not for the same reasons his subordinate wanted them back. Cheetham's main concern, ahead of their welfare, was that he considered their rescue essential for the morale of the settlers who had taken news of the Stirling Castle's demise hard.

To his credit, Cheetham had insisted on attending the meeting that was about to start, and he was now surveying the assembled as the captain stood up to begin proceedings.

When Marsden was sure everyone who counted was present, he opened the meeting without preamble. "Gentlemen," he said, eyeing the assembled, "you have no doubt by now heard rumours that the brig the Stirling Castle has foundered, and my daughter and Missus Eliza Fraser are being held by natives on Great Sandy Island."

The soldiers nodded, indicating they had heard. Many of them glanced at the map Marsden had placed on a free-standing noticeboard alongside him. The island had been circled in red.

"I can assure you they are not rumours," Marsden said. Nodding at Lieutenant Otter, he said, "The lieutenant brought in a survivor who confirmed the information you now have." Pausing to assemble his thoughts, he continued, "The purpose of this meeting is to finalise the rescue mission we plan to mount."

Marsden then outlined what he and Cheetham had discussed earlier, explaining that he personally would lead a contingent comprising thirty foot soldiers. He hadn't forgotten the problems he'd encountered using horses on the previous raid on the Kabi. "We depart by sea at first light tomorrow," he said. Although there was no vessel berthed at Moreton Bay at present, he was aware a ship was scheduled to arrive at dusk. The vessel concerned had been sighted a short while ago out in the bay, so he was confident she would arrive as per schedule. Looking at the assembled, he asked, "Any questions?"

There were no questions so Marsden spent the next fifteen minutes discussing manpower, firepower and provisions required for the mission ahead. Before the meeting adjourned, the thirty soldiers tasked with rescuing the captives had been selected, and every man present knew what needed to be done. Even the clerks and others not going on the mission had related duties to perform, and they hurried off to attend to these. No mention was made of Barega accompanying the soldiers, but he and the captain both knew he'd be going. Some things didn't need to be spelt out.

The tracker had an extra spring in his step when he left the room. He loved the thrill of the hunt and couldn't wait for tomorrow. He also loved the fact his masters considered him indispensable. Almost without realising it, he'd started emulating the whites he worked for—even to the extent of wearing boots to go with his European clothing when he was off duty.

Outside, Barega quickened his step when he thought of Orana waiting for him in their love nest in the annex behind the Marsdens' cottage. Their lovemaking always had some extra spice on the eve of a hunt. Before he knew it, he was running toward the cottage, his long gait covering the ground with effortless ease and his silver crucifix bobbing up and down on his chest.

When Marsden and Cheetham finally had the meeting room to themselves, the commandant lit up a cigar and then asked, "How do you propose finding the women, Tom?" Before Marsden could answer, he commented, "It's a big island and the Kabi move about constantly. It will be like trying to find a needle in a haystack."

The captain had already considered that. Even though it went against the grain, he planned to take John on the search. Looking at his superior, he said, "The Irishman will help us find them."

Cheetham almost choked on the cigar he was smoking. "Surely you don't mean John Graham?" he asked.

"I surely do, even though it pains me to admit it," Marsden said.

The commandant pondered this. He slowly came round to Marsden's way of thinking. "Well, I must admit he knows these people . . . as well as they know themselves perhaps," he conceded.

"And he knows the island," Marsden said, encouraged by Cheetham's turnaround. "He has been there at least three or four times to my knowledge." He hesitated. "However, there is no guarantee he will help us, of course. He thinks of the Kabi as his people now."

"Yes it is quite fascinating. A thief, a murderer . . . and now he has gone native . . ." Cheetham studied his cigar for a moment then looked slyly at his opposite. "I have yet to meet a man who isn't open to persuasion . . . Perhaps we could dangle a carrot . . ."

"An incentive would be good," Marsden agreed.

"I believe he had some kind of relationship with your daughter?" Cheetham asked innocently.

Marsden immediately bristled. "My daughter hardly knows the man!" he objected.

Cheetham realised he'd overstepped the mark. He began to mumble a hasty apology.

Interjecting, Marsden said, "My Lord mentions the man as a savage in one breath and then implies my daughter—"

"I meant no offence," Cheetham said.

"Well I take offence," Marsden informed him. "I thought a man of your stature would be above slanderous gossip."

Now it was Cheetham's turn to be offended. Marsden had never addressed him in such fashion. "Tom," he said soothingly, "I imagine I am usually the last to hear any gossip around this place, but even I have heard that Helen has taken a shine to the Irishman . . . So even if that is only half true, let us use that to our advantage and see if he can be persuaded to help find your daughter."

Marsden felt deflated to learn that Helen's relationship with John was an open secret in the settlement. Cheetham was right when he indicated if he'd heard the rumours they must be circulating far and wide. He guessed James Whitelock must have mentioned Helen's late night visit to John's cell to someone, and he made a mental note to withhold yet another week's pay from the wayward Northerner. Turning his attention back to the matter at hand, he asked, "What do you suggest?"

Cheetham savoured a draw on his cigar then said, "Get Graham in here. I think I have an offer he will find hard to turn down."

Minutes later, as the afternoon shadows lengthened, a barefoot, shackled John found himself standing before Cheetham and Marsden. Both officials thought the clean-shaven, fit-looking Irishman appeared considerably better groomed and more presentable than the last time they'd seen him, but they kept that to themselves.

The two guards who had escorted the prisoner stood just inside the doorway. Marsden ordered them to wait outside, and to close the door behind them, and they did as told at once.

Now alone with the officials, John looked them up and down disdainfully.

These two pompous bastards are the reason you're in solitary, Graham.

Cheetham, who was now pretending to study an official-looking document he'd pulled from a desk drawer moments before John arrived, looked up. "Nice of you to join us, Graham. I have some news for you"—he glanced at the document—"and I wanted to deliver it in person."

Marsden glanced at his superior and wondered what was coming next.

Cheetham continued, "This document"—he waved it in front of John's face—"is a letter from the Governor, ordering that you be hung." When he saw he now had the prisoner's full attention, he added, "The Governor advised he does not think it is a good look to allow a convict with your record to live. Not even if you are in solitary confinement. And so he has overturned the original sentence and ordered that you be hung."

96

JOHN WAS SHOCKED, BUT HE kept his composure. He didn't want to give the officials the satisfaction of knowing he was rattled.

Cheetham turned to Marsden who, he noticed, had done a very good job in hiding his surprise. He asked, "When do you intend to hang him, Captain?"

"Tomorrow morning, my Lord," Marsden said, playing along with the lie.

"Very well." Looking back at John, Cheetham asked, "Any last words, Graham?"

"Not for you there aren't," a defiant John said.

Resisting the temptation to order that the Irishman be flogged for his insubordination, Cheetham said, "There may be a way to have this hanging overturned, Graham." When John didn't respond, he continued, "A vessel has foundered on the north coast. At the cost of many lives, I might add."

The Irishman assumed a disinterested look.

Cheetham could see right through the prisoner's adopted nonchalance. The commandant knew John was hanging on to his every word. He continued, "We have learned the master's wife, Eliza Fraser, survived and is being held captive on Great Sandy Island by your old friends, the Kabi." He added, "God help her."

John could contain his air of indifference no longer. "The master's wife has a much better chance of surviving than if a Kabi woman were detained here!" he said.

"Enough!" Cheetham could contain his anger no longer. "You are to be transported to Great Sandy Island at first light. There, you will negotiate Missus Fraser's release. The hanging order will be reversed and you will be able to serve out the remainder of your sentence in solitary."

Hearing that he was about to be hung had left John feeling stunned and confused, and it took him a moment to remember that Helen had left Moreton Bay on the same vessel as Eliza. His blood ran cold at the thought the young woman could be dead. "Who . . . ah . . . Did anyone else survive the sinking?" he asked.

Cheetham caught Marsden's eye then looked back at the prisoner. He said, "Yes, Captain Marsden's daughter survived, and she, too, is being held captive on the island."

John hid his elation and tried to marshal his thoughts. His mind was in a whirl, but somewhere, deep down, he sensed an opportunity. "I want no part of this," he said at length.

"What sort of an answer is that?" Marsden asked, butting into the two-way conversation. "*You* are their only hope," he said.

John pretended to consider his options. He already knew what he wanted. Finally, he said, "In return for helping you to find the women, I would want a full pardon and my ticket of leave."

"Out of the question, Graham!" Cheetham said. "We will commute your death sentence, that is all." He added, "You can count yourself lucky. You deserve to have your neck stretched because you and your Kabi friends killed many good soldiers."

"And those raiders killed my wife and son!" John fired back.

Cheetham couldn't hide his amusement. "Your wife and son?" he asked. "Good Lord! You really did go native, didn't you?"

John clenched his fists and took a step toward the commandant.

Marsden stepped between the pair, his hand on his pistol. Staring John down, he said, "You have our offer, Graham. Help us or hang."

John returned the captain's stare. "I'll not hunt my own people," he said.

Marsden sighed. "Guards!" he shouted, and the two guards waiting outside the door burst in. "Take him back to his cell," he ordered. Before the guards could execute his order, the captain looked back at John. "We will stop at nothing to rescue those women," he said. "Without your help, we will send in every available soldier, and you can guarantee the Kabi will be wiped out because we won't be taking any prisoners."

John pretended to have second thoughts. Then he said, "You have my answer . . . I will help you . . . in return for a full pardon and my ticket of leave."

Angry, Marsden looked at the guards. "Get him out," he ordered.

The guards marched John from the room. As they escorted the prisoner along the corridor, Marsden and Cheetham just looked at each other, listening to the clink of chains.

It was Marsden who spoke first. "We have to give him what he wants," he said. He was prepared to give John anything to get his daughter back, and Eliza, too. He just hoped his superior felt the same way.

Cheetham didn't speak for a long time. Deep in thought, he closed his eyes as he drew on his cigar. Finally, he said, "I am afraid you are right, Tom." He added, "That Irish bastard could be the difference between success and failure . . . and we want to get those women back."

Marsden breathed a sigh of relief. "Thank you, Bertie," he said.

Cheetham waved his cigar dismissively. "But let's not make it too easy for the Irish bastard," he said. "Let him think he is going to hang a while longer. He may have a change of heart."

While John was preparing for what he fully expected would be his last night in his cell, and, indeed, his last night on Earth, on Great Sandy Island Helen and Eliza were helping the Kabi clan members to prepare their respective encampments for the night ahead. It was already dusk, and darkness was coming quickly.

After a full day's trek, Helen's party were still some distance from the eastern shore they were heading for. They were preparing a campsite alongside a freshwater lake.

Eliza's party had already reached their destination—an often-used encampment nestled between two giant sand-dunes at the northern end of the island.

Both women were exhausted, and a full day beneath a hot sun had done nothing for their sunburn. After half a day's paddle in a canoe, Eliza's blistered shoulders felt like they were on fire; and after a full day's trek without the benefit of a hat or any sort of shade, Helen was suffering sunstroke, and was quite dizzy even before being tasked with collecting firewood and branches for the clan members' bivouacs.

Each wondered whereabouts on the island the other was, and each prayed for rescue.

That night, alone in his cell, John waited for the guards to come for him again. He was confident Cheetham and Marsden were bluffing. *They need me more than I need them,* he told himself. As the hours passed, he wondered if he'd misread the situation.

Unable to contain himself any longer, he began hammering on his cell door. "Guard!" he shouted. "Guard!" Moments later, the eye-level panel slid open and he saw a pair of eyes staring back at him in the darkness. "Who's that?" he asked.

"It's me." the reply came back. "Who the fuck do you think it is?" Jessie Farrow's Cockney accent left no doubt who it was.

"What time is it, Jessie?" John asked.

"About two hours to midnight. Why?"

"No reason." John resumed his earlier pacing. Behind him, he heard the panel shut with a bang and he heard Farrow cursing all Irishmen as he walked away.

John decided he'd give it another hour until he asked to see Marsden. The prisoner had decided at the outset, whilst still in the meeting room, that he *would* agree to help find the captured women. He would help them even if the army was going to make him serve out his time in solitary. That's how badly he wanted to save Helen. John felt sorry for the Scottish woman, too, but he didn't know her. He did know Helen, and he'd do anything for her. However, he still believed there was a chance to secure his freedom outright, so he'd give it another hour.

John didn't have to wait an hour. Less than thirty minutes later, his door opened and the same two guards who had called for him earlier were standing there again.

"Come with us, Graham," the older guard said.

Five minutes later, John found himself in front of Cheetham and Marsden once more. They were in Marsden's office this time.

Cheetham came straight to the point. "Last chance, Graham," he said. "Do you want to help us or do you want to hang?"

John had half expected to be presented with the hanging option a second time. He hoped the commandant was bluffing. "My terms are as before," he said resolutely. "Commute my sentence and give me my ticket of leave, and I will help you."

Cheetham glared at him then glanced at Marsden who shrugged his shoulders. "You take it from here, Captain," he said.

Marsden looked at the prisoner. "Very well, Graham," he said resignedly. "We agree to your terms."

John inwardly rejoiced, but he remained outwardly impassive. "I want that in writing," he said.

Annoyed, Marsden glanced at Cheetham who nodded almost unperceptively. "Very well," he said, reaching for a piece of paper."

"Not you," John said. Pointing to Cheetham, he said, "I want *him* to sign it. And I want it on official army letterhead."

Marsden looked ready to fly into a rage, but the commandant motioned to him to remain calm. "I will do it," Cheetham grumbled. "You write it, Captain, and I will sign it."

Seething, Marsden selected an army letterhead, complete with seal at the top, then dipped a quill into an open ink bottle and began writing. As soon as he finished, he handed it to Cheetham who quickly checked it then signed it.

After blowing on the ink to dry it, the commandant handed it to John. "Good enough?" he asked.

John checked it. He couldn't believe his eyes. It was all there. Subject to helping find the women, his sentence would be commuted and he would receive his ticket of leave.

I'm feckin' free!

Remaining nonchalant, he nodded and said, "Good enough."

Cheetham held his hand out for the document, but John kept hold of it. Blowing on it until he was certain the ink was dry, he folded it and then carefully inserted it into his shirt pocket. "It is mine I believe," he said.

The commandant and the captain glanced at each other. Both seemed uncertain and neither seemed to know what to say next. For the moment, it was almost as if the power in the room had been transferred to John. The Irishman looked at them both and smiled. It was a smile of triumph.

John wouldn't have been so cocky had he known what Cheetham was planning. The commandant had no intention of honouring the transaction the prisoner had just negotiated. There was no duplicate copy of the ticket of leave John had in his possession. Nor were there any witnesses to the agreement they'd reached other than Marsden—and judging by the look of anger on Marsden's face, Cheetham was confident his subordinate would go along with what he planned.

97

DECEPTIVELY LARGE SWELLS ENSURED A steady stream of soldiers visited the American schooner's starboard or portside rail throughout the day to puke over the side—much to the amusement of the vessel's master and crew. *The New Yorker* was well suited to the Pacific Ocean swells, but that was no consolation to the many landlubbers who had found themselves aboard her.

John had been feeling queasy since the two-masted schooner departed Moreton Bay at dawn, though he had avoided having to part with his breakfast—unlike many of his fellow voyageurs.

The New Yorker had berthed at Moreton Bay as scheduled late the previous day. She was a first-time visitor to the bay and had been charged with delivering cargo and mail from Melbourne and Sydney Town. Her master, Captain Arthur Rayburn, an American from Boston, had not been at all accommodating when Marsden had suggested he interrupt his busy schedule to transport troops to Great Sandy Island. The offer of generous compensation had overcome any hesitation on the visiting captain's part, and the terms had been quickly finalised for the expedition ahead.

The thirty soldiers under Marsden's command had boarded the schooner before dawn along with Cheetham, Doctor Andrews, a cook, Barega and half a dozen Quandamooka trackers.

John had been escorted on board at first light, still shackled. Ticket of leave or no ticket of leave, it was obvious to him that he still wasn't trusted. Marsden had made it clear he would remain shackled until the missing women's whereabouts was known.

With so many passengers on board—in addition to the eight mainly American crewmembers and their captain—*the New Yorker* was sailing low in the water. Below deck was off limits to the passengers, except for Cheetham who had secured private sleeping quarters for himself courtesy of negotiating an additional bonus with the vessel's master prior to departure.

The half dozen Quandamooka trackers with Barega had been brought along in anticipation of difficulties in locating Helen and Eliza. Having visited the island previously, Marsden was acutely aware how big it was and how easy it would be for the Kabi, or anyone for that matter, to remain hidden if they didn't want to be found. Like Barega, who had dispensed with his adopted European clothing, the Quandamooka wore only their loincloths and carried spears and woomeras and other traditional weapons. And, like many of the soldiers on board, they and Barega were making regular visits to the nearest rail to spew over the side.

Barega wasn't happy about the presence of Quandamooka on board. He despised them and their tribe, and he made no secret of it. For their part, they despised *and*

571

feared Barega—more feared than despised—and they weren't at all happy about having to take orders from him.

The Aborigines sat at the schooner's bow, away from everyone else except John who had been ordered to sit with them. Every now and then Barega would turn around and stare at John. Once, he caught the Irishman looking at the silver crucifix he wore, and he flashed a grin his way. Staring back at the tracker, John repeated the promise he'd made to himself before, that he would slit Barega's throat at the first available opportunity. Right now however, everyone's attention was on Great Sandy Island, which was looming up straight ahead. Even from a distance, its towering sand-dunes looked mighty impressive—especially to those visiting the island for the first time.

Captain Rayburn was heading for a point that would put the schooner midway between the island's northern and southern tips. The plan was for the soldiers to establish a beachhead on its western shoreline while the trackers scoured the island, looking for the two women. As soon as the trackers made a sighting, they would report back to the beachhead and John would then be sent to negotiate the women's release with their Kabi captors.

That was the plan at least, but as the designers of that plan well knew, the best laid plans of mice and men often went askew.

Cheetham and Marsden, who had spent the entire voyage refining the plan, were at that very moment discussing what options they had for the remaining daylight hours. They were ensconced in the commandant's private quarters below deck. Smoke from Cheetham's specially tailored cigars filled the small cabin, and the aroma of marijuana was overpowering.

Cheetham was all for sending soldiers out with the trackers as soon as the schooner berthed whereas Marsden had other ideas.

"Our men will only slow the trackers down," Marsden protested. "Besides, we need to keep the soldiers together in case of attack." Memories of the Kabis' fighting abilities were still firmly etched on his mind.

"Perhaps you are right," Cheetham conceded. "Very well," he said, "we will do it your way."

Marsden was thankful he hadn't had to pull rank to get his own way. Just as Captain Rayburn had the final say regarding what happened on board his ship, he, Marsden, had the final say on operational matters. When the soldiers were in the field, he had the last word. That was written in the army's rule book plain and clear, and Cheetham knew the rules as well as anyone. "I had best check topside," Marsden said, excusing himself. He was as anxious to escape the cigar smoke as he was to see how close they were to the island.

Emerging above deck, Marsden saw the island was close now. Its towering dunes were basking in a golden glow in the late afternoon sun. Pristine, white sand beaches showed signs of recent human life—the remains of cooking fires, abandoned bivouacs, discarded tools and other bits and pieces—while beyond the dunes, the smoke from two cooking fires could be seen curling up into the blue sky.

Marsden sought out Captain Rayburn. As expected, he found him in the vessel's wheelhouse.

"I thought I would berth there," Rayburn said when he saw Marsden. He was pointing to a bay less than a mile distant.

Marsden saw at once it was a sheltered bay and an obvious safe anchorage. "That will do us fine, thank you, Captain," he said.

The remaining daylight hours were needed to ferry the soldiers and trackers ashore together with their supplies, and to erect tents and establish a defensively sound beachhead. Marsden then organised a round-the-clock roster system for sentries. He insisted on four men being rostered on at all times during daylight hours and six at night. They were to be relieved every two hours. And all soldiers were to bear arms at all times whilst ashore. The captain was taking no chances.

While the soldiers were securing the beachhead and the cook was preparing the evening meal, Barega and the other trackers were scouring their immediate surroundings, looking for signs of life. They were ordered to report back at dusk or shortly after. Depending on their findings, they would be sent out at dawn next day to scour the whole island.

Marsden was aware the search for the missing women could take many days or even weeks. His trackers were good—very good—but they had a lot of ground to cover, and they would need some luck if they were to find the women quickly. The captain hoped they would befriend those Kabi they encountered, and learn from them where the women were being held.

Barega didn't share Marsden's optimism. Other than the fact he despised any native not of his tribe, he had no particular beef with the Kabi. However, he knew the Quandamooka were traditional enemies of the Kabi, and it was very unlikely they would learn anything from them. In fact, he knew the Kabi well enough to know they didn't treat trespassers well. And the expedition members would all be viewed as trespassers, of that he was in no doubt. The tracker had tried to convey this to Marsden, but he wasn't sure he'd gotten through to him.

While all this was going on, John was confined to the schooner. He would be brought ashore only when the women's exact whereabouts was known, and not before. Marsden wasn't taking any chances with the Irishman. Until then, John intermittently dozed on deck or chatted with those crewmen who bothered to talk to him.

Though he appreciated escaping the confines of his cell—this was after all the first time in three years he'd spent the entire day outside—he was nervous about what lay ahead. The thought of seeing his Kabi brothers and sisters again under such complex circumstances was not the sort of reunion he'd yearned for, and he wondered whether he could actually go through with what Marsden and Cheetham were asking of him. Added to that, he wasn't sure he was ready to learn that Carravanty was in fact dead.

The trackers began drifting back to the beach singly or in pairs as dusk fell. Barega was the last to return, and his report was no more positive than the others had been. Kabi clan members had been seen, but no contact had been made with them and there had been no sign of the women.

It was agreed the trackers would resume the search at dawn. Each would head off in a different direction, and between them they would cover the whole island. They were to report back to Marsden at least once every two or three days, and they weren't to stop searching until they found the women or until the search was called off.

Marsden prayed they would find the women quickly. He didn't intend to return to Moreton Bay until they did.

98

TIME SLOWED AS THE FIRST two days on Great Sandy Island passed without result. On shore, those soldiers not on sentry duty passed the time cleaning their rifles, sharpening their bayonets, practising parade ground drills and, when Marsden wasn't around, snoozing or playing cards.

Aboard *the New Yorker*, Captain Rayburn kept his crew occupied with cleaning and maintenance tasks above and below deck, while John passed the time doing whatever caught his fancy. The hot, sunny days lent themselves to snoozing and sunbathing on deck, and he did plenty of that. However, he also wanted to continue the fitness regime he'd adopted in solitary, so he spent many an hour pacing the schooner's deck and performing press-ups and chin-ups—all to the amusement of the crewmembers who were intrigued by the sight of the shackled Irishman in their midst.

In the course of his travels around the deck, the *clink* of John's shackles signalled to one and all his whereabouts at any one time. The banter from amused crewmen was relentless, but, to their added amusement, he threw the banter right back at them. By the end of day two at anchor, the Irishman had been accepted by the others.

John's acceptance by the crew yielded some immediate benefits. For a start, they made sure the cook fed him well, and if he ever wanted a second helping of food at mealtimes, all he had to do was ask. And ask he did. He also made some good friends amongst the crewmembers who were only too pleased to include him in their card games, drinking sessions and other activities whenever they were off duty.

Throughout all this, however, Helen was never far from his mind. John wondered how the Kabi were treating her and the Scottish woman. He wondered, too, whether Carravanty was still alive and, if he was, whether he was also on the island.

Thinking of them reminded him what he was here for, and that motivated him to exercise longer and harder than ever. He had a feeling he'd need all his strength for what lay ahead.

On shore, atop one of the two giant sand-dunes that overlooked the bay the schooner and the soldiers occupied, two Kabi clan members observed the soldiers who, at that moment, were milling about on the beach, enjoying a drinks break. The soldiers were drinking mugs of hot tea the unit's cook had prepared.

Gabirri, John's friend, and Yarran, the Noosa clan leader, had crawled to the top of one of the dunes after the sentry based there had returned to the beach for the drinks break. From here, even lying down, they had an uninterrupted view of the bay.

575

"It is as Karadji prophesised," Gabirri murmured, referring to the clan's young shaman. "He predicted the land would be over-run by white spirits."

Yarran grunted in acknowledgement.

"They bring their smoking weapons," Gabirri said.

Yarran guessed Gabirri referred the soldiers' rifles. He had never seen firearms before, but he had seen the damage they could cause when the survivors of the raid on Gabirri's clan had sought out the security of his own clan. That was nearly five years ago. Since then, the expanded clan had largely kept to the northern end of their territory, such was their determination to remain as far from European settlement as possible. They'd heard about the settlement at Moreton Bay, but none had dared go near it. Great Sandy Island was the farthest south they generally ventured these days. "They are here for the white women," Yarran said with certainty.

Gabirri nodded. They had always known it would be a risk holding the two whites in captivity, which was why he and some other clan members had opposed keeping them prisoner. Some even wanted them dead. However, Yarran had insisted they be kept alive, and, as senior elder, his desires swayed the majority; and, as always, the majority rule prevailed.

Switching their attention to the schooner out in the bay, the pair studied the activity on board. Even though she was a good hundred yards offshore, and perhaps a hundred and fifty yards from where they lay, they could see what was going on. Squinting into the sun, they watched as crewmen scrubbed the deck and riggers clambered over fore and aft masts, doing running repairs.

The sight of a shackled man at the stern of the vessel caught Gabirri's attention. He didn't realise he was looking at John. The Irishman was hanging from an overhead rail and performing chin-ups—an exercise made even more difficult by the shackles he wore. With each movement, the shackles glinted in the sunlight.

Gabirri and Yarran began crawling backwards when they noticed a sentry heading up the dune whose summit they occupied. When they were satisfied they couldn't be seen, they stood up and began running back toward their current encampment. Even though they had a long run ahead of them, they set a fast pace, oblivious to the sun which beat down on their bare backs.

The shadows were lengthening when a weary Helen noticed Yarran and Gabirri run into the camp. She was gathering firewood in the dense rainforest that bordered the site that the clan members had reached earlier that afternoon.

Helen watched as the two new arrivals met with other men in the centre of the encampment. She could see the pair were glistening with sweat and were breathing hard, and she wondered what news they had that was so important.

A firm hand on one sunburnt shoulder made her wince. She turned around to see Alba, the healer's toothless woman, motioning to her to keep working. Alba jabbered away at Helen who gleaned that her self-appointed chaperone wanted her to stop watching the menfolk and to work harder. "Alright, alright!" she protested, hurrying off to pick up more branches.

Sunburn, thirst, weariness and an over-zealous chaperone weren't the young

English woman's only problems. Her feet were killing her. She was still wearing the semi-formal, leather shoes she'd worn aboard the brig, and, while they were ideal for shipboard life, they were totally unsuitable for trekking through the wilderness. She had discovered that very early on when her feet became badly blistered. Since then, her feet had toughened up, but in recent days they had swollen in the heat, which effectively meant her shoes were now too small for her. She had tried walking barefoot for a while, but that was even more painful. The soles of her Anglo Saxon feet were too tender to tolerate the rough ground and hot sand. And so she persevered with her shoes.

To take her mind off her own problems, she thought of Eliza and wondered how she was coping.

That night, the Kabi elders sat around a campfire, discussing the disturbing report two of their number had made that very afternoon. Yarran and Gabirri repeated in more detail to their concerned audience what they'd observed. Their report tallied with the sighting of two Quandamooka trackers elsewhere on the island that morning. At the time, the presence of trackers from another tribe on the island had made no sense. Now, unfortunately, it did.

"The Quandamooka are working for the white spirits," Yarran said with absolute certainty.

Karadji, the young shaman, agreed. "It is as I said," he reminded the assembled. "The world as we know it is changing. The white spirits are coming, and they will spread over our lands like ants."

The elders nodded. They had dismissed the shaman's prophesy before. Now they could see it happening before their very eyes.

At length, Yarran said, "We must leave a message for the white spirits. To discourage them from searching for their women, and to discourage them from staying on our island."

The assembled listened intently as the senior elder explained the message he had in mind.

The Quandamooka trackers began drifting back to the soldiers' beachhead early afternoon the following day—day three of the search for Helen and Eliza. By dusk, all except Barega had shown up.

The returned trackers reported to Marsden that they had sighted several Kabi encampments, but there had been no sign of the missing women. Two of them reported having spoken to Kabi clan members they'd encountered, but both indicated the clan members were unhelpful and unfriendly.

It was with increasing alarm that Marsden listened to his trackers' reports. He had hoped by now to at least have confirmation Helen and Eliza were still on the island. Every day that passed without finding them increased the likelihood they had been relocated to the mainland by their captors. If that was the case, he well knew, they would likely never be found.

The captain had renewed hope when he saw that Barega had finally returned to the beachhead. His hope was dashed when the tracker advised he'd had no more luck than the Quandamooka had. He'd observed three Kabi encampments, but there had been no sign of the women at any of them.

Marsden resigned himself to the fact the search was going to take longer than he'd hoped.

99

DAY FOUR FOLLOWED THE SAME pattern as the first three days—as did days five and six. While the trackers scoured the island for some sign of Helen and Eliza, the soldiers on the beachhead continued with their mindless drills and the crewmen aboard the schooner continued with their thankless maintenance tasks.

If time had slowed for the soldiers and crewmen during the first three days, now it seemed to be standing still.

For Marsden, the waiting was torture. With each passing hour, he'd been tempted to give in to Cheetham's wishes that he order his soldiers to join with the trackers in searching for the women. The commandant, who until now had remained aboard *the New Yorker,* puffing on his never-ending supply of cigars, had argued convincingly that the thirty soldiers could be split into three squads of ten men and cover the island much more effectively than seven trackers could.

Though tempted, Marsden had resisted despatching his soldiers. He agreed with John's warning that armed soldiers would inflame the Kabi and likely result in their harming the women, or worse.

By the end of the sixth day, all but two of the Quandamooka trackers had returned and all reported no better result than they'd had earlier.

An impatient Cheetham was now increasing the pressure on Marsden to order the soldiers to join the hunt. The captain promised he would consider that in the morning. Meanwhile, he still held out faint hope that the two Quandamooka trackers yet to report back had some good news.

That night, Eliza slept fitfully. Since being separated from Helen several days earlier, the Scotswoman's physical condition had further deteriorated.

Today had been the worst day yet. After being transferred by canoe along with Turo's extended family to the northern end of the island, she'd been put to work immediately alongside the other women. If they had known Eliza was exhausted and still suffering from the sunstroke she'd incurred after working a full day outside the previous day, they gave no sign. She'd been tasked with cleaning pelts out in the open without the benefit of any shade. That entailed beating the pelts with a branch to rid them of dust. The pelts had been hung up on a makeshift clothesline. It was hard, dusty work, and Eliza was done in before the day was even half over. Her captors had toiled until dusk, and they expected her to do the same. So spent was she, she avoided the evening meal in favour of retiring to the bivouac she'd been allocated to rest her weary body. There, she cried herself to sleep.

Unfortunately, the sleep didn't last. The mosquitoes saw to that. And now she lay wide awake, scratching her insect bites and listening to the sounds of the night.

Somewhere, in the distance, a dingo barked. Eliza shuddered. When she finally went back to sleep, she dreamed of the baby she'd lost.

At first light next morning, the soldiers on the beach emerged from their tents to a ghoulish sight. There, atop the two sand-dunes towering above them, were the Quandamooka trackers who hadn't reported back the previous night. The pair's naked, mutilated bodies had been tied to planks of timber. The planks, which had been recovered from an old shipwreck, had been arranged to resemble crosses, and they rose tree-like from the summits of the dunes. To those on the beach, the scene resembled a crucifixion.

The half dozen soldiers now scrambling up the nearest dune to investigate would soon discover the two sentries who had been patrolling the summit had also been killed. Under cover of darkness, they'd been run through with spears and their bodies had been thrown down the other side of the dune.

The first Marsden was aware something was askew was when he heard shouts coming from outside the tent he shared with Lieutenant Otter.

"Wha . . . what's that?" a half-awake Otter asked as Marsden stuck his head out the tent's flap.

Marsden was lost for words as he scrambled from the tent and looked up at the crucified trackers.

"Christ!" Otter gasped when he saw what it was his commanding officer was looking at.

The soldiers climbing up to investigate were making hard work of it. For every two paces they took, they slid back one, so steep was the dune. Private Askew, a survivor of the Kabi raid, was among them. Only when they reached the summit did they see the sentries' bodies. They lay face down in the sand and their attackers' spears still protruded from their backs, so it was obvious how they'd died.

Private Askew was the first soldier to report back to Marsden who, by now, was standing at the foot of the dune.

"Both sentries were killed, Captain," a breathless Askew said.

Even though it was barely light, Marsden could see the soldier was sweating profusely. "How did they die, Private Askew?" he asked.

"They were run through with spears, Captain." As he spoke, he and his superior saw soldiers carrying the sentries' bodies down the dune. The spears had been removed.

"And what of the two trackers?"

"Both dead, sir."

"I can see that, man! I mean how did they die?"

"Unknown without the benefit of an autopsy, Captain," Askew said. "But they were both badly mutilated. Eyes gouged out, ears, noses and tongues cut off, finger and toe nails removed, fingers broken . . ."

As Askew reeled off the list of atrocities the trackers had suffered, Marsden didn't need to wonder at the message the Kabi were sending him. They were telling him to depart the island and stop searching for Helen and Eliza. That much was clear.

Later that morning, after the two sentries had been buried on a grassy ledge further along the beach, Marsden sent the remaining trackers on their way with unchanged orders; they were to continue searching for the two women and, in the event they had no luck, they were to report back to the beachhead three days hence.

Barega had set out alone and without so much as a word. However, the remaining four Quandamooka had needed some convincing after seeing what happened to their fellow trackers. Only the promise of doubling their rum ration on their return to Moreton Bay convinced them to persevere. Even so, it was with considerable trepidation they headed out again.

Marsden had decided against committing his soldiers to join the search just yet. Even though they were champing at the bit, and Cheetham was agitating for their involvement, he preferred to err on the side of caution.

John's warning still rang loud in his ears.

Armed soldiers would inflame the Kabi and likely result in their harming the women, or worse.

The captain wasn't prepared to do anything that could make Helen's situation any worse than it was already. Or Eliza's for that matter.

On board *the New Yorker*, as the morning sun rose high in the sky, John was only just awaking from his slumbers. Three days earlier, the schooner's carpenter had rigged up a hammock for him on deck, in a semi-private area toward the stern, and ever since he'd slept like a king.

"Oh look who's decided to join us!" a New York accent announced as the Irishman climbed from his hammock. The voice belonged to a rigger who had been working in the rigging of the aft mast since before dawn, and who had just noticed John was finally up and about.

"Careful up there!" John shouted to the rigger.

"What do you care?" the rigger asked.

"Now that I think about it . . . I don't!" John replied.

Chuckling to himself, the rigger flashed a crude sign the Irishman's way and carried on with his work.

John wandered below deck to the schooner's galley and sought out the cook. He ordered his usual—bacon and eggs—and stayed to chat with the friendly cook whilst his meal was prepared. The cook, a beefy guy from New Jersey, had taken a shine to the cheeky Irishman and didn't mind going out of his way for him. John suspected his new friend wanted more than to be just friends, but he didn't mind—as long as *Cooky*, as he called him, kept his hands to himself.

Days of eating, sleeping, sunbathing and exercising had done wonders for John's physical and mental wellbeing. He couldn't believe his change of fortune, and he prayed it would continue. However, always at the back of his mind was the knowledge that two women on the island now directly to starboard of the schooner would soon need his help. He just hoped he was up to it.

100

THE NEXT THREE DAYS WENT the way of the last three, and the three before that.

By nightfall on the ninth day, only two of the remaining four Quandamooka trackers had returned to the beachhead. An hour after dark, Barega returned with the news that he had stumbled across the mutilated body of one of the missing trackers several miles inland. He'd suffered the same fate as the pair who had been crucified.

That was the last thing the other Quandamooka wanted to hear, and they threatened to pull out of the search. Marsden convinced them to delay their decision until morning, by which time, he hoped, the missing tracker would show up. Perhaps he would have some good news, he told them.

However, come morning there was still no sign of the missing tracker. That was the final straw for the surviving Quandamooka who informed the captain they were pulling out immediately. Marsden offered to triple their rum ration, and when that didn't work he threatened to leave them on the island if they didn't keep searching. To no avail. They had made up their minds and not even the offer of a hundred voluptuous virgins each would have changed their minds.

It was at this time that Cheetham poked his nose in. He chose the very moment Marsden was remonstrating with the trackers to step ashore, having just been rowed out from the schooner in the longboat that ferried fresh supplies to the soldiers each morning.

The commandant had avoided coming ashore until three days earlier. Since then, he'd come ashore twice more—a sure sign that his impatience was growing.

"What is going on, Captain?" Cheetham asked as he joined his subordinate on the beach.

Marsden quickly brought the commandant up to date with the latest news.

"What are you planning to do?" Cheetham asked.

"It is time for John Graham to enter the search," Marsden said. He'd been thinking about his next step all night, and he was sure what needed to be done. "Barega will go with him," he added.

"What about the soldiers?" Cheetham asked. Before Marsden could answer, he said, "It is time to let them loose. Three squads of ten men. They will cover a lot more ground."

Marsden shook his head. He wanted to give the Irishman his shot at finding the women before he let his men loose. Looking at Cheetham, he said, "No, I have made my decision."

The commandant fired up at that. "Tom"—he was dispensing with formalities to drive home his point—"I have let you do it your way for nine days now. Without success. It is time to do it my way." Marsden went to respond, but Cheetham talked over him. "I would remind you who the commandant is here," he said.

Marsden had hoped it wouldn't come to this, but it was obvious the time had come to pull rank. Although he was Cheetham's subordinate at Moreton Bay, the chain of command was upended when he was operational. And he was on active duty now, which meant he was operational.

The captain called Lieutenant Otter to his side, explaining to the commandant that he wanted a witness to what he was about to say. As soon as Otter had joined them, Marsden quoted to Cheetham word for word the relevant passage in the British Army's rule book. The passage clearly defined when the senior military officer—emphasis on the word *military*—had the final say in any debate, argument or disagreement with any non-commissioned officer or civilian, regardless of the status of said persons.

Marsden had memorised the ruling only because he thought he might need to recite it back to Cheetham one day. That day had arrived, and he was thankful he'd taken the trouble. Looking at his opposite, he said, "I can fetch the rule book if you require verification, my Lord." He knew he couldn't fetch it because it was in his desk drawer in his office back at Moreton Bay, but he gambled that the commandant wouldn't demand to see it.

"Not necessary," a miffed Cheetham grumbled. Realising he was stumped for the moment, he mumbled his goodbyes and returned to the nearby longboat. The craft had been emptied of its supplies, and its four oarsmen were waiting to return the commandant to the schooner.

Marsden and Otter shared a knowing glance behind Cheetham's back.

"Accompany the commandant back to the schooner, if you would, Lieutenant," Marsden said. "I would like you to bring John Graham ashore. It is time we put him to use."

"Aye, Captain," Otter said.

After exchanging salutes, they separated. Otter hurried over to the longboat while Marsden went off to find Barega.

A still shackled John observed the approaching shoreline with interest as the longboat ferried him and Otter out from the schooner.

"You are going to start earning your keep, Irishman," the lieutenant advised him.

John ignored his fellow passenger, and he studied the soldiers ashore. Those who weren't carrying out various tasks observed him with more than a little curiosity as the longboat nosed up onto the beach. The Irishman knew what they were thinking.

You're thinking how can I find the women when everyone else has failed.

He flashed a grin at the nearest soldiers. None quite knew how to react to the cheeky Irishman and some of them looked away.

As soon as John's bare feet hit the sand, he noticed Marsden approaching with Barega in tow.

Without preamble Marsden said, "You will be introduced to the search today, Graham." Motioning to Barega who had pulled up behind him, he added, "The tracker will accompany you."

John shook his head. "No deal, Captain," he said. "The tracker stays."

Otter was about to discipline John, but Marsden flashed him a look that told him he'd handle it.

"I call the tune here, Graham," Marsden said. "Not you."

"Well, that depends."

"On what?"

John could see the captain was losing his patience. Adopting what he hoped was a reasonable tone, he said, "It depends on whether you wish to see your daughter again." When he saw he had Marsden's undivided attention, he added, "My Kabi friends won't show themselves if *he's* with me." He glared at the tracker. "Our chances will be one hundredfold better if I'm on my own."

Marsden considered his choices. He could threaten to reverse the decision to give the prisoner his ticket of leave and risk him refusing to help, or he could agree to his demands. If he met his demands, he knew full well John could escape into the wilds and remain free forever more. And if that happened, he feared he'd never see Helen again.

John seemed to read his mind. The Irishman looked into Marsden's eyes and said, "I give you my word I will keep searching for your daughter until I find her, Captain."

"Your word?" the captain asked, more than a little sceptical.

John nodded and extended his right hand. "My word," he said.

Marsden hesitated, but only for a moment. He clasped John's hand and the two old adversaries stood there, unmoving, for several drawn-out moments. Finally, they shook hands and stepped apart. "Very well, Graham," he said. "We do it your way."

John noticed that throughout all this Barega feigned disinterest, but he could tell the tracker was taking in every word. As always, the Irishman's eyes were drawn to the silver crucifix resting against the tracker's chest. He silently vowed the crucifix would be his before this little excursion was over.

"This way, Graham," Marsden ordered, walking toward a nearby tent.

Otter and Barega followed the captain. When the lieutenant noticed the Irishman hadn't moved he said, "You heard the captain, Graham."

John looked pointedly at his shackles. They made walking quite arduous in the soft sand, and he had no intention of taking another step while shackled.

Otter drew Marsden's attention to the predicament. Selecting a key from a heavy key ring he wore on his belt, the captain strode back to John's side, and, after some fumbling, unlocked the restraints.

On reaching the tent that the captain led him to, John discovered it was the stores tent. He waited alongside Otter while Marsden disappeared inside. Barega stood nearby, looking more bored than ever.

Otter studied the tracker for a moment then turned to John and asked, "So tell me, Graham, what are these Kabi chaps like?"

John ignored the lieutenant as he'd been doing for the past half hour.

Undeterred, Otter asked, "I mean, are they like Captain Marsden's tracker here?" He glanced at Barega.

"They're nothing like him," John assured the lieutenant.

The tracker flashed a sly smirk John's way.

"I see," Otter remarked. "Well, what are they—"

Before the lieutenant could finish his latest question, Marsden emerged from the tent. He was followed by a soldier who carried a pack he'd filled with food provisions and a variety of wilderness survival items.

The captain took the pack from the soldier and handed it to John. "There's sufficient provisions in this to last you three days, Graham," he said. "I want you to report back here every couple of days—for as long as it takes to find the women."

Again, John shook his head. "I will report back only when I have found the women," he said.

Marsden was about to remonstrate with the argumentative Irishman, but thought better of it. At this point, he was aware John was calling all the shots. The captain nodded curtly. He then spent the next half hour summarising the results of the search to date, explaining, with the aid of a map, which parts of the island had been searched and where Kabi clan members and encampments had been seen.

John listened intently, asking questions only when necessary. Few questions were needed. The captain had memorised the details the trackers had provided him with over the preceding days, and his delivery of the facts was clear and concise. Twice he had to seek clarification from Barega, but by the time he'd finished the briefing, the Irishman knew as much as anyone about the search and the ground covered thus far.

When John realised the briefing was over, he turned to leave.

"One minute," Marsden said.

John looked around and saw the captain was staring at his bare feet.

"Do you need boots?" Marsden asked.

John just shook his head and headed off toward the southern end of the island. Free of his shackles, he savoured the feeling of freedom he experienced as he strode out along the beach, but still he couldn't shake the feeling of foreboding that enveloped him.

Marsden watched John as he grew ever smaller. Only when he finally disappeared from view did the captain realise he'd never before depended as much on someone else as he did now. He just hoped the Irishman was good for his word.

101

JOHN'S PLAN WAS TO WALK to the southern tip of the island—not far beyond the place where the Gureng had attacked the Kabi on one of the clan's previous visits. He had no concrete reason to head south except his gut told him to go that way, and so that's what he was doing.

Once there, he decided, he would head north, criss-crossing from coast to coast until he reached the island's northern tip. If that yielded no result, he would zig-zag south again, all the while hoping the Songlines would guide him.

How long it would take to trek from one end of the island to the other like that he could only guess. He imagined it would take all of two weeks—more if the terrain proved difficult. He just hoped the Kabi weren't planning to return to the mainland any time soon.

As he continued along the shoreline, his path bordered by sparkling ocean on his right and towering dunes on his left, he checked the contents of the pack Marsden had given him. He saw it included a variety of food items he recognised as typical army rations—all very boring compared to the beautiful meals Cookie had been serving up of late.

In addition to the food, the pack contained a compass, a sheathed hunting knife, several rolls of toilet paper, a compact first aid kit, a light raincoat, several bars of chocolate, two water bottles—both full—and a sheet of canvass large enough to serve as a bed mat or a makeshift tent. "Everything a man could need," John told himself as he inserted the knife, sheath and all, into a loop in his belt, and hung one of the water bottles from a loop on the underside of his pack for easy access.

Lengthening his stride, he tried to make sense of the feelings that were coursing through him at that moment. Undeniable feelings of exhilaration were tempered by a fear of the unknown.

Inevitably, his thoughts turned to Carravanty. He prayed the boy was alive, and he prayed he'd find him as well as the two women.

It was late the following morning before John reached the rainforest clearing that was the site of the bloody clash with the Gureng all those years ago. Memories of that brief but violent event came flooding back to him.

The encampment, in a clearing in the rainforest that bordered the beach, was largely overgrown, but the skeletons of slaughtered Gureng raiders still lay scattered about. John marvelled that the bones remained despite the bodies having been burnt. The Irishman thought he identified the skeletons of two raiders he and Mirritji had despatched. He recalled the elder had bashed one of the raiders to the ground with his shield and had clubbed the other with his nulla nulla, and then John had joined the fray and helped finish them off with one of two makeshift tomahawks he'd armed himself with.

The Irishman was also reminded of the shoulder wound he received in that skirmish. It still troubled him now and he reflexively rubbed it.

Looking around, he saw the remains of some of the bivouacs the Kabi clan members had used. He recognised the leafy rear wall of the bivouac he and Mamba had overnighted in with Murrowdooling and Carravanty, and could still identify the very spot where he and Mamba had made love. How he wished they could relive that night.

Walking back down to the nearby beach, he studied the place above the high water mark where the Kabi had cremated their dead before hurriedly quitting the island. That had been the start of his problems, he recalled.

Putting the memories behind him, he struck off along the beach again, always alert for signs of human life. So far, he'd seen no-one. He thought that strange as he knew it was likely all the Kabi clans occupied Great Sandy Island at the present time. They usually congregated on the island for a coroboree at this time of year.

Searching back into his memory, he recalled on one of his visits the clans met in the centre of the island for their coroboree. He rebuked himself for only now remembering that. *What did they call it?* he asked himself. Then he remembered.

The place of totems.

It was a valley hemmed in by steep, rain-forested hills. "That's where they'll be," he muttered.

The Irishman strode out as he remembered it was still several hours' walk from here to the end of the island. He vowed if he didn't find the women there, he would head straight for the place of totems.

It was mid-afternoon before John neared the island's southern-most point. For the past three hours—since leaving the site of the Gureng raid—he'd had the feeling he was being followed. He kept glancing behind him, but couldn't see anyone. Twice he lay in wait behind rocks, ready to surprise anyone who may be following, to no avail.

John was beginning to regret he hadn't taken Marsden up on his suggestion that he wear boots. Although he had gone without footwear whilst in solitary, that hadn't prepared him for the rigours of walking barefoot for long distances outdoors. The abrasiveness of the hot sand underfoot was causing the soles of his feet to blister. It didn't help, either, that every so often the sandy shorelines gave way to rocks, and he had to scramble over them, losing skin from the soles of his feet in the process.

The Irishman was discovering also that his fitness regime aboard the schooner, and in solitary before that, hadn't fully prepared him for hours of walking non-stop. One hour's exercise in the prison courtyard every second day was hardly ideal for what he was putting himself through now. So he paced himself, slowing his gait and conserving his energy as best he could.

Something made him look out to sea. Some two or three miles behind him he saw *the New Yorker*. Close to shore, she was being pushed along ahead of a brisk northerly, and appeared to be making good speed.

Within minutes of his sighting the schooner, he noticed a puff of smoke belch out from the single cannon that was mounted at her bow. Seconds later, that was followed by the *boom* of the cannon. Even from this distance, it was loud and made the Irishman flinch.

John thought the cannon must have been fired to attract his attention. That was confirmed moments later when flashes of reflected sunlight came from someone standing at the bow. They were obviously using a mirror to ensure they had his attention.

Standing in the shallows, he waved both arms above his head until he was sure they knew he'd seen them.

John wondered what could be so important the schooner had followed him along the coast. He also wondered what could be so important the canon was used to attract his attention. "If the Kabi didn't know we were here before, they do now," he muttered. He assumed it could only be news of the missing women, and he watched with interest as the vessel drew level with him. Moments after she anchored, the longboat was launched.

The longboat's oarsmen steered straight for John. When he saw there were no passengers with them, he realised they were coming to collect him and return him to the schooner. For one brief moment, he wondered whether he should flee.

After the longboat transferred him from shore to the schooner, John was greeted on deck by Marsden. Even before the captain could say anything, the Irishman noticed all the soldiers were now back on board along with all their weapons and equipment.

"We have news of a sighting," Marsden informed the new arrival. "The tracker spoke to two Noonuccal fishermen this morning who confirmed they'd seen a white woman at a Kabi encampment at the opposite end of the island."

"Which woman?" John asked, hoping it was Helen.

"From the description it sounds like Missus Fraser," the captain said, hiding his own disappointment. He added, "The fishermen said they made the sighting late yesterday, so we are hoping she is still there . . . or better still they are both still there."

Marsden didn't mention that he'd fallen out with Cheetham over his decision to sail south to collect John rather than sailing straight to the Kabis' encampment to the north. He'd only gotten his way after yet again reminding Cheetham of the army's rules, and, as a result, the two officials were no longer talking to each other. Marsden remained convinced he needed the Irishman for this tricky operation.

Looking around for the tracker, John asked, "Where is Barega?"

"He is travelling on foot to find and reconnoitre the encampment to confirm whether one or both women are where the Noonuccal say they are," Marsden said.

"He will rendezvous with us south of the encampment."

John absorbed that. He didn't like the idea of the tracker being left to his own resources on this assignment, but the matter was out of his hands for the moment.

The schooner weighed anchor and it wasn't long before John noticed she was sailing north via the island's east coast, which was a first for him as he'd never visited the far side of the island. He soon discovered the east coast was every bit as picturesque as the west coast.

Darkness fell before the rendezvous could be made with Barega, so *the New Yorker* anchored several miles offshore to await the dawn.

Before the evening meal was served, John spent an hour on deck sitting with his blistered feet immersed in a bucket of vinegar. It was a trick he'd learned from the soldiers who regularly used vinegar to treat blisters during and after forced marches. They swore the vinegar also helped prevent infection and, they claimed, it had the added benefit of toughening the feet.

After eating, a weary John adjourned to his personal hammock for a good night's sleep.

Contact was made with Barega within an hour of *the New Yorker* setting sail next morning. The tracker was where he'd said he would be, on a rocky headland some ten miles from the last known location of the Kabi encampment. Marsden didn't want to risk sailing further north for fear of alerting the natives.

Within minutes of coming ashore, John and Marsden had established that a white woman was being held by the Kabi, and Barega's description confirmed it was indeed Eliza. It also confirmed that she wasn't coping at all well with her captivity.

While the three unlikely allies talked, the twelve soldiers who had accompanied John and Marsden ashore unloaded supplies from the longboat, which then headed back to the schooner to collect more soldiers.

It was obvious to John the captain planned to establish another beachhead here. He wondered at the wisdom of having such a military presence so close to the Kabis' encampment. Looking at Marsden, he said, "You realise every Aborigine on the island knows we are here now?" Before Marsden could respond, he added, "And they know why we are here."

Marsden nodded somewhat ruefully. "I am aware of that," he said.

John glanced knowingly at *the New Yorker* at anchor not a hundred yards away. "She *is* rather hard to miss," he said. He had no doubt the Kabi had been observing the schooner since her arrival nearly two weeks earlier, and they had followed her every move since.

Marsden was only too aware of the truth in what his opposite said. He fired some orders to the soldiers nearby then turned back to John. "Here's the plan," he said. "Barega will guide you to the encampment . . ." He stopped when he noticed the Irishman was shaking his head.

"We have already been through that," John reminded him.

Marsden grimaced as if he was in pain. It irked him that the Irishman continued to call the shots, but he had learned it was futile to argue.

"This will only work if I do it alone," John said.

"Very well," the captain muttered. "Go it alone . . . but we will be here if you need us." When he saw John was satisfied with that, he ordered the tracker to explain how to find the encampment.

Barega obliged, using a stick to draw in the sand to help clarify the verbal directions he delivered in pigeon English.

From what John gathered, the encampment was around eight miles up the coast and a further one or two miles inland. A complicating factor was the beach between here and there was being used by the Kabi fishermen, and so John would have to travel via an inland route Barega recommended.

John informed Marsden he planned a night-time rescue. First, though, he wanted to reconnoitre the encampment in daylight hours to establish exactly where Eliza was being held and what sort of protection she had around her. He was in no doubt her captors would be aware someone would be coming for her, and for Helen, too.

Marsden suggested he send soldiers in the longboat after dark to await John and Eliza at a beach closer to the Kabi encampment. John thought that an excellent idea. A lengthy trek overland would be a problem for Eliza given her physical state—more so if they were being pursued by angry clan members.

So it was agreed the longboat would be despatched after dark in time for a midnight rendezvous, and John was to escort the Scotswoman to the nearest beach and then walk south along the shoreline until they came across their rescuers. If they were unable to keep tonight's rendezvous, the same arrangement would apply tomorrow night and the following night if necessary.

When he was satisfied he had the arrangements fixed in his mind, John, who was now wearing boots, slipped his pack over his back and struck off inland. Ahead of him, he estimated he had a good half day trek. Barega had warned there were Kabi hunters and lookouts in the area so he would have to sacrifice speed for caution if he was to remain unseen and carry out a successful rescue.

John was prepared to show himself to his Kabi kinfolk if all else failed, but he much preferred a clandestine approach for he wasn't at all sure what sort of reception he'd receive if he made his presence known to them.

102

THE KABI ENCAMPMENT WAS ALONGSIDE a freshwater lake on a grassy plain surrounded by bush-covered hills. From his hiding place on a hillside overlooking the site, John estimated it was home to at least a hundred and fifty clan members. That didn't surprise him as he'd sighted quite a few hunters and lookouts during his trek from the coast.

To avoid being seen, he'd had to rely on every last bit of bush craft and knowledge he'd acquired during his years with the Kabi. He was surprised how quickly it had all come back to him. Mentally at least. Physically, he was feeling decidedly weary. All the trekking he'd done over the past three days was taking its toll. To make matters worse, he now had fresh blisters from the new boots he was wearing.

John had sighted Eliza almost as soon as he'd arrived at the encampment earlier that afternoon. He'd been alarmed at her sorry state. The near-naked Scotswoman was in an even worse state than Barega had indicated. Even from fifty yards away, he could see she was so weak she struggled to perform the tasks her female escorts gave her. Barefoot, she was hobbling quite badly. That didn't fill John with confidence for what lay ahead.

This doesn't augur well for the return journey.

As the hours passed, he recognised numerous clan members. He saw Turo heading out to hunt with one of his sons; he saw Mirritji watching rowdy youths playing burinjoin; he saw Mamba's aunt Jiba minding young children; he saw Turo's second wife Ekala talking to friends; he saw many others whose names he couldn't recall, but whose faces were very familiar.

The familiar faces evoked a flood of memories. Sighting Ekala made him think of Carravanty. After Mamba's death, the boy had often stayed with her when John was away hunting. To his disappointment, he saw no sign of him. Nor did he see Helen. He guessed they were at a different encampment. At least he hoped they were.

As dusk approached, he still hadn't had an opportunity to attract Eliza's attention. Not without his risking being seen. He'd hoped to let her know he was here and arrange an after-dark rendezvous. At one stage, whilst collecting firewood, she'd come to within thirty yards of his hiding place, but there were half a dozen women around her, so the opportunity went begging.

With the onset of darkness almost upon him, John cautiously retreated to a cave he'd found earlier. It was half a mile or so from the encampment—far enough removed to reduce the likelihood of his being discovered. He was resigned to laying low until tomorrow when he would try once more to make contact with the

Scotswoman.

By mid-afternoon the following day, John was starting to despair that he'd ever get the chance to contact Eliza. Several times throughout the day, she'd come close to his hideout—even closer than she had the previous day—but so well guarded was she, he never had the opportunity to reveal his presence without alerting clan members.

That changed when the Scotswoman received permission to walk to the nearby lake for a drink of water. The lake was close to John's hiding place. The bush that concealed his presence continued all the way to the water's edge, and the Irishman took advantage of that.

As Eliza drank greedily to assuage her thirst, John threw a stone, which landed just in front of her. "Psst!" he hissed.

Eliza looked around and started when she saw John staring at her from a bush not ten feet away. Before she could scream or otherwise attract attention to herself, John placed his forefinger over his lips to indicate that she should keep quiet. The startled woman only just managed to keep her composure.

John realised he must look a sight. He deliberately hadn't shaved since departing Moreton Bay, and he knew by now he probably resembled the wild man of Borneo. Smiling to signal he meant the woman no harm, he waved her over to him.

Eliza glanced behind her and saw that no-one was watching. She hesitated a moment longer then hobbled as fast as she could into the bush John was hiding in.

"Missus Fraser, I presume?" John asked when Eliza joined him.

"Yes, who are you?" Eliza asked, still unable to believe she was standing before a fellow European. Only now did she remember she wore only a petticoat, and she made a pathetic attempt to cover herself with her hands.

"I am John Graham, from Moreton Bay, at your service, Missus," John said, ignoring Eliza's vain attempts at modesty. "And Captain Marsden has sent me to rescue you."

Eliza was overcome with joy. She had prayed rescuers would come. "Have you found Helen?" she asked hopefully.

"No," John said. "Do you know where she is?"

The Scotswoman shook her head. "They took her to another camp several days ago," she said.

John looked at Eliza's feet. They were swollen and badly blistered, and in a far worse state than his own. "Where are your shoes?" he asked.

"Someone took them," she said. "No matter, my feet were too swollen to wear them." Although in obvious pain, she didn't complain.

John wished he'd thought to bring replacement footwear for her. He made a mental note to take spare shoes for Helen. Realising it wouldn't be long before someone came looking for Eliza, he said, "Captain Marsden and his men are waiting for us on the coast, but we cannot leave before dark."

"Why not?" Eliza asked, alarmed. She'd hoped they could leave at once.

"That's not important," John said. He didn't have time to explain that the Kabi would find them long before they reached the coast if they set off now in broad daylight. "You will need to come to me after dark," he explained. "*After* everyone beds down for the night."

"How will I do that?" Eliza asked.

"You will think of something," John assured her. "If challenged, you could indicate you need a drink or you need to relieve yourself." Ignoring the doubtful look on Eliza's face, he said, "Come straight here. I'll be waiting." Before Eliza could question him further, John turned and ran back up the hill. He didn't want to tempt fate any more than he already had.

Eliza emerged from the bush and returned to the encampment where the womenfolk awaited her. The despair she'd felt up until five minutes ago had been replaced with hope. She couldn't wait for nightfall.

When darkness finally descended, John crept back down the hill to the same bush he'd hidden in earlier. He hoped Eliza followed his instructions and didn't attempt to come to him until the clan members were asleep. Any earlier would be too risky.

One hour stretched out to two, and still she hadn't made her move.

"C'mon Missus," John murmured. "Don't leave it too late." The last of the cooking fires scattered throughout the encampment had long-since burnt out. Only their embers glowed in the darkness.

The Irishman was thankful there was no moon this night. The only light in the heavens came from the stars that appeared briefly and disappeared just as quickly as clouds scudded across the sky. However, it was sufficient to allow him to see Eliza when she emerged from the bivouac she occupied. He was relieved to see she walked normally so as not to attract suspicion. That's to say she walked as normally as she could given the state of her feet. Her bivouac was dead centre in the middle of the encampment, which meant she had some distance to walk between other bivouacs before reaching the bush beyond.

Plenty of time for a wide awake clan member or an alert lookout to see her.

Eliza reached John's hiding place without incident. Even though it appeared no-one else had seen her, she had the presence of mind to pretend she was removing her undergarments as she stooped to enter the bushes. She hoped an observer would think she was about to relieve herself.

Even though Eliza had been expecting to find John, she gasped when she actually saw him.

"Shhh!" John warned. Taking her firmly by the arm, he led her deeper into the bush.

As soon as he was satisfied they were far enough away from the encampment, John reached into his backpack and withdrew the spare water bottle he'd brought. He handed it to Eliza who gratefully drank from it. "Drink it slowly," John warned. "It may be the last drink you have for a while." He then pulled out the light raincoat from his pack and this he draped around Eliza's badly sunburnt shoulders.

She grimaced as the coat aggravated her sunburn.

"It will protect your shoulders from the branches and thorns," John explained.

"Thank you, Mister Graham," Eliza murmured.

John could see she was overcome with gratitude. His heart went out to her, knowing what she'd endured these past few months since her husband's ship foundered. Putting that aside, he took her arm once more and said, "Come." He led her through the bush toward the coast. This time, he took the direct route.

They hadn't gone more than fifty yards when John suddenly pulled up. There, in the dark, a native had stepped from out of the trees not ten yards ahead of them. He held a spear in the throwing position, and he was looking straight at John.

"What is it?" Eliza asked. She still hadn't yet seen the native.

John clamped his hand over Eliza's mouth. He knew she'd scream as soon as she saw the shadowy figure, and sure enough she did, or at least she tried to.

103

NOTHING HAPPENED FOR WHAT SEEMED a lifetime, but may only have been a few heartbeats. The native stared at the two whites, and they stared back at him.

Finally, John said, "I bring you goodwill." He spoke the language of the Kabi.

"Moilow?" came the answering reply.

"Mirritji?" John asked.

It was Mirritji. "I accept your goodwill," the elder said when he realised who it was he confronted. Lowering his spear, he stepped forward.

John released his grip on Eliza and went forward to greet Mirritji. The two old friends stopped a foot apart and looked solemnly at each other. Mirritji glanced from John to Eliza and back to the younger man, and waited for him to speak.

"I came to take her back to her people," John said, looking at Eliza. The expression on her face told him she was amazed to hear him speaking in the Kabi tongue.

Mirritji nodded. "She belongs with her people," he said. He'd been against those clan members who had decided to keep Eliza and Helen captive, but he'd been out-voted.

John was relieved to hear that. "Do you know where they keep the other white woman?" he asked.

"No," the elder said, "but all the clans and families will meet for a corroboree in two days." He added, "The other woman will be there."

"Where is the corroboree to be held?" John asked.

"At the place of totems," Mirritji said, referring to the sacred meeting place in the middle of the island. He then reached out and place one hand on John's shoulder. It was the hand of friendship. "Go in peace, Moilow," he murmured. "That is my blessing for you." The elder turned to do, but the Irishman restrained him.

"What of Carravanty?" John asked. He held his breath, not sure if he wanted to know the answer.

"He is well," Mirritji said at length.

Relief flooded through John. Until this moment, he hadn't known whether Barega had killed the boy that fateful day he'd been captured.

Mirritji continued, "Carravanty lives with Turo's extended family, but he is away hunting at present." With that, the elder disappeared into the darkness.

John's shoulder felt warm where his old friend's hand had been moments earlier. Unaccountably warm, and yet comforting. Without a word, he led Eliza deeper into the bush. His heart was filled with joy, and he now walked with a spring in his step.

"Who was that savage?" the Scotswoman asked when she'd gotten over her surprise.

"No talking!" John whispered. He wanted Eliza to conserve her energy for the trek ahead. Besides, he thought, lengthy explanations could wait until they were both safely on board the waiting schooner.

Half a mile from the Kabi encampment, Eliza could walk no further. A quick inspection of her feet revealed they were a bloody mess. Long days going barefoot had finally taken their toll.

"I am sorry, Mister Graham," she sobbed. "I cannot take another step."

"Don't you worry, Missus," John said, lifting her off her feet, "Only a mile or so to go." He was surprised how light she felt in his arms. The ordeal she'd suffered had virtually reduced her to skin and bones, and she now weighed little more than a child.

The Irishman's estimate of how far they had to go was pretty accurate. However, the route he took traversed some of the most difficult terrain on the island. It consisted of a series of steep, rain-forested hills separated by deep valleys, most of which had fast-flowing streams running their full length. Some of these proved quite a challenge to cross, more so because Eliza was now a mere passenger and John had to do the work for both of them. Several times they were almost swept away, and only John's strength and confidence in the water saved them from drowning or from being swept far downstream at least.

After two hours' trekking, Eliza felt as heavy as an overweight adult in his arms. To add to his difficulties, the presence of Kabi lookouts forced him to detour constantly. He spotted four lookouts on the journey to the coast, but he sensed there were more around. It was the ones he didn't see he most worried about. Those he did see, he gave a wide berth, and this slowed them down considerably.

It was with great relief to them both that they arrived at the coast without incident. No sooner had they emerged from the rainforest and stepped onto the beach than Barega appeared before them, spear in hand.

"Who is that?" Eliza asked, alarmed.

"He is one of us," John assured her, lowering her onto the sand to ease his aching arms. He regretted his choice of words immediately.

Never in a million years could he be considered one of us.

Without a word, the tracker motioned to them to follow him. He set off running south along the beach.

John flexed his arms a couple of times then picked Eliza up and began hurrying after Barega. The tracker slowed his pace every now and then so that the Irishman wouldn't lose sight of him.

The fifteen minutes it took to reach the waiting longboat seemed more like an hour to John. He was breathing hard, and his arms and legs felt like they were about to drop off. "Thank God!" he gasped when he saw the soldiers standing beside the beached craft.

The soldiers—twelve in all—looked alert with rifles at the ready and bayonets fixed. Marsden was among them. So, too, was Doctor Andrews who stood apart from the others with his medical bag in hand.

When Eliza saw the reception party she wept tears of joy.

Marsden and Andrews strode forward to greet John and Eliza as soon as they saw them.

"Welcome back to civilisation, Missus Fraser," the captain said, ignoring her rescuer.

"Thank you, Captain Marsden," Eliza sobbed as John lowered her onto the sand. "It is wonderful to see you and your men." She pulled the raincoat tight around her, and was thankful she had it in the presence of so many soldiers.

Looking at John, the captain wanted to say, "Well done, Mister Graham," but he couldn't bring himself to compliment the Irishman. Instead, he nodded curtly in John's direction then returned his attention to Eliza who was now being fussed over by the doctor. "Do your examination on board, Phillip," he said. "We don't want to tempt our luck any longer." He was afraid the Kabi may have followed John to the coast, and he didn't fancy a skirmish here, exposed as he and his men were, on the beach.

Two minutes later, everyone on the beach was seated in the longboat, which quickly pulled away from the shore as the oarsmen bent their backs and dipped their oars in well-practised unison. Behind the oarsmen, not seventy-five yards offshore, the shadowy outline of *the New Yorker* could just be seen by those passengers who were facing forward. John was one of those, and already he was thinking of the fine meal Cooky would soon be serving him. He decided he'd wash the food down with a double serving of rum.

Eliza was greeted effusively by Cheetham as soon as she was lifted aboard the schooner. "My dear Eliza," the commandant gushed, "how wonderful to have you back."

The Scotswoman was so tired she could barely raise a smile.

Doctor Andrews, who was holding tight to his patient to stop her from falling, told Cheetham he needed to examine Eliza straight away. His tone let the older man know the pleasantries could wait.

"Of course," Cheetham said. "I have vacated my quarters so that Missus Marsden can stay there." The quarters he referred to, of course, were Captain Rayburn's requisitioned quarters, which the commandant had commandeered.

As Andrews assisted Eliza below deck, Cheetham turned to Marsden and insisted they debrief John immediately. He wanted to know everything that had happened and, more to the point, what Marsden planned to do next.

The three men adjourned to the same private area at the stern that the Irishman occupied at night when aboard ship. His hammock lay folded nearby on the deck where he'd left it.

"Now," Cheetham said, eyeing John, "tell me everything." He lit up a cigar as the

Irishman related everything of importance that had transpired over the past couple of days. When John finished, the commandant looked to Marsden for confirmation that he was satisfied the prisoner—for that's how he still viewed the Irishman—had been telling the truth. The captain nodded, indicating he believed it was as John said.

John listened as the two men discussed strategies for Helen's rescue. He didn't like the way the discussion was going, but he said nothing for the moment.

Cheetham agreed with his subordinate that soldiers should accompany John ashore this time—a necessary precaution, according to the commandant, given all the Kabi clan members would be assembled at the site they called the place of totems, making the Irishman's task all the more challenging.

John bided his time before voicing his opposition to the plan. Even though they never said as much, he knew both men wanted payback for the disastrous Kabi raid all those years earlier. And he was in no doubt if soldiers accompanied him to the place of totems there would be unnecessary violence and quite possibly a bloodbath. Much as he wanted to save Helen, he didn't want another massacre on his conscience.

Looking at the Irishman, Cheetham asked, "Where is this corroboree taking place?"

"That's for me to know," John said.

The commandant nearly swallowed his cigar. Angry, he glanced at Marsden.

The captain shrugged. "He refuses to tell me the location," he said.

Cheetham rounded on John. "I am ordering you to tell me the location, Graham!" he shouted.

John just grinned, further infuriating the commandant.

Cheetham then threatened to rescind John's ticket of leave and to reinstate the death penalty.

"You won't do that, Bertie," John said, deliberately baiting the older man. Enjoying the expressions of anger on the faces of both officials, he quickly added, "You won't do that because I have already rescued Missus Fraser and you know I *will* rescue the captain's daughter." He paused to add emphasis to that last comment, then he said, "And I have your signature guaranteeing my ticket of leave." Looking at Marsden, but still addressing Cheetham, he added, "*And* I have a witness to your signature, Bertie."

Marsden couldn't hold John's gaze. He looked away, knowing his daughter's rescue was entirely in the hands of the lippy Irishman.

Cheetham, who was now lost for words, looked to his subordinate for some sort of guidance.

After assembling his thoughts, Marsden said, "We have no choice but to do it his way, my Lord."

Cheetham wasn't happy about that, but he held his tongue.

Marsden continued, "We will do it his way"—he nodded toward John—"and we will send him out alone tomorrow night to rescue Helen."

On hearing that, John looked out into the darkness. He didn't see Marsden wink at his superior behind his back.

That night, or what little was left of it, *the New Yorker* sailed around Great Sandy Island's northern tip and headed for the same bay she had anchored in upon arrival at the island. The rationale being the vessel would be closer to the mainland and therefore closer to Moreton Bay.

During the short voyage, as John slept soundly in his hammock, two decisions were made that would have alarmed him had he known about them.

Firstly, Cheetham and Marsden decided between themselves they *would* send soldiers ashore to assist in Helen's rescue. After much soul-searching, Marsden had agreed with the commandant there was too much at stake to entrust the success of the rescue mission entirely to John Graham. His daughter's life was far too precious to gamble with. Secondly, the two men decided that Barega would track John to the Kabis' meeting place and then return to guide the soldiers to it.

104

THE FOLLOWING NIGHT, AFTER A restful day aboard *the New Yorker,* John was ferried back to the island aboard the longboat as arranged. The Irishman was the only passenger on this occasion, and he spent the duration of the short journey checking the contents of his pack, which, he was pleased to see, included a few delicacies amongst the fresh food provisions. He guessed Cookie had had something to do with that.

As soon as he was ashore, he struck off toward the centre of the island while the oarsmen manning the longboat rowed back to the waiting schooner. Ahead of him was a two-day walk. He would travel only by night; by day he would hide—just as he did when he rescued Eliza.

John was satisfied Marsden had made the right decision in allowing him to attempt the rescue of Helen alone. He was also happy that the captain had agreed to arrange for the schooner to sail off until she was out of sight once he was ashore. That had been a last minute request, which Marsden had readily agreed to—the rationale being the Kabi would believe the soldiers had given up on rescuing Helen, and that would make the Irishman's job that much easier.

John had no idea that Barega was already ashore and was tracking him at that very moment. Nor did he realise Marsden and Cheetham planned to double-cross him.

The route he followed from the island's western shoreline was foreign to him. In the past, he'd only ever approached it from the north or south. And walking only under the cover of darkness made the going that much harder. Several times he realised he was heading the wrong way and had to change direction. He just hoped he could find the place of totems.

As he came to the end of yet another dead-end gully, he found himself humming a tune. It bothered him that it seemed so familiar and yet he couldn't remember where he'd heard it before. Then he remembered.

Mamba used to sing it!

John recalled it was one of the tunes Mamba often sang or hummed while trekking through the wilderness. He had laughed at her when she claimed singing or humming enabled her to hear the Songlines, which would guide her to her destination. But he knew different now.

The Irishman resumed humming the tune. This time, however, he listened hard for the Songlines. Nothing came to him until he left behind the gully he'd entered earlier. Then he heard it. Faint at first, it gradually grew louder. It was Mamba.

She's singing to me!

Mamba was putting words to the tune he was humming. Slowly, the words came back to him and he sang along with her. Striding out, he headed off in a different direction, all the while listening to Mamba. Now he realised he was no longer lost. He was following the Songlines.

Next morning, as the first signs of the new day dawned, John found a suitable place to hole up. It was inside a cleft beneath an overhang near the top of a high, bush-covered hill. Screened from prying eyes by thorny bushes, it was an ideal hiding place.

Before retiring into the cleft, he glanced behind him. From up here, he had a commanding view of the sea.

He did a double take when he saw *the New Yorker* still at anchor. "Damn you, Marsden!" he muttered. He hadn't expected to see hide nor hare of the schooner. The captain had gone back on their agreement that the schooner would be gone by daybreak.

Eliza didn't emerge from her temporary quarters aboard *the New Yorker* until early afternoon. She had been so exhausted she'd spent the previous day in her bunk, catching up on lost sleep. Today, she'd slept in until lunchtime, and then, at Doctor Andrews' insistence, had remained in her cabin to enjoy a meal served to her in bed.

When she did finally emerge on deck, the improvement in her colour and alertness was immediately noticeable to all. She now wore a dress and sun bonnet selected from a wardrobe that had been stowed on board for Helen and herself. The dress all but concealed the over-sized slippers she now wore. The slippers were necessary because her damaged feet had been bandaged, which prevented her from wearing normal shoes.

"My dear Eliza," Cheetham enthused as he hurried forward to greet her, "you look wonderful today." He ushered the Scotswoman to a chair that had been brought up from below. In her present condition, she couldn't walk more than a few paces.

"Thank you, Bertie," Eliza smiled as she sat down, "but I am sure you exaggerate."

"Not at all," Cheetham insisted. Turning to Marsden, who was talking to Lieutenant Otter nearby, he said, "Isn't that so, Tom."

The captain left his lieutenant's side and walked over to join Cheetham. Looking down at Eliza, he said, "It certainly is. And I am sure the salt air will do wonders for you as well."

"You are both too kind," Eliza said. After some more chit-chat between the three, she looked up at the men. "Gentlemen, I am given to understand John Graham is a convict from Moreton Bay," she said. Doctor Andrews had confirmed that much during one of his visits to her cabin.

"Yes, my dear," Cheetham confirmed.

"What will happen to Mister Graham?" Eliza asked, concerned for the welfare of the man who had risked his life for her.

"As it stands, he will serve out his sentence in Moreton Bay," Cheetham said. He made no mention of the fact John had received his ticket of leave and a promissory note overturning his sentence. Neither he nor Marsden had any intention of honouring that arrangement.

"But he knowingly put himself in great danger to rescue me," Eliza protested. "Surely he deserves his freedom."

Cheetham left his subordinate to answer that curly question.

"I am sure the Governor will take that into account, Eliza," Marsden said, neatly sidestepping the question.

Taking his cue, Cheetham hurriedly added, "Yes, the question of overturning any convict's sentence lies squarely with Sir Ralph . . . I will take it up with him as soon as we return to Moreton Bay."

"Oh, that would be good, Bertie," Eliza said. "Mister Graham so deserves some latitude."

While Eliza enjoyed her visit topside aboard the schooner, John woke from a restless sleep in his hiding place on the island. His first thought was for *the New Yorker,* and he wondered whether she had sailed off since he'd last checked at around mid-morning. He crawled to the entrance of the crevice and was disappointed to see the vessel was still there.

Bastards!

He was now more certain than ever that Marsden and Cheetham planned to send soldiers ashore—if they hadn't already. The plan had been that they sail off so that the Kabi would believe they'd given up on rescuing Helen, but that arrangement had clearly been discarded.

John began to suspect a double-cross.

If they can't honour that arrangement, will they honour my ticket of leave?

He patted his shirt pocket to confirm the signed letter was still there.

John found the place of totems just before dawn the following day after having trekked through a second night. It was as he remembered—a broad, grassy plain ringed by high, rain-forested hills in the dead centre of the island.

As the name suggested, the sacred site was distinguished by ancient rock drawings of kangaroos, emus, snakes, dingoes, lizards, eagles and other totems revered by the Kabi. Most of these were hidden from view, concealed as they were in the many caves that dotted the area, but some were out in the open for all to see.

John's trek had been no more eventful than the first night. He had been pleasantly surprised how few lookouts he'd come across. He'd counted three in all, and he put the slack security down to the fact that the Kabi believed there was safety in numbers. He knew from experience that hundreds of clan members converged on the place of totems each year, and they were supremely confident their swollen numbers and combined strength would be more than a match for any who dared challenge them.

The Irishman observed the Kabi encampment from the cover of the rainforest. The light of a full moon revealed all the clan members were sleeping. All except for a handful of lookouts who patrolled the site's outskirts. The bivouacs were too many to count, but John estimated most of the tribe's members were present. That meant at least five hundred clan members were on site.

John found himself wondering if Carravanty was here or whether he was still away hunting. He prayed he would see the boy at least once before he departed. He needed to confirm with his own eyes that he was still alive.

As for which bivouac accommodated Helen, he hadn't a clue. He hoped to spot her during daylight hours when everyone was up and about.

That is if she's even here.

John was under no illusions the task ahead was challenging. With so many clan members here for the corroboree, it would be difficult to communicate with Helen without being seen.

As for the two of us making it back to the coast, that may be too much to hope for.

The more he thought about it, the more he became resigned to having to show himself to the clan members and hope that, first and foremost, they had fond memories of him, and secondly they would allow him to depart with Helen. However, he decided to think on that some more. In the meantime, he realised dawn was approaching and he needed to find a hiding place. He cautiously retraced his steps deeper into the rainforest.

It was mid-day before John finally saw Helen. The Irishman was hiding amongst the upper branches of a tree from where he had a commanding view of the encampment. He'd managed to sleep for a couple of hours in his new hiding place, and had only missed seeing the young Englishwoman head out earlier with other women to collect berries by a matter of minutes.

While waiting, he had seen many more familiar faces, including most of those he'd seen at the other site three days earlier as well as his close friend Gabirri and clan leader Yarran.

On sighting Gabirri, he had to consciously restrain himself from shouting out to him. The strapping native hadn't changed one bit. He looked as imposing as ever.

Gabirri and Yarran were heading out with a large party of hunters. All carried spears and woomeras, and all looked keen for the hunt. They seemed very aware they had hundreds of mouths to feed at tonight's corroboree, and they were hoping to make many kills in the hours ahead.

Watching them run off into the trees on the other side of the encampment, John wished he was with them. It was a long time since he'd experienced the thrill of the hunt.

As before, he looked around for Carravanty, but still there was no sign of him. He prayed he'd see him soon.

When Helen finally returned to camp, John saw her immediately. Her blonde hair made her hard to miss. His first impression was she had thus far survived her captivity considerably better than Eliza had. That didn't surprise him for she was younger and more used to Australia's harsh conditions—and she hadn't given birth recently, or ever for that matter. Not to his knowledge at least.

However, on closer inspection he saw Helen was as badly sunburnt as Eliza had been. That didn't surprise him because she wore nothing but a bodice and petticoat—and, like the Scotswoman, she was being forced to work with the other women outside in the sun. She, too, was hobbling around barefoot. Each and every step caused her obvious pain. "Poor girl," John murmured. Despite her sorry condition, he saw she still exuded an inner beauty and poise that were impossible to miss.

Then and there, he repeated the earlier vow he'd made to himself, and to Marsden, that he would rescue Helen. Exactly how he was going to achieve that, he wasn't sure.

By late afternoon, John still hadn't had an opportunity to make contact with Helen. There were so many clan members around, he realised it would be impossible to make a move without being seen by one of them. He decided to retire to his hiding place for a snooze before returning tonight.

The Irishman was about to descend the tree when a commotion beyond the encampment caught his attention. He watched as the same hunters he'd observed earlier emerged from the rainforest. They were carrying one of their own. Some were shouting to attract the attention of others.

Only when they entered the encampment did John see they were carrying Yarran. The clan leader wasn't moving. He appeared to be either unconscious or dead. As they came closer to John's position, it became evident that Yarran was dead.

Female relatives began wailing when the identity of the dead hunter became known. A crowd quickly gathered around Yarran, but not before John saw the bloody chest wound he'd received. The Irishman would learn later he'd been accidentally speared by a fellow hunter who had mistaken him for a big red roo. He would also learn the hunter responsible had been tied to an ant hill and left to die a slow and painful death—as Kabi custom dictated when a clan member killed an elder regardless of whether it was accidental or not.

The burial rites for Yarran began that afternoon and continued through to the following afternoon. When the clan's former leader was eventually buried—in one of the caves above the encampment—the corroboree finally began, and it continued well into the night.

In all that time, John hadn't had a single opportunity to communicate with Helen. He saw her often, but couldn't get near her. And so he resigned himself to waiting another day.

That night, while John slept in the rainforest near the place of totems, Barega, Lieutenant Otter and twenty-four of his men slept in the same rainforest only a day's march away. With the tracker leading the way, the soldiers hoped to reach the Kabi encampment by nightfall the following day.

Barega had reported back to Marsden as soon as he'd returned from his trek into the interior. He'd followed John all the way to the encampment without the Irishman having realised he was being tracked. On arriving back on board *the New Yorker,* the tracker had discovered Marsden had been laid low with dysentery, which had also swept through most of the crew. Fortunately, none of the other soldiers had caught it, and nor had Cheetham, Andrews or Eliza thus far.

Marsden had handed over temporary command of the soldiers to Otter, and it was the lieutenant who was now leading them cross country to rescue the captain's daughter.

Otter's brief was to provide whatever support was required to help John Graham rescue Helen. Before the lieutenant had departed the schooner, Cheetham had taken him aside and made it clear the *support* Marsden referred to meant he should use all the resources at his disposal. How he construed that, the commandant advised, was over to him, but it was clear to Otter that Cheetham would have no objection if he went in with all guns blazing. Having never seen action before, he was excited by the prospect.

Upon going ashore, the lieutenant's first task had been to establish a secure beachhead for his men to return to. Otter ordered five soldiers to remain with the longboat and its oarsmen to ensure the craft was protected and ever-ready to facilitate a quick departure if necessary.

The main squad, with Otter at their head, spent the full day following Barega deeper into the hills. Most of the men, like the lieutenant, had never seen action. And, like the lieutenant, they, too, were excited by the prospect.

105

C LAN MEMBERS SLEPT IN LATE when the new day dawned. *Late* for them was an hour after sun-up, or, in some cases, two hours after sun-up. It was little wonder they'd slept in given the corroboree had gone on into the wee small hours, and that on top of the lengthy and emotionally draining ceremonies that followed Yarran's untimely death.

The late start suited John because he had roused himself to observe the encampment during the night and hadn't gotten back to sleep until shortly before dawn.

By mid-morning, life was returning to normal in the encampment. Men headed out to hunt, women minded their young children and performed their daily tasks, and boys practised throwing boomerangs and indulged in play fights, which all too often weren't so playful.

From the same hiding place atop the same tree, John observed the women. He soon picked Helen out. She was collecting branches to reinforce some of the flimsier bivouacs. Her escort on this occasion was a big woman John had never seen before. She kept berating Helen, and it took all the Irishman's control not to rush out and whack her. It seemed the woman wanted her charge to work harder despite the fact the barefoot Helen was in some pain.

John's attention switched back to the boys who were now playing burinjoin. He noticed a group of youths had stopped to watch them. Armed with spears, they were obviously about to head out to hunt. A familiar face amongst the youths caught his eye.

Carravanty!

The Irishman nearly lost his grip on the branch he was holding so delighted was he to see the boy. Studying Carravanty, he realised why he hadn't seen him until now. He'd been looking out for a spindly fifteen-year-old, for that's how old Carravanty was when he last saw him, but the youth he was looking at now was eighteen and already a man.

He's the spitting image of Murrowdooling!

John's first reaction was one of immense relief. He knew for sure now that it was as Mirritji had said.

He's alive and well.

John looked on with pride as Carravanty led the banter the youths directed at the boys playing burinjoin. "That's my boy," John chuckled. It seemed only yesterday that Carravanty was one of those boys, and his older brother was heckling him from the side-lines as he played.

Studying the young man more closely, John saw he had undergone the scarification ritual. Prominent welts covered Carravanty's limbs and torso, adding to his mature persona and signifying that he'd survived the same testing passage into manhood that Murrowdooling had survived.

Carravanty and the other youths soon tired of the banter and headed off into the rainforest. John watched them until they disappeared.

Staring at the place where Carravanty had been moments earlier, the Irishman realised he felt content now. He suddenly felt more confident about what lay ahead.

As the morning dragged on, John slowly reached a decision he'd hoped to avoid. *I have to show myself.*

Already it was approaching mid-day, and he could see today going the way of the past two days. He feared he would never get the chance to communicate with Helen without being seen by the others.

Watching the young woman being abused by her minders, and then seeing Carravanty—the boy he considered his son—had been the last straw. He knew he had to throw caution to the wind and reveal his presence or he could be here forever and a day, talking to himself and acting like a voyeur.

Before he showed himself, he had something to do. He quietly descended the tree and, keeping to the cover of the rainforest, crept around to the far side of the encampment where he'd noticed freshly skinned roo pelts had been hung out to dry.

It took him thirty minutes to work his way around to where the pelts were hanging. They were draped over a line that had been strung up in the open just in front of the rainforest. Fortunately, the pelts concealed his presence from the clan members as he dashed forward and removed one of them. He was back in the trees in a matter of seconds, and, it seemed, no-one had noticed.

Withdrawing deeper into the rainforest, John stopped only when he considered he'd ventured a safe distance from the encampment. He soon found what he was looking for—a flat, grassy area he could lay the pelt out on. Then, drawing his knife from its sheath, he set about fashioning a loincloth for himself.

The Irishman wanted to stack the odds a little more in his favour before he showed himself to the Kabi. He knew the more he looked like the old Moilow and the less he looked like a European the better. Hence the loincloth he was now making.

That done, he removed his shirt, boots, breeches and undershorts, stuffed them into his pack, and then fixed the loincloth around him to hide his nakedness. He then fashioned a belt from the remaining section of the roo pelt and tied it around his waist, inserting his knife through a loop in the makeshift belt. "There, I am now Moilow," he told himself as he crammed the remains of the pelt in his pack. He repeated the refrain, louder this time, as if to convince himself he was the white spirit the Kabi once believed him to be.

Now, as he trekked barefoot back toward the encampment, he felt silly. *I must look like a bloody galah!* he thought. That was confirmed when he came across a billabong he'd passed earlier. Looking into its still waters, his mirror image confirmed for him that he did indeed look like a galah. Sunburnt face aside, his body was as pasty white as to be expected of someone who had spent three years in solitary confinement. He stroked his two-week-old beard as he looked for some redeeming features in the face that stared back at him. Finding none, he resumed his walk toward the encampment feeling a little less confident than before.

As he neared the camp, he began to have misgivings about what he was about to do. *What if they don't recognise me?* He quickly dismissed that thought. *Of course they'll recognise me. After all, I recognised them.* His greater concern was whether they would welcome him.

They'll know I'm here for the woman.

Standing just inside the rainforest, he surveyed the encampment. Most of the clan members were now sitting around cooking fires, eating their mid-day meal. Some were already sleeping off their tucker in the shade of their bivouacs. He looked for Helen and was alarmed to see her minder had kept her working. The young woman was staggering beneath the weight of a new load of branches she'd collected, and was hobbling toward a partially collapsed bivouac on the far side of the encampment.

John removed his pack and hid it in a hole in the trunk of a towering fig tree. He then steeled himself for what he was about to do. "Here we go," he muttered. "I hope you know what you're doin' Graham."

The Irishman stepped out from the cover of the trees and walked as casually as he could toward the centre of the camp. He hadn't gone more than a few yards than he was challenged by a spear-wielding lookout, a young native he'd never seen before. The lookout's shouts attracted other clan members, and it wasn't long before John found himself surrounded by hostile men. He recoiled as the tips of their spears prodded none too gently into his back and chest.

"I am Moilow!" John announced in the Kabi tongue. "I bring you goodwill." His utterance momentarily silenced those around him.

"I accept your goodwill," a voice boomed out.

John recognised Gabirri's voice, though he couldn't see his friend for he was concealed behind other clan members for the moment.

Gabirri finally managed to force his way through the others. Stopping before John, he turned to his fellow clan members and said, "He is who he claims to be. He is Moilow." The two old friends shared a look that signalled to each they were still friends.

Those closest to John hesitantly lowered their spears. He heard the term *white spirit* being whispered amongst the assembled. Some, he noted, looked at him in awe; some looked at him in fear and a few looked at him with undisguised anger.

Arguing broke out amongst the assembled. "He comes for the white woman!" one native said. "He is not a white spirit!" another shouted. "He is one of us!" yet another insisted.

"He is Moilow," a voice came from behind the men. It was Carravanty. He'd returned to the encampment ahead of his fellow hunters. The youth pushed his way to the front of the throng and looked straight at John. He said, "He is my father."

106

A HUSH FELL OVER THE assembled as John and Carravanty sized each other up. The two kin locked eyes. In that moment, the Irishman knew he'd made the right decision. He walked quickly over to his boy and hugged him. "You have grown up," he smiled. Only now did he realise Carravanty was almost as tall as him.

"You have stayed away a long time," Carravanty said with all the honesty of youth.

John didn't know how to respond to that. He hugged the boy again. Beyond the assembled, he suddenly noticed Helen staring at him. The expression of disbelief on her face told him she had only just seen him. He shook his head once, indicating she should not react. She quickly recovered her composure and resumed working.

Looking at the clan members before him, John noticed their ranks suddenly part. He realised they were making way for Mirritji who had just joined them.

Now that Yarran was dead, Mirritji was the clan's senior elder, and as such he received all the respect due a leader and spokesman. Mirritji made no attempt to pretend he was surprised to see John. After their recent encounter at the other encampment, he'd fully expected to see him here. In fact, he'd expected to see him a lot earlier. Looking at the white, he said, "You took your time arriving here, Moilow."

John grinned. "The Songlines caused me to lose my way a few times," he joked.

Mirritji didn't see the humour. "If you listen to the Songlines, you will never lose your way," he said. "I have told you that."

John knew the elder was chastising him. He cursed himself for making light of the Songlines, and for not remembering that the Kabi never joked about them or the Dreamtime.

Looking over to where Helen was working, Mirritji asked, "Is it true you come for the woman?" He already knew the answer.

John wished the old man wasn't so direct. "Yes," he said simply. Then he had an epiphany. Almost without thinking, he added, "She is my woman." His thinking was he would have more ownership of Helen if the Kabi believe she belonged to him.

Mirritji gave no indication whether he believed him or not. "Did you bring white invaders with you?" he asked.

"No, I insisted they stay on board the boat," John said, meeting the elder's level gaze. He quickly added, "You cannot keep the white woman. If you do, the soldiers will come for her and the Kabi will suffer."

"The Kabi are not like the Gureng!" a native shouted. "We are not scared of the invader."

John looked at the native and couldn't place him. He was evidently from another clan—as were the majority of his fellows. "You did not witness the destruction the soldiers brought upon the Kabi when they came once before," he said with certainty. Looking around, he added, "Your brothers who did witness that awful event know the truth in what I say. Next time the soldiers come, they will come in greater numbers and the Kabi's losses will be much higher than before."

More arguing erupted as the clan members discussed the white's prediction.

John sensed his immediate future, and Helen's, too, was in the balance. He felt he needed to take the initiative now, or it would be too late. He caught Mirritji's eye and indicated he had something else to say.

The elder held up his hand and the voices gradually quietened. When he had everyone's attention, he said, "The white spirit wishes to speak."

Heartened that Mirritji still referred to him as the *white spirit,* John said, "As I have said before, I am not Moilow."

This revelation was news to some, and more angry murmurings arose.

Undeterred, the Irishman continued, "My name is John Graham. The white men brought me to your country from Ireland"—he quickly rephrased it—"from . . . a land far across the sea. I escaped, and that is when the Kabi found me."

The clan members now listened intently. Those seeing him for the first time couldn't help but be impressed by his mastery of their language.

John continued, "I let you believe I was Moilow because I was scared. For this I am sorry. But as the seasons passed, I grew to love the Kabi. And for that I am not sorry."

Faces amongst the assembled began to soften.

The Irishman noticed more and more clan members were joining the assembled, swelling their numbers. Women and children were among them. Emboldened, he said, "I am not Moilow, but I am Kabi. Husband of Mamba, father to Murrowdooling"—he looked at Carravanty and placed his hand on the youth's head—"and father to Carravanty."

Carravanty smiled for the first time. John winked at him and then looked around at the other clan members. He wasn't sure if he'd won them over or not. Some of the men especially still looked at him with suspicion and wariness. All the while, he could feel Helen's eyes on him, but he deliberately didn't look at her.

No-one spoke for some time.

Finally, Turo stepped forward from amongst the assembled. He'd remained hidden until now. The big native looked at John solemnly and said, "You are even whiter than you were when you were a white spirit." Before the Irishman could answer, he asked, "Are you hungry, Moilow?"

Grinning, John said, "Hungry as ever, my friend."

"Come," Turo commanded. He turned and strode off toward his bivouac where one of his wives was tending a cooking fire.

John and Carravanty followed Turo, chatting away as if they'd never been separated. As they neared Turo's bivouac, the white glanced around at the other clan members and saw that most of them had gone back to doing what they'd been doing before he'd shown himself. He breathed a sigh of relief. His gamble had paid off—so far.

They arrived at the bivouac to find Turo's second wife, Ekala, had all but finished preparing a hot meal. She and Turo shared a knowing glance, confirming for John what he'd always suspected—that she was his friend's favourite wife.

During the meal that followed, John learned what Turo and his fellow clan members had been up to in recent years. He also learned that Carravanty had acquitted himself well as a hunter and provider, and had proven himself in skirmishes with enemy tribes—the Noonuccal and Gureng in particular—and, according to Turo, was shaping up to be a future leader.

Looking at Carravanty, John asked, "Are you married yet, boy?" He was aware many youths his age were already married.

Carravanty shook his head. "I am still looking," he said. The look on his face told John that he wanted to change the subject.

Ekala, who had been following the conversation with interest, leaned over to the Irishman and said, "He is too busy planting his seed to worry about taking a wife."

John chuckled. A sheepish Carravanty looked away.

Taking over from where his wife left off, Turo looked at John and said, "Your boy has no shortage of marriage prospects, Moilow." He added, "The clan's available women beat a steady path to his bivouac most nights."

"And some of the clan's *unavailable* women do, too," Ekala smiled.

The men laughed. Only Carravanty didn't see the funny side, preferring to focus his attention on the brazed brush turkey leg he was chewing on.

Before the meal was over, it felt to John as if he'd never been away.

After the meal, the Irishman circulated amongst the clan members, renewing old friendships and acquaintances. All the while, he kept one eye on Helen who, he noticed, was about to accompany several other women into the bush on a food-gathering expedition. He realised he needed to act now.

If they believed me when I said she is my woman she should be with me.

John marched over to Helen just in time to prevent her leaving. "Play along," he hissed as he dragged a startled Helen away by the arm. "I know what I'm doing." He was gambling on the fact that clan members would expect him to reclaim ownership of Helen if she was, as he said, his woman. They would think less of him if he allowed her to keep working as someone else's slave. Better if she were his slave.

Helen was too shocked to ask her rescuer what was going on, and she allowed him to pull her along behind him.

John dragged her over to a disassembled bivouac he'd noticed earlier. Hoping it had been vacated, he said, "This is our new home."

"What?" Helen asked. She couldn't work out what was going on. Everything was happening so fast.

John turned the young woman around so that she was facing him. "Listen to me," he said grimly, "and listen hard." When he saw he had her full focus, he said, "I am going to order you to do something, and you are going to refuse."

"Pardon?" Helen asked, still confused.

"Concentrate!" John snapped. "When you refuse, I'm going to hit you, and I want you to fall down crying. Understand?"

Helen didn't really understand, but she nodded anyway.

"Good," John said. He then pointed at the remains of the bivouac and shouted, "Do as I say and fix it!"

"No," Helen said, playing along.

John smacked her face with the palm of his hand—not too hard, but not too soft either. Helen fell to the ground as instructed. When she scrambled to her feet, she was crying, and, if her assailant wasn't mistaken, her tears were for real. The smack had left an imprint on her sunburnt face and John could see she was in pain. "Sorry," he whispered. Shouting once more, he pointed at the broken bivouac, raised his hand threateningly and repeated his order of a few moments earlier.

This time Helen hurried to attend to the bivouac's repairs.

Glancing around, John was pleased to see nearly everyone in the encampment had seen the incident.

If there was ever any doubt she's my woman there should be none now.

He was aggrieved to see the incident had also been witnessed by Carravanty, and he made a mental note to explain his actions to the youth later.

Turning his attention back to Helen, he saw she was making hard work of the repairs. He quickly knelt down beside her and showed her how to weave the leafy branches together and how to secure them with the flax ties the previous owners had left behind. As they worked side by side, he murmured, "Thanks for playing along, Miss Marsden."

"Thank you for coming to find me, Mister Graham," Helen whispered. By this time, she had worked out that John was playing some sort of game for the benefit of her captors. She couldn't help smiling to show how relieved she was to see him.

"Don't smile!" John warned. "They are still watching us." He wasn't sure whether the clan members were still watching them, but he wasn't prepared to take chances.

A moment later, Helen asked, "Did you find Eliza?"

John nodded. "She is safe now," he said.

Helen couldn't hide her relief. "Thank God," she murmured. "Is she well?" she asked.

"As well as could be expected," John said.

The young Englishwoman then looked pointedly at John's loincloth. "I almost didn't recognise you"—this time she *had* to smile—"in that outfit."

John struggled to hide his embarrassment. He looked at the dirty, torn bodice and petticoat Helen was wearing and muttered, "Nor I you." To her credit, he observed, she didn't try to cover up her near-nakedness. Nor did she even look embarrassed.

When the bivouac's repairs were completed, the Irishman suggested Helen go to a nearby billabong to quench her thirst. He could see she was dehydrated and, if he wasn't mistaken, had a touch of sunstroke to go with her thirst and sunburn. Helen gratefully hobbled over to the watering hole.

John watched her as she drank her fill and began hobbling back toward him. Though weak and hindered by her blistered feet, he could tell she remained unbowed by her captivity, and her spirit remained undaunted.

Maybe this will be an easier rescue than Missus Fraser's.

When Helen returned, John motioned to her to sit down next to him. Over the next short while he told her all about Eliza, and he explained that her father awaited her aboard *the New Yorker.*

For the young woman, the news got better and better. Her eyes were shining with hope by the time he'd finished. "Thank God, you came," she said. "I feared I would be with these savages forever."

"They aren't savages, Helen," John advised her. He could see she wasn't convinced. "Don't forget, the last whites these people saw, before you and Eliza ended up in their midst, was when your father's men attacked the clan." He added, "Many clan members lost loved-ones that day."

Helen made no comment, but John could see she was considering the wisom of his words. "There's something else you should know," he said at length.

"Oh?"

"Yes. They think you are my woman."

Helen's eyes opened wide at that news. "And why would they think that?" She didn't mind them thinking she was his, but she wasn't going to give him the satisfaction of knowing that.

Before John could answer, Carravanty wandered over toward them.

"Let me introduce you to my son," John said to Helen when he saw the young man.

"Your son?" Helen asked.

Next moment, Carravanty was standing before them. The Irishman did the introductions, and then acted as translator as Helen and the youth conversed. It wasn't long before the pair were chatting like old friends.

Later that afternoon, John found himself conversing with Mirritji in the shade of the elder's bivouac.

"We thought you were dead, Moilow," Mirritji told him. He referred to the day Barega tracked him to the Kabis' encampment and overpowered him whilst he was in the bush teaching Carravanty how to make fire.

"I thought I was dead, too," John said. He then brought the elder up to date with all that had transpired since that fateful day.

While the white spoke, Mirritji observed him through all-knowing eyes. "Moilow," he said, insisting on using the name he'd always used, "I am an old man. Soon we will need a new leader."

There was a long pause, and John wondered what was coming next.

Finally, Mirritji said, "When I am gone, Gabirri will take my place."

He and John glanced over at Gabirri who was at that moment teaching a group of young boys how to skin a wallaby he'd speared a short while earlier.

"He will be a great leader," John said.

The old man nodded wisely. "Gabirri will need your counsel," he said. John went to speak, but the elder quickly said, "Mirritji knows the white invaders will keep coming. Soon there will be more. The shaman said it was so." He looked back at John. "The clan needs someone who knows the white man's way . . . Moilow knows the white man's way."

John let his eyes wander over to Helen who, he saw, was watching them intently from the shade of their newly repaired bivouac.

"There is a connection between you and the white woman," Mirritji observed.

"As I said, she is my woman," John reminded him.

Mirritji smiled.

John wasn't sure whether the elder was acknowledging his statement as fact or whether he was humouring him. He suspected the latter. Still looking at Helen, John said, "I must return her to her people. If not, many soldiers will come for her and many Kabi will die."

Mirritji thought on this carefully for a long time. Eventually, he said, "The woman will be your wife and she will be a mother to Carravanty. If the invaders come for her, or for you, Moilow, we will fight them together, as one . . . Mirritji has spoken." With that, the elder stood up and strode off atop his now impossibly bandy legs.

A somewhat disillusioned John wandered back to join Helen. His talk with Mirritji hadn't gone as well as he'd wanted. He had been hoping to receive the elder's blessing to take Helen away—especially now that the old man was effectively the clan's leader. His blessing would have cleared the way for the Englishwoman's rescue. Now he feared he'd have to do it the hard way.

Only now did he notice many of the clan members were quitting the encampment and preparing to head off to other parts of the island. He stopped to observe them go, and was relieved to see without exception they headed east, toward the coastline farthest away from *the New Yorker* and the soldiers he still believed were aboard her.

That'll make my task easier.

John guessed the departing Kabi were headed for the canoes that would return them to the mainland. He was fairly certain they must have hidden their craft somewhere on the island's eastern shore because *the New Yorker* had sailed the full length of the western shoreline during daylight hours and, to his knowledge, had not sighted a single canoe.

The Irishman resumed walking. When he reached Helen, he stood looking down at her. "We leave tonight," he said.

107

DUSK DESCENDED AT THE PLACE of totems, and daylight was replaced by the flickering light of scores of cooking fires throughout the Kabi encampment. John, Helen and Carravanty sat with Gabirri and his extended family around one of the fires as Gabirri's two wives served portions of brazed kangaroo meat to the assembled.

Looking around, John estimated the clan members' numbers had been reduced by about half following the departure of so many that afternoon. Even so, he reckoned, a good two hundred and fifty still remained.

There was much laughter and hilarity—all of which went over Helen's head. John was in the middle of relating to their Kabi hosts his experiences over the past three years. The tale took a while to relate because he had to stop frequently to field questions and to translate for Helen's benefit.

Mirritji, Turo and several other men drifted over to Gabirri's group to see what all the hilarity was about.

Before long, the group's numbers had swollen to about fifty. Some of the men began to dance to the sounds of a didgeridoo and the drumming of sticks, attracting still more clan members. Carravanty joined them. The men mimicked the jerky movements of the dingo and the emu, and it was soon evident they were becoming entranced by the mesmerising effect of the accompaniment.

"Why do they do that?" Helen asked. She had to lean close to John and repeat herself to make herself heard.

John grinned. "I would need all night to explain it," he said.

Before Helen could question him further, the Irishman jumped up and joined in the dancing. Astonished, the young woman watched as her would-be rescuer became Kabi-like before her very eyes. It slowly dawned on her that he belonged here.

Sitting opposite Helen, on the other side of the cooking fire, Mirritji observed the young woman's reactions and smiled to himself.

When the dancing ended, John returned to Helen's side. He saw she was nearly falling asleep. "Time to bed down," he said, leading her away to their bivouac. He was pleased to see, the other clan members were preparing to retire for the night. Their cooking fires had almost burnt themselves out.

Some four miles away, in a clearing in the rainforest, Lieutenant Otter listened intently as Barega briefed him on what he'd observed at the Kabi encampment less than an hour earlier. Nearby, the lieutenant's men sat around a large fire, talking quietly.

Breathless after his recent exertions, the tracker said, "The Irish and white woman . . . both there."

"You are sure it was them?" Otter asked.

Barega nodded, placing the two spears he'd been carrying on the ground.

"What were they doing?"

"Corroboree," the tracker said.

The lieutenant had been in the colony long enough to know what a corroboree was. He'd witnessed a few. "Security?" he asked.

Barega looked puzzled.

"How many lookouts were posted around the camp?" Otter asked, rephrasing the question.

"Only few, Mister."

Otter was grateful for that. He assumed the Irishman must have convinced Helen's captors that the soldiers wouldn't bother them.

As the briefing came to an end, Barega looked beyond Otter into the darkness. He hadn't seen or heard anything, but he sensed watchful eyes upon the lieutenant and himself at that moment.

Otter returned to the soldiers who were still huddled around the fire, leaving his tracker to his own resources as always.

Barega picked up his spears then turned and headed back into the rainforest. He was even more certain now someone was watching them from the far side of the clearing. As soon as he was out of sight, he quickly and quietly doubled around to where he'd sensed the presence of others. He arrived just in time to make out two shadowy figures. They hadn't seen him.

Studying the pair, the tracker knew they were Kabi even though it was too dark to make out any distinguishing features. He had tracked and observed Kabi for so long now he could tell immediately who they were just by their attitude, their weapons and even their smell. Barega prided himself on being able to smell his fellow Man. He'd lived with nature for so long now he had all the instincts of a wild animal.

The first the shadowy pair knew they were themselves being observed was when a spear thudded into the back of one of them. His companion sprinted off before the assailant could loose another spear in his direction.

Barega took off after the escapee, satisfied the man's companion was already dead. The spear had struck him exactly where he'd intended, between the shoulder blades.

The race through the rainforest took less than ten minutes, which was considerably longer than the tracker expected. He had yet to meet his equal in a footrace, but on this occasion his quarry had given him a run for his money for a while at least. He'd caught up to him in a dead-end gully. When the fleeing Kabi clan member saw he had nowhere to go, he'd drawn his nulla nulla and turned to meet his enemy. Barega's second spear had struck him in the belly, felling him immediately.

On seeing his prey was still alive, the tracker had been content to use the native's own nulla nulla to smash both his knee caps. He wanted to leave him to a slow, painful death, but he didn't want to risk him crawling back to his clan to sound the alarm. Before returning to the soldiers, he smashed both his victim's ankles to make doubly sure he didn't go anywhere.

John and Helen sat talking to each other in the darkness of their bivouac. It was so dark only the whites of their eyes, and occasionally the whites of their teeth, were visible. There was an undercurrent of tension in the confined space for each knew they would soon be making a bid for freedom.

Every now and then, the Irishman glanced out the shelter's small opening to see if the clan members were asleep. He was keen to make an early start, but he didn't want the alarm to go up before they'd even departed the encampment. And so he bided his time.

"Tell me why the men dance like that?" Helen asked. She had been intrigued by the strange, ritualistic dancing she'd observed earlier.

"I would need all night to explain," John said, "and all tomorrow, too." He couldn't see the flash of impatience that registered on Helen's face, but he sensed it. "Very well," he sighed. "The dancers imitate the actions of animals . . . animals they hold sacred to them . . . like the dingo . . . and they do that to . . . ah . . . to tell a story."

"A story? What kind of story?"

"About the Dreamtime."

"I have heard Orana talk—"

"Orana?"

"Our maid. I have heard her talk about the Dreamtime."

"Oh." John recalled the maid she referred to. Continuing, he said, "They also call it the Dreaming." Anticipating his one-woman audience's next question, he said, "The Dreaming is another story for another day."

The silence between them stretched out. Sitting here, so close to each other in total privacy, was a surreal experience for both of them. The unrequited feelings each had for the other were still there, very close to the surface, and yet each knew, deep down, theirs was a relationship that could never be.

John glanced outside once more and was relieved to see no movement other than a lookout pacing up and down on the far side of the encampment. He knew it would be prudent to wait a while longer, but he was mindful that every minute counted because the Kabi would come for them as soon as their absence was noted. And it would be noted at sun-up at the very latest, of that he was sure.

"Are they sleeping yet?" Helen asked.

John nodded. Remembering she couldn't see him in the dark, he said, "Yes." He added, "It's time to go." With that, he grabbed her arm and led her from the bivouac. They crawled out on all fours.

Outside, they slowly stood up and looked around. All was quiet. The Kabi were sleeping.

"This way," John whispered as he led Helen around behind the bivouac and toward the shelter of the nearby trees.

108

EVEN BEFORE THEY REACHED THE rainforest, John could see Helen was hobbling badly. "Hop on board," he insisted, bending forward to allow her to climb onto his back.

Giggling, Helen did as she was told.

"Shhh!" John warned her.

"Sorry," Helen whispered. After they'd gone a few paces piggyback style through the rainforest, she said, "We won't get far like this."

John didn't mention they didn't have far to go before their first stop, and it was only a matter of a minute or so before he pulled up in front of the towering fig tree in which he'd hidden his pack the previous day. "Hop off," he ordered.

"What is it?" Helen asked, concerned, as she slid to the ground.

Without explaining, John reached into the hole in the tree's trunk to retrieve the pack. He quickly pulled his hand out when a black snake slithered out of the hole. If he'd been a fraction slower, the deadly reptile would have bitten him. He glanced around and saw that Helen hadn't noticed the near miss, and he decided there was no need to alarm her so he didn't draw her attention to it. Checking the contents of the pack to ensure the snake's mate wasn't inside it, he pulled out his boots and threw them away.

The significance of that act wasn't lost on Helen. It was obvious to her that the Irishman was most comfortable when barefoot and dressed like his Kabi friends.

John then pulled out the replacement raincoat he'd brought with him and handed it to Helen. "You'll need this," he said, advising her as he had Eliza that it would protect her sunburnt shoulders in the rainforest. He didn't see any need to add that it would also allow her some modesty.

Helen gratefully donned the lightweight coat and watched with interest as John pulled out the remains of the roo pelt he'd salvaged after making his loincloth. He then drew out his knife and cut the pelt in two, placing the pieces in front of his companion's bare feet. "Place your foot on that," he said, tapping Helen's left foot.

The young woman did as she was told and watched as her rescuer bound her foot so that the pelt now resembled a moccasin. "Clever man," she murmured. She watched with growing admiration as he repeated the process with her right foot.

When both feet were bound, John reached up and pulled several sizeable leaves from the fig tree. He then used these to fashion protective soles to reinforce Helen's improvised footwear.

"You are a wasted talent, John Graham," she whispered.

Ignoring her, John then produced two small strips of flax, which he'd had the foresight to scavenge from the bivouac they'd just vacated, and these he used to secure the leaves to the moccasins. "There you go," he whispered. "Good as new." He motioned to her to try walking a little distance.

Helen walked ten yards or so with little discomfort. Delighted, she looked back at him. "Thank you, kind sir," she smiled as she returned to his side.

John then pulled from his pack one of the two full water bottles he'd brought with him, and handed it to Helen. "You'll need this, too." He waited while she took a quick swig from the bottle. "Let's go," he urged. "No time to waste."

Helen saw he'd already slipped his pack over his shoulders and was heading deeper into the rainforest. She had to hurry to catch up to him.

⋅⋅⋅

"You okay?" John asked as he assisted Helen down a steep, slippery incline.

"Yes," Helen said as she leaned on her rescuer to avoid falling. "How far to go?" she asked.

John chuckled. "We've only been walking an hour," he pointed out.

"I know, but how much further?"

"Two days' trek."

"Two days?" Helen was shocked. She'd imagined they were a lot closer to the coast.

"And that's if we're lucky," John added. "We will hole up during daylight hours."

"Hence the two days," Helen said.

"Aye."

On reaching the bottom of the incline, they walked in silence for a while.

Never one to remain quiet for too long, Helen finally asked, "How did you find me?"

"Mirritji told me where you were."

"Oh . . . but how did you *actually* find me?"

"The Songlines guided me." John immediately regretted divulging that little piece of information. He knew he was about to be extensively grilled just as he had been about the Dreaming earlier.

"Songlines?" Helen asked. "What Songlines?"

John sighed to himself.

Here we go.

He couldn't even adequately explain the Songlines to his own satisfaction. Nevertheless he knew he had to try to answer the question because the inquisitive Miss Marsden wouldn't let up. "The Songlines are tracks the Kabis' spirit ancestors made when they created the land," he said.

Helen let him speak without interrupting for once. Although she had many questions, she wanted to let him explain things in his own time, in his own words.

As he explained the Songlines, it occurred to her the affection he had for the Kabi was evident in everything he said, even in the tone of his voice. As before, she was slightly taken aback by this realisation.

When John finally finished, she asked, "Are the Songlines related to the Dreaming?"

"Yeah," John said. "If they sing certain songs and perform certain ceremonies at sacred places along the spirit ancestors' tracks, they will eventually be led to their spirit world."

"To the Dreaming," Helen said.

"To the Dreaming," John confirmed. He was about to expand on that when he suddenly pulled up, causing his companion to bump into him.

"What?" Helen asked, alarmed.

John didn't answer.

Helen looked at him and saw that he was staring straight ahead into the darkness. It took her a few moments before she saw what he'd seen. A native was standing not twenty yards away, looking at them. He was holding two spears. Helen didn't know it, but John and Eliza had had a very similar experience, except this time it wasn't Mirritji standing there in the dark.

"He is with us," John whispered. Even in the dark, the Irishman had recognised Barega. The tracker's impressive physique and abnormally long legs were a dead giveaway. Looking at Barega, he asked, "Did you come alone?"

Barega shook his head. "Soldiers come for you and woman," he said.

That wasn't what John wanted to hear. News that the soldiers were coming confirmed that Cheetham and Marsden had gone back on their word. More worryingly, the presence of soldiers anywhere on the island increased the possibility of bloodshed. "Where are they?" he asked.

The tracker pointed behind him. "They sleep now . . . four mile . . . that way," he said.

"Damn," John muttered. They were much too close to the Kabi encampment for comfort.

"What is it?" Helen asked.

John translated for Helen's benefit what the tracker had just told him, and he explained he feared another bloodbath if the soldiers reached the encampment. Looking at Barega, he said, "Take us to them . . . Quickly."

The tracker turned and began striding back the way he'd come. John and Helen hurried after him.

It was after midnight when they came across the soldiers. Otter had posted five sentries around the campsite, and it was one of them who greeted the new arrivals.

"Halt!" the sentry ordered, pointing his rifle at the trio. In the dark they were but shadows to him. "Who goes there?" he asked.

John could tell the sentry was nervous, and he hoped the man wasn't trigger-happy. He thought he recognised his voice. "Private Withers?" he enquired. He remembered the young soldier used to chaperone Lord Cheetham around the penal settlement on a horse-drawn cart.

"*Corporal* Withers now," Withers informed him. The sentry sounded less nervous than he had a moment earlier. He asked, "Is that . . ." His voice trailed off when he noticed Helen amongst the three standing before him.

"Yes, you can advise Captain Marsden his daughter is safe and sound," John said.

Withers stepped forward to inspect the two whites more closely. He was as John remembered him except his once hairless face now sported a beard. The look on his face told him the sentry didn't know what to make of the white man standing before him in a loincloth.

The sentry turned to Helen. "Your father will be pleased to see you, Miss," he said.

"I should hope so," Helen said brightly. "Is he here?"

"Ah . . . no, Miss," Withers said. "I believe he is waiting for you at the beachhead. Lieutenant Otter is our senior officer."

"Well, best take us to him then," John suggested. The edge in his voice suggested they didn't have all night to stand around chatting.

Withers took the hint and escorted the pair into the camp. Barega had already left them to it, disappearing into the night.

The site Otter had chosen to overnight in was a small clearing in the rainforest. It was only just big enough to accommodate the twenty-four soldiers under his command.

John's first impression was that Otter had shown a lack of judgement in choosing the site. It was, in his opinion, nigh on indefensible with trees and dense undergrowth pressing in on all sides, leaving the soldiers exposed to a surprise attack. In the event of an attack, he could see, there was no cover for the defenders.

Otter and those soldiers not on sentry duty were fast asleep. In the darkness, they were but shadowy figures lying around the remains of a campfire which had long since burnt itself out.

Withers walked over to the lieutenant and woke him. To his credit, Otter came fully alert almost immediately. His first reaction upon seeing who the corporal had brought to him was one of disappointment. He'd been planning to attack the Kabi encampment at dawn to rescue Helen. Just moments earlier he had been dreaming of the hero's welcome he'd receive when he returned as a successful warrior to the beachhead with his superior's daughter. Hiding his disappointment, he dismissed Withers then smiled at Helen and extended his hand. "How wonderful to see you again, Miss Marsden," he said.

"Thank you, Lieutenant," Helen smiled, accepting Otter's hand. Glancing at John, she added, "It is because of Mister Graham's heroism that I am here."

Only now did Otter look at John. "I hardly recognised you, Graham," he said, glancing pointedly at the Irishman's loincloth. He added, "Thought you were a bloody Abo for a moment there."

Ignoring Otter's sarcasm, John said, "I am sure Miss Marsden would like to rest now, and she needs something for her sore feet. *And* we could both do with something to eat."

"Of course," Otter jumped to do as John suggested. The lieutenant realised to do otherwise would appear churlish in Helen's eyes. As he hurried off, John suggested he find some clothes and footwear for Helen as well. Otter cursed the Irishman under his breath.

John and Helen claimed one of the few patches of grass not already occupied by the sleeping soldiers or their supplies, and waited while Otter woke two of his men and ordered them to look after the new arrivals.

One soldier rustled up some food rations while the other—a sleepy young private who doubled as the expedition's medic—fetched ointment and bandages for Helen's feet. Unsure what was expected of him, the young private handed the items to her.

"Thank you, Private," Helen smiled as she removed her makeshift moccasins and began rubbing the ointment onto her blistered feet.

Blushing, the young soldier said, "We brought a change of clothes for you—and some shoes for you as well, Miss. I'll see if I can find them." He hurried off, returning moments later with the items he'd referred to. "I'd best bandage your feet, Miss," the soldier suggested.

"Leave that until daylight," a thoughtful Helen said.

The private smiled, grateful that he could now get back to sleep. "Thank you, Miss," he mumbled, leaving the new arrivals to themselves.

Taking advantage of the darkness, Helen quickly discarded her petticoat and donned the garments she'd received.

John and Helen sat down on the plastic sheet the Irishman had recovered from his pack, and they tucked into the food rations the other soldier had supplied them with. When they finished eating, they lay down and prepared for sleep. Around them, all except for the sentries were now fast asleep.

"Goodnight, John Graham," Helen murmured.

Even though it was still dark, John could tell she was smiling. "Goodnight, Miss Marsden," he said.

The sound of their breathing in the still night air reminded each that only a few inches separated them.

An hour later, John and Helen were still wide awake. Whether it was their close proximity to each other or the excitement of having quit the Kabi encampment without being challenged, neither was sure.

"Are you awake?" Helen asked, knowing full well he was. She could tell by his breathing pattern.

"Yes," John murmured.

Helen took a deep breath. She had something to ask, and she wasn't sure how to put it. At length she asked, "May I ask you a personal question?" She hurriedly added, "You don't have to tell me if you don't want to." She spoke quietly so as not to wake the soldiers around them.

"Alright," a hesitant John said. He wasn't sure what was coming.

"I . . . ah, my father said you weren't transported to Australia just for stealing from your employer . . . is that correct?" she asked.

John didn't answer her immediately. He tried not to revisit his distant past these days, preferring to focus on his future, or what was left of it. There were things in his past he'd rather forget. Things he wasn't proud of. Finally, he said, "I killed him . . . stabbed him to death, Helen." *There it is,* he thought. *Now she knows.*

After a long, long silence, Helen asked, "Why?"

She spoke so quietly, John wondered if he'd heard her correctly. "Why?" he asked. When the young Englishwoman said nothing, he said, "I have asked myself the same question these past ten years . . . and I still have no satisfactory answer."

Still Helen said nothing.

John continued, "I was a young man . . . full of anger toward a system that kept poor people like me and my máthair downtrodden while the wealthy lauded it over our kind . . . When my employer didn't pay me wages due, I overlooked it . . . When that happened again . . . and again . . . and again, I . . . I struck out." John was on a roll now. After having bottled it up inside him for so long, it was a huge relief to share it with someone. He said, "When I finally acted . . . I didn't even realise I'd killed him. I never meant to . . . it . . . it just happened." Only now, as he unburdened himself, did he realise he was crying silent tears of guilt and shame.

Sensing John's pain, Helen reached out and placed her hand on his arm. A moment later, he placed his hand over hers and kept it there.

Eventually, the events of the day caught up with them both and they began to drift off to sleep.

Just before Helen fell asleep, she whispered, "That was the past. You are a good man now, John Graham." She didn't know if he'd heard her.

He did hear her, and it brought him comfort.

109

LIEUTENANT OTTER'S MEN COULDN'T KEEP their eyes off the two new arrivals who had ended up in their midst unbeknown to most of them during the night. One of those new arrivals, John, joined them as they tucked into their first meal of the day around a roaring fire. The other, Helen, remained fast asleep nearby.

Word had quickly spread that the Englishwoman they'd come to liberate had been rescued by the Irishman who was now eating alongside them. Like their commanding officer, many of them were disappointed that they wouldn't be seeing action—and there was no small amount of resentment that John had done their job for them.

Although it was not yet dawn, there was sufficient light to alert the soldiers to the fact that the Irishman who was now eating alongside them wore only a loincloth.

"It appears we are in the company of a bloody Abo," one wag observed.

"Aye," a Scottish corporal said, looking pointedly at John's loincloth. "Looks like the Irishman's gone native on us!"

His companions rowdily agreed with him.

Unfazed, John eyed the Scotsman. "If it's alright for your countrymen to wear tartan dresses in the highlands, Scottie, it's alright for me to wear a loincloth out here in the colonies," he replied, effectively silencing the Scotsman.

The banter subsided, but only momentarily.

"I know what he reminds me of," a Welsh private said, pointing at John.

"What's that?" someone asked.

"He reminds me of a stick insect in a nappy!" the Welshman said, sparking loud guffaws.

Quick as a flash, John responded, "Well Taffy, when me nappy next needs changing I'll be sure to come to you." This prompted more raucous laughter.

"Quiet, men!" Lieutenant Otter shouted from the other side of the clearing where he stood conversing with one of the sentries. He added, "Don't dally you lot because we need to be gone by sunrise."

The soldiers quietened, but only but only for a little while. They just couldn't contain themselves. The Irishman in the loincloth was too tempting a target for bored men, and the jibes started all over again.

To Helen's amusement, John took it all in good grace, throwing the banter back at his antagonists until they finally tired of the game. The rowdy repartee had awoken her a few moments earlier, but she gave no sign that she was awake. She was enjoying the pre-dawn entertainment too much, and feared the men would behave themselves if they knew she'd woken.

The soldiers were relieved to be able to let off some steam. Like their commanding officer, they'd been looking forward to seeing some action. Helen's unexpected arrival in their midst had put paid to that, and they were resigned to not being able to satisfy their bloodlust or put their bravery and their marksmanship to the test.

No-one was more disappointed about the latest turn of events than Otter. It was eating away at him that he'd been deprived of his chance for glory. On waking, he'd come close to disobeying orders and confronting the Kabi even though there was now no reason to. It was only with extreme self-discipline that he resisted the temptation to act on his desires.

Finally, Helen stirred, and the men noticed. The same young private who had assisted the new arrivals just hours earlier held true to his word when he approached Helen to bandage her feet. His task wasn't made easy by his fellow soldiers who directed suggestive comments his way, and he blushed when Helen informed him he should ignore the others because they were only jealous.

The private hurried off as soon as he'd completed his task, leaving Helen to try on the shoes that had been brought for her. To her disappointment, she found they wouldn't fit her bandaged feet. John immediately came to the rescue, securing the makeshift moccasins to her feet once more. She took a few steps and was relieved to find her footwear was even more comfortable now that her feet were bandaged. "Perfect," she said.

"Best get something to eat," John suggested. "We will be heading out soon."

"I will join you in a moment," Helen said. She needed to pee. After retreating a little way into the surrounding trees, she re-joined John who had resumed eating and was once more exchanging banter with the soldiers.

The men fell silent when Helen joined them. Lieutenant Otter aside, none quite knew how to behave when in the company of such a beautiful and sophisticated young woman. So, to a man, they opted for silence, focussing their attention on the last of the food they were devouring. One by one, they stood and packed their overnight gear away in preparation for the long trek back to the beachhead.

John and Helen had talked little since the Irishman's confession of a few hours earlier. It was Helen who broke the strained silence that now existed between them. "What are you planning to do when you receive your ticket of leave, John?" she asked. He'd already told her he had a signed ticket of leave from Cheetham.

"Honestly, I don't know," John said.

After another long silence, Helen asked, "Would you stay here?" When the Irishman didn't respond, she said, "Perhaps you belong here, John."

◦€⸱———⸱3◦

Mirritji looked around the place of totems. The sun was already a finger's span above the eastern horizon, and most clan members had eaten and were preparing for the day ahead. His attention was drawn to a group of youths heading out to hunt. Carravanty was leading the way. The provisions he and his companions carried indicated they could be away for a day or two.

Seeing Carravanty reminded Mirritji of John and Helen. He looked over at the bivouac the couple had retired to the previous evening, and thought it spoke volumes that they hadn't arisen yet. The old man considered waking them, but he could well imagine they needed extra sleep after a night of energetic lovemaking. So he left them to it.

Closer to the couple's bivouac, Gabirri was having similar thoughts. However, he wasn't as considerate as Mirritji. He strode over to the bivouac and looked inside it. On realising the whites weren't there, he immediately suspected they'd run off, and he reported his discovery to Mirritji.

After urgent discussion with other elders, it was decided to send three trackers to hunt the couple down and return them to the encampment. After all, the clan members had decreed that John and Helen belonged to the clan.

While the Kabi trackers tracked John and Helen, Marsden himself was anxiously awaiting news of his daughter at the beachhead that had been established on the island's western shore. The captain had recovered from his bout of illness and was currently inspecting the beachhead, which had been further fortified in anticipation of an attack.

In addition to the remaining four enlisted men on duty, four armed crewmen from *the New Yorker* had been rostered on to provide extra firepower in case it was required. The schooner's master had needed some cajoling before he agreed to releasing the crewmembers from normal duties, but Marsden had convinced him by increasing the bonus he and his crew could expect on their return to Moreton Bay. The four crewmen also doubled as oarsmen for the longboat, which they guarded with their lives. A sensible precaution given their lives may well depend on it.

Marsden was pleased to see the crewmen looked as alert and capable as his soldiers—even if they were still suffering the lingering after-effects of the dysentery that had laid them and him low. Though he didn't expect trouble this far from the Kabis' last reported encampment, he believed in being prepared.

The sight of a skiff making its way from the schooner to shore caught Marsden's eye. He cursed to himself when he identified its solitary passenger as Cheetham. The captain had enough on his plate without having to engage in small talk with the commandant.

Hiding his frustration, Marsden stepped forward to greet his superior when the skiff beached close to the longboat. "Good morning, my Lord," he said, assisting Cheetham from the skiff. "What brings you ashore?"

"I just wanted to check the beachhead for myself, Captain," the older man said, casting his eye over the soldiers and crewmen nearby as he lit up a cigar. He and Marsden always observed formalities when the soldiers were within earshot. "Any news?" he asked.

Marsden shook his head. "No, my Lord."

Cheetham looked up at the giant sand-dunes towering above the beach as if expecting to see Lieutenant Otter and his men appear with John and Helen. Turning back to Marsden, he said, "They should be back by now."

"They would only be back by now if they marched non-stop with barely a pause to rest," Marsden said, barely able to control his growing impatience. He was aware Cheetham was trying to exert his superiority, and was conveniently ignoring the fact that the chain of command in the field didn't rest with him.

Cheetham shook his head as if to signify he was dealing with a novice then looked back to the top of the sand-dunes.

Both men knew there was every chance the soldiers would return without Helen. And both knew if that transpired decisions would need to be made—the main one being whether to keep looking or return to Moreton Bay. Cheetham already knew the answer. As for Marsden, that was an eventuality he wasn't prepared to consider yet.

Barega, who had taken it upon himself to watch out for any Kabi who may be pursuing John and Helen, saw the three trackers Mirritji had despatched long before they saw him. They'd evidently tracked the couple to the clearing the soldiers had overnighted in, in the rainforest, and now were having no problems tracking their quarry as they continued toward the coast. Trampled undergrowth, bent and broken branches, discarded military rations and a myriad of other signs made the trio's task ridiculously simple.

One of the trackers trailed his companions by some distance—and it was him that Barega struck first. The well-placed spear that felled the unfortunate native entered his back and pierced his heart before exiting out his chest. He was dead before he could utter anything other than a startled grunt.

Barega paused only long enough to retrieve his spear as he set off after the other two.

The surviving trackers were running so close to each other that Barega couldn't kill one of them without his companion knowing. He noticed only the closest of them carried spears. The other carried a nulla nulla. Throwing caution to the wind, Barega launched one of his own spears at the nearest tracker, felling him in identical fashion to his first victim. The other tracker instinctively threw himself to one side, just managing to avoid the second spear Barega had thrown his way.

Barega drew his own nulla nulla and advanced on the surviving tracker. What the Kabi lacked in skill, he made up for in strength, and he struck his attacker a glancing blow that staggered Barega. Had it struck his head, the fight would have been over. As it was, it had struck his right shoulder, leaving it temporarily out of action. Barega was forced to transfer his nulla nulla to his left hand.

Sensing he had the advantage, the Kabi tracker attacked, swinging his weapon around his head and forcing his assailant to back-peddle. Barega bided his time until one mighty swing of the nulla nulla caused the Kabi to momentarily lose balance. That was the opening Barega was waiting for, and he struck with the speed of a snake, clubbing his opposite over the head.

Stunned, the Kabi tracker dropped his nulla nulla and fell onto all fours. Barega watched as he desperately tried to regain his feet, but his limbs wouldn't oblige. His arms gave way and he fell on his face. The next blow shattered his spine and rendered him unconscious.

Barega sat down and waited for his victim to come round. It took a little while, but when the Kabi recovered consciousness, he was horrified to see his assailant sitting nearby, watching him. Barega looked on in amusement as his victim tried to crawl away. Only now, as he tried to stand up, did the poor fellow realise he was paralysed.

After what seemed an eternity to the injured native, Barega stood up and walked over to him. Using his left arm, for his right arm was still numb from the earlier blow he'd received, he brought his nulla nulla down on his victim's right arm, shattering the bone. The Kabi screamed, startling a small flock of parrots which had been nesting in nearby trees. The parrots flew off in search of a more peaceful nesting place.

Satisfied the Kabi tracker was in no condition to return to his clan, Barega sauntered off to collect his spears and then catch up to Lieutenant Otter and his men. He smiled to himself as the Kabi's agonised groans carried to him.

110

I T WAS EARLY AFTERNOON BEFORE Barega caught up to the soldiers. He was breathing hard, having run non-stop since ambushing the Kabi trackers hours earlier.

Barega reported straight to Otter who was at the head of the column of soldiers. John and Helen were further back in the column, and they watched the pair converse. The Irishman wished he could hear what was being said.

Otter was interested to learn about Barega's altercation with the Kabi trackers. "There were only three of them you say?" he asked.

"Only three, Mister," Barega confirmed. The tracker then reported that he'd returned earlier to the Kabi encampment and had observed that many clan members had departed since his first visit.

"How many are left?" Otter asked, suddenly interested.

Barega shrugged. So large a number was beyond his linguistic abilities or understanding.

"How many, man?" a frustrated Otter asked.

Barega drew out his hunting knife and laboriously proceeded to draw symbols on the ground. "Bivouacs," he explained. He drew forty in all.

"Bivouacs?" Otter asked.

The tracker nodded.

Otter counted the symbols. "Forty bivouacs?"

Barega nodded again even though the number ten represented the limit of his understanding of the white man's numerals.

The lieutenant did some quick math in his head. Based on each bivouac accommodating an average of five people, forty bivouacs represented two hundred clan members in total. That was considerably less than the number Barega had indicated two or three days earlier.

Otter then grilled the tracker on the encampment's defences and the number of lookouts posted, and he was relieved to learn the site's security was lax. Barega said it was obvious the Kabi did not believe they were in any danger of being attacked.

This was music to the lieutenant's ears. All morning he'd been brooding about returning to the beachhead without having blooded his men, or himself for that matter. He yearned to taste action, and it had been eating away at him that he wouldn't get his chance.

Barega's report helped Otter reach a decision. He and his men would attack the encampment; they would avenge the deaths of their fellow soldiers at the hands of the Kabi, and they would return to Moreton Bay as heroes.

Encouraged by his tracker's report, and emboldened by the fact he knew Cheetham would back him even if Marsden didn't, Otter called his men to him. He quickly informed them of his intentions, taking care not to be overheard by John or Helen, and then he ordered two privates to escort the pair the rest of the way to the beachhead. The privates weren't at all happy that they would be missing out on the action, but their superior wasn't in the mood to listen to their grumbles.

Otter then approached John and Helen. "Two of my men will escort you back to the beachhead," he informed them.

"Why is that, Lieutenant?" a suspicious John asked.

"The tracker reports that the Kabi have sent natives out to prevent Miss Marsden from returning to the beachhead," Otter responded without hesitation, "so I am establishing a rear-guard with my men to ensure none get through."

That made good tactical sense to John, and yet he felt uneasy. Before he could question the lieutenant further, Otter returned to his men.

John and Helen, along with the two privates charged with escorting them to the beachhead, could only watch as Barega led the lieutenant and his men back the way they'd just come.

"Are we safe, John?" a concerned Helen asked.

"The Kabi can't get past so many soldiers with rifles," John assured her. Smiling, he added, "Besides, they don't want to hurt you." He could see she wasn't convinced, but there was no time for further discussion. The two remaining soldiers were making it clear they were anxious to get back to the relative safety of the beachhead.

As the four resumed their trek, John pondered Otter's decision.

If Barega's report was correct then it makes sense to establish a rear-guard.

And yet he was bothered by Otter's decision. Exactly why, he wasn't certain.

With every passing mile, John's concerns grew. Otter's enthusiasm to engage the Kabi had been almost gleeful. His enthusiasm had been infectious, too, and his men had seemed equally elated. Their attitude, to the Irishman's way of thinking, didn't match that of soldiers tasked with establishing a straightforward, defensive rear-guard. If he wasn't mistaken, they had the bloodlust. He recognised the signs.

Not for the first time, John's thoughts returned to the army's first bloody engagement with the Kabi.

At the place of totems, Mirritji and other elders walked separately amongst the clan members, advising them the decision had been made to depart for the mainland the following day. The decision, which had been made moments earlier, was greeted with the stoicism of people well used to uprooting themselves and relocating to new hunting and fishing grounds. They'd been doing it for thousands of years.

Only Mirritji's clan members, along with a few others from related clans, still remained at the encampment. The other remaining Kabi had left in dribs and drabs throughout the day, leaving around a hundred and sixty still to make the trek back to the island's east coast. There, they would retrieve their hidden canoes and paddle around the island and then back to the mainland. It was another routine they were well used to.

As he ambled from one bivouac to the next, Mirritji stopped and surveyed the surrounding rainforest. The afternoon shadows were lengthening and he'd expected by now to see at least one of the three trackers he'd sent out after John and Helen. In fact, he'd expected to see all three by now along with the two whites they'd been tasked with recapturing.

One part of Mirritji hoped John and Helen had eluded the trackers. Deep down, he sensed they belonged to each other, and to their own kind.

For John and Helen, their second night in the rainforest started much as their first night had. After eating army rations supplied by their escorts, they lay down—a little away from the two soldiers—on the same canvas sheet they'd used the previous night. And, as before, sleep eluded them.

John had good reason not to sleep. He was now convinced Otter planned to attack the Kabi, and he cursed himself that he hadn't realised that earlier.

"Penny for your thoughts," Helen murmured.

"I must go back," John whispered at length. He didn't need to whisper for the snores of the two privates told him they were fast asleep. Even so, he didn't want to risk waking them. When Helen didn't comment, he asked, "Did you hear me?"

"Yes," Helen said. After a long silence, she added, "I knew you would go back . . . You belong with the Kabi."

John thought she sounded sad, though he couldn't be sure. He propped himself up on one elbow then leaned over and kissed the young woman's cheek. "Bless you, Helen," he whispered. "You will make some lucky man a good wife one day."

Before she could respond, he was gone.

John forced himself to run hard through the rainforest. More certain than ever that Otter planned to attack the Kabi, he just hoped he'd be in time to alert the clan members before they were slaughtered. He knew the soldiers would attack either at dusk or dawn as those were the optimum times for a surprise raid, and he prayed they would opt for dawn.

If they attacked at dusk then I'm already too late.

Putting himself in Otter's shoes, he sensed the lieutenant would wait until dawn. That would give his men time to prepare and time to recover from their trek inland.

Even if Otter was planning a dawn raid, John knew it would be touch and go whether he'd arrive in time to sound the alarm. The thought of arriving too late drove him to run harder.

He didn't know how long he'd been running when he almost literally stumbled over the body of one of the Kabi trackers Barega had killed. It was Barega's first victim, and the dead native's spears and woomera still lay where he'd dropped them close by. John scooped them up without breaking stride and continued on his way.

Later that night, Otter surveyed the Kabi encampment from the cover of the rainforest while his men—or those not assigned to sentry duty at least—slept. The lieutenant was satisfied their presence hadn't been noted by the Kabi. Barega had assured him he'd dealt with the two lookouts the clan had posted, and he could see for himself the clan members were asleep.

Otter planned a dawn raid. Unlike Marsden's raid on the Kabi years earlier, his troops wouldn't be charging into the camp. The British Army had learned much since that doomed engagement. Rather than engaging the enemy, his men would surround the site and then open fire from the cover of the trees. That, he was certain, would ensure victory was achieved with minimum casualties. His reasoning was a bunch of spear-wielding savages couldn't kill what they couldn't see no matter how good they were in battle.

Looking up at the night sky, Otter estimated dawn was only an hour away. Already he could feel his excitement arising. He crept back into the rainforest to ready his men for what lay ahead.

John was breathing hard as he ran along a dry creek bed. The return journey to the centre of the island had taken him longer than expected. Dawn was already breaking and by his reckoning he was still an hour or more from the Kabi encampment.

A foreign sound carried to him. He stopped running and cocked his head to listen.

There it is again.

At first, he thought it was thunder. Then he realised it was gunfire. "God, no!" he shouted. He began sprinting along the creek bed.

The gunfire continued unabated, like rolling thunder, for all of ten minutes. Each and every individual shot made the Irishman grimace. With each shot, the faces of Kabi friends and loved-ones flashed before his eyes. Carravanty, Mirritji, Gabirri, Turo, Ekala, Karadji and many, many more.

Gradually, the gunfire dissipated. Soon there was only the occasional shot to be heard—and then silence.

For John, the silence was the worst. It signalled the end of the slaughter and the demise of the clan. He couldn't imagine anyone surviving such genocide.

The Irishman stopped running. He realised there was no point in hurrying. He knew he was too late to prevent the attack, and he knew what he'd find when he finally reached the encampment.

John experienced the same sharp pangs of guilt he felt the last time soldiers attacked the Kabi. The difference this time was he sensed many more clan members had died. "All because of me," he cursed.

In the grey light of dawn, John sat down on the baked earth of the creek bed and cried. He couldn't remember ever feeling so desolate—not since Mamba and Murrowdooling had been taken from him at least.

Finally, when he had no tears left, he stood up and resumed walking toward the encampment. He walked trance-like. He was in no rush now.

John didn't know how long he'd been walking when he heard voices coming from the trees up ahead. Gruff European voices.

Soldiers!

He quickly hid in a dense patch of bush just off the track he'd been following. As the soldiers approached, he could tell they were in a buoyant mood. Various lewd comments were greeted with bawdy laughter.

It wasn't long before John could make out what they were saying.

"We must've killed thirty of the bastards in the first fuckin' volley!" a Cockney soldier said.

"More like forty!" a fellow Cockney countered.

"Those boongas didn't know what hit 'em," a Devonshire corporal announced. This sparked more laughter.

"Keep it down to a dull roar, lads," Otter ordered from the front of the column.

John risked a peek as the first of the returning soldiers filed past his hiding place. The lieutenant was the first familiar face he saw. He couldn't help but notice the look on Otter's face was one of smug contentment.

Barega followed close behind the lieutenant. In addition to the spears and other weapons he carried, he now wore a colourful cloak over his loincloth. John recognised it. Made from the pelt of a roo, it belonged to Karadji, the shaman. The distinctive cloak didn't hide the silver crucifix the tracker still wore. It glinted in the early morning sunlight.

John switched his attention back to the soldiers. At first, he thought they had all been wounded as their uniforms were covered in blood. It took him a few moments to realise the blood was mainly that of their victims. Some soldiers had minor wounds, but it appeared all have survived. This confirmed what the Irishman had feared since hearing the gunfire: it had been a slaughter.

He wasn't to know, but his assessment of the recent conflict was very accurate.

By the time the soldiers had filed past his hiding place, he'd been able to form a picture of what had happened just by listening to their running commentary as they relived their moment of glory. It appeared they had surrounded the encampment and then, as dawn broke, simultaneously opened fire on the unsuspecting Kabi. The gunfire was so intense many clan members had died whilst still in their bivouacs. Some had even died in their sleep. It seemed those who ventured out into the open were quickly cut down. Only when victory was assured did Otter give the order to advance. The soldiers advanced with bayonets fixed and finished off the wounded. That also tallied with what John had observed: the soldiers' bayonets were covered in congealed blood.

No mention was made of survivors. Nor did the soldiers mention Barega's contribution to the slaughter. The tracker had taken it upon himself to finish off any clan members who managed to flee into the rainforest. In this task, he'd been spectacularly successful, killing all but a few who had escaped the initial gunfire. John didn't know this, but he could well imagine Barega had enthusiastically participated in the massacre.

The Irishman did a quick head count as the soldiers walked past his hiding place. He counted twenty-three in all, including Otter. At first he thought they'd lost two men because he recalled there were twenty-five in total. Then he remembered the two privates who were escorting Helen back to the beachhead. He wondered how she was coping without him.

When he was satisfied the last of the soldiers had passed by, John emerged from his hiding place and began running toward the encampment. He prayed he'd find survivors. He prayed especially for Carravanty.

111

THE SIGHT THAT GREETED JOHN upon arrival at the place of totems was déjà vu. Bodies lay strewn throughout the encampment—men, women, children and babies. Many had been bayonetted. Some of their wounds were too gory to look at.

A quick glance was all the shocked Irishman needed to establish the Kabi death toll this time was many times higher than the aftermath of the raid Marsden led.

One consolation for John was there were survivors. He hadn't expected to find any. The survivors—he counted eight in all—walked like zombies amongst the fallen. All but two were men. He recognised the survivors by sight, and he identified Mirritji, Gabirri and Turo amongst them. Like the others, they'd all suffered wounds of varying degrees and were bleeding badly.

The two women, who were also bloodied, were sitting together in the centre of the encampment, comforting each other as they wailed and chanted to the spirits of their ancestors. The only other sound was the unrelenting buzzing of the flies that hovered over the bodies.

John walked over to join the men. They saw him approach, but were too dazed to even acknowledge him. To reach them, he had to walk around and over bodies. He counted the dead as he walked. By the time the count reached seventy, he estimated he'd still only counted half the dead so he gave up. It was too depressing.

On reaching Mirritji's side, he said, "I bring you goodwill, Mirritji." As soon as he said it, he regretted opening his mouth. His words sounded hollow even to his ears.

The dazed elder just nodded by way of acknowledgement.

Studying Mirritji, John could see he was in pain. He'd suffered a bayonet wound to his right side, and it was bleeding profusely. "Let me help you," the Irishman said, reaching out to the older man.

Mirritji refused his help. "Moilow was right," he mumbled. "The white man came. I should have listened."

John had no words of comfort to offer, so he didn't respond.

Looking around at the dead, Mirritji said, "I need to be with my people." He wandered over to where a group of youths lay huddled together in death. They lay in a tangled heap of legs and arms, and it was evident all had been shot and bayonetted. Mirritji knew all by name, and he stood over them, chanting.

John recognised the chant. It was a prayer to the spirits of the youths' ancestors, asking that they guide the deceased to the Dreaming.

Looking around, he saw Turo was wandering aimlessly amongst the remains of the bivouacs, which, until this morning had accommodated his extended family. It appeared he'd lost them all—all five wives and eight children.

Gabirri, it seemed, had fared no better. Both his wives had died along with their three children. As for their parents and grandparents, they were all dead, too.

A movement in the trees behind Gabirri caught John's eye. A young woman appeared with her two young children—one a small boy whom she dragged along by the hand and the other a baby she clasped to her breast. They weren't alone either. Over the course of the day, more survivors drifted into the encampment in ones and twos. It seemed they'd escaped death by fleeing into the rainforest and by somehow avoiding Barega.

John kept an eye out for Carravanty. A search of the encampment had confirmed his boy was not amongst the dead. The Irishman wasn't to know that he and his friends were still away hunting.

It was late morning when Helen and her two escorts arrived at the army's beachhead on the island's western shore. The Englishwoman was nearly out on her feet by the time she scaled one of the towering dunes that separated the rainforest from the beach. Now, standing on the dune's summit, she cried for joy when she saw her father amongst those waiting by the longboat at the water's edge. She vaguely noticed *the New Yorker* anchored offshore, but she only had eyes for her dear papa.

Despite her sore feet and her exhaustion, she ran down the side of the dune, falling over twice before reaching the bottom. Her father was there to greet her as she finally staggered onto the beach, covered in sand. "Oh, papa," she said, "I feared I would never see you again!"

Marsden was too choked up to speak. He swooped his daughter up in his arms and held her tight.

Soon, they were both laughing and crying all at once.

Finally, Marsden lowered Helen onto the sand. Scowling at her with mock severity, he said, "You have led us on a merry dance these past few weeks, young lady."

"I am sure you don't hold me accountable for that, father," Helen smiled.

"No, I don't," the captain said.

"How is Eliza?" Helen asked.

"Missus Fraser is well, my dear girl." It was Cheetham who answered.

In her joy at seeing her father, Helen hadn't noticed Cheetham standing behind him. The commandant stepped forward and planted a kiss on the top of her head. He reeked of cigar smoke and marijuana, but she wasn't complaining. She was so happy to be reunited with her father. And she was so happy to be free.

"Where is John Graham and the rest of the men?" Marsden asked, looking around at the nearer of the two privates who had returned his daughter to the beach.

"Ah . . . Graham slipped away from us during the night, Captain," the young soldier said.

"And the others?" Marsden asked, not unduly alarmed to hear that the Irishman had run off. Helen's safe return rendered other concerns less worrisome than they might otherwise be.

The soldier said, "The tracker reported that the savages were coming for your daughter so Lieutenant Otter took the other men to mount a rear-guard action to prevent them getting through, sir."

"When was this?" Cheetham asked.

"Ah . . ." the young soldier looked at his companion.

"It was early yesterday afternoon, my Lord," the other private said.

Cheetham looked at Marsden. "They should be back by now," he grumbled.

Marsden nodded. "I can understand Lieutenant Otter's reasoning in mounting a rear-guard action if Barega's report was accurate, but I can think of no reason why he hasn't returned yet," he said.

"Unless they struck problems," Cheetham suggested.

"Or unless . . ." Marsden didn't finish his sentence, but he could tell the commandant knew what he was thinking.

It was Helen who finally cleared the air. "John . . . ah . . . Mister Graham feared the lieutenant was planning to attack the Kabi encampment," she said. "That is why he ran off . . . to try to prevent bloodshed."

"Did he tell you that?" Marsden asked.

"No," Helen said, "but I knew what he was thinking."

Marsden didn't ask her how she knew what the Irishman was thinking, though he was sorely tempted to. Then something else occurred to him. He looked at Cheetham to see if he had anything to offer. The commandant studiously avoided his gaze. Marsden knew then that there was something Cheetham wasn't telling him. He suspected Otter was after glory. He also suspected the commandant may have had a private word with his lieutenant before the latter had departed the beachhead. Hiding his anger, he turned to Helen, "We best get you back on board the schooner," he said. "You look like you could do with a wash and a good meal."

"And a good sleep," Helen smiled. "I haven't had a full night's sleep in weeks."

Marsden immediately made arrangements with the longboat's oarsmen to ferry his daughter back to *the New Yorker.* Cheetham decided to accompany her. He was looking forward to sharing an afternoon tipple or two with the schooner's master. It was a little on-board routine they'd gotten into in recent days.

By late that afternoon, at the place of totems, the trickle of survivors returning to the site ended. John did the math. Twenty-one clan members, it seemed, had survived; a hundred and forty, give or take, had died. Mirritji's clan, to all intents and purposes, was finished.

John kept an eye out for Carravanty, but there was no sign of him. At least the young man wasn't amongst the dead in the encampment. Twice now, the Irishman had inspected every single body and determined once and for all that Carravanty wasn't here. He hoped he'd escaped unscathed into the rainforest.

The surviving menfolk had finally begun the awful task of burning the dead.

There were too many bodies to bury, so the men—or those of them who were physically able at least—piled the corpses in heaps and then set fire to them, using branches, dry grass and leaves as fuel. The gruesome bonfires soon took, and it wasn't long before the encampment was hidden beneath smoke; the sickly smell of burning human flesh pervaded the atmosphere for miles around.

Those few women who had survived chanted to their ancestors' spirits, pleading for a safe passage to the Dreaming for their loved-ones.

Later, as the smoke cleared and night fell, John found himself sitting alongside Gabirri and Turo. Like the other survivors, the two natives were beside themselves with grief. They'd lost all their loved-ones, and they remained in a state of shock. They rarely spoke, and when they did they spoke in monosyllables.

John was in shock, too. He was also feeling extremely guilty. Guilty that yet again he and he alone was responsible for the tragedy that had befallen the Kabi. But above all else, he was feeling angry. Angry that the soldiers had acted as they did. Not for the first time, he wondered whose was the civilised world—the soldiers' world or the Kabis.' He believed he now knew the answer to that.

As the evening progressed, he could feel his anger building. It gradually spiralled into something else altogether. Something he didn't recognised at first. And then he realised what it was: it was hatred. Pure, blind hatred. Hatred toward those who had done this to his kin—for that's how he viewed his Kabi friends more than ever.

Almost without thinking, John began arming himself with weapons. There were plenty to choose from. They lay scattered all around where clan members had dropped them. It wasn't long before he had a bundle of spears, a woomera and two nulla nullas to complement the knife he carried.

Gabirri and Turo watched the white spirit as he prepared to head out. It was obvious to them what he was planning.

The two friends looked gravely at each other. Turo nodded almost unperceptively. Gabirri didn't miss the gesture. He pushed himself to his feet and extended his hand to Turo. His friend clasped the other's hand and hauled himself up to his feet. They stood there staring at each other for a moment and then set about arming themselves, too.

John had already started jogging toward the rainforest when Gabirri caught his attention and motioned to him to wait. He didn't have to wait long. It was only a few moments before the pair joined him. Between the three of them, they looked ready for war. They carried a dozen spears, five nulla nullas and three knives in total.

Only now did they notice Mirritji staring at them from the other side of the encampment.

The elder could see at a glance what the three men intended. How he wished he could join them. Unfortunately, his wounds and injuries prevented his participation in any such physical activity. He contented himself with a wave of his hand in the trio's direction.

Turo acknowledged Mirritji and then turned to John. "You lead the way, Moilow," he said.

John was happy to oblige. Although his friends were better trackers than he'd ever be, he knew the route the soldiers were following back to the beachhead so it made sense for him to lead. Besides, it was too dark to see any tracks.

They set a steady pace as they ran through the darkness. Each man ran alone with his thoughts. Each had his heart set on vengeance.

112

IT WAS IN THE EARLY hours of the morning that the trio caught up to the soldiers. John wasn't surprised to find them sleeping in the same campsite they occupied when Barega had guided Helen and himself to the soldiers three nights earlier.

Creatures of routine.

The Irishman quietly described the layout of the rainforest clearing to Gabirri and Turo, and warned them to expect at least two sentries on duty if Lieutenant Otter was true to form. When they discovered only one sentry on patrol, John guessed the lieutenant was confident he'd eliminated any threat of attack.

Turo dealt with the solitary sentry with a mighty swing of one of the two nulla nullas he carried. John was tempted to commandeer the dead sentry's rifle, but he resisted the temptation, preferring the benefits the Kabi's traditional weapons offered over the soldiers' firearms. For the task ahead, he knew the quiet, stealthy approach would win out over modern firepower—especially against so many.

They decided on a quick hit-and-run attack. It was agreed they would each aim to take out two soldiers before vanishing into the rainforest. Thereafter, they would pick the surviving soldiers off one by one as they continued their trek to the coast.

The three allies separated.

John worked his way quietly around to the far side of the campsite. Once there, he waited for Turo's signal. It had been agreed the native would give the call of the masked owl so common to these parts.

While he waited, John was reminded how critical he'd been of the lack of judgement shown by Otter in choosing the small clearing as a campsite. The rainforest pressed close in on all sides, allowing outsiders to get close to the sleeping soldiers. The nearest soldiers were so close he felt he could reach out and touch them. In the dark, they were little more than shadowy shapes on the ground. Their snores signalled they were asleep.

The Irishman tensed when he heard the rasping screech of a masked owl. That was the signal he and Gabirri had been waiting for. Without hesitation all three simultaneously crept out from the undergrowth and went to work, quickly despatching the nearest soldiers. The two Kabi wielded their nulla nullas, crushing the skulls of their victims, while John used his knife to slit the throat of his first victim.

As expected, the sudden violence woke some of the soldiers and they reacted immediately, lunging for their rifles. Their shouts and cries of distress shattered the silence.

John had time to club another soldier to death with one of his nulla nullas before self-preservation determined that he retreat into the rainforest. Gabirri and Turo, he noted, had fared at least as well as himself, notching up kills of their own.

The three raiders vanished into the darkness as quickly as they'd appeared, leaving behind four dead soldiers, two mortally wounded and another seriously disabled. The latter's pelvis had been shattered courtesy of a blow from Gabirri's nulla nulla.

Behind them, they left the campsite in chaos and the surviving soldiers in a state of panic. Screaming, shouting and hasty rifle shots rang out in tandem, creating one almighty din. This continued for some time before Otter restored some semblance of order. By this time, the raiders were well away.

•⟨•———•⟩•

John, Gabirri and Turo met at a pre-arranged rendezvous—a freshwater lake they'd passed earlier a mile from the soldiers' campsite.

"The first blow has been struck," Turo said breathlessly as the trio came together.

"The first of many," John said.

"What is next?" Gabirri asked.

"Next, we sleep," John said. Noting the looks of surprise on his friends' faces, he added, "The soldiers will be ready for us now. Let them have a sleepless night and then let us pick them off one by one in the daylight."

The two natives saw the wisdom in the white spirit's words.

"They will be asleep on their feet then," Turo smiled.

All three immediately set about making themselves comfortable for the night on a hastily arranged but nevertheless cosy bed of leaves.

Before drifting off, John wondered why they hadn't seen Barega at the soldiers' campsite. He wasn't to know that since he last saw the tracker, Otter had sent him back to the beachhead to report on the successful raid on the Kabi encampment.

•⟨•———•⟩•

Otter saw to it that his men resumed their trek to the coast at first light. He and the others were in a high state of anxiety. Overnight, two of the wounded had died, reducing their number from twenty-three men to sixteen. The third wounded soldier was in such a bad state he had to be stretchered out. The men agreed to take turns to carry their disabled comrade. His shattered pelvis caused him to cry out in agony as his stretcher-bearers negotiated the difficult terrain.

As they trekked along the floor of a narrow valley sandwiched between two bush-covered ranges, Otter wondered how many natives had participated in the raid on the campsite. Some of his men reckoned as many as a dozen had been involved, but he had his doubts. He estimated half a dozen at most had participated. Any more than that and they'd have been sighted. As it was, no-one had identified any attackers other than one or two fast-moving shadows. It was as if they'd been attacked by ghosts, and this had unsettled the men. They were willing enough to confront an enemy head on, but combatting shadows that came and went at will was something else altogether.

As the first rays of the morning sun pierced the canopy of the trees above, Otter also wondered how long it would be before the natives struck again. He had a feeling he wouldn't have long to wait.

John knew the soldiers would be expecting their enemies to attack from the rear so he persuaded his two allies to target the front of the column. "They won't be expecting that," he assured them.

Gabirri and Turo weren't so sure, but they bowed to John's proven tactical nous.

It didn't take them long to work their way around to the front of the column of soldiers. They stopped atop a high bluff to observe their enemies. The route the soldiers were taking would lead them along the cliff-face directly below the trio.

"Avoid hand-to-hand fighting this time," John cautioned. He added, "Spears only . . . and then run like the wind."

Gabirri and Turo both nodded. They could see that to engage an enemy at close quarters so close to the cliff-face would be to invite disaster. One slip and it would be all over. Below them was a drop of at least five hundred feet.

As the soldiers neared, John was disappointed to see that Otter had drifted back in the column. He'd planned to take him out, but the lieutenant had inconsiderately chosen this moment to check on the soldiers bringing up the rear. *You'll keep, Otter,* the Irishman promised himself. He held the smug officer personally accountable for the previous day's slaughter.

John and his companions waited until the leading soldiers were directly below the bluff they occupied before showing themselves. Together, they leapt to their feet and unleashed their spears in one deadly volley. Three spears hurtled through the air, and three spears found their mark. Two of the wounded soldiers fell screaming over the edge of the cliff; the third, who died instantly, was only prevented from following the other two by the quick thinking of another soldier who grabbed him before he could fall.

Gabirri and Turo had each fitted another spear to their woomeras before the soldiers had recovered from their surprise. They unleashed their weapons and, as before, the spears found their mark. Another two soldiers fell.

John, who was not as skilled with the Kabis' weapons as his companions, took longer to ready his second spear. By the time he'd inserted it into his woomera and lined up his target, the soldiers had recovered their composure and were starting to shoot back. He felt the wind from the gunshot as it whizzed past his ear. Consequently, his throw was rushed, and his spear missed its target by a country mile. That was all the motivation he needed to get the hell out of there.

As he ducked back out of view of the soldiers and ran for the trees, he saw Gabirri and Turo were following close behind. Even though all three of them were now out of sight and therefore out of the line of fire, the panic-stricken soldiers kept shooting up at the bluff their attackers had occupied just moments before.

The shooting continued until well after the trio had reached the cover of trees. It was obvious to all three they'd well and truly spooked the soldiers. The shooting only stopped when Otter managed to exert his authority over the men.

John smiled to himself.

Five more soldiers down. Eleven to go.

⋯⋯⋯⋯⋯

For the surviving soldiers, the expedition had turned into a nightmare. Their glorious victory of the previous morning was now all but forgotten. All they could think of was staying alive until they reached the safety of the beachhead.

For Otter, the expedition was worse than a nightmare; it was a personal disaster. He knew, beyond doubt, his career was finished. Any support he could have expected from Cheetham for going against Marsden's orders wouldn't materialise now. Of that he was certain. Since last night he'd lost more than half his men, and he knew Cheetham wouldn't countenance that. He fully expected he'd be court-martialled.

What most galled the lieutenant was the losses, it seemed, had been caused by so few assailants. After today's attack, his men had exaggerated the number of their attackers—just as they had after the attack in the night. However, he knew different. He'd had a good view of the action today, and he only counted three assailants. The biggest surprise, however, was that one of them was John Graham.

Thinking on that, he realised the Irishman's involvement was a further nail in his own coffin. If he'd obeyed orders and personally escorted John back to the beachhead, the bloodshed would have been avoided. As it was, there was little doubt John had organised the hit-and-run attacks his men were now being subjected to. And there was no doubt the army would take that into account at his court-martial.

113

J OHN AND HIS COMPANIONS FOLLOWED the soldiers for the remainder of the day, looking for opportunities to launch another attack or to at least pick off one or two stragglers. However, Otter shrewdly kept his men in open country, avoiding dense vegetation where possible and limiting the likelihood of another ambush while they resolutely pressed on. As a result, their enemies never had another chance to strike.

That all changed as the day drew to a close. The approaching dusk coincided with the end of the open countryside. Ahead of the soldiers was more dense rainforest. The lieutenant knew he should make camp for the night in the open, where his enemies had nowhere to hide, but he was keen to knock off some more miles before making camp, and so ordered his men to press on.

Watching the soldiers from a mile or so distant, John couldn't believe it when they entered the rainforest. "It could be a trap," he muttered to himself in English.

Gabirri and Turo looked at him strangely.

Switching to Kabi, John said, "It could be a trap."

The two natives agreed. Between the three of them, they decided to enter the rainforest some distance from where the soldiers had ventured in, and then circle around to intercept them.

It was almost dark before the trio located their quarry. The soldiers had established their latest campsite in a large clearing this time. It was half the size of a football field, and Otter had taken the precaution of setting up barricades, using fallen trees and sturdy branches his men had hauled into the camp. He had ensured the makeshift fort was sited in the dead centre of the clearing, as far from the trees as possible. As an added precaution, he'd rostered four sentries to patrol the site's perimeter at all times.

"He's learning," John said. He and his companions watched as Otter supervised the strengthening of the barricades. It was evident those not on sentry duty would sleep inside the barricaded area.

"We should wait for dark," Turo said.

"No," John countered. "I want to try something while there is still some light." He quickly explained his plan and then, when he was sure his companions understood, he set off alone, working his way over to the far side of the campsite where two of the four sentries were stationed. There, he placed all his weapons on the ground and prepared to show himself.

Here goes.

"Don't shoot!" he shouted in clear English. "Don't shoot," he repeated. "I'm alone." He raised his hands above his head in the surrender position and stepped out from the trees.

"Halt!" the nearest sentry said, pointing his rifle at John.

"Who goes there?" the sentry's companion asked.

John recognised him as the young private who had bandaged Helen's feet after they'd fled the Kabi encampment. "It's John Graham . . . Who do you bloody think it is?" he asked. Less than thirty yards separated him from the two sentries. Beyond them, on the far side of the site, he could see the other two sentries had seen him as well and were looking every bit as anxious as their comrades.

That's it lads, keep your attention on me.

Looking at the pair closest to him, he prayed they wouldn't shoot him. Even in the deepening gloom, he could see the fear in their eyes. They obviously thought they were about to be attacked. Smiling to allay their fears, he said, "I've had enough of running. I want to surrender." By now he saw he had the attention of everyone in the campsite. The other soldiers could be seen running about, gathering up their rifles and preparing for the attack they believed inevitable.

John looked for some sign of Gabirri and Turo in the rainforest opposite. He considered this the optimum time, while every eye was on him, to execute what they'd planned.

Do it now!

Then he saw them. The two natives emerged, running at full speed from the rainforest. They ran crouched over, their spears already in their woomeras and ready to launch. Even though he'd been expecting them, he could barely see them in the dark. He just hoped no-one else thought to look in their direction. Addressing the sentries again, he shouted, "Please don't shoot! I'm unarmed!" He wasn't even thinking what he was saying. He just wanted to keep them and their fellow soldiers focussed on him.

"Approach slowly," the nearest sentry ordered.

John did as he was told, but he was ready to flee. The Irishman knew when his friends' presence was noted, there was a good chance he'd be shot before he could retreat into the rainforest.

Turo was first to release his spear. It felled the nearest of the two sentries on the far side of the encampment. Before the sentry's companion could react, he was felled by Gabirri's spear. Death for both was instantaneous. At such close range, especially when propelled by the woomeras the Kabi favoured, the spears' velocity was devastating.

Only now was the plight of the sentries noticed by their fellow soldiers. Gunfire shattered the stillness of the evening as the men fired their rifles at the two natives who were still out in the open.

John thought the gunfire was for him. The fear of being shot lent strength to his legs and he ran faster than he thought possible to reach the relative safety of the trees. Once inside the rainforest, he gathered up his weapons and returned to the edge of the campsite to see what unfolded. He was alarmed to see Gabirri and Turo were still out in the open. "Bloody idiots!" he muttered. He could only watch as his friends ran backwards and forwards, taunting the soldiers.

At first he couldn't work out what the pair were up to. They were dicing with death, gambling that the soldiers' marksmanship was off. Then it made sense.

It's a distraction!

He realised they were trying to keep the soldiers occupied to give him the chance to inflict some damage of his own.

John saw the two sentries who had challenged him were both preoccupied, shooting at Gabirri and Turo. He lined the nearest sentry up and launched one of his spears. From twenty yards he couldn't miss. The spear thudded into the sentry's back, causing the soldier to fall forward onto his face. He was dead before he hit the ground.

The attack had been so silent, the sentry's companion hadn't even noticed. Even so, some sixth sense made him look around.

John had been about to launch a second spear when he saw the sentry bringing his rifle around toward him. He realised then that it was the young soldier who had attended to Helen. Unwilling to push his luck any further, he ran off into the trees before the sentry could line him up in his sights. There, he sheltered behind a tree trunk while the soldier emptied his rifle, firing blindly into the rainforest.

When the firing stopped, John ran off to meet up with his allies at yet another pre-arranged rendezvous. He just hoped they hadn't gotten themselves shot in the meantime.

That night, John and his companions observed the soldiers' campsite from a safe distance. There was little to observe because Otter had banned any cooking fires or lighting of any kind. The lieutenant had obviously worked out that the darkness was his ally as much as it was his enemy's.

"We wait until morning," John said.

Gabirri and Turo grunted by way of acknowledgement.

"We should eat," Turo grumbled.

He got no opposition on that score. The trio had eaten little other than a few bunya nuts, berries and grubs they'd gathered along the way, and their bellies were starting to rumble.

Gabirri had speared a wallaby earlier and had left it in a cave they'd identified was a good place to overnight. So it was with a sense of anticipation they returned to the cave. There, they wasted no time in setting up a cooking fire and heating the wallaby over the flames.

Later, after downing the last remaining morsels of meat, they sat in companionable silence and watched as the cooking fire slowly burnt itself out. The dying flames cast flickering shadows over the faces of the three men. None of them said much, but they didn't have to. There were no words to explain what they'd shared these past few days.

After a long silence, it was John who finally spoke. "I blame myself for the tragedy that befell the clan," he murmured.

Gabirri nodded cautiously. Honest to a fault, he, too, blamed John, but only in part. Summarising the reasons for the massacre of the clan members, as he saw it at least, he said, "The white men came to the place of totems because of you and the woman"—John knew he referred to Helen—"but you did not invite them to slaughter our people."

"Why did they do that, do you think?" John asked. He already knew the answer. He knew the soldiers attacked the Kabi because they had the bloodlust, and because Otter wanted his day of glory. However, he wanted to hear what Gabirri thought.

Gabirri was at a loss to answer the question. He couldn't imagine why white men—men from another world—would slaughter so many innocents. He looked at Turo, hoping he could provide some clue.

"They did that because Karadji said it would be so," Turo said with certainty.

Again Gabirri nodded. "The shaman said the white man would cover our lands . . . like ants," he said.

"Yes," Turo agreed. "Like stars in the sky . . . Karadji said that."

John remembered the shaman's prophesy.

How right you were, Karadji.

The conversation turned to the loved-ones Gabirri and Turo had lost. Rather than the mood being morbid and sad, it was warm and happy as the trio shared favourite memories of friends and family members who were among the departed. Once, this would have surprised John, but he'd lived with the Kabi long enough to realise they derived real pleasure from knowing recently departed loved-ones were on their way to the Dreaming. Sometimes, he imagined they envied the fate of their loved-ones.

"I hope Carravanty is alright," John said during a lull in the conversation.

Gabirri placed his hand on the Irishman's arm. "He is a survivor . . . like you, Moilow," he said.

Turo agreed. He assured John the young man survived.

John prayed they were right.

By now, the fire had burnt itself out. All that remained were the embers, and their glow cast a warm light over the three friends.

114

THE NEW DAY BEGAN AS the previous day had for the soldiers and for the three men tracking them. Otter ensured his men were on their way by sun-up. As they marched west, they were unaware their enemies were already some distance ahead of them, searching for a suitable place to launch another ambush.

John and Gabirri identified suitable spots for an ambush, but Turo disagreed with both suggestions. In typical Kabi fashion, all three needed to agree before any final decision was made.

They came to a river. Wide and slow-moving with rainforest hugging its far bank, all agreed it offered potential for an ambush.

It was John who found the ideal spot—a ford he thought the soldiers would likely use because it appeared to be the only crossing for a mile in either direction. The riverbank opposite was steep and muddy, and he could see the soldiers would find it quite difficult to climb. Better still, the dense vegetation offered plenty of hiding places. The trees were so close to the bank their branches extended out over the water. John pointed to the trees directly opposite. "We can wait there," he said.

He and Gabirri looked at Turo, and to their relief the big man agreed.

Without further discussion, they forded the river, scaled the bank—with some difficulty—and then hid in the trees.

A quarter a mile away, to the east, the soldiers were a miserable lot as they trekked ever westward. Now numbering only eight men, including their commanding officer, their glorious campaign had been reduced to a battle for their very survival. At all times, two of them were needed to serve as stretcher-bearers for their injured comrade while the others had to remain on high alert in case of further attack. Remaining vigilant mile after mile, hour after hour was beginning to take its toll. Some of the men were already talking mutiny.

Otter was very aware of the soldiers' low morale. He didn't blame them. God knows he felt the same way, but as their commanding officer he daren't show any sign of weakness. So, he constantly cajoled them and urged them to keep moving and to remain alert. To ensure they didn't shirk, he warned them to expect another attack at any moment.

When the soldiers reached the river, they soon found the ford. Otter prevaricated for some time before ordering his men across, and it was with extreme caution and nervousness that they entered the water. Even the most inexperienced soldier could see this was an ideal place for an ambush.

The two soldiers tasked with acting as stretcher-bearers for their injured comrade had trouble keeping their footing in the river. Not that the water was fast-flowing, but it was quite deep, reaching the waist of a man of average height, and it was rocky underfoot. Twice the stretcher-bearers stumbled, and twice their injured comrade ended up saturated. He groaned in pain and cursed his helpers.

From the trees on the far bank, the reception party watched as their quarry drew ever closer. They could see the soldiers were clearly expecting trouble. They had their rifles at the ready and their heads moved left and right as they searched the rainforest for some sign of their enemies.

John, Gabirri and Turo were hiding in trees on either side of what appeared to be the only place the soldiers could scale the bank when they finally emerged from the river. Elsewhere, upriver and down, the bank was too steep to scale without the use of ropes.

Otter had warned his men that if an ambush was to occur, it would likely happen whilst they were scaling the bank, and so they were hyper-alert as they prepared to emerge from the water.

John could see the soldiers had discussed what they needed to do. Those closest stood knee-deep in the shallows, their rifles pointing up into the trees, as the lieutenant scaled the bank. Otter slipped a couple of times, but he soon reached the top. There, he unshouldered his rifle and stood, with his back to the river, ready for whatever came his way.

What came his way was a spear travelling so fast he didn't even see it. It struck him in his stomach and propelled him backwards. He scrambled to keep his feet, but couldn't prevent himself from toppling into the river.

At the sight of their commanding officer ending up back in the water with a spear protruding from his belly, the soldiers began shooting wildly into the trees.

Gabirri, who was responsible for Otter's current predicament, released a second spear from his hiding place. It struck one of the stretcher-bearers. The wounded soldier let go his grip on the stretcher, tipping his injured comrade into the water. The screams of both men were all but drowned out by the crescendo of gunfire the others were directing into the trees above them. The gunfire momentarily kept their attackers at bay.

On the bank above the soldiers, all three attackers had to shelter behind trees to avoid being hit. Lead was flying in all directions.

It was Turo who struck next. He'd lined up the other stretcher-bearer, and he released his spear with full force. Its tip buried itself in the soldier's chest, killing him instantly. That prompted another prolonged volley of gunfire.

Now it was John's turn. He'd been waiting for the opportunity to finish off Otter who, he observed, was being kept afloat by one of his men. When he had a clear view of the wounded lieutenant, he released his spear. Its tip passed right through Otter's exposed throat and embedded itself in the forearm of the young private who was supporting him. Only now did John identify him as one of the sentries he'd confronted the previous night. The private cried out in pain and released his grip on Otter, leaving him to float away.

The sight of their commanding officer's body floating downstream on his back with two spears protruding from him was too much for the four remaining able-bodied soldiers. Panic-stricken, they began running downstream to elude the death that rained down on them from above. One was so frightened he threw his rifle away as he ran.

Gabirri and Turo both threw spears at the fleeing soldiers, but they were hindered by the branches that extended out over the river, and their hasty efforts yielded no further result.

Now that there was no danger of being shot, the trio emerged from the trees to survey the results of their handiwork.

Four soldiers could be seen drifting downstream. Otter and one of the stretcher-bearers were already dead. The other stretcher-bearer, by the looks, would soon be dead. He was having trouble keeping his head above water, and it was evident he was drowning. Spears protruding from those three made them easy to spot in the river. The other soldier—the injured man whose pelvis had been shattered—had a little more life in him, but he was also clearly drowning. His cries were growing fainter as he struggled to keep his head above water.

John was anxious to set out after the four surviving soldiers before they managed to climb out of the river. The Irishman was mindful their beachhead was only four or five hours' trek away, and he wanted to finish them off before they reached it or before Marsden sent his remaining soldiers to look for their comrades. He turned to go, but hesitated when he realised his companions were showing no inclination to follow.

"It is time to go back to the place of totems," Gabirri said simply.

"But our work isn't finished!" John said, pointing downstream in the direction the soldiers fled. "We can kill them all."

"Our work is finished, Moilow," Turo said. He added, "It is as Gabirri said. It is time to go back."

Before John could further object, Gabirri said, "There has been enough killing. We need to return to our people . . . or what is left of them."

With that, Gabirri and Turo scrambled down the bank and began wading across the river. Neither looked back. They knew the white spirit would not follow them. Not yet at least. He had the bloodlust, and it would not be satisfied until he'd killed every last soldier.

John watched his friends until they disappeared into the rainforest on the other side of the river. It crossed his mind that may well be the last he ever saw of them.

Resigned to completing the mission alone, he began running hard along the riverbank, more determined than ever to complete what he'd set out to do. Only then—if ever—could he assuage the guilt that wracked him or rid the anger than coursed through his veins.

John was too late to prevent the soldiers climbing from the river, but he soon found where they'd re-entered the rainforest. He had no trouble following them. Their tracks were still fresh in the soft ground underfoot. The space between each stride revealed they were running to distance themselves from their enemies. John could imagine they were still in panic mode, and that brought him no small amount of pleasure.

It was mid-morning before he caught up to the stragglers. He'd been running fast for the past hour, and was breathing hard. His haste was inspired not by any need to kill the surviving soldiers quickly—he was enjoying prolonging their fear—but he was aware they would reach the safety of the beachhead if he dallied. If one solitary soldier made it back, he'd consider his mission a failure and, he knew, it would eat away at him for the rest of his days.

By his reckoning the coast was only two or three miles away. He could see the ocean now, blue and beckoning beyond the summits of the mighty dunes that ringed much of the island. Rainforest was giving way to rolling bush country, and the terrain looked very familiar. He increased his pace. It was mainly downhill now.

Some two hundred yards ahead of him, a flash of light caught his eye. He identified it as sunlight reflecting off the barrel of a soldier's rifle. Then he saw the soldier through the foliage. A heavy man, slightly overweight, he was clearly on his last legs and could only manage a slow shuffle. There was no sign of the other three. John guessed they were each making their own way to the beachhead. He could imagine in their panic it was every man for himself.

The Irishman quickly closed the gap on his prey. When he launched his spear, he didn't even break stride. The spear flew true, and the power generated by the woomera ensure the weapon's barbed tip passed right through the soldier's back and exited out the front of his chest. The Scotsman saw the spear, or its bloodied tip at least, before he felt the pain. Such was the suddenness of the assault. He looked around in surprise. Only then did the pain register. Before he could scream or utter a sound, his attacker clubbed him with one of his nulla nullas.

John delayed only long enough to pull his spear from his victim's back before resuming his downhill run through the bush. He stopped every now and then to listen. Somewhere, away to his left, he heard the faint sound of someone crashing through the undergrowth. He ran toward the sound.

This time, his quarry saw him coming. The soldier, a tall, gangly Welsh corporal, had been looking behind him every few strides ever since he'd left the river, so fearful was he of being overtaken. When he saw John, he began running for all he was worth.

The Irishman recognised him as the soldier who had thrown his rifle away in fright. He looked to be around his own age. As he closed on him, he could see the only weapon the gangly soldier had was a knife, which he was holding in his right hand.

Breathless, the corporal stopped running and turned to face his pursuer when he realised he couldn't escape him.

John dropped his spears and drew both his nulla nullas before pressing his attack.

One knife proved no match for two deadly clubs, and the corporal soon found himself on his back, both arms shattered from two savage blows. "Spare me!" he gasped, looking up at his attacker.

"You didn't spare those women and children, did you, Corporal?" John asked, looking down at his broken opponent.

"Please!" the injured man pleaded. His misery was ended by one well-placed blow that crushed his skull.

"That one was for the women," John murmured as he blithely scraped away the blood and brain matter that had ended up splattered over his bare chest and stomach. He then picked up his spears and woomera, and resumed the chase.

Another one down, two to go.

Marsden made no attempt to hide his anxiety as he paced up and down in front of the soldiers and seamen who manned the beachhead he'd established. The captain had been beside himself with concern ever since Barega had reported back the previous day. He'd expected Otter and his men to be with the tracker. Instead, Barega had returned alone; worse, he'd advised him the lieutenant and his men had attacked the Kabi encampment.

News of the success of the surprise raid hadn't done anything to soften the anger Marsden felt at learning Otter had disobeyed orders and attacked the encampment when there was no earthly reason to. "He knew Helen was safe by then" the captain muttered to himself.

Equally concerning to Marsden was Cheetham's reaction upon learning of the unauthorised raid. The commandant hadn't been able to hide his pleasure when he heard the Kabi had all but been annihilated without the loss of a single soldier, confirming for Marsden that he and Otter were in cahoots.

With every passing hour, the captain's anxiety increased. The sun's position told him it was closing in on mid-day, and Otter's men should have returned by now. His soldier's instincts told him some misfortune had befallen the overdue soldiers. He decided he'd order Barega to look for them if they weren't back by early afternoon.

Thinking of Barega prompted him to glance down the beach. He saw the tracker was spearing fish from the rocks a hundred yards or so away, filling in time until he was next called upon.

John almost didn't see the ambush that had been set for him. He'd been so intent on running down his quarry, it didn't occur to him they would have the presence of mind to set a trap for him.

It was the glint of sunlight on yet another rifle barrel that saved his life. He threw himself to one side just as the shot rang out, shattering the silence. More shots followed in quick succession—too quick and too many for one rifle. He could tell both the surviving soldiers were shooting at him.

John was thankful for the rock that shielded him from the gunfire. He had rolled behind it as soon as he'd seen the tell-tale reflection. If it wasn't for the rock, he knew he'd be dead because the shooting was pretty accurate.

The gunfire subsided and silence returned to the bush.

As one minute became two, and two minutes became five, John pondered his situation.

If I stay here, one of them could work his way round behind me and pick me off.

He decided to make a run for it. Discarding all but one of the spears he carried, he leapt to his feet and sprinted toward a grove of gum trees, all the while expecting to be shot.

He needn't have bothered. The soldiers had decided to bolt as soon as the Irishman had ducked for cover. They'd sensed they were close to the beachhead, and were keen to reach it without further delay. They also feared John's two friends were still around.

After establishing his quarry had fled, John resumed the pursuit—a little more cautiously now. He didn't want to blunder into another ambush. His caution was tempered by the need to make haste. He desperately wanted to prevent them from escaping the fate he had planned for them.

It didn't take him long to catch up to the slower of the two soldiers. An English corporal, he was hampered by a calf strain he'd sustained when clambering out of the river where four of his fellow soldiers had perished. With every mile, the muscle had tightened up to the point he could barely run.

On sighting John coming up fast behind him, he put his pain aside and ran for his dear life. Unfortunately, he wasn't fast enough to avoid the spear that flew through the air and thudded into his back. His first thought was he couldn't believe he'd been hit. His attacker had been all of seventy-five yards away when he'd thrown the spear. His second thought was he was dying. He was lying face down in the dirt, and was struggling to breathe. He only just had the strength to turn his head so that he could suck in a lung-full of air.

When John arrived, he found the corporal barely alive. He quickly pulled the spear from his victim's back. Blood spewed simultaneously from the wound and from the corporal's mouth.

The Irishman watched impassively as his latest victim choked to death on the blood that filled his lungs. "That one was for the children," he said a moment before the corporal breathed his last.

John turned and resumed the chase.

Another one down, one to go.

115

JOHN CAUGHT UP TO THE last surviving soldier in dense rainforest just a mile or so from the beachhead on the western shore. He recognised him as the young sentry he'd encountered at the soldiers' campsite the previous evening, and again in the river earlier this morning. The wound he'd sustained in his arm whilst trying to save his commanding officer was still bleeding badly. Since then, he'd scraped it against thorns and branches, causing it to bleed even more.

The Irishman decided against using a spear to deliver the coup de grace this time. He wanted this particular soldier to suffer. So, he discarded his spears and woomera, and drew out one of his nulla nullas as he closed the gap between himself and his quarry.

The young soldier noticed John too late to shoot him. As it was, he barely had time to bring his rifle up to parry the blow his attacker had aimed at his skull. The nulla nulla was wielded with such force it slid down the rifle's barrel and shattered his left shoulder. He fell to the ground, screaming in pain.

Standing astride the young soldier, John raised his weapon above his head and prepared to deliver the death blow. Beneath him, his victim lay clutching his shoulder, groaning and staring up at him.

The Irishman hesitated. This was the moment he'd been waiting for, to satisfy his bloodlust and to assuage the guilt he felt, but now that the time had come he found he couldn't find it in himself to go through with it.

Gabirri's words came back to him.

There has been enough killing.

John looked into the young soldier's eyes. He saw sheer terror in them, but still the soldier didn't plead to be spared. Ever so slowly, the Irishman lowered his arm and threw the nulla nulla aside. "What's your name, soldier?" he asked.

"Private Harry Hershaw," the young man stammered, scarcely able to comprehend that he was still alive. His accent was that of a working class Londoner.

Unaccountably, John felt sudden compassion for the soldier. He bent down, grasped him by the shirt collar and lifted him to his feet. "East End?" he asked.

A bemused Hershaw nodded, confirming he was from London's East End.

"Well, Private Harry Hershaw from the East End, this is your lucky day," he smiled. With that, he pushed Hershaw away—in the direction of the beachhead—and watched as he stumbled off downhill, clutching his injured shoulder. When he noticed the soldier was heading too far south, he shouted, "To your right a little, Hershaw!"

The grateful soldier changed direction slightly.

"That'll do it!" John shouted. "Not far to go now." He continued to watch Hershaw until he disappeared from sight.

Then, for the first time since departing the place of totems, the Irishman wondered what he was going to do next.

Marsden was still pacing up and down, his anxiety growing by the minute. The sight of the schooner's skiff approaching the shore distracted him. He was annoyed to see Helen aboard it. He'd told her that it was potentially too dangerous for her or Eliza to come ashore. Helen waved at him, and, despite his annoyance, he returned the wave. He never could stay mad at her for long, he reminded himself as he walked down to the water's edge to greet her.

As the skiff nosed up onto the beach, Marsden couldn't help but marvel at how quickly Helen had recovered from her recent ordeal. Sleep, rest and good food had done wonders for her—physically at least. And the doctor had treated her sunburn and scratches, and her blistered and bruised feet, and he'd assured Marsden his daughter would make a full recovery.

Eliza was in a poorer state, physically and mentally, but she, too, was recovering.

"Good morning, papa," Helen smiled as her father helped her from the small craft.

"I thought I told you to stay on board the schooner," a stern Marsden reminded her.

"Oh, I completely forgot," Helen said innocently. Before her father could say any more, she held up a picnic basket and blanket she'd brought with her. "Cookie prepared lunch for us," she announced gaily.

Despite himself, Marsden couldn't hide his pleasure at seeing her. Besides, he'd missed breakfast and he was hungry.

Helen turned to the two oarsmen who had rowed her ashore. "You can go now," she advised them.

"Wait up," Marsden ordered, looking at the oarsmen. He said, "My daughter will be returning to the schooner as soon as we have eaten, so you may as well wait."

The oarsmen glanced at each other, anxious not to get caught up in any disagreement between father and daughter. They looked at Helen and were relieved to receive a nod of approval from her.

Smiling, Helen turned to her father. "I was hoping to spend more time ashore, but I see that doesn't suit," she said.

"You know the rules, my dear," Marsden mumbled. He added, "But I can break the rules this once if it means dining with you."

"Oh, goodie," Helen said. "Wait until you see what Cookie has prepared." With that she put her arm through Marsden's and led him off up the beach. When she considered they were far enough removed from the prying eyes of the soldiers and seamen, she chose a flat area of sand to spread the picnic blanket out on. "This should do nicely," she said.

The captain looked on with increasing admiration as his daughter laid out the food and refreshments the schooner's cook had prepared for the two of them. Any guilt or embarrassment he felt at indulging himself so in front of his men was eased when he set eyes on the delicious food. The aroma reminded him how hungry it was. "You are a lifesaver, you know," he said, smiling at last.

"I know," Helen said as she selected a fresh-cut sandwich for her father. "And I know you haven't eaten since last night."

They ate in silence for a while, each savouring the meal.

Marsden didn't know it, but Helen had an ulterior motive for coming ashore. She had seen Barega report to her father on his return to the beachhead the previous day, and she'd overheard Cheetham just that morning advising the schooner's master that Otter's men should have returned by now, so she was keen to learn if there was any news. In particular, she wanted to know if there was any news of John. "Papa," she said.

Marsden smiled to himself. He knew his daughter better than she realised, and he knew what was coming. "Yes, my dear?" he asked.

"Is there any news of Lieutenant Otter?"

The captain debated whether to tell her what he knew. In the end, he decided to tell her because she'd find out soon anyway. "The lieutenant and his men disobeyed orders and attacked the Kabis' camp," he said, scowling.

"Oh . . ." Helen was perturbed to learn that. She thought of the young clan members, and the elderly, too, and hoped no harm had come to them.

"It was a slaughter by all accounts," Marsden said, anticipating her next question.

"No survivors?" Helen asked, scarcely able to comprehend what she was hearing.

"Not many from what I hear."

Helen was struck dumb. Although she had few fond memories of the natives who had made captives of Eliza and herself, she wished them no harm. After a long silence, she asked, "And what of Mister Graham?"

"Nowhere to be seen," her father answered abruptly. He added, "I doubt we will ever see him again."

The remainder of the meal was eaten in silence. Helen had lost her appetite, and she didn't object when her father suggested she return to the schooner. She quickly gathered up her things.

A short while later, as Marsden prepared to help his daughter climb into the skiff, they were distracted by a commotion behind them. They turned to see the others looking up at the nearby sand-dunes. The pair saw it was Private Hershaw who had caught their attention. The young soldier was now stumbling down the side of the nearest dune. Clutching his injured shoulder, he was clearly distressed and in pain. Two soldiers ran to assist him. He tripped, falling face down in the sand just before his fellow soldiers reached him. They lifted him up between them and half carried him to the beachhead.

"What happened, Private Hershaw?" Marsden asked as the other soldiers sat the new arrival down on an upturned crate and proceeded to make him as comfortable as they could.

"The Irishman did this!" Hershaw gasped as he fought against the pain and feelings of faintness that threatened to overwhelm him. He grabbed a water bottle a fellow soldier gave him and drank his fill, coughing and spluttering in the process.

"Where are the others?" Marsden asked, looking up at the dunes as if expecting to see Otter and the other men appear.

"All dead, Captain," Hershaw sobbed in between swigs from the bottle.

Marsden thought he was hearing things. "All dead?" he asked.

Hershaw nodded. Lowering the water bottle, he said, "He . . . he hunted us down . . . like . . . like rabbits."

"Who?" Marsden asked.

"John Graham . . . the Irishman," Hershaw said. He was crying now.

Marsden noticed Helen had joined them. She was looking sympathetically at Hershaw, and she gestured to her father that he should see that the private's injury was attended to before he questioned her further. Ignoring her, he looked back at Hershaw and asked, "One man killed all your comrades?"

The captain's tone left the young soldier in no doubt his superior didn't believe him. Summonsing up what little energy he still had, he said, "There were three of them to start with . . . Graham and two natives. We thought there were more . . . many more . . . but there were only three . . . to start with."

"To start with?" Marsden asked.

Hershaw nodded. "Until this morning . . . after they ambushed us in the river," Hershaw mumbled. The memory of that incident prompted fresh tears. Between sobs, he said, "Then there was only the Irishman . . . He . . . he tracked us from the river . . . to the coast . . . and picked us off one by one."

On hearing that John had followed the soldiers to the coast, Marsden looked sharply around at the dunes. "Graham followed you to the coast?" he asked.

Ignoring the question, Hershaw sobbed, "He . . . he let me live!"

"Where was he when you last saw him, Private?" Marsden asked. It took all his control not to reach out and shake Hershaw, such was his desire to learn the Irishman's whereabouts.

Pointing directly inland, Hershaw said, "Maybe one mile away . . . maybe less."

Capturing John to make him pay for the carnage he'd caused was now Marsden's sole focus in life. He spun around looking for the tracker. "Barega!" he shouted. He needn't have shouted. The tracker was standing just behind him.

"Here, Mister," Barega said.

"We leave in five minutes," Marsden muttered.

Barega grinned. He still didn't know exactly how long five minutes was, but he was sufficiently familiar with the term to know it wasn't long. Long enough, if he wasn't mistaken, to bring his lover Orana to a climax, or long enough to skin a wallaby perhaps. He quickly ran off to collect his weapons for the coming chase.

Marsden then turned to address the other soldiers. "You men remain here on high alert," he ordered. "Expect an attack at any time." He personally didn't believe an attack was likely. Not if Barega was correct when he reported that Otter's men had as good as annihilated the Kabi. However, with John Graham still on the loose, he knew anything was possible.

Helen tried to get her father's attention. "Father," she said, touching his arm.

Ignoring her, Marsden turned to the four American seamen responsible for the safekeeping and operation of the longboat, which was resting in the shallows behind them. "I can't tell you gentlemen what to do," he said, "but it would be appreciated if you would remain here in case my men need to make a quick getaway."

The senior oarsman assured him their master had ordered them to do whatever possible to ensure the safety of the soldiers on shore. He and his fellow oarsmen were still armed, and, by the looks of them, none were strangers to conflict.

Heartened by that, Marsden then turned to the two oarsmen who had brought Helen ashore in the skiff. He noticed Private Hershaw already occupied one of its two seats. "You men have another passenger to return to the schooner," he said, referring to his daughter. As the seamen prepared to push the skiff into the water, he turned to Helen. "Now, what did you want?" he asked.

Helen grabbed her father's arm and led him away from the others. When she was satisfied they were out of earshot, she asked, "What have you done, father?"

"What have *I* done?" a surprised Marsden asked. "Don't you mean what has your Irishman done?"

"I am not excusing Mister Graham's actions, father," Helen said. "I am asking why *your* men saw fit to slaughter innocent men, women and children." Before the captain could reply, Helen added, "Because surely you can see Mister Graham's actions were a direct result of . . . of that . . . that unforgiveable event."

Marsden was done with talking. He steered Helen back to the skiff and firmly sat her on the spare passenger seat in front of the injured private. Turning to the oarsmen, he said, "Ensure my daughter remains on the schooner and does not return to the beach. Understood?"

"Yessir," the older of the two seamen said. His southern drawl left no doubt which part of America he hailed from.

Helen suddenly stood up in the skiff, her hands on her hips and her jaw set determinedly. "Father," she said, "if you kill John Graham, I shall never forgive you!"

Father and daughter stared at each other as the oarsmen rowed the skiff steadily away from shore. Only when the craft was thirty or so yards offshore did Helen finally sit down.

When Marsden was satisfied his daughter was out of harm's way, he informed his soldiers that he and Barega were going after the Irishman. He looked around for the tracker and saw him standing atop the same dune Hershaw had descended a short time earlier. Barega carried his usual assortment of spears and other weaponry, and he looked eager for the hunt. He reminded Marsden of a hunting hound straining at the leash.

Without another word, the captain set off up the dune, his rifle over his shoulder, his pistol in its holster and his mind set on resolving the John Graham problem once and for all.

116

SINCE SENDING PRIVATE HERSHAW ON his way an hour or so earlier, John had wandered aimlessly in the hills above the beachhead. He'd lost any desire for more bloodshed, and had discarded all his weapons except for his hunting knife and one of his two nulla nullas. These he retained more out of habit than any thought of further violence.

Walking through scrubby bush country, he tried to make sense of his actions these past couple of days. Try as he may, he couldn't. The most disconcerting thing was, the revenge killings of so many soldiers had done nothing to assuage the guilt he felt over the massacre of the Kabi clan members. If anything, he felt even more guilty.

Now I have the deaths of soldiers on my conscience as well.

Tired, anxious and depressed, he sat down in a bush clearing to ponder his situation and to weigh his options. Once he focussed his mind, it didn't take him long to work out that his options were extremely limited.

The Irishman realised the Moreton Bay authorities would no longer honour his ticket of leave. Not that they ever intended to honour it, but he didn't know that. He also realised without a shadow of a doubt if they ever recaptured him they'd hang him for what he'd done.

For a brief moment he wondered if he'd done the right thing in sparing Private Hershaw. If he hadn't, Marsden would never know he was responsible for the soldiers' deaths. However, he knew deep within that even if he had his time over again he couldn't have killed the young East Ender.

That would have been one death too many.

The bloodlust had truly been satisfied by the time it came to kill Hershaw.

The sight of a flock of bush pigeons flying just above the treetops distracted him. He watched the pigeons as they flew inland toward the middle of the island. And then it dawned on him.

I must return to the place of totems.

John slowly pushed himself to his feet. He needed to return to the place of totems and find out if Carravanty had shown up yet. Until he discovered whether the boy— his boy—had survived, he knew he'd never find peace.

John had only walked a hundred yards when he came across the last soldier he'd killed. The English corporal lay where he'd left him after removing the spear from his back. Rigor mortis had already set in, and his limbs had stiffened at angles that left no doubt the man was dead. His face remained forever frozen in pain.

The Irishman turned away and dry-retched. He glanced back at the body and could scarcely believe he'd done that to the man.

What's become of you, Graham?

John quickly set off for the interior, striding out to remove himself from the sight of the dead soldier. It was as if leaving him behind would help him forget what he'd done. He soon realised the futility of that and he immediately slowed his pace. Somewhere up ahead, he remembered, were the bodies of another twenty-three soldiers—men he and his Kabi friends had killed.

Marsden stopped walking long enough to take a well-earned swig from his water bottle. It was mid-afternoon and the sun was at its zenith. He and Barega had been tracking John for a couple of hours now. They were having no problem following him: the Irishman was basically retracing his steps as he headed inland. "Returning to the scene of the crime," Marsden muttered to himself.

So far, he and the tracker had come across three of John's victims. With each discovery, the captain's anger grew.

When he'd set out after the Irishman, his intention had been to capture him and return him to Moreton Bay to hang. Now, as he saw first-hand the results of John's handiwork, he was intent on killing him.

Marsden noticed Barega was running back toward him.

"Irish not far now," the tracker said, pointing behind him.

"How far?"

"Not far."

Marsden glared at his tracker. He knew that was all he was going to get from him for the moment. He asked, "What do you suggest?"

"I go ahead, Mister," Barega said. "Find Irish . . . wait you catch up."

"Alright," the captain said. "Make sure you do wait for me." He asked, "How will I find you?"

The tracker turned and pointed due east, toward the summit of a small, bush-covered hill some two miles distant. "I wait there," he said.

Marsden nodded and Barega took off, running at speed. Watching him go, he marvelled at the native's physicality. He almost felt sorry for John Graham.

117

JOHN WAS ALONE WITH HIS thoughts as he trekked inland. He walked, eyes down, thinking of Carravanty and praying the boy was still alive. At this point in his life, he realised, Carravanty was all he had. He'd lost everything else.

The Irishman was following a dirt track through scattered bush country. He looked up only to ensure that the way was clear and he wasn't about to walk into a tree or step over the edge of a cliff.

As he crested a small rise in the track, he froze. There, not thirty yards ahead of him, was Barega. The tracker had found Carravanty, and he was holding his long-bladed knife to the boy's throat. Barega grinned when he saw John's shocked reaction.

John thought of reaching for his own knife then resisted the urge when he realised Carravanty's life was in the balance. Carravanty, he noticed, was looking at him impassively. There was no fear in his eyes. It was as if he accepted whatever it was that fate had in store for him. "Don't hurt the boy!" John pleaded, extending a hand out toward Barega.

The tracker's grin broadened and he tightened his grip on Carravanty. "Throw weapons away, Irish," Barega ordered.

John's mind was racing as he calculated his options. He realised the native had him by the short and curlies, but he didn't want to discard his weapons for he knew if he did that neither he nor Carravanty would have much hope of survival. He wondered how Barega had found the boy, and he guessed, correctly, that Carravanty had come looking for him and had simply ended up in the wrong place at the wrong time.

"Irish throw weapons away!" an impatient Barega repeated.

John decided to try to stall for time. "Can't we talk about this?" he asked. Before he could do anything or say anything more, the tracker drew the point of his blade lightly across Carravanty's throat—not hard enough to inflict permanent injury, but hard enough to leave a faint line in the skin and to draw a drop of blood. "Nooo!" John screamed, fearing the boy's throat had been slit.

"Throw weapons!" Barega repeated.

Relieved Carravanty was unharmed, John quickly drew out his knife and nulla nulla, and threw them as far as he could into the undergrowth. "There," he said, "now let the boy go!"

Barega's next actions almost caught John off guard. In one fluid movement, the tracker drew his own nulla nulla and struck Carravanty over the head, knocking him out, and then charged the Irishman.

John back-peddled just in time to avoid a crushing blow of the tracker's nulla nulla. Barega quickly following up with a thrust of his knife, the blade nicking his opponent's forehead. Although it was a small nick, a surprising volume of blood streamed into John's eyes, causing him to blink furiously in an attempt to clear his vision. Grinning, the tracker kept pressing John, causing him to back up furiously to avoid being struck by the nulla nulla Barega wielded in his left hand or stabbed by the knife he held in his right hand.

All the while, the Irishman was conscious of Carravanty who he could see at the far edge of his peripheral vision. The boy was lying motionless and, to all intents and purposes, appeared dead.

John just managed to evade another swipe of Barega's nulla nulla. He sensed he was on borrowed time. His evasive tactics were never going to prevail. He knew that.

It's only a matter of time.

Sure enough, one of Barega's blows landed. It was the nulla nulla that caused the damage this time. Fortunately, it was only a glancing blow that struck John's head, but it was sufficiently hard to send him sprawling and leave him dazed. He only just regained his senses in time to roll away, narrowly avoiding another blow that would have crushed his skull had it connected. Barega had put so much force behind it he lost his grip on the weapon when it thudded into a rock where his opponent's head had been a moment earlier. The nulla nulla flew through the air and ended up at the base of a tree some ten yards away.

The two combatants eyed the weapon, which lay near enough equidistant from each. If anything, John estimated, it was perhaps a yard closer to Barega. The tracker had reached the same conclusion. He moved first, lunging for the nulla nulla he'd inadvertently discarded.

John was content to let his opponent get to it first. He knew he'd never beat Barega to the weapon. His eyes were on the tracker, not the nulla nulla, and he lunged for Barega. His knees thudded into the tracker's exposed ribs just as Barega's fingers closed around the nulla nulla. John heard two of his assailant's ribs snap.

Barega screamed in agony. In that instant, he forgot all about reclaiming his nulla nulla. All he could think of was the agony that gripped him as one of his broken ribs pierced a lung, taking the pain to an even higher level *if* that was even possible. It was worse than anything he'd experienced. He dropped his weapons and curled up into a ball, holding his knees to his chest for he instinctively found that's what he needed to do to ease the pain that coursed through his rib cage.

John was on his feet by now. He, too, disregarded the fallen weapons, preferring to deliver savage kicks to Barega's ribs. With each kick, he felt another rib bend or break beneath the impact. Blood was beginning to pour from the tracker's mouth. He was clearly finished.

Breathing hard, John stood back and wiped blood from his eyes. Blinking, he looked over at Carravanty and was relieved to see he wasn't dead. The boy was now sitting up, looking around as he tried to make sense of where he was. Blood flowed from the blow he'd received to his head, but he was alive and that was all that mattered.

Turning back to Barega, John stooped and picked up one of the discarded nulla nullas. When Barega saw what his intentions were, he tried to speak, but no words came.

Before John could deliver the killer blow, Barega's eyes clouded over as blood filled his lungs, depriving him of air. Within moments he was dead.

The Irishman almost felt cheated. He'd have smashed the dead tracker's skull with the nulla nulla had Carravanty not been there.

Remembering the boy, he turned around and saw he was now standing. "Carravanty!" he said. He hurried over to him and hugged him tight. Standing back, he asked, "Are you alright?"

Carravanty nodded, assuring him he was.

"How did you end up here . . . I mean . . . how did you find me?" John asked, looking at the boy in wonderment. He still couldn't believe they'd been reunited.

"I saw Turo and Gabirri," Carravanty said. "They said you were coming to this side of the island."

John was about to ask if he'd been back to the encampment at the place of totems, but he didn't need to: the look in the boy's eyes told him he knew of the horror that had occurred there.

Carravanty and his friends had seen the aftermath of the massacre when they'd returned from their hunting trip the previous afternoon. He'd set out after John as soon as Turo and Gabirri had told him where he was headed.

John hugged Carravanty again and then turned back to Barega. His gaze fastened on the silver crucifix around the tracker's neck. He strode over to the native and slid the silver necklace that secured the crucifix over Barega's head. "You won't be needing this anymore," he murmured. Pausing only to wipe a smear of blood from the crucifix, he slipped the necklace over his own head, and then smiled to himself when he felt the crucifix resting against his chest—back where it belonged.

"Moilow," Carravanty said, his tone urgent.

John looked up and saw that the boy was staring intently at something behind him. The Irishman looked around and tensed when he saw what it was that had caught Carravanty's attention. It was Marsden. The captain was standing only twenty-five yards away, his rifle pointed straight at John's chest.

John's first thought was for Carravanty. Moving slowly, so as not to pre-empt anything and cause the captain to shoot him, he reached out and manoeuvred the boy so that he was concealed behind him. He and Marsden then stared at each other grimly. Neither man spoke. They didn't need to: there was nothing to say.

◈———◈

At the same time, not one hundred yards distant, a small mob of kangaroos drank from a billabong. Their leader, a big buck, kept a wary eye on the others in his mob—and for good reason: they were all jills, or females, and there was no shortage of horny bucks in the neighbourhood who would like to usurp his ownership claims.

Two deafening rifle shots rang out in quick succession, and the mob scattered. Moments later, aside from some flattened grass around the billabong, it was as if the roos were never there.

EPILOGUE

THOSE ABOARD *THE NEW YORKER* not involved in readying her for departure watched as Marsden and the remaining soldiers drew near in the longboat. Standing at the starboard rail alongside Captain Rayburn, the schooner's master, were Cheetham, Doctor Andrews, Helen and Eliza. They'd been there ever since one of the sailors had noticed Marsden's arrival at the now dismantled beachhead a short time earlier.

Though the assembled—Helen in particular—were pleased to see Marsden had returned unharmed, the mood on board was sombre as the longboat drew alongside. Helen feared for John's welfare, and she was still in shock over the recent catastrophic loss of lives both black and white; Eliza still mourned the loss of her husband and baby; and Captain Rayburn feared that the bonuses promised by Cheetham wouldn't compensate for the extra time over and above the original estimate that his vessel had been side-lined for this mission. Time that would have been better spent carrying lucrative cargo to faraway ports.

However, their fears, grief and misgivings were nothing compared to Cheetham's. Since learning of the slaughter of Lieutenant Otter and the soldiers under his command, the commandant knew that his career, like Marsden's, was over. This failed mission would, he realised, be one black mark too many on a copybook already blighted by an earlier failed raid that resulted in soldiers' lives being lost—not as many lives as this time maybe, but enough to ensure a red flag was placed next to his name in the corridors of power.

After his opium addiction had been brought to the Governor's attention, Sir Ralph had personally warned him there would be no more second chances. Even though he'd managed to defy the medical experts and kick his addiction, he realised that would hold no sway. Not after this latest disaster. He was finished.

Cheetham blamed one man for his misfortune: John Graham. Watching Marsden scale the rope ladder hanging over the schooner's side, he hoped the captain had one piece of good news for him at least.

When Marsden's feet finally landed on the deck, he looked directly at Cheetham. "It is done," he said simply.

Cheetham smiled. That was the news he'd been waiting for. Turning to Rayburn, he said, "Weigh anchor, Captain. Time to go."

"Yessir," Rayburn said. The schooner's master walked off, barking orders at his crew.

Marsden avoided Helen's eyes when he saw her. He stepped forward to hug her, but she turned her back on him. She had overheard what he said to Cheetham.

Helen glanced at Eliza and saw that she also drawn her own conclusions.

"Poor Mister Graham," Eliza murmured. She, too, had overheard Helen's father.

Behind them, Cheetham lit up a cigar as he questioned Marsden. "Did the tracker make it?" he asked.

Marsden shook his head.

"No loss," the commandant said. "Plenty more where he came from."

A cloud of cigar smoke enveloped Helen and Eliza.

"I do wish he would stop smoking those ghastly cigars," Eliza whispered.

Helen raised her eyes, indicating she couldn't agree more.

"Vile beasts those Aborigines," Cheetham announced for all to hear. "Absolute savages," he grumbled. He was in full flight now, determined to vocalise his frustrations and happy to let the natives share some of the blame for his failures. "Best we wipe them all out and start rebuilding the colony from there," he said. "Eradication, that's the answer."

"Oh, shut up, Bertie!" Helen said, rounding on Cheetham. She'd had enough of the pompous man's arrogance and racial attitudes, and she wasn't about to hold back. "You are insufferable, you pompous little man!"

Cheetham was shocked into silence. He would have choked on his cigar had he not removed it from his mouth. Angry beyond words, he turned to Marsden, expecting him to put Helen in her place.

Marsden turned his back on the commandant and returned to the starboard rail where he stood staring at the island that had claimed so many lives in recent days.

That was the final straw for Cheetham. He threw his cigar overboard and stormed off below deck, muttering to himself.

Helen glanced at Eliza and saw the Scotswoman was smiling at her. It was clear she approved of her little outburst.

Nearby, Doctor Andrews caught Helen's eye and winked at her. "That was long overdue," he said before walking away.

Helen excused herself and left Eliza to join her father. She still couldn't bring herself to talk to him, and he wasn't sure what to say to her, so they just stood there, side by side, watching Great Sandy Island as the schooner began to sail off.

Helen's eyes were drawn to the towering sand-dunes above the beachhead the soldiers had occupied a short time earlier. The last rays of the setting sun bathed the dunes in golden light.

A movement on the summit of the highest of the dunes caught her attention. She looked closer, and her heart missed a beat. There, standing shoulder to shoulder, were John and Carravanty. They seemed to be looking straight at her. Sunlight glinted off the silver crucifix the Irishman wore.

Suppressing the joy that coursed through her, Helen resisted the urge to wave. She glanced at her father to see whether he'd seen the pair.

The captain didn't say anything, but he didn't need to. The gleam in his eye told Helen he'd seen them.

Father and daughter shared a precious moment.

Atop the sand-dune, John looked at Helen for the last time and then slowly turned and led Carravanty away from the coast.

"Where are we going?" Carravanty asked.

"Home," John smiled.

As they walked down the far side of the dune, the Irishman marvelled at the turn of events that had seen him get a second chance at life.

Why Marsden hadn't shot him when he had the opportunity, he couldn't imagine. When the captain had pulled the trigger, not once but twice, John was certain he and Carravanty were dead. It wasn't until Marsden began walking away that the Irishman realised they were both still alive. For reasons known only to himself, Marsden had aimed high and spared them.

At the place of totems, in the centre of the island, the few surviving Kabi clan members slept—except for Mirritji, Gabirri and Turo. They sat in front of a small fire, enjoying its warmth and each other's company.

The men preferred the nights. The darkness prevented them from seeing how desolate the encampment was now that the clan's numbers had been so decimated. It also hid from them the sight of the ashes of their loved-ones. At night, they could imagine the place as it was only a few days ago: a vibrant, happy place that resonated to the laughter of children and the vitality of a thriving community.

Gabirri threw a log on the fire. The flames flared briefly, illuminating the features of the three men.

"I hope Carravanty found Moilow," Turo said.

No-one commented for a while.

Finally, Mirritji said, "He did. . . . He found him."

The other two didn't doubt him.

After a long silence, Gabirri looked at the elder. "Do you think Moilow will return to the place of totems?" he asked.

Mirritji didn't answer.

A short while later, a movement on the edge of the firelight caught the old man's eye. A dingo and his pup appeared briefly, just thirty yards away, and then disappeared just as quickly.

Finally, Mirritji looked at Gabirri. "Moilow will return soon," he said with certainty.

THE END

Authors' notes follow over page . . .

AUTHORS' NOTES

❦————❧

SURPRISINGLY, JOHN GRAHAM'S STORY is not well known—certainly not as well known or as infamous as that of Eliza Fraser whose life is integrally and forever linked with the Irishman's. That's surprising, to us at least, because John's adventures in the wilds of an untamed Australia must surely rank with the most incredible true-life tales of survival. Not only Down Under, in Australia, but anywhere in the world.

In writing this novel, we were helped in no small way by 'John Graham, Convict,' a historical narrative penned and illustrated by one Robert Gibbings, and first published in 1937. Inclusive of (copies of) documents written in John's own hand, it proved a valuable research aid and is recommended reading for those of you who resonated with our novel.

Above: Cover of Robert Gibbings' document on Graham.

Though *White Spirit* is first and foremost a novel and therefore a work of fiction, many of the adventures described herein happened—exactly as related in some cases, and with some embellishments for drama's sake in others. We refer, for example, to the inhumane treatment of convicts at Moreton Bay; John's daring escape from the penal settlement, his subsequent trek north and his capture by the Kabi; his marriage to Mamba; his eventual return to Moreton Bay and the role he played in securing Eliza Fraser's freedom. All verified in the main by official reports and, in a few cases, by John Graham himself in the aforementioned documents.

Incidentally, Mamba *did* identify John as her dead, departed husband Moilow; Mamba's sons Murrowdooling and Carravanty *did* exist in real life; and the Kabi clan members *did* spare the Irishman because they believed him to be a white spirit.

To say the Moreton Bay penal settlement, and others like it throughout the colony, was hell on earth would be an understatement, and it is true that convicts committed suicide rather than serve out their sentences.

If anything, we downplayed the cruelty of the authorities and the ill treatment of the convicts in our novel. For example, the records show that for a time Moreton Bay's convicts were forced to work in all weather without clothes or boots. Naked in other words! And in their huts all too often it was standing room only, which meant the occupants had to sleep standing up if that's even possible.

The records also show that between February and October 1828, some two hundred floggings were ordered for a total of eleven thousand one hundred lashes, and, when the settlement's crops failed (in 1828–29) the worst months saw dozens of convicts die from hunger and from dysentery and other illnesses. Fortunately for John, he was living with the Kabi at that most terrible of times.

In that same dreadful period, some one hundred and twenty-six convicts are said to have fled south from Moreton Bay, but not one of those poor souls is known to have gotten clean away. Those who didn't perish in the bush were dragged back to face up to three hundred strokes of the dreaded cat o' nine tails—a punishment many didn't survive.

Above: Moreton Bay Penal Settlement.

Not dramatized was our account of the fate that befell the unfortunate Joseph Sudds, the misguided soldier who broke the rules in the hope he'd be released from military service. He really was sentenced to do hard labour alongside the convicts, and he really did die a horrible death when the spiked, steel collar he was forced to wear suffocated him.

Our account of the dreaded treadmill, or waterwheel, is authentic, too. Convict manpower was used to operate it, and the convicts really did consider it the ultimate torture machine.

Oh, and our reference to *Old Bumble,* the chief flogger, is also authentic. Dear Old Bumble really did exist, *and,* if the official reports are accurate, he really did stagger along like a bumble bee when he walked, *and,* after floggings, he really did soak his bloodied cat o'nine tails in a can of water and then drink the contents . . . Charming!

In reality, John's story was so unbelievably remarkable it needn't have been dramatized. However, we are first and foremost novelists, and, as such, couldn't resist embellishing certain events and concocting others to suit our storyline.

Our creation of Helen Marsden is a good example of this. To our knowledge there never was such a person at the Moreton Bay penal settlement. Her character was added simply to add some spice and to help balance the preponderance of males who resided in that part of the world at that particular time.

Barega, the tracker, was another figment of our imagination, but the British Army did employ Aboriginal trackers, and with great success. Indigenous Australians were, and are, superb trackers. (More about these remarkable people later in our notes).

We took liberties also with the officials stationed at Moreton Bay, oftentimes replacing true-life figures with fictional figures. This better enabled us to deviate from the known history where required—again to suit the storyline. A good example of this was the creation of the cruel and eccentric Lord Cheetham who, in fact, was loosely fashioned on the true-life and, by all accounts, equally cruel Captain Patrick Logan who, according to the history books, was both hated and feared by the convicts.

Other deviations include the two verses quoted from the popular ballad, *The Convict's Lament,* in a scene set in 1827. While the verses were accurately quoted to the best of our knowledge, historians would be aware the ballad wasn't penned until a later date. However, we felt the verses very appropriate, hence our cheeky decision to make use of them.

History also tells us that not too long after John Graham secured his freedom, the Kabi were displaced by European settlement and ultimately absorbed into other tribes, but our tale ends before that sad event transpired.

Australians and some others will be aware that this novel is almost entirely set in what is known today as the State of Queensland, *not* New South Wales. Queensland wasn't formed until 1859—twenty-two years after our story ends. Hence our frequent references to New South Wales. And the river we so often refer to (at Moreton Bay) is, in fact, Brisbane River. Brisbane City, the state capital, now occupies the site that was the Moreton Bay penal settlement and the adjoining settlement known as Brisbane Town.

In similar vein, the Kabi's territory is the tourist mecca still referred to today as the Sunshine Coast, and Great Sandy Island is now appropriately called Fraser Island, named after Eliza.

Above: Portrait of Eliza Fraser (1798–1858).

You may be interested to know that after Eliza's rescue, she sailed back to her homeland Scotland, returning to Australia years later. She died in Melbourne in 1858.

Brisbane-ites will know there are no crocodiles to be found in Brisbane River these days as they no longer venture that far south. However, crocs did frequent the river in John's time, hence our occasional reference to them early on.

Having lived in south east Queensland almost six years (1986–92), and having regularly visited the Kabis' former domain (the Sunshine Coast) during that unforgettable period in our lives, we can only marvel at John Graham's bravery, endurance, fortitude and gumption. How he could survive all those months alone in that unforgiving environment (after escaping the penal settlement) beggars belief; and how he not only survived but flourished all those years living with the Kabi we can't begin to imagine. Talk about the luck o' the Irish!

Returning to those Indigenous Australians, we sincerely hope we have done justice to these unique people in our writing. We strived for accuracy and balance in our portrayals: we show the cruelty the Aborigines were capable of, and we show their love for family, their community-mindedness, their incredible hunting and tracking skills, and their ability to survive in the most unforgiving of environments.

History now tells us the First Australians have had around fifty thousand years to familiarise themselves with the continent that is Australia. John wouldn't have known that, but if he had we imagine he wouldn't have been surprised: he was after all well placed to observe their oneness with the land over a long period of time.

Unfortunately, there is no record of John Graham's life after he gained his freedom in 1837. Perhaps he returned to family and friends in Ireland. Possibly he decided to seek his fortune elsewhere in Australia, or even in New Zealand.

We prefer to believe he resumed his former life with the Kabi . . .

If you liked this book, the authors would greatly appreciate a review from you on Amazon.

OTHER BOOKS BY
LANCE & JAMES MORCAN
PUBLISHED BY STERLING GATE BOOKS . . .

HISTORICAL FICTION:

Into the Americas (A novel based on a true story)

World Odyssey (The World Duology, #1)

Fiji: A Novel (The World Duology, #2)

THRILLERS:

The Ninth Orphan (The Orphan Trilogy, #1)

The Orphan Factory (The Orphan Trilogy, #2)

The Orphan Uprising (The Orphan Trilogy, #3)

NON-FICTION:

DEBUNKING HOLOCAUST DENIAL THEORIES: Two Non-Jews Affirm the Historicity of the Nazi Genocide

The Orphan Conspiracies: 29 Conspiracy Theories from The Orphan Trilogy

GENIUS INTELLIGENCE: Secret Techniques and Technologies to Increase IQ (The Underground Knowledge Series, #1)

ANTIGRAVITY PROPULSION: Human or Alien Technologies? (The Underground Knowledge Series, #2)

MEDICAL INDUSTRIAL COMPLEX: The $ickness Industry, Big Pharma and Suppressed Cures (The Underground Knowledge Series, #3)

The Catcher in the Rye Enigma: J.D. Salinger's Mind Control Triggering Device or a Coincidental Literary Obsession of Criminals? (The Underground Knowledge Series, #4)

INTERNATIONAL BANKSTER$: The Global Banking Elite Exposed and the Case for Restructuring Capitalism (The Underground Knowledge Series, #5)

BANKRUPTING THE THIRD WORLD: How the Global Elite Drown Poor Nations in a Sea of Debt (The Underground Knowledge Series, #6)

UNDERGROUND BASES: Subterranean Military Facilities and the Cities Beneath Our Feet (The Underground Knowledge Series, #7)